ALAN FURST
Three Great Novels

Also by Alan Furst

Spies of the Balkans
The Spies of Warsaw
The Foreign Correspondent
Dark Voyage
Blood of Victory
Red Gold
The World at Night
Night Soldiers

ALAN FURST is the author of ten highly acclaimed espionage novels, including *The Foreign Correspondent, Red Gold* and *The World at Night*. He has lived for long periods in France, especially in Paris, and has travelled as a journalist in Eastern Europe and Russia. He has written extensively for *Esquire* and the *International Herald Tribune*.

Alan Furst

Three Great Novels

Kingdom of Shadows
Dark Star
The Polish Officer

Weidenfeld & Nicolson
LONDON

This omnibus edition first published in Great Britain in 2010
by Weidenfeld & Nicolson
An imprint of the Orion Publishing Group
Orion House, 5 Upper St Martin's Lane, London WC2H 9EA

An Hachette UK Company

1 3 5 7 9 10 8 6 4 2

Kingdom of Shadows first published in Great Britain in 2000 by Victor Gollancz
Dark Star first published in Great Britain in 1991 by Grafton
The Polish Officer first published in Great Britain in 1995 by HarperCollins

A CIP catalogue record for this book is available
from the British Library

ISBN 978 0 297 86328 1

Typeset at The Spartan Press Ltd,
Lymington, Hants

Printed and bound in Great Britain by
Clays Ltd, St Ives plc

The Orion Publishing Group's policy is to use papers that
are natural, renewable and recyclable products and
made from wood grown in sustainable forests. The logging
and manufacturing processes are expected to conform to
the environmental regulations of the country of origin.

www.orionbooks.co.uk

Contents

Kingdom of Shadows

'This nation has already paid for its sins, past and future'
Hungarian National Anthem

In the Garden of
the Baroness Frei

On 10 March 1938, the night train from Budapest pulled into the Gare du Nord a little after four in the morning. There were storms in the Ruhr Valley and down through Picardy and the sides of the *wagons-lits* glistened with rain. In the station at Vienna, a brick had been thrown at the window of a first-class compartment, leaving a frosted star in the glass. And later that day there'd been difficulties at the frontiers for some of the passengers, so in the end the train was late getting into Paris.

Nicholas Morath, travelling on a Hungarian diplomatic passport, hurried down the platform and headed for the taxi rank outside the station. The first driver in line watched him for a moment, then briskly folded his *Paris-Midi* and sat up straight behind the wheel. Morath tossed his bag on the floor in the back and climbed in after it. 'L'avenue Bourdonnais,' he said. 'Number eight.'

Foreign, the driver thought. *Aristocrat.* He started his cab and sped along the *quai* towards the seventh arrondissement. Morath cranked the window down and let the sharp city air blow in his face.

Number eight, avenue Bourdonnais. A cold, *haut bourgeois* fortress of biscuit-coloured stone block, flanked by the legations of small countries. Clearly, the people who lived there were people who could live anywhere, which was why they lived there. Morath opened the gate with a big key, walked across the courtyard, used a second key for the building entry. '*Bonsoir*, Séléne,' he said. The black Belgian shepherd belonged to the concierge and guarded the door at night. A shadow in the darkness, she came to his hand for a pat, then sighed as she stretched back out on the tile. *Séléne*, he thought, *goddess of the moon.*

Cara's apartment was the top floor. He let himself in, his footsteps echoed on the parquet in the long hallway. The bedroom door was open, by the glow of a street lamp he could see a bottle of champagne and two glasses on the dressing table; a candle on the rosewood chest had burned down to a puddle of golden wax.

'Nicky?'

'Yes.'

'What time is it?'

'Four-thirty.'

'Your wire said midnight.' She sat up, kicked free of the quilts. She had fallen asleep in her lovemaking costume, what she called her '*petite chemisette*', silky and black and very short, a dainty filigree of lace on top. She leaned forward and pulled it over her head, there was a red line across her breast where she'd slept on the seam.

She shook her hair back and smiled at him. 'Well?' When he didn't respond she said, 'We are going to have champagne, aren't we?'

Oh, no. But he didn't say it. She was twenty-six, he was forty-four. He retrieved the champagne from the dressing table, held the cork and twisted the bottle slowly until the air hissed out. He filled a glass, gave it to her, poured one for himself.

'To you and me, Nicky,' she said.

It was awful, thin and sweet, as he knew it would be; the *caviste* in the rue St Dominique cheated her horribly. He set his glass on the carpet, went to the closet, began to undress.

'Was it very bad?'

Morath shrugged. He'd travelled to a family estate in Slovakia where his uncle's coachman lay dying. After two days, he died. 'Austria was a nightmare,' he said.

'Yes, it's on the radio.'

He hung his suit on a hanger, bundled up his shirt and underwear and put them in the hamper. 'Nazis in the streets of Vienna,' he said. 'Truck-loads of them, screaming and waving flags, beating up Jews.'

'Like Germany.'

'Worse.' He took a fresh towel off a shelf in the closet.

'They were always so nice.'

He headed for the bathroom.

'Nicky?'

'Yes.'

'Come sit with me a minute, then you can bathe.'

He sat on the edge of the bed. Cara turned on her side, pulled her knees up to her chin, took a deep breath and let it out very slowly, pleased to have him home at last, waiting patiently for what she was showing him to take effect.

Oh well. Caridad Valentina Maria Westendorf – the grandmother – de Parra – the mother – y Dionello. *All five feet, two inches of her.* From one of the wealthiest families in Buenos Aires. On the wall above the bed was a charcoal nude of her, drawn by Pablo Picasso in 1934 at an atelier in the Montmartre, in a shimmering frame, eight inches of gold leaf.

Outside, the street lamp had gone out. Through a sheer curtain he could see the ecstatic grey light of a rainy Parisian morning.

Morath lay back in the cooling water of the bathtub, smoking a Chesterfield and tapping it, from time to time, into a mother-of-pearl soap dish. *Cara my love.* Small, perfect, wicked, slippery. 'A long, long night,' she'd told him. Dozing, sometimes waking suddenly at the sound of a car. 'Like blue movies, Nicky, my fantasies, good and bad, but it was you in every one of them. I thought, he isn't coming, I will pleasure myself and fall dead asleep.' But she didn't; said she didn't. *Bad* fantasies? About him? He'd asked her but she only laughed. Slave-master? Was that it? Or naughty old Uncle Gaston, leering away in his curious chair? Perhaps something from de Sade – *and now you will be taken to the abbot's private chambers.*

Or, conversely, what? The 'good' fantasies were even harder to imagine. The Melancholy King? *Until tonight, I had no reason to live.* Errol Flynn? Cary Grant? The Hungarian Hussar?

He laughed at that, because he had been one, but it was no operetta. A lieutenant of cavalry in the Austro-Hungarian army, he'd fought Brusilov's cossacks in the marshes of Polesia, in 1915 on the eastern front. Outside Lutsk, outside Kovel and Tarnopol. He could still smell the burning barns.

Morath rested his foot on the gold-coloured spigot, staring down at the puckered pink and white skin that ran from ankle to knee. Shrapnel had done that – a random artillery round that blew a fountain of mud from the street of a nameless village. He had, before passing out, managed to shoot his horse. Then he woke in an aid station, looking up at two surgeons, an Austrian and a Pole, in blood-spattered leather aprons. 'The legs come off,' said one. 'I cannot agree,' said the other. They stood on either side of a plank table in a farmhouse kitchen, arguing while Morath watched the grey blanket turn brown.

The storm that had followed him across Europe had reached Paris; he could hear rain drumming on the roof. Cara came plodding into the bathroom, tested the water with her finger and frowned. 'How can you stand it?' she said. She climbed in and sat facing him, rested her back against the porcelain and turned the hot water on full blast. He handed her the Chesterfield and she took an elaborate puff – she didn't actually smoke – blowing out a dramatic stream of smoke as though she were Marlene Dietrich. 'I woke up,' she said. 'Couldn't go back to sleep.'

'What's wrong?'

She shook her head.

They'd certainly played long and hard – it was what they did best – night love and morning love tumbled up together, and when he'd left the bedroom she'd been out cold, mouth open, breathing sonorous and hoarse. Not snoring, because, according to her, she never snored.

In the light of the white bathroom he could see that her eyes were shining, lips pressed tight – *portrait of a woman not crying*. What was it? Sometimes women just felt sad. Or maybe it was something he'd said, or done, or not done. The world was going to hell, maybe it was that. Christ he hoped it wasn't that. He stroked the skin of Cara's legs where they wrapped around his, there wasn't anything to say and Morath knew better than to try and say it.

The rain slackened, that afternoon, Paris a little *triste* in its afternoon drizzle but accustomed to weather in the spring season and looking forward to the adventures of the evening. Count Janos Polanyi – properly von Polanyi de Nemeszvar but beyond place cards at diplomatic dinners it hardly ever appeared that way – no longer waited for evening to have his adventures. He was well into his sixties now, and the *cinq-à-sept affaire* suited the rhythm of his desire. He was a large, heavy man with thick, white hair, almost yellow in lamplight, who wore blue suits cut by London tailors and smelled of *bay rhum*, used liberally several times a day, cigar smoke, and the Burgundy he drank with lunch.

He sat in his office in the Hungarian legation, crumpled up a cable and tossed it in the waste basket. Now, he thought, it was actually going to happen. *A leap into hell*. The real thing, death and fire. He glanced at his watch, left the desk and settled in a leather chair, dwarfed by immense portraits hanging high on the walls: a pair of Arpad kings, Geza II and Bela IV, the heroic general Hunyadi hung beside his son, Matthias Corvinus, with customary raven. All of them dripping furs and bound in polished iron, with long swords and drooping moustaches, attended by noble dogs of breeds long vanished. The portraits continued in the hall outside his office, and there would have been more yet if they'd had room on the walls. A long and bloody history, and no end of painters.

Five-twenty. She was, as always, subtly late, enough to stir anticipation. With the drapes drawn the room was almost dark, lit only by a single, small lamp and firelight. Did the fire need another log? No, it would do, and he didn't want to wait while the porter climbed three flights of stairs.

Just as his eyes began to close, a delicate knock at the door followed by the appearance of Mimi Moux – the *chanteuse* Mimi Moux as the gossip writers of the newspapers had it. Ageless, twittering like a canary, with vast eyes and carmine lipstick – a theatrical face – she bustled into his office, kissed him on both cheeks and touched him, somehow, damned if he knew how she did it, in sixteen places at once. Talking and laughing without pause – you could enter the conversation or not, it didn't matter – she hung her afternoon Chanel in a closet and fluttered around the room in expensive and pleasantly exhilarating underwear.

'Put on the Mendelssohn, my dear, would you?'

Arms crossed over her breasts, a mock play on modesty, she twitched her way over to an escritoire with a victrola atop it and, still talking – 'You can imagine, there we were, all dressed for the opera, it was simply *insupportable*, no? Of course it was, one couldn't do such a thing in ignorance, or, at least, so we thought. Nonetheless' – put the First Violin Concerto on the turntable and set the needle down, returned to the leather chair, and curled herself up in Count Polanyi's commodious lap.

Eventually, just at the moment – of their several underappreciated virtues, he mused, the French possessed the purest sense of timing in all Europe – she settled on her knees in front of his chair, unbuttoned his fly with one hand and, at last, stopped talking. Polanyi watched her, the record came to an end, the needle hissed back and forth in an empty groove. He had spent his life, he thought, giving pleasure to women; now he had reached a point where they would give pleasure to him.

Later, when Mimi Moux had gone, the legation cook knocked lightly on his door and carried in a steaming tray. 'A little something, your excellency,' she said. A soup made from two chickens, with tiny dumplings and cream, and a bottle of 1924 Echézeaux. When he was done, he sat back in his chair and breathed a sigh of great contentment. Now, he noted, his fly was closed but his belt and trousers button were undone. *Really just as good*, he thought. *Better?*

The café Le Caprice lurked in the eternal shadows of the rue Beaujolais, more alley than street, hidden between the gardens of the Palais Royal and the Bibliothèque Nationale. His uncle, Morath had realized long ago, almost never invited him to the legation, preferring to meet in unlikely cafés, or, sometimes, at the houses of friends. 'Indulge me, Nicholas,' he would say, 'it frees me from my life for an hour.' Morath liked Le Caprice, cramped and grimy and warm. The walls had been painted yellow in the nineteenth century, then cured to a rich amber by a hundred years of cigarette smoke.

Just after three in the afternoon, the lunch crowd began to leave and the regulars drifted back in to take their tables. *The mad scholars*, Morath thought, who spent their lives in the Bibliothèque. They were triumphantly seedy. Ancient sweaters and shapeless jackets had replaced the spotted gowns and conical hats of the medieval alchemists, but they were the same people. Morath could never come here without recalling what the waiter, Hyacinthe, had once said about his clientele. 'God forbid they should actually ever *find* it.' Morath was puzzled. 'Find what?' Hyacinthe looked startled, almost offended. 'Why, *it*, monsieur,' he said.

Morath took a table vacated by a party of stockbrokers who'd walked over from the Bourse, lit a cigarette, ordered a *gentiane* and settled in to wait for his uncle. Suddenly, the men at the neighbouring table stopped arguing, went dead silent and stared out at the street.

A very grand Opel Admiral had pulled up in front of Le Caprice. The driver held the back door open, a tall man in black SS uniform emerged, followed by a man in a raincoat, followed by Uncle Janos. Who talked and gesticulated as the others listened avidly, expectant half-smiles on their faces. Count Polanyi pointed his finger and scowled theatrically as he delivered what was obviously a punchline. All three burst into laughter, just faintly audible inside the café, and the SS man clapped Polanyi on the back – *that was a good one!*

They said goodbye, shook hands, and the civilian and the SS man returned to the Opel. *Here's something new*, Morath thought. You rarely saw SS men in uniform in Paris. They were everywhere in Germany, of course, and very much in the newsreels; marching, saluting, throwing books into bonfires.

His uncle entered the café and took a moment to find him. Somebody at the next table made a remark, one of his friends snickered. Morath stood, embraced his uncle, and they greeted each other – as usual, they spoke French together in public. Count Polanyi took off his hat, gloves, scarf and coat and piled them up on the empty chair. 'Hmm, that went over well,' he said. 'The two Roumanian businessmen?'

'I haven't heard it.'

'They run into each other on the street in Bucharest, Gheorgiu is carrying a suitcase. "Where are you off to?" Petrescu asks. "Cernauti," his friend says. "Liar!" Petrescu shouts. "You tell me you're going to Cernauti to make me think you're going to Jassy, but I've bribed your office boy and I know you're going to Cernauti!" '

Morath laughed.

'You know von Schleben?'

'Which one was he?'

'Wearing a raincoat.'

Hyacinthe appeared. Polanyi ordered a Ricon.

'I don't think so,' Morath said. He wasn't completely sure. The man was tall, with pale, fading hair a little longer than it should be, and something about the face was impish; he had the sly grin of the practical joker. Quite handsome, he could have played the suitor – not the one who wins, the one who loses – in an English drawing-room comedy. Morath was sure he'd seen him somewhere. 'Who is he?'

'He works in the diplomatic area. Not a bad sort, when all is said and done. I'll introduce you some time.'

The Ricon arrived and Morath ordered another *gentiane*. 'I never did get lunch,' his uncle said. 'Not really. Hyacinthe?'

'Monsieur?'

'What's for lunch today?'

'*Tête de veau.*'

'How is it?'

'Not too bad.'

'I think I'll have some. Nicholas?'

Morath shook his head. He placed a small packet on the table. The size of a hand, it was wrapped in very old, yellowed muslin, perhaps a piece cut from a curtain a long time ago. He unfolded the fabric, revealing a silver cross on a faded ribbon, black and gold, the colours of Austria-Hungary. 'This he sent to you.'

Polanyi sighed. 'Sandor,' he said, as though the coachman could hear him. He picked up the medal, let it lie flat on his open hand. 'A Silver Cross of Valour. You know, Nicholas, I'm honoured, but this is worth something.'

Morath nodded. 'I offered it to the daughter, with your kindest sympathies, but she wouldn't hear of it.'

'No. Of course not.'

'When is it from?'

Polanyi thought for a time. 'The late eighties, as near as I can work it out. A Serbian rising, down in the Banat. Sandor was a sergeant, in the regiment raised in Pozsony. It was Pressburg, then.'

'Bratislava, now.'

'The same place, before they gave it to the Slovaks. Anyhow, he used to talk about it now and then. The Serbs gave them a hard time – some villages had to be burned down. They had snipers up in the caves, on the hillsides. Sandor's company spent a week, dealing with that, and he got the cross.'

'He wanted you to have it.'

Polanyi nodded that he understood. 'Is anything left, up there?'

'Not much. They stripped the house, after the border moved. Door knobs, windows, the good floors, fireplace brick, chimneys, whatever pipe they could get out of the walls. The livestock's long gone, of course. Some of the vineyard remains. The older fruit trees.'

'*Nem, nem, soha,*' Polanyi said. No, no, never – the Hungarian rejection of Trianon, the treaty that took away two-thirds of its land and people after the Austro-Hungarian army was defeated in the Great War. There was more than a touch of irony in Polanyi's voice when he said it, a shrug, *all we can do is whine,* but that wasn't all. In some sense, complex, possibly obscure, he meant it.

'One day, perhaps, it comes back.'

The group at the next table had been attentive. One pugnacious little man, balding, nostrils flared, the reek of his mildewed room floating over their apéritifs, said, '*Revanchiste.*' He didn't say it to them, quite, or to his friends; perhaps he meant it for the world at large.

They looked at him. *Revanchist, irredentist Hungarian fascists,* he meant, seething with Red Front indignation. But Morath and Polanyi were not that, they were of the Hungarian Nation, as the nobility was called, Magyars with family histories that went back a thousand years, and they were quite prepared, with chair leg and wine bottle, to throw the whole crowd out into the rue Beaujolais.

When the group at the next table had returned, ostentatiously, to minding its own business, Polanyi carefully folded the medal back into its wrapping and put it in the inside pocket of his jacket.

'He spent a long time dying,' Morath said. 'Not in pain, and he wasn't sad – he just had a hardheaded soul, it didn't want to go.'

From Polanyi, a tender little snort of pleasure as he tasted the veal.

'Also,' Morath went on, 'he wanted me to tell you something.'

Polanyi raised his eyebrows.

'It had to do with the death of his grandfather, who was ninety-five, he thought, and who had died in the same bed. The family knew the time had come, they were all gathered around. Suddenly, the old man became agitated and started to talk. Sandor had to lean close in order to hear him. "Remember," he whispered, "life is like licking honey . . ." He said it three or four times, and Sandor could tell there was more. At last, he managed: ". . . licking honey off a thorn."'

Polanyi smiled, acknowledging the story. 'It's been twenty years', he said, 'since I saw him. When it was no longer Hungary, I didn't want anything to do with it, I knew it would be destroyed.' He took a sip of the wine, then more. 'You want some, Nicholas? I'll have them bring a glass.'

'No, thank you.'

'I wouldn't go up there,' Polanyi said. 'That was weak. And I knew it.' He shrugged, forgiving himself.

'He didn't hold it against you.'

'No, he understood. His family was there?'

'All sorts. Daughters, a son, nieces and nephews, his brother.'

'Ferenc.'

'Yes, Ferenc. They had all the mirrors turned around. One old lady – immense, she cried, she laughed, she cooked me an egg – couldn't stop talking about it. When the soul leaves, it mustn't ever be allowed to see itself in the mirror. Because, she said, if it did, it might like looking at itself and then it would be back again and again.'

'I don't think mine would. Did they put out the tub of water?'

'By the door. For death to wash his scythe. Otherwise he would have to go all the way down to the creek, and somebody else in the house would die within the year.'

Polanyi daintily ate a chunk of bread he'd soaked in the sauce. When he looked up, the waiter was passing by. 'Hyacinthe, *s'il vous plaît*, a glass for my nephew here. And, while you're at it, another carafe.'

They walked in the Palais Royal gardens after lunch. A dark afternoon, perpetual dusk, Polanyi and Morath like two ghosts in overcoats, moving slowly past the grey branches of the winter parterre.

Polanyi wanted to hear about Austria – he knew that Wehrmacht units were poised on the borders, ready to march in to suppress the 'riots' organized by the Austrian Nazis. 'If Hitler gets his *Anschluss*, there will be war in Europe,' he said.

'The trip was a nightmare,' Morath said. A nightmare that began with an absurdity – a fistfight in the corridor of the first-class car between two German harmonica salesmen. 'Imagine, two stout men, both with moustaches, screaming insults at each other and flailing away with their little white fists. By the time we got them separated, they were bright red. We made them sit down, gave them water. We were afraid one of them would drop dead, and the conductor would have to stop the train and call for the police. Nobody, *nobody* in the car wanted that.'

'It started in Bucharest, no doubt,' Polanyi said. Roumania, he explained, had been forced to sell its wheat harvest to Germany, and the Reich Finance Ministry refused to pay in marks. They would only barter. For, exclusively, aspirin, Leica cameras, or harmonicas.

'Well, that was just the beginning,' Morath said. 'We were still in western Hungary.' While the train stood in the station in Vienna, a man approximately Morath's age, pale, trembling, had taken the seat across from him. When the family that occupied the rest of the compartment went off to the dining car, they had started to talk.

The man was a Viennese Jew, an obstetrician. He told Morath that the Jewish communities of Austria had been destroyed in a day and a night. It was, he said, sudden, chaotic, not like Berlin. By which he meant, Morath knew, a certain style of persecution – the slow, meticulous grinding of civil servants. *Schreibtischtäter*, he called them, 'desk-murderers'.

The mobs had run wild in the city, led by Austrian SS and SA, hauling Jews out of their apartments – identified by the building custodians – and forcing them to scrub the walls free of slogans for Schuschnigg, the elected chancellor, in the plebiscite that Hitler refused to allow. In the wealthy Jewish suburb of Wahring, they made the women put on their fur coats and forced them to clean the streets on their hands and knees, then stood over them and urinated on their heads.

Morath grew worried; the man was coming apart before his eyes. Would he care for a cigarette? No, he didn't smoke. Perhaps a brandy? Morath offered to go to the dining car and bring it back. The man shook his head; what was the point. 'We are finished,' he said. Eight hundred years of Jewish life, ended in one night. At the hospital, an hour before he'd made a run for it, a woman with a newborn child had taken it in her arms and jumped out of a window on the top floor. Other patients crawled from their beds and fled into the streets. A young intern said he'd seen a man standing at a bar, the night before, who took a razor from his pocket and cut his throat.

'Was there no warning?' Morath said.

'Anti-Semites in political office,' the man said. 'But you don't sell your house because of that. A month ago, more or less, a few people left the country.' Of course there were some, he added, who'd gotten out in 1933, when Hitler came to power. He'd said, in *Mein Kampf*, that he meant to unite Austria with Germany. *Ein Volk, ein Reich, ein Führer!* But reading the political future was like reading Nostradamus. His wife and children he'd put on a Danube steamer to Budapest, thank God, two weeks earlier. 'It was her brother who did that. He came to the house, said we should leave, insisted. There was an argument, my wife in tears, bad feelings. In the end, I was so angry I let him have his way.'

'But you stayed on,' Morath said.

'I had patients.'

They were silent for a moment. Outside, boys with swastika flags were running down the platform, screaming some kind of rhymed chant, their faces wild with excitement.

*

Polanyi and Morath sat on a bench in the gardens. It seemed very quiet there. A few sparrows working at the crumbs of a *baguette*, a little girl in a coat with a velvet collar, trying to play with a hoop and a stick while a nursemaid watched her.

'In the town of Amstetten,' Morath said, 'just outside the station, they were waiting at a road crossing so they could throw rocks at the trains. We could see the police, standing around with their arms folded; they'd come to watch. They were laughing, it was a certain kind of joke. The whole thing had, more than anything, a terrible strangeness to it. I remember thinking, they've wanted this for a long time. Under all the sentiment and *schlag* was this.'

'Their cherished *Wut*,' Polanyi said. 'You know the word.'

'Rage.'

'Of a particular kind, yes. The sudden burst of anger that rises from despair. The Germans believe it lies deep within their character; they suffer in silence, and then they explode. Listen to Hitler speak – it's always, "How much longer must we endure . . ." whatever it is. He can't leave it alone.' Polanyi paused for a moment. 'And now, with *Anschluss*, we will have the pleasure of their company on *our* border.'

'Will anything happen?'

'To us?'

'Yes.'

'I doubt it. Horthy will be summoned to meet with Hitler, he'll bow and scrape, agree to anything. As you know, he has beautiful manners. Of course, what we actually do will not be quite what we've agreed to, but, even so, when it's all over, we won't keep our innocence. It can't be done. And we will pay for that.'

For a time, they watched the people walking along the gravel paths, then Polanyi said, 'These gardens will be lovely in the spring. The whole city.'

'Soon, I hope.'

Polanyi nodded. 'You know,' he said, 'they fight wars, the French, but their country, their Paris, is never destroyed. Do you ever wonder how they do that?'

'They are clever.'

'Yes, they are. They are also brave. Foolish, even. But that's not, in the end, how they save what they love. That they do by crawling.'

The eleventh of March, Morath thought. Too cold to sit in a garden, the air damp, sharp, as though chilled in wet earth. When it began to sprinkle rain, Morath and Polanyi rose and walked in the covered arcade, past a famous milliner, a store that sold expensive dolls, a dealer in rare coins.

'And the Viennese doctor?' Polanyi said.

'Reached Paris, long after midnight. Although he did have trouble at the German border. They tried to send him back to Vienna, something not quite right with his papers. A date. I stood next to him throughout the whole filthy business. In the end, I couldn't keep out of it.'

'What did you do, Nicholas?'

Morath shrugged. 'Looked at them a certain way. Spoke to them a certain way.'

'And it worked.'

'This time.'

4 April 1938.

Théâtre des Catacombes. 9.20 p.m.

'Know him? Yes, I know him. His wife makes love to my wife every Thursday afternoon.'

'Really? Where?'

'In the maid's room.'

Lines not spoken from the stage – *would that they had been*, Morath thought – but overheard in the lobby during the intermission. As Morath and Cara worked their way through the crowd they were noticed, the glances polite, covert. A dramatic couple. Cara's face was not her best feature – it was soft and plain, hard to remember. Her best features were long, honey-gold hair, beautiful scarves, and the ways she found to make people want her. For an evening of avant-garde theatre she had added a gypsy skirt, with appropriate hoop earrings, and soft leather boots with the tops folded over.

Morath seemed taller than he was. He had black hair, thick, heavy, combed back from the forehead, a certain tightness around the eyes, 'green' on his passport but very close to black, and all that darkness made him seem pale, a fin-de-siècle decadent. He'd once met a film producer, introduced by a mutal friend at Fouquet. 'I usually make gangster films,' the man told him with a smile. 'Or, you know, intrigue.' But, at the moment, a costume epic was soon to go into production. A large cast, a new version of *Taras Bulba*. Had Morath ever acted? He could play, possibly, 'a chieftain'. The producer's friend, a scrawny little man who looked like Trotsky, added, 'A khan, maybe.'

But they were wrong. Morath had been eighteen years in Paris and the émigré life, with its appetizing privacy, and immersion in the city, all passion, pleasure and bad philosophy, had changed the way he looked. It meant that women liked him more, meant that people didn't mind asking him for directions in the street. Still, what the producer had seen remained, somewhere, just below the surface. Years earlier, towards the end of a brief love affair, a French woman said to him, 'Why, you're not at all cruel.' She had sounded, he thought, slightly disappointed.

Act II. *A Room in Purgatory – The Following Day.*

Morath shifted his weight, a pointless effort to get comfortable in the diabolical chair. Crossed his legs, leaned the other way. Cara clutched his arm – *stop it.* The row of seats, fixed on a wooden frame, went twelve across. Where did Montrouchet get them? he wondered. From some long-dead institution, no doubt. A prison? A school for horrible children?

On stage, the Seven Deadly Sins were harassing a gloomy Everyman. Poor soul, seated on a stool, wearing a grey shroud. 'Ahh, but you slept through her funeral.' This well-meaning woman, no longer young, was probably Sloth, though Morath had been wrong two or three times when he'd actually tried watching the play. They had soft edges, the Sins. Either the playwright's fault or Satan's – Morath wasn't sure. Pride was angry, it seemed to him, and Covetousness upstaged Envy every chance he got. But then, Covetousness.

On the other hand, Gluttony wasn't so bad. A plump young man, come to Paris from the provinces, trying for a career in theatre or the movies. Trouble was, the playwright hadn't given him much to do. What could he say to poor, dead Everyman? You ate too much! Well, he made the best of what had been given him; perhaps a prominent director or producer would come to watch the play, one never knew.

But one did know. Morath looked down at the programme in his lap, the only permissible distraction to the white fog that rolled in from the stage. The back cover was given over to promotion. The critic from *Flambeau Rouge,* Red Torch, had found the play 'Provocative!' Below that a quote from Lamont Higson of the *Paris Herald*: 'The Théâtre des Catacombes is the only Parisian theatre in recent memory to present plays of both Racine and Corneille in the nude.' There followed a list of sponsors, including one Mlle Cara Dionello. Well, he thought, why not? At least a few of those poor beasts in Argentina, trudging down the ramp to the abattoir, added more to life than roast beef.

The theatre lay deep in the heart of the fifth arrondissement. Originally, there'd been a plan for Montrouchet to stage his performances at the catacombs themselves, but the municipal authority had been mysteriously cool to the possibility of actors capering about in the dank bone-rooms beneath the Denfert/Rochereau Métro stop. In the end, he had had to make do with a mural in the lobby: piles of clown-white skulls and femurs sharply picked out in black.

'What? You forgot? That night by the river?' Morath returned from dreamland to find Lust, typecast, maybe seventeen, whispering her line as she slithered on her belly across the stage. Cara took his arm again, gentle this time.

Morath did not sleep at the avenue Bourdonnais that night. He returned to his apartment in the rue d'Artois, then left early the following morning to catch the Nord Express up to Antwerp. This was a no-nonsense train; the conductors brisk and serious, the seats filled with soldiers of commerce on the march along the ancient trade route. Beyond the rhythm of the wheels on the track, the only sound in Morath's compartment was the rustle of newsprint as a turned-over page of *Figaro* was snapped into place.

In Vienna, he read, the *Anschluss* was to be formalized by a plebiscite – the Austrian voter now understanding that the alternative to saying *Ja* was getting his teeth knocked out. This was, Hitler explained in a speech on 9 April, God's work.

There is a higher ordering, and we are all nothing else than its agents. When on March 9 Herr Schuschnigg broke his agreement then in that second I felt that now the call of Providence had come to me. And that which then took place in three days was only conceivable as the fulfilment of the wish and will of Providence. I would now give thanks to Him who let me return to my homeland in order that I might now lead it into the German Reich! Tomorrow may every German recognize the hour and measure its import and bow in humility before the Almighty, who in a few weeks has wrought a miracle upon us.

So, Austria ceased to exist.

And the Almighty, not quite satisfied with His work, had determined that the fuddled Doktor Schuschnigg should be locked up, guarded by the Gestapo, in a small room on the fifth floor of the Hotel Metropole.

For the moment, Morath couldn't stand any more. He put the paper down and stared out the window at tilled Flemish earth. The reflection in the glass was Morath the executive – very good dark suit, sober tie, perfect shirt. He was travelling north for a meeting with Monsieur Antoine Hooryckx, better known, in business circles, as 'Hooryckx, the Soap King of Antwerp'.

In 1928, Nicholas Morath had become half-owner of the Agence Courtmain, a small and reasonably prosperous advertising agency.

This was a sudden, extraordinary gift from Uncle Janos. Morath had been summoned to lunch on one of the restaurant-boats, and, while cruising slowly beneath the bridges of the Seine, informed of his elevated status. 'You get it all eventually,' Uncle Janos said, 'so you may as well have the use of it now.' Polanyi's wife and children would be provided for, Morath knew, but the real money, the thousand kilometres of wheatfield in the Puszta with villages and peasants, the small bauxite mine and the large portfolio of Canadian railroad stock, would come to him, along with the title, when his uncle died.

But Morath was in no hurry, none of that 'race you up the stairs, Grampa' stuff for him. Polanyi would live a long time, that was fine with his nephew. The convenient part was that, with a steady income assured, if Count Polanyi needed Nicholas to help him out, he was available. Meanwhile, Morath's share of the profits kept him in apéritifs and mistresses and a slightly shabby apartment at a reasonably *bonne adresse.*

The Agence Courtmain had a very *bonne adresse* indeed but, as an advertising agency, it had first of all to advertise its own success. Which it did, along with various lawyers, stock brokerages and Lebanese bankers, by renting an absurdly expensive suite of offices in a building on the avenue Matignon. More than likely owned, Courtmain theorized – the title of the *société anonyme* gave no indication – 'by an Auvergnat peasant with goatshit in his hat'.

Sitting across from Morath, Courtmain lowered his newspaper and glanced at his watch.

'On time?' Morath said.

Courtmain nodded. He was, like Morath, very well dressed. Emile Courtmain was not much over forty. He had white hair, thin lips, grey eyes, and a cold, distant personality found magnetic by virtually everybody. He smiled rarely, stared openly, said little. He was either brilliant or stupid, nobody knew, and it didn't seem terribly important. What sort of life he may have had after seven in the evening was completely unknown. One of the copywriters claimed that after everybody left the office Courtmain hung himself up in the closet and waited for daylight.

'We aren't going to the plant, are we?' Morath said.

'No.'

Morath was grateful. The Soap King had taken them to his plant, a year earlier, just making sure they didn't forget who they were, who he was, and what made the world go round. They didn't forget. Huge, bubbling vats of animal fat, mouldering piles of bones, kettles of lye boiling gently over a low flame. The last ride for most of the cart and carriage horses in northern Belgium. 'Just give your behind a good wash with that!' Hooryckx cried out, emerging like an industrial devil from a cloud of yellow steam.

They arrived in Antwerp on time and climbed into a cab outside the station. Courtmain gave the driver complicated instructions – Hooryckx's office was down a crooked street at the edge of the dockside neighbourhood, a few rooms in a genteel but crumbling building. 'The world tells me I'm a rich man,' Hooryckx would say. 'Then it snatches everything I have.'

In the back of the cab, Courtmain rummaged in his briefcase and produced a bottle of toilet water called Zouave; a soldier with fierce moustaches stared imperiously from the label. This was also a Hooryckx product, though not nearly so popular as the soap. Courtmain unscrewed the cap, splashed some on his face, and gave the bottle to Morath. 'Ahh,' he said, as the heavy fragrance filled the air, 'the finest peg-house in Istanbul.'

Hooryckx was delighted to see them. 'The boys from Paris!' He had a vast belly and a hairstyle like a cartoon character that sticks his finger in a light socket. Courtmain took a coloured drawing from his briefcase. Hooryckx, with a wink, told his secretary to go and get his advertising manager. 'My daughter's husband,' he said. The man showed up a few minutes later, Courtmain laid the drawing on a table and they all gathered around it.

In a royal blue sky, two white swans flew above the legend *Deux Cygnes* . . . This was something new. In 1937, their magazine advertising had shown an attractive mother, wearing an apron, showing a bar of *Deux Cygnes* to her little girl.

'Well,' said Hooryckx. 'What do the dots mean?'

'Two swans . . .' Courtmain said, letting his voice trail away. 'No words can describe the delicacy, the loveliness of the moment.'

'Shouldn't they be swimming?' Hooryckx said.

Courtmain reached into his briefcase and brought out the swimming version. His copy chief had warned him this would happen. Now the swans made ripples in a pond as they floated past a clump of reeds.

Hooryckx compressed his lips.

'I like them flying,' the son-in-law said. 'More chic, no?'

'How about it?' Hooryckx said to Morath.

'It's sold to women,' Morath said.

'So?'

'It's what they feel when they use it.'

Hooryckx stared, back and forth, from one image to the other. 'Of course,' he said, 'swans sometimes fly.'

After a moment, Morath nodded. *Of course.*

Courtmain brought forth another version. Swans flying, this time, in a sky turned aquamarine.

'Phoo,' Hooryckx said.

Courtmain whipped it away.

The son-in-law suggested a cloud, a subtle one, no more than a wash in the blue field. Courtmain thought it over. 'Very expensive,' he said.

'But an excellent idea, Louis,' Hooryckx said. 'I can see it.'

Hooryckx tapped his fingers on the desk. 'It's good when they fly, but I miss that curve in the neck.'

'We can try it,' Courtmain said.

Hooryckx stared for a few seconds. 'No, better this way.'

After lunch, Courtmain went off to see a prospective client and Morath headed for the central commercial district – to a shop called Homme du Monde, Man about Town, its window occupied by suave mannequins in tuxedos. Much too warm inside, where a clerk was on her knees with a mouth full of pins, fitting a customer for a pair of evening trousers.

'Madame Golsztahn?' Morath said.

'A moment, monsieur.'

A curtain at the rear of the shop was moved aside and Madame Golsztahn appeared. 'Yes?'

'I came up from Paris this morning.'

'Oh, it's you,' she said. 'Come through.'

Behind the curtain, a man was pressing trousers, working a foot pedal that produced a loud hiss and a puff of steam. Madame Golsztahn led Morath down a long rack of tuxedos and tail-coats to a battered desk, its cubby holes packed with receipts. They had never met before but Morath knew who she was. She'd been famous for love affairs, in her younger days in Budapest, the subject of poems in little journals, the cause of two or three scandals and a rumoured suicide from the Elizabeth Bridge. He felt it, standing next to her. A ruined face and stark, brick-red hair above a dancer's body in a tight black sweater and skirt. *Like the current in a river.* She gave him a tart smile, read him like a book, wouldn't have minded, then swept the hair back off her forehead. There was a radio playing, Schumann maybe, violins, something exceptionally gooey, and, every few seconds, a loud hiss from the steam press. 'So then,' she said, before anything actually happened.

'Should we go to a café?'

'Here would be best.'

They sat side by side at the desk, she lit a cigarette and held it between her lips, squinting as the smoke drifted into her eyes. She found one of the receipts, turned it over and smoothed it flat with her hands. Morath could see a few letters and numbers, some circled. 'Mnemonics,' she said. 'Now all I have to do is decipher it.'

'All right,' she said at last, 'here is your uncle's friend in Budapest, to be known as "a senior police official". He states that "as of the tenth of March, evidence points to intense activity among all sectors of the *nyilas* community".' *Neelosh* – her voice was determinedly neutral. It meant the Arrow Cross, pure Hitlerite fascists; the EME, which specialized in bomb attacks against Jewish women; the *Kereszteny Kurzus*, Christian Course, which meant so much more than 'Christian', and various others, great and small.

' "On the fifth of March," ' she said, ' "a fire in a shed in the Eighth District, *Csikago*" ' – Chicago, as in factories and gangsters – ' "police inspectors were called when rifles and pistols were found to have been stored there." '

She coughed, covering her mouth with the back of her hand, and rested the cigarette among a line of brown scars on the edge of the desk. ' "An Arrow Cross member, by trade a cabinet-maker, detained for defacing public property, was found in possession of the home telephone number of the German economic attaché. A police informer in Szeged, murdered on the sixth of March. Eight young men, members of the *Turul* student association, observed carrying out a surveillance of the army barracks at Arad. A furniture mover's truck, parked in an alley by the south railway station, was searched by police on information received from the estranged wife of the driver. A Berthier heavy machine gun was found, with eighty-five belts of ammunition." '

'I'm going to have to make notes,' Morath said.

Golsztahn's eyes met his. 'You aren't going anywhere, are you?' She paused. 'East?'

Morath shook his head. 'Just to Paris. Tonight.'

She handed him an unused rental receipt. 'Use the back. The police official notes that "a report of these events has been routed, in the customary way, to the office of Colonel Sombor in the Hungarian legation in Paris".'

'A minute,' Morath said. He had almost caught up Sombor had something to do with security at the legation – the same name as the head of the secret police, taken from a town in the south of Hungary. This usually meant Hungarians of German, Saxon, ancestry.

When he looked up, she continued. ' "An Arrow Cross informant reports that several of his colleagues are preparing to send their families out of the city during the first week in May. And . . ." ' She peered closely at the top of the receipt. 'What?' she said, then, 'Oh. "Two known agents of the German intelligence service, the SD, had in their room at the Hotel Gellert photographs of the architectural blueprints of the Water District police station and the Palace of Justice." The police official states finally that there are further instances of this kind of activity, some three dozen, that point to a political action in the near future.'

It was quiet on the evening train to Paris. Courtmain worked, jotting notes on a tablet, and Morath read the newspaper. The leading stories continued to focus on Austria and the *Anschluss*. The British politician Churchill, a member of the Tory Opposition, was quoted by a political columnist on the editorial page, from a speech given in Parliament at the end of February: 'Austria has now been laid in thrall, and we do not know whether Czechoslovakia will suffer a similar fate.'

Well, somebody will.

Morath touched the receipt in his pocket. Golsztahn had burned hers in a coffee cup, then poked the ashes apart with the end of a pencil.

Of all of them, perhaps Otto Adler loved Paris the most. He had arrived in the winter of 1937, installed his life – a wife, four children, two cats and an editorial office – in a big, draughty old house in St Germain-en-Laye where, from a window in his study, he could look out over miles of Parisian rooftops. *Paris – the best idea mankind ever had.*

'Third time lucky!' was the way his wife put it. Otto Adler had grown up in Koenigsberg, the capital of East Prussia, in the Baltic German community. After university in Berlin, he came home a Marxist, then spent the decade of his thirties becoming a Social Democrat, a journalist, and a pauper. 'When you are that poor,' he'd say, 'the only thing left for you is to start a magazine.' So, *Die Aussicht, The Outlook,* was born. Not so popular, it turned out, in the tight, *Volksdeutsch* world of Koenigsberg. 'This failed postcard painter from Linz will destroy German culture,' he said of Hitler in 1933. Two broken windows for that, his wife cursed in the butcher's shop, and, soon enough, a big, draughty old apartment in Vienna.

Otto Adler fitted in much better there. 'Otto, darling, I think you were born to be Viennese,' his wife said. He had a round, hairless, rosy face, a beaming smile – he wished the world well – one of those big-hearted people who can be benign and angry at once and laugh at himself into the bargain. Somehow, he kept publishing the magazine. 'We should probably call it *The Ox*, it plods along in all weathers.' And in time, a little Viennese money – from progressive bankers, Jewish businessmen, union leaders – began to come his way. As *Die Aussicht* gained credibility, he managed to obtain an article by one of the gods of German literary culture, Karl Kraus, the savage, brilliant satirist whose disciples – readers, students – were known as *Krausianer*.

In 1937, *Die Aussicht* published a brief *reportage* by an Italian journalist, the wife of a diplomat, who'd been present at one of Hermann Goering's infamous dinners at Schorfheide, his hunting lodge. The usual Nazi merriment, with the soup and the fish, but before the main course arrived, Goering left the table and returned wearing a rawhide shirt, with a bearskin thrown over his shoulders – a warrior costume from the old Teutonic tribes. Not nearly, of course, enough. Goering was armed with a spear, and led a pair of hairy bison, harnessed in chains, around and around the room while the guests roared. Still not enough. The entertainment concluded with the mating of the bison. 'A party to remember,' it said in *Die Aussicht*. Adler's children were expelled from school, a swastika chalked on his door, the maid quit, the neighbours ceased to say, '*Gruss Gött.*'

It was a big, draughty old house they found in Geneva. But nobody was very happy there. What the *Volksdeutsch* and the Austrians did with party operatives, the Swiss did with clerks. Nobody actually said anything about the magazine; he could, apparently, publish whatever he wanted in democratic Switzerland, but life was a spider's web of rules and regulations that controlled mailing permits, alien residence, and, it seemed to Adler, the very air they breathed.

It was a little quiet around the dinner table when Adler informed the family they had to move. 'A necessary adventure,' he said, beaming away. Under the table, his wife put her hand on his knee. So, December of 'thirty-seven, Paris. St Germain-en-Laye was a classic of the exile's geography, it turned out, a time-honoured refuge for princes unwelcome in many lands. There was a grand Promenade Anglais where one could walk for hours, just right for a bittersweet contemplation of the lost crown, castle, or homeland. Adler found a sympathetic printer, made contacts in the community of liberal, German émigrés and went back to work hammering the fascists and the Bolsheviks. Such was the destiny of the Social Democrat, and who was that man in the raincoat by the newspaper kiosk?

Meanwhile, Adler fell in love with the public gardens of Paris. 'What sort of lunatic takes a train to go to the park?' The kind who filled his briefcase with books; Schnitzler, Weininger, Mann, maybe von Hoffmansthal, two pens, and a cheese sandwich, then sat in the Jardin du Luxembourg and watched the dappled light of the plane trees playing on the gravel path. A few centimes to the old dragon who kept watch on the chairs and one could spend the afternoon in a painting.

At first he went in nice weather, later in light rain. It became his habit. As time went by, as the spring of 1938 worked its way towards whatever summer had in store, Otto Adler, fountain pen scratching out a new editorial, or, for a moment, just snoozing, was almost always to be found in the park.

The note from the Baroness Frei invited 'My dearest Nicholas' to call at her house at five in the afternoon on 16 April. Morath took a taxi to the Sèvres-Babylone Métro stop and from there walked to the rue de Villon.

Buried deep in a maze of narrow lanes that crisscrossed the border between the sixth and seventh arrondissements it was, like paradise everywhere, damned hard to find. Taxi drivers thumbed through their city directories, then sped off to the rue Francois Villon, named for the medieval robber-poet, in a distant neighbourhood where, on arrival, it was immediately clear to both driver and patron that this was not the right street *at all.*

The one true rue de Villon could be entered only through a vaulted alley – the impasse Villon – a tunnel of perpetual dusk that dared the courageous *automobiliste* to try his luck. It could sometimes be done, depending on the model and year of the machine, and was always a matter of centimetres, but it did not *look* like it could be done. The alley gave no indication of what lay beyond it; the casual passer-by tended to do exactly that, pass by, while the truly self-confident tourist peered defiantly down the tunnel and then went away.

On the other side, however, light from heaven poured down on a row of seventeenth-century houses, protected by wrought-iron palings, that dead-ended at a garden wall: 3 rue de Villon to 9 rue de Villon in a sequence whose logic was known only to God and the postman. In the evening, the tiny street was lit by Victorian gas lamps which made soft shadows of a vine that twisted its way along the top of the garden wall. The garden belonged to number three – a faint impression of the number could be found on a rusty metal door, the width of a carriage – which was owned by the Baroness Lillian Frei. She did not know her neighbours. They did not know her.

A maid answered the door and led Morath to the garden. Sitting at the garden table, the baroness put her cheek up to be kissed. 'Dearest love,' she said. 'I am so happy to see you.' Morath's heart warmed; he smiled like a five-year-old and kissed her with pleasure.

The Baroness Frei was possibly sixty. She was bent over in a lifelong crouch, one side of her back humped far above her shoulder. She had shimmering blue eyes and soft, snow-white hair and a radiance like the sun. She was, at the moment, as always, surrounded by a pack of Viszla dogs – not one of which could Morath distinguish from another but which, as the baroness liked to tell her guests, belonged to a vast, capricious, bumptious family who lived out an unending romantic epic in the house and garden. Korto, bred to Fina, loved Malya, his daughter by the gallant and long-departed Moselda. Of course, for the integrity of the line, they could never 'be together', so, in heat, the exquisite Malya was sent to live in the kitchen whilst poor Korto lay about on the garden gravel with his chin slumped atop his forepaws, or stood on his hind legs, peered myopically through the windows and barked until the maid threw a rag at him.

Now they stormed around Morath's legs and he bent to run his hands along the satin skin of their sides.

'Yes,' said the baroness, 'here's your friend Nicholas.'

The Viszlas were fast. Morath got a wet kiss on the eye and never saw it coming.

'Korto!'

'No, no. I'm flattered.'

The dog smacked his forepaws against the ground.

'What, Korto, you want to hunt?'

Morath roughed him up a little and he mewed with pleasure.

'Go to the forest?'

Korto danced sideways – *chase me.*

'A bear? That would be best?'

'He would not run away,' the baroness said. Then, to the dog, 'Would you?'

Korto wagged his tail. Morath stood up, then joined the baroness at the table.

'Pure courage,' she said. 'And the last five minutes of his life would be the best.' The maid approached, pushing a glass-topped cart with a squeaky wheel. She set a tray of pastries on the table, poured a cup of tea and set it down by Morath. Silver tongs in hand, the baroness looked over the pastries. 'Let's see . . .'

A doughy roll, folded over itself, with walnuts and raisins. The lightly sugared crust was still warm from the oven.

'And so?'

'Like Ruszwurm. Better.'

For that lie, a gracious nod from the baroness. Below the table, many dogs. 'You must wait, darlings,' the baroness said. Her smile was tolerant, infinitely kind. Morath had once visited at midmorning, counted twenty pieces of buttered toast on the baroness's breakfast tray.

'I was in Budapest last week,' she said.

'How was it?'

'Tense, I should say, underneath all the usual commotion. I saw your mother and sister.'

'How are they?'

'They're well. Teresa's oldest girl may go to school in Switzerland.'

'Maybe for the best.'

'Maybe. They send you their love. You will write to them.'

'I will.'

'Your mother told me that Eva Zameny has left her husband.' She and Morath had, long ago, been engaged to marry.

'I am sorry.'

The baroness's expression indicated she wasn't. 'For the best. Her husband was a hound. And he gambled terribly.'

A bell – the kind worked by pulling a cord – rang in the house. 'That will be your uncle.'

There were other guests. The women in hats with veils, bolero jackets, and the black and white polka-dot dresses that were popular in springtime. Former citizens of the Dual Monarchy, the guests spoke the Austrian dialect with High German flourishes, Hungarian and French, shifting effortlessly between languages when only a very particular expression would say what they meant. The men were well barbered and used good cologne. Two of them wore decorations, one a black and gold ribbon beneath a medal marked KUK – *Kaiser und Königlich*, meaning 'Imperial and Regal', the Dual Monarchy – the other awarded for service in the Russo-Polish War in 1920. A refined group, polite and attentive, it was hard to tell who was rich and who wasn't.

Morath and Polanyi stood by a large boxwood at a corner of the garden wall, holding cups and saucers.

'Christ, I'd like a drink,' Polanyi said.

'We can go somewhere, after this.'

'I'm afraid I can't. I have cocktails with the Finns, dinner with the Venezuelan foreign minister. Flores, up in the sixteenth.'

Morath nodded, sympathetic.

'No, not Flores.' Polanyi compressed his lips, annoyed at the lapse. 'Montemayor, I should've said. Flores is, pfft.'

'Any news of home?'

'Nothing good. It's as you described, in the notes you made in Antwerp. And worse.'

'Another Austria?'

'Not quite. We are not *Ein Volk*, one people. But the pressure is growing. *You will be our allies, or else.*' He sighed, shook his head. 'Now comes the real nightmare, Nicholas, the one where the monster walks towards you but you can't run away, you're frozen in place. I think, more and more, that these people, this German aggression, will finish us, sooner or later. The Austrians pulled us into war in 1914 – perhaps some day somebody will tell me precisely *why* we had to do all that. And now it begins again. In the next day or so, the newspapers will announce that Hungary has come out in favour of the *Anschluss*. In return, Hitler will guarantee our borders. Quid pro quo, very tidy.'

'You believe it?'

'No.' He took a sip of tea. 'I'll amend that. To "maybe". Hitler is intimidated by Horthy, because Horthy is everything Hitler always wanted to be. Old nobility, aide-de-camp to Franz Josef, war hero, polo player, married into the cream of society. And they both paint. In fact, Horthy has lasted longer than any other leader in Europe. That has to count for something, Nicholas, right?'

Polanyi's face showed exactly what it counted for.

'So the current unrest . . . will be dealt with?'

'Not easily, and maybe not at all. We're facing insurrection. Conservatives out, fascists in, liberals *au poteau.*' The phrase from 1789 – to the guillotine.

Morath was surprised. In Budapest, when the Arrow Cross men dressed up in their black uniforms and strutted about the city, the police forced them to strip and sent them home in their underwear. 'What about the police? The army?'

'Uncertain.'

'Then what?'

'If Daranyi means to stay as premier, he'll have to give them something. Or there will be blood in the streets. So, at the moment, we find ourselves negotiating. And we will be forced, among other things, to do favours.'

'For whom?'

'Important people.'

Morath felt it coming. Polanyi, no doubt, meant him to feel it. He set his cup and saucer on a table, reached in his pocket, took a cigarette from a tortoiseshell case and lit it with a silver lighter.

The last nights of April, but no sign of spring. The weather blew hard across the Métro staircase, wind and rain and fog with a taste of factory smoke. Morath held his overcoat closed and walked next to the buildings. Down a dark street, down another, then a sharp left and a blinking, blue neon sigh, *Balalaika.* The cossack doorman, with sheepskin tunic and fierce moustache, peered out from the shelter of the doorway, in his hand a black umbrella in the final hours of life on a windy night.

The doorman growled good evening, his Russian accent thick and melodramatic. 'Welcome, sir, to Balalaika, the show is now just starting.'

Inside, thick air; cigarettes glowed in the darkness. Red plush walls and a stunning hat-check girl. Morath gave her a generous tip and kept his coat. Here, too, they wore their decorations. The maitre d', six and a half feet tall with a sash and high boots, had a bronze medal pinned to his blouse, earned in service as mercenary and palace guardsman to King Zog of Albania.

Morath went to the bar and sat at the far end. From there he caught a glimpse of the stage. The gypsy trio was sawing away in sentimental agony, a dancer in sheer pantaloons and halter showed, in the blue klieg lights, just exactly what her faithless lover was giving up, while her partner stood to one side, hands clasped in fruitless longing, a red light bulb in his trousers going on and off in time to the music.

Morath ordered a Polish vodka and, when it arrived, offered the barman a cigarette and lit it for him. He was a short, compact man with narrow eyes deeply lined at the corners, from laughing, maybe, or squinting into the distance. Beneath his red jacket he wore a shirt washed so often it was the pastel of an unknown colour.

'Are you Boris?' Morath said.

'Now and then.'

'Well, Boris, I have a friend . . .' A little cloud of irony hung over the phrase and the barman smiled appreciatively. 'He was in trouble, he came to you for help.'

'When was that?'

'Last year, around this time. His girlfriend needed a doctor.'

The barman shrugged. A thousand customers, a thousand stories. 'I can't say I remember.'

Morath understood, a bad memory was a good idea. 'Now, it's another friend. A different kind of problem.'

'Yes?'

'A passport problem.'

The barman used his rag to wipe down the zinc surface, then paused and had a good look at Morath. 'Where are you from, if you don't mind my asking?'

'Budapest.'

'Emigré?'

'Not really. I came here after the war. I'm in business here.'

'You were in the war?'

'Yes.'

'Where was that?'

'Galicia. Up into Volhynia for a time . . .'

'Then back to Galicia.' The barman was laughing as he finished Morath's sentence. 'Oh yes,' he said, '*that* shithouse.'

'You were there?'

'Mm. Likely we shot at each other. Then, autumn of 'seventeen, my regiment took a walk. Same again?'

'Please.'

The clear liquor came exactly to the rim.

'Will you join me?'

The barman poured himself a vodka and raised his glass. 'To poor shooting, I guess.' He drank in the Russian manner – with grace, but all gone.

From the nightclub tables, rhythmic clapping, growing louder as the patrons grew bolder, some of them yelling 'Hey!' on the beat. The male dancer, squatting on the stage with his arms folded across his chest, was kicking his legs out.

'Passports,' the barman said, suddenly gloomy. 'You can get into real trouble fooling with that. They lock you up, here, if they catch you. It goes on, of course, mostly among the refugees, the Jews and the political exiles. Once you get run out of Germany, you aren't legal anywhere unless you've got a visa. That takes time, and money, you can't afford to be in a hurry. But you are – with the Gestapo after you, you have to do whatever it takes. So you sneak out. Now, you're a "Stateless Person". You slip into Czechoslovakia, or Switzerland, hide out for a week if you know the right rooming house, then they catch you and send you across the Austrian border. After a week or two in jail, the customs officers walk you back across the frontier, at night, in the woods, and the whole thing starts again. Here it's a little better. If you stay out of trouble, the *flics* don't care that much, unless you try to work.' He shook his head slowly, in sorrow.

'How did you manage?'

'Nansen. We were lucky. Because we were the first wave, we got the League of Nations passports, we got the work permits, we got the jobs the French didn't want. That was 1920 or so. Revolution over, civil war winding down, then the Cheka comes around. "We hear you were a friend of Ivanov." So, time to run. Next, when Mussolini's boys got to work, came the Italians. Then luck was pretty much the same as ours – you used to be a professor of theoretical physics, now you're a real waiter. *Thank God* you're a waiter. Because, starting in 'thirty-three, here come the Germans. They have passports, most of them, but no work permits. They peddle, sell needles and thread from little suitcases on the boulevards, work the tourists, starve, beg, sit in the offices of the refugee organizations. It's the same for the Spaniards, running from Franco, and now we have the Austrians. No papers, no work permits, no money.'

'This friend, Boris, has money.'

The barman had known that all along. After a time he said, 'You're a detective, right?'

'With my accent?'

'Well, maybe you are, maybe you aren't. Either way, I'm not the man you want. You have to go where the refugees are, to the Café Madine, the Grosse Marie, places like that.'

'A question? Personal question.'

'I'm an open book.'

'Why did *you* run?'

'Because they were chasing me,' he said, laughing again.

Morath waited.

'I was a poet. Also, to be honest, a criminal. When they came after me, I was never really sure which one it was.'

The Café Madine was in the eleventh arrondissement, just off the place de la République, between a butcher that sold *halal* meat to Arabs and kosher meat to Jews, and a repair shop for musical instruments called Szczwerna. It was easy, maybe too easy, to make contact at Madine. He showed up in the late afternoon, stood at the counter, ordered a beer, stared out at the throbbing street life of the quarter. A man tried to sell him a ring, Morath looked it over – he was there to buy, let them see a buyer. A small, red stone set in gold, University of Heidelberg, 1922.

'How much?'

'Worth three hundred, more or less.'

'I'll think about it. Actually, I'm here because a friend of mine in Paris lost his passport.'

'Go to *Préfecture.*'

From Morath a look, *if only one could.* 'Or?'

'Or nothing.'

Back the next day. Ten in the morning, deserted, silent. A shaft of sunlight, a sleeping cat, the *patron* wore his glasses down on his nose. He took his time with Morath's *café au lait*, there was no skin on the boiled milk, the coffee was powerful and fresh, and he sent his little boy off to the bakery to get fresh bread for a *tartine.*

The contact was a tough old bird, once upon a time a timber

merchant in the Ukraine, though Morath had no way of knowing that. He tipped his hat, asked Morath to join him at a table. 'You're the fellow with the passport difficulties?'

'Friend of mine.'

'Naturally.'

'What's the market like, these days?'

'Seller's market, obviously.'

'He needs the real thing.'

'The real thing.' Maybe in other times he would have found it funny enough to laugh at. Morath got it, he thought. *Borders, papers, nations –* made-up stuff, politicians' lies.

'As much as possible.'

'A man who buys the best.'

Morath agreed.

'Twenty-five hundred francs. A figure like that scares you, perhaps.'

'No. For good value, you pay.'

'Very reasonable, this gentleman.' He spoke to an invisible friend. Then he told Morath where to be, and when.

Two days later, a Friday afternoon at the Louvre. Morath had to work to find the right room – up the stairs here in order to go down the stairs there, past Napoleon's swag from Egypt, past rooms of small, puzzling Roman things, around a corner and down an endless corridor of British schoolboys. At last, *the room with the Ingres portrait.* A luminous nude, seated at a table, her back curved and soft.

A man rose from a bench against the wall, smiled, and spread his hands in welcome. He knew who Morath was, had probably looked him over at the café. A handsome gentleman, portly, with a Vandyke beard and a tweed suit. Something like, Morath thought, the owner of a prosperous art gallery. He had, apparently, a colleague, standing on the other side of the room and staring at a painting, hands clasped behind his back. Morath saw them exchange a glance. White as chalk, this man, as though missing a lifelong beard. He wore a black Homburg set square on a shaved head.

The man who looked like an art dealer sat next to Morath on the wooden bench. 'I'm told that you are seeking a document of the finest quality,' he said. He spoke French like an educated German.

'I am.'

'That would be a corpse.'

'All right.'

'You are buying from the family of the deceased, naturally, and they will want twenty-five hundred francs. For our work, for the change of identity, it is another thousand francs. Can we agree?'

'Yes.'

The art dealer opened a newspaper, revealing a report of a polo match in the Bois de Boulogne and a passport in a cardboard folder. 'The family wishes to sell immediately. The nationality of the passport is Roumanian, and has seventeen months to run.' The head in the identification photograph was of a man in middle years, formal, self-satisfied, his dark moustache carefully clipped and groomed. Below it, the name: Andreas Panea.

'I will pay you now, if you like.'

'Half now. Half when we give you the finished product. Your photo goes in place of the deceased, the raised lettering on the photo is provided by the technician. The physical description is washed out and your own put in. The one thing that can't be changed is the place of birth – that's on the seal. So, the bearer of the document will be called this name, is of Roumanian nationality and was born in Cluj.'

'What happened to him?'

The art dealer stared for a moment. *Why are you concerned with that?* Then said, 'Nothing dramatic.' And, a moment later, 'He came to the end of caring. It is quite common.'

'Here's the photograph,' Morath said.

The art dealer was mildly surprised. It wasn't Morath. A man in his twenties, a hard, bony face made even more severe by steel-rimmed spectacles and hair cut back to a colourless inch and brushed flat. A student, perhaps. At best, that. Given a passing grade by his professors whether he attended the lectures or not. The art dealer turned the photo over. Stamped on the back was the name of the photography studio, in Serbo-Croatian, and the word 'Zagreb'.

The art dealer signalled to his friend, who joined them on the bench, took the photograph and studied it for a long minute, then said something in Yiddish. Morath, who spoke fluent German, would ordinarily have got the sense of it but this was argot of some kind, spoken rapidly, the tone sarcastic.

The art dealer nodded, almost smiled.

'Can the bearer work?' Morath asked.

'In Roumania. Not here. Here he could apply to work, but . . .'

'And, if it should be checked with the Roumanian authority?'

'Why would it be checked?'

Morath didn't answer.

The man wearing the Homburg took a stub of pencil from his pocket and asked a question, again in Yiddish.

'He wants to know, how tall, how much does he weigh?'

Morath gave him the numbers – lean, shorter than average.

'Eyes?'

'Grey. The hair is blond.'

'Identifying marks?'

'None.'

'Profession?'

'Student.'

The photograph was put away. The art dealer turned a page of the newspaper to reveal an envelope. 'Take this to the washroom down the hall. Put seventeen hundred and fifty francs in here, tuck the newspaper under your arm and leave the museum. Use the exit on the rue Coligny. Stand on the top step and wait for a few minutes. Then, tomorrow at noon, go back there. You'll see somebody you recognize, follow that person and the exchange will be made someplace where you can have a good look at what you're buying.'

Morath did as he was told. Counted hundred-franc notes into the envelope, then waited at the entrance. Ten minutes later, a woman waved and came towards him, smiling, trotting up the museum steps. She was well dressed, wore pearl earrings and white gloves. She kissed him lightly on the cheek, slid the newspaper from beneath his arm, and left in a waiting taxi.

The night before the train.

It had become something of a tradition for Nicky and Cara, a *Kama Sutra* evening – farewell my love, something to remember. They sat around the bedroom in candlelight and drank a bottle of wine. Cara wore black underwear, Morath a dressing gown. Sometimes they played records – Morath owned two kinds, Ellington and Lee Wiley – or listened to '*les beeg bands*' on the radio. One night they'd journeyed up to Pigalle, where Cara waited in a taxi while Morath bought picture books. Then they'd hurried back to the avenue Bourdonnais and looked at the pictures. Sepia couples, trios, quartets, heavy women with wide hips and soft smiles, the book printed in Sofia.

Cara teased him, sometimes, with 'Tales of the Convent School'. She'd spent three years in such a place, on a grand estate outside Buenos Aires. 'It was just as you would suppose, Nicky,' she'd say, a little breathless and wide-eyed. 'All these girls, beauty of every type. Dark. Fair. Passionate, shy, some of them so naïve they knew *nothing*, not even what to *touch*. And all of them locked up together at night. Imagine!'

He did.

But, closer to the truth, he suspected, were the daylight recollections of 'cold hands and smelly feet', and the diabolical nuns who forced them to learn, among other things, French. It was the only language she and Morath had in common, but Cara couldn't forgive. 'God, how they terrified us,' she'd say. Would clap her hands – as the teaching nun apparently did – and sing out, '*Traduction, les jeunes filles!*' Next they would be confronted by some unfathomable horror, a grammar monster, and allowed only five minutes for translation.

'I remember once,' Cara told him, 'who was it? Sister Modeste. She wrote on the board: "What if they should never have united themselves in that, over there?"' Cara had started to laugh, remembering the moment. 'Panic! *Se joindre*, a homicidal verb. It's much simpler in Spanish. And then my friend Elena, after the sister wrote out the answer, leaned across the aisle and whispered, "Well, I'm certainly glad I know how to say *that*!"'

Morath poured out the last of the wine, Cara finished hers, put the glass on the floor and wound herself around him. He kissed her, reached over and undid her bra, she shrugged her shoulders, he tossed it on a chair. Some time later, he hooked a finger in the waistband of her panties and slid them down her legs, slow and easy, until she pointed her feet so he could get them off.

Then, for a time, they lay still. She took his hand and held it against her breast – she wouldn't let him move – as though this was sufficient, no need to go further. He wondered what might be nice to do, his mind wandering idly through the repertoire. Was she thinking about that? Or something else? *He loves me*? Morath opened his eyes and saw that she was smiling.

All very good to think about, in the morning, cast adrift in the cold world. She didn't wake up when he left, sleeping with her mouth open, a hand trapped under the pillow. Somehow he could look at her and know she'd made love the night before. He almost dozed, as the train left the empty streets and moved through the countryside. *Her tits, her bum, looking up at her, looking down, fucking*. She whispered sometimes, talking to herself. He could never actually hear what she was saying.

It was a very slow train, that left at dawn. Going east it crawled, as if it really didn't want to get there. It would go through Metz and Saarbrucken, then on to Wurzburg, where passengers could change for the train to Prague, with connections to Brno, to Kosice, and to Uzhorod.

*

Eastern France, a lost season, not winter, not spring. The sky was low and heavy, the wind colder than it should have been, the train crawling endlessly through dead, weedy fields.

A pleasant countryside, once upon a time, small farms and villages. Then 1914 came along and war turned it into grey mud. It would never really heal, people said. A few years earlier, when the snow melted, a farmer had come upon what had, evidently, once been a trench. Where a squad of French soldiers, heading into battle, had been suddenly buried by the explosion of an enormous artillery shell. Then, years later, with the spring thaw, the farmer saw a dozen bayonet points thrust out of the earth, still in marching order.

Morath lit a cigarette and went back to reading – Nicholas Bartha's *Land of the Kazars*, published in Hungarian in 1901.

The sovereign stag should not be disturbed in its family affairs. What is a Ruthenian compared with it? Only a peasant. The hunting period lasts two weeks. For this pastime, 70,000 Ruthenians must be doomed to starvation by the army of the officials. The deer and the wild boar destroy the corn, the potatoes and the clover of the Ruthenians (the whole harvest of his tiny lot of half an acre). Their whole yearly work is destroyed. The people sow and the deer of the estate harvest. It is easy to say the peasant should complain. But where and to whom? Those who have the power he sees always together. The village chief, the deputy sheriff, the sheriff, the district judge, the tax officer, the forester, the steward and the manager, all are men of the same education, of the same social pleasures, and of the same standard. From whom could he hope for justice?

When Morath had learned he'd be going to Ruthenia, he'd borrowed the book from the Baroness Frei's enormous library – purchased by the baron from Hungarian institutions that fell, after 1918, within the borders of other nations. 'Saved from the fire,' he'd say. Morath smiled at the memory of him. A short, fat man with mutton-chops who never knew himself just how much money he made with his 'schemes'. For Morath's sixteenth birthday, the baron had taken him on an 'educational ramble' to the casino at Monte Carlo. Bought him a pair of diamond cufflinks and a cadaverous blonde.

He'd sat by the baron's side at the *chemin de fer* table and watched him write, at four in the morning, a cheque with an alarming number of zeros. Pale but smiling, the baron stood, lit a cigar, winked at Morath and headed off towards the marble staircase. Ten minutes later, a black-suited *fonctionnaire* floated to his side, cleared his throat and said, 'The

Baron Frei has gone into the garden.' Morath hesitated, then stood and went quickly into the casino garden, where the baron was discovered urinating on a rosebush. He would die, ten years later, of a tropical disease contracted in the jungles of Brazil, where he'd gone to buy industrial diamonds.

Morath glanced up at the luggage rack above the seat, making sure of his leather satchel. Inside, a passport he'd received at the Louvre, sewn into the lining of a wool jacket. *Pavlo*, Polanyi called the man, a man he said he'd never met. *The student.* Who had got himself into the town of Uzhorod and couldn't get out. 'A favour for a friend,' Polanyi said.

In midafternoon, the train slowed for the Moselle bridges and the station at Metz, the buildings dark with soot from the mills. Most of Morath's fellow passengers got off – not many people travelling into Germany just then. Morath took a walk on the platform and bought a newspaper. At twilight, the train halted for the French border control. No problem for Morath, officially a *résident* of France.

Two hours later, the train crossed the frontier at Saarbrucken. No problem there either. The officer who knocked on the door of Morath's compartment was pleased to see the Hungarian passport. 'Welcome to the Reich,' he said. 'I know you will enjoy your stay.'

Morath thanked him graciously, and tried to settle down for the night. The border station was floodlit, a brilliant white: wire strung on stanchions, officials, sentries, machine guns, dogs. This is for you, it said, and Morath didn't like it. It recalled a certain Hungarian saying, 'One should never voluntarily enter a room or a country the door of which cannot be opened from the inside.'

Somewhere down the line he was joined by a pair of SS officers and spent the night drinking cognac and discussing the old Europe, the new Germany, and how to lay Hungarian women. The two young officers – political intellectuals who'd gone to university together in Ulm – had a fine time. They talked and laughed, polished their spectacles, got drunk, and fell asleep. Morath was relieved to arrive in Wurzburg, where he slept overnight at the railway hotel and left the next morning on the train to Prague.

The Czech border police weren't quite so happy to see him. Hungary ran espionage networks in several cities and the Czechs knew it.

'How long', the border guard asked him, 'do you plan to stay in Czechoslovakia?'

'A few days.'

'Your business here, sir?'

'To buy woodland, if possible, on behalf of a group of investors in Paris.'

'Woodland?'

'In Ruthenia, sir.'

'Ah. Of course. You are travelling to . . . ?'

'Uzhorod.'

The guard nodded, tapped Morath's passport with the end of a pencil. 'I will stamp a one-week visa for you. Please apply at the Uzhorod préfecture if you need to extend that.'

He ate a ghastly *blutwurst* in the dining car, finished Bartha, managed to buy a copy of *EST*, the evening edition brought in from Budapest, at the station buffet in Brno. Clearly, political life was heating up. Two members of parliament had come to blows. At a workers' march in the Tenth District, bricks thrown, people arrested. *To the Editor. Sir: How can we let these liberal pansies run our lives?* An editorial called for 'strength, firmness, singleness of purpose. The world is changing, Hungary must change with it.' A coffee house by the university had burned down. TENS OF THOUSANDS CHEER HITLER SPEECH IN REGENSBURG. With photograph, on page one. *Here they come*, Morath thought.

Outside the window, a strange countryside. Low hills, pine forest. Sudden rivers at spring flood, the sound of the locomotive sharpening as it passed through an open gorge. At the station in the Slovakian town of Zvolen, the train stood midway between Warsaw to the north and Budapest to the south. Next stop, Kosice, a border town before 1918. On the platform, women holding straw baskets, their heads covered with black kerchiefs. The train climbed through snow-patched meadows, came to a village with domed churches painted lime green. In the late afternoon haze, Morath could see the Carpathians on the far horizon. An hour later he got off in Uzhorod.

The stationmaster told him there was a place he could stay in Krolevska Street. It turned out to be a yellow brick building with a sign that said 'Hotel'. The proprietor had a white eye, wore a greasy silk waistcoat and a knitted yarmulke. 'Our finest room,' he said. 'The finest.' Morath sat on the straw mattress, picked the stitching from the lining of his wool jacket, and extracted the passport. *Andreas Panea.*

Late in the afternoon he walked to the post office. The Czech postal clerks wore blue uniforms. On an envelope he had written *Malko, Poste Restante, Uzhorod.* Inside, a meaningless note – a sister had been ill, now she was better. The actual message was the return address: the same as 'Malko's', with a different name.

Now, to wait.

Morath lay on the bed, stared out of the cloudy window. The finest room was bent at a strange angle: a low ceiling of wooden boards, whitewashed long ago, went in one direction, then another. When he stood up, it was only a few inches above his head. In the street, the steady sound of horses' hooves on cobblestone. Ruthenia. Or, affectionately, Little Russia. Or, technically, Sub-Carpathian Ukraine. A Slavic nibble taken by the medieval kings of Hungary, and ever since a lost land in the northeast corner of the nation. Then, after the Great War, on a rare day when American idealism went hand in hand with French diplomacy – what Count Polanyi called 'a frightening convergence' – they stuck it on to Slovakia and handed it to the Czechs. Somewhere, Morath speculated, in a little room in a ministry of culture, a Moravian bureaucrat was hard at work on a song. 'Merry old Ruthenia/Land we love so well.'

At dinner, the proprietor and his wife served him jellied calf's foot, buckwheat groats with mushrooms, white cheese with scallions, and pancakes with redcurrant jam. A bottle of cherry brandy stood on the plank table. The proprietor nervously rubbed his hands.

'Very good,' Morath said, pretending to wipe his mouth with the napkin – it had certainly been a napkin, once – and pushed his chair away from the table. He'd meant the compliment, however, and the proprietor could see that.

'Another blini, sir? Uhh, *Pannküchen? Crêpe? Blintz?*'

'Thank you, but no.'

Morath paid for the dinner and returned to his room. Lying there in the darkness, he could feel the countryside. There was a stable attached to the hotel, and sometimes the horses whickered and moved around in their stalls. The aroma, manure and rotted straw, drifted up to Morath's room. Still cold, at the end of April. He wrapped himself up in the worn blanket and tried to sleep. Out on Krolevska Street, somebody got drunk in a tavern. Singing at first, then the argument, then the fight. Then the police, a woman crying and pleading as her man was taken away.

Two days later, a letter at the post office, an address on the edge of Uzhorod, he had to take a droshky. Down streets of packed dirt lined with one-storey log houses, each with a single window and a thatched roof. A woman answered his knock on the door. She was dark, with black, curly hair, wore crimson lipstick and a tight, thin dress. Perhaps

Roumanian, he thought, or gypsy. She asked him a question in a language he didn't recognize.

He tried her in German. 'Is Pavlo here?'

She'd expected him, he could sense that; now he'd arrived and she was curious, looked him over carefully. Morath heard a door slam in the house, then a man's voice. The woman stood aside and Pavlo came to the door. He was one of those people who look very much like their photograph. 'Are you the man from Paris?' The question was asked in German. Not good, but serviceable.

'Yes.'

'They took their time, getting you here.'

'Yes? Well, here I am.'

Pavlo's eyes swept the street. 'Maybe you'd better come inside.'

The room was crowded with furniture, heavy chairs and couches covered in various patterns and fabrics, much of it red, some of the fabric very good, some not. Morath counted five different mirrors on the walls. The woman spoke quietly to Pavlo, glanced over at Morath, then left the room and closed the door.

'She is packing her suitcase,' Pavlo said.

'She's coming with us?'

'She thinks she is.'

Morath did not show a reaction.

Pavlo took that for disapproval. 'Try it some time,' he said, his voice a little sharp, 'life without a passport.' He paused, then, 'Have you money for me?'

Morath hesitated. Maybe somebody was supposed to give Pavlo money, but it wasn't him. 'I can let you have some,' he said, 'until we get to Paris.'

This wasn't the answer Pavlo wanted, but he was in no position to argue. He was perhaps a few years older than Morath had thought, in his late twenties. He had on a stained blue suit, colourful tie, and scuffed, hardworn shoes.

Morath counted out a thousand francs. 'This should tide you over,' he said.

It would do much more than that, but Pavlo didn't seem to notice. He put eight hundred francs in his pocket and looked around the room. Under a shimmering aquamarine vase with a bouquet of satin tulips in it was a paper doily. Pavlo slid two hundred-franc notes beneath the doily so the edges were just visible.

'Here's the passport,' Morath said.

Pavlo looked it over carefully, held it up to the light, squinted at the photograph and ran a finger over the raised lettering on the edge. 'Why Roumanian?' he said.

'That's what I could get.'

'Oh. Well, I don't speak it. I'm Croatian.'

'That won't be a problem. We're going across the Hungarian border. At Michal'an. Are you carrying another passport? I don't think we have to worry about it, but still . . .'

'No. I had to get rid of it.'

He left the room. Morath could hear him talking to the woman. When he reappeared he was carrying a briefcase. Walking behind him, the woman held a cheap valise in both hands. She'd put on a hat, and a coat with a ragged fur collar. Pavlo whispered something to her and kissed her on the forehead. She looked at Morath, her eyes suspicious but hopeful, and sat on a couch, the valise between her feet.

'We're going out for an hour or so,' Pavlo said to Morath. 'Then we'll be back.'

Morath wanted no part of it.

Pavlo closed the door. Out in the street, he grinned and cast his eyes to heaven.

They walked for a long time before they found a droshky. Morath directed the driver back to the hotel, then Pavlo waited in the room while Morath went to see the proprietor in a tiny office behind the kitchen where he was labouring over a bookkeeper's ledger. As Morath counted out Czech kroner to pay the bill he said, 'Do you know a driver with a car? As soon as possible – I'll make it worthwhile.'

The proprietor thought it over. 'Are you going', he said delicately, 'some distance away from here?'

He meant, *borders*.

'Some.'

'We are, as you know, blessed with many neighbours.'

Morath nodded. Hungary, Poland, Transylvanian Roumania.

'We are going to Hungary.'

The proprietor thought it over. 'Actually, I do know somebody. He's a Pole, a quiet fellow. Just what you want, eh?'

'As soon as possible,' Morath repeated. 'We'll wait in the room, if that's all right with you.' He didn't know who was looking for Pavlo, or why, but railway stations were always watched. Better a quiet exit from Uzhorod.

The driver appeared in the late afternoon, introduced himself as Mierczak, and offered Morath a hand like tempered steel. Morath sensed a powerful domesticity. 'I'm a mechanic at the flour mill,' he said. 'But I also do this and that. You know how it is.' He was ageless, with a receding hairline and a genial smile and a British shooting jacket, in hound's-tooth check, that had somehow wandered into this region in an earlier age.

Morath was actually startled by the car. If you closed one eye it didn't look so different from the European Fords of the 1930s, but a second look told you it wasn't anything like a Ford, while a third told you it wasn't anything. It had lost, for example, all its colour. What remained was a shadowy tone of iron, maybe, that faded or darkened depending on what part of the car you looked at.

Mierczak laughed, jiggling the passenger side door until it opened. 'Some car,' he said. 'You don't mind, do you?'

'No,' Morath said. He settled down on the horse blanket that had, a long time ago, replaced the upholstery. Pavlo got in the back. The car started easily and drove away from the hotel.

'Actually,' Mierczak said, 'it's not mine. Well, it's partly mine. Mostly it is to be found with my wife's cousin. It's the Mukachevo taxi, and, when he's not working at the store, he drives it.'

'What is it?'

'What is it?' Mierczak said. 'Well, some of it is a Tatra, built in Nesseldorf. After the war when it became Czechoslovakia. The Type Two, they called it. Some name, hey? But that's that company. Then it burned. The car, I mean. Though, now that I think about it, the factory also burned, but that was later. Next, it became a Wartburg. We had a machine shop in Mukachevo, back then, and somebody had left a Wartburg in a ditch, during the war, and it came back to life in the Tatra. But – we didn't really think about it at the time – it was an *old* Wartburg. We couldn't get parts. They didn't make them or they wouldn't send them or whatever it was. So it became then a Skoda.' He pressed the clutch pedal to the floor and revved the engine. 'See? Skoda! Like the machine gun.'

The car had used up the cobblestone part of Uzhorod and was now on packed dirt. 'Gentlemen,' Mierczak said. 'We're going to Hungary, according to the innkeeper. But I must ask if you have a particular place in mind. Or maybe it's just "Hungary". If that's how it is, I perfectly understand, believe me.'

'Could we go to Michal'an?'

'We could. It's nice and quiet there, as a rule.'

Morath waited. 'But. . . ?'

'But even quieter in Zahony.'

'Zahony, then.'

Mierczak nodded. A few minutes later, he turned a sharp corner on to a farm road and shifted down to second gear. It sounded like he'd swung an iron bar against a bathtub. They bumped along the road for a time, twenty miles an hour, maybe, until they had to slow down and work their way around a horse cart.

'What's it like there?'

'Zahony?'

'Yes.'

'The usual. Small customs post. A guard, if he's awake. Not any traffic to speak of. These days, most people stay where they are.'

'I imagine we can pick up a train there. For Debrecen, I guess, where we can catch the express.'

Pavlo kicked the back of the seat. At first, Morath couldn't believe he'd done it. He almost turned around and said something, then didn't.

'I'm sure there's a train from Zahony,' Mierczak said.

They drove south in the last of the daylight, the afternoon fading away to a long, languid dusk. Staring out of the window, Morath had a sudden sense of home, of knowing where he was. The sky was filled with torn cloud, tinted red by the sunset over the Carpathian foothills, empty fields stretched away from the little road, boundary lines marked by groves of birch and poplar. The land turned to wild meadow, where the winter grass hissed and swayed in the evening wind. It was very beautiful, very lost. *These blissful, bloodsoaked valleys*, he thought.

A tiny village, then another. It was dark now, cloud covered the moon and spring mist rose from the rivers. Midway through a long, slow curve, they caught sight of the bridge over the Tisza and the Zahony border station. Pavlo shouted, 'Stop!' Mierczak stamped on the brake as Pavlo hung over the top of the seat and punched the button that turned off the lights. 'The bitch,' he said, his voice tight with fury. He was breathing hard, Morath could hear him.

In the distance they could see two khaki-coloured trucks, river fog drifting through the beams of their lights, and a number of silhouettes, possibly soldiers, moving about. In the car it was very quiet, the idling engine banging away, the smell of petrol strong in the air.

'How can you be sure it was her?' Morath asked.

Pavlo didn't answer.

'Maybe they are just there,' Mierczak said.

'No,' Pavlo said. For a time, they watched the trucks and the soldiers. 'It's my fault. I knew what to do, I just didn't do it.'

Morath thought the best thing would be to drive south to Berezhevo, find a rooming house for a day or two, and take a train into Hungary.

Or, maybe better, drive west into the Slovakian part of the country – away from Ruthenia, land of too many borders – and then take the train.

'You think they saw our lights?' Mierczak said. He swallowed once, then again.

'Just turn around and get out of here,' Pavlo said.

Mierczak hesitated. He hadn't done anything wrong, but if he ran away that changed.

'Now,' Pavlo said.

Reluctantly, Mierczak yanked the gearshift into reverse and got the car turned around. He drove a little way in the darkness, then put the lights back on. Pavlo watched through the rear window until the border post disappeared around the curve. 'They're staying put,' he said.

'How far is it to Berezhevo?' Morath said. 'Maybe the best thing now is to take the train.'

'An hour. A little more at night.'

'I'm not getting on a train,' Pavlo said. 'If your papers don't work, you're trapped.'

Stay here, then.

'Is there another way across?' Pavlo said.

Mierczak thought it over. 'There's a footbridge, outside the village of Vezlovo. It's used at night, sometimes.'

'By who?'

'Certain families – for avoiding the import duties. A trade in cigarettes, mostly, or vodka.'

Pavlo stared, couldn't believe what he'd heard. 'So why didn't you take us there in the first place?'

'We didn't ask him to do that,' Morath said. Even in the cool night air, Pavlo was sweating. Morath could smell it.

'You have to go through a forest,' Mierczak said.

Morath sighed, he wasn't sure what he wanted to do. 'At least we can take a look,' he said. *Maybe the trucks were there by chance.* He was wearing a sweater, a tweed jacket and flannels – dressed for a country hotel and a train. Now he was going to have to crawl around in the woods.

They drove for an hour. There were no other cars on the road. The land, field and meadow, was dark, empty. At last they came upon a village – a dozen log houses at the edge of the road, windows lit by oil lamps. A few sheds and barns. The dogs barked at them as they went past.

'It's not far from here,' Mierczak said, squinting as he tried to peer into the night. The car's headlights gave off a dull, amber glow. Where the countryside turned to forest, Mierczak stopped the car, got out and walked up the road. A minute later, he returned. He was grinning again. 'Believe in miracles,' he said. 'I found it.'

They left the car, Morath carrying a satchel, Pavlo with his briefcase, and the three of them started walking. The silence was immense, there was only the wind and the sound of their footsteps on the dirt road.

'It's right there,' Mierczak said.

Morath stared, then saw a path in the underbrush between two towering beech trees.

'About a kilometre or so,' Mierczak said. 'You'll hear the river.'

Morath opened his wallet and began to count out hundred-kroner notes.

'That's very generous of you,' Mierczak said.

'Would you agree to wait here?' Morath asked him. 'Maybe forty minutes. Just in case.'

Mierczak nodded. 'Good luck, gentlemen,' he said, clearly relieved. He hadn't realized what he was getting himself into – the cash in his pocket proved that he'd been right to be scared. He waved as they walked into the forest, glad to see them go.

Mierczak was right, Morath thought. Almost from the moment they entered the forest they could hear the river, hidden, but not far away. Water dripped from the bare branches of the trees, the earth was soft and spongy underfoot. They walked for what seemed like a long time, then got their first view of the Tisza. About a hundred yards wide and running at spring flood, heavy and grey in the darkness, with plumes of white foam where the water surged around a rock or a snag.

'And where is this bridge?' Pavlo said. *This supposed bridge.*

Morath nodded his head – up the path. They walked for another ten minutes, then he saw a dry root at the foot of a tree, sat down, gave Pavlo a cigarette and lit one for himself. Balto, they were called; he'd bought them in Uzhorod.

'Lived in Paris a long time?' Pavlo asked.

'A long time.'

'I can see that.'

Morath smoked his cigarette.

'You seem to forget how life goes, over here.'

'Take it easy,' Morath said. 'We'll be in Hungary soon enough. Find a tavern, have something to eat.'

Pavlo laughed. 'You don't believe the Pole is going to wait for us, do you?'

Morath looked at his watch. 'He's there.'

Pavlo gave Morath a sorrowful look. 'Not for long. He'll be going home to his wife, any minute now. And on the way he'll stop and have a word with the police.'

'Calm down,' Morath said.

'Over here, it's about one thing, and one thing only. And that is money.'

Morath shrugged.

Pavlo stood. 'I'll be right back,' he said.

'What are you doing?'

'A few minutes,' he said, over his shoulder.

Christ! Morath heard him heading back the way they'd come, then it was quiet. Maybe he'd gone, really gone. Or he was going to check on Mierczak, which made no sense at all. *Well, he must have value to somebody.* When Morath was growing up, his mother went to Mass every day. She often told him that all people were good, it was just that some of them had lost their way.

Morath stared up at the tops of the trees. The moon was in and out, a pale slice among the clouds. A long time since he'd been in a forest. This was an old one, probably part of a huge estate. Prince Esterhazy had three hundred thousand acres in Hungary, with eleven thousand people in seventeen villages. Not so unusual, in this part of the world. The nobleman who owned this property no doubt intended his grand-children to cut the slow-growing hardwood, mostly oak and beech.

It occurred to Morath then that he hadn't actually lied to the Czech customs officer. He'd said he was going to look at woodland; well, here he was, looking at it. In the distance, two pops, and, a moment later, a third.

When Pavlo returned, he said only, 'Well, we should be getting on our way.' What needed to be done was done, why talk about it? The two of them walked in silence and, a few minutes later, they saw the bridge. A narrow, rickety old thing, the water sucked into deep eddies around the wooden poles that held it up, the surface maybe ten feet below the walkway. As Morath watched the bridge, it moved. The far end was sharp against the sky – a broken shard of railing thrust out towards the Hungarian side of the river. And, by moonlight, he could make out the blackened char pattern on the wood, where the part that had been set on fire – or dynamited, or whatever it was – had fallen into the water.

Morath was already so sickened at what Pavlo had done that he hardly cared. He'd seen it in the war, a dozen times, maybe more, and it brought always the same words, never spoken aloud. *Pointless* was the important one, the rest never mattered that much. *Pointless, pointless.* As though anything in the world might happen as long as somebody, somewhere, could see the point of it. A rather black joke, he'd thought at the time. The columns riding through the smoking villages of Galicia, a cavalry officer saying *pointless* to himself.

'They'll have a way to get across,' Pavlo said.

'What?'

'The people who go back and forth across the border at night. Will have a way to do it.'

He was probably right. A boat, another bridge, something. They worked their way towards the bank of the river, were within a few metres of it when they heard the voice. A command. In Russian, or maybe Ukrainian. Morath didn't speak the language but, even so, the intention was clear and he started to stand up. Pavlo grabbed him by the shoulder and forced him down, into the high reeds along the riverbank. 'Don't do it,' Pavlo whispered.

Again the voice, mock-polite, wheedling. *We wouldn't hurt a fly.*

Pavlo tapped his lips with his forefinger.

Morath pointed behind them, at the relative safety of the forest. Pavlo thought it over, and nodded. When they started to crawl backwards, somebody shot at them. A yellow spark in the woods, a report that flattened out over the water. Then a shout in Russian, followed, rather thoughtfully, by a version in Hungarian, *fuck you, stand up*, being the general idea, and a snicker.

Pavlo picked up a stone and threw it at them. At least two guns responded. Then a silence, then the sound of somebody lurching through the underbrush, a crash, an oath, and a raucous bellow that passed for laughter.

Morath never saw where it came from – the briefcase? But a heavy, steel-coloured revolver appeared in Pavlo's hand and he squeezed off a round in the direction of the noise.

That *wasn't* funny. That was unconscionably rude. Somebody screamed at them, and Morath and Pavlo went flat as a fusillade whizzed over the reeds. Morath made a hand sign, stay still. Pavlo nodded. From the darkness, a challenge – *come out and fight, you cowards.* Followed by shouted dialogue between two, then three, voices. All of them drunk, mean, and very angry.

But that was it. Pavlo's single shot had made an eloquent statement, had altered the social contract: sorry, no free killing tonight. It took a long time, thirty minutes, of yelling, shooting, and what Morath guessed were meant to be intolerable insults. Still, Pavlo and Morath managed to tolerate them, and, when the gang went away, knew enough to wait the requisite fifteen minutes for the final shot, when they sent somebody back to ruin the victory celebration.

4.40 a.m. The light pearl grey. The best moment to see and not to be seen. Morath, wet and cold, could hear birds singing on the Hungarian side of the river. He and Pavlo had walked upstream for an hour, soaked by the heavy mist, looking for a boat or another bridge, had found nothing and returned to the bridge.

'Whatever they use, they've hidden it,' Pavlo said.

Morath agreed. And this was not the morning for two strangers to walk into an isolated village. The Czech police would be interested in the murder of a Polish taxi driver, the Ukrainian gang more than curious to know who'd been shooting at them the night before. 'Can you swim?' Morath said.

Very slowly, Pavlo shook his head.

Morath was a strong swimmer, and this would not be the first time he'd been in a fast river. He'd done it in his teens, with daring friends. Jumped into spring current holding a piece of log, floated downstream until he could fight his way to the far shore. But, this time of year, you had only fifteen minutes. He'd seen that too, during the war, in the Bzura and the Dniester. First an agonized grimace at the cold, next a silly smile, then death.

Morath would take his chances, the problem was what to do with Pavlo. It didn't matter what he felt – he had to get him across. *Strange, though, a lot of folklore on this issue.* Endless foxes and roosters and frogs and tigers and priests and rabbis. A river to be crossed – why was it always the cunning one that couldn't swim?

And there weren't any logs. Maybe they could break off a piece of the burned railing, but they'd only know that once they got to the far end of the bridge. Morath decided to abandon his satchel. He was sorry to lose the copy of Bartha; he would find a way to replace it. For the rest, razor and socks and shirt, goodbye. The Ukrainians could have it. As for Pavlo, he unbuckled his belt and looped it through the handle of the briefcase. 'Put your passport in your mouth,' Morath said.

'And money?'

'Money dries.'

Flat on his belly, Morath worked his way across the bridge. He could hear the water as it rushed past, ten feet below, could feel it – the damp, chill air that rose from heavy current. He did not look back, Pavlo would either find the nerve to do this, or he wouldn't. Crawling over the weathered planks, he realized that a lot more of it had burned than was evident from the shoreline. It smelled like old fire, and his lamb's wool sweater from a shop on the rue de la Paix – 'Not that green, Nicky, *this* green' – already caked with mud, was now smeared with charcoal.

Long before he reached the end, he stopped. The support poles had burned, part of the way, anyhow, leaving black sticks to hold up the bridge. Morath realized he would be going into the river a little earlier than he'd planned. The bridge trembled and swayed each time he moved, so he signalled to Pavlo to stay where he was and went ahead on his own.

He reached a bad place, hung on, felt himself start to sweat in the cold air. Would it be better to dive in here? No, it was a long way to the other shore. He waited for the bridge to stop wobbling, then curled his fingers around the edge of the next board and slid forward. Waited, reached out, pulled, and slid. Resting his face against the wood, he saw a pair of white egrets flying over the water, their wings beating as they passed above him.

By the time he reached the end – or as close as he could get to it; beyond a certain point the wood was so burned away it wouldn't hold a cat – he had to take a minute to catch his breath. He motioned for Pavlo to come along. As he waited, he heard voices. He turned, saw two women, in black skirts and kerchiefs, standing by the river's edge and staring at him.

When Pavlo arrived they studied the far bank, a good forty yards away. In the growing daylight, the water was brown with earth swept down from the mountain streams. Lying next to him, Pavlo was the colour of chalk.

'Take off your tie,' Morath said.

Pavlo hesitated, then, reluctantly, pulled the knot apart.

'I'm going into the water, you follow. You hold on to one end of the tie, I'll swim across and pull you with me. You do the best you can. Kick your feet, paddle with your free arm. We'll manage.'

Pavlo nodded.

Morath looked down at the water, ten feet below him, dark and swirling. The far shore seemed a long distance away, but at least the bank was low.

'Wait a minute,' Pavlo said.

'Yes?'

But there was nothing to say, he just didn't want to go into the water.

'We'll be fine,' Morath said. He decided to try for the next pole, something he could hang on to while he coaxed Pavlo to jump in after him. He pulled himself along, felt the planks beneath him quiver, then shift. He swore, heard a beam snap, was turned on his side, and dropped. He fought the air, then landed with a shock that knocked him senseless. It wasn't the icy jolt of the water, he was waiting for that. It was the rock. Smooth and dark, about two feet below the surface. Morath found himself on his hands and knees, no pain yet but he could feel it coming, the river churning around him. *Hidden causeway.* The oldest trick in the world.

Pavlo came crawling towards him, tie held in his hand, passport clenched in his teeth, steel spectacles askew, and laughing.

They walked to Zahony, following first the river, then a cart-track through the woods that turned into a road. It took all morning but they didn't care. Pavlo was pleased not to be drowned, and his money wasn't all that wet. He peeled the bills apart, Austrian, Czech, French, blew gently on the various kings and saints, then put it away in his briefcase.

Morath had hurt his wrist and knee, but not as badly as he'd feared, and had a bruise by his left eye. A plank, most likely, he never felt it happen. In time, the sun came out and light sparkled on the river. They passed a woodcutter, a tramp, and two boys fishing for the small sturgeon that ran in the Tisza. Morath spoke to them in Hungarian. 'Any luck?' A little, yes, not too bad. They seemed not very surprised when two men in muddy clothes walked out of the forest. That's what comes from living on a frontier, Morath thought.

They found a restaurant in Zahony, ate cabbage stuffed with sausage and a plate of fried eggs, and got on a train that afternoon. Pavlo fell asleep, Morath stared out of the window at the Hungarian plain.

Well, he'd kept his word. Promised Polanyi he would bring this, this whatever-he-was to Paris. *Pavlo.* Certainly an alias – *nom de guerre*, code name, impersonation. Something. He claimed he was a Croat and that, Morath thought, just might be true. Perhaps a Croatian Ustachi. Which meant *terrorist* in some neighbourhoods and *patriot* in others.

Croatia, a province of Hungary for centuries and her access to the sea – which was how Miklos Horthy came to be Admiral Horthy – had stewed up quite a bit of political history since becoming part of a manufactured kingdom, Yugoslavia, in 1918. The founder of the Ustachi, Ante Pavelic, had found celebrity by turning to a political opponent in the Croatian Chamber of Deputies and shooting him in the heart. Six months later, Pavelic returned from hiding, walked into the lobby of the chamber carrying a shotgun, and killed two more.

Under Mussolini's protection, Pavelic moved to a villa in Turin, where he kept a guiding hand on the political philosophy of his organization: over forty train wrecks in ten years, numberless buildings bombed, hand grenades thrown into soldiers' cafés, and five thousand

Croatian and Serbian officials murdered. The money came from Mussolini, the assassins from IMRO, the Internal Macedonian Revolutionary Organization, with headquarters in Bulgaria. It had been IMRO operatives who assassinated King Alexander of Yugoslavia in 1934, in Marseilles. They had been trained in camps in Hungary which, in service of an alliance with Italy, also provided military instructors and false papers. Papers issued, quite often, in the name of Edouard Benes, the hated president of Czechoslovakia. A certain sense of humour at work there, Morath thought.

'*Balkan, Balkan,*' they said in French, of a pimp slapping a whore or three kids beating up a fourth – anything barbarous or brutal. In the seat across from Morath, Pavlo slumbered away, arms crossed protectively over his briefcase.

The passport formalities at the Austrian border were, mercifully, not too drawn out. For *Andreas Panea*, the Roumanian, that particular masked rudeness of central Europe – you practically had to be Austrian to know you'd been insulted. For everybody else it took a day or two, and by then you'd left the country.

A long time on the train, Morath thought, anxious to be back in the life he'd made in Paris. Hungarian plain, Austrian valley, German forest, and, at last, French fields, and the sun came out in Morath's heart. By evening, the train chugged through the Ile de France, wheatfields and not much else, then the conductor – who was all French train conductors, broad and stocky with a black moustache – announced the final stop, a hint of a song in his voice. Pavlo grew attentive, peering out of the window as the train slowed for the villages outside the city.

'You've been to Paris?' Morath said.

'No.'

On 4 May 1938, the night train from Budapest pulled into the Gare du Nord a little after midnight. It was, on the whole, a quiet evening in Europe, cloudy and warm for the season, rain expected towards dawn. Nicholas Morath, travelling on a Hungarian diplomatic passport, stepped slowly from the first-class car and headed for the taxi rank outside the station. As he left the platform he turned, as though he were about to say something to a companion but, on looking back, he discovered that whoever he'd been with had disappeared into the crowd.

Von Schleben's Whore

The bar of the Balalaika, 3.30 p.m., the dusty, tired air of a nightclub on a spring afternoon. On the stage were two women and a man, dancers, in tight, black clothing, harassed by a tiny Russian wearing a pince-nez, hands on hips, stricken with all the hopelessness in the world. He closed his eyes and pressed his lips together, a man who'd been right about everything since birth. 'To leap like a gypsy', he explained, 'is to leap like a gypsy.' Silence. All stared. He showed them what he meant, shouting 'Hah!' and throwing his arms into the air. He thrust his face towards them. 'You, *love*, life!'

Boris Balki was leaning on his elbows, the stub of a blunt pencil stuck behind his ear, a half-completed crossword puzzle in a French newspaper spread out on the bar. He looked up at Morath and said, '*Ça va?*'

Morath sat on a stool. 'Not too bad.'

'What can I get for you?'

'A beer.'

'Pelforth all right?'

Morath said it was. 'Have one with me?'

Balki got the bottles from beneath the counter, opened one and poured the beer against the side of a tilted glass.

Morath drank. Balki filled his own glass, studied the puzzle, flipped the page, glanced at the headlines. 'Why I keep buying this rag I don't know.'

It was one of the friskier Parisian weeklies: sexy gossip, risqué cartoons, photos of lurid chorus girls, pages of racing news from Auteuil and Longchamps. His name had once, to his shame and horror, appeared in it. The year before he met Cara he'd been going around with a second-rank movie star and they'd called him 'the Hungarian playboy Nicky Morath'. There'd been neither a duel nor a lawsuit, but he'd considered both.

Balki laughed. 'Where do they get this stuff? "There are currently twenty-seven Hitlers locked up in Berlin insane asylums." '

'And one to go.'

Balki flipped the page, took a sip of his beer, read for a few moments. 'Tell me, you're Hungarian, right?'

'Yes.'

'So what goes on with this new law? You can't wait to be like Germany, is that it?'

The last week in May, the Hungarian parliament had passed a law restricting Jewish employment, in private companies, to twenty per cent of the workforce.

'Shameful,' Balki said.

Morath nodded. 'The government had to do something, something symbolic, or the Hungarian Nazis would have staged a *coup d'état.*'

Balki read further. 'Who is Count Bethlen?'

'A conservative. Against the radical right.' Morath didn't mention Bethlen's well-known definition of the anti-Semite as 'one who detests the Jews more than necessary'.

'His party fought the law. Alongside the liberal conservatives, and the Social Democrats. The "Shadow Front", they call it here.'

'The law is a token,' Morath said. 'Nothing more. Horthy brought in a new prime minister, Imredy, to get legislation passed that would keep the lunatics quiet, otherwise . . .'

From the stage, a record of gypsy violins. One of the women dancers, a ginger blonde, raised her head to a haughty angle, held a hand high and snapped her fingers. 'Yes,' the tiny Russian cried out. 'That's good, Rivka, that's *Tzigane!*' He made his voice husky and dramatic. 'What man will dare to take me.' Morath, watching the dancer, could see how hard she was trying.

'And the Jews?' Balki said, raising his voice above the music. 'What do they think about this?'

'They don't like it. But they see what's going on in Europe, and they can look at a map. Somehow, the country has to find a way to survive.'

Disgusted, Balki flipped back to the crossword and took the pencil from behind his ear. 'Politics,' he said. Then, 'A wild berry?'

Morath thought it over. 'Maybe, *fraise de bois?*'

Balki counted the spaces. 'Too long,' he said.

Morath shrugged.

'And you? What do you think?' Balki said. He was back to the new law.

'Of course I'm against it. But one thing we all know is that if the Arrow Cross ever takes power, then it *will* be like Germany. There will be another White Terror, like 1919. They'll hang the liberals, the traditional right *and* the Jews. Believe me, it will be like Vienna, only worse.' He paused a moment. 'Are you Jewish, Boris?'

'I sometimes wonder,' Balki said.

It wasn't an answer Morath expected.

'I grew up in an orphanage, in Odessa. They found me with the name "Boris" pinned to a blanket. "Balki" means ditch – that's the name they gave me. Of course, Odessa, almost everybody's *something*. Maybe a Jew or a Greek or a Tartar. The Ukrainians think it's in the Ukraine, but people in Odessa know better.'

Morath smiled, the city was famously eccentric. He remembered reading, in 1920, when elements of various European armies tried to intervene in the civil war, that the border between the French and Greek sectors of the city was marked by a line of kitchen chairs.

'I basically grew up in the gangs,' Balki said. 'I was a Zakovitsa. Age eleven, a member of the Zakovits gang. We controlled the chicken markets in the Moldavanka. That was mostly a Jewish gang. We all had knives, and we did what we had to do. But, for the first time in my life, I had enough to eat.'

'And then?'

'Well, eventually the Cheka showed up. Then *they* were the only gang in town. I tried going straight, but you know how it is. Zakovits saved my life. Got me out of bed one night, took me down to the dock and put me on a Black Sea freighter.' He sighed. 'I miss it sometimes, bad as it was.'

They drank their beer. Balki working on the puzzle, Morath watching the dance rehearsal.

'It's a hard world,' Morath said. 'Take, for instance, the case of a friend of mine.'

Balki looked up. 'Always in difficulties, your friends.'

'Well, that's true. But you have to try to help them out, if you can.'

Balki waited.

'This one friend of mine, he has to do business with the Germans.'

'Forget it.'

'If you knew the whole story, you'd be sympathetic, believe me.' He paused, but Balki was silent. 'You lost your country, Boris. You know what that feels like. We're trying not to lose ours. So, it's what you just said, we're doing what we have to do. I'm not going to be a *conard* and offer you money, but there is money in this, for somebody. I can't believe you won't put them in the way of it. At least, find out what the offer is.'

Balki softened. Everybody he knew needed money. There were

women, out in Boulogne where the Russian émigrés lived, going blind from doing contract embroidery for the fashion houses. He gestured with his hands, helpless. *Je m'en fous* – I'm fucked no matter what happens.

'It's the old story,' Morath said. 'German officer in Paris, needs girlfriend.'

Balki was offended. 'Someone told you I was a pimp?'

Morath shook his head.

'Tell me,' Balki said. 'Who are you?' He meant, *What are you?*

'Nicholas Morath. I'm in the advertising business in Paris. You can look me up in the telephone book.'

Balki finished his beer. 'Oh, all right.' He gave in, more to some fate he thought he had than to Morath. 'What's the rest of it?'

'Pretty much as I said.'

'Monsieur Morath – Nicholas, if you don't mind – this is Paris. If you want to fuck a camel, all it takes is a small bribe to the zookeeper. Whatever you want to do, any hole you can think of and some you can't, it's up in Pigalle, out in Clichy. For money, anything.'

'Yes, I know. But remember what happened to Blomberg and Fritsch.' Two generals Hitler had got rid of, one accused of a homosexual affair, the other married to a woman rumoured to have been a prostitute. 'This officer can't be seen to have a mistress. Boris, I don't know the man, but my friend tells me he has a jealous wife. They both come from stodgy old Catholic families in Bavaria. He can be ruined. Still, here he is in Paris, it's everywhere, it's all around him, in every café, on every street. So he's desperate to arrange something, a *liaison*. But it must be discreet. For the woman, for the woman who tells absolutely nobody, and understands what's at stake without being told too much, and makes him happy in the bargain, there's a monthly arrangement. Five thousand francs a month. And, if everybody's satisfied, more over time.'

That was a lot of money. A schoolteacher earned twenty-five hundred francs a month. Balki's face changed, Morath saw it. No more Boris the bartender. Balki the Zakovitsa.

'I don't handle the money.'

'No.'

'Then maybe,' Balki said. 'Let me think it over.'

Juan-les-Pins, 11 June.

Her breasts, pale in the moonlight.

Late at night, Cara and her friend Francesca, holding hands, laughing, rising naked from the sea, shining with water. Morath sat on the sand, his trousers rolled to mid-calf, feet bare. Next to him, Simon something, a British lawyer, said, 'My God,' awed at the Lord's work running up the beach towards them.

They came down here every year, around this time, before the people showed up. To what they called 'Juan'. Where they lived by the sea in a tall, apricot-coloured house with green shutters. In the little village where you could buy a Saint-Pierre from the fishermen when the boats returned at midday.

Cara's crowd. Montrouchet from the Théâtre des Catacombes, accompanied by Sloth. A handsome woman, ingeniously desirable. Montrouchet called her by her proper name but to Morath she was Sloth and always would be. They stayed at the Pension Trudi, in the pine forest above the village. Francesca was from Buenos Aires, from the Italian community in Argentina, the same as Cara, and lived in London. Then there was Mona, known as Moni, a Canadian sculptor, and the woman she lived with, Marlene, who made jewellery. Shublin, a Polish Jew who painted fire, Frieda, who wrote small novels, and Bernhard, who wrote poems about Spain. And others, a shifting crowd, friends of friends or mysterious strangers, who rented cabins in the pines or took cheap rooms at the Hotel du Mer or slept under the stars.

Morath loved the Cara of Juan-les-Pins, where the warm air heated her excessively. 'We will be up very late tonight,' she would say, 'so we will have to rest this afternoon.' A wash in the sulphurous, tepid water that trickled into the rust-stained bath, then sweaty, inspired love on the coarse sheet. Half asleep, they lay beneath the open window, breathing the pine resin on the afternoon wind. At dusk the cicadas started, and went on until dawn. Sometimes they would take a taxi to the restaurant on the *moyenne* corniche above Villefranche, where they brought you bowls of garlicky *tapenade* and pancakes made of chickpea flour and then, finding you at peace with the world and unable to eat another bite, dinner.

Too proud and Magyar for beach sandals, Morath ran to the sea at noon, burning his feet on the hot pebbles, then treading water and staring out at the flat horizon. He would stay there a long time, numb as a stone, as happy as he ever got, while Cara and Francesca and their friends stretched out on their towels and glistened with coconut oil and talked.

'Half past eight at Juan-les-Pins, half past nine in Prague.' You heard that at the Bar Basque, where people went in the late afternoon to drink white rum. So the shadow was there, darker on some days, lighter on others, and if you didn't care to take measurements for yourself, the newspapers would do it for you. Going to the village shop for a *Nice Matin* and a *Figaro*, Morath joined the other addicts, then went to the café. The sun was fierce by nine in the morning, the shade of the café umbrella cool and secret. 'According to Herr Hitler,' he read, ' "The Czechs are like bicycle racers – they bow from the waist but down below they never stop kicking." ' In June, that was the new, the fashionable, place for the war to start, Czechoslovakia. The *Volksdeutsch* of the old Austrian provinces, Bohemia and Moravia – the Sudetenland – demanded unification with the Reich. And the *incidents*, the fires, the assassinations, the marches, were well under way.

Morath turned the page.

Spain was almost finished now, you had to go to page three. The Falange would win, it was only a matter of time. Off the coast, British freighters, supplying Republican ports, were being sunk by Italian fighter planes flying from bases in Majorca. The *Figaro* had reproduced a British editorial cartoon: Colonel Blimp says, 'Gad sir, it is time we told Franco that if he sinks another hundred British ships, we shall retire from the Mediterranean altogether.'

Morath looked out to sea, a white sail in the distance. The fighting was heavy seventy kilometres north of Valencia, less than a day's drive from the café where he drank his coffee.

Shublin had gone to Spain to fight, but the NKVD kicked him out. 'The times we live in,' he said at the Bar Basque one evening. 'The rule of the invertebrates.' He was in his thirties, with curly blond hair, a broken nose, and tobacco-stained fingers with oil paint under the nails. 'And King Adolf will sit on the throne of Europe.'

'The French will smash him.' Bernhard was German. He had marched in a Communist demonstration in Paris and now he couldn't go home.

'Still,' said Simon the lawyer. The others looked at him, but he wasn't going to make a speech. A sad smile, that was it.

The table was at the edge of the dance floor, which was liberally dusted with sand and pine needles brought in by the wind. It blew hard off the sea, smelled like a jetty at low tide, and fluttered the tablecloths. The little band finished playing '*Le Tango du Chat*' and started up on '*Begin the Beguine*'.

Bernhard turned to Moni. 'You have danced this "*Beguine*"?'

'Oh yes.'

'You have?' Marlene said.

'Yes.'

'When was that?'

'When you weren't there to see.'

'Oh yes? And when was *that*?'

'Dance with me, Nicky,' Sloth said and took him by the arm. They did something not unlike a foxtrot and the band – 'Los Hermanos' was printed in script on the bass drum – slowed down to accommodate them. She leaned against him, heavy and soft. 'Do you stay up late, when you're here?'

'Sometimes.'

'I do. Montrouchet drinks at night, then he sleeps like the dead.'

They danced for a time.

'You're lucky to have Cara,' she said.

'Mm.'

'She must be exciting to you. I mean, she just is that way, I can feel it.'

'Yes?'

'Sometimes I think about the two of you, in your room.' She laughed. 'I'm terrible, aren't I.'

'Not really.'

'Well, I don't care if I am. You can even tell her what I said.'

Later, in bed, Cara sat back against the wall, sweat glistening between her breasts and on her stomach. She took a puff of Morath's Chester-field and blew out a long stream of smoke. 'You're happy, Nicky?'

'Can't you tell?'

'Truly?'

'Yes, truly.'

Outside, the fall of waves on the beach. A rush, a silence, then the crash.

The moon was down, hazy gold, waning, in the lower corner of the window but not for long. Cautiously, careful not to wake Cara, he reached for his watch on a chair by the bed. 3.50. *Go to sleep.* 'That knits up the ravelled sleeve of care.' Well, it would take some considerable knitting.

Cara was on to him, but that was just too bad. He was doomed to live with a certain heaviness of soul; not despair, but the tiresome weight of pushing back against it. It had cost him a wife, long ago, an engagement that never quite led to marriage, and had ended more than one affair since then. If you made love to a woman it had better make you happy – or else.

Maybe it was the war. He was not the same when he came back; he knew what people could do to each other. It would have been better not to know that, you lived a different life if you didn't know that. He had read Remarque's book, *All Quiet on the Western Front*, three or four times. And certain passages again and again.

> *Now if we go back we will be weary, broken, burned out, rootless, and without hope. We will not be able to find our way any more . . . Let the months and the years come, they bring me nothing, they can bring me nothing. I am so alone and so without hope that I can confront them without fear.*

A German book. Morath had a pretty good idea what Hitler was mining in the hearts of the German veterans. But it was not only about Germany. They had all, British, French, Russian, German, Hungarian and the rest, been poured into the grinding machine. Where some of them died, and some of them died inside themselves. Who, he wondered, survived?

But who *ever* did? He didn't know. The point was to get up in the morning. To see what might happen, good or bad, a red/black wager. But, even so, a friend of his used to say, it was probably a good idea that you couldn't commit suicide by counting to ten and saying *now*.

Very carefully he slid out of bed, put on a pair of cotton trousers, crept downstairs, opened the door and stood in the doorway. A silver line of wave swelled, then rolled over and vanished. Somebody laughed on the beach, somebody drunk who didn't care. He could see, barely, if he squinted, the glow of a dying fire and a few silhouettes in the gloom. A whispered shout, another laugh.

Paris, 15 June.

Otto Adler settled in a chair in the Jardin du Luxembourg across from the round pool where children came with their sailboats. He folded his hands behind his head and studied the clouds, white and towering, sharp against the perfect sky. Maybe a thunderstorm by late afternoon, he thought. It was hot enough, unseasonal, and he would have looked forward to it but for the few centimes it would cost him to seek refuge in the café on the rue de Médicis. He couldn't afford a few centimes.

This would be his first full summer in France, it would find him poor and dreamy, passionate for dark, lovely corners – alleys and churches – full of schemes and opinions, in love with half the women he saw, depressed, amused, and impatient for lunch. In short, Parisian.

Die Aussicht, like all political magazines, didn't quite live and didn't quite die. The January issue, out in March, had featured an article by Professor Bordeleone, of the University of Turin, *Some Notes on the*

Tradition of the Fascist Aesthetic. It hadn't quite the elevated depth his readers expected, but it did have the epic sweep – reaching back into imperial Rome and marching forward past nineteenth-century architecture to D'Annunzio. A gentle, twinkling sort of man, Bordeleone, now professor emeritus of the University of Turin, after a night of interrogation and castor oil at the local police station. But, thank God, at least Signora Bordeleone was rich and they would survive.

For the winter issue, Adler had grand ambitions. He had received a letter from an old Koenigsberg friend, Dr Pfeffer, now an émigré in Switzerland. Dr Pfeffer had attended a lecture in Basel, and at the coffee hour following the talk, the lecturer had mentioned that Thomas Mann, himself an émigré since 1936, was considering the publication of a brief essay. For Mann, that could mean eighty pages but Adler didn't care. His printer, down in Saclay, was – to date, anyhow – an idealist in matters of credit and overdue bills, and, well, *Thomas Mann.* 'I wondered aloud,' said Pfeffer in his letter, 'ever so gently, whether there was any indication of a *topic*, but the fellow simply coughed and averted his eyes. Would you ask Zeus what he had for breakfast?' Adler smiled, remembering the letter. Of course, the topic was completely beside the point. In order to have that name in *Die Aussicht* he would have published the man's laundry bill.

He unbuckled his briefcase and peered inside: a copy of Schnitzler's collected plays, a tablet of cheap writing paper – the good stuff stayed in his desk back in St Germain-en-Laye – yesterday's *Figaro*, gathered, he thought of it as *rescued*, on the train that brought him to Paris, and a cheese sandwich wrapped in brown paper. '*Ah, mais oui, monsieur, le fromage de champagne!*' The lady who owned the local *crémerie* had quickly figured out that he had no money, but, French to the bone, had a small passion for seedy intellectuals and sold him what she called, with a curious mixture of pride and cruelty, *cheese of the countryside.* Nameless, yellow, plain, and cheap. But, Adler thought, bless her anyhow for keeping us alive.

He took the tablet from his briefcase, hunted around until he found a pencil, and began to compose. '*Mein Herr Doktor* Mann.' Could he do better with the honorific? Should he try? He let that sit, and went on to strategy. '*Mein Herr Doktor* Mann: As I have a wife and four children to feed and holes in my underwear, I know you will want to publish an important essay in my little magazine.' Now, how to say that without saying it. 'Perhaps not widely known but read in important circles'? Phooey. 'The most substantive and thoughtful of the émigré political magazines'? Limp. 'Makes Hitler shit!'

Now, he thought, there he was on to something. What if, he thought, for one manic second, he actually came out and said such a thing?

His gaze wandered, from the paper to the deep green of the chestnut trees on the other side of the pool. No children this morning, of course, they would be suffering through a June day in a schoolroom.

A stroller in the park came towards him. A young man, clearly not at work, perhaps, sadly, unemployed. Adler looked back down at his tablet until the man stood beside his chair. '*Pardon, monsieur,*' he said. 'Can you tell me the time?'

Adler reached inside his jacket and withdrew a silver pocket watch on a chain. The minute hand rested precisely on the four.

'It is just . . .' he said.

Monsieur Coupin was an old man who lived on a railway pension and went to the park to read the newspaper and look at the girls. He told his story to the *flics* standing outside the Jardin du Luxembourg, then to the detectives at the Préfecture, then to a reporter from the *Paris Soir*, then to two men from the Interior Ministry, and, finally, to another reporter, who met him at his local café, bought him a *pastis*, then another, seemed to know more about the event than any of the others, and asked him a number of questions he couldn't answer.

He told them all the same story, more or less. The man sitting across from the pond, the man in the blue suit and the steel-rimmed spectacles who approached him, and the shooting. A single shot and a *coup de grâce*.

He did not see the first shot, he heard it. 'A sharp report, like a firecracker.' That drew his attention. 'The man looking at his watch dropped it, then leapt to his feet, as though he had been insulted. He swayed for a moment, then toppled over, taking the chair with him. His foot moved once, after that he was still. The man in the blue suit leaned over him, aimed his pistol and fired again. Then he walked away.'

Monsieur Coupin did not shout, or give chase, or anything else. He stayed where he was, motionless. Because, he explained, 'I could not believe what I had seen.' And further, doubted himself when the assassin 'simply walked away. He did not run. He did not hurry. It was, it was as though he had done nothing at all.'

There were other witnesses. One described a man in an overcoat, another said there were two men, a third reported a heated exchange between the assassin and the victim. But almost all of them were further away from the shooting than Monsieur Coupin. The exception was a couple, a man and a woman, strolling arm in arm on a gravel path. The detectives watched the park for several days but the couple did not reappear, and, despite a plea in the story that ran in the newspapers, did not contact the Préfecture.

'Extraordinary,' Count Polanyi said. He meant a soft waffle, folded into a conical shape so that a ball of vanilla ice cream rested on top. 'One can eat it while walking.'

Morath had met his uncle at the zoo, where a *glacier* by the restaurant offered the ice cream and waffle. It was very hot; Polanyi wore a silk suit and a straw hat. They strolled past a llama, then a camel, the zoo smell strong in the afternoon sun.

'Do you see the papers, Nicholas, down there?'

Morath said he did.

'The Paris papers?'

'Sometimes *Figaro*, when they have it.'

Polanyi stopped for a moment and took a cautious taste of the ice cream, holding his pocket handkerchief under the waffle so it didn't drip on his shoes. 'Plenty of politics, while you were away,' he said. 'Mostly in Czechoslovakia.'

'I read some of it.'

'It felt like 1914 – events overtaking politicians. What happened was this: Hitler moved ten divisions to the Czech border. At night. But they caught him at it. The Czechs mobilized – unlike the Austrians, who just sat there and waited for it to happen – and the French and British diplomats in Berlin went wild. *This means war!* In the end, he backed down.'

'For the time being.'

'That's true, he won't give it up, he hates the Czechs. Calls them "a miserable pygmy race without culture". So, he'll find a way. And he'll pull us in with him, if he can. And the Poles. The way he's going to sell it, we're simply three nations settling territorial issues with a fourth.'

'Business as usual.'

'Yes.'

'Well, down where I was, nobody had any doubts about the future. War is coming, we're all going to die, there is only tonight . . .'

Polanyi frowned. 'It seems a great indulgence to me, that sort of thing.' He stopped for a moment, ate some of his ice cream. 'By the way, have you had any luck, finding a companion for my friend?'

'Not yet.'

'As long as you're at it, it occurs to me that the lovebirds will need a love nest. Very private, of course, and discreet.'

Morath thought it over.

'It will have to be in somebody's name,' Polanyi said.

'Mine?'

'No. Why don't you ask our friend Szubl?'

'Szubl and Mitten.'

Polanyi laughed. 'Yes.' The two men had shared a room, and the hardships of émigré life, for as long as anyone could remember.

'I'll ask them,' Morath said.

They walked for a time, through the ménagerie, into the gardens. They could hear train whistles from the Gare d'Austerlitz. Polanyi finished his ice cream. 'I've been wondering,' Morath said, 'what became of the man I brought to Paris.'

Polanyi shrugged. 'Myself, I make it a point not to know things like that.'

Morath wrote a note to Szubl and Mitten and invited them to lunch. A Lyonnais restaurant, he decided, where a *grand déjeuner* would keep you going for weeks. The two men were famously poor. A few years earlier, there'd been a rumour that only one of them could go out at night, since they shared ownership of a single, ash-black suit.

Morath got there early, Wolfi Szubl was waiting for him. A heavy man, fifty or so, with a long, lugubrious face and red-rimmed eyes and a back bent by years of carrying sample cases of ladies' foundation garments to every town in *Mitteleuropa*. Szubl was a blend of nationalities – he never said exactly which ones they were. Herbert Mitten was a Transylvanian Jew, born in Cluj while it was still Hungary. Their papers, and their lives, were like dead leaves of the old empire, for years blown aimlessly up and down the streets of a dozen cities. Until, in 1930, some good soul took pity on them and granted them Parisian residence permits.

Morath ordered apéritifs, then chatted with Szubl until Mitten returned, the skin of his face ruddy and shining, from the WC. Good God, Morath thought, he hadn't *shaved* in there, had he? 'Ah, Morath,' he said, offering a soft hand and a beaming theatrical smile. A professional actor, Mitten had performed in eight languages in the films of five nations and played always the same character, best defined by his most recent appearance as Mr Pickwick in a Hungarian version of *The Pickwick Papers*. Mitten had the figure of a nineteenth-century cartoon, wide at the middle and tapering at either end, with hair that stood out from his head like a clown wig.

They ordered. Copiously. It was a family restaurant – thick china bowls and heavy platters. Bearing sausage, some of it in oil, slices of white potato fried in butter, fat roasted chickens, salads with *haricots blancs* and salads with lardons of bacon. Mont d'or cheese. And strawberries. Morath could barely see the tablecloth. He spent money on the wine – the '26 Burgundies – exciting the red-faced *patron* to smiles and bows.

They walked afterwards, down the dark, narrow streets that ran from the back of the fifth arrondissement to the river. 'An apartment,' Morath said, 'for a clandestine love affair.'

Szubl thought it over. 'A lover who won't rent his own apartment.'

'Very romantic,' Mitten said.

'Very clandestine, anyhow,' said Szubl.

Mitten said, 'What are they, prominent?'

'Cautious,' Morath said. 'And rich.'

'Ah.'

They waited. Morath said, 'Two thousand francs a month for the love nest. Five hundred for you. One of you signs the lease. If they need a maid, you hire her. The concierge knows you, only you, the friend of the lovers.'

Szubl laughed. 'For the five hundred, do we have to believe this?'

'For the five hundred, you know better.'

'Nicholas,' Mitten said, 'people like us don't get away with spying.'

'It isn't spying.'

'We get put against a wall.'

Morath shook his head.

'So, God willing, it's only a bank robbery.'

'Love affair,' Morath said.

'Six hundred,' Mitten said.

'All right. Six hundred. I'll give you money for the furniture.'

'Furniture!'

'What kind of love affair is this?'

They were, to Morath's surprise, good at it. Quite good.

Somehow, in a week's time, they managed to unearth a selection of love nests. To start, they took him up to Mistress Row, the avenue Foch area, where gorgeous shop girls luxuriated on powder-puff sofas behind windows draped in pink and gold. In the apartment they took him to, the most recent *affaire* had evidently ended abruptly, an open tin of caviar and a mossy lemon left in the little refrigerator.

Next they showed him a large room, formerly servants' quarters, up in the eaves of an *hôtel particulier* in the fourth arrondissement, where nobody ever went. 'Six flights of stairs,' Mitten said.

'But very private.'

And for an actual love affair, Morath thought, not the worst choice. A quiet neighbourhood, last popular in 1788, and deserted streets. Next, a taxi to Saint-Germain-des-Prés, to a painter's atelier on the rue Guénégaud, with a pretty, blue slice of the Seine in one of the windows. 'He paints, she models,' Szubl said.

'And then, one afternoon, Fragonard!'

Morath was impressed. 'It's perfect.'

'For a Parisian, I'm not so sure. But if the lovers are, perhaps, *foreign*, well, as you see, it's pure MGM.'

'*Très chic*,' Szubl said.

'And the landlord's in prison.'

Their final choice was, obviously, a throwaway. Perhaps a favour for a friend: another Szubl, a different Mitten, penniless and awash in a Gallic sea. Two rooms, barely, at the foot of the ninth arrondissement, near the Chaussée-d'Antin Métro stop, halfway down the side street – the rue Mogador – behind the Galeries Lafayette department store. The streets were full of people, shopping at the Galeries or working there. At Christmas, children were brought here to see the mechanical Père Noël in the window.

The apartment was on the third floor of a nineteenth-century tenement, the exterior dark with soot and grime. Inside, brown walls, a two-burner stove, toilet in the hall, limp net curtains yellow with age, a table covered with green oilcloth, a couch, and a narrow bed with a page of an illustrated Hungarian calendar tacked to the wall above the pillow – *Harvest in Esztergom*.

'Well, Morath, here it is!'

'Gives you a stiff pencil just to *see* this bed, right?'

'*Ma biche, ma douce*, that army blanket! That coat rolled up for a pillow! Now is our moment! Undress – if you dare!'

'Who's your friend?'

'Laszlo.'

'Nice Hungarian name.'

'Nice Hungarian man.'

'Thank him for me. I'll give you some money to take him to dinner.'

'So then, it's the first one, right? The pink boudoir?'

'Or the atelier. I have to think it over.'

They left the apartment, walked downstairs. Morath headed towards the street door but Mitten took his elbow. 'Let's go the other way.'

Morath followed, through a door at the opposite end of the hallway, across a narrow courtyard in perpetual shadow, then in another door and down a corridor where several men and women were talking and smoking cigarettes.

'Where the hell are we?'

'The Galeries. But not the part the public sees. It's where the clerks go for a cigarette. Sometimes it's used for deliveries.'

They came to another door, Szubl opened it and they were on the street floor of the department store, amid crowds of well-dressed people carrying packages.

'Need anything?' Szubl said.

'Maybe a tie?'

'*Salops!*' Morath was smiling.

'Laszlo wants twenty-five hundred.'

Balki called him a week later.

'Perhaps you'd like to meet a friend of mine.'

Morath said he would.

'So tomorrow. At the big café on the rue de Rivoli, by the Palais Royal Métro. Around four. She'll be wearing flowers. You'll know who she is.'

'Four o'clock.'

'Her name is Silvana.'

'Thank you, Boris,' Morath said.

'Sure,' Balki said, his voice hard. 'Any time.'

The café was exceptionally neutral ground: tourists, poets, thieves, anybody at all could go there. On a steaming day in July, Silvana wore a dark suit, with a tiny corsage pinned to the lapel. Back straight, knees together, legs angled off to one side, face set in stone.

Morath had very good manners, not once in his life had he remained seated when a woman came to a table. And a very good heart; people tended to know that about him right away. Even so, it did not go easily between them. He was pleased to meet her, he said, and went on a little, his voice quiet and cool and far more communicative than whatever words it happened to be saying. *I know how hard life can be. We all do the best we can. There is nothing to fear.*

She was not unattractive – that was the phrase that occurred to him when he first saw her. Thirty-five or so, with brass-coloured hair that hung limp around her face, an upturned nose, generous lips, and olive, slightly oily skin. Not glamorous, particularly, but sulky, that kind of look. Prominent breasts, very pert in a tight sweater, narrow waist, hips not too wide. From somewhere around the Mediterranean, he guessed. Was she Marseillaise? Maybe Greek, or Italian. But cold, he thought. Would von Schleben actually make love to her? For himself, he wouldn't, but it was impossible to know what other people liked in bed.

'Well then,' he said. 'An apéritif? A Cinzano – would that be good? With *glaçons* – we'll drink like Americans.'

She shook a stubby Gauloise Bleue loose from its packet and tapped the end on her thumbnail. He lit a match for her, she cupped the back of his hand with hers, then blew out the flame. 'Thank you,' she said. She inhaled eagerly, then coughed.

The drinks came, there was no ice. Looking over Silvana's shoulder, he happened to notice that a small, neat man seated at a corner table was watching her. He had thin hair combed flat and wore a bow tie, which made him look like – Morath had to search for it – the American comedian Buster Keaton. He met Morath's eyes for a moment, then went back to reading his magazine.

'My friend is German,' Morath said. 'A gentleman. From the nobility.'

She nodded. 'Yes, Balki told me.'

'He would like you to join him for dinner, tomorrow night, at the Pré Catalan. At eight-thirty. Of course, he'll send his car for you.'

'All right. I stay at a hotel on the rue Georgette, in Montparnasse.' She paused. 'It's just the two of us?'

'No. A large dinner party, I believe.'

'And where did you say?'

'Pré Catalan. In the Bois de Boulogne. It's very *fin de siècle*. Champagne, dancing till dawn.'

Silvana was amused. 'Oh,' she said.

Morath explained about Szubl and Mitten, the apartment, the money. Silvana seemed vaguely detached, watched the smoke rise from the end of her cigarette. They had another Cinzano. Silvana told him she was Roumanian, from Sinaia. She'd come to Paris in the winter of '36 with 'a man who made a living playing cards'. He'd got into some sort of trouble, then disappeared. 'I expect he's dead,' she said, then smiled. 'Of course, with him you never know.' A friend found her a job in a shop, in a *confiserie*, but it didn't last. Then, down on her luck, she'd been hired as the hat-check girl at the Balalaika. She shook her head ruefully. '*Quelle catastrophe.*' She laughed, exhaling Gauloise smoke. 'Couldn't do it at all, and poor Boris got the blame.'

It was the end of the afternoon, cool and dark beneath the arches that covered the rue de Rivoli. The café was jammed with people, and very loud. A street musician showed up and started to play the concertina. 'I think I'll go home,' Silvana said. They stood and shook hands, then she unchained a bicycle from the lamp-post on the corner, climbed on, waved to Morath, and pedalled away into traffic.

Morath ordered a Scotch.

An old woman came around, selling newspapers. Morath bought a *Paris Soir* to see what was at the movies; he was going to spend the evening by himself. The headlines were thick and black: GOVERNMENT DECLARES COMMITMENT TO DEFEND CZECHOSLOVAKIA 'INDISPUTABLE AND SACRED'.

The man who looked like Buster Keaton left the café, giving Morath a glance as he went. Morath thought, for a moment, that he'd nodded. But, if it happened at all it was very subtle, or, more likely, it was just his imagination.

Juillet, Juillet. The sun hammered down on the city and the smell of the butchers' shops hung like smoke in the dead air.

Morath retreated to the Agence Courtmain, not the first time he'd sought refuge there. On the run from summer, on the run from Uncle Janos and his politics, on the run from Cara, lately consumed by vacation manias. The sacred *mois d'Août* approached; one either went to the countryside or hid in one's apartment and didn't answer the phone. What troubled Cara was, should they go to the Baroness Frei in Normandy or to her friend Francesca and her boyfriend in Sussex? It wasn't the same, not at all, and one had to shop.

At Agence Courtmain they had big, black fans that blew the heat around, and sometimes a breeze from the river worked its way up avenue Matignon and leaked in the window. Morath sat with Courtmain and his copy chief in her office, staring at a tin of cocoa.

'They have plantations in Africa, on the southern border of the Gold Coast,' the copy chief said. Her name was Mary Day – a French mother and an Irish father. She was close to Morath's age, and had never married. One line of gossip had it that she was religious, formerly a nun, while another speculated that she made extra income by writing erotic novels under a pen-name.

Morath asked about the owner.

'It's a big provincial family from around Bordeaux. We deal with the general manager.'

'A Parisian?'

'Colonial,' Courtmain said. '*Pied-noir,* with barbered whiskers.'

The tin had a red label with 'CASTIGNAC' printed in black across the top. Down below it said *Cacao Fin.* Morath pried up the metal cap, touched a finger to the powder and licked it. Bitter, but not unpleasant. He did it again.

'It's supposedly very pure,' Mary Day said. 'Sold to *chocolatiers,* here and in Turin and Vienna.'

'What do they want us to do?'

'Sell more cocoa,' Courtmain said.

'Well, new art,' Mary Day said. 'Posters for bakeries and grocery stores. And he told us that now, with the war winding down, they want to sell in Spain.'

'Do Spaniards like chocolate?'

She leaned forward, to say 'of course', then realized she didn't know.

'Can't get enough,' Courtmain said. *They do in this agency.*

Morath held the tin up to the window. Outside, the sky was white, and there were pigeons cooing on a ledge. 'The label's not so bad.' There was a decorative strand of intertwined ivy leaves around the border, nothing else.

Courtmain laughed. 'It's perfection,' he said. 'We'll sell it back to them in ten years.'

Mary Day took several sheets of art paper from a folder and pinned them up on the wall. 'We're going to give them Cassandre,' she said. A.M. Cassandre had done the artwork for the popular 'Dubo/Dubon/Dubonnet' image in three panels.

'In-house Cassandre,' Courtmain said.

The art was sumptuous, suggesting the tropics. Backgrounds in renaissance ochres and chrome yellows, with figures – mostly tigers and palm trees – in a span of Venetian reds.

'Handsome,' Morath said, impressed.

Courtmain agreed. 'Too bad about the name,' he said. He made a label in the air with his thumb and index finger. '*Palmier,*' he suggested, meaning 'palm tree'. '*Cacao fin!*'

'*Tigre?*' Morath said.

Mary Day had a very impish smile. '*Tigresse,*' she said.

Courtmain nodded. He took an artist's chalk from a cup on the desk and stood to one side of the drawings. 'That's the name,' he said. 'With this tree.' It curved gently, with three fronds on top. 'And this tiger.' A front view. The animal sat on its haunches, revealing a broad expanse of white chest.

Morath was excited. 'Do you think they'll do it?'

'Not in a thousand years.'

He was at Cara's when the telephone rang, three-thirty in the morning. He rolled out of bed, managed to fumble the receiver free of the cradle. 'Yes?'

'It's Wolfi.' Szubl was almost whispering.

'What is it?'

'You better go to the apartment. There's big trouble.'

'I'll be there,' Morath said, and hung up the phone.

What to wear?

'Nicky?'

He'd already put on a shirt and was trying to knot his tie. 'I have to go out.'

'*Now?*'

'Yes.'

'What's going on?'

'A friend in trouble.'

After a silence, 'Oh.'

He buttoned his trousers, shrugged a jacket on, forced his feet into his shoes while smoothing his hair back with his hands.

'What friend?' Now the note was in her voice.

'A Hungarian man, Cara. Nobody you know.'

Then he was out the door.

The streets were deserted. He walked quickly towards the Métro at Pont d'Alma. The trains had stopped running three hours earlier, but there was a taxi parked by the entrance. 'Rue Mogador,' Morath told the driver. 'Around the corner from the Galeries.'

The street door had been left open. Morath stood at the foot of the staircase and peered up into the gloom. Thirty seconds, nothing happened, then, as he started up the stairs, he heard the click of a closing door somewhere above him. *Trying not to make a noise.* Again he waited, then began to climb.

On the first-floor landing he stopped again. 'Szubl?' He said it in a low voice, not a whisper, just barely loud enough to be heard on the floor above.

No answer.

He held his breath. He thought he could hear light snoring, a creak, then another. Normal for a building at four in the morning. Again he climbed, slowly, standing for a moment on every step. Halfway up, he touched something sticky on the wall. What was *that?* Too dark to see. He swore, and rubbed his fingers against his trousers.

On the second floor he went to the end of the hall and stood in front of the door. The smell was not strong – not yet – but Morath had fought in the war and knew exactly what it was. *The woman.* His heart sank. He had known this would happen. Somehow, mysteriously, he'd known it. And he would settle with whoever had done it. Von Schleben, somebody else, it didn't matter. His blood was racing; he told himself to calm down.

Or, maybe, Szubl. No, why would anyone bother?

He put his index finger on the door and pushed. It swung open. He could see the couch, the bed, a dresser he didn't remember. He smelled paint, along with the other smell, stronger now, and the burned, bittersweet odour of a weapon fired in a small room.

When he stepped inside, he could see the table covered with oilcloth. At one end, a man was sitting in a chair, his legs spread wide, his head hanging, almost upside down, over the back, his arms dangling at his sides.

Morath lit a match. Boots and trousers of a German officer's uniform. The man was wearing a white shirt and braces, his jacket hung carefully on the chair and now pinned in place by his head. A grey face, well puffed up, one eye open, one eye shut. The expression – and he had seen this before – one of sorrow mixed with petty irritation. The hole in the temple was small; the blood had dried to brown, on the face and down the arm. Morath knelt, the Walther side arm had dropped to the floor beneath the hand. On the table, the wallet. A note? No, not that he could see.

The match started to burn his fingers, Morath shook it out and lit another. He opened the wallet: a photograph of a wife and grown children, various Wehrmacht identity papers. Here was Oberst – Colonel – Albert Stieffen, attached to the German general staff at the Stahlheim barracks, who'd come to Paris and shot himself in the kitchen of von Schleben's love nest.

A soft tap at the door. Morath glanced at the pistol, then let it lie there. 'Yes?'

Szubl came into the room. He was sweating, red-faced. 'Christ,' he said.

'Where were you?'

'Over at the Gare St-Lazare. I used the phone, then I stood across the street and watched you come inside.'

'What happened?'

Szubl spread his hands apart, *God only knows*. 'A man called, about two-thirty in the morning. Told me to come over here and take care of things.'

' "Take care of things." '

'Yes. A German, speaking German.'

'Meaning it happened here, so it's our problem.'

'Something like that.'

They were silent for a time. Szubl shook his head, slow and ponderous. Morath exhaled, a sound of exasperation, ran his fingers through his hair, swore in Hungarian – mostly to do with fate, shitting pigs, saints' blood – and lit a cigarette. 'All right,' he said, more to himself than to Szubl. 'So now it disappears.'

Szubl looked glum. 'It will cost plenty, that kind of thing.'

Morath laughed and waved the problem away. 'Don't worry about that,' he said.

'Really? Well, then you're in luck. I have a friend.'

'*Flic?* Undertaker?'

'Better. A desk man at the Grand Hotel'

'Who is he?'

'One of us. From Debrecen, a long time ago. He was in a French prisoner-of-war camp in 1917, somehow managed to get himself to the local hospital. Long story short, he married the nurse. Then, after the war, he settled in Paris and worked in the hotels. So about a year ago, he tells me a story. Seems there was a symphony conductor, a celebrity, staying in the luxury suite. One night, maybe two in the morning, the phone at the desk rings. It's the maestro, he's frantic. My friend rushes upstairs – the guy had a sailor in the room, the sailor died.'

'Awkward.'

'Yes, very. Anyhow, it was taken care of.'

Morath thought it over. 'Go back to St-Lazare,' he said. 'Call your friend.'

Szubl turned to leave.

'I'm sorry to put you through this, Wolfi. It's Polanyi, and his . . .'

Szubl shrugged, adjusted his hat. 'Don't blame your uncle for intrigue, Nicholas. It's like blaming a fox for killing a chicken.'

From Morath, a sour smile, Szubl wasn't wrong. *Although*, he thought, *'blaming' isn't what's usually done to a fox*. The stairs creaked as Szubl went down, then Morath watched him through the window. The dawn was grey and humid, Szubl trudged along, head down, shoulders hunched.

The desk man was tall and handsome, *dashing*, with a cavalry moustache. He arrived at five-thirty, wearing a red uniform with gold buttons. 'Feeling better?' he said to the corpse.

'Two thousand francs,' Morath said. 'All right?'

'Could be more, by the time it's done, but I trust Wolfi for it.' For a moment, he stared at the dead officer. 'Our friend here is drunk,' he said to Morath. 'We're going to get his arms around our shoulders and carry him downstairs. I'd ask you to sing, but something tells me you won't. Anyhow, there's a taxi at the door, the driver is in on it. We'll put our friend here in the back seat, I'll get in with the driver and that's that. The jacket, the gun, the wallet, you find a way to get rid of those. If it was me, I'd burn the papers.'

Eventually Morath and the desk man had to carry Stieffen downstairs

– the pantomime played only from the street door to the taxi and they barely made it that far.

A blue car – later he thought it was a big Peugeot – pulled to the kerb in front of him. Slowly, the back window was lowered and the little man in the bow tie stared out at him. 'Thank you,' he said. The window was rolled back up as the car pulled away, following the taxi. Morath watched as they drove off, then returned to the apartment where Szubl, stripped to his underwear, was scrubbing the floor and whistling a Mozart aria.

Polyani outdid himself, Morath thought, when he chose a place to meet. A nameless little bar in the quarter known as the *grande truanderie,* the thieves' palace, buried in the maze of streets around Montorgueil. It reminded Morath of something Emile Courtmain had once told him: 'The truth of lunch is in the choice of the restaurant. All that other business, eating, drinking, talking, that doesn't mean very much.'

Polanyi sat there, looking very sorrowful and abused by the gods. 'I'm not going to apologize,' he said.

'Do you know who he was? Colonel Stieffen?'

'No idea. And no idea why it happened. To do with honour, Nicholas – if I had to bet, I'd bet on that. He puts his wallet on the table, meaning this was who I was, and does it in a secret apartment, meaning this is where I failed.'

'Failed at what?'

Polanyi shook his head.

They were sitting at one of the three tables in the room. The fat woman at the bar called out, 'Say, boys, let me know when you're ready for another.'

'We will,' Polanyi said.

'Who's the man with the bow tie?'

'He is called Dr Lapp.'

'Dr Lapp?'

'A name. Certainly there are others. He is an officer in the Abwehr.'

'Oh well, that explains it, then. I've become a German spy. Should we stay for lunch?'

Polanyi took a sip of wine. He was like, Morath thought, a man going to work. 'They're going to get rid of him, Nicholas. It's dangerous for me to tell you that, and dangerous for you to know it, but this Colonel Stieffen has opened a door and now I have, against my better judgment, *believe* me, to let you inside.'

'To get rid of who?'

'Hitler.'

No answer to that.

'If they fail, we will have war, and it will make the last one look like a tea party. The fact is, if you hadn't called me, I was going to call you. I believe it's time for you to think seriously about how to get your mother, and your sister, out of Hungary.'

It had a life of its own, the war, like an immense rumour that wound its way through the newspapers, the cafés and the markets. But somehow, in Polanyi's voice, it was fact, and Morath, for the first time, believed it.

Polanyi leaned forward, his voice low. 'Hitler is going to *settle*, as he puts it, with the Czechs. The Wehrmacht will invade, probably in the autumn – the traditional time, when the harvest is in and the men from the countryside become soldiers. Russia is pledged to defend Czechoslovakia if France does. The Russians will march through Poland, with or without the Poles' permission, but she'll invade us. You know what that means – Mongolian cavalry and the Cheka and all the rest of it. France and England will invade Germany through Belgium – this is no different than 1914. Given the structure of treaties in Europe, the alliances, that is exactly what is going to happen. Germany will bomb the cities, fifty thousand casualties every night. Unless they use phosgene gas, then it's more. Britain will blockade the ports, central Europe will starve. The burning and the starving will go on until the Red Army crosses the German border and destroys the Reich. Will they stop there? "God lives in France", as the Germans like to say, perhaps Stalin will want to go and see Him.'

Morath looked for contradictions. He couldn't find them.

'This is what worries me, this is what ought to worry you, but it means very little to the OKW, the Oberkommando Wehrmacht, the army's General Staff. Those people – the map people, the logistics people, the intelligence people – have always been accused, by operational commanders, of thinking more than is good for them, but this time they've got it right. If Hitler attacks Czechoslovakia, which is easy for Germany since the *Anschluss*, they surround the Czechs on three sides, England, France and Russia will come into the war. Germany will be destroyed. But, more important, to the OKW, the *army* will be destroyed. Everything they've worked for, since the ink dried on the treaties in 1918, will be torn to pieces. Everything. They can't let that happen. And they know, with Hitler protected by the SS, that only the army has the strength to remove him.'

Morath thought for a time. 'In a way,' he said, 'this is the best thing that could happen.'

'If it happens, yes.'

'What can go wrong?'

'Russia fights only if France does. France, and England, will fight only if Germany invades, and the Czechs resist. Hitler can only be removed for starting a war he can't win.'

'Will the Czechs fight?'

'They have thirty-five divisions, about three hundred and fifty thousand men, and a defensive line of forts that runs along the Sudetenland border. Said to be good – as good as the Maginot Line. And, of course, Bohemia and Moravia are bordered by mountains, the Shumava. For the German tanks, the passes, especially if they are defended, will be difficult. So, certain people in the OKW are making contact with the British and the French, urging them to stand firm. Don't give Hitler what he wants, make him fight for it. Then, when he fights, the OKW will deal with him.'

' "Making contact", you said.'

Polanyi smiled. 'You know how it's done, Nicholas, it's not a lone hero, crawling through the desert, trying to save the world. It's various people, various approaches, various methods. Connections. Relationships. And, when the OKW people need a quiet place to talk, away from Berlin, away from the Gestapo, they have an apartment in the rue Mogador – where that rogue von Schleben sees his Roumanian girlfriend. Who knows, it might even be a place to meet a foreign colleague, over from London for the day.'

'A setting provided by their Hungarian friends.'

'Yes, why not?'

'And, similarly, the man we brought into Paris.'

'Also for von Schleben. He has many interests, many projects.'

'Such as . . .'

Polanyi shrugged. 'He didn't explain, Nicholas. I didn't insist.'

'And Colonel Stieffen?' Now they'd ridden the merry-go-round back to where they'd started. Morath might have got the brass ring, he wasn't sure.

'Ask Dr Lapp,' Polanyi said. 'If you feel you have to know.'

Morath, puzzled, stared at his uncle.

'If you should happen to see him, I meant to say.'

On Saturday mornings, Cara and Nicky went riding in the Bois de Boulogne on the Chemin des Vieux Chênes, or around the Lac Inférieur. They rode big chestnut geldings, the sweat white and foamy above the horses' hocks in the midsummer heat. They rode very well, came, each of them, from a country where horseback riding was part of life, like marriage or religion. Sometimes Morath found the bridle paths a little tame – he had galloped into machine gun positions and jumped horses over barbed wire – but the feel of it brought him a peace he could find no other way.

They nodded to the other couples, everyone smart in their jodhpurs and handmade boots, and trotted along at a good, stiff pace in the shade of the oak trees.

'I have a letter from Francesca,' Cara told him. 'She says the house in Sussex is lovely, but small.'

'If you'd prefer something grand, we'll go to the baroness's place.'

'That's what you'd like, right, Nicky?'

'Well,' Morath said. He really didn't care, but pretended in order to please Cara. 'Maybe Normandy's better. Cool at night, and I like to swim in the sea.'

'Good. I'll write this afternoon. We can see Francesca when she comes in the autumn. For the clothes.'

Boris Balki telephoned and asked him to come to the nightclub. The Balalaika was closed for the August vacation, the tables covered with old bedsheets. There was no beer to drink, so Balki opened a bottle of wine. 'They won't miss it,' he said. Then, 'So, you must be leaving soon.'

'A few days. The great migration.'

'Where do you go?'

'Normandy. Just outside Deauville.'

'That must be nice.'

'It's all right.'

'I like the time off,' Balki said. 'We have to paint, fix the place up, but at least I don't have to make jokes.' He reached in a pocket, unfolded a page of cheap writing paper covered with small Cyrillic characters. 'It's from a friend of mine, in Budapest. He writes from Matyas Street.'

'Not much there. The prison.'

Balki's answer was a grim smile.

'Oh.'

'He's an old friend, from Odessa. I thought, maybe, if somebody knew somebody . . .'

'Matyas is the worst – in Budapest, anyhow.'

'He says that, as much as he can get it past the censor.'

'Is he in for a long time?'

'Forty months.'

'Long enough. What'd he do?'

'Bonds.'

'Hungarian?'

'Russian. Railway bonds. The 1916 kind.'

'Somebody *buys* that?'

Balki nodded, then, despite himself, started laughing. 'Poor Rashkow. He's tiny. "Look at me," he used to say. "If I tried to hold somebody up they'd stuff me in a drawer." So he sells things. Sometimes jewellery, sometimes paintings, even manuscripts. Tolstoy! His unfinished novel! But, lately, it's railway bonds.'

They both laughed.

'You see why I love him,' Balki said.

'They're not actually *worth* anything, are they?'

'Well, Rashkow would say, not *now*. But think of the future. "I sell hope," he used to say. "Hope for tomorrow. Think how important that is, hope for tomorrow."'

'Boris,' Morath said, 'I'm not sure I can help.'

'Well, anyhow, you'll try.' The *after all, I tried for you* was unspoken, but not difficult to hear.

'Of course.'

'Before you go away?'

'Even if I can't do that, I won't wait for September. They have telephones in Deauville.'

'Semyon Rashkow.' Balki held the letter up to the light and squinted. Morath realized he needed glasses. 'Number 3352–18.'

'Just out of curiosity, who wrote Tolstoy's unfinished novel?'

Balki grinned. 'Wasn't bad, Morath. Really. It wasn't.'

The last place he wanted to be, in Colonel Sombor's office on the top floor at the Hungarian legation. Sombor sat erect at his desk, reading a dossier, using the end of a pencil to guide his eyes along a typewritten line. Morath stared out of the open window. Down below, in the garden, a porter, an old man in a grey uniform and a grey peaked cap, was raking the gravel. The sound was sharp in the silent courtyard.

He had to help, he felt he had to help. Balki wasn't an affable barman, Balki was him, Morath, in the wrong country, in the wrong year, forced to live the wrong life. A man who hated having to be grateful for a job he hated.

Morath had tried his uncle first, was told he was not in Paris, then reached Sombor at his office. 'Of course, come tomorrow morning.' Sombor was the man who could help, so Morath went to see him, knowing it was a mistake every step of the way. Sombor had a title, something innocuous, but he worked for the secret police and everybody knew it. There was an official spy at the legation, Major Fekaj, the military attaché, and there was Sombor.

'I don't see you enough,' he complained to Morath, closing the dossier. Morath found it hard to look at him. He was one of those people whose hair looks like a hat – a polished, glossy black hat – and, with his sharp, slanted eyebrows, he suggested a tenor made up to play the devil in a comic opera.

'My uncle keeps me busy.'

Sombor acknowledged Polanyi's position with a gracious nod. Morath certainly wanted it to be gracious.

'Yes, I can believe it,' Sombor said. 'Also, I'm sure, this wonderful city. And its opportunities.'

'That too.'

Sombor touched his lips with his tongue. Leaned forward, lowered his voice. 'We're grateful, of course.'

From a man who'd been forced, in 1937, to remove a portrait of Julius Gombos from his wall – Gombos was widely credited with having invented the philosophies of Adolf Hitler – not necessarily what Morath wanted to hear. 'Good of you to say it.' *Grateful for what?*

'Not the kind of thing you can allow,' Sombor said.

Morath nodded. What in hell's name had Polanyi told this man? And why? For his own good? Morath's? Some other reason? What he did know was that this conversation was not, not if he could help it, going to turn frank and open.

'Someone who has done a favour for me, for us' – Morath smiled, so did Sombor – 'needs a favour in return.'

'Favours . . .'

'Well, what is one to do?'

'Quite.'

A contest of silence. Sombor ended it. 'So, exactly what sort of favour are we talking about?'

'An old friend. Locked up in Matyas.'

'For?'

'Selling worthless bonds.'

'*Beszivargok?*' Infiltrator. Which meant, for Sombor and others, Jew. Morath thought it over. Rashkow? 'I don't think so,' he said. 'Not from the name.'

'Which is?'

'Rashkow.'

Sombor took a tablet of white paper and unscrewed the cap of his pen and carefully wrote the name down on the paper.

The *Month in the Country* gathered momentum, preparation on the avenue Bourdonnais proceeded at a fever pitch. The baroness had been written to, then telephoned, then telephoned again. Cara's MG had been washed, waxed, and filled with water, oil and petrol, the seats rubbed with saddlesoap, the walnut dashboard polished to a soft glow. The picnic hamper was ordered from Pantagruel, then Delbard, then Fauchon. Did Morath like sliced beef tongue in aspic? No? Why not? The tiny folding table purchased, taken back to the store, replaced with a green horse blanket, then a fine wool blanket, brown with a grey stripe, which could also be used on the beach. Cara brought home a bathing suit this little, then this little, and then this little; the last one springing a seam as Morath whipped it off. And she should be damned glad, he thought, that there weren't toothmarks in it – take *that* back to Mademoiselle Ninette on the rue Saint-Honoré.

Saturday morning, Morath had a long list of errands, carefully saved up as a pretext for the evasion of Cara's packing. He stopped at Courtmain, at the bank, at the *tabac*, at the bookstore, where he bought Freya Stark's *The Valley of the Assassins* and Hemingway's *A Farewell to Arms*, both in French translation. He already had a Gyula Krudy novel. Krudy was in essence the Hungarian Proust – 'Autumn and Budapest were born of the same mother' – and Morath had always liked him. In fact, the baroness's houses were stacked to the ceilings with books, and Morath knew he would fall in love with some exotic lost masterpiece and never turn a page of whatever he'd brought with him.

When he got back to the avenue Bourdonnais, he discovered there'd been a blizzard of underwear and shoes and crinkly pink paper. On the kitchen table was a vase with a dozen yellow roses. 'These are not from you, Nicky, are they?'

'No.'

'I didn't think so.'

'Is there a card?'

'Yes, but it's in Hungarian. I can't read it.'

Morath could read it. A single word written in black ink on a florist's card. *Regrets.*

Three-thirty when Cara's phone rang, and a man's voice asked him, very politely, if it would be altogether too much trouble to walk to the newspaper kiosk by the Pont d'Alma Métro.

'I'm going to get the paper,' he said to Cara.

'What? *Now?* For God's sake, Nicky, I—'

'Back in a minute.'

Dr Lapp was in a black Mercedes. His suit was blue, his bow tie green, his face as sad as Buster Keaton's. There was really nothing to discuss, he said.

This was a privilege, not a sacrifice.

*

Still, Morath felt terrible. Perhaps if he'd been able to say something, to explain, maybe it wouldn't have been so bad.

'*Messieurs et Mesdames.*'

The conductor had opened the door of the compartment and the rhythmic hammering of the wheels on the track grew suddenly louder. Morath rested the Freya Stark book on his knee.

The conductor held the first-class passenger list in his hand. ''*Sieurs et 'dames*, the dining car will open in thirty minutes, you may reserve for the first or second seating.'

He went around the compartment: businessman, middle-aged woman, mother and little boy – possibly English – then Morath. 'Second, please,' Morath said.

'And that would be?'

'Monsieur Morath.'

'Very good, sir.'

'Can you tell me, what time we expect to be in Prague?'

'The timetable says four-thirty, *monsieur*, but, of course, these days . . .'

2 August 1938. Marienbad, Czechoslovakia.

Six-twenty in the evening, Morath came down the marble staircase and walked across the lobby. Grand hotels in spa towns were all of a type and the Europa was no different – miles of corridors, chandeliers, everywhere mahogany. Frayed carpets, frayed respectability, the former much rewoven, the latter a faint but detectable presence in the air, like the smell of the kitchen.

Two women in leather chairs smiled at him, widow and unmarried daughter, he guessed, come husband-hunting in Marienbad. Morath had been at the Europa for only a night and a day and they had flirted with him twice. They were handsome and well fleshed. *Good appetites*, he thought, *of all sorts*. Not unusual in that part of the world. The Czechs felt life owed them a little pleasure; they happily embraced the Protestant virtues but just as happily embraced each other. If a proposal of marriage were not forthcoming then, mother or daughter, rolling around in a creaky hotel bed might not be the worst thing in the world.

Morath walked out the door, into a genteel lane lit with gas lamps. There were mountains in the distance, dark shapes in the failing light. He walked for a long time, glancing at his watch every few minutes. He had once, dragged off to Evian-les-Bains by Cara's predecessor, actually tried the treatment – packed in mud by laughing girls, then hosed down by a stern woman wearing a hairnet. Victorian medicine. Victorian eroticism? Victorian *something*.

He reached the edge of the town, a black, dense forest of pine, rolling up a hillside above the street. Down below, the gas lamps twinkled. There were several orchestras at work and he could hear, when the wind was right, the violins. It was very romantic. Through the trees, a glimpse of the toy train that puffed its way up the mountain to the station called Marianske Lazne. Marienbad, in the Austro-Hungarian days. Hard to think of it any other way. The wind shifted, the distant violins floated up to him. Along with a faint smell of gunnery, artillery shells.

Now it was 7.10. There were candles on the tables of the tearoom in Otava Street. Morath studied the menu, mounted in a brass frame on a stand by the door. Inside, a Czech army officer watched him for a moment, then rose from his chair, leaving an uneaten pastry on his plate. To get to his feet, the officer used a stick, a good one, Morath saw, with a brass tip and an ivory head. He was not far from Morath's age, with a soldier's face and a neatly trimmed beard, blond and grey and red.

They shook hands in the street. 'Colonel Novotny,' the officer said, with a motion of the head somewhere between a nod and a bow.

'Morath.'

An exchange of pleasantries. We are like, Morath thought, two provincial officials, meeting in the sleepy days of the old empire.

Novotny had a military car: the least expensive Opel, something like a Parisian taxi cab, painted olive green. 'We are going up towards Kreslice,' he said. 'About forty kilometres from here.'

Morath opened the passenger door. On the seat was a holstered automatic pistol in a leather belt. 'Oh, just put that on the floor,' Novotny said. 'We're in the Sudetenland here – it's wiser to have something in the car.'

They drove on mountain roads, darker as they climbed, the beams of the headlights alive with moths. Novotny squinted through the windshield, the narrow dirt path twisted and turned and disappeared into the night. Twice they had to put branches under the wheels, and when they crossed bridges over mountain streams – built for wagons and oxen – Morath got out and walked ahead of the car with a torch. They passed one house only, a woodcutter's hut. Up on the crest, something ran away from them; they could hear it, crashing through the underbrush.

'I brought my dog along once,' Novotny said. 'She went crazy. Ran back and forth across the seat, scratching the windows with her paws.'

'What do you have?'

'Pointer bitch.'

'I've had them – couldn't wait to go to work.'

'That's her. She was crying because I wouldn't let her out of the car. I've seen bear up here, and stag. Wild boar. The peasants say there's lynx – kills their animals.'

Novotny slowed to a crawl, worked the car carefully around a hairpin curve. Morath could hear a stream, a long way below them. 'A shame, really,' Novotny said. 'When we start fighting here, well, you know what happens to the game.'

'I know. I was in the Carpathians, in 'fifteen.'

'This is, of course, where we want them.'

'In the mountains?'

'Yes. We watched them mobilize, back in May. Very educational. Tanks, trucks, cars, motorcycles. Big petrol tankers. It's not a secret, what they mean to do – read Guderian's book, and Rommel's. Everything's motorized, that's the sharp edge of the axe. After the first wave, of course, it's all horses and artillery limbers, like everyone else. So, the logic goes, run them up the mountains, or make them go through the valleys.'

'Enfilade.'

'Yes. With registered mortars. And machine guns on the hillsides.'

'When will it start?'

'In the autumn. We hold them two months, it starts to snow.' The road ahead was cut into wagon ruts. When it grew steeper, Novotny shifted into a whining first gear. 'What did you do, last time?'

'Hussars. The Sixteenth Corps, in the Second Army.'

'Magyar.'

'Yes, that's right.'

'I was in the Seventh. First under Pflanzer, then Baltin.'

'Down in Moldavia.'

'To start with. Eventually – I'm an artillery officer – they sent me over to Russian Poland. Lemberg, and Przemsyl.'

'The forts.'

'Twenty-eight months,' Novotny said. 'Lost them, got them back.'

Morath had never fought alongside the Czechs. The Austrian army spoke ten languages – Czech, Slovak, Croatian, Serb, Slovene, Ruthenian, Polish, Italian, Hungarian and German – and was normally divided into regiments based on nationality. But the history of the soldiers who defended the forts was well known. Twice they'd been surrounded and cut off, but the hundred and fifty thousand men in the blockhouses and bunkers had held out for months, while Russian dead piled up beneath their guns.

It was well after nine when they reached the Kreslice barracks – a set of long, low buildings in the imperial style, built of the honey-coloured sandstone so loved by Franz Josef's architects. 'We can probably get something for dinner,' Novotny said, sounding hopeful. But there was a feast laid on for Morath in the officers' mess. Roast goose, red cabbage with vinegar, beer from a small brewery in Pilsen, and a lieutenant-general at the head of the table.

'To friendship between our nations!'

'To friendship!'

Many of the officers were bearded, the style among artillerymen, and many had served on the eastern front in 1914. Morath saw the medals. Most decorated of all, the general: short and thick and angry. And fairly drunk, Morath thought, with a flushed face and a loud voice. 'It gets harder and harder to read the goddamn newspapers,' he said. 'Back in the winter, they couldn't love us enough, especially the French. Czechoslovakia – new hope! Liberal democracy – example for Europe! Masaryk and Benes – statesmen for the ages! Then something happened. In July, I think it was, there was Halifax, in the House of Lords, talking about "impractical devotion to high purpose". "Oh shit," we said, "now look what's happened."'

'And it continues,' Novotny said. 'The little minuet.'

The general took a long drink of beer and wiped his mouth with a linen napkin. 'It encourages him, of course. The Reichsführer. The army's the only thing he ever liked, but he's got tired of watching it march. Now he wants to see it fight. But he's coming to the wrong neighbourhood.'

'Because you'll fight back.'

'We'll give him a good Czech boot up his Austrian arse, is what we'll do. This *Wehrmacht*, we have films of their manoeuvres, they're built to roll across the plains of Europe. It's the Poles who ought to worry, and the Russians. Down here, we'll fight in the mountains. Like the Swiss, like the Spaniards. He can beat us, he's bigger than we are, no way to change that, but it will take everything he has. When he does that, he leaves the Siegfried Line wide open, and the French can march in with a battalion of café waiters.'

'If they dare.' There was laughter at the table.

The general's eyes glowed. Like Novotny's pointer bitch, he couldn't wait to get at the game. 'Yes, if they dare – *something's* gone wrong with them.' He paused for a moment, then leaned towards Morath. 'And what about Hungary? It's all plains, like Poland. You don't even have a river.'

'God only knows,' Morath said. 'We barely have an army. For the moment, we depend on being smarter than they are.'

'Smarter,' the general said. He thought it over; it didn't seem like much. 'Than all of them?'

'Hitler killed off the really smart ones, or chased them out of the country. So, for the moment, that's what we have.'

'Well then, may God watch over you,' the general said.

They gave him a room of his own – above the stables, the horses restless down below – a hard bed, and a bottle of plum brandy. At least, he thought, they didn't send along 'the stableman's daughter'. He drank some of the brandy, but still he couldn't sleep. It was thunder that kept him awake, from a storm that never rained, yet never moved away. He looked out the window now and then, but the sky was all stars. Then he realized that the Czechs were working at night. He could feel it in the floor. Not thunder, dynamite, the explosions rolling back and forth across the high valleys. It was the engineers who kept him awake, blowing the faces off their mountains, building fortifications.

Two-thirty. Three. Instead of sleeping, he smoked. He had felt, since he came to the barracks, a certain, familiar undercurrent. *Together we live, together we die, and nobody cares which way it goes.* He hadn't felt it for a long time. It wasn't that he liked it, but thinking about it kept him awake.

Just after dawn they were back on the mountain roads, this time in an armoured car, accompanied by the general and a pale, soft civilian in a dark suit, quite sinister, with tinted eyeglasses and very little to say. *A spy*, Morath thought. At least, a spy in a movie.

The road was newly made, ripped out of the forest with bulldozers and explosives, then surfaced with sawn tree trunks at the low spots. It would break your back but it wouldn't stall your car. To make matters worse, the armoured car rode as though it were sprung with steel bars. 'Better keep your mouth closed,' Novotny said. Then added, 'No offence meant.'

Morath never saw the fort until they were almost on top of it: cement walls, broken by firing slits, built into the mountainside, and independent blockhouses hidden in the natural sweep of the terrain. The general, clearly proud of the work, said, 'Now you see it, now you don't.'

Morath was impressed, and showed it.

The spy smiled, pleased with the reaction.

Inside, the raw smell of new cement and damp earth. As they went down endless flights of stairs, Novotny said, 'They have elevators in the Maginot Line. For people, elevators. But here, only the ammunition gets to ride.' A shaft had been carved out of the rock, Morath could see, with a steel platform on cables that could be operated electrically, or cranked by hand.

The spy's German was atrocious. 'So many forts are blown up from their own magazines. It need not happen.'

Novotny was joined by a group of officers who manned the fort. As they moved down a long corridor, the general put out a hand so that Morath stayed back from the group. 'How do you like my engineer?'

'Who is he?'

'A fortifications expert, artist is a better word. From the Savoy. They've been building these things since the renaissance – tradition of Leonardo, all that.'

'He's Italian?'

The general spread his hands. 'French by passport, Italian by culture, though he would say Savoyard, and a Jew by birth.' The Savoy, a mountain country between France and Italy, had managed to keep its independence until 1860. 'They've always permitted Jews to serve as officers,' the general said. 'This one was a major. Now he works for me.'

At the end of a cement chamber, under a six-foot ceiling, an embrasure opened out above a forest valley. The Czech officers stood apart, hands clasped behind their backs, as the general and the spy and Morath approached the opening.

'Find a river,' the spy said.

This took time. A pale summer sky, then a ridge-line dense with trees, then a green mountainside and a narrow valley that led to the upward slope where the fort had been built. Finally, Morath caught sight of a blue ribbon that wound through the pine trees.

'You have it?'

'Yes.'

'Here. Take.'

He handed Morath a fist-sized wad of cotton. Two soldiers rolled a 105-millimetre mountain gun up to the opening and ran a shell into the breech. Morath tore pieces of cotton from the wad and stuffed his ears, then covered them with his hands. Everyone in the room did the same. Finally, the general mouthed the word, 'Ready?' Morath nodded and the floor trembled as a tongue of flame leapt from the barrel of the cannon. Even with the cotton, the report was deafening.

Down range, a flash and a drift of dirty grey smoke. In the river, Morath thought, though he didn't actually see it happen. Other guns began firing, some from the floor below them, some from the block-houses, and puffs of smoke floated over the mountainside. The general handed him a pair of binoculars. Now he could see fountains of dirt blown forty feet in the air, trees torn from the ground or sheared in two. There was, in fact, a small road that led down to the river. As he watched, a cloud of orange tracers floated past his vision and churned up a storm of dirt spouts on the road.

The spy pointed to his ears. Morath took the cotton out; the room still rang with concussion. 'Do you see?' the spy said.

'Yes.'

'All the firing lines intersect, and the forts cover each other, so an attempt to storm will be very costly.' He reached in the inside pocket of his jacket and produced a few sheets of paper and a sharpened pencil. 'Please,' he said. 'Do the best you can.'

The general said, 'I can't give you blueprints, of course, but we don't mind if you sketch.'

The spy smiled. 'My father always wanted to teach the espionage drawing. "So terrible," he would say.'

They left him to work; only Novotny stayed behind. 'Well, now you've met our expert.'

'He seems a little, odd, maybe.'

'Yes. He is very odd. But a genius. An architect, a mathematician, a gunnery expert. Also he knows geology, and mining science.' Novotny shook his head. 'Likely there's more, we just haven't found out about it.'

Morath sketched. He wasn't very good. He concentrated on showing how the fort and its independent firing points were fitted tight into the mountainside. They would be hard to bomb, he realized. Even a Stuka would have to fly directly at them, with machine guns tracking it the minute it appeared over the crest of the mountain.

'Draw the room,' Novotny said. 'Don't forget the elevator for the shells.'

His day had barely begun. They drove him to other forts. At one of them, overlooking a paved road that ran south from Dresden, the spy took a stick and drew semicircles in the dirt to show overlapping fields of fire. Morath crawled into two-man pillboxes, sighted along machine guns aimed down mown strips of cornfield, saw tank traps to fall in, and tank traps of cement posts, 'dragon's teeth', wound in generous tangles of barbed wire. He squinted through Swiss sniperscopes fitted to Steyr rifles, and fired a ZGB 33, the Czech machine gun made in Brno – used as the model for the British Bren, *Brno/Enfield* – assassinating eight feather pillows gathering for an attack at the far end of a wheatfield. 'Good shooting,' Novotny said.

Morath reloaded; the curved-box magazine locked in place with a loud metallic snap.

'When you talk about your trip to the mountains,' Novotny said, 'don't forget to mention that Europe would be better off if Adolf did not have control of the Czech machine shops.'

Morath agreed. 'Of course,' he said, 'if it should come to that, I imagine the workers here would be – prone to error.'

But his conspiratorial smile was not returned. 'Just between us,' Novotny said, 'if it should happen that we are betrayed by those who claim to be our friends, we may not be so quick to give our lives in their service. That sort of business is bloody, Morath. There is always interrogation, always reprisal – you can only create a resistance movement when people don't care about their lives.'

Novotny drove him back to the Europa that evening. A fine summer dusk, flights of swallows swooping and climbing in the sky above the hotels. In the lobby, the mother-and-daughter smiled at him, warmer than ever. *Who would know?* On a leather couch, a man in mutton-chop whiskers and mountaineering costume was reading the *Volkischer Beobachter*. CZECH POLICE BURN SUDETEN FARMS, went the headline. DOZENS INJURED. Animals confiscated. Dogs shot. Three young women missing.

Dr Lapp, wearing a flat-brimmed straw boater at a jaunty angle, was waiting for him in the room, fanning himself with a room-service menu.

'I didn't hear you knock,' Morath said.

'Actually, I did knock,' Dr Lapp said, slightly amused. 'Of course, I'll be happy to apologize, if you wish.'

'Don't bother.'

Dr Lapp stared out of the window. The street lamps were on, couples strolling in the mountain air. 'You know, I cannot abide these people, the Czechs.'

Morath hung up his jacket, then began undoing his tie. He did not want there to be a war in Europe, but he was going to take a bath.

'They have no culture,' Dr Lapp said.

'They think they do.'

'What, Smetana? Perhaps you like Dvořàk. Good God.'

Morath took off his tie, looped it over a hanger, sat on the edge of the bed and lit a Chesterfield.

'I should mention,' Dr Lapp said, 'that I saw Count Polanyi, not so long ago, and that he sends his best regards. He said that you were considering, at one time, a vacation in Britain. Is it so?'

'Yes.'

Dr Lapp nodded. 'Can you still go?'

Morath thought about Cara. 'Maybe,' he said. 'Maybe not.'

'I see. Well, if you can, you should.'

'I'll try,' Morath said.

'They're weakening, the British. This morning's London *Times* says that the Czech government ought to grant "self-determination" to the Sudeten Germans, "even if it should mean their secession from Czechoslovakia". I would suppose that comes from Chamberlain's office. We know he met American correspondents at a lunch at Lady Astor's a few weeks ago and told them that Britain thought the Sudetenland ought to be turned over to Germany. In the interest of world peace, you understand. What his problem really is is that he doesn't trust the French, he doesn't trust the Russians, and he fears, politically, the possibility that Britain might have to fight alone.'

'He doesn't trust the French?'

Dr Lapp's laugh was dry, and delicate, and very brief.

It was almost dark. They sat in silence for a long time. Finally, Dr Lapp stood. 'There is something I want you to look at,' he said. 'I'll send it along tomorrow, if you don't mind.'

He closed the door silently behind him. Morath left the room in darkness. He went into the bathroom and turned on the water. There was a bright green mineral stain below the spout. *Good for the health.* If you believed in it, he thought. The water ran slow, and Morath waited patiently and listened to the distant thunder.

He booked a call to Paris early the next morning, the hotel operator rang his room an hour later. 'So much traffic, sir,' she apologized. 'Not usual for August.'

In Paris, a very elegant voice: 'Good morning, this is Cartier.'

Polanyi liked to say that the great fault of poets was that they never sang of the power of money in affairs between men and women. 'So for that we are left to the mercy of cynics – bartenders, novelists, or lubricious aunts.' Amusing when he said it, but not so amusing in real life. Morath didn't like himself for making this telephone call, but he could think of nothing else. The other possibility was flowers, and flowers weren't enough.

He found himself telling the saleswoman almost everything. 'I under-stand,' she said. Thought a moment, then added, 'We have just com-pleted a new design, a bracelet, which might be exactly right for

Madame. A little exotic – emeralds set in silver and black onyx, but very personal. And not at all the usual thing. Do you think she would like that?'

'Yes.'

'She would be the first in Paris to have it – it's a new style, for us. Would she like *that*?'

He knew she would. The saleswoman explained that the size was easily adjusted, so the bracelet could be sent by Cartier messenger to the residence. 'And finally, monsieur' – now there was a different note in her voice, she was, for a moment, speaking from the heart – 'the card.'

'Just say, "Love, Nicky".'

Later on, he was able to get through to an officer at the Crédit Lyonnais. A bank draft would be sent over to Cartier that afternoon.

Novotny showed up at eleven and they worked most of the day, spending much of the time in the car, driving east on the northern borders of Moravia and Bohemia. More fortifications, more barbed wire, more artillery pointed towards Germany. 'What happens to all this,' Morath asked, 'if the Sudetenlands are granted independence?'

Novotny laughed. 'Then it belongs to Hitler,' he said. 'With good, flat roads running straight to Prague. A hundred kilometres, more or less, about two hours.'

By nightfall they had turned back to the west, headed for the Kreslice barracks and a regimental dinner – a farewell dinner – with the general in attendance. 'There may be a speech,' Novotny said.

He paused a moment, peering into the darkness to find his way. They rattled over the crest of a mountain, then Novotny rode the brakes down the steep grade on the other side. 'Decin,' he said – a cluster of lights in the trees. This was, Morath thought, one last demonstration: that Czech forces could move east and west without returning to the roads in the valleys. They'd improved the old village paths, used mostly for cows and goats. In the beams of the headlights he could see where holes had been filled with small stones and packed down flat.

'And then, after the general's speech . . .' Novotny said.

'Yes?' *Oh no, he would refuse.*

'Perhaps you would consider . . . ?'

Morath was blinded. An explosion of yellow light, then blackness, with the dazzling after-image of a fiery star. He pressed his hands against his eyes but it wouldn't fade. Something had burned the air in front of his face, then gone whizzing away into the trees. Novotny yelled – apparently in Czech. Morath didn't understand. He shoved the door open, then reached for Novotny, who seemed frozen in place. As he grabbed hold of a sleeve there were two pings, metal on metal, and another tracer bullet, this one on the other side of the windshield. Morath could hear the machine gun, firing disciplined five-round bursts. When he smelled petrol he pulled with all his strength, dragging Novotny across the seat and out of the passenger door.

Lying flat on the ground, he rubbed his eyes as the star began to fade.

'Can you see?' Novotny was back in German.

'Not much.'

From the front of the car, a loud bang as a round hit the engine block, followed by the sharp smell of steam from the radiator. 'Christ,' Morath said. He began to crawl away from the road, pulling Novotny with him. He fought his way into a tangle of vines and branches, a thorn raked him across the forehead. He could now see grey shapes, resolving into trees and forest. He took a deep breath. A burned retina meant blindness for life and Morath knew it.

'What about you?' he said.

'Better.' Novotny probed his hairline with an index finger. 'The thing actually burned me,' he said.

The machine gunner wouldn't leave the car alone. He stitched frosted holes in the window glass, then blew out the tyres on the traverse. Morath could hear gunfire in the distance, and an orange light flickered on a cloud above the town.

'Is it the invasion?' Morath said.

Novotny snorted with contempt. 'It's the oppressed Sudeten Germans,' he said. 'Crying out for justice and equality.'

Morath got to his knees. 'We'll be better off in Decin.'

'I can't,' Novotny said. 'Without the stick.'

Morath crawled to the car, opened the back door, lay flat on the seat and retrieved the walking stick and the holstered pistol. Novotny was glad to have both. He staggered to his feet, held the butt of the pistol, unsnapped the holster with his teeth and swept the belt over his shoulder as the pistol slid free. 'Now let them come,' he said, laughing at himself and the whole stupid business.

They walked through the woods, Novotny limping along and breathing hard but keeping up with Morath. As it turned out, they were fortunate he was in uniform. A sixteen-year-old militiaman with a machine pistol almost cut them down as they reached Decin.

Headed for the police station, they kept to the alleys, the walls pocked and chipped from small-arms fire. 'I knew there was trouble here,' Morath said. 'Marching and rioting, you see it in the newsreels. But nothing like this.'

From Novotny, a sour smile. 'These are commando units, armed and trained by the SS. You won't see that in the newsreels.'

The alley ended at a side street. Morath and Novotny crouched at the edge of a stucco wall. To their left, on the other side of a broad avenue, the town school was on fire, bursts of red sparks blown up into the night sky. There were two bodies lit by the firelight, their faces pressed into the angle between the street and the pavement. One of them had a bare foot.

'Go ahead,' Morath said. There was a touch of nobility in this – 'First across the road' was a sacred axiom under fire. The enemy gunners saw the first, shot the second.

'Thanks just the same,' Novotny said. 'We'll go together.'

Even so, Morath took the side towards the gunfire, ran out of bravado midway across, grabbed Novotny around the waist and the two of them galloped to cover – a three-legged race – laughing like madmen as bullets sang past them.

It took them twenty minutes to reach the police station, where a shredded Czech flag hung limp above the barred windows. 'Poor fucking thing,' said the Decin chief of police. 'These fucking people keep *shooting* it.'

A strange scene at the station house. Policemen, some off-duty when the attack came – one of them firing a rifle out of the window with a forgotten napkin tucked in his belt – a few soldiers, local citizens. In the corner, lying flat on a desk, holding a compress to a bloody head wound, was a tall, spare man in a high collar and cutaway coat. One of the lenses in his eyeglasses was cracked in half.

'Our Latin teacher,' the police chief explained. 'They beat him up. Forced their way into the school, started throwing Czech schoolbooks out in the street, set them on fire, started *singing*, you know, and set the school on fire. Then they marched around the neighbourhood chanting, "Teach our children in German" while a newsreel cameraman filmed from the roof of a car.

'We did – nothing. We're under orders up here, don't let them provoke you. So we stood there and smiled, unprovoked, got the nurse over here to paste the Latin teacher back together, and everything was just perfectly lovely.

'But, of course, *they* were under orders to provoke us or else, so they went and took a shot at a policeman. He shot back, everyone ran away, and now we have this.'

'You radioed the army?' Novotny said.

The policeman nodded. 'They're coming. In armoured cars. But they've got four or five of these things to deal with so it might not be right away.'

'You have weapons for us,' Morath said. It wasn't a question.

Before the police chief could answer, Novotny spoke to him in rapid Czech. Then, later on, he explained as they moved towards the safe end of town. 'I'm sorry,' he said. 'But they would kill me if I let anything happen to you.'

But the safe end of town wasn't all that safe. At the bottom of a winding street they found the milkman's horse and cart, the milkman himself lying face down on the cobblestones, the back of his jacket flung up over his head. The blinkered horse, standing patiently with his wagonload of milk cans, turned and stared at them as they went past.

The chief of police had directed them to a three-storey brick monstrosity, perhaps the grandest house in Decin, on a broad boulevard shadowed by linden trees. The building was guarded by two policemen wearing French-style helmets and armed with rifles. They followed one of them to an overstuffed parlour on the top floor, the walls crowded with oil portraits of very fat people in very expensive clothing. As Morath and Novotny settled in, a local functionary came puffing up the stairs carrying two ledgers, a clerk and a secretary close behind him with two more. Still wheezing, he stopped dead, bowed politely, then spun on his heel and hurried off.

'His honour the mayor,' said the policeman. 'The Germans keep trying to burn the town hall, so he brings the tax records here.'

' "Keep trying"?'

The policeman nodded grimly. 'Third time since March.'

From the parlour window, Morath looked out over Decin. According to the policeman, the German units held several buildings – garages and small workshops on the north side of the town – and the railway station. Morath saw them once or twice as they changed positions: shapeless forms in peaked caps and jackets, bent low, running close to the walls. Once he got a clear view of a machine gunner and his helper, caught for an instant in the glow of a street lamp, one carrying a Maxim gun, the other its tripod and belts. Then they scurried away into the darkness, disappearing between the deserted office buildings on the other side of the boulevard.

Midnight. The crackle of small-arms fire intensified. Then the town lights went out, and a few minutes later, a call came on the radio and Novotny and the senior policeman returned to the station. The other policeman came upstairs, took his helmet off and sat on a sofa. He was young, Morath saw, not much more than twenty. 'The armoured cars should come soon,' he said.

Morath stared out into the street. It was hard to see, the warm, misty night darkened by smoke from the burning buildings. The distant firing slowed, then stopped, replaced by heavy silence. Morath looked at his watch. Two-twenty. Cara likely asleep, by now, on the avenue Bourdonnais, unless she'd gone out somewhere. The bracelet would have arrived that afternoon. Strange, how far away that seemed. *Not so far.* He remembered the bars on the Mediterranean beach, the crash of the waves, people saying, 'Half-past eight in Juan-les-Pins, half-past nine in Prague.'

A low, distant rumble, resolving, as Morath listened, to the throb of heavy engines. The policeman leapt to his feet. He was openly relieved – Morath hadn't realized how frightened he'd been. 'Now we'll see,' he said, running his hand over a cowlick of wheat-coloured hair. 'Now we'll see.'

Two of the armoured cars crept up the boulevard, going no more than ten miles an hour. One of them broke off and headed for the north side of the town, the other stood in the middle of the street, its turret turning slowly as the gunner looked for a target. Somebody – somebody not very bright, Morath thought – shot at it. The response was a blast of the turret cannon, a yellow flare and a ragged boom that rolled over the empty streets.

'Idiot.'

'A sniper,' the policeman said. 'He tries to fire into the aiming port of the turret.'

They both stood at the window. As the armoured car moved forward, there was a second shot.

'Did you see it?'

Morath shook his head.

'Sometimes you can.' Now, quite excited, he spoke in a loud whisper. He knelt in front of the window, rested the rifle on the sill and sighted down the barrel.

The armoured car disappeared. From the other end of town, a serious engagement – cannon and machine gun fire. Morath, leaning out of the window, thought he could see flicks of light from the muzzle flashes. Something exploded, an armoured car sped past, headed in the direction of the fighting. And something was on fire. Very slowly, the outlines of the buildings sharpened, touched with orange light. Downstairs, in the kitchen, an angry burst of static from the radio. The policeman swore softly, under his breath, as he ran off to answer it.

*

Four in the morning. The policeman was snoring away on the couch while Morath kept watch. The policeman had apologized for being so tired. 'We spent two days in the street,' he said. 'Fighting them with batons and shields.' Morath smoked to stay awake, making sure to keep well away from the window when he lit a match, masking the end of the cigarette with his hand. At one point, to his amazement, a freight train came through the town. He could hear it from a long way off. It didn't stop, the slow chuffing of the locomotive moved from east to west, and he listened to it until the sound faded away into the distance.

A silhouette.

Morath came wide awake, crushed the cigarette out on the floor, snatched the rifle from the corner and rested it on the windowsill.

Was it there? He didn't think so. A ghost, a phantom – *the same phantoms we saw in Galicia.* Until the dawn.

But no. Not this time.

A shape, on one knee, tight to the wall of a building across the boulevard and very still. It stood, ran a few feet, and stopped again. It held, Morath thought, something in its hand.

He touched the bolt of the rifle, making sure it was locked, then let his finger rest gently against the trigger. When he squinted over the open sight he lost the shape until it moved again. Then he tracked it as it stood, ran, and knelt down. Stood, ran, knelt down. Stood, ran.

Tracked, squeezed.

The policeman cried out and rolled off the couch. 'What happened?' he said, breathless. 'Are they here?'

Morath shrugged. 'I saw something.'

'Where is it?' The policeman knelt by his side.

Morath looked, there was nothing there.

But it was there an hour later, in grey light, when they crossed the boulevard. 'A runner!' the policeman said. 'To supply the sniper.'

Maybe. Not much more than a kid, he'd been knocked backwards and tumbled into a cellar entry and died there, halfway down the steps, arms flung out to stop his fall, a sandwich wrapped in newspaper dropped on the pavement.

At daybreak they walked over to the police station but it wasn't there any more. What remained was a burned-out shell, blackened beams, smoke rising from the charred interior. One corner of the building had been blown out – a hand grenade, Morath thought, or a homemade bomb. There was no way to know, there was nobody left to tell the story. He stayed for a while, talking to the firemen as they wandered around and looked for something to do. Then an army captain showed up and drove them back to the hotel. 'It wasn't only Novotny,' he said. 'We lost three others: they bicycled in from an observation post when they heard a call on the radio. Then there was the police chief, several officers, militia. At the end, they let the drunks out of the cells and gave them rifles.' He shook his head, angry and disgusted. 'Somebody said they tried to surrender, when the building caught on fire, but the Germans wouldn't let them.' He was silent for a time. 'I don't know, that might not be true,' he said. 'Or maybe it doesn't matter.'

Back at the Europa, there was a spray of gladioli in a silver vase on a table in the lobby. In the room, Morath slept for an hour, couldn't after that. Ordered coffee and rolls, left most of it on the tray, and called the railway station. 'Of course they're running,' he was told. As he hung up the phone, there was a knock at the door. 'Fresh towels, sir.'

Morath opened the door and Dr Lapp settled himself in the easy chair.

'Well, where are my towels?'

'You know, I once actually *did* that. Back when. In a maid's uniform, pushing the little trolley.'

'There must have been – at least a smile.'

'No, actually not. The man who answered the door was the colour of wood ash.'

Morath started to pack, folding underwear and socks into his valise.

'By the way,' Dr Lapp said. 'Have you met the two women who sit in the lobby?'

'Not really.'

'Oh? You didn't, ah, avail yourself?'

A sideways glance. *I told you I didn't.*

'They were arrested last night, is the reason I ask. In this very room, as it happens. Taken through the lobby in handcuffs.'

Morath stopped dead, a pair of silver hairbrushes in his hands. 'Who were they?'

'Sudeten Germans. Likely working for the Sicherheitsdienst, SD, the SS intelligence service. It caused quite a stir downstairs. *In Marienbad! Well!* But the women hardly cared – they were laughing and joking. All the Czechs can do is keep them overnight in the police station, and they barely dare to do that.'

Morath slipped the brushes through loops in a leather case, then zipped it closed.

Dr Lapp reached in his pocket. 'As long as you're packing.' He handed over a cellophane envelope, an inch square. Fitted neatly within was a photographic negative cut from a strip of film. Morath held it up to the light and saw a typed document, in German.

A death sentence. He'd put his drawings of the mountain fortifications in a manila folder and slid it down the side of the valise. He could, he thought, get away with that, even if he were searched. Could say it was a property for sale, or a sketch for a planned ski lodge. But not this.

'What is it?'

'A memorandum, on Oberkommando Wehrmacht stationery. From General Ludwig Beck, who has just resigned as head of the OKW, to his boss, General von Brauchitsch, the commander-in-chief of the German army. It says that Hitler "must abandon the intention of solving the Czech question by force". Actually he said a great deal more, in person, to do with getting rid of the Gestapo and the Nazi party bosses and returning Germany to "probity and simplicity". Then, in protest, he quit. And his successor, General Halder, believes these things even more strongly than Beck did.'

'I will be asked how I came to have it.'

Dr Lapp nodded. 'The Abwehr, military intelligence, is part of the OKW. We go to the same meetings, then, at night, to the same dinner parties.' He crossed his legs, tapped the heel of his shoe, and gave Morath a look that said, *of course you know where to put that.* He leaned over the table, took the Hotel Europa butter knife from the tray, held it to the light and studied its edge, then handed it to Morath.

Morath took off his shoe and went to work on the heel. He was very tired and sick of the world and had to force himself to be patient and careful. He prised up a corner of the heel and slid the negative in. It didn't work; he could see the space easily enough and he could feel it when he walked.

Dr Lapp shrugged. 'Improvisation,' he said, letting his voice trail away into a sigh.

Morath finished packing, pulled the straps tight on his valise and buckled them.

'I don't know who you'll find to talk to, Herr Morath, but the more powerful the better. We're opening as many lines of communication as we can, surely one of them will work.' From his voice, he didn't believe it, sounded as though he were trying to persuade himself that two and two was five. 'All we ask of the English is that they do nothing.' He looked up at Morath. 'Is that asking too much?'

Morath glanced at his watch, lit a cigarette and sat down to wait until it was time to leave for the train. It was quiet in the hotel; muffled voices in the hall, the sound of a maid's vacuum cleaner.

'My poor country,' Dr Lapp said. He hunted around in the inner pocket of his jacket, took out a pair of spectacles in a leather case, then a small metal box. 'Perhaps you'd better have this.'

Morath opened it and found a gold swastika pin. He fastened it to his breast pocket and went to look at himself in the bathroom mirror.

'Use it when you reach the German border,' Dr Lapp said, one hand on the door knob. 'But please do remember to take it off before you cross into France.'

'The two women,' Morath said. 'Were they after me, in particular?'

Dr Lapp shook his head slowly and looked sad. 'God knows,' he said. 'I don't.'

17 August. Bromley-on-Ware, Sussex.

Morath stood at the end of a gravel driveway as a taxi rattled off down the lane. Francesca's friend, Simon the lawyer, came smiling towards him, walking across the saintly lawn. He wore shorts and sandals, a white shirt with the cuffs folded back, a jacket thrown over his shoulders, a pipe clenched in his teeth and a newspaper under his arm. Behind him, a brick house with many chimneys, a blue sky, a white cloud.

Simon took his bag with one hand and his arm with the other, said, 'So pleased you could come, Nicholas,' in English, then moved into French.

There was a terrace; women in polka-dot dresses, men with white hair, a glass of Scotch whisky. A hug from Cara, who'd arrived a few days earlier, and some words in his ear. He wasn't exactly forgiven, but she was relieved to have him back safely. Also, he saw in the next few minutes, she was having a good time.

'How do you do, name's Bromley.'

So then it is your village, and your castle, and your peasants. 'Good afternoon, Mr Bromley.'

'Heh, heh, that's Bramble!'

'Mr Bramble?'

'No, no. *Bram*-well. Yes. Hmm.'

Cara's bare behind was blue in the Sussex moonlight. 'Not so loud,' she hissed.

'The bed squeaks – I can't help it.'

'*Méchant!* We can't make noise like that. Here, lie on your back.'

The bank of the river lay on the other side of a cow pasture. 'Mind the cowpats,' Simon told him.

They sat on a bench by a huge willow, where the sun sparkled on the water as it left the shadow of the tree. 'I have an old friend,' Morath said. 'When he heard I was coming to England for the August vacation, he asked me to take along some papers.'

'Oh?' Simon had thought the 'private conversation' would be about Cara, women, that sort of thing. 'Papers?'

'Confidential papers.'

'Oh.' Simon had a mop of brown hair that he pushed back off his forehead. 'Are you a spy then, Nicholas?'

'No. Just someone who doesn't like Hitler,' Morath said. 'Doesn't like Hitlers.' He told Simon about the Czechoslovakian mountain defence, and the memorandum from General Beck. 'My friend believes', he explained, 'that Hitler cannot be overthrown unless he fails. If your government holds firm, he will. One way or another.'

Simon took a minute to think it over. 'It's difficult, you see, because there are two sides to this. Like all politics, really. On one side, the side that wants to give the Sudetenland to Hitler, is Nevile Henderson, the ambassador to Germany. Very pro-German – pro-Nazi, it is said – and very anti-Czech. But Chamberlain *does* listen to him. Then, on the other side, there are people like Vansittart, the adviser to the foreign secretary, who'd be more in Churchill's camp. So the question is, who do we talk to? For me, you see, Vansittart is the hero, and Henderson the villain.' An *homme néfaste*, Simon called him. A man who does harm.

'But then,' Simon continued, 'if I find you a friend who can talk to Vansittart, eventually, aren't you simply preaching to the choir?'

Morath thought Simon was in his late twenties, but it sometimes amused him to be younger, to be terribly silly. Now, however, he seemed suddenly older, much older.

Simon stared down at the slow water. 'So then,' he said. 'What to do.'

Morath didn't know. The serenity of the countryside – of the country itself – was like the airs of springtime; it made the continent and its intrigues seem foolish and brutal and distant.

In the end, Simon got on the telephone and had a word with a friend of a friend.

Who stopped by for a drink that very evening. Left alone on the terrace with the family spaniel, they stumbled along in a combination of Morath's hesitant English and the friend-of-a-friend's university French. Still, they managed. Morath explained the defences, handed over the memo and passed along Dr Lapp's message as strongly as he could.

He did somewhat better the following day, when friend-of-a-friend – very good suit and military rank – brought along a smiling gnome who spoke Hungarian, Budapest Hungarian.

'We can always use a friend in Paris,' they said to him.

Morath declined with a smile.

They were never quite rude, after that. Inquisitive. How did *he* come to be involved with this? Was he simply an officer in the VK-VI, the Hungarian intelligence service? Had he met *Germans*? But it was none of their business and he didn't tell them and was rescued, in the end, by Simon's mother, who came out on the terrace and talked and laughed and flirted at them until they went away.

August 1938, everybody said it was the summer before the war. At night, the wireless crackled and the cicadas whirred. The Czechs mobilized, the British fleet mobilized, Benes offered Henlein and the Sudetenlanders everything either of them could think of – starting with complete autonomy and going on from there. But, not enough. In England, gas masks were issued and air-raid trenches dug in London parks. 'But what will become of *you*, Nicholas?' Simon's mother asked him at the lunch table.

He'd thought about that. More than he wanted to. He supposed he would be called back to duty, told to report to the regimental barracks in Budapest, amid the chubby stockbrokers and the balding lawyers, and ordered to fight alongside the Wehrmacht.

He discovered Cara, one night, wearing the Cartier bracelet, face down on the bedspread, weeping into the pillow. 'I shall tell my father', she whispered, 'that we must sell one of the *estancias*, because I am going to buy a villa in Lugano.'

At drinks the next day he was, *attacked* was the only word for it, by a neighbour in an army officer's uniform, fierce, and crimson with anger. The man had a totally incomprehensible accent – his words disappeared in a thick, black moustache – and Morath took a step back and had no idea what to do. It was Simon who saved him, whisking him away because he simply must meet the uncle from Perth. They were terribly, almost violently, kind to him at the house in Sussex. One rainy afternoon, when everyone but Morath and Cara played bridge, they dug deep in a chest and extracted a faded jigsaw puzzle. *The Defeat of the Spanish Armada.*

Speaking of which:

On the twenty-sixth the wireless reported Admiral Horthy's visit to the Reich, to Kiel, ostensibly as the last commander-in-chief of the Austro-Hungarian navy, to christen a new German battleship, the *Prinz Eugen*, and to have, the BBC said, 'private consultations with Chancellor Hitler'. Nobody in the room looked at Morath; all eyes found something else infinitely more interesting.

What the BBC didn't say, Count Polanyi did, three weeks later when they met in Paris. The whole business was staged so that Hitler could tell Horthy this: 'If you want to join in the meal, you must help with the cooking.'

It took two cars to get them to the station, the maids and the gardener stood by the door when they drove away. The thirty-first of August turned out to be, of course, a diabolically perfect day. The sky chalk blue, the children's-book clouds with chiselled edges, the little train from another time. Simon shook his hand and said, 'We'll hope for the best, right?' Morath nodded. Cara dabbed at her eyes with a hand-kerchief and held on to Francesca as the train pulled in. And Simon's mother took Morath's hands in hers. She had cool grey eyes and gave him a good long look. 'I'm so glad you could come,' she said. 'And we do want you to come back, Nicholas. You'll try, won't you?'

He promised he would, and held her hands.

Night Train
to Budapest

Paris that September was tense and brooding, on the edge of war, darker than Morath had ever known it. The *retour*, the return to daily life after the August vacation, was usually a sweet moment in Parisian life, but not that autumn. They came back to the office, the dinner party, the love affair, but Hitler was screaming at them from every newspaper stand and they had no taste for any of it. At Morath's morning café the waiter said, 'Let them come and drop their bombs, I'm tired of waiting.'

They couldn't bear it, the idea of another war; they'd never really recovered from the last one. The man who came home from the trenches and made love to his wife on the day the war ended, in 1918, now had a nineteen-year-old son, just the right age for the army. On 6 September, the morning papers wondered if the Sudeten issue was really worth a world war. The next day, a *Times* of London editorial supported partition.

In Germany, the annual Nazi party rally in Nuremberg began on the sixth and would end on the twelfth, with torchlight parades, gymnastic maidens, and the grand finale, a speech in the colossal Hall of the Fifty Thousand, where the Führer promised to reveal what he had in mind for the Czechs.

On the tenth, Parisian radio reported Roosevelt's statement that it was 'one hundred per cent wrong' to assume the USA would join Britain and France in a war over Czechoslovakia. On the eleventh, the proprietor of the stationery shop in the rue Richelieu showed Morath his old Lebel revolver from the Great War. 'Well, here is *my* answer,' he said. Which answer was that? Suicide? Shooting a German tourist? Sniping at the Wehrmacht?

'He has us where he wants us,' Polanyi said, at lunch on the quai de la Tournelle. 'Did you see the newsreel of Horthy's arrival at Kiel Station?' Morath hadn't. 'You get a glimpse of me, just over Count Csaky's shoulder.' Then he described how Hungary had been offered a return of disputed territories if she would agree to march into Slovakia when Hitler attacked the Czechs.

'Horthy declined. On the basis that we barely have an army, and what we have barely has guns and bullets,' Polanyi said, then went on to repeat Hitler's remark about the meal and the cooking.

They were eating *blanquette de veau* at a table on the terrace of a Norman restaurant. Polanyi waited while two young men hurried past. 'So naturally,' he said, 'some units are being recalled to service. But I made sure you weren't included in *that*.' He ran a forkful of fried potatoes through a dish of mayonnaise, then paused before eating and said, 'I trust I did the right thing?'

Morath didn't bother to answer.

'Why waste your life in a barracks?' Polanyi said. 'And besides, I need you with me.'

Eight-thirty in the morning on 14 September – Chamberlain had flown to Berchtesgaden to consult with Hitler – the phone rang in Morath's apartment. It was Cara, in a voice he'd never heard her use. 'I hope you will come over and say goodbye to me,' she said.

He started to say 'What—?' but she hung up on him.

Twenty minutes later he was there. The door was open, he walked in. Two men in blue smocks were packing Cara's clothing in the drawers of a large steamer trunk, its wardrobe side already crammed with dresses on little hangers. A third man, bigger than the others, stood and watched them, his arms folded across his chest. A chauffeur or a bodyguard, Morath thought, with a dark, heavy face and a collarless jacket. When Morath came into the room he took a half step towards him and let his arms hang by his sides.

Cara was sitting on the edge of the bed, the Picasso nude in its gold frame held on her knees. 'Monsieur Morath,' she said, her voice dull and flat, 'allow me to present my father, Señor Dionello.'

A short man, sitting in the bedroom chair, got to his feet. He had a black and white moustache and wore a double-breasted suit with black and white stripes and a black, borsalino-style hat. He said, 'Señor,' tipped his hat and shook hands. It was clear to Morath that he was not pleased to meet his daughter's forty-four-year-old lover, Hungarian lover, Parisian lover, but he would agree not to make a scene if Morath didn't.

Morath sought Cara's eyes – *what do you want me to do?* Family was family, but he was not going to allow her to be abducted against her will.

She shook her head and closed her eyes. It was subtle, a small, fragile gesture of surrender, but she'd told him what he needed to know.

His heart sank; he'd lost her.

Señor Dionello spoke to her in rapid Spanish, his voice not unkind.

'It's the war, Nicky,' Cara said. 'My father expresses his regrets, but my mother and grandmother are sick with worry, he says, that I will be hurt.'

Señor Dionello smiled ruefully at Morath as Cara spoke, in his expression a plea for understanding, a plea that he not be forced to use power or money to get his way.

'My father is staying at the Meurice. I am to join him there for a few days, until the boat leaves.'

Morath nodded to Señor Dionello, forcing himself to be as gracious as he could.

Señor Dionello spoke again, and smiled at Morath. 'My father would be pleased if you would join us for dinner at the hotel.' She hesitated, then said, 'It's a lot for him, Nicky.'

Morath declined. Cara translated, then said, '*Un momentito, por favor.*'

As they went out into the hall, Señor Dionello made a small gesture and the bodyguard stayed where he was.

In the hall, Cara clenched his shirt in her fists and sobbed, silently, with her face pressed against him. Then she pushed him away, wiped the tears off with her hand, took two steps towards the door, looked at him one last time, and went back into the apartment.

On 21 September, Chamberlain tried again. Flew to Bad Godesberg and offered Hitler what he said he wanted. The Sudetenland, with French and British approval, would become a German possession. But the Führer didn't quite work the way Chamberlain thought he did. Once he got what he wanted, he wanted more. Now it was military occupation, by 1 October.

Or else, war.

So, on the twenty-ninth, Chamberlain flew back to Germany, this time to Munich, and agreed to the occupation. The Czechoslovakian army abandoned its forts, and moved back from the mountains.

18 October.

Morath stared out of the train window, a tiny village slid away down the track. Was it called Szentovar? Maybe. Or that was another place. A hundred kilometres and a hundred years away from Budapest, where the peasants still rubbed garlic on barn doors to keep the vampires from milking the cows at night.

On the road, a gypsy wagon. The driver looked up as Morath's window went by. Prosperously fat, with three chins and clever eyes, perhaps a *primas*, a clan leader. He held the reins loosely in his hands, turned and said something to the women in the wagon behind him. Morath never saw their faces, simply the red and yellow colours of their clothing as the train clattered past.

October was a dead month, he thought. The brutal politics played out in the newspapers. The French relaxed, congratulated themselves on having done the right thing, the *smart* thing, for once in their dreamy lives. Morath smoked too much and stared out of the window when he woke up in the morning.

He was surprised at his broken heart. He had always told himself that the love affair with Cara was a passing thing that stayed. But now she was gone, he missed what he'd taken for granted, and he ached for what she'd lost. 'When I lived in Paris,' she would say to her friends in Buenos Aires.

Count Polanyi didn't care for this mood and let Morath know it. 'We've all been thrown off the horse,' he said. 'The thing to do is get back in the saddle.' When that didn't work, he tried harder. 'This is no time to feel sorry for yourself. Need something to do? Go back to Budapest and save your mother's life.'

Keleti Palyuadvar. The *east* railway station where, this being Hungary, all important trains arrived from the west. There were cabs in the street but Morath decided to walk – in the late afternoon of an autumn day, what else. *It is your nose that tells you you're home*, he thought. Burned coffee and coal dust, Turkish tobacco and rotten fruit, lilac water from the barber shops, drains and damp stone, grilled chicken. And more; unknown, unimagined. A deep breath, another – Morath inhaled his childhood, his country, the exile returned.

He walked for a long time, taking the cobbled alleys, heading more or less across the city, towards a villa in the hills of the Third District, on the Buda side of the Danube. He dawdled, stopped to look in shop windows. As always, this time of day, a melancholy, speculative idleness settled over the city and Morath slowed down to meet its rhythm. At five-thirty, when the sun hit the windows of a tenement on Kazinczy Avenue and turned them flaming gold, Morath took the Number Seven tram across the Chain Bridge and went home.

*

They didn't really talk until the next morning. In the living room, the rugs were still up for the summer, so when his mother spoke there was a faint echo. She sat, perfectly composed, on a spindly chair in front of the French doors, a silhouette in garden light. She was, as always, slim and lovely, with ice-coloured hair set in steel and pale skin that showed in the vee of her silk dress.

'And do you see Lillian Frei?' she asked.

'Now and then. She always asks after you.'

'I miss her. Does she still wear the suits from de Pinna?'

'Where?'

'A store on Fifth Avenue, in New York.'

Morath shrugged politely, he had no idea.

'In any event, you'll kiss her for me.'

Morath drank a sip of coffee.

'Would you care for a pastry, Nicholas? I can send Malya to Gundel's.'

'No, thank you.'

'Bread and butter, then.'

'Really, just coffee.'

'Oh Nicholas, what a *Parisian* you are. You're sure?'

Morath smiled. He'd never in his life been able to eat anything before noon. 'How long has it been, *anyuci*, since you've seen Paris?' This was 'mother', very much her preference. She had never been 'mama'.

His mother sighed. 'Oh, a long time,' she said. 'Your father was alive, the war just over. Nineteen-nineteen – could that be right?'

'Yes.'

'Has it changed? People say it has.'

'There are more automobiles. Electric signs. Cheap restaurants on the boulevards. Some people say it's not as nice as it was.'

'Here it is the same.'

'*Anyuci?*'

'Yes?'

'Janos Polanyi feels that, with the situation in Germany, you, and perhaps Teresa, should consider, should find a place . . .'

When she smiled, his mother was still incredibly beautiful. 'You haven't come all the way here for *that*, I hope. Ferenc Molnar has moved to New York. He is living at the Plaza and is said to be utterly miserable.'

A long look, mother and son.

'I won't leave my house, Nicholas.' *And how can you not have known it?*

*

They went to the movies in the afternoon. A British comedy, dubbed in Hungarian, from the 1920s. It had a cruise ship, nightclubs with shiny floors, a hound called 'Randy', a hero with patent-leather hair called 'Tony', a blonde with kiss curls that they fought over called 'Veronica', which sounded very strange in Hungarian.

Morath's mother loved it – he glanced over and saw her eyes shining like a child's. She laughed at every joke and ate caramels from a little bag. During a song-and-dance sequence at the nightclub, she hummed along with the music.

> *Akor mikor, Lambeth utodon*
> *Bar melyek este, bar melyek napon,*
> *Ugy találnád hogy mi mind is*
> *Sétalják a Lambeth Walk. Oi!*
>
> *Minden kis Lambeth leany*
> *Az ö kis, Lambeth parjával*
> *Ugy találnád hogy ök*
> *Sétalják a Lambeth Walk. Oi!*

Afterwards, they went to the tearoom of the Hotel Gellert and had acacia honey and whipped cream on toasted cake.

Three-thirty in the morning. In the rambling, iron-gated gardens of the villa district, some people kept nightingales. Other than that, he could hear wind in the autumn leaves, a creak in a shutter, a neighbour's fountain, a distant rumble of thunder, north, he thought, in the mountains.

Still, it was hard to sleep. Morath lay in his old bed and read Freya Stark. This was the third time he'd started it, a travel narrative, adventures in the wild mountain valleys of Persia.

He'd always stayed up late in this house, his father's very own son. He used to hear him, sometimes, as he paced around the living room. Often he would play records on the victrola while he worked in his office – sliding stamps into glassine envelopes with silver tweezers.

They weren't rich, but his father never worked for money. He had been one of the great philatelists of Hungary, very strong in both nineteenth-century Europe and colonials. Morath supposed his father had traded in the international markets, perhaps he'd made some money that way. Then too, before the war, nobody really had to work. At least, nobody they knew.

But, after Trianon, everything changed. Families lost the income they'd had from land in the countryside. Even so, most of them managed; they simply had to learn to improvise. It became fashionable to say things like, 'If only I could afford to live the way I live.'

Then, on a June day in 1919, the communists killed his father.

In the spasms of political chaos that followed the loss of the war, there came a Soviet Republic of Hungary – a government born of a national desperation so deluded it persuaded itself that Lenin and the Red Army would save them from their enemies, the Serbs and the Roumanians.

The Soviet was led by a Hungarian journalist named Bela Kun who, while serving in the Austro-Hungarian army, had deserted to the Russians during the war. Kun, his henchman Szamuelly and forty-five commissars, began a rule of 133 days, and shot and burned and hanged their way from one end of Hungary to the other. They were then chased out of the country – across the border and, eventually, into the Lubianka – by a Roumanian army, which occupied Budapest, wandered aimlessly about the countryside, and spent its days in desultory looting until it was shooed back across the border by a Hungarian army led by Miklos Horthy. The counter-revolution then gave birth to the White Terror, which shot and burned and hanged its way from one end of Hungary to the other, paying particular attention to the Jews, since Jews were Bolsheviks (or bankers), and Kun and a number of his comrades were Jewish.

It was one of Kun's wandering bands who did for Morath's father. He had gone, one weekend, to the country house in the Carpathian foothills. The communist militia rode into the yard at dusk, demanded jewellery for the oppressed masses, then bloodied the farm manager's nose, threw Morath's father into a horse trough, took three stamp albums – 1910 commemoratives from Luxembourg – all the cash they could find, several shirts, and a lamp. They chased the servant girls into the woods but couldn't catch them, and, in one corner of the kitchen, set a fire, which burned a hole in the pantry wall and went out.

Morath's father dried himself off, calmed the servant girls, put a cold spoon on old Tibor's neck to stop the bleeding, then poured a glass of plum brandy and sat down in his favourite chair where, with his glasses folded up and held gently in one hand, he died.

Morath went to his sister's house for dinner. A new villa, also in the Third District, but up in the newly elegant quarter known as Rose Hill. His sister, in a low-cut dress and red felt boots with tiny mirrors on them – oh, Cara – gave him a sexy hug and a warm kiss on the lips. 'I'm so happy to see you, Nicholas. I am.' She didn't let him go until a maid came into the room.

This was not new. She was three years older than Morath. When he was nine and she was twelve, she liked to comb his hair, would slip into his bed during a scary thunderstorm, would always know when he was melancholy and be tender to him.

'Teresa,' he said. 'My only love.' They both laughed.

Morath looked around. There was too much furniture in the Duchazy house, much too expensive and much too new. How his sister could have married that idiot Duchazy was beyond him. They had four children, including a ten-year-old Nicholas – the absolute image of that idiot Duchazy.

Still, Teresa had married him, and her days of worrying about money were long over. The Duchazy family owned flour mills; thirty years earlier there'd been more mills in Budapest than any other city in the world. Morath's mother, who disliked Duchazy even more than he did, would refer to him in private as 'the miller'.

Not the typical miller. He strode towards Morath and embraced him, a sinewy man with uncomfortably stiff posture, a pencil moustache, and strange, pale green eyes. Well then, how was Paris? Still in the advertising business? Still a bachelor? What a life! The children were brought out, shown off, and put away. Duchazy poured Scotch whiskies and had the fire lit.

The conversation wandered here and there. The Duchazy family was not exactly *nyilas*, but close enough. Teresa warned him with a glance, more than once, when he was headed into a sensitive area. By the end of the second Scotch, Duchazy had thrown a second oak log on the fire, which blazed merrily in a newly installed surround of yellow tile.

'Janos Polanyi thinks mother ought to leave Budapest,' Morath said.

'Why is that?' Duchazy was annoyed.

'War,' Morath said.

Teresa shrugged. 'She won't go.'

'Maybe if you two suggested it, she might.'

'But we won't,' Duchazy said. 'We're patriots. Besides, I think it's going to go on this way for a long time.' He meant diplomacy, marches, street fighting – the sort of thing they'd seen in the Sudetenland. 'Hitler means to dominate the Balkans,' he continued. 'Someone's going to, it might as well be him. And he wants it quiet in Hungary and south of here – that's the granary, and the oil fields. I don't think the British dare to fight him but, if it comes to that, he'll need the wheat and the oil. Anyhow, if we're smart, we'll stay in his good graces, because the borders are going to start moving.'

'They already have,' Teresa said.

That was true. Hungary, having supported the occupation of the Sudetenland, was to be rewarded with the return of some of its northern territory, especially in lower Slovakia, where the population was eighty-five per cent Magyar.

'Laszlo's brother is fighting up in Ruthenia,' Teresa said.

Morath found this puzzling. Duchazy gave his wife the look that meant *you've been indiscreet.*

'Really?' Morath said.

Duchazy shrugged. 'Nothing's secret around here.' He meant, Morath thought, the house, Budapest, the nation itself.

'In Ruthenia?'

'Near Uzhorod. We're in it with the Poles. They have irregulars, in the north, and we have the Rongyos Garda.' The Ragged Guard.

'What's *that*?'

'Arrow Cross men, the street-corner boys and what have you, led by a few army officers in civilian clothing. They're fighting the Sich, the Ukrainian militia. The next thing is, local Hungarians demand an end to the instability, and we send in the regular army. This used to be Hungary, after all, why should it belong to the Czechs?'

Jackals, Morath thought. Now that the prey was down they'd tear off a piece for themselves.

'The world's changing,' Duchazy said. His eyes sparkled. 'And about time.'

Dinner was exceptional. Devilled carp with onions, cabbage stuffed with ground pork, and a Médoc from the Duchazy estates near Eger.

After dinner, Teresa left the men to themselves and Morath and Duchazy sat by the fire. Cigars were lit, and for a time they smoked in companionable silence. 'One thing I did want to ask you,' Duchazy said.

'Yes?'

'A few of us have got together to support Szalassy. Can I put you down for a contribution?' Szalassy was one of the leaders of the Arrow Cross.

'Thank you for asking, but not right now,' Morath said.

'Mmm. Oh well, I promised some people I'd ask.'

'I don't mind.'

'Do you ever see Colonel Sombor, at the legation?'

'I'm hardly ever there.'

'Oh. He asked after you. I thought maybe you were friends.'

Tuesday. In the late afternoon, Morath took a trolley to the Kobanya District, where factory walls rose high above the track on both sides of the street. There was a smoky haze, as evening came on, and a light rain dappled the surface of the river. A young woman sat across from him. She had the liquid radiance of some Hungarian girls, and long hair that blew across her face as the trolley went around a curve. She swept it back with one hand, and glanced at Morath. The trolley stopped in front of a brewery, the girl got off in a crowd of workmen. Some of them knew her, called her by name, and one of them gave her a hand down from the high step.

The slaughterhouse was at the next stop, where a metal sign bolted to the brickwork said 'Gersoviczy'. When Morath got off the trolley the air was like ammonia and made his eyes water. It was a long way to the entrance that led to the office, past loading docks with open doors where he could see red carcasses hung on hooks and butchers in leather aprons. One of them rested a sledgehammer in the sawdust, the iron head beaten flat at both ends, while he took a minute to smoke a cigarette.

'The office?'

'Upstairs. Keep going till you see the river.'

In the Gersoviczy brothers' office there was a desk with a telephone and an adding machine, an ancient safe in one corner, a clothes tree behind the door. The brothers were waiting for him. They wore black Homburgs and heavy suits and silver ties, and they had the long sidelocks and beards of orthodox Jews. On the wall was a Hebrew calendar with a picture of a rabbi blowing a ram's horn. Across the top it said, in Hungarian, 'Gersoviczy Brothers Wish You A Happy And Prosperous New Year'.

A soot-blackened window looked out over the river, lights twinkling on a hill above the far bank. The brothers, both smoking oval cigarettes, peered at Morath through the gloom of the unlit office.

'You are Morath *uhr*?' He used the traditional form of address, Morath Sir.

'Yes. Count Polanyi's nephew.'

'Please do sit down. I'm sorry we cannot offer you anything.'

Morath and the older brother, his beard streaked with silver, took the two wooden swivel chairs; the younger brother half sat on the edge of the desk. 'I am Szimon Gersoviczy,' he said. 'And this is Herschel.' The older brother gave him a stiff nod.

Szimon spoke heavily accented Hungarian. 'We're Polish,' he explained. 'From Tarnopol, twenty years ago. Then we came down here. Half of Galicia came here, a hundred years ago. We came for the same reason, to get away from the pogroms, to get a little opportunity.

And it worked out like that. So, we stayed, and we Magyarized the name. It used to be just Gersovicz.'

The older brother finished his cigarette and stubbed it out in a tin ashtray. 'Your uncle came to us for help, that was in September. I don't know if he told you.'

'Not then, no.'

'Well, he did. Through our brother-in-law, in Paris. He asked if we would help, help the country. He saw the handwriting on the wall, as they say.'

He paused a moment. Ouside, the drumming of a tugboat engine, hauling a line of barges north on the river.

'We don't *ask* for anything,' he went on, 'but now Polanyi knows, and you know, so . . .'

Szimon went over to the safe and began to work the combination. Then he pulled the handles to the up position and swung the doors open. Herschel leaned close to Morath. He smelled strong; of sweat and onions, cigarettes.

'It's in pengo,' he said. 'Maybe if the community was more involved, we could make it in something else. But the count wanted it kept close, so it's only a few people. Szimon and me, our family, you know, one or two others, but mostly us.'

Szimon began stacking piles of pengo on the desk, each fifty notes pinned at the corner. He flipped the ends of the stacks, wet his thumb, then counted in Yiddish as he shuffled through the bills. Herschel laughed. 'For some reason,' he said, 'it's hard to do that in Hungarian.'

Morath shook his head. 'Nobody ever thought it would come to this,' he said.

'Forgive me, sir, but it always comes to this.'

'*Zvei hundrit toizend*,' Szimon said.

'What will you call it?'

'I don't know. The Free Hungary Committee – something like that.'

'In Paris?'

'Or London. If the country is occupied, the best place is the closest place. Closest safe place.'

'So, do you like New York?'

'God forbid.'

Szimon finished counting, then squared the stacks off by tapping the edges on the desk. 'Four hundred thousand pengo,' he said. 'About the same in French francs. Or, in case God doesn't forbid, eighty thousand dollars.'

'Tell me one thing,' Herschel said. 'Do you think the country will be occupied? Some people say sell and get out.'

'And lose everything,' Szimon said. He slid the money across the desk
– thousand-pengo notes, wider than French currency, with black and
red engravings of St Istvan on one side and a castle on the other.
Morath opened a briefcase, placed the stacks on the bottom, put Freya
Stark on top.

'Don't we have rubber bands?' Herschel said.

Morath pulled the straps tight and buckled them. Then he shook
hands, very formally, with each of the brothers. 'Go with God,' Herschel
said.

That night he met Wolfi Szubl at the Arizona, a *nachtlokal* in Szint Josef
Alley on Margaret Island. Szubl wore a pale blue suit and a flowery tie
and smelled of heliotrope. 'You never know,' he said to Morath.

'Wolfi,' Morath said, shaking his head.

'There's someone for everyone,' Szubl said.

Szubl led him to a table on a platform by the wall, then pressed a
button which raised them ten feet. 'Here it's good.' They shouted down
to a waiter for drinks, Polish vodkas, that came up on a mechanical tray.

The orchestra was dressed in white tuxedos, and played Cole Porter
songs to a packed dance floor, which sometimes disappeared into the
basement to a chorus of shrieks and laughter from the dancers.

A naked girl floated past in a harness, dark hair streaming out behind
her. Her pose was artistic, lofty, an insouciant hand rested against the
wire that hung from the ceiling.

'Ahh,' Szubl said.

'You like her?'

Szubl grinned – who wouldn't?

'Why "Arizona"?' Morath said.

'The couple who own it got an unexpected inheritance, a fortune,
from an uncle in Vienna. Decided to build a nightclub on Margaret
Island. When they got the telegram they were in Arizona, so . . .'

'No. Really?'

Szubl nodded. 'Yes,' he said. 'Tucson.'

The drinks came. The girl went by again, headed the other way. 'You
see? She ignores us,' Szubl said.

'She just happened to fly past, naked on a wire. Don't make
assumptions.'

Szubl raised his glass. 'To the Free Hungary Committee.'

'May it never exist.'

Morath liked Polish vodka, potato vodka. It had a ghost of a taste he
could never quite understand. 'So, how did you do?'

'Not bad. From the Salon Kitty, on Szinyei Street, two hundred and fifty thousand pengo. Most of it from Madame Kitty, but she wanted us to know that three of the girls contributed. Then, from the nephew of the late, lamented minister of finance, another one hundred and fifty.'

'That's all? His uncle would steal the wool from a sheep.'

'Too late, Nicholas. The casino got most of it – he's a candidate for the boat.'

The citizens of Budapest were partial to suicide, so the municipal authority maintained a boat tied up below the Ferenc Josef Bridge. A riverman waited in the bow with a long pole, ready to haul in the night's jumpers before they drowned.

'What about you?' Szubl said.

'Four hundred thousand from the Gersoviczy brothers. I go out to Koloszvar tomorrow.'

'Shooting animals?'

'Christ, I hadn't thought of that.'

'I'm to see Voyschinkowsky.'

' "The Lion of the Bourse". He lives in Paris, what's he doing here?'

'Nostalgia.'

'Waiter!'

'Sir?'

'Two more, please.'

A big redhead came gliding by. She blew a kiss, put her hands beneath her breasts and wobbled them, then raised an eyebrow.

'Let me buy her for you, Wolfi. All night, my treat.'

They drank their vodkas, ordered doubles. The dance floor re-appeared. The leader of the orchestra had shiny black hair and a little moustache and smiled like a saint as he waved his baton.

'When you begin-n-n-n, the beguine.' Szubl took a deep breath, and sighed. 'You know,' he said, 'what I really like is to look at naked women.'

'You do?'

'No, Nicholas, don't make fun of me, I'm serious. I mean, I really don't like anything else. If I could have begun this at fourteen, as my life's work, as the only thing I did day and night, there never would have been a reason for me to disturb the world in any other way.

'But, of course, they wouldn't let me do that. So now I crowd into trains, make telephones ring, throw orange peels into trash cans, make women buy girdles, ask for change, it doesn't stop. And, worst of all, on a lovely day when you're happy and calm you go out in the street – and there I am! Really, there's no end to it. And it won't stop until I take up the space in the graveyard you wanted for your mother.'

The orchestra played the 'Tango du Chat'. Morath remembered the song, from the bar on the beach in Juan-les-Pins. 'Tell you what,' he said to Szubl. 'We'll go over to Szinyei Street, to Kitty's. Order a parade around the parlour, every girl in the house. Or a game of tag. No, wait, hide-and-seek!'

'Nicholas. You know, you're a romantic.'

Later Morath went to the WC, met an old friend, gossiped for a few minutes. When he came back the redhead was sitting on Szubl's lap, playing with his tie and laughing. Wolfi's voice floated down from the platform. 'Good night, Nicholas. Good night.'

At Koloszvar railway station, a bright, cold morning.

There were two other Hungarians who left the train with him. Hunters, with shotguns under their arms. The conductor on the platform wished him good morning, in Hungarian, as he got off the train. And the two women mopping the floor in the station waiting room bantered in Hungarian and, in fact, laughed in Hungarian. A pleasant, Magyar world, it just happened to be in Roumania. Once Koloszvar, now Cluj. *Nem, nem, soha.*

A journey to the estate of Prince Hrubal turned out to be infernally complicated to arrange. It had required, in the end, several medieval phone calls, three telegrams – one of which went, inexplicably, to Wales – a verbal message taken to the castle by a gamekeeper's daughter, and a personal intervention by the village mayor. But, in the end, it worked.

In the street outside the station, Prince Hrubal's head groom was waiting for him, mounted on a bay gelding and holding the reins of a dock-tailed chocolate mare. This was, Morath knew, much the best way. You could try the road by car, but you spent more time digging than driving, and the trip by horse and carriage would hammer your teeth flat. That left walking and riding, and riding was faster.

He swung up into the saddle and tucked his briefcase under his arm. He'd made sure, in Budapest, to wear boots for the journey.

'Your excellency, I kiss your hands,' said the groom.

'Good morning to you,' Morath said, and they were off.

The good road in Cluj led to the bad road outside Cluj, then on to a road paved long ago, at the direction of some nameless dreamer/bureaucrat, and soon forgotten. This was northern Transylvania, mountainous and lost, where for generations Hungarian nobles ruled the lives of Roumanian serfs. There were, now and then, savage *jacqueries*, peasant risings, and the looting and burning would go on until the army arrived, coils of rope hung on their saddles. The trees were already there. Now, for the moment at least, it was quiet. Very quiet. Out in the countryside, a ruined castle broke the line of a mountain crest, then there was only forest, sometimes a field.

It took Morath back to the war. They'd been no different than any of the armies who came down these roads on mornings in the fall. He remembered wisps of autumn mist caught on the barbed wire, the sound of wind in the stubble of the rye fields, the creak of harness, crows wheeling in the sky and laughing at them. Sometimes they saw geese flying south, sometimes, when it rained at dawn, they only heard them. A thousand horses' hooves rang on the paved roads – their coming was no secret, and the riflemen waited for them. Once there was a sergeant, a Croat, adjusting a stirrup in the shade of an oak tree. The air cracked, an officer shouted. The sergeant put a hand over his eye, like a man reading an eye chart. The horse reared, galloped down the road a little way, and began to graze.

Prince Hrubal owned forests and mountains.

A servant answered Morath's knock and led him to the great hall – stag heads on the wall and tennis racquets in the corner. The prince showed up a moment later. 'Welcome to my house,' he said. He had merciless eyes, black, depthless, and cruel, a shaven head, a drooping Turkish moustache, the nickname 'Jacky', acquired during his two years at Cornell, a taste for Italian fashion models, and a near manic passion for charity. His bookkeeper could barely keep track of it: broom factories for the blind, orphanages, homes for elderly nuns, and, lately, roof repairs on ancient monasteries. 'This may do it for me, Nicholas,' he said, a heavy arm draped around Morath's shoulders. 'I've had to sell my sugar contracts in Chicago. But, still, the contemplative life must be lived, right? If not by you and me, by *somebody*, right? We can't have wet monks.'

The Baroness Frei once told Morath that the prince's life was the story of an aristocrat of the blood seeking to become an aristocrat of the heart. 'Hrubal's a little mad,' she said. 'And it remains to be seen if his wealth can accommodate his madness. But, whatever happens, these are thrilling races to watch, don't you agree? Poor man. Thirty generations of ancestors, brutal and bloody as the day is long, roasting rebels on iron thrones and God knows what, and only one lifetime for redemption.'

The prince led Morath outside. 'We've been moving boxwood,' he said. He wore high boots, corduroy field trousers and a peasant blouse; a pair of cowhide gloves in his back pocket. At the end of the lawn, two peasants waited for him, leaning on their shovels.

'And Janos Polanyi,' Hrubal said. 'He's in good form?'

'Always up to something.'

Hrubal laughed. 'The King of Swords – that's his tarot card. A leader, powerful, but dark and secretive. His subjects prosper, but regret they ever knew him.' The prince laughed again, fondly, and patted Morath's shoulder. 'Hasn't killed you yet, I see. But have no fear, Nicky, he will, he will.'

Dinner for twelve. Venison from Hrubal's forest, trout from his stream, sauce from his redcurrants and sauce from his figs, a traditional salad – lettuce dressed with lard and paprika – and burgundy, Bull's Blood, from the Hrubal vineyards.

They ate in the small dining room, where the walls were lined with red satin, sagging, here and there, in melancholy folds, and well spotted with champagne, wax and blood. 'But it proves the room,' Hrubal said. 'Last burned in 1810. A long time, in this part of the world.' Dinner was eaten by the light of two hundred candles. Morath felt the sweat running down his sides.

He sat close to the head of the table, between Annalisa, the prince's friend from Rome, pale as a ghost, with long, white hands, last seen in the April *Vogue*; and the fiancée of the Reuters correspondent in Bucharest, Miss Bonington.

'It is miserable, now,' she said to Morath. 'Hitler is bad enough, but the local spawn are worse.'

'The Iron Guard.'

'They are everywhere. With tiny bags of earth around their necks. Sacred earth, you see.'

'Come to Rome,' Annalisa said. 'And see them strut, our *fascisti*. Chubby little men, they think it's their *time*.'

'What are we supposed to do?' Miss Bonington said, her voice shrill. 'Vote?'

Annalisa flipped a hand in the air. 'Be worse than they are, I suppose, that's the tragedy. They have created a cheap, soiled, empty world, and now we are to have the pleasure of living in it.'

'Well, personally, I never imagined—'

'*Basta*,' Annalisa said softly. 'Hrubal is looking at us; to talk politics with food is against the rules.'

Miss Bonington laughed. 'What then?'

'Love. Poetry. Venice.'

'Dear man.'

The three of them turned their eyes to the head of the table.

'I loved the life there,' Hrubal said. 'On Saturday afternoon, the big game. That's what they called it – the big game! As for me, well, I was their sabre champion, what else, and only our girlfriends came to the matches. But we all went to see the football. I had a giant horn, for cheering.'

'A giant horn?'

'Damn. Somebody . . .'

'A megaphone, I think,' said the Reuters man.

'That's it! Thank you, years I've wanted to remember that.'

A servant approached the table and whispered to Hrubal. 'Yes, very well,' he said.

The string quartet had arrived. They were shown into the dining room and the servants went for chairs. The four men smiled and nodded, wiping the rain from their hair and drying their instrument cases with their handkerchiefs.

When everyone had gone to their rooms, Morath followed Hrubal to an office high in a crumbling turret, where the prince opened an iron box and counted out packets of faded Austrian schillings. 'These are very old,' he said. 'I never know quite what to do with them.' Morath converted schillings to pengo as the money went into the briefcase. Six hundred thousand, more or less. 'Tell Count Janos', Hrubal said, 'that there's more if he needs it. Or, you know, Nicholas, whatever it might be.'

Later that night, Morath heard a soft tapping and opened his door. *After venison from Prince Hrubal's forest and trout from his stream, a servant girl from his kitchen.* They never spoke a word. She stared at him with grave, dark eyes and, when he'd closed the door, lit the candle by his bedside and pulled her shift over her head. She had a faint moustache, a lush body, and wore knitted, red wool stockings which came to midthigh.

A sweet morning, Morath thought, riding through the brown leaves on the floor of the forest. Delicately, the mare walked across a wide stream – a few inches of fast, silver water – then down a series of rocky ledges. Morath kept the reins loose, let her find her own way. It was an old Magyar cavalryman who'd taught him that a horse can go anywhere a man can go without using his hands.

Morath kept his weight balanced, steadied the briefcase on the saddle, tugged a gentle reproach when the mare saw something she wanted for breakfast. 'Manners,' he whispered. Did she speak Hungarian? A Transyivanian horse, she must.

Up ahead, Hrubal's head groom rode his bay gelding. Morath pulled up for a moment and whistled softly; the groom half turned in the saddle to look back at him. He thought he'd heard other horses, not far away, but, when he listened, they weren't there. He rode up to the groom and asked him about it.

'No, your excellency,' the groom said. 'I believe we are alone.'

'Hunters, perhaps.'

The groom listened, then shook his head.

They rode on. Morath watched a bank of mist as it drifted over the side of a mountain. He looked at his watch: a little after noon. The groom carried a picnic hamper of sandwiches and beer. Morath was hungry, but decided to ride for another hour.

In the forest, somewhere above him on the gentle slope, a horse whickered, then stopped, abruptly, as though someone had put a hand over its muzzle.

Again Morath rode up to the groom. 'Surely you heard that.'

'No, your excellency. I did not.'

Morath stared at him. He had a sharp face, with hair and beard cut short, and there was something in his voice, subtle, but there, that suggested defiance: *I chose not to hear it.*

'Are you armed?'

The groom reached under his shirt, held up a large revolver, then put it away. Morath wanted it.

'Are you able to use it?' he asked.

'Yes, your excellency.'

'May I see it for a moment?'

'Forgive me, your excellency, but I must decline.'

Morath felt the heat in his face. He was going to be murdered for this money and he was very angry. He threw the reins over hard and dug his heels in the horse's side. She sped off, dead leaves whispering beneath her hooves as she galloped down the slope. Morath looked back and saw that the groom was following him, his horse easily keeping pace. But there was no revolver to be seen, and Morath let the mare slow to a walk.

'You can leave now,' he called out to the groom. 'I'll go on by myself.' He was breathing hard, after the gallop.

'I cannot, your excellency.'

Why don't you shoot me and get it over with? Morath let the mare walk downhill. Something made him look back once more, and he saw, through the bare trees, a horse and rider, then another, some way up the slope. When they realized he'd seen them they walked their horses into cover, but seemed to be in no great hurry. Morath thought of tossing the briefcase away, but by then he knew it wouldn't matter. He called to the groom, 'Who are your friends?' his voice almost mocking, but the man wouldn't answer.

A few minutes later he came to the road. It had been built in Roman times, the stone blocks hollowed and cracked by centuries of horse and wagon traffic. Morath turned towards Koloszvar. When he looked up into the forest, he caught an occasional glimpse of the other riders, keeping pace with him. Directly behind him was the groom, on the bay gelding.

When he heard the car, sputtering and tapping, he stopped, and stroked the mare on her heaving side. A gentle animal, she'd done her best; he hoped they wouldn't shoot her. It was an old Citroën that appeared from a grove of birch trees by the side of the road. There was mud spattered on the doors and the wheel guards, a brown sweep across the windshield where the driver had tried to clear the dust with the single wiper.

The Citroën stopped with a loud squeak from the brakes and two men climbed out, both of them heavy and short. They wore straw hats, dark suits, and soiled white shirts buttoned at the throat. *Siguranza*, he thought. Roumanian secret police. Obviously they'd been waiting for him.

'Get down from there,' the driver said. It was Hungarian, badly spoken. Morath took longer to dismount than they liked. The man on the passenger side of the car opened his jacket, showing Morath the handgrip of an automatic pistol in a shoulder holster. 'If you need to be shot, we'll be happy to oblige you,' he said. 'Maybe it's a matter of honour, or something.'

'Don't bother,' Morath said. He got off the horse and held her by the bridle. The driver approached and took the briefcase. Something about him made the mare nervous, she tossed her head and stamped her hooves on the stone blocks. The driver unbuckled the briefcase and had a look inside, then he called out to the groom, 'You can go home now, Vilmos. Take his horse.'

'Yes, your excellency,' the groom said. He was very frightened.

'And keep your mouth shut.'

Morath watched as he rode into the forest, leading the mare by the reins.

The Siguranza men tied his wrists with a length of cord and shoved him into the back seat of the car, then made jokes as the starter motor whined and faded until the engine caught. They talked for a moment more – Morath didn't understand Roumanian but caught the word 'Bistrita', a small town north of Koloszvar. As the car bounced along the road, the passenger opened the briefcase and divided up Morath's underwear and shaving kit. The two men argued briefly over Morath's spare shirt but the driver gave in almost immediately. The passenger then turned in his seat and stared at Morath. He hadn't shaved for several days, the stubble on his face black and grey.

He leaned over the seat and slapped Morath in the face. Then did it again, harder. The driver laughed, the passenger stretched sideways until he could see himself in the rear-view mirror and adjusted the brim of his hat.

Morath did not feel pain where he'd been slapped, he felt it in his wrists, where he'd tried to break the cord as the Siguranza man hit him. Later on, when he managed to twist around and get a covert look, he saw that he was bleeding.

Bistrita had been part of the Ottoman Empire until 1878 and not that much had changed. Dusty streets and lime trees, stucco buildings painted yellow and pale green, with fishscale roofing on the better houses. The Catholic crosses were mounted on the domes of the former mosques; the women on the street kept their eyes lowered, and so did the men.

The Citroën pulled up in front of the police station and they hauled Morath out by the elbow and kicked him through the door. He made a point of not falling. Then they beat him down the stairs, along a hallway, and to the door of a cell. When they cut the cord on his wrists, the knife sliced through the back of his jacket. One of them made a joke, the other one snickered. Then they cleaned out his pockets, took his boots and socks, jacket and tie, threw him in the cell, slammed the iron door, shot the bolt.

Black dark in the cell, no window, and the walls breathed cold air. There was a straw mattress, a bucket, and a pair of rusted, ancient brackets in the wall. Used for chains – in 1540, or last night. They brought him a salt herring, which he knew better than to eat – he would suffer terribly from thirst – a lump of bread, and a small cup of water. He could hear, in the room directly above him, somebody pacing back and forth.

Heidelberg. Half-timbered houses, the bridge over the Neckar. When he was at Eotvos they'd gone over there for Schollwagen's lectures on Aristophanes. And – it was late February – just to be somewhere else. In a *Weinstube*, Frieda. Curly hair, broad hips, a wonderful laugh. He could hear it.

A two-day love affair, and long ago, but every minute of it stayed in his memory and, now and then, he liked to go back over it. Because she liked to make love in every possible way and shivered with excitement.

He was nineteen, he thought that women did such things as favours, maybe, when they loved you, on your birthday, or you paid whores a special rate.

There was a thump above him. *A sack of flour thrown on the floor.* Cara had no particular interest in *choses affreuses.* She would have done them – would have done anything, to be sophisticated and chic, that's what excited Cara. Did she do it with Francesca? She liked to tease him that she did, because she knew it interested him. *Another sack of flour.* This one cried out when it hit the floor.

Fuck you, he told them.

He'd thought about seeing Eva Zameny in Budapest, his former fiancée, who'd left her husband. Jesus, she'd been so beautiful. No other country made women who looked like that. Not much to remember with Eva – passionate kisses, in the vestibule of her house. Once he had unbuttoned her blouse. She had wanted, she told him, to become a nun. Went to Mass twice a day because it gave her peace, she said, and nothing else did.

Married to Eva, two children, three, four. To work as a lawyer, spend his days with wills and contracts. Friday night dinner at his mother's house, Sunday lunch at hers. Make love on Saturday night under a feather quilt in the Hungarian winter. Summer cabin on Lake Balaton. He'd have a coffee house, a gentlemen's club, a tailor. Why had he not lived his life in this way?

Really, why?

He wouldn't be in a Roumanian dungeon, if he had. Who'd sold him? he wondered. And would he – God grant! – have a chance to square that account? Was it somebody at Hrubal's house? Duchazy?

Stop it. Here is Frieda: curly hair, broad hips, sweet laugh.

'Bad luck, Monsieur Morath. For you and for us. God only knows how we are going to get this straightened out. What, in the name of heaven, were you thinking of?'

This one was also from the Siguranza, Morath thought, but much higher up. Well shaven, well pomaded, and well spoken, in French.

The man rested his elbows on the desk and steepled his fingers. Told Morath he was guilty of technical crimes, no question, but who really cared. He didn't. Still, what the hell was he doing with all that *money?* Playing Hungarian – minority – politics? In Roumania? 'Couldn't you have murdered somebody? Robbed a bank? Burned down a church? No. You had to make my life complicated, on Saturday morning, when I'm supposed to play golf with my father-in-law.' Yes, it was Roumania, *douce décadence, Byzance après Byzance*, it was all too true. Still, they had laws.

Morath nodded, he knew. But what law, exactly, had he broken?

Overwhelmed, the Siguranza officer barely knew what to say – too many, too few, old ones, new ones, some we're just now making up. 'Let's talk about Paris. I've told them to bring you coffee and a brioche.' He looked at his watch. 'They've gone to the café across the square.'

Now here he really envied Morath, he might as well admit it. A man of his class and connection, taking the pleasures of that delightful city. One would know, don't bother denying it, the most stimulating people. French generals, Russian émigrés, diplomats. Had he met Monsieur X, Herr Y, Señor Z? What about, Colonel Something at the British embassy? Don't know him? Well, really you ought to meet him. He is, one hears, an amusing fellow.

No, Morath told him.

No? Well, why not? Morath was certainly the sort of gentleman who could meet anybody he liked. What could be – oh, was it money? Not to be indelicate, but the bills did pile up. Annoying people sent annoying letters. Being in debt could be a full-time occupation.

A lifelong hobby. But Morath didn't say it.

Life didn't have to be so hard, the officer told him. He himself had, for example, friends in Paris, businessmen, who were always seeking the advice and counsel of somebody like Morath. 'And for them, believe me, money is no problem.'

A policeman brought in a tray with two cups, a zinc coffee pot, and a large brioche. Morath tore a strip off the fluted brioche, yellow and sweet. 'I'll bet you have this every morning, at home,' the officer said.

Morath smiled. 'I am travelling, as you know, on a Hungarian diplomatic passport.'

The officer nodded, brushing a crumb off his lapel.

'They will want to know what's become of me.'

'No doubt. They will send us a note. So we will send them one. Then they will send us one. And so on. A deliberate sort of process, diplomacy. Quite drawn out.'

Morath thought it over. 'Still, my friends will worry. They'll want to help.'

The officer stared at him, made it clear he had a bad, violent temper. Morath had offered him a bribe, and he didn't like it. 'We have been very polite to you, you know.' *So far.*

'Thank you for the coffee,' Morath said.

The officer was again his affable self. 'My pleasure,' he said. 'We're not in a hurry to lock you up. Twenty years in a Roumanian prison won't do you any good. And it doesn't help us. Much better, put you over the border at Oradea. Goodbye, good luck, good riddance. But, it's up to you.'

Morath indicated he understood. 'Perhaps I need to think it over.'

'You must do what's best for you,' the officer said. 'I'll be back tomorrow.'

In the room above him, the pacing never stopped. Outside, a storm. He heard the thunder, and the drumming of the rain. A slow seep of water covered the floor, rose an inch, then stopped. Morath lay on the straw mattress and stared at the ceiling. *They didn't kill me and take the money.* For the Siguranza thugs who'd arrested him it was a fortune, a life on the French Riviera. But this was Roumania, 'kiss the hand you cannot bite', and they had done what they'd been told to do.

He slept, sometimes. The cold woke him, and bad dreams. Even when he woke up, bad dreams.

In the morning they took him to a room on the top floor, likely the office, he thought, of the chief of the Bistrita police. There was a calendar on the wall, scenic views of Constanta on the Black Sea coast. A framed photograph on the desk, a smiling woman with dark hair and dark eyes. And an official photograph of King Carol, in white army uniform with sash and medals, hung on the wall.

Out the window Morath could see life in the square. At the stalls of the market place, women were buying bread, carrying string bags of vegetables. In front of the fountain there was a Hungarian street singer. A rather comic fat man who sang like an opera tenor, arms thrown wide. An old song of the Budapest *nachtlokals*:

> *Wait for me, please wait for me,*
> *even when the nights are long,*
> *my sweet, my only dove,*
> *oh please, wait for me.*

When somebody dropped a coin in the battered hat on the ground in front of him, he smiled and nodded gracefully and somehow never missed a beat.

It was Colonel Sombor who entered the office, pulling the door shut behind him. Sombor, with glossy black hair like a hat and slanted eyebrows, in a sharp green suit and a tie with a gold crown on it. Very tight-lipped and serious, he greeted Morath and shook his head – *now look what you've done.* He took the swivel chair at the police chief's desk, Morath sat across from him. 'I flew right over when I heard about it,' Sombor said. 'Are you, all right?'

Morath was filthy, unshaven, and barefoot. 'As you see.'

'But they haven't *done* anything.'

'No.'

Sombor took a pack of Chesterfields from his pocket, laid it on the desk, put a box of matches on top. Morath tore the foil open, extracted a cigarette and lit it, blowing out a long, grateful stream of smoke.

'Tell me what happened.'

'I was in Budapest. I came over to Roumania to see a friend, and they arrested me.'

'The police?'

'Siguranza.'

Sombor looked grim. 'Well, I'll have you out in a day or two, don't worry about that.'

'I would certainly appreciate it.'

Sombor smiled. 'Can't have this sort of thing happening to our friends. Any idea what they're after?'

'Not really.'

Sombor looked around the office for a moment, then he stood, walked to the window and stared out at the street. 'I've been wanting to talk to you,' he said.

Morath waited.

'This job I have', Sombor said, 'seems to grow more demanding every day.' He turned back towards Morath. 'Europe is changing. It's a new world, we're part of it, whether we want to be or not, and we can win or lose, depending how we play our cards. The Czechs, for instance, have lost. They trusted the wrong people. You'll agree to that, I think.'

'Yes.'

'Now look, Morath, I have to be frank with you. I understand who you are and what you think – Kossuth, civil liberty, democracy, all that cosy shadow-front idealism. Perhaps I don't agree, but who cares? You know the old saying, "Let the horse worry about politics, his head is bigger." Right?'

'Right.'

'I have to see the world in a practical way, I don't have time to be a philosopher. Now I have the greatest respect for Count Polanyi, he too is a realist, perhaps more than you know. He does what he needs to do, and you've helped him do it. You're not a virgin, is what I mean.'

Sombor waited for a response. 'And so?' Morath said it quietly.

'Just as I've come to help you, I would like you to help me. Help your country. That, I trust, would not be against your principles.'

'Not at all.'

'You will have to get your hands dirty, my friend. If not today, tomorrow, whether you like the idea or don't like it. Believe me, the time has come.'

'And if I say "no"?'

Sombor shrugged. 'We will have to accept your decision.'

It didn't end there.

Morath lay on the wet straw and stared into the darkness. Outside, a truck rumbled past, driving slowly around the square. A few minutes later it returned, paused briefly in front of the station, then drove off.

Sombor had gone on at length. Whatever light there'd been in his eyes had blown out like a candle but his voice never changed. *Getting you out may not be so easy. But don't you worry. Do our best. The prison at Iasi. The prison at Sinaia. Forced to stand with his nose touching the wall for seventy-two hours.*

For supper, they'd brought him another salt herring. He broke off a tiny piece, just to see what it tasted like. Ate the bread, drank the cold tea. They'd taken his cigarettes and matches when they put him back in the cell.

'I flew right over when I heard about it.' Said casually enough. The legation in Paris had two Fiesler-Storch aeroplanes, sold to Hungary by the Germans after endless, agonizing negotiation and God only knew what favours. *I'm more important than you think*, Sombor meant. I command the use of the legation aeroplane.

When Sombor got up to leave, Morath said, 'You'll let Count Polanyi know what's happened.'

'Naturally.'

Polanyi would never know. *Nacht und nebel*, Adolf Hitler's phrase, night and fog. A man left his home in the morning and was never heard of again. Morath worked hard, *think only of the next hour*, but despair rose in his heart and he could not make it go away. Petoffi, Hungary's national poet, said that dogs were always well looked after and wolves starved, but only wolves were free. So here, in this cell or those to come, was freedom.

They came for him at dawn.

The door opened and two guards took him under the arms, ran him down the hall and hauled him up the long staircase. It was barely daylight, but even the soft gloom hurt his eyes. They gave him back his boots, then shackled him at the wrists and ankles, and he shuffled out the front door to a waiting truck. There were two other prisoners in there, one a gypsy, the other perhaps a Russian, tall, with sheared white hair and blue tears tatooed at the corners of his eyes.

Only the women who swept the street saw him leave. They paused for a bare moment, their brooms, made of bundles of brown reeds, resting on the ground. *Poor boys. God help you.* Morath never forgot it.

The truck bounced on the cobbles. The gypsy caught Morath's eye and sniffed the air. They'd driven past a bakery. It wasn't a long ride, maybe fifteen minutes. Then they were at the station where trains, Morath understood perfectly, left for towns like Iasi, or Sinaia.

Three men in chains and six policemen. That was something worth looking at when your train stopped in Bistrita. Passengers lowered the tops of their windows to see the show. A commercial traveller, from the look of him, peeling an orange and throwing the rind on the station platform. A woman in a pillbox hat, the dark veil hiding her eyes, white hands resting atop the window. Other faces, pale in the early light. A man made a joke, his friend laughed. A child, who watched Morath with wide eyes, knowing she was allowed to stare. A man in an overcoat with a velvet collar, stern, elegant, who nodded to Morath as though he knew him.

Then, chaos. Who were they? For slow-motion moments the question raced through Morath's mind. They came from nowhere. Moving too fast to count, shouting in – was it Russian? Polish? The policeman at Morath's side was hit. Morath heard the impact, then a yelp, then he staggered off somewhere, groping at his holster. A man in a soft hat stepped from a cloud of steam vented by the locomotive. A cool, frosty morning, he'd wrapped a muffler around his throat, tucked the ends inside his jacket, and turned up the collar. He studied Morath carefully, for what seemed like a long time, then swung his shotgun a little to one side and fired both barrels. Several passengers gasped; the sound, to Morath, was clear as a bell.

The Russian prisoner knew. Maybe too much, Morath thought later. He stretched out full length on the platform and covered his head with his shackled hands. A lifelong convict, perhaps, who knew that this business was, sadly, not for him, his gods weren't that powerful. The gypsy cried out to a man with a handkerchief tied over his face, extended his wrists. Free me! But the man pushed him aside. He almost fell, then tried to run away, taking tiny steps, his ankle chain scraping along the concrete.

In the killing, they almost forgot Morath. He stood alone at the centre of it. A detective, at least a man in a suit holding a revolver, ran past, then turned towards Morath, his face anxious, uncertain, the right thing must be done. He hesitated, started to raise his pistol, closed his eyes, bit his lip, and sat down. Now he knew what to do but it was too late. The pistol moved only a few inches, a red gash opened in his forehead and, very slowly, he collapsed. A few yards away, the train conductor was lying back against a wheel of the coal car. In his eyes, a look Morath knew. He was dying.

Now a black car came driving, very slowly, along the platform. Driven by a young boy, no more than thirteen, hands white on the wheel, face knotted with concentration. He stopped the car, while the man in the soft hat dragged another man by the collar of his jacket, sliding him up to the rear door of the car. He opened the door and threw him in the back seat. In the middle of it all, screams and shots, Morath could hardly believe that anybody could be that strong.

'Move, dumb ox!' The words in German, the Slavic accent so thick it took Morath a moment to understand. The man gripped his arm like a steel claw. A hook nose, dark face, an unlit cigarette in his lips. 'To the *truck*, yes?' he said. '*Yes?*

Morath walked as fast as he could. Behind him, from the train, a cry in Hungarian. A woman, cursing, enraged, screaming, telling them all, brutes, devils, to cease this fouling of the world and go and burn in hell. The man at Morath's side lost all patience – the rise and fall of distant sirens coming nearer – and dragged Morath towards the truck. The driver reached over and helped him and he sprawled across the passenger seat, then fought his way upright.

The driver was an old man with a beard and a scar that cut across his lips. He pressed the gas pedal, gingerly; the engine raced, then died back. 'Very good,' he said.

'Hungarian?'

The man shook his head. 'I learn in war.'

He pressed the clutch pedal to the floor as the man in the soft hat ran towards the truck and violently waved his shotgun. *Go. Move.* 'Yes, yes,' the driver said, this time in Russian. He shoved the gear lever forward and, after a moment, it engaged. He gave Morath an inquisitive look. Morath nodded.

They drove away slowly, into the street behind the station. A police car was idling at the corner, both doors open. Morath could hear the train moving out of the station – the engineer at last come to his senses. A black sedan came flying past and, tyres squealing, cut in front of them, then slowed down. A hand came out of the driver's window and beckoned them forward. The sedan accelerated and, at the next street, turned sharply and sped away.

*

They were quickly out of Bistrita, the road narrowed, turned to dirt, wound past a few dilapidated farms and villages, then climbed into the Transylvanian forest. At sunset, despite the cold iron on his wrists and ankles, Morath slept. Then woke in darkness. Out of the window, a field painted in frost and moonlight. The old man was bent over the wheel, squinting to see the road.

'Where are we?' Morath said.

From the old man, an eloquent shrug. He took a scrap of brown paper from atop the dashboard and handed it to Morath. A cross-hatch of lines, drawn in blunt pencil, with notes in Cyrillic script scrawled along the margin. 'So, where we are?'

Morath had to laugh.

The old man joined him. Maybe they would find their way, maybe not, so life went.

The truck worked its way up a long hill, the wheels slipping in the frozen ruts, the old man restlessly shifting gears. 'Like tractor,' he said. In the distance, Morath saw a dull glow that appeared and disappeared through the trees. This turned out to be, a few minutes later, a low, stone building at the junction of two ancient roads, its windows lit by oil lamps. An inn, a wooden sign hung on chains above the door.

The old man smiled in triumph, let the truck roll to a stop in the cobblestone yard and honked the horn. This produced two barking mastiffs, galloping back and forth in the headlights, and an innkeeper wearing a leather apron, a blazing pitch-pine torch held high in one hand. 'You are welcome in this house,' he said, in formal Hungarian.

A deliberate man, round and genial. He led Morath to the stable, set the torch in a bracket, and, with hammer and chisel, broke the shackles and took them off. As he worked, his face grew sorrowful. 'So my grandfather,' he explained, repositioning the chain atop an anvil. 'And his.'

When he was done he led Morath to the kitchen, sat him in front of the fire, and served him a large glass of brandy and a thick slice of fried cornmeal. When Morath had eaten, he was shown to a room off the kitchen, where he fell dead asleep.

When he woke, the truck was gone. The innkeeper gave him an old jacket and a peaked cap and, later that morning, he sat next to a farmer on a wagon and entered Hungarian territory by crossing a hayfield.

Morath had always liked the Novembers of Paris. It rained, but the bistros were warm, the Seine dark, the lamps gold, the season's new love affairs still new. The 1938 November began well enough, *tout Paris* ecstatic that it wouldn't have to go to war. But then, *Kristallnacht*, on the night of 9 November, and in the shimmering tons of shattered Jewish glass could be read, more clearly than anybody liked, what was coming. Still, it wasn't coming *here*. Let Hitler and Stalin rip each other's throats out, went that week's thinking, we'll go up to Normandy for the weekend.

Morath arranged to meet his uncle at some *cuisine grandmère* hole-in-the-wall out in Clichy. He'd spent ten days in Budapest, collecting money, listening to poor Szubl's misadventures with the redheaded chorus girl he'd met at the nightclub. Then the two of them had hidden the cash in a cello and taken the night express back to Paris. For the moment, Morath was a man with well over two million pengo in his closet.

It was obvious to Morath that Count Polanyi had got an early start on lunch. Trying to sit down, he lurched into the neighbouring table, very nearly causing a soup accident and drawing a sharp glance from the *grandmère*. 'It seems the gods are after me today,' he said, in a gust of cognac fumes.

It wasn't the gods. The pouches beneath his eyes had grown alarmingly, and darkened.

Polanyi peered at the chalked menu on the blackboard. '*Andouillette*,' he said.

'I hear you've been away,' Morath said.

'Yes, once again I'm a man with a house in the country, what's left of it.' On 2 November, the Vienna Commission – Hitler – had awarded Hungary, in return for supporting Germany during the Sudeten crisis, the Magyar districts of southern Czechoslovakia. Twelve thousand square miles, a million people, the new border running from Pozsony/Bratislava all the way east to Ruthenia.

The waiter arrived with a carafe of wine and a plate of snails.

'Uncle Janos?'

'Yes?'

'How much do you know about what happened to me in Roumania?'

From Polanyi's expression it was clear he didn't want to talk about it. 'You had difficulties. It was seen to.'

'And that's that.'

'Nicholas, don't be cross with me. Basically, you were lucky. Had I left the country two weeks earlier you might have been gone for good.'

'But, somehow, you heard about it.'

Polanyi shrugged.

'Did you hear that Sombor appeared? At the Bistrita police station?'

His uncle raised an eyebrow, speared a snail on the third try and ate it, dripping garlic butter on the table. 'Mmm? What'd he want?'

'Me.'

'Did he get you?'

'No.'

'So where's the problem?'

'Perhaps Sombor is a problem.'

'Sombor is Sombor.'

'He acted like he owned the world.'

'He does.'

'Was he responsible for what happened to me?'

'Now that's an interesting idea. What would you do if he was?'

'What would you suggest?'

'Kill him.'

'Are you serious?'

'Kill him, Nicholas, or don't ruin my lunch. Choose one.'

Morath poured himself a glass of wine, and lit a Chesterfield. 'And the people who rescued me?'

'*Très cher*, Nicholas.'

'Who shall I thank for it?'

'Somebody owed me a favour. Now I owe him one.'

'Russian? German?'

'Eskimo! My dear nephew, if you're going to be inquisitive and difficult about this . . .'

'Forgive me. Of course I'm grateful.'

'Can I have the last snail? That grateful?'

'At least that.'

Polanyi jammed the tiny fork into the snail and frowned as he worked it free of its shell. Then, for a moment, he looked very sad. 'I'm just an old, fat Hungarian man, Nicholas. I can't save the world. I'd like to, but I can't.'

The last days of November, Morath pulled his overcoat tight and hurried through the streets of the Marais to the Café Madine. It was, Morath thought, frozen in time. Empty, as before, in the cold morning light, a cat asleep on the counter, the *patron* with his spectacles down on his nose.

The *patron*, Morath suspected, remembered him. Morath ordered a *café au lait*, and, when it came, warmed his hands on the bowl. 'I was here once before,' he said to the *patron*. 'Last March, I think it was.'

The *patron* gave him a look. *Really?*

'I met an old man. I can't recall his name, I don't think he mentioned it. At the time, a friend of mine had difficulties with a passport.'

The owner nodded. Yes, that sort of thing did happen, now and then. 'It's possible. Somebody like that used to come here, once in a while.'

'But not any more.'

'Deported,' the owner said. 'In the summer. He had a little problem with the police. But for him, the little problem became a big problem and they sent him back to Vienna. After that, I can't say.'

'I'm sorry to hear it,' Morath said.

'He is also sorry, no doubt.'

Morath looked down, felt the height of the wall between him and the *patron*, and understood there was nothing more to be said. 'He had a friend. A man with a Vandyke beard. Quite educated, I thought. We met at the Louvre.'

'The Louvre.'

'Yes.'

The *patron* began drying a glass with a cloth, held it up to the light and put it back on the shelf. 'Cold, today,' he said.

'With snow tonight.'

'You think so?'

'You can feel it in the air.'

'Maybe you're right.' He began wiping the bar with the cloth, lifting Morath's bowl, scooping up the cat and setting it gently on the floor. 'You must let me clean, Sascha,' he said.

Morath waited, drinking his coffee. A woman with a baby in a blanket went past in the street.

'It's quiet here,' Morath said. 'Very pleasant.'

'You should come more often, then.' The *patron* gave him a tart smile.

'I will. Perhaps tomorrow.'

'We'll be here. God willing.'

It took a half-hour, the following morning. Then a woman – the woman who had picked up the money, and, Morath remembered, kissed him on the steps of the Louvre – appeared at the café. 'He'll see you,' she told Morath. 'Try at four-fifteen tomorrow, in the Jussieu Métro station. If he can't get there, try the next day at three-fifteen. If that doesn't work, you'll have to find another way.'

He wasn't there, on the first try. The station was crowded, and if somebody was taking a look at him, making sure there were no detectives around, Morath never saw it. On the second day, he waited forty-five minutes, then gave up. As he climbed the stairs to the street, the man fell in step with him.

Not so portly as Morath remembered him, he still wore the Vandyke beard and the tweed suit, and something about him suggested affinity with the world of commercial culture. *The art dealer.* He was accompanied, as before, by a man with a white, bony face who wore a hat set square on a shaven head.

'Let's take a taxi,' the art dealer said. 'It's too cold to walk.'

The three of them got in the back of a taxi that was idling at the kerb. 'Take us to the Ritz, driver,' said the art dealer.

The driver laughed. He drove slowly down the rue Jussieu and turned into the rue Cuvier.

'So,' the art dealer said. 'Your friends still have problems with their papers.'

'Not this time,' Morath said.

'Oh? Then what?'

'I would like to meet somebody in the diamond business.'

'You're selling?'

'Buying.'

'A little something for the sweetheart.'

'Absolutely. In a velvet box.'

The driver turned up the hill on the rue Monge. From the low sky, a few drops of rain; people on the street opened their umbrellas. 'A substantial purchase,' Morath said. 'Best would be somebody in the business a long time.'

'And discreet.'

'Very. But please understand, there's no crime, nothing like that. We just want to be quiet.'

The art dealer nodded. 'Not the neighbourhood jeweller.'

'No.'

'Has to be in Paris?'

Morath thought it over. 'Western Europe.'

'Then it's easy. Now, for us it's a taxi ride and, maybe tomorrow, a train ride. So, we'll say, five thousand francs?'

Morath reached into his inside pocket, counted out the money in hundred-franc notes, and put the rest away.

'One thing I should tell you. The market in refugee diamonds is not good. If you bought in Amsterdam a year ago and went to sell in Costa Rica tomorrow, you'd be badly disappointed. If you think a thousand carats of value is a thousand carats of value, like currency in a normal country somewhere, and all you'll have to do is carve up the heel in your shoe, you're wrong. People think it's like that but it isn't. Since Hitler, the gem market is a good place to lose your shirt. *F'shtai?*'

'Understood,' Morath said.

'Say, want to buy a Vermeer?'

Morath started to laugh.

'No? A Hals then, a little one. Fits in a suitcase. *Good,* too. I'll vouch for it. You don't know who I am, and I'd rather you never did, but I know what I'm talking about.'

'You're serious.'

'Yes.'

'You need somebody rich.'

'Not this week, I don't.'

Morath smiled regret.

The chalk-white man took off his hat and ran his hand over his head. Then said, in German, 'Stop. He's moral.'

'Is that it?' the art dealer said. 'You don't want to take advantage of a man who's a fugitive.'

The driver laughed.

'Well, if you ever, God forbid, have to run for your life, then you'll understand. It's beyond *value,* by then. What you'll be saying is, "Take the picture, give the money, thank you, goodbye." Once you only plan to live till the afternoon, you'll understand.'

For a time, there was silence in the cab. The art dealer patted Morath on the knee. 'Forgive me. What you need today is a name. That's going to be Shabet. It's a Hasidic family, in Antwerp, in the diamond district. There's brothers, sons, all sorts, but do business with one and you're doing business with all of them.'

'They can be trusted?'

'With your life. I trusted them with mine, and here I am.' The art dealer spelled the name, then said, 'Of course I need to certify you to them. What should I call you?'

'André.'

'So be it. Give me ten days, because I have to send somebody up there. This is not business for the telephone. And, just in case, you and I need a confirmation signal. Go to the Madine, ten days from now. If you see the woman, it's settled.'

Morath thanked him. They shook hands. The chalk-white man tipped his hat. 'Good luck to you, sir,' he said in German. The driver pulled over to the kerb, in front of a *charcuterie* with a tin statue of a pig by its doorway, inviting customers inside with a sweep of his trotter. '*Voilà le Ritz!*' the driver called out.

Emile Courtmain sat back in his swivel chair, clasped his hands behind his head and stared out at the avenue Matignon. 'When you first think about it, it should be easy. But then you start to work, and it turns out to be very difficult.'

There were forty wash drawings set out around the office – pinned to the walls, propped up on chairs. *French life*. Peasant couples in the fields, or the doorways of farmhouses, or sitting on wagons. Like Millet, perhaps, a benign, optimistic sort of Millet. Then there were Parisian *papas* and *mamans* out for a Sunday stroll, by a carousel, at the Arc de Triomphe. A pair of lovers on a bridge over the Seine, holding hands, she with bouquet, he in courting suit – *facing the future*. A soldier, home from the front, seated at the kitchen table, his good wife setting a tureen in front of him. This one wasn't so bad, Morath thought.

'Too gentle,' Courtmain said. 'The ministry will want something with a little more clenched fist in it.'

'Any text?'

'A word or two. Mary's going to join us in a minute. Something like, "In a dangerous world, France remains strong." It's meant to dispel defeatism, especially after what happened at Munich.'

'Exhibited where?'

'The usual places. Métro, street kiosk, post office.'

'Hard to dispel defeatism in a French post office.'

Morath sat down in a chair across from Courtmain. Mary Day knocked lightly on the frame of the open door. 'Hello, Nicholas,' she said. She pulled up a chair, lit a Gitanes, and handed Courtmain a sheet of paper.

' "France will win," ' he read. Then, to Morath, 'That's not poor Mary's line.' From Courtmain, an affectionate grin. Mary Day had the smart person's horror of the fatuous phrase.

'It's the little man at the Interior Ministry,' she explained. 'He "had an idea".'

'I hope they're paying.'

Courtmain made a face. *Not much*. 'Advertising goes to war – you can't say no to them.'

Mary Day took the paper back from Courtmain. ' "France for ever." '

'*Bon Dieu*,' Courtmain said.

' "Our France." '

Morath said, 'Why not just "La France"?'

'Yes,' Mary Day said. 'The *Vive* understood. That was my first try. They didn't care for it.'

'Too subtle,' Courtmain said. He looked at his watch. 'I have to be at RCA at five.' He stood, opened his briefcase and made sure he had what he needed, then adjusted the knot of his tie. 'I'll see you tomorrow?' he said to Morath.

'About ten,' Morath said.

'Good,' Courtmain said. He liked having Morath around and wanted him to know it. He said goodbye to each of them and went out the door.

Which left Morath alone in the room with Mary Day.

He pretended to look at the drawings, and tried to think of something clever to say. She glanced at him, read over her notes. She was the daughter of an Irish officer in the Royal Navy and the French artist Marie D'Aumonville – an extraordinary combination, if you asked Morath, or anybody. A light sprinkle of freckles across the bridge of the nose; long, loose, brown hair, and pleading brown eyes. She was flat-chested, amused, impish, absent-minded, awkward. 'Mary's a certain type,' Courtmain had once told him. When she was sixteen, he suspected, the boys would have died for her but they were afraid to ask her to the movies.

Morath sensed she knew he was staring at her and turned towards the window. A moment later she looked up and said, 'Well, I suppose we'd better get on with work.'

Morath agreed.

'And then, you'll take me for a drink.' She started to gather up her papers. 'Right?'

Morath stared; did she mean it? 'With pleasure,' he said, retreating into formality. 'At seven?'

Her smile was, as always, rueful. 'You don't have to, Nicholas.' She was just teasing him.

'I want to,' he said. 'Fouquet, if you like.'

'Well,' she said. 'That would be nice. Or the place around the corner.'

'Fouquet,' he announced. 'Why not?'

A comic shrug – don't know why not. 'Seven,' she said, a little startled at what she'd done.

They hurried through the crowds, up the Champs Elysées, a few flakes of snow in the night air. She walked with big strides, shoulders hunched over, hands thrust in the pockets of what Morath thought was a very odd coat – three-quarter length, maroon wool with big buttons covered in brown fabric.

Fouquet was packed and noisy, throbbing with life, they had to wait for a table. Mary Day rubbed her hands to get warm. Morath gave a waiter ten francs and he found them a tiny table in the corner. 'What would you like?' Morath said.

She thought it over.

'*Garçon*, champagne!'

She grinned. 'A vermouth, maybe. Martini *rouge*.'

Morath ordered a *gentiane*, Mary Day changed her mind and decided

to have the same thing. 'I like it, I just never remember to ask for it.'
She spent a long moment watching the people around them – Parisian
theatre of the night – and from the look on her face took great pleasure
in it. 'I wrote something about this place, back when, a piece for
the *Paris Herald*. Restaurants with private rooms – what really goes
on?'

'What does?'

'Balzac. But not as much as you'd like to think. Most of the time it's
anniversary parties. Birthday. First Communion.'

'You worked for the *Herald*?'

'Freelance. Anything and everything, as long as they'd pay for it.'

'Such as . . .'

'Wine festival in Anjou! Turkish foreign minister fêted at the
Lumpingtons!'

'Not so easy.'

'Not hard. You need stamina, mostly.'

'Somebody at the office said you wrote books.'

She answered in the tough-guy voice from American gangster
movies. 'Oh, so you found out about that, did ya?'

'Yes, you're a novelist.'

'Oh, sort of, maybe. Naughty books, but they pay the rent. I got tired
of wine festivals in Anjou, believe it or not, and somebody introduced
me to an English publisher, he's got an office in the place Vendôme. The
kindest man in the world. A Jew, I think, from Birmingham. He was in
the textile business, came to France to fight in the war, discovered Paree,
and just couldn't bear to go home. So he started to publish books. Some
of them famous, in a certain set, but most of it comes in plain brown
wrappers, if you know what I mean. A friend of mine calls them "books
one reads with one hand".'

Morath laughed.

'Not so bad, the best of them. There's one called *Tropic of Cancer*.'

'Actually, I think the woman I used to live with read it.'

'Pretty salty.'

'That was her.'

'Then maybe she read *Suzette*. Or the sequel, *Suzette Goes Boating*.'

'Are those yours?'

'D. E. Cameron is what the jacket says.'

'What are they like?'

' "She slipped the straps from her white shoulders and let the shift fall
to her waist. The handsome lieutenant . . ." '

'Yes? What did he do?'

Mary Day laughed and shook her hair back. 'Not much. Mostly it's about underwear.'

The *gentianes* arrived, with a dish of salted almonds.

They had two more. And two more after that. She touched his hand with the tips of her fingers.

An hour later they'd had all of Fouquet they wanted and went off to find dinner. They tried Lucas Carton but it was *complet* and they didn't have a reservation. Then they wandered along the rue Marboeuf, found a little place that smelled good, and ate soup and omelettes and Saint Marcellin.

They gossiped about the office. 'I have to travel, now and then,' Morath said, 'but I like the time I spend in the office, I like what we do – the clients, what they're trying to sell.'

'It can take over your life.'

'That's not so bad.'

She tore a piece of bread in half and put some crumbly Saint Marcellin on it. 'I don't mean to pry, but you said "the woman I used to live with". Is she no more?'

'She left, had to leave. Her father came all the way from Buenos Aires and took her away. He thought we'd be at war by now.'

She ate the bread and cheese. 'Do you miss her?'

It took Morath a moment to answer. 'Of course I do, we had a good time together.'

'Sometimes that's the most important thing.'

Morath agreed.

'I lost my friend a year ago. Maybe Courtmain told you.'

'He didn't, it's mostly all business with us.'

'It was very sad. We'd lived together for three years. We were never going to get married, it wasn't like that. But we were in love, most of the time. He was a musician, a guitarist, from a town near Chartres. Classically trained, but he got to playing in the jazz clubs in Montparnasse and fell in love with the life. Drank too much, smoked opium with his friends, never went to bed until the sun rose. Then, one night, they found him dead in the street.'

'From opium?'

She spread her hands, *who knows?*

'I am sorry,' Morath said.

Her eyes were shining; she wiped them with a napkin.

They were silent in the taxi, going back to her apartment. She lived on the rue Guisarde, a quiet street in the back of the sixth arrondissement.

He came around to her side of the cab, opened the door and helped her out. Standing in the doorway she raised her face for the goodnight *bisou* on the cheek but it became a little more than that, then a lot, and it went on for a long time. It was very tender, her lips dry and soft, her skin warm beneath his hand. He waited in the doorway until he saw her light go on, then he went off down the street, heart pounding.

He was a long way from home but he wanted to walk. *Too good to be true*, he told himself. Because the light of day hit these things and they turned to dust. *A folie*, the French would say, an error of the heart.

He'd been very low since he came back to Paris. The days in Bistrita, the cell, the railway station – it didn't go away. He woke up at night and thought about it. So he'd sought refuge, distraction, at the Agence Courtmain. And then, an office romance. Everybody was half in love with Mary Day, why not him?

The streets were cold and dark, the wind hit him hard as he crossed the Pont Royal. On the boulevard, an empty taxi. Morath climbed in. Go back to her apartment? 'The rue Richelieu,' he told the driver.

But the next morning, in the light of day, she was wearing a black dress with buttons up the front and a belt that tied, a dress that showed her in a certain way and, when their eyes met for the first time, he knew.

So the letter waiting for him in his mailbox that night brought him down to earth in a hurry. Préfecture de Police, Quai du Marché Neuf, Paris 1^{ier}. The *Monsieur* was printed, on the form letter, the *Morath, Nicholas* written in ink. Would he please present himself at *la salle 24* of the Préfecture on *le 8 Décembre*, between the hours of *9 et 12 du matin*.

Veuillez accepter, Monsieur, l'expression de nos sentiments distingués.

This happened, from time to time. The summons to the Préfecture – a fact of life for every foreigner, a cold front in the bureaucratic weather of the city. Morath hated going there: the worn linoleum and green walls, the gloomy air of the place, the faces of the summoned, each one with its own particular combination of boredom and terror.

Room 24. That was not his usual room, good old 38, where resident foreigners with mild diplomatic connections were seen. What did *that* mean? he wondered, putting on his best blue suit.

It meant a serious inspector with a hard, square face and military bearing. Very formal, very correct, and very dangerous. He asked for Morath's papers, made notations on a form. Asked if there had been any changes in his *situation*: residence, employment, marital status. Asked if he had recently travelled to Roumania.

Morath felt the thin ice. Yes, at the end of October.

Exactly where, in Roumania?

In the district of Cluj.

And?

That was all.

And, please, for what purpose?

For a social engagement.

Not for business?

Non, monsieur l'inspecteur.

Very well, would he be so good as to wait in the *réception?*

Morath sat there, the lawyer part of his mind churning away. Twenty minutes. Thirty. *Bastards.*

Then the inspector, Morath's papers in his hand. Thank you, monsieur, there will be no further questions. At this time. A long instant, then, '*Vos papiers, monsieur.*'

Polanyi looked like he hadn't slept. Rolled his eyes when he heard the story. *Lord, why me.* They met that afternoon, in the office of an elegant shop on the rue de la Paix that sold men's accessories. Polanyi spoke to the owner, exquisitely dressed, and barbered, in Hungarian. 'May we have the use of your office, Kovacs *uhr,* for a little while?' The man nodded eagerly, wrung his hands, there was fear in his eyes. Morath didn't like it.

'I don't believe they will pursue this,' Polanyi said.

'Can they extradite me to Roumania?'

'They can, of course, but they won't. A trial, the newspapers, that's not what they want. Two things I would suggest to you: first of all, don't worry about it; second of all, don't go to Roumania.'

Morath stubbed out a cigarette in the ashtray.

'Of course, you are aware that relations between France and Roumania have always been important to both governments. French companies hold concessions in the Roumanian oilfields at Ploesti. So, you have to be careful.'

Polanyi paused for a moment, then said, 'Now, as long as we're here, I need to ask you a question. I have a letter from Hrubal, who wonders if I would find out from you what became of Vilmos, his head groom, who never returned from escorting you to the Cluj railway station.'

'Obviously they killed him.'

'Did they? Perhaps he simply ran away.'

'It's possible. Does Hrubal know that his money vanished?'

'No. And he never will. I had to go to Voyschinkowsky who, without anything like a real explanation, agreed to make it good. So Prince

Hrubal's contribution to the national committee will be made in his name.'

Morath sighed. 'Christ, it never ends,' he said.

'It's the times we live in, Nicholas. Cold comfort, I know, but it's been worse in the past. In any event, I don't want you losing sleep over any of this. As long as I'm here to protect you, you're reasonably safe.'

To follow the art dealer's instructions, Morath had to go to the Café Madine that morning, but he went first of all to the office. Which he found silent and deserted – he was too early. Then, suddenly, a swirl of activity. Mary Day with an apprentice copy writer, Mary Day with Léon, the artist, Mary Day talking to Courtmain through his open door. In a white, angelic sweater, she glanced at him as he hurried past like a man who actually had something to do. Morath retreated to his office, looked at his watch, came out, went back in. Finally, she was alone at her desk, head in hands over five words typed on a sheet of yellow paper. 'Mary,' he said.

She looked up. 'Hello,' she said. Where have you been?

'I tried to call, last night, I couldn't find your number.'

'Oh that's a long story,' she said. 'The apartment is actually . . .' She looked around. People everywhere. 'Damn, I'm out of pencils.'

She rose brusquely and he followed her to the supply room, a large closet. He pulled the door closed behind them. 'Here it is,' she said, writing it down.

'I want to see you.'

She handed him a slip of paper, then kissed him. He put his arms around her, held her for a moment, inhaled her perfume. 'Tomorrow night?' she said.

Morath calculated. 'By ten, I think.'

'There's a café on the corner of the rue Guisarde.' She pressed her hand against the side of his face, then grabbed a handful of pencils. 'Can't get caught mugging in the supply room,' she said, laughing.

He followed her swinging skirt down the hall, she disappeared into the bookkeeper's office, looking back over her shoulder as she closed the door.

At the Café Madine, Morath stood at the counter and had his usual coffee. Twenty minutes later – somebody, somewhere was watching, he decided – the woman showed up. She ignored Morath, sat at a table by the wall, read her copy of Le Temps.

So then, Antwerp. He went to see Boris Balki at the nightclub.

'Still at it?' Balki said, pouring two Polish vodkas.

'I guess I am,' Morath said.

'Well, I should say thank you.' Balki raised his glass in a silent toast and drank the vodka. 'My friend Rashkow's out of prison. They brought him his clothes in the middle of the night, took him to the back gate, gave him a good kick in the arse and told him not to come back.'

'I'm glad I could help.'

'Poor little Rashkow,' Balki said.

'I need to go to Antwerp,' Morath said. 'I'm hoping you'll come with me.'

'Antwerp.'

'We'll need a car.'

At dawn, Morath stamped his feet to keep warm and pulled his overcoat tight, waiting in a white fog by the entry to the Palais Royal Métro station. A splendid car, Morath thought. It came, very slowly, up the rue Saint-Honoré, a 201 Peugeot, ten years old, painted deep forest green and glowing with polish and affection.

They drove north, following lines of trucks, into Saint Denis. Morath directed Balki through a maze of winding streets to a park behind a church where, working hard at the reluctant latches, they took out the back seat 'Please, Morath,' Balki said. 'Don't hurt anything. This is somebody's life, this car.' He wore a stiff brown suit, white shirt, no tie, and a peaked cap; a bartender on his day off.

Morath opened his valise and stuffed thick packets of pengo under the wire coils in the seat. Balki was grim, shook his head as he saw all the money.

Route 2, headed north and east of Paris, went through Soissons and Laon, with signs for Cambrai and Amiens, the flat, weedy plain where they'd always fought the Germans. In the villages, smoke rose from the chimneys, women opened their shutters, glanced up at the sky, and put the pillows and blankets out to air. There were kids going to school, their dogs trotting along beside them, shop assistants raising the metal shutters of their shops, milkmen setting bottles on the doorsteps.

Outside the French town of Bettignies, the Belgian police at the border post were busy smoking and leaning against their shed and couldn't be bothered looking at the Peugeot as it drove past.

'Half done,' Balki said, relief in his voice.

'No, that's it,' Morath said as the shed disappeared in the rear-view mirror. 'Once we get to Antwerp, we're tourists. Probably I should've just taken the train.'

Balki shrugged. 'Well, you never know.'

They turned off the road, drove out into the farmland and put the money back in the valise.

It was slow going through Brussels. They stopped for eels and *frites* in a bar on the outskirts, then drove along the Schelde river into Antwerp. They could hear a foghorn in the distance as a freighter worked its way out of the harbour. The diamond district was in van Eykelai Street, in a luxurious neighbourhood by a triangular park. 'I'll walk from here,' Morath said. Balki pulled over, wincing as a tyre scraped against the kerb.

'Shabet? Two stalls down,' they told him. He'd found the diamond exchange on Pelikanstraat – long tables of diamond brokers, with the cutters' offices on the floor above. The Shabet he found was in his thirties, balding and worried. 'I think you'd better see my uncle,' he said. Morath waited by the table while a phone call was made and, ten minutes later, the uncle showed up. 'We'll go to my office,' he said.

Which was back in van Eykelai Street, on the second floor of an imposing grey stone building, and rather splendid. Persian carpets, a vast mahogany break-front crowded with old books, an ornate desk with a green baize inset.

The elder Shabet settled himself at the desk. 'So then, how can we help you?'

'An acquaintance in Paris gave me your name.'

'Paris. Oh, are you Monsieur André?'

'It's the name I asked him to use.'

Shabet looked him over. He was in his sixties, Morath thought, with fine features and silver hair, a white silk yarmulke on the back of his head. A comfortable man, wealthy, and confident in what he knew about the world. 'The times we live in,' he said, forgiving Morath the small deception. 'Your friend in Paris sent someone to see me. Your interest is, I believe, investment.'

'More or less. The money is in Hungarian pengo, about two million.'

'You don't interest yourself in shape or quality, that you leave to us. Simply a question of conversion.'

'To diamonds.'

Shabet folded his hands on the desk, his thumbs pressed together. 'The stones are available, of course.' He knew it wasn't that simple.

'And once we own them, we would like them sold.'

'By us?'

'By your associates, perhaps family associates, in New York. And the money paid into an account in America.'

'Ah.'

148

'And if, to save the expense of shipping, the firm in New York were to use its own inventory, stones of equal value, that would not concern us.'

'You have in mind a letter, I think. Us to them, and the accounting worked out within the family, is that it?'

Morath nodded, and handed Shabet a sheet of cream-coloured writing paper.

Shabet took a pince-nez from his breast pocket and settled it on the bridge of his nose. '"United Chemical Supply,"' he read. '"Mr J. S. Horvath, treasurer." At the Chase National Bank, the Park Avenue branch.' He laid the paper on the desk and put the pince-nez back in his pocket.

'Monsieur André? What sort of money is this?'

'Donated money.'

'For espionage?'

'No.'

'What then?'

'For certain funds. To be available in case of national emergency.'

'Am I doing business with the Hungarian government?'

'You are not. The money is given by private donors. It is not fascist money, not expropriated, not extorted, not stolen. The politics of this money is the politics of what the newspapers call the "Shadow Front". Which is to say, liberals, legitimists, Jews, intellectuals.'

Shabet wasn't pleased; he frowned, the look of a man who might want to say no but can't. 'It's a great deal of money, sir.'

'We ask only this single transfer.'

Shabet glanced out of the window, a few flakes of snow drifted through the air. 'Well, it's a very old method.'

'Medieval.'

Shabet nodded. 'And you trust us to do this? There will be no receipt, nothing like that.'

'You are, we believe, an established firm.'

'I would say we are, Monsieur André. I would have to say we are. Since 1550.'

Shabet took the sheet of paper from his desk, folded it in half, and slipped it in the desk drawer. 'There was a time', he said, 'when we might have suggested you do business with somebody else. But now—' It wasn't necessary to finish the sentence, and Shabet didn't bother. 'Very well,' he said, 'you have the money with you?'

It was dusk by the time they tried to find their way out of Antwerp. They had a city map, apparently drawn by a high-spirited Belgian anarchist, and argued with each other as the Peugeot wound through the narrow streets, Morath stabbing his finger at the map and telling Balki where they were, Balki looking at the street signs and telling Morath where they weren't.

The windshield wipers squeaked as they swept wet snow back and forth across the cloudy glass. In one street, a fire, it took for ever to back the car out. They turned into the next street behind a junkman's horse and wagon, then tried another, which led to a statue of a king and a dead end. Balki said, '*Merde*,' got the car going in the opposite direction, took the next left.

Which was, for some reason, vaguely familiar to Morath, he'd been there before. Then he saw why – the shop called *Homme du Monde*, Madame Golsztahn's tuxedo rental business. But there was no mannequin in the window. Only a hand-lettered sign saying *Fermé*.

'What is it?' Balki said.

Morath didn't answer.

Maybe the Belgian border guards didn't care who came and went, but the French customs inspectors did. 'The watch, monsieur. Is it, ah, new?'

'Bought in Paris,' Balki told them.

It was hot in the customs shed, an iron stove glowed in one corner, and it smelled of wet wool from the inspectors' capes. *A Russian? And a Hungarian? With residence permits? Work permits? The Hungarian with a diplomatic passport? In a borrowed car?*

So then, exactly what kind of *business* had them crossing the border in a snowstorm? Perhaps we'll have a look in the boot. The key, monsieur, if you please.

Morath began to calculate time. To be at the café on the rue Guisarde at ten o'clock, they should have left this hell an hour earlier. Outside, a truck driver honked his horn. The traffic began to back up as one of the inspectors tried to reach the Paris Préfecture on the telephone. Morath could hear the operator's voice as she argued with the inspector, who held his hand over the receiver and said to his supervisor, 'She says there's a line down in Lille.'

'Our calls don't go through Lille, she of all people should know that!'

Morath and Balki exchanged a look. But the chief officer grew bored with them, a few minutes later, and sent them on their way with an imperious flip of the hand. If they insisted on being foreigners it certainly wasn't *his* fault.

Out on Route 2, snow.

The Peugeot crawled behind an old Citroën *camionette* with the name of a Soissons grocery painted on the rear door. Balki swore under his breath and tried to pass, the wheels spun, the Peugeot began to fishtail, Balki stamped on the brake, Morath saw the white, furious face of the *camionette's* driver as it skidded past, the Peugeot spun in a circle, then ploughed into a field, wheels bouncing on ruts beneath the snow.

They came to rest a few feet from a large plane tree, its trunk scarred by the indiscretions of past motorists. Balki and Morath stood in the falling snow and stared at the car. The right rear tyre was flat.

Ten minutes to midnight, the rue Guisarde white and silent in the whispering snow, the lights of the café an amber glow at the end of the street. He saw her right away, the last customer, looking very sorrowful and abandoned, sitting hunched over a book and an empty cup of coffee.

He sat down across from her. 'Forgive me,' he said.

'Oh, it doesn't matter.'

'A nightmare, out on the roads. We had to change a tyre.'

He took her hands.

'You're wet,' she said.

'And cold.'

'Maybe you should go home. It hasn't been a good night.'

He didn't want to go home.

'Or you could come to the apartment. Dry your hair, at least.'

He rose. Took a few francs from his pocket and put them on the table for the coffee.

A very small apartment, a single room with a bed in an alcove and a bathroom. He took off his overcoat, she hung it by the radiator. Put his jacket in the armoire and his soaked shoes on a sheet of newspaper.

They sat on an elaborate old sofa, a Victorian horror, the sort of thing that, once it came up five flights of stairs, was never going anywhere again. 'Dear old thing,' she said affectionately, smoothing the brown velvet cushion with her hand. 'She often plays a role in the D. E. Cameron novels.'

'Field of honour.'

'Yes.' She laughed and said, 'Actually, I was lucky to find this place. I'm not the legal tenant, that's why my name isn't in the phone book. It belongs to a woman called Moni.'

'Moni?'

'Well, I think she's officially Mona but, if you're Mona, I guess the only pet name is Moni.'

'Short and dark? Likes to stir up trouble?'

'That's her. She's an artist, from Montreal, lives with her girlfriend over by Bastille somewhere. Where did you meet Moni?'

'Juan-les-Pins. She was one of Cara's friends.'

'Oh. Well, anyhow, she was a godsend. When Jean-Marie died, I swore I was going to stay in that apartment, but I couldn't bear it. I miss a refrigerator, in the summer, but I have a hotplate, and I can see St Sulpice.'

'It's quiet.'

'Lost in the stars.'

She took a bottle of wine from the windowsill, opened it and poured him a glass, and one for herself. He lit a cigarette and she got him a Ricon ashtray.

'It's Portuguese,' she said.

He took a sip. 'Very good.'

'Not bad, I'd say.'

'Not at all.'

'I like it.'

'Mm.'

'Garrafeira, it's called.'

Christ it's a long way across this couch.

'What was it you were reading, in the café?'

'Babel.'

'In French?'

'English. My father was Irish, but I had to learn it in school. My mother was French, and we lived in Paris and spoke French at home.'

'So, officially, you're French.'

'Irish. I've only been there twice, but on my eighteenth birthday I had to pick one or the other. Both my parents wanted me to be Irish – something my mother wanted for my father, I think that's what it was. Anyhow, who cares. Citizen of the world, right?'

'Are you?'

'No, I'm French, my heart is, I can't help it. My publisher thought I wrote in English, but I lied about it. I write in French and translate it.'

Morath walked over to the window, stared down at the snow floating past the street lamps. That did it. Mary Day came across the room and leaned against him. He took her hand.

'Did you like Ireland?' His voice was soft.

'It was very beautiful,' she said.

It was a relief to get it over with, the first time, because God only knew what could go wrong. The second time was much better. She had a long, smooth body, silky and lean. Was a little shy to begin with, then not.

The bed was narrow, not really meant for two, but she slept in his arms all night so it didn't matter.

Christmas Eve. A long-standing tradition, the Baroness Frei's Christmas party. Mary Day was tense in the taxi – this was a party they hadn't quite fought over. He had to go, and he didn't want to leave her home alone on Christmas Eve. 'Something new for you,' he'd said. 'A Hungarian evening.'

'Who will I talk to?'

'Mary, *ma douce*, there is no such thing as a Hungarian who speaks only Hungarian. The people at the party will speak French, perhaps English. And if, God forbid, you are presented to somebody only to discover that you cannot say a single comprehensible word to each other, well, so what? A smile of regret, and you escape to the buffet.'

In the end, she went. In something black – and very faintly strange, like everything she wore – but she looked even more heartbreaking than usual. She was of course delighted at the impasse Villon, and the house. And the servant who bowed when they came to the door and whisked away their coats.

'Nicholas?' she whispered.

'Yes?'

'That was a liveried footman, Nicholas.' She looked around. The candles, the silver, the hundred-year-old créche above the fireplace, the men, the women. In a distant room, a string quartet.

The Baroness Frei was pleased to see him accompanied, and obviously approved of his choice. 'You must come and see me some time, when we can talk,' she said to Mary Day. Who stayed on Morath's arm for only ten minutes before a baron took her away.

Morath, glass of champagne in hand, found himself in conversation with a man introduced as Bolthos, an official at the Hungarian legation. Very refined, with grey hair at the temples, looking, Morath thought, like an oil painting of a 1910 diplomat. Bolthos wanted to talk politics. 'Hitler is enraged with them,' he said of the Roumanians. 'Calinescu, the interior minister, made quick work of the Iron Guard. With the king's approval, naturally. They shot Codreanu, and fourteen of his lieutenants. "Shot while trying to escape", as the saying goes.'

'Perhaps we have something to learn from them.'

'It was a message, I think. Keep your wretched trash out of our country, Adolf.'

Morath agreed. 'If we joined with Poland and Roumania, even the Serbs, and confronted him, we might actually survive this.'

'Yes, the Intermarium. And I agree with you, especially if the French would help.'

The French had signed a treaty of friendship with Berlin two weeks earlier – Munich reconfirmed. 'Would they?' Morath said.

Bolthos had some champagne. 'At the last minute, perhaps, after we've given up hope. It takes the French a long time to do the right thing.'

'The Poles won't have any Munich,' Morath said.

'No, they'll fight.'

'And Horthy?'

'Will slither, as always. In the end, however, it may not be enough. Then into the cauldron we go.'

Bolthos's stunning wife joined them, all platinum hair and diamond earrings. 'I hope I haven't caught you talking politics,' she said with a mock scowl. 'It's *Christmas*, dearest, not the time for duels.'

'Your servant, sir.' Morath clicked his heels and bowed.

'There, you see?' Madame Bolthos said. 'Now you'll have to get up at dawn, and serves you right.'

'Quick!' said a young woman. 'It's Kolovitzky!'

'Where?'

'In the ballroom.'

Morath followed her as she cut through the crowd. 'Do I know you?'

The woman looked over her shoulder and laughed.

In the ballroom, the eminent cellist Bela Kolovitzky stood on the raised platform and grinned at the gathering crowd. His colleagues, the remainder of the string quartet, joined them. Kolovitzky tucked a handkerchief between his neck and shoulder and settled himself around a violin. He'd been famous and successful in Budapest then, in 1933, had gone to Hollywood.

' "Flight of the Bumblebee"!' somebody called out, clearly joking.

Kolovitzky played a discordant bleat, then looked between his feet. 'Something else?'

Then he began to play: a slow, deep, romantic melody, vaguely familiar. 'This is from *Enchanted Holiday*,' he said.

The music grew sadder. 'Now Hedy Lamarr looks up at the steamship.'

And now, wistful. 'She sees Charles Boyer at the railing . . . he is searching for her . . . among the crowd . . . she starts to raise her hand . . . halfway up . . . now back down . . . no, they can never be together . . . now the steamship blows its horn,' he made the sound on the violin, 'Charles Boyer is frantic . . . where is she?'

'What *is* that?' a woman asked. 'I almost know it.'

Kolovitzky shrugged. 'Something midway between Tchaikovsky and Brahms. Brahmsky, we call him.' He began to speak English, in a comic Hungarian accent. 'It muzt be zo tender, ro-*man*-tic, zenti-*men*tal. Zo lovely it makes . . . Sam Goldwyn cry . . . and makes . . . Kolovitzky . . . rich.'

Morath wandered through the party, looking for Mary Day. He found her in the library, sitting by a blazing fire. She was leaning forward on a settee, a thumb keeping her place in a book as she listened earnestly to a tiny white-haired gentleman in a leather chair, his hand resting on a stick topped with a silver ram's head. At Mary Day's feet lay one of the Viszlas, supine with bliss as Mary Day's ceaseless stroking of its velvety skin had reduced it to a state of semi-consciousness. 'Then, from that hill,' said the white-haired gentleman, 'you can see the temple of Pallas Athena.'

Morath sat on a spindly chair by a French door, eating cake from a plate balanced on his knee. The Baroness Frei sat close to him, back curved in a silk evening gown, face, as always, luminous. *One could say*, Morath thought, *that she is the most beautiful woman in Europe.*

'And your mother, Nicholas, what did she say?'

'She will not leave.'

'I will write to her,' the baroness said firmly.

'Please,' he said. 'But I doubt she'll change her mind.'

'Stubborn! Always her way.'

'She did say, just before I left, that she could live with the Germans, if she had to, but if the country was to be occupied by the Russians, I must find a way to get her out. "Then," she told me, "I will come to Paris."'

He found Mary Day and took her out into the winter garden; dead leaves plastered to the iron chairs and table, bare rose canes climbing up through the trellis. The frozen air made the sky black and the stars white and sharp. When she started to tremble, Morath stood behind her and wrapped her in his arms. 'I love you, Nicholas,' she said.

Intermarium

11 March 1939.

Amen. The world in chaos, half the armies in Europe mobilized, diplomats in constant motion, popping up here and there like tin monkeys in shooting galleries. Very much, Morath thought, like tin monkeys in shooting galleries.

Crossing the Pont Royal on his way to lunch, late, unhurried, he stopped and leaned on the stone parapet. The river ran full and heavy, its colour like shining slate, its surface roughed up by the March wind and the spring currents. In the western sky, white scud blew in from the channel ports. *The last days of Pisces*, he thought, dreams and mysteries, the equinox in ten days. When it rained in the middle of the night they woke up and made love.

He looked at his watch – Polanyi would be waiting for him – was there any way to avoid this? From here the Seine flowed north, to Rouen, to Normandy, to the sea. *Escape.*

No, lunch.

Thirty minutes later, the Brasserie Heininger. A white marble staircase climbed to a room of red plush banquettes, painted cupids, gold cords on the draperies. Waiters in mutton-chop whiskers ran back and forth, carrying silver trays of pink *langoustes*. Morath was relieved. No more Prévert, 'the beauty of sinister things', the Count von Polanyi de Nemeszvar had apparently risen from the lower depths, tempted by sumptuous food and a wine list bound in leather.

Polanyi greeted him formally in Hungarian and stood to shake hands.

'I'm sorry to be late.'

A bottle of Echézeaux was open on the table, a waiter scurried over and poured Morath a glass. He took a sip and stared at the mirrored panel above the banquette. Polanyi followed his eyes.

'Don't look now, but there's a bullet hole in the mirror behind you,' Morath said.

'Yes. The infamous Table Fourteen, this place has a history.'

'Really?'

'Two years ago, I think. The head waiter was assassinated while sitting on the toilet in the ladies' bathroom.'

'Well he won't do *that* again.'

'With a machine gun, it's said. Something to do with Bulgarian politics.'

'Oh. And in his memory . . .'

'Yes. Also, the story goes, some kind of British spy-mistress used to hold court here.'

'At this very table.'

The waiter returned, Polanyi ordered mussels, and a *choucroute royale*.

'What's "royale"?' Morath asked.

'They cook the sauerkraut in champagne instead of beer.'

'You can taste the champagne? In sauerkraut?'

'An illusion. But one likes the idea of it.'

Morath ordered *suprêmes de volaille*, chicken breast in cream, the simplest dish he could find.

'Have you heard what's happened at the French Air Ministry?' Polanyi said.

'Now what?'

'Well, first of all, they let a contract for building fighter planes go to a furniture manufacturer.'

'Somebody's brother-in-law.'

'Probably. And then they decided to store their secret papers at a testing facility outside Paris. Stored them in a disused wind tunnel. Only they forgot to tell the technicians, who turned the thing on and blew the papers all over the neighbourhood.'

Morath shook his head; there was a time when it would have been funny. 'They'll have Adolf in the Elysée Palace, if they don't watch out.'

'Not in our lifetime,' Polanyi said, finishing off his wine and refilling the glass. 'We think Adolf is about to make a mistake.'

'Which is?'

'Poland. Lately he's been screaming about Danzig – "is German, has always been German, will always be German". His radio station tells Germans in the city to "keep a list of your enemies, soon the German army will help you to punish them". So what must happen now is a pact, between the Poles, the Roumanians, and us – the Yugoslavs can join if they like. The Intermarium, so – called, the lands between the seas, the Baltic and the Adriatic. Together, we're strong. Poland has the largest land army in Europe, and we can deny Hitler Roumanian wheat and oil. If we can make him back down, call his bluff, that will be the end of him.'

Polanyi saw that Morath was sceptical. 'I know, I know,' he said. 'Ancient hatreds and territorial disputes and all the rest of it. But, if we don't do something, we'll all go the way of the Czechs.'

The lunch arrived, the waiter announcing each dish as he set it down.

'And what does Horthy think about all this?'

'Supports it. Perhaps you know the background of political events in February, perhaps you don't. Officially, Imredy resigned and Count Teleki became the prime minister. In fact, Horthy was told that a Budapest newspaper was about to publish proof, obtained in Czecho-slovakia, that Dr Bela Imredy, the rabid anti-Semite, was Jewish. Had, at least, a Jewish great-grandfather. So Imredy didn't jump, he was pushed. And when he resigned, Horthy chose to replace him with Teleki, an internationally prominent geographer, and a liberal. Which means Horthy supports at least some resistance to German objectives as the best means of keeping Hungary out of another war.'

'With Great Britain and France. And, sooner or later, America. We'll surely win that one.'

'You forgot Russia,' Polanyi said. 'How's your chicken?'

'Very good.'

Polanyi took a moment, using a knife to pile a small mound of sauerkraut atop a bite of frankfurter on his fork, then added a dab of mustard. 'You don't mind the Poles, do you, Nicholas?'

'Not at all.'

'Lovely countryside. And the mountains, the Tatra, sublime. Especially this time of year.'

'So it's said.'

'Nicholas!'

'Yes?'

'Can it be possible that you've never been there? To the majestic Tatra?'

A memorandum on his desk at the Agence Courtmain requested that he have a look at the file on Betravix, a nerve tonic made of beetroot. And there he found a postcard of a wild-eyed Zeus, beard blown sideways by a thundercloud above his head, about to ravish an extraordinarily pink and naked Hera he'd got hold of by the foot. On the back of the card, a drawing, in red crayon, of a heart pierced by an exclamation mark.

He sat through a meeting with Courtmain, then, back in his office, found a second message, this one scrawled on a slip of paper: *Your friend Ilya called. M.*

He walked down the hall to her office, a glassed-in cubicle by a window. 'I liked your card,' he said. 'Is this the sort of thing that goes on when you take Betravix?'

'I wouldn't, if I were you.' The late afternoon sun slanted in on her hair. 'Did you get your telephone message?'

'I did. Who's Ilya?'

'A friend, he said. He wants you to meet him.' She thumbed through a stack of notes on her desk. 'For a drink. At the café on rue Maubeuge, across from the Gare du Nord. At six-fifteen.'

Ilya? 'You're sure it was for me?'

She nodded. 'He said, "Can you tell Nicholas." '

'Is there another Nicholas?'

She thought about it. 'Not in this office. He sounded nice enough, very calm. With a Russian accent.'

'Well, who knows?'

'You'll go?'

He hesitated. Unknown Russians, meetings at station cafés. 'Why did he call *you*?'

'I don't know, my love.' She looked past him, to her doorway. 'Is that it?'

He turned to see Léon with a sketch of a woman in a fur stole. 'I can come back later, if you're busy,' Léon said.

'No, we're done,' Morath said.

For the rest of the day he thought about it. Couldn't stop. Almost called Polanyi, then didn't. Decided, finally, to stay away. He left the office at five-thirty, stood for a moment on the avenue Matignon, then waved at a taxi, intending to go back to his apartment.

'Monsieur?' the driver said.

'The Gare du Nord.' *Je m'en fous*, the hell with it.

He sat in the café, an unread newspaper beside his coffee, staring at people as they came through the door. Was it something to do with the diamond dealer in Antwerp? Somebody Balki knew? Or a friend of a friend – *call Morath when you get to Paris*. Somebody who wanted to sell him insurance, maybe, or a stockbroker, or an émigré who needed a job. A Russian client? Who wanted to advertise his – shoe store?

Anything, really, but what he knew it was.

Morath waited until seven, then took a taxi to Mary Day's apartment. They drank a glass of wine, made love, went out for *steak-frites*, walked home, curled up together under the blankets. But he woke up at three-thirty, and again at five.

And, when the phone rang in his office the following morning, waited three rings before he picked it up.

'My apology, Monsieur Morath. I hope you will forgive.' A soft voice, heavily accented.

'Who are you?'

'Just Ilya. I'll be, tomorrow morning, at the open market at Maubert.'

'And this concerns—?'

'Thank you,' he said. In the background, somebody called out, '*Un café allongé.*' There was a radio playing, a chair scraped a tile floor, then the phone was hung up.

A big market, at the place Maubert, on Tuesdays and Saturdays. Cod and red snapper on chipped ice. Cabbages, potatoes, turnips, leeks, onions. Dried rosemary and lavender. Walnuts and hazelnuts. A pair of bloody pork kidneys wrapped in a sheet of newspaper.

Morath saw him, waiting in a doorway. *A spectre.* Stared for a moment, got a nod in return.

They walked among the stalls, breaths steaming in the cold air.

'Do I know you?' Morath asked.

'No,' Ilya said. 'But I know you.'

There was something subtly mismade about him, Morath thought, perhaps a trunk too long for the legs, or arms too short. A receding hairline, with hair sheared so close he seemed at first to have a high forehead. A placid face, waxy and pale, which made a thick black moustache even blacker. And in his bearing there was a hint of the doctor or the lawyer, the man who trained himself, for professional reasons, not to show emotion. He wore a sad, old overcoat, olive green, perhaps a remnant of somebody's army, somewhere, so soiled and frayed that its identity had long ago faded away.

'Did we meet, somewhere?' Morath asked him.

'Not quite. I know you from your dossier, in Moscow. The sort of record kept by the special services. It is, perhaps, more complete than you would expect. Who you know, what you earn. Political views, family – the usual things. I had a choice of hundreds of people, in Paris. Various nationalities, circumstances. Eventually, I chose you.'

They walked in silence, for a time. 'I am in flight, of course. I was due to be shot, in the purge of the Foreign Directorate. My friends had been arrested, had vanished, as is the normal course of things there. At the time I was in – I can say, Europe. And when I was recalled to Moscow – to receive a medal, they said – I knew precisely what medal that was, nine grams, and I knew precisely what was in store for me before they got around to using the bullet. So, I ran away, and came to Paris to hide. For seven months I lived in a room. I believe I left the room three times in that period.'

'How did you live?'

Ilya shrugged. 'The way one does. Using the little money I had, I bought a pot, a spirit stove, and a large sack of oats. With water, available down the hall from my room, I could boil the oats and make *kasha*. Add a little lard and you can live on that. I did.'

'And me? What do you want of me?'

'Help.'

A policeman walked past, his cape drawn around him for warmth. Morath avoided his glance.

'There are things that should be known,' Ilya said. 'Perhaps you can help me to do this.'

'They are looking for you, of course.'

'High and low. And they will find me.'

'Should you be out on the street?'

'No.'

They passed a *boulangerie*. 'A moment,' Morath said, entered the shop and emerged with a *bâtard*. He tore a piece off the end and handed the rest to Ilya.

Morath chewed on the bread for a long time. His mouth was very dry and it was hard to swallow.

'I've put you in danger, I know,' Ilya said. 'And your woman friend. For that I must apologize.'

'You knew to call me through her, where she works?'

'I followed you, monsieur. It isn't so very hard to do.'

'No, I suppose it isn't.'

'You can walk away, of course. I would not bother you again.'

'Yes. I know.'

'But you do not.'

Morath didn't answer.

Ilya smiled. 'So,' he said.

Morath reached in his pocket and handed Ilya whatever money he had.

'For your kindness, I thank you,' Ilya said. 'And, for anything more, if God wills, please keep in mind that I don't have very much time.'

Morath took Mary Day to the movies that night, a gangster film, as luck would have it, detectives chasing a handsome bank robber down alleys in the rain. A noble savage, his dark soul redeemed by love in the previous reel, but the *flics* didn't know that. The white scarf in his hand when he died in a puddle under a street lamp – that belonged to dear, good, stunning, tight-sweatered Dany. No justice, in this world. A covert sniffle from Mary Day, that was all he got. When the newsreel came on – coal mine cave-in at Lille, Hitler shrieking in Regensburg – they left.

Back on the rue Guisarde, they lay in bed in the darkness. 'Did you find your Russian?' she said.

'This morning. Over in the Maubert market.'

'And?'

'A fugitive.'

'Oh?'

She felt light in his arms, fragile.

'What did he want?' she said.

'Some kind of help.'

'Will you help him?'

For a moment he was silent, then he said, 'I might.'

He didn't want to talk about it, slid his hand down her stomach to change the subject. 'See what happens when I take my Betravix?'

She snickered. 'Now that is something I *did* see. A week after I was hired, I think it was. You were off someplace – wherever it is you go – and this strange little man showed up with his tonic. "For the nerves," he said. "And to increase the vigour." Courtmain was anxious to take it on. We sat in his office, this green bottle on his desk, somewhere he'd found a spoon. I took the cap off and smelled it. Courtmain looked inquisitive but I didn't say anything – I'd only been there a few days and I was afraid to make a mistake. Well, nothing scares Courtmain, he poured himself a spoonful and slugged it down. Then he turned pale and went running down the hall.'

'Betravix – keeps you running.'

'The look on his face.' She snorted at the memory.

The Ides of March. On the fifteenth, German motorized infantry, motorcycles, halftracks and armoured cars entered Prague in a heavy blizzard. The Czech army did not resist, the airforce stayed on the ground. All day long, the Wehrmacht columns wound through the city, headed for the Slovakian border. The following morning, Hitler addressed a crowd of Volksdeutsch from the balcony of Hradcany Castle. Over the next few days there were five thousand arrests in Czechoslovakia, and hundreds of suicides.

Two weeks earlier, Hungary had joined the Anti-Comintern Pact – Germany, Italy and Japan – while simultaneously initiating a severe repression of fascist elements throughout the country. *We will oppose the Bolsheviks,* the action seemed to say, *and we can sign any paper we like, but we will not be ruled by Nazi surrogates.* In a certain light, a dark, tormented kind of light, it made sense. Even more sense when, on the fourteenth, the Honved, the Royal Hungarian army, marched across the border and occupied Ruthenia. Slowly, painfully, the old territories were coming back.

In Paris, the driving snow in Prague fell as rain. The news was alive on the streets. Under black, shining umbrellas, crowds gathered at the kiosks where the headlines were posted. *Betrayal.* Morath could feel it in the air. As though the beast, safely locked in the basement at the time of Munich, had kicked the door down and started smashing the china.

The receptionist at the agency answered the phone while dabbing at her eyes with a handkerchief. A subdued Courtmain showed Morath a list of younger men in the office who would likely be mobilized – how to get along without them? In the hallways, conversations in urgent whispers.

But, when Morath left the office at midday, nobody was whispering. In the streets, at the café and the bank and everywhere else, it was *merde* and *merde* again. And *merdeux, un beau merdier, merdique, emmerdé,* and *emmerdeur.* The Parisians had a lot of ways to say it and they used them all. Morath's newspaper, violently pessimistic about the future, reminded its readers what Churchill had said in response to Chamberlain's 'peace-with-honour' speeches at the time of Munich: 'You were given the choice between war and dishonour. You chose dishonour, and you will have war.'

On 28 March, Madrid fell to Franco's armies, and the Spanish republic surrendered. Mary Day sat on the edge of the bed in her flannel nightshirt, listening to the voice on the wireless. 'You know I once had a friend,' she said, close to tears. 'An Englishman. Tall and silly, blind as a bat – Edwin Pennington. Edwin Pennington, who wrote *Annabelle Surprised,* and *Miss Lovett's School.* And then one day he went off and died in Andalusia.'

For Morath, at work that morning, a *petit bleu,* a telegram delivered via the pneumatic tube system used by the Parisian post offices. A simple message: 'Notre Dame de Lorette. 1.30.'

The church of Notre Dame de Lorette was out in the scruffy ninth arrondissement – the whores in the neighbourhood known as *Lorettes.* In the streets around the church, Ilya would not seem especially noticeable. Morath's best instincts told him not to go. He sat back in his chair, stared at the telegram, smoked a cigarette, and left the office at one.

It was dark and busy in the church, mostly older women, that time of day. *War widows*, he thought, dressed in black, early for the two o'clock Mass. He found the deepest shadow, towards the back, away from the stained-glass windows. Ilya appeared almost immediately. He was tense, the small bravado of the Maubert market was no more. He sat down, then took a deep breath and let it out, as though he'd been running. 'Good,' he said, speaking softly. 'You are here.'

'You see what happens in Prague,' he said, 'and next is Poland. You don't need me to tell you that. But what is not known is that the directive is *written*, the war plan is made. It has a name, *Fall Weiss*, Case White, and it has a date, any time after the first of September.'

Morath repeated the name and the date.

'I can prove,' Ilya said, excited, losing his French. 'With papers.' He paused a moment, then said, 'This is good Chekist work, but it must go – up high. Otherwise, war. No way to stop it. Can you help?'

'I can try.'

Ilya stared into his eyes to see if he was telling the truth. 'That is what I hope.' He had enormous presence, Morath thought. Power. Even battered and hungry and frightened, he had it.

'There's somebody I can go to,' Morath said.

Ilya's expression said, *If that's what I can get I'll take it.* 'The Poles are in the middle of this thing,' he said. 'And they are difficult, impossible. In the five-man junta that runs the country, only Beck and Rydz-Smigly matter – Beck for foreign policy, Rydz-Smigly for the army – but they are all Pilsudski's children. When he died, in 1935, they inherited the country, and they have the same experience. They fought for independence in 1914, and got it. Then they beat the Russians, in 1920, before the gates of Warsaw, and now they want nothing to do with them. Too many wars, the last hundred years. Too much blood spilled. There's a point where, between nations, it's too late. That's Russia and Poland.

'Now, they think they can beat Germany. Jozef Beck's background is in clandestine service. He was expelled from France in 1923 when he served as Polish military attaché, suspected of spying for Germany. So, what he knows of Russia and Germany he knows from the shadows, where the truth is usually to be found.

'What the Poles want is alliance with France and Britain. Logical, on the surface. But how can Britain help them? With ships? Like Gallipoli? It's a joke. The only nation that can help Poland, today, is Russia – look at a map. And Stalin wants the same thing the Poles want, alliance with Britain, for the same reason, to keep Hitler's wolves away from the door. But we are despised by the British, feared, hated, Godless communists and murderers. That's true, but what is also true, even more true, is that we are the only nation that can form, with Poland, an eastern front against the Wehrmacht.

'Chamberlain and Halifax don't like this idea, and there is more than a little evidence that what they do like is the idea of Hitler fighting Stalin. Do they think Stalin doesn't know it? Do they? So here is the truth: if Stalin can't make a pact with the British, he will make one with Germany. He will have no choice.'

Morath didn't answer, trying to take it all in. The two o'clock Mass had begun, a young priest serving in the afternoon. Morath thought he would hear about bloody crimes; famines, purges. Ilya wasn't the only defector from the Russian secret service – there was a GRU general, called Krivitsky, who'd written a bestseller in America. Ilya, he assumed, wanted protection, refuge, in return for evidence that Stalin meant to rule the world.

'You believe?' Ilya said.

'Yes.' More or less, from a certain angle.

'Your friend can approach the British?'

'I would think he could. And the papers?'

'When he agrees, he'll have them.'

'What are they?'

'From the Kremlin, notes of meetings. NKVD reports, copies of German memoranda.'

'Can I contact you?'

Ilya smiled and, slowly, shook his head. 'How much time do you need?'

'A week, perhaps.'

'So be it.' Ilya stood. 'I will go first, you can leave in a few minutes. Is safer, that way.'

Ilya headed for the door. Morath stayed where he was. He glanced at his watch, followed along with the priest's Latin phrases. He'd grown up with it, then, when he came home from the war, stopped going.

Finally he rose and walked slowly to the back of the church.

Ilya was standing inside the door, staring out into the rain. Morath stood beside him. 'You're staying here?'

He nodded towards the street. 'A car.'

In front of the church, a Renault with a man in the passenger seat.

'For me, maybe,' Ilya said.

'We'll go together.'

'No.'

'Out the side door, then.'

Ilya looked at him. They're waiting at only one door? He almost laughed. 'Trapped,' he said.

'Go back to where we were, I'll come and get you.'

Ilya hesitated, then walked away.

Morath was furious. *To die in the rain on Tuesday afternoon!* Out in the street, he hunted for a taxi. Hurried along the rue Peletier, then rue Druot. At the corner, an empty taxi pulled up in front of a small hotel. As Morath ran for it, he saw a portly gentleman with a woman on his arm come out of the lobby. Morath and the portly gentleman opened the rear doors at the same moment and stared at each other across the back seat. 'Forgive me, my friend,' the man said, 'but I telephoned for this taxi.' He offered the woman his hand and she climbed in.

Morath stood there, water running down his face.

'Monsieur!' the woman said, pointing across the street. 'What luck!'

An empty taxi had stopped in traffic, Morath thanked the woman and waved at it. He got in and told the driver where to go. 'I have a friend waiting,' he said.

At the church, Morath found Ilya and hurried him to the door. The taxi was idling at the foot of the steps, the Renault had disappeared. 'Quickly,' Morath said.

Ilya hesitated.

'Let's go,' Morath said, his voice urgent. Ilya didn't move, he seemed frozen, hypnotized. 'They're not going to kill you here.'

'Oh yes.'

Morath looked at him. Realized it was something he knew, had seen. Had, perhaps, done. From the taxi, an impatient bleat of the horn.

He took Ilya by the arm and said, '*Now.*' Fought the old instinct to stay low and sprint, and they trotted down the steps together.

In the taxi, Ilya gave the driver an address and, as they drove away, turned around and stared out of the back window.

'Was it somebody you recognized?' Morath said.

'Not this time. Once before, maybe. And once, certainly.'

For long minutes, the taxi crawled behind a bus, the rear platform crowded with passengers. Suddenly, Ilya called out, 'Stop here, driver!' He leapt from the taxi and ran down the entry of a Métro station. Chausée-d'Antin, Morath saw, a busy *correspondance* where riders could transfer from one line to another.

The driver watched him go, then twisted an index finger against his temple, which meant 'crazy' in taxi sign language. He turned and gave Morath a sour look. 'And now?' he said.

'Avenue Matignon. Just off the boulevard.'

That was a long way from Chausée-d'Antin, especially in the rain. Taking people from one place to another was fundamentally an imposition – clearly that was the driver's view. He sighed, rammed the gearshift home and spun his tyres as he took off. 'What goes on with your friend?' he said.

'His wife is chasing him.'

'Woof.' Better him than me.

A few minutes later he said, 'Seen the papers?'

'Not today.'

'Even old *J'aime Berlin* is giving it to Hitler now.' He used the Parisian pun on Chamberlain's name with great relish.

'What's happened?'

'A speech. "Maybe Adolf wants to rule the world".'

'Maybe he does.'

The driver turned to look at Morath. 'Just let him take his army up into *Poland*, and that'll be the end of that.'

'I forbid you to see him again,' Polanyi said. They were at a café near the legation. 'Anyhow, there's a part of me wants to tell you that.'

Morath was amused. 'You sound like a father in a play.'

'Yes, I suppose. Do you buy it, Nicholas?'

'Yes and no.'

'I have to admit that everything he says is true. But what troubles me is the possibility that someone on Dzerzhinsky Street sent him here. After all, anybody can buy an overcoat.'

'Does it matter?'

Polanyi acknowledged that it might not. If diplomats couldn't persuade the British, maybe *a defector* could. 'These games,' he said. ' "Hungarian diplomats in contact with a Soviet operative." '

'He said he had papers to prove it.'

'Papers, yes. Like overcoats. Any way to get back in touch with him?'

'No.'

'No, of course not.' He thought for a moment. 'All right, I'll mention it to somebody. But if this blows up, in some way we can't see from here, don't blame me.'

'Why would I?'

'Next time he calls, if he calls, I'll see him. For God's sake don't tell *him* that, just accept the meeting and leave the rest to me.'

Polanyi leaned forward and lowered his voice. 'You see, whatever else happens now, we must not do anything that will compromise the prime minister. Teleki's our only way out of this mess – that little man's a *knight*, Nicholas, a hero. Last week he paid some boys in Budapest to rub garlic on the doors of the Foreign Office, with a note that said, "German vampires keep out".'

'Amen,' Morath said. 'How could contact with a defector damage Teleki?'

'I won't know until it's too late, Nicholas – that's the way things are now. Sad, but true.'

Sad, but true for Morath was, on the last day of March, another letter from the Préfecture. Once again, Room 24, and six days, until the appointment, to worry about it. The Roumanians, he guessed, would not go away, but it wasn't a good guess.

They kept him waiting outside the inspector's office for forty-five minutes. *Calculated*, he thought, but he felt it working on him anyhow. The inspector hadn't changed; sitting at attention, square-faced and predatory, cold as ice. 'You'll forgive us for troubling you again,' he said. 'A few things we're trying to clarify.'

Morath waited patiently.

The inspector had all the time in the world. Slowly, he read over a page in the dossier. 'Monsieur Morath. Have you, by chance, ever heard of a man called Andreas Panea?'

The name on the passport he'd obtained for Pavlo. He took a moment to steady himself. 'Panea?'

'Yes, that's right. A Roumanian name.'

Why this? Why now? 'I don't believe I know him,' he said.

The inspector made a note in the margin. 'Please be certain, monsieur. Think it over, if you like.'

'Sorry,' he said. Graciously.

The inspector read further. Whatever was in there, it was substantial. 'And Dr Otto Adler? Is that name known to you?'

Able this time to tell the truth, Morath was relieved. 'Once again,' he said, 'someone I don't know.'

The inspector noted his response. 'Dr Otto Adler was the editor of a political journal – a socialist journal. An émigré from Germany, he came to France in the spring of 1938 and set up an editorial office in his home, in St Germain-en-Laye. Then, in June, he was murdered. Shot to death in the Jardin du Luxembourg. A political assassination, no doubt, and these are always difficult to solve, but we pride ourselves on keeping at it. Murder is murder, Monsieur Morath, even in times of – political turmoil.'

The inspector saw it hit home – Morath thought he did. 'Once again,' Morath said, regret in his voice, 'I don't believe I can help you.'

The inspector seemed to accept what he'd said. He closed the dossier. 'Perhaps you'll try to remember, monsieur. At your leisure. Something may come back to you.'

Something had.

'If that should be the case,' the inspector went on, 'you can always get in touch with me here.' He handed Morath his card, Morath looked at it and put it in his pocket. The inspector's name was Villiers.

He called Polanyi. He called Polanyi from the café just across the Seine – the first public telephone you came to when you left the Préfecture. They made a living from their neighbour, Morath thought, pushing a *jeton* into the slot. The refugees were easy to spot: a couple celebrating with wine they couldn't afford, a bearded man with his head in his hands.

'The Count Polanyi is not available this afternoon,' said a voice at the legation. Morath hung up the phone, a woman was waiting to use it. Polanyi would never decline to talk to him, would he?

He went to the Agence Courtmain but he couldn't stay there. Saw Mary Day, for a moment. 'Everything all right?' she said. He went to the WC and looked in the mirror – what had she seen? He was perhaps a little pale, nothing more. But the difference between Cara at twenty-six and Mary Day at forty, he thought, was that Mary Day understood what the world did to people. Sensed, apparently, that it had done something to Morath.

She didn't mention it, that evening, but she was immensely good to him. He couldn't say exactly how. Touched him more than usual, maybe that was it. He was sick at heart, she knew it, but didn't ask him why. They went to bed, he fell asleep, eventually, woke long before dawn, slid out of bed as quietly as he could and stood at the window, watching the night go by. *Nothing you can do, now.*

He didn't get to his apartment until noon of the following day, and the letter was waiting for him there. Hand delivered, there was no stamp.

A clipping, from the 9 March edition of the newspaper that served the German community in Sofia. He supposed it was in the Bulgarian papers as well, some version of it, but the anonymous sender knew he could read German.

A certain Stefan Gujac, the story went, a Croat, had apparently hanged himself in his cell in a Sofia jail. This Gujac, using the false passport of a deceased Roumanian named Andreas Panea, was suspected, by the security agencies of several Balkan countries, of having taken part in more than a dozen political assassinations. Born in Zagreb, Gujac had joined the fascist Ustashi organization, and had been arrested several times in Croatia – for agitation and assault – and had served time in jail, three months, for robbing a bank in Trieste.

At the time of his arrest in Sofia, he had been sought for questioning by authorities in Salonika after a café bombing which killed seven people, including E.X. Patridas, an official in the Interior Ministry, and injured twenty others. In addition, police in Paris had wanted to question Gujac with regard to the murder of a German émigré, editor of a political journal.

Gujac's arrest in Sofia resulted from the attempted assassination, thwarted by an alert police sergeant, of a Turkish diplomat in residence at the Grand Hotel. He had been questioned by Bulgarian police, who suspected the plot against the diplomat had been organized by Zveno, the terrorist gang based in Macedonia.

Gujac, twenty-eight years old, had hung himself by fashioning a noose from his underwear. Sofia authorities said the suicide remained under investigation.

Polanyi agreed to see him later that afternoon, in the café near the Hungarian legation. Polanyi read his face when he walked in and said, 'Nicholas?'

Morath wasted no time. Recounted his interrogation at the Préfecture, then slid the newspaper clipping across the table.

'I didn't know,' Polanyi said.

From Morath, a bitter smile.

'At the time it happened, I didn't know. Whatever you want to believe, that's the truth. I found out later, but by then the thing was done and there was no point in telling you. Why? What good would it have done?'

'Not your fault, is that it?'

'Yes. That is it. This was von Schleben's business. You don't understand what goes on in Germany now – the way power works. They trade, Nicholas, trade in lives and money and favours. The honourable men are gone. Retired mostly, if not murdered or chased out of the country. Von Schleben abides. That's his nature. He abides, and I deal with him. I must deal with somebody, so I deal with him. Then it's my turn to trade.'

'A reciprocal arrangement.' Morath's voice was cold.

'Yes. I assume an obligation, then I pay it off. I'm a banker, Nicholas, and if, at times, a sorrowful banker, so what?'

'So reluctantly, but owing favours, you organized this killing.'

'No. Von Schleben did that. Maybe it was a favour, a debt he had to pay, I don't know. Perhaps all *he* agreed to do was bring this, this *thing*, to Paris. I can't say who gave him his instructions once he got here, I don't know who paid him. Someone in the SS, start there, you'll find the culprit. Though I suspect you know that long before you find him he'll find you.'

Polanyi paused a moment, then said, 'You see, some days von Schleben is a king, some days a pawn. Like me, Nicholas. Like you.'

'And what I did in Czechoslovakia? Whose idea was that?'

'Again von Schleben. On the other side, this time.'

A waiter brought them coffee, the two cups sat untouched. 'I'm sorry, Nicholas, and more concerned with the Préfecture business than who did what to whom last year, because what's done is done.'

'Done for the last time.'

'Then farewell and Godspeed. I would wish it for myself, Nicholas, but I can't resign from my country, and that's what this is all about. We can't pick up the nation and paste it on Norway. We are where we are, and everything follows from that.'

'Who set the Préfecture on me?'

'The same person who sent the clipping. Sombor, both times.'

'You know?'

'You never know. You assume.'

'To gain what?'

'You. And to damage me, who he sees as a rival. That's true – he's in the hands of the Arrow Cross, I most decidedly am not. What's going on here is Hungarian politics.'

'Why send the clipping?'

'*It's not too late*, he means. So far, the Préfecture only knows this much. Do you want me to tell them the rest? That's what he's asking you.'

'I have to do something,' Morath said. 'Go away, perhaps.'

'It may come to that. For the moment, you will leave it to me.'

'Why?'

'I owe you at least that much.'

'Why not have von Schleben deal with it?'

'I could. But are you prepared to do what he asks in return?'

'You're sure he *would* ask?'

'Absolutely. After all, you are already in debt to him.'

'I am? How?'

'Lest you forget, when the Siguranza had you in Roumania, he saved your life.'

Polanyi reached across the table and took his hand. 'Forgive me, Nicholas. Forgive, forgive. Try to forgive the world for being what it is. Maybe next week Hitler drops dead and we all go out to dinner.'

'And you'll pay.'

'And I'll pay.'

*

In April, the *grisaille*, the greyness, settled on Paris as it always did. Grey buildings, grey skies, rain and mist in the long evenings. The artist Shublin had told him, one night in Juan-les-Pins, that in the spring of the year the art-supply stores could not keep the colour called Payne's Grey in stock.

The city didn't mind its grey – found all that bright and sunny business in late winter a little too cheerful for its comfort. For Morath, life settled into a kind of brooding peace, his fantasy of 'the ordinary life' not so sweet a reality as he liked to imagine. Mary Day embarked on a new novel, *Suzette* and *Suzette Goes Boating* now to be followed by *Suzette at Sea*. A luxury liner, its compass sabotaged by an evil competitor, wandering lost in the tropics. There was to be a licentious captain, a handsome sailor named Jack, an American millionaire, and the oily leader of the ship's orchestra, all of them scheming, one way or another, for a glimpse of Suzette's succulent breasts and rosy bottom.

Mary Day wrote for an hour or two every night, on a clackety typewriter, wearing a vast, woolly sweater with its sleeves pushed up her slim wrists. Morath would look up from his book to see her face in odd contortions, lips pressed together in concentration, and schemed for his own glimpse, which was easy to come by when writing was done for the night.

The world on the wireless drifted idly towards blood and fire. Britain and France announced they would defend Poland if she were attacked. Churchill stated that 'There is no means of maintaining an eastern front against Nazi aggression without the active aid of Russia.' A speaker in the House of Commons said, 'If we are going in without the help of Russia we are walking into a trap.' Morath watched as people read their newspapers in the cafés. They shrugged and turned the page, and so did he. It all seemed to happen in a faraway land, distant and unreal, where ministers arrived at railway stations and monsters walked at night. Somewhere in the city, he knew, Ilya hid in a tiny room, or, perhaps, he had already been beaten to death in the Lubianka.

The chestnut trees bloomed, white blossoms stuck to the wet streets, the captain peeked through Suzette's keyhole as she brushed her long blonde hair. Léon, the artist from the Agence Courtmain, went to Rome to see his fiancée and returned with a bruised face and a broken hand. Lucinda, the Baroness Frei's sweetest Viszla, gave birth to a litter of puppies and Morath and Mary Day went to the rue Villon to eat *sachertorte* and observe the new arrivals in a wicker basket decorated with silver *passementerie*. Adolf Hitler celebrated his fiftieth birthday. Under German pressure, Hungary resigned from the League of Nations.

Morath went to a shop on the rue de la Paix and bought Mary Day a silk scarf, golden loops and swirls on a background of Venetian red. Wolfi Szubl called, clearly in great distress, and Morath left work and journeyed out to a small dark apartment in the depths of the fourteenth arrondissement, on a street where Lenin had once lived in exile.

The apartment smelled like boiled flour and was everywhere corsets. Violet and lime green, pale pink and rose, white and black. A large sample case lay open on the unmade bed.

'Forgive the mess,' Szubl said. 'I'm taking inventory.'

'Is Mitten here?'

'Mitten! Mitten's rich. He's on location in Strasbourg.'

'Good for him.'

'Not bad. *The Sins of Doktor Braunschweig.*'

'Which were—'

'Murders. Herbert is stabbed to death in the first ten minutes, so it's not a big part. With a knitting needle. Still, the money's good.'

Szubl picked up a typed sheet of yellow paper and ran his finger down the page. 'Nicholas, there's a bustier on the radiator, can you see the label?'

'This?' It was silver, with buttons up the back and garter snaps on the bottom. As Morath looked for the label he thought he smelled lavender bath powder. 'Marie Louise,' he said.

Szubl made a check mark on the list.

'Women try these on? The samples?'

'Now and then. Private fittings.' He began to count through a small mound of girdles on the edge of the bed. 'I just heard they want to promote me,' he said.

'Congratulations.'

'Disaster.'

'Why?'

'The company is in Frankfurt, I'd have to live in Germany.'

'So turn it down.'

'It's the son – the old man got old and the son took over. "A new day," he says. "New blood in the home office." Anyhow, I can deal with him. This is why I called.'

He took a folded paper from his pocket and handed it to Morath. A letter from the Préfecture, summoning *Szubl, Wolfgang* to Room 24.

'Why this?' Szubl said.

'An investigation, but they don't know anything. However, they *will* try to scare you.'

'They don't have to try. What should I say?'

'Don't know, wasn't there, never met him. You aren't going to make them like you, and don't start talking to fill up the silence. Sit.'

Szubl frowned, a pink girdle in his hand. 'I knew this would happen.'

'Courage, Wolfi.'

'I don't want to break rocks.'

'You won't. You'll have to keep the appointment, this time, because they sent you the letter, it's official. But it won't go on. All right?'

Szubl nodded, unhappy and scared.

Morath called Polanyi and told him about it.

Count Janos Polanyi sat in his office in the Hungarian legation. It was quiet – sometimes a telephone, sometimes a typewriter, but the room had its own particular silence, the drapes drawn over the tall windows keeping the weather and the city outside. Polanyi stared down at a stack of cables on his desk, then pushed them aside. Nothing new, or, at least, nothing good.

He poured some apricot brandy into a glass and drank it down. Closed his eyes for a moment and reminded himself who he was, where he came from. *Riders in the high grass, campfires on the plain.* Idle dreams, he thought, romantic nonsense, but it was still there, some-where, rattling around inside him. At least he liked to think it was. In his mind? No, in his heart. *Bad science, but good metaphysics.* And that, he thought, was pretty much who he'd always been.

Count Janos Polanyi had two personal telephone books, bound in green leather. A big one, that stayed in his office, and a small one, that went wherever he did. It was the small one he opened now, and placed a telephone call to a woman he knew who lived, in very grand style, in an apartment in the Palais Royal. *White and fine,* was the way he thought of her, *like snow.*

As the phone rang he looked at his watch. Four-twenty-five. She answered, as she always did, after many rings – condescended to answer, from the tone of her voice. There followed an intricate conversation. Oblique, and pleasantly devious. It concerned certain friends she had, women, some a little younger, others more experienced. Some quite outgoing, others shy. Some ate well, while others were slim. So varied, people nowadays. Fair. And dark. From foreign lands, or the sixteenth arrondissement. And each with her own definition of pleasure. Miracu-lous, this world of ours! One was stern, prone to temper. Another was playful, didn't care what as long as there was a laugh in it.

Eventually, they came to an agreement. A time. And a price.

Business before pleasure. A vile saying. He sighed, stared up at the huge portraits on his wall, Arpad kings and their noble hounds, and had a little more brandy, then a little more. *The Magyar Chieftian Prepares for Battle.* He mocked himself, an old habit, but then they all did that, an instinct of the national consciousness – irony, paradox, seeing the world inside out, amused by that which was not supposed to be amusing. Likely that was why the Germans didn't much care for them, Polanyi had always believed. It was the Austrian Archduke Franz Ferdinand who said of the Hungarians, 'It was an act of bad taste on the part of these gentlemen ever to have come to Europe.' Well, here they were, whether the neighbours liked it or not.

Polanyi once again looked at his watch. For a few minutes yet he could postpone the inevitable. His evening pleasure was not to arrive until six; he'd put it back an hour later than usual. *And speaking of pleasure, business before it.* He took a moment and swore merrily, various Hungarian anathemas. Really, *why* did he have to do this? *Why* did this Sombor creature have to come swooping down on to his life? But, here he was. Poor Nicholas, he didn't deserve it. All he wanted was his artists and actors and poets, had thought, in 1918, that he'd done his fighting. And done it well, Polanyi knew; it was there in the regimental history. A hero, his nephew, and a good officer, a miser with the lives of his men.

He put the brandy bottle away in the bottom drawer. Stood, straightened his tie, and left the office, closing the door carefully behind him. He walked along the corridor, past a vase of fresh flowers on a hall table with a mirror behind it. Greeted Bolthos, who hurried past with a courier envelope under his arm, and climbed up a flight on the marble staircase.

The floor above was busier, noisier. The commercial attaché in the first office, then the economic man, then Sombor. Polanyi rapped twice and opened the door. Sombor looked up when he entered and said, 'Your excellency.' He was busy writing – transferring jotted notes to a sheet of paper that would be retyped as a report.

'Colonel Sombor,' Polanyi said. 'A word with you.'

'Yes, your excellency. In a moment.'

This was pure rudeness and they both knew it. It was Sombor's place to rise to his feet, offer a polite greeting, and attempt to satisfy the wishes of a superior. But, he as much as said, the business of state security took precedence. Now and for ever. Polanyi could stand there and wait.

Which, for a time, he did.

Sombor's gold fountain pen scratched across the paper. *Like a field mouse in the granary.* He made eternal notes, this man with leather hair and sharp ears. Scratch, scratch. *Now where did I put that pitchfork?* But he did not have a pitchfork.

Sombor felt it. 'I'm sure it is most important, your excellency. I mean to give it my full attention.'

'Please, sir,' Polanyi said, his voice barely under control. 'I must tell you that certain confidential information, pertaining to my office, has been made available to the Paris Préfecture.'

'Has it. You're certain?'

'I am. It may have been done directly, or through the services of an informant.'

'Regrettable. My office will definitely take an interest in this, your excellency. Just as soon as we can.'

Polanyi lowered his voice. 'Stop it,' he said.

'Well, I must certainly try to do that. I wonder if you would be prepared to address a report to me, on this matter.'

'A report.'

'Indeed.'

Polanyi stepped close to the edge of the desk. Sombor glanced up at him, then went back to writing. Polanyi took a small silver pistol out of his belt and shot him in the middle of the head.

Sombor sprang to his feet, furious, eyes hot with indignation, unaware that a big drop of blood had left his hairline and was trickling down his forehead. 'Cur!' he shouted. Leapt into the air, clapped his hands to his head, spun around in a circle, and went crashing backward over his chair. Screamed, turned blue, and died.

Polanyi took the white handkerchief from his breast pocket, wiped off the grip of the pistol, and tossed it on the floor. In the hall, running footsteps.

The police arrived almost immediately, the detectives followed half an hour later. The senior detective questioned Polanyi in his office. Over fifty, Polanyi thought, short and thick, with a small moustache and dark eyes.

He sat across the desk from Polanyi and took notes on a pad. 'Colonel Sombor was, to your knowledge, despondent?'

'Not at all. But I saw him only on official business, and then only rarely.'

'Can you describe, monsieur, exactly what happened?'

'I went to his office to discuss legation business, nothing terribly urgent, in fact I was on my way to see the commercial attaché and I decided to stop in. We spoke for a minute or two. Then, when I had turned to go, I heard a shot. I rushed to his assistance, but he was gone almost immediately.'

'Monsieur,' the detective said. Clearly he'd missed something. 'The last words he spoke, would you happen to recall them?'

'He said goodbye. Before that, he'd asked for a written report on the matter we'd discussed.'

'Which was?'

'Pertained to, to an internal security matter.'

'I see. So, he spoke normally to you, you turned to leave the office, at which time the deceased extended his arm to its fullest length – I'm guessing here, pending a report from the coroner, but the nature of the wound implies, um, a certain *distance*. Extended his arm to its fullest length, as I said, and shot himself in the top of the head?'

He was on the verge of bursting into laughter, as was Polanyi.

'Apparently,' Polanyi said. He absolutely could not meet the detective's eyes.

The detective cleared his throat. After a moment he said, 'Why would he do that?' It wasn't precisely a police question.

'God only knows.'

'Do you not consider it' – he searched for a word – 'bizarre?'

'Bizarre,' Polanyi said. 'Without a doubt.'

There were more questions, all according to form, back over the ground, and back again, but the remainder of the interview was desultory, with the truth in the air, but not articulated.

So then, take me to jail.

No, not for us to be involved in these kinds of politics. Très Balkan, *as we say.*

And the hell with it.

The inspector closed his notebook, put his pen away, walked to the door and adjusted the brim of his hat. Standing in the open doorway he said, 'He was, of course, the secret police.'

'He was.'

'Bad?'

'Bad enough.'

'My condolences,' the inspector said.

Polanyi arranged for Morath to know about it right away. A telephone call from the legation. 'Colonel Sombor has tragically chosen to end his life. Would you care to donate to the fund for floral tributes?'

The end of April. Late in the evening on the rue Guisarde, the lissome Suzette winding down for the night. Plans to stage a King Neptune ball had inspired the passengers, getting rather restless after days of being lost at sea. Even more inspired was Jack the handsome sailor, who'd been kind enough to steady the ladder while Suzette climbed to the top to tack up decorations in the ballroom.

'No underpants?' Morath said.

'She forgot.'

A knock at the door produced Moni. Looking very sorrowful and asking if she could spend the night on the couch.

Mary Day brought out the Portuguese wine and Moni cried a little. 'It's my fault,' she said. 'I stomped out, in the middle of an argument, and Marlene locked the door and wouldn't let me back in.'

'Well, you're welcome to stay,' Mary Day said.

'Just for the night. Tomorrow, all will be forgiven.' She drank some wine and lit a Gauloise. 'Jealousy,' she said. 'Why do I do these things?'

They sent Morath out for more wine and when he returned Moni was on the telephone. 'She offered to go to a hotel,' Mary Day told him quietly. 'But I asked her to stay.'

'I don't mind. But maybe she'd prefer it.'

'Money, Nicholas,' Mary Day said. 'None of us has any. Really, most people don't.'

Moni hung up the telephone. 'Well, it's the couch for me.'

The conversation drifted here and there – poor Cara in Buenos Aires, Montrouchet's difficulties at the Théâtre des Catacombes, Juan-les-Pins – then settled on the war. 'What will you do, Nicholas, if it happens?'

Morath shrugged. 'I would have to go back to Hungary, I suppose. To the army.'

'What about Mary?'

'Camp follower,' Mary Day said. 'He would fight, and I would cook the stew.'

Moni smiled, but Mary Day met Morath's eyes. 'No, really,' Moni said. 'Would you two run away?'

'I don't know,' Morath said. 'Paris would be bombed. Blown to pieces.'

'That's what everybody says. We're all going to Tangiers – that's the plan. Otherwise, doom. Back to Montreal.'

Mary Day laughed. 'Nicholas in a djellaba.'

They drank both bottles Morath had brought back and, long after midnight, Moni and Mary Day fell dead asleep lying across the bed and it was Morath who wound up on the couch. He lay there for a long time, in the smoky darkness, wondering what would happen to them. Could they run away somewhere? Where? Budapest, maybe, or New York. Lugano? No. Dead calm by a cold lake, a month and it was over. *A Paris love affair, it won't transplant.* They couldn't live anywhere else, not together they couldn't. *Stay in Paris, then.* Another week, another month, whatever it turned out to be, and die in the war.

He had an awful headache in the morning. When he left the apartment, taking the rue Mabillon towards the river, Ilya emerged from a doorway and fell in step with him. He'd changed the green overcoat for a corduroy jacket, in more or less the same shape as the coat.

'Will your friend see me?' he said, his voice urgent.

'He will.'

'Everything has changed, tell him that. Litvinov is finished – it's a signal to Hitler that Stalin wants to do business.' Litvinov was the Soviet foreign minister. 'Do you understand it?'

He didn't wait for an answer. 'Litvinov is a Jewish intellectual – an old-line Bolshevik. Now, for this negotiation, Stalin provides the Nazis with a more palatable partner. Which is perhaps Molotov.'

'If you want to see my friend, you'll have to say where and when.'

'Tomorrow night. Ten-thirty. At the Parmentier Métro stop.'

A deserted station, out in the eleventh arrondissement. 'What if he can't come?' Morath meant *won't* and Ilya knew it.

'Then he can't. And I either contact you or I don't.'

Moving quickly, he turned, walked away, disappeared.

For a time, Morath considered letting it die right there. Suddenly, Ilya *knew things.* How? This wasn't hiding in a room with a sack of oats. Could he have been caught? Then made a deal with NKVD? But Polanyi had said, 'Leave it to me.' He was no fool, would not go unprotected to a meeting like this. *You have to let him decide,* Morath told himself. Because, if the information was real, it meant Hitler didn't have to worry about three hundred Russian divisions, and that meant war in Poland. This time, the British and the French would have to fight, and that meant war in Europe.

When Morath reached the Agence Courtmain, he called the legation.

'A fraud,' Polanyi said. 'We are being used – I don't exactly understand why, but we are.'

They sat in the back of a shiny black Grosser Mercedes, Bolthos in front with the driver. On the sixth day of May, benign and bright under a windswept sky. They drove along the Seine, out of the city at the Porte de Bercy, headed south for the village of Thiais.

'You went alone?' Morath said.

Polanyi laughed. 'A strange evening at the Parmentier Métro – heavyset men reading Hungarian newspapers.'

'And the documents?'

'Tonight. Then *adieu* to Comrade Ilya.'

'Maybe it doesn't matter, now.' Litvinov had resigned two days earlier.

'No, we must do something. Wake up the British, it's not too late for the diplomats. I would say that Poland is an autumn project, after the harvest, before the rains.'

The car moved slowly through the village of Alfortville, where a row of dance halls stood side by side on the quai facing the river. Parisians came here on summer nights, to drink and dance till dawn. 'Poor soul,' Polanyi said. 'Perhaps he drank in these places.'

'Not many places he didn't,' Bolthos said.

They were on their way to the funeral of the novelist Josef Roth, dead of delirium tremens at the age of forty-four. Sharing the back seat with Polanyi and Morath, a large, elaborate wreath, cream-coloured roses and a black silk ribbon, from the Hungarian legation.

'So then,' Morath said, 'this fugitive business is a fraud.'

'Likely it is. Allows the people who sent him to deny his existence, maybe that's it. Or perhaps just a minuet in the Soviet style – deceit hides deception and who knows what. One thing that does occur to me is that he is being operated by a faction in Moscow, people like Litvinov, who don't want to do business with Hitler.'

'You will take care, when you see him again.'

'Oh yes. You can be sure that the Nazi secret service will want to keep any word of a Hitler–Stalin negotiation a secret from the British. They would not like us to be passing documents to English friends in Paris.' He paused, then said, 'I'll be glad when this is over, whichever way it goes.'

He seemed tired of it all, Morath thought. Sombor, the Russians, God only knew what else. Sitting close together, the scent of *bay rhum* and brandy was strong in the air, suggesting power and rich, easy life. Polanyi looked at his watch. 'It's at two o'clock,' he said to the driver.

'We'll be on time, your excellency.' To be polite, he sped up a little.

'Do you read the novels, Nicholas?'

'*Radetzky March*, more than once. *Hotel Savoy. Flight without End.*'

'There, that says it. An epitaph.' Roth had fled from Germany in 1933, writing to a friend that 'one must run from a burning house'.

'A Catholic burial?' Morath said.

'Yes. He was born in a Galician *shtetl* but he got tired of being a Jew. Loved the monarchy, Franz Josef, Austria-Hungary.' Polanyi shook his head. 'Sad, sad, Nicholas. He hated the émigré life, drank himself to death when he saw the war coming.'

They arrived at Thiais, twenty minutes later, and the driver parked on the street in front of the church. A small crowd, mostly émigrés, ragged and worn but brushed up as best they could. Before the Mass began, two men wearing dark suits and decorations carried a wreath into the church. 'Ah, the Legitimists,' Polanyi said. Across the wreath, a black and yellow sash, the colours of the Dual Monarchy, and the single word 'Otto', the head of the House of Habsburg and heir to a vanished empire. It occurred to Morath that he was witness to the final moment in the life of Austria-Hungary.

In the graveyard by the church, the priest spoke briefly, mentioned Roth's wife Friedl, in a mental institution in Vienna, his military service in Galicia during the war, his novels and journalism, and his love of the church and the monarchy. *We all overestimated the world*, Morath thought. The phrase, written to a friend after Roth fled to Paris, was from an obituary in the morning paper.

After the coffin was lowered into the grave, Morath took a handful of dirt and sprinkled it on top of the pinewood lid. 'Rest in peace,' he said. The mourners stood silent while the gravediggers began to shovel earth into the grave. Some of the émigrés wept. The afternoon sun lit the tombstone, a square of white marble with an inscription:

> *Josef Roth*
> *Austrian Poet*
> *Died in Paris in Exile*

On the afternoon of 9 May, Morath was at the Agence Courtmain when he was handed a telephone message. 'Please call Major Fekaj at the Hungarian legation.' His heart sank. Polanyi had told him, on the way back from Thiais, that Fekaj now sat in Sombor's office, his own replacement due from Budapest within the week.

Morath put the message in his pocket and went off to a meeting in Courtmain's office. Another poster campaign – a parade, a pageant, the ministries preparing to celebrate, in July, the hundred and fiftieth anniversary of the revolution of 1789. After the meeting, Courtmain and Morath treated a crowd from the agency to a raucous lunch in an upstairs room at Lapérouse, their own particular answer to the latest valley in the national morale.

By the time he got back to the avenue Matignon, Morath knew he had to call. Either that or brood about it for the rest of the day.

Fekaj's voice was flat and cold. He was a colourless man, precise, formal and reserved. 'I called to inform you, sir, that we have serious concerns about the well-being of his excellency Count Polanyi.'

'Yes?' Now what?

'He has not been seen at the legation for two days, and does not answer his telephone at home. We want to know if you, by any chance, have been in contact with him.'

'No, not since the sixth.'

'Did he, to your knowledge, have plans to go abroad?'

'I don't think he did. Perhaps he's ill.'

'We have called the city hospitals. There is no record of admission.'

'Have you gone to the apartment?'

'This morning, the concierge let us in. Everything was in order, no indication of – anything wrong. The maid stated that his bed had not been slept in for two nights.' Fekaj cleared his throat. 'Would you care to tell us, sir, if he sometimes spends the night elsewhere? With a woman?'

'If he does he doesn't tell me about it, he keeps the details of his personal life to himself. Have you informed the police?'

'We have.'

Morath had to sit down at his desk. He lit a cigarette and said, 'Major Fekaj, I don't know how to help you.'

'We accept . . .' Fekaj hesitated, then continued, 'We understand that certain aspects of Count Polanyi's work had to remain – out of view. For reasons of state. But, should he make contact with you, we trust that you will at least let us know that he is, safe.'

Alive, you mean. 'I will,' Morath said.

'Thank you. Of course, you'll be notified if we hear anything further.'

Morath held the receiver in his hand, oblivious to the silence on the line after Fekaj hung up.

Gone.

He called Bolthos at his office, but Bolthos didn't want to speak on the legation telephone and met him, after dark, in a busy café.

'I spoke to Fekaj,' Morath said. 'But I had nothing to tell him.'

Bolthos looked haggard. 'It's been difficult,' he said. 'Impossible. Because of our atrocious politics, we're cursed with separate investigations. Officially, the *nyilas* are responsible, but any real work must be done by Polanyi's friends. Fekaj and his allies won't involve themselves.'

'Where do you think he is?'

A polite shrug. 'Abducted.'

'Murdered?'

'In time.'

After a moment Bolthos said, 'He wouldn't jump off a bridge, would he?'

'Not him, no.'

'Nicholas,' Bothos said. 'You're going to have to tell me what he was doing.'

Morath paused, but he had no choice. 'On Tuesday, the sixth, he was supposed to meet a man who said he had defected from the Soviet special services, which Polanyi did not believe. He didn't run, according to Polanyi, he was sent. But, even so, he came bearing information that Polanyi thought was important – Litvinov's dismissal, a negotiation between Stalin and Hitler. So Polanyi met him, and agreed to a second, a final, meeting. Documents to be exchanged for money, I suspect.

'But, if you're looking for enemies you can't stop there. You have to consider Sombor's colleagues, certainly suspicious of what went on at the legation, and capable of anything. And you can't ignore the fact that Polanyi was in touch with the Germans – diplomats, spies, Wehrmacht staff officers. And he also had some kind of business with the Poles; maybe Roumanians and Serbs as well, a potential united front against Hitler.'

From Bolthos, a sour smile. 'But no scorned mistress, you're sure of that.'

They sat in silence while the café life swirled around them. A woman at the next table was reading with a lorgnette, her dachshund asleep under a chair.

'That was, of course, his work,' Bolthos said.

'Yes. It was.' Morath heard himself use the past tense. 'You think he's dead.'

'I hope he isn't, but better that than some dungeon in Moscow or Berlin.' Bolthos took a small notebook from his pocket. 'This meeting, will you tell me where it was supposed to take place?'

'I don't know. The first meeting was at the Parmentier Métro station. But in my dealings with this man he was careful to change time and location. So, in a way, the second meeting would have been anywhere *but* there.'

'Unless Polanyi insisted.' Bolthos flipped back through the notebook. 'I've been working with my own sources in the Paris police. On Tuesday the sixth, a man was shot somewhere near the Parmentier Métro station. This was buried among all the robberies and domestic disturbances, but there was something about it that caught my attention. The victim was a French citizen, born in Slovakia. Served in the Foreign Legion, then discharged for political activity. He crawled into a doorway and died on the rue St-Maur, a minute or so away from the Métro.'

'A phantom,' Morath said. 'Polanyi's bodyguard – is that what you think? Or maybe his assassin. Or both, why not? Or, more likely, nobody, caught up in somebody's politics on the wrong night, or killed for a ten-franc piece.'

Bolthos closed the notebook. 'We have to try,' he said. He meant he'd done the best he could.

'Yes. I know,' Morath said.

Temetni Tudunk, a Magyar sentiment, complex and ironic – 'how to bury people, that is one thing we know'. It was Wolfi Szubl who said the words, at a Hungarian nightclub in the cellar of a strange little hotel out in the seventeenth arrondissement. Szubl and Mitten, the Baroness Frei escorted by a French film producer, Bolthos and his wife and her cousin, Voyschinkowsky and Lady Angela Hope, the artist Szabo, the lovely Madame Kareny, various other strays and aristocrats who had floated through Janos Polanyi's complicated life.

It wasn't a funeral – there was no burial, thus Szubl's ironic twist on the phrase, not even a memorial, only an evening to remember a friend. 'A difficult friend' – Voyschinkowsky said that, an index finger wiping the corner of his eye. There was candlelight, a small gypsy orchestra, platters of chicken with paprika and cream, wine and fruit brandy and, yes, it was said more than once as the evening wore on, Polanyi would have liked to be there. During one of the particularly heartbreaking songs, a pale, willowy woman, supremely, utterly *Parisienne* and rumoured to be a procuress who lived in the Palais Royal, stood in front of the orchestra and danced with a shawl. Morath sat beside Mary Day and translated, now and then, what somebody said in Hungarian.

They drank to Polanyi, 'wherever he is tonight', meaning heaven or hell. 'Or maybe Palm Beach,' Herbert Mitten said. 'I guess there's nothing wrong in thinking that if you care to.'

The bill came to Morath at two in the morning, on a silver tray, with a grand bow from the *patron*. Voyschinkowsky, thwarted in his attempt to pay for the evening, insisted on taking Morath and Mary Day home in his chauffeur-driven Hispano-Suiza car.

We have to try – Bolthos had said it for both of them. Which meant, for Morath, one obvious but difficult strand, really the only one he knew, in what must have been a vast tangle of shadowy connections.

He went to the Balalaika the following afternoon and drank vodka with Boris Balki.

'A shame,' Balki said, and drank 'to his memory'.

'Looking back, probably inevitable.'

'Yes, sooner or later. This type of man lives on borrowed time.'

'The people responsible', Morath said, 'are perhaps in Moscow.'

A certain delicacy prevented Balki from saying what he felt about that, but the reaction – Balki looked around to see who might be listening – was clear to Morath.

'I wouldn't even try to talk to them, if I were you,' Balki said.

'Well, if I thought it would help.'

'Once they do it it's done,' Balki said. 'Fated is fated, Slavs know all about that.'

'I was wondering,' Morath said. 'What's become of Silvana?'

'Living high.' Balki was clearly relieved to be off the subject of Moscow. 'That's what I hear.'

'I want to talk to von Schleben.'

'Well . . .'

'Can you do it?'

'Silvana, yes. The rest is up to you.'

Then, the last week in May, Morath received a letter, on thick, creamy paper, from one Auguste Thien, summoning him to the Thien law offices in Geneva 'to settle matters pertaining to the estate of Count Janos von Polanyi de Nemeszvar'.

Morath took the train down from Paris, staring out at the green and gold Burgundian countryside, staying at a silent Geneva hotel that night, and arriving at the office, which looked out over Lac Léman, the following morning.

The lawyer Thien, when Morath was ushered into his office by a junior member of the staff, turned out to be an ancient bag of bones held upright only by means of a stiff, iron-coloured suit. He had a full head of wavy silver hair, parted in the middle, and skin like parchment. 'Your excellency,' the lawyer said, offering his hand. 'Will you take a coffee? Something stronger?'

Morath took the coffee, which produced the junior member carrying a Sèvres service, countless pieces of it, on an immense tray. Thien himself served the coffee, his breathing audible as he worked.

'There,' he said, when Morath at last had the cup in his hands.

On the desk, a metal box of the kind used in safe deposit vaults. 'These papers comprise a significant proportion of the Polanyi de Nemeszvar estate,' Thien said, 'which, according to my instructions, now, in substance, pass to you. There are provisions made for Count Polanyi's surviving family, very generous provisions, but the greatest part of the estate is, as of this date, yours. Including, of course, the title, which descends to the eldest surviving member of the male line – in this case the son of Count Polanyi's sister, your mother. So, before we proceed to more technical matters, it is my privilege to greet you, even in a sad hour, as Nicholas, Count Morath.'

Slowly, he stood and came around the desk to shake Morath's hand.

'Perhaps I'm ignorant of the law,' Morath said, when he'd sat back down, 'but there is, to my knowledge, no death certificate.'

'No, there is not.' A cloud crossed Thien's face. 'But our instructions preclude the necessity for certification. You should be aware that certain individuals, in their determination of a final distribution of assets, may presuppose, well, any condition they choose. It is, at least in Switzerland, entirely at their discretion. We are in receipt of a letter from the Paris Préfecture, an *attestation*, which certifies, to our satisfaction, that the legator has been officially declared a missing person. This unhappy eventuality was, in fact, foreseen. And this office, I will say, is known for the most scrupulous adherence to a client's direction, no matter what it might entail. You have perhaps heard of Loulou the circus elephant? No? Well, she now lives in splendid retirement, on a farm near Coimbra, in compliance with the wishes of the late Senhor Alvares, former owner of the Circus Alvares. In his last will and testament, he did not forget his faithful performer. So this elephant will, one might say, never forget Senhor Alvares. And this law firm, Count Morath, will never forget the elephant!'

The lawyer Thien smiled with satisfaction, took from his drawer a substantial key, opened the metal box, and began to hand Morath various deeds and certificates.

He was, he learned, very rich. He'd known about it, in a general way, the Canadian railroad bonds, the estates in Hungary, but here it was in reality. 'In addition,' Thien said, 'there are certain, specified accounts held in banks in this city, which will now come into your possession. My associate will guide you in completing the forms. You may elect to have these funds administered by any institution you choose, or they can remain where they are, in your name, with payment instructions according to your wishes.

'This is, Count Morath, a lot to absorb in a single meeting. Are there, at present, any points you would care to have clarified?'

'I don't believe so.'

'Then, with your permission, I will add this.'

He took from his drawer a sheet of stationery and read aloud. ' "A man's departure from his familiar world may be inevitable, but his spirit lives on, in the deeds and actions of those who remain, in the memories of those left behind, his friends and family, whose lives may reflect the lessons they have learned from him, and that shall become his truest legacy." '

After a pause, Thien said, 'I believe you should find comfort in those words, your excellency.'

'Certainly I do,' Morath said.

Bastard. You're alive.

On his return to Paris there was, of course, an ascension-to-the-title party, attended, as it happened, solely by the Count and the Countess Presumptive. The latter provided, from the *pâtisserie* on the corner, a handsome cake, on top of which, in consultation with the baker's wife and aided by a dictionary, a congratulatory phrase in Hungarian was rendered in blue icing. This turned out to be, when Morath read it, something like *Good Feelings Mister Count*, but, given the difficulty of the language, close enough. In addition – shades of Suzette! – Mary Day had pinned paper streamers to the wall of the apartment, though, unlike Jack the handsome sailor, Morath was not there to steady the ladder. Still, he saw far more than Jack was ever going to and got to lick frosting off the countess's nipples into the bargain.

There followed a night of adventure. At three, they stood at the window and saw the moon in a mist. Across the rue Guisarde, a man in an undershirt leaned on his windowsill and smoked a pipe. A spring wind, an hour later, and the scent of fields in the countryside. They decided they would go to the Closerie de Lilas at dawn and drink champagne, then Mary Day fell asleep, hair plastered to her forehead, mouth open, sleeping so peacefully he didn't have the heart to wake her.

They went to the movies, that night, at one of the fancy Gaumont theatres over by the Grand Hotel. *The loveliest fluff*, Morath thought. A French obsession – how passion played itself out into romantic intrigue, with everybody pretty and well dressed. His beloved Mary Day, hard-headed as could be in so many ways, caved in completely. He could feel it, sitting next to her, how her heart beat for a stolen embrace.

But in the lobby on the way out, all chandeliers and cherubs, he heard a young man say to his girlfriend, '*Tout Paris* can fuck itself blue in the face, it won't stop Hitler for a minute.'

Thus the Parisian mood that June. Edgy but resilient, it fought to recover from the cataclysms – Austria, Munich, Prague – and tried to work its way back to normality. But the Nazis wouldn't leave it alone. Now there was Danzig, with the Poles giving as good as they got. Every morning it lay waiting in the newspapers: customs officers shot, post offices burned, flags pulled down and stamped into the dirt.

Meanwhile, in Hungary no rioting or burning, but the same political war that refused to die. The parliament had passed new anti-Semitic laws in May, and when Morath was solicited by Voyschinkowsky for a subscription to a fund for Jews leaving the country, he wrote out a cheque that startled even 'the Lion of the Bourse'. Voyschinkowsky raised his eyebrows when he saw the number. 'Well, this is *terribly* generous of you, Nicholas. Are you sure you want to do all that much?'

He was. He'd had a letter from his sister. Life in Budapest, Teresa said, was 'spoiled, ruined'. Endless talk of war, suicide, an incident during a performance of *Der Rosenkavalier.* 'Nicholas, even at the *opera.*' Duchazy was up to 'God only knows what'. Plots, conspiracies. 'Last Tuesday, the phone rang twice after midnight.'

Morath took Mary Day to afternoon tea at the Baroness Frei's house, the official celebration of summer's arrival in the garden. The stars of the show were two roses that spread across the brick walls that enclosed the terrace: *Madame Alfred Carrière,* white flowers touched with pale pink – 'a perfect noisette', the baroness told Mary Day, 'planted by the baron with his own hands in 1911', and *Gloire de Dijon,* soft yellow with tones of apricot.

The baroness held court in an ironwork garden chair, scolding the Viszlas as they agitated for forbidden morsels from the guests, and beckoning her friends to her side. Seated next to her was an American woman called Blanche. She was the wife of the cellist Kolovitzky, a vivid blonde with black eyebrows, tanned skin from a life spent by Hollywood pools, and an imposing bosom on a body that should have been Rubenesque but was forced to live on grapefruit and toast.

'Darling Nicholas,' the baroness called out to him. 'Come and talk to us.'

As he headed towards her he saw Bolthos in the crowd and acknowledged his glance with a friendly nod. He was, for a moment, tempted to say something of his suspicions but immediately thought better of it. *Silence,* he told himself.

Morath kissed Lillian Frei on both cheeks. 'Nicholas, have you met Blanche? Bela's wife?'

'That's Kolovitzky, not Lugosi,' the woman said with a laugh.

Morath laughed politely along with her as he took her hand. Why was this funny?

'At the Christmas party,' Morath said. 'It's good to see you again.'

'She was at the Crillon,' Baroness Frei said. 'But I made her come and stay with me.'

Kolovitzky's wife started to talk to him in English, while Morath tried to follow along as best he could. The baroness saw that he was lost and began to translate into Hungarian, holding Blanche's right hand tightly in her left and moving both hands up and down for emphasis as the conversation continued.

This was, Morath saw right away, a bad, potentially fatal, case of money madness. On the death of an aunt in Johannesburg, the cellist who scored Hollywood films had inherited two apartment houses in Vienna. 'Nothing fancy, you know, but solid. Respectable.'

Kolovitzky's friends, his lawyer and his wife had laughed at the absurdity of Kolovitzky going back to Austria to claim the inheritance. Kolovitzky laughed right along with them, then flew to Paris and took a train to Vienna.

'He was poor as a child,' Blanche said. 'So money is never enough for him. He goes around the house and turns off the lights.'

She paused, found a handkerchief in her purse, and dabbed at her eyes. 'Excuse me,' she said. 'He went to Vienna three weeks ago, he's still there. They won't let him out.'

'Did someone encourage him to go?'

'See? He knows,' Blanche said to the baroness. 'A scoundrel, a lawyer in Vienna. "Don't worry about a thing," he said in his letter. "You're an American, it won't be a problem."'

'He's a citizen?'

'He's got papers as a resident alien. I had a letter from him, at the Crillon, and the story was that once he gave them the buildings – that laywer's in cahoots with the Nazis, *that's* what's going on – he thought they'd let him go home. But maybe it isn't so simple.'

The baroness stopped dead on 'cahoots', and Blanche said, 'I mean, they're all in it together.'

'Did he go to the American embassy?'

'He tried. But they don't interest themselves in Jews. "Come back in July", they told him.'

'Where is he, in Vienna?'

She opened her purse and brought out a much-folded letter on thin paper. 'He says here—' she hunted for her glasses and put them on. 'Says here, the Schoenhof. Why I don't know – he was at the Graben, which he always liked.' She read further and said, 'Here. He says, "I have put the buildings, for tax purposes, in Herr Kreml's name." That's the lawyer. "But they tell me that further payments may be required." Then he says, "I can only hope it will be acceptable, but please speak with Mr R. L. Stevenson at the bank and see what can be done." That too is odd, because there is no Mr Stevenson, not that I know about.'

'They won't let him out,' the baroness said.

'May I have the letter?' Morath said.

Blanche handed it to him and he put it in his pocket.

'Should I send money?'

Morath thought it over. 'Write and ask him how much he needs, and when he'll be coming home. Then say that you're annoyed, or show it, with how he's always getting into trouble. Why can't he learn to respect the rules? The point is, you'll bribe, but the bribe has to work, and you'll say later that it was all his fault. They're sensitive about America, the Nazis, they don't want stories in the newspapers.'

'Nicholas,' the baroness said. 'Can anything be done?'

Morath nodded. 'Maybe. Let me think it over.'

The Baroness Frei looked up at him, eyes blue as the autumn sky.

Blanche started to thank him, and had already said too much and was about to mention money, when the baroness intervened.

'He knows, darling, he knows,' she said gently. 'He has a good heart, Count Nicholas.'

Seen from a private box in the grandstand, the lawns of Longchamps racetrack glowed like green velvet. The jockeys' silks were bright in the sunshine, scarlet and gold and royal blue. Silvana tapped the end of a pencil against a racecard. 'Coup de Tonnerre?' she said. Thunderbolt. 'Was that the one with the blond mane? Horst? Do you remember?'

'I think it was,' von Schleben said, peering at the programme. 'Pierre Lavard is riding, and they let him win once a day.' He read further. 'Or maybe Bal Masqué. Who do you like, Morath?'

Silvana looked at him expectantly. She wore a print silk dress and pearls, her hair now expensively styled.

'Coup de Tonnerre,' Morath said. 'He took third place, the last time he ran. The odds are attractive.'

Von Schleben handed Silvana a few hundred francs. 'Take care of it for us, will you?' Morath also gave her money. 'Let's try Count Morath's hunch.'

When she'd gone off to the betting window, von Schleben said, 'Too bad about your uncle. We had good times together, but that's life.'

'You didn't hear anything, did you? After it happened?'

'No, no,' von Schleben said. 'Into thin air.'

As the horses were walked to the starting line, there were the usual difficulties; a starter's assistant leaping out of the way to avoid being kicked.

'There's a lawyer in Vienna I'd like to get in touch with,' Morath said. 'Gerhard Kreml.'

'Kreml,' von Schleben said. 'I don't think I know him. What is it that interests you?'

'Who he is. What kind of business he does. I think he has connections with the Austrian party.'

'I'll see what I can do for you,' von Schleben said. He handed Morath a card. 'Call me, first part of next week, if you haven't heard anything. Use the second number, there, on the bottom.'

The race began, the horses galloping in a tight pack. Von Schleben raised a pair of mother-of-pearl opera glasses to his eyes and followed the race. 'Take the rail, idiot,' he said. The horses' hooves drummed on the grass. At the halfway point, the jockeys began to use their whips. '*Ach scheisse*,' von Schleben said, lowering the glasses.

'This Kreml,' Morath said. 'He has a client in Vienna, a friend of a friend, who seems to be having tax problems. There's a question of being allowed to leave the country.'

'A Jew?'

'Yes. A Hungarian musician, who lives in California.'

'If he pays the taxes there should be no problem. Of course, there are special situations. And if there are, irregularities, well, the Austrian tax authority can be infernally slow.'

'Shall I tell you who it is?'

'No, don't bother. Let me find out first who you're dealing with. Everything in Vienna is – a little more complicated.'

The winners of the race were announced. 'Too bad,' von Schleben said. 'Maybe better luck next time.'

'I would hope.'

'By the way, there's a man called Bolthos, at the legation. Friend of yours?

'Yes. An acquaintance, anyhow.'

'I've been trying to get in touch with him, but he's hard to get hold of. Very occupied, I suppose.'

'Why don't I have him call you?'

'Could you?'

'I'll ask him.'

'I'd certainly appreciate it. We have interests in common, here and there.'

Silvana returned. Morath could see she'd freshened her lipstick. 'I'll be on my way,' he said.

'Expect to hear from me,' von Schleben said. 'And again, I'm sorry about your uncle. We must hope for the best.'

Shoes off, tie pulled down, a cigarette in one hand and a glass of wine by his side, Morath stretched out on the brown velvet sofa and read and reread Kolovitzky's letter.

Mary Day, wrapped in one towel with another around her head, came fresh from her bath, still warm, and sat by his side.

'Who is R. L. Stevenson?' Morath said.

'I give up, who is he?'

'It's in this letter. From Kolovitzky, who played the violin at the baroness's Christmas party. He managed to get himself trapped in Vienna, and they allowed him to write to his wife – just once, I think, there won't be another – to see if they can get anything more out of him before they throw him in a canal.'

'Nicholas!'

'I'm sorry, but that's how it is.'

'The name is in the letter?'

'Code. Trying to tell his wife something.'

'Oh, well, then it's the writer.'

'What writer?'

'Robert Louis Stevenson.'

'Who's that?'

'He wrote adventure novels. Terrifically popular. My father had all the books, read them when he was growing up.'

'Such as?'

'*Treasure Island.*' She unwound the towel from her head and began drying her hair. 'You've never heard of it?'

'No.'

'Long John Silver the pirate, with a wooden leg and a parrot on his shoulder. Avast there, maties! It's about a cabin boy, and buried treasure.'

'I don't know,' he mused. 'What else?'

'*The Master of Ballantrae?*'

'What happens there?'

She shrugged. 'Never read it. Oh, also *Kidnapped.*'

'That's it.'

'He's telling her he's been kidnapped?'

'Held for ransom.'

8.30 p.m. The Balalaika was packed, smoky and loud, the gypsy violins moaning, the customers laughing, and shouting in Russian, the man down the bar from Morath weeping silently as he drank. Balki glanced at him and shook his head. '*Kabatskaya melankholia,*' he said, mouth tight with disapproval.

'What's that?'

'A Russian expression – tavern melancholy.'

Morath watched while Balki made up a *diabolo,* a generous portion of grenadine, then the glass filled with lemonade. Balki looked at his watch. 'My relief should be here.'

A few minutes later the man showed up and Balki and Morath headed for a bar in the place Clichy. Earlier, during a lull in business, Morath had laid out the details of Kolovitzky's letter and the two of them had discussed strategy, coming up with the plan that couldn't go wrong and what to do once it did.

In the bar, Balki greeted the owner in Russian and asked him if they could use the telephone.

'Maybe we should go to the railway station,' Morath said.

'Save yourself the trip. Half the White Russians in Paris use this phone. Mercenaries, bomb throwers, guys trying to put the Czar back on the throne, they all come here.'

'The Czar is dead, Boris.'

Balki laughed. 'Sure he is. So?'

Morath asked for the international operator and got the call through to Vienna almost immediately. The phone rang for a long time, then a man said, 'Hotel Schoenhof.'

'Good evening. Herr Kolovitzky, please.'

The line hissed for a moment, then the man said, 'Hold on.'

Morath waited, then a different voice, sharp and suspicious, said, 'Yes? What do you want with Kolovitzky?'

'I just want to talk to him for a minute.'

'He's busy right now, can't come to the phone. Who's calling?'

'Mr Stevenson. I'm in Paris at the moment, but I might come over to Vienna next week.'

'I'll tell him you called,' the man said, and hung up.

He called von Schleben from the Agence Courtmain. A secretary said he wasn't available but, a few minutes later, he called back. 'I have the information you wanted,' he said. 'Gerhard Kreml is a smalltime lawyer, basically crooked. Barely made a living before the *Anschluss*, but he's done very well since.'

'Where is he located?'

'He has a one-room office in the Singerstrasse. But he's not your problem, your problem is an Austrian SS, Sturmbannführer Kammer. He and Kreml have a swindle going where they arrest Jews who still have something left to steal. I suspect your friend was lured back to Vienna, and I should also tell you that his chances of getting out are not good.'

'Is there anything you can do?'

'I don't think they'll give him up – maybe if it was Germany I could help. Do you want me to try? There would have to be a quid pro quo, of course, and even then there's no guarantee.'

'What if we pay?'

'That's what I would do. You have to understand, in dealing with Kammer you're dealing with a warlord. He isn't going to let somebody come into his territory and take what belongs to him.'

Morath thanked him and hung up.

'*Liebchen*.'

Wolfi Szubl said it tenderly, gratefully. Frau Trudi turned at the wall, gave him a luscious smile, and walked across the room, her immense behind and heavy thighs wobbled as she swung her hips. When she reached the end of the room she turned again, leaned towards him, shook her shoulders and said, 'So, what do you see?'

'Paradise,' Wolfi said.

'And my discount?'

'*Big* discount, *liebchen*.'

'Yes?' Now her face beamed with pleasure. *Even her hair is fat*, he thought. A curly, auburn mop, she'd brushed it out after wriggling into the corset and it bounced up and down, with all the glorious rest of her, as she walked for him.

'I take all you have, Wolfi. The *Madame Pompadour*. My ladies will swoon.'

'Not just your ladies. What is that I see? Did you drop something, over there?'

'Did I? Oh dear.' Hands on hips she walked like a model on the runway, a shoulder thrust forward with every step, chin high, mouth set in a stylish pout. 'Two dozen? Sixty per cent off?'

'You read my mind.'

At the wall, she bent over and held the pose. 'I don't *see* anything.'

Szubl rose from his chair, came up behind her and began to unsnap the tiny buttons. When he was done she ran to the bed with baby steps and lay on her stomach with her chin propped on her hands.

Szubl began to undo his tie.

'Wolfi,' she said softly. 'Not a day goes by I don't think about you.'

Szubl took off his underpants and twirled them around his finger.

The apartment was above her shop, also *Frau Trudi*, on the Prinzstrasse next to a bakery, and the smell of pastries in the oven drifted up through the open window. A warmish day in Vienna, the beastly *Föhn* not blowing for a change, Frau Trudi's canary twittering in its cage, everything peaceful and at rest. By now it was twilight, and they could hear the bell on the door of shop below them as the customers went in and out.

Frau Trudi, damp and pink after lovemaking, nestled against him. 'You like it here, Wolfi? With me?'

'Who wouldn't?'

'You could stay for a while, if you liked.'

Wolfi sighed. If only he could. 'I wonder,' he said, 'if you know anybody who needs to make a little money. Maybe one of your ladies has a husband who's out of work.'

'What would he have to do?'

'Not much. Lend his passport to a friend of mine for a week or so.'

She propped herself on her elbow and looked down at him. 'Wolfi, are you in trouble?'

'Not me. The friend pays five hundred American dollars for the loan. So I thought, well, maybe Trudi knows somebody.'

He watched her. Fancied he could hear the ring of a cash-register drawer as she converted the dollars into schillings. 'Maybe,' she said. 'A woman I know, her husband could use it.'

'How old?'

'The husband?' She shrugged. 'Forty-five, maybe. Always problems – she comes to me for a loan, sometimes.'

'Is it possible tonight?'

'I suppose.'

'I'll give you the money now, *liebchen*, and I'll stop by tomorrow night for the passport.'

28 June. A fine day with bright sunshine, but not a ray of it reached the hunting lodge. Three storeys, thirty rooms, a grand hall; all sunk in dark, musty gloom. Morath and Balki had hired a car in Bratislava and driven up into the wooded hills north of the Danube. They were in historical Slovakia – Hungarian territory since 1938 – and only a few miles from the Austrian border.

Balki looked around him in a kind of dispirited awe – trophy heads on every wall, their glass eyes glittering in the forest light. Tentatively, he settled himself on the leather cushion of a huge wooden chair with hunting scenes carved into the high back.

'Where giants sat,' he said.

'That's the idea.'

The old empire lived on, Morath thought. One of the baroness's pet aristocrats had agreed to loan him the hunting lodge. 'So very *private*,' he'd said with a wink. It was that. In the Little Carpathians, thick with pines, by a rushing brook that wound past the window and a pictur-esque waterfall that foamed white over a dark outcropping.

Balki wandered about, gazed up at the terrible paintings. Sicilian maidens caught as they filled amphorae from little streams, gypsy girls with tambourines, a dyspeptic Napoleon with his hand on a cannon. At the far end of the room, between the stuffed heads of a bear and a tusky wild boar, he stood before a gun cabinet and tapped his fingers on the oiled stock of a rifle. 'We're not going to play with these, are we?'

'We are not.'

'No cowboys and Indians?'

Emphatically, Morath shook his head.

There was even a telephone. Of a sort – easy to imagine Archduke Franz Ferdinand calling his taxidermist. A wooden box on the kitchen wall, with the earpiece on a cord and a black horn in the centre into which one could speak. *Or shout, more likely.* He lifted the earpiece from the cradle, heard static, put it back. Looked at his watch.

Balki took off his workman's cap and hung it on an antler. 'I'll come along if you like, Morath.'

That was pure bravery – a Russian going into Austria. 'Guard the castle,' Morath said. 'Enough that you took vacation days for this, you don't have to get arrested into the bargain.'

Once again, Morath looked at his watch. 'Well, let's try it,' he said. Morath lit a cigarette, put the telephone receiver to his ear and tapped the cradle. From the static, an operator speaking Hungarian.

'I'd like to book a call to Austria,' Morath said.

'I can get through right away, sir.'

'In Vienna, 4025.'

Morath heard the phone, a two-ring signal. Then: 'Herr Kreml's office.'

'Is Herr Kreml in?'

'May I say who's calling?'

'Mr Stevenson.'

'Hold the line, please.'

Kreml was on immediately. A smooth, confident, oily voice. Saying that it was good of him to call. Morath asked after Kolovitzky's health.

'In excellent spirits!' Well, perhaps a little, how to say, *oppressed*, what with his various tax difficulties, but that could soon be put right.

'I'm in contact with Madame Kolovitzky, here in Paris,' Morath said. 'If the paperwork can be resolved, a bank draft will be sent immediately.'

Kreml went on a little, lawyer's talk, then mentioned a figure. 'In terms of your American currency, Herr Stevenson, I think it would be in the neighbourhood of ten thousand dollars.'

'The Kolovitzkys are prepared to meet that obligation, Herr Kreml.'

'I'm so pleased,' Kreml said. 'And then, in a month or so, once the draft has been processed by our banks, Herr Kolovitzky will be able to leave Austria with a clear conscience.'

'A month, Herr Kreml?'

'Oh, at least that, the way things are here.' The only way to expedite matters, Kreml said, would be to use a rather obscure provision of the tax code, for payments in cash. 'That would clear things up immediately, you see.'

Morath saw. 'Perhaps the best way,' he said.

Well, that was up to the Kolovitzkys, wasn't it? 'Herr Stevenson, I do want to compliment you on your excellent German. For an American—'

'Actually, Herr Kreml, I was born in Budapest, as Istvanagy. So, after I emigrated to California, I changed it to Stevenson.'

Ah! Of course!

'I will speak with Madame Kolovitzky, Herr Kreml, but please be assured that a cash payment will reach you within the week.'

Kreml was *very* pleased to hear that. They chattered on for a time. The weather, California, Vienna, then started to say goodbye.

'Oh yes,' Morath said, 'there is one more thing. I would very much like to have a word with Herr Kolovitzky.'

'Naturally. Do you have the number of the Hotel Schoenhof?'

'I called there. He seems always to be unavailable.'

'Really? Well, you know, that doesn't surprise me. An amiable man, Herr Kolovitzky, makes friends everywhere he goes. So I would suppose he's in and out, being entertained, sitting in the pastry shops. Have you left a message?'

'Yes.'

'Then what's the problem? He'll call you back, the minute he gets a chance. Then too, Herr Stevenson, the telephone lines between here and Paris – it can be difficult.'

'Likely that's it.'

'I must say goodbye, Herr Stevenson, but I look forward to hearing from you.'

'Be certain that you will.'

'Goodbye, Herr Stevenson.'

'Goodbye, Herr Kreml.'

They drove to Bratislava the next morning, where Morath meant to take the train to Vienna, but it was not to be. Chaos at Central Station, crowds of stranded travellers, all the benches taken, people out on Jaskovy Avenue sitting on their suitcases. 'It's the Zilina line,' the man at the ticket window explained. All passenger trains had been cancelled to make way for flatbed cars carrying Wehrmacht tanks and artillery, moving east in a steady stream. Morath and Balki stood on the platform and stared, in the midst of a silent crowd. Two locomotives pulled forty flatbeds, the long snouts of the guns thrust out from beneath canvas tarpaulins. Twenty minutes later, a trainload of horses in cattle cars, then a troop train, soldiers waving as they went by, a message chalked beneath the coach windows: 'We're going to Poland to beat up the Jews.'

The town of Zilina lay ten miles from the Polish frontier. It would have a hospital, a hotel for the general staff, a telephone system. Morath's heart sank as he watched the trains; this was hope slipping away. It could be intimidation, he thought, a feint, but he knew better. Here was the first stage of an invasion. These were the divisions that would attack from Slovakia, breaking through the Carpathian passes into southern Poland.

Morath and Balki walked around Bratislava, drank beer at a café, and waited. The city reminded Morath of Vienna in '38 – Jewish shop windows smashed, 'Jew Get Out!' painted on building walls. The Slovakian politicians hated the Czechs, invited Hitler to protect them, then discovered that they didn't like being protected. But it was too late. Here and there somebody had written *pro tento krat* on the telephone poles, 'for the time being', but that was braggadocio and fooled nobody.

Back in the station restaurant, Morath sat with his valise between his feet, ten thousand dollars in Austrian schillings packed inside. He asked a waiter if the Danube bridge was open – in case he decided to drive across – but the man looked gloomy and shook his head. 'No, you cannot use it,' he said, 'they've been crossing for days.'

'Any way into Austria?'

'Maybe at five they let a train through, but you have to be on the platform, and it will be – very crowded. You understand?'

Morath said he did.

When the waiter left, Balki said, 'Will you be able to get back out?'

'Probably.'

Balki nodded. 'Morath?'

'Yes?'

'You're not going to get yourself killed, are you?'

'I don't think so,' Morath said.

He had two hours to wait, and used a telephone in the station to place a call to Paris. He had to wait twenty minutes, then the call went through to the Agence Courtmain. The receptionist, after several tries, found Mary Day at a meeting in Courtmain's office.

'Nicholas!' she said. 'Where are you?' She wasn't exactly sure what he was doing. 'Some family business,' he'd told her, but she knew it was more than that.

'I'm in Bratislava,' he said.

'Bratislava. How's the weather?'

'Sunny. I wanted to tell you that I miss you.'

After a moment she said, 'Me too, Nicholas. When are you coming back?'

'Soon, a few days, if all goes well.'

'It will, won't it? Go well?'

'I think so, you don't have to worry. I thought I'd call, to say I love you.'

'I know,' she said.

'I guess I have to go, there are people waiting to use the phone.'

'All right. Goodbye.'

'A few days.'

'The weekend.'

'Oh yes, by then.'

'Well, I'll see you then.'

'Goodbye, Mary.'

The waiter had been right about the passenger train. It pulled in slowly, after six-thirty, people jammed in everywhere. Morath forced his way on, using his strength, smiling and apologizing, making a small space for himself on the platform of the last car, hanging on to a metal stanchion all the way to Vienna.

He called Szubl at his hotel and they met in a coffee house, the patrons smoking and reading the papers and conversing in polite tones. A city where everyone was sad and everyone smiled and nothing could be done – it had always seemed that way to Morath and it was worse than ever that summer night in 1939.

'I have what you want,' Szubl said, and handed him a passport under the table. Morath looked at the photo. An angry little man glared up at him, moustache, glasses, *nothing ever goes right.*

'Can you fix it?' Szubl said.

'Yes. More or less. I took a photo from some document his wife had with her, I can paste it in. But, with any luck at all, I won't need it.'

'Did they look at your bag, at the border?'

'Yes. I told them what the money was for, then they went through everything else. But it was only the usual customs inspectors, not SS or anything.'

'I took the stays out of a corset. You still want them?'

'Yes.'

Szubl handed him a long envelope, hotel stationery. Morath put it in his pocket. 'When are you getting out of here?'

'Tomorrow. By noon.'

'Make sure of that, Wolfi.'

'I will. What about the passport?'

'Tell her your friend lost it. More money for Herr X, and he can go and get another.'

Szubl nodded, then stood up. 'I'll see you back in Paris, then.'

They shook hands, and Morath watched him leave, heavy and slow, even without the sample case, a folded newspaper under one arm.

'Would you go once around the Mauerplatz?'

'If you like.' The taxi driver was an old man with a cavalry moustache, his war medals pinned to the sun visor.

'A sentimental journey,' Morath explained.

'Ah, of course.'

A small, cobbled square, people strolling on a warm evening, old linden trees making leaf shadows in the light of the street lamps. Morath rolled the window down and the driver took a slow tour around the square.

'A lady and I stayed here, a few years ago.'

'At the Schoenhof?'

'Yes. Still the same old place?'

'I would think. Care to get out and take a look? I don't mind.'

'No, I just wanted to see it again.'

'So, now to the Landstrasse?'

'Yes. The Imperial.'

'Come to Vienna often?'

'Now and again.'

'Different, this past year.'

'Is it?'

'Yes. *Quiet*, thank God. Earlier we had nothing but trouble.'

Eight-fifteen. He would try one last time, he decided, and made the call from a phone in the hotel lobby.

'Hotel Schoenhof.'

'Good evening. This is Doktor Heber, please connect me with Herr Kolovitzky's room.'

'Sorry. Herr Kolovitzky is not available.'

'Not in his room?'

'No. Goodnight, Herr Doktor.'

'This is urgent, and you will give him a message. He took some tests, in my clinic here in Wahring, and he must return as soon as possible.'

'All right, I'll let him know about it.'

'Thank you. Now would you be so kind as to call the manager to the phone?

'I'm the manager.'

'And you are?'

'The manager. Goodnight, Herr Doktor.'

The next morning Morath bought a briefcase, put the money and his passport inside, explained to the desk clerk that he would be away for a week, paid for his room until the following Thursday, and had the briefcase put in the hotel safe. From the art dealer in Paris he had a new passport – French, this time. He returned to his room, gave his valise a last and very thorough search and found nothing out of the ordinary. Then he took a taxi to the Nordbannhof, had a cup of coffee in the station buffet, went outside and hailed a taxi.

'The Hotel Schoenhof,' he told the driver.

In the lobby, only men.

Something faintly awkward in the way they were dressed, he thought, as though they were used to military uniform. *SS in civilian clothing.* Nobody saluted, or clicked his heels, but he could sense it – the way their hair was cut, the way they stood, the way they looked at him.

The man behind the desk was not one of them. The owner, Morath guessed. In his fifties, soft and frightened. He met Morath's eyes for a moment longer than he needed to. *Go away, you don't belong here.*

'A room, please,' Morath said.

One of the young men in the lobby strolled over and leaned on the desk. When Morath looked at him he got a friendly little nod in return. Not at all unpleasant, he was there to find out who Morath was and what he wanted. No hard feelings.

'Single or double?' the owner said.

'A single. On the square, if you have it.'

The owner made a show of looking at his registration book. 'Very well. For how long, please?'

'Two nights.'

'Your name?'

'Lebrun.' Morath handed over the passport.

'Will you be taking the demi-pension?'

'Yes, please.'

'Dinner is served in the dining room. At seven promptly.'

The owner took a key from a numbered hook on a board behind him. Something odd about the board. The top row of hooks, he saw, had no keys. 'Four zero three,' the owner said. 'Would you like the porter to take your valise up?' His hand hovered over a bell.

'I can manage,' Morath said.

He walked up four flights of stairs, the carpet old and frayed. Just a commercial hotel, he thought. Like hundreds in Vienna, Berlin, Paris, anywhere one went. He found 403 and unlocked the door. An edelweiss pattern on the limp curtains and the coverlet on the narrow bed. Pale green walls, a tired carpet, and hardly a sound to be heard. *Very quiet in this hotel.*

He decided to take a walk, let them have a look at his valise. He handed the key to the owner at the desk and went out on to the Mauerplatz. At a newsstand he glanced at the headlines. POLAND THREATENS BOMBARDMENT OF DANZIG! Then bought a sports magazine, youths playing volleyball on the cover. A genteel neighbourhood, he thought. Sturdy, brick apartments, women with baby carriages, a trolley line, a school where he could hear children singing, a smiling grocer in the doorway of his store, a little man who looked like a weasel sitting at the wheel of a battered Opel. Back at the Schoenhof, Morath retrieved his key and walked upstairs, past the fourth floor, up to the fifth. In the corridor, a heavy man with a red face sat on a chair leaned back against the wall. He stood when he saw Morath.

'What do you want up here?'

'I'm in room 403.'

'Then you're on the wrong floor.'

'Oh. What's up here?'

'Reserved,' the man said, 'get moving.'

Morath apologized and hurried away. *Very close,* he thought. Ten rooms on the fifth floor, Kolovitzky was a prisoner in one of them.

Three in the morning. Morath lay on the bed in the dark room, sometimes a breeze from the Mauerplatz moved the curtains. Otherwise, silence. After dinner there'd been a street musician on the square, playing an accordion and singing. Then he'd listened to the wireless on the night table, Liszt and Schubert, until midnight, when the national radio station went off the air. Not completely off the air – they played the ticking of a metronome until dawn. *To reassure people,* it was said.

Morath gazed at the ceiling. He'd been lying there for three hours with nothing to do but wait, had thought about almost everything he could think of. His life. Mary Day. The war. Uncle Janos. He missed Polanyi, it surprised him how much. Echézeaux and *bay rhum*. The amiable contempt he felt for the world he had to live in. And his final trick. *Here, you try it.*

He wondered about the other guests in the hotel – the real ones, not the SS. They'd been easy enough to spot in the dining room, trying to eat the awful dinner. He'd mostly pushed noodles from one side of his plate to the other, kept an eye on the waiter, and figured out how the downstairs worked. As for the guests, he believed they would survive. Hoped they would.

From a church, somewhere in the neighbourhood, the single chime for the half-hour. Morath sighed and swung his legs off the bed. Put on his jacket, pulled his tie up. Then he took the stays from the envelope Szubl had given him. *Celluloid.* Made of soluble guncotton and camphor.

He took a deep breath and slowly turned the knob on his door, listened for twenty seconds, and stepped out into the hallway. He descended the staircase one slow step at a time. Somebody coughing on the third floor, a light under a door on the second.

A few steps from the bottom – the reception area – he stared out into the gloom. There had to be a guard. Where? Finally he made out part of a silhouette above the back of a couch, and heard the shallow breathing that meant light sleep. Morath moved cautiously around the newel post at the foot of the staircase, entered the dining room, then the hallway where the waiter had appeared and disappeared during dinner.

Finally, the kitchen. He lit a match, looked around, then blew it out. There was a street lamp in the alley, not far from the windows, enough light for Morath to see what he was doing. He found the sinks, big, heavy tubs made of zinc, knelt on the floor below them and ran his fingertips over the cement. Found the grease trap, realized he'd have trouble prying up the lid, and abandoned the idea.

Next he tried the stove, and here he found what he needed. In a cabinet next to the oven door, a large metal can that had once contained lard was now used to store the grease poured from cooking pans. It was surprisingly heavy, maybe twenty pounds of yellow, rancid fat, mostly congealed, with an inch or so of oil floating on top. *Sausages, butter, bacon*, he thought. *Roast goose.*

He looked around, saw an iron ring above the stove where implements were hung, carefully removed a giant ladle, and served up a heaping scoop of thick fat. Took a handful, and smeared it on the wooden countertop. Worked it on to the walls and the window frames and the doors of the cabinets. Then he laid the can on its side in one corner, sunk the corset stays halfway into the fat, lit a match, and tossed it in.

The celluloid caught immediately; a hot, white flash, then the fat sputtered to life and a little river of liquid fire ran across the floor and began to burn its way up the wall. A few moments later, he saw the ceiling start to turn black.

Now he had to wait. He found a broom closet by the entrance to the kitchen, stepped inside and closed the door. Barely room for him in there, he discovered. He counted eleven brooms. What the hell were they doing with so many brooms?

He told himself to stay calm, but the crackling sound from the kitchen and the smell of fire made his pulse race. Tried to count to a hundred and twenty, as he'd planned, but he never got there. He did not mean to die in a Viennese broom closet. He threw the door open and hurried down the hallway through a haze of oily smoke.

He heard a shout from the guard in the lobby, then another. Christ, there'd been *two* of them in there. 'Fire!' he yelled as he ran up the stairs. He could hear doors opening, running footsteps.

Second floor. Third floor. Now he had to trust that the Austrian SS guards changed shifts like everybody else. Halfway up the stairs to the fifth floor he started yelling, 'Police! Police!'

A bullet-headed man in his shirtsleeves came charging down the corridor, a Luger in his hand. 'What's happening?'

'Open these doors. The hotel's on fire.'

'What?' The man backed up a step. *Open the doors?*

'Hurry up. You have the keys? Give them to me. Go, now, run, for God's sake!'

'I have to—'

Morath the policeman had no time for him. Grabbed him by the shirt and ran him down the hall. 'Go wake up your officers. *Now.* We don't have time for monkey business.'

That, for whatever reason, did it. The man shoved the Luger into a shoulder holster and went bounding down the steps, shouting 'Fire!' as he went.

Morath started opening doors – the room numbers, thank God, were on the keys. The first room was empty. In the second, one of the SS men, who sat up in bed and stared at Morath in terror. 'What? What is it?'

'The hotel's on fire. You better get out.'

'Oh.'

Relieved that it was only the hotel on fire. What had he thought?

There was smoke in the hallway. The SS man trotted past, he was wearing candy-striped pyjamas and carrying a machine pistol by its strap. Morath found another empty room, then, next door, Kolovitzky, struggling to open the window.

'Not like that,' Morath said. 'Come with me.'

Kolovitzky turned towards him. He wasn't the same man who'd played the violin at the baroness's party, this man was old and tired and frightened, wearing braces and a soiled shirt. He studied Morath's face – was he playing some new trick, one they hadn't tried on him yet?

'I came here for you,' Morath said. 'I burned down this hotel for you.'

Kolovitzky understood. 'Blanche,' he said.

'Are they holding anyone else up here?'

'There were two others, but they left yesterday.'

Now they heard sirens and they ran, coughing, hands over mouths, down the stairs through the rising smoke.

The street in front of the Schoenhof was utter confusion. Fire engines, firemen hauling hoses into the hotel, policemen, crowds of onlookers, a man wearing only a blanket, two women in bathrobes. Morath guided Kolovitzky across the Mauerplatz, then down a side street. As they approached, the driver of a battered Opel started his car. Kolovitzky got in the back seat, Morath in front.

'Hello, Rashkow,' Morath said.

'Who is he?' Kolovitzky asked later that morning, while Rashkow watered a tree by the roadside.

'He's from Odessa,' Morath said. 'Poor little Rashkow', Balki had called him, who'd sold Czarist railway bonds and Tolstoy's unfinished novel and wound up in a Hungarian prison. Morath had gone to Sombor to get him out of jail.

'The way he looks,' Kolovitzky said, 'he should come to Hollywood.'

Rashkow drove on farm roads through the Austrian countryside. A day in July, the beetroot and potatoes sprouted bright green in the rolling fields. It was only forty miles to the Hungarian border at Bratislava. Or Pressburg, if you liked, or Pozsony. In the back seat, Kolovitzky stared at the Austrian passport with his photo in it. 'Do you think they're looking for me?'

'They are.'

They stopped well short of the Danube bridge, in Petrzalka, once a Czech border point, now in the Slovakian Protectorate. Abandoned the car. Went to a rented room above a café, where all three changed into dark suits. When they came downstairs, a Grosser Mercedes with Hungarian diplomatic registration was waiting for them, driven by the chauffeur of one of Bolthos's diplomatic colleagues in Budapest.

There was a swarm of Austrian SS gathered at the border crossing, smoking, laughing, strutting about in their high, polished boots. But the chauffeur ignored them. Rolled to a smooth stop at the customs building, handed four passports out of the window. The border guard put a finger to the visor of his cap, glanced briefly into the car, then handed them back.

'Welcome home,' the chauffeur said to Kolovitzky, as they crossed to the Hungarian side of the river.

Kolovitzky wept.

A midnight supper on the rue Guisarde.

Mary Day knew the trains were late, crossing Germany, so she'd planned for it. She set out a plate of sliced ham, a vegetable salad and a *baguette*. 'And this was delivered yesterday,' she said, taking a bottle of wine from the cupboard and a corkscrew from the kitchen drawer. 'You must have ordered it by telephone,' she said. 'Very thoughtful of you, in the middle of – whatever it was, to think of us.'

A 1922 Echézeaux.

'It's what you wanted?'

'Yes,' he said, smiling.

'You are really very good, Nicholas,' she said. 'Really, you are.'

Dark Star

'You may not be interested in war, but war is interested in you.' *Lev Bronshtein, known as Trotsky, June 1919*

Silence in
Prague

In the late autumn of 1937, in the steady beat of North Sea rain that comes with dawn in that season, the tramp freighter *Nicaea* stood at anchor off the Belgian city of Ostend. In the distance, a berthing tug made slow progress through the harbour swell, the rhythm of its engine distinct over the water, its amber running lights twin blurs in the darkness.

The *Nicaea*, 6,320 gross tonnes, of Maltese registry, had spent her first thirty years as a coastal steamer in the eastern Mediterranean, hauling every imaginable cargo from Latakia to Famagusta, back to Iskenderun, down to Beirut, north to Smyrna, then south to Sidon and Jaffa – thirty years of blistering summers and drizzling winters, trading and smuggling in equal proportion, occasionally enriching, more typically ruining, a succession of owner syndicates as she herself was slowly ruined by salt, rust, and a long line of engineers whose enthusiasm far exceeded their skill. Now, in her final years, she was chartered to Exportkhleb, the Soviet Union's grain-trading bureau, and she creaked and groaned sorrowfully to lie at anchor in such cold, northern seas.

Riding low in the water, she bore her cargo gracelessly – principally Anatolian wheat bound for the Black Sea port of Odessa, a city that had not seen imported grains for more than a century. She carried, as well, several small consignments: flax-seed loaded in Istanbul, dried figs from Limassol, a steel drum of Ammonal – a mining explosive made of TNT and powdered aluminium – en route to a sabotage cell in Hamburg, a metal trunk of engineering blueprints for an Italian submarine torpedo, deftly copied at a naval research station in Brindisi, and two passengers: a senior Comintern official using a Dutch passport with the alias Van Doorn, and a foreign correspondent of the newspaper *Pravda* travelling under his true name, André Szara.

Szara, hands thrust deep in pockets, hair blown about by the offshore gale, stood in the shelter of a passageway and silently cursed the Belgian tug captain who, from the methodical chug of the engine, was taking his own sweet time attending to the *Nicaea*. Szara knew harbourmen in this part of the world; stolid, reflective pipe smokers who were never far from the coffeepot and the evening paper. Unshakable in crisis, they spent the rest of their days making the world wait on their pleasure. Szara shifted his weight with the roll of the ship, turned his back to the wind, and lit a cigarette.

He had boarded the freighter nineteen days earlier, in Piraeus, having been assigned a story on *the struggle of the Belgian dockworkers*. That was one assignment; there was another. Killing time in a dockside tavern as the *Nicaea* was eased into moorage, he had been approached by the World's Plainest Man. Where, he wondered, did they find them? Russia marked people: deformed most, made some exquisite, at the very least burned itself deep into the eyes. But not this one. His mother was water, his father a wall. 'A small favour,' said the world's plainest man. 'You'll have a fellow passenger, he is travelling on Comintern business. Perhaps you will find out where he is stopping in Ostend.'

'If I can,' Szara had said. The word *if* could not really be used between them, but Szara pretended it could be and the NKVD operative – or GRU or whatever he was – graciously conceded his right to suggest he had a choice in the matter. Szara, after all, was an important correspondent.

'Yes. If you can,' he'd said. Then added, 'Leave us a little note at the desk of your hotel. To Monsieur Brun.'

Szara spelled it, to make sure he'd got it right. Defiance was over for the day.

'Just so,' said the man.

There was ample time to do the small favour; the *Nicaea* had been at sea for nineteen days, an eternity of icy, seawater showers, salt cod for dinner, and the smell of coal fumes from the freighter's rusting stack as she butted through the October seas. Squinting through the darkness at the lights of the wallowing tug, Szara ached for something sweet, sugar after salt, a cream cake, rain in a pine forest, a woman's perfume. He had, he thought, been too long at sea. An ironist, he heard the theatrical echo of the phrase and grinned privately. *La mélancolie des paquebots* – that said it better. He'd come across the phrase in Flaubert and it had stayed with him; it was all in those four words, the narrow cabin with a light bulb swaying on a cord, the seaweed reek of harbours, slanting rains, a column of black smoke from a funnel on the horizon.

The ship's bell sounded once. Four-thirty. The tug's amber lights grew brighter.

The Comintern man known as Van Doorn stepped from his cabin carrying a leather valise and joined Szara at the railing. He was swaddled in clothing like a child dressed for a winter day, woollen muffler crossed precisely at his throat, cap set low on his head, overcoat buttoned to the very top. 'One hour, eh? And we'll be down the gangplank. What is your view, André Aronovich?' Van Doorn was, as always, wryly deferential towards 'the famous journalist Szara'.

'If the port officer makes no difficulties, I would agree,' Szara said.

'That will not happen. He is *nash*.' The word meant *ours, we own him*, and the tone suggested Szara's great fortune in having such iron-fisted types as Van Doorn to watch out for him in the real world.'

'Well, then . . .' Szara said, acknowledging superior strength.

It happened that Szara knew who Van Doorn was; one of his friends in the Foreign Department of the NKVD had once pointed him out, with a sneer, at a party in Moscow. Szara's NKVD friends were, like himself, Russified Polish Jews or Latvians, Ukrainians, Germans, all sorts, and typically intellectuals. They constituted his *khvost* – the word fell somewhere between clique and gang. Van Doorn, in fact Grigory Khelidze, was from a different crowd: Georgians, Armenians, Russified Greeks and Turks, a *khvost* with roots in the southeast corner of the empire led by Beria, Dekanozov, and Alexei Agayan. It was a smaller group than the Poles and Ukrainians but easily its equal in power. Stalin came from down there; they knew what he liked and how he thought.

From the tugboat's silhouette, a high shape against the rain-softened glow of the city, a blinkered signal light began to operate. This was progress. Khelidze rubbed his hands to warm them up. 'Not long now,' he said merrily. He gave Szara a lecher's grin; in no time at all he'd be with his 'perfect dumpling'.

Thank heaven for the dumpling, Szara thought. Without her he might never have managed the small favour. Khelidze wasn't much to look at, a fattish man in his forties with pale hair worn well brushed and pomaded. His hands were small and chubby, endlessly fussing with a pair of silver-rimmed spectacles of which he was very proud. But he fancied himself a ladies' man. 'I envy you, André Aronovich,' he'd said one night when they were alone in the ship's wardroom after dinner. 'You move in exalted circles. The way it is with my job, well, the best I can hope for is the frau of some German shop steward, a big Inga with red hands, and then, likely as not, all a man gets is an extra potato and a stolen cuddle in the kitchen. Ah, but a man in your position – for you it's professors' daughters and lawyers' wives; those hot, skinny bitches that can't leave a journalist alone. Isn't it so?'

Szara had brought vodka to the feast, also brandy. The vast, green ocean rolled beneath them, the *Nicaea*'s engines coughed and grumbled. Khelidze rested his elbows on the faded oilcloth and leaned forward in expectation, a man who wanted to hear every detail.

Szara obliged. His talent, set alight by alcohol, burned and flamed. A certain lady in, ah, Budapest. Gold earrings like a Gypsy – but no Gypsy, an aristocrat who affected British tweeds and wore a silk scarf, the colour of a cloud, knotted at her throat. Hair dark red, like autumn, Magyar cheekbones, long, delicate fingers. Szara, a good storyteller, took his time. He cast about for a name, came up with Magda, thought it commonplace, but could do no better. Magda, then. The husband was a lout, ignorant, *nye kulturny* – a man of no culture who exported wool. So Szara had the wife. Where? In the stables? On straw? No, in the apartment, a *cinq-à-sept affaire* by lamplight. The husband was . . . hunting wild boar. Szara watched the level in the brandy bottle on the table. As it descended, so did the pants. And there, the most delicate little triangle, also dark red, like autumn. And fine blue veins beneath the milky skin. The green silk divan was ruined. Khelidze's ears were scarlet. Later it came to Szara that he'd been describing his private musings on a particular secretary he sometimes encountered at the Yugoslav Ministry of Posts and Telegraph.

Khelidze was drunk. He polished his glasses with a handkerchief, his eyes watery and vague. Yes well, he said, one sometimes imagined. For himself, well it was all a matter of taste in this life wasn't it? He had, in all confidence, 'a perfect dumpling' in Ostend, resident at the Hotel Groenendaal in the street of the same name. 'A fat little thing. They dress her up like a child, with a bow and a party dress of white satin. My God, André Aronovich, how we carry on! Such a grand little actress she is, pouting, sulking, tossing her curls about, whining for biscuits and milk. But she can't have them. No, definitely not! Because, well, there's something she must do first. Oh no, she wails. Oh yes.' Khelidze sat back in his chair, put his glasses on, and sighed. 'A marvel,' he said. 'She'll suck ten years off a man's life.'

By the time they went singing off to bed, holding each other upright in the passageway that rolled with the motion of the ship, the dark surface of the sea was turning grey with dawn.

Szara's hotel in Ostend was all flowers: on the wallpaper, heavy cabbage roses on a sombre field; on the bedspread, a jungle of vines and geraniums; and in the park below his window, frostbitten asters, dusty purple and faded pink. And the place was called the Hotel Blommen. *Ignore this stern, northern, Flemish light, here we have flowers.* Szara stood at the window and listened to the foghorns from the harbour and the rattle of dead leaves as the wind swept them through the deserted park. He folded the note and creased it between thumb and index finger: 'M. Van Doorn will be visiting the Hotel Groenendaal.' He put it in an envelope, licked and sealed it, and wrote 'M. Brun' on the front. He didn't know what it meant, why a journalist was asked to report on a Comintern operative. But there was a reason, a single reason that lately explained anything you wanted explained: the purge had shuddered to a halt in '36, now another had begun. The first had taken politicians, Stalin's opposition, and more than a few journalists. This one, it was said, had gone to work on the intelligence services themselves. Szara, beginning in 1934, had learned to live with it: he was careful what he wrote, what he said, who he saw. Not yet what he thought – *not yet*, he told himself now and then, as though it needed to be said. He took the note down to the reception desk and handed it to the old man behind the counter.

The knock on the door was discreet, two taps with a knuckle. Szara had fallen asleep, still wearing shirt and trousers, on top of the bedspread. He sat up and pulled the damp shirt away from his back. It was a grey dawn outside the window, fog hanging in the tree branches. He looked at his watch – a little after six. The polite knock came a second time and Szara felt his heart accelerate. A knock at the door meant too much, nobody did that in Moscow any more, they phoned first. 'Yes, a moment,' he said. Somewhere within, a small, urgent voice: *out the window*. He took a breath, staggered to his feet, and opened the door. It was the old man from the hotel desk, holding a coffee and a newspaper. Had he left a call to be woken up? No.

'Good morning, good morning,' said the old man tartly. It never really was, but one had to pretend. 'Your friend was kind enough to leave you the newspaper,' he added, putting it at the foot of the bed.

Szara fumbled for change and handed over a few coins. Drachmas, he thought. He'd bought Belgian francs in Athens; where were they? But the old man seemed happy enough, thanked him and left. The coffee was cooler than he would have liked, the boiled milk a little sour, but he was grateful for it. The front page of the newspaper was devoted to anti-Jewish riots that had broken out in Danzig, with a photo of shouting, black-shirted Nazis. In Spain the Republican government, under pressure from Franco's columns, had fled from Valencia to Barcelona. On page 6, the misfortunes of Ostend's soccer team. Printed down the margin in pen, in a fine Cyrillic hand, were detailed instructions for a noon meeting. The 'small favour' had started to grow.

*

Szara walked down the hall, locked the door of the bathroom, and started to wash. The instructions in the newspaper frightened him; he was afraid of being forced into a car and taken away. The purge sometimes worked like that – the security *apparat* worked quietly when it took public figures. Senior NKVD officers were called to meetings in small towns just outside Moscow, then arrested as they got off the train, a tactic that kept friends and family from trying to intervene. A foreign country, he reasoned, would be even more convenient. Should he run? Was now the time? There was a part of him that thought so. *Go to the British consulate*, it said. *Fly for your life. Call the friends in Moscow who protect you. Buy a gun.* Meanwhile, he shaved.

Then he sat in the park, where a nursemaid with a baby carriage flirted with him. *Go with her*, he told himself, *hide in her bed. She will do anything you want.* Perhaps it was true. He very well knew, at the age of forty, somewhat past illusion, what she saw. The longish black hair he combed back with his fingers, the tight line of the jaw, a concentration of personality in the eyes. These were hooded, knowing, of a grey-green sea colour that women had more than once called 'strange', and often read as both expectant and sorrowful, like dogs' eyes. His features were delicate, skin colourless, made to seem pallid by a permanent beard shadow. It was, taken altogether, a sad, attentive presence, anxious for happiness, certain of disappointment. He dressed the role of worldly intellectual, favouring soft clothing: thick grey cotton shirts, monochromatic ties in the sombre tones of basic colours. He was, in the world's mirror, a man you could take seriously, at least for a time. Then, later, there would be affection or intense dislike, a strong reaction whichever way it went.

The nursemaid, in a starched cap, plain, hand mindlessly rocking the carriage where some other woman's baby slept, had no doubts at all. He need only rescue her, from boredom, servitude, chapped hands, and she would do whatever was necessary. Below a broad forehead her eyes were frank. *Don't be frightened. I can fix anything.*

Just before ten-thirty he stood, pulled his raincoat tightly about him, and walked away. Glancing back, he easily read her expression: *Then no? Stupid man.*

A series of tram lines took him to a neighbourhood of worker tenements, the narrow streets smelled like fish, urine, fried onions. The November day was cool in the shadow of the buildings. Was he followed? He thought not. They had something better, a kind of invisible cable, the method the psychologist Pavlov used with laboratory animals. It was called – he had to look for the word – conditioning. His last day on earth, yet he did what he was told. His mind stood off and watched the scene: a man of intellect, independence, delivering himself to the *apparat.* Pitiful. Contemptible. Szara glanced at his watch. He didn't want to be late.

At a small market he stopped and bought fruit, then paid a few sous extra for a paper bag. The market woman wore a shawl over her head; her glance was suspicious. What was he, a foreigner, doing in this part of the city? Szara walked another block, made sure nobody was watching, and left most of the fruit in an alley. He watched the street behind him in a shop window where wooden soldiers were for sale. Then he moved off again, entering a small square lined by plane trees cut back to rounded pollard shapes for the coming winter. A driver slept in a parked taxi, a man in *bleu de travail* sat on a bench and stared at his feet, the war memorial fountain was dry: the square at the end of the world. A small brasserie, Le Terminus, had no patrons on its glassed-in *terrasse.*

Szara, more and more now the critic of his own abduction, was struck by the normalcy of the scene. What a placid, ordinary place they'd chosen. Perhaps they liked the name of the brasserie, Le Terminus – the terminal, the end of the line. Was the choice ironic? Were they that clever? Perhaps Pavlov was not, after all, the day's guiding spirit; perhaps that honour belonged to Chekhov, or Gorky. He searched for a terminal, for tramways, a railway station, but there was nothing he could see.

The interior of the brasserie was enormous and silent. Szara stood in the foyer as the door behind him bumped back and forth until it came to rest. Behind the zinc bar a man in a white shirt with cuffs turned back was aimlessly stirring a coffee, a few patrons sat quietly with a glass of beer, one or two were eating. Szara felt himself swept by intuition, a sense of loss, a conviction that this still life of a brasserie in Ostend was a frozen image of what had been and would now vanish forever: amber walls, marble tables, a wooden fan slowly turning on the smoke-darkened ceiling, a florid-faced man with a handlebar moustache who rattled his newspaper into place, the scrape of a chair on the tile floor, the cry of a seagull from the square, the sound of a ship's horn from the harbour.

There was an old weather glass on one wall; beneath it sat a woman in a brown, belted raincoat with buttoned epaulettes on the shoulders. She glanced at him, then went back to eating, a plate of eels and *pommes frites;* Szara could smell the horse fat the Belgians used for frying. A red wool scarf was looped over the top of an adjacent chair. The glass and the scarf were the recognition signals described in the margin of the newspaper.

The woman was perhaps in her late thirties. She had strong hands with long fingers – the knife and fork moved gracefully as she ate. She wore her chestnut hair cut close and short, a strand or two of grey caught the light when she moved. Her skin was pale, with the slight reddening at the cheekbones of a delicate complexion chapped by a sea breeze. *An aristocrat*, he thought. *Once upon a time.* Something fine and elegant in her had been discouraged, she wished to be plain, and almost was. Russian she was not, he thought. German perhaps, or Czech.

When he sat down across from her he saw that her eyes were grey and serious, with dark blushes of fatigue beneath them. The nonsense greetings of the *parol*, the confirmation passwords, were exchanged, and she lowered the edge of the paper bag he'd carried to make sure there was an orange inside.

Isn't this all absurd, I mean, oranges and a red scarf and . . . But these were words he never got to say. Just as he leaned towards her, to make contact, to let her know that they were the sort of people who could easily bridge the nonsense a foolish world imposed on them, she stopped him with a look. It made him swallow. 'I am called Renate Braun,' she said. *Called* meant what? An alias? Or simply a formal way of speaking. 'I know who you are,' she added. The notion *and that will suffice* was unstated but clear.

Szara liked women and they knew it. All he wanted to do, as the tension left him, was chatter, maybe make her laugh. They were just people, a man and a woman, but she wasn't buying. Whatever this was, he thought, it was not an arrest. Very well, then a continuation of the business he did with the NKVD from time to time. Every journalist, every citizen outside the Soviet Union, had to do that. But why make it into a funeral? Internally, he shrugged. She was German, he thought. Or Swiss or Austrian – one of those places where position, station in life, excluded informality.

She put a few francs on the waiter's saucer, retrieved her scarf, and they went outside into a hard, bright sky and a stiff wind. A boxy Simca sedan was now parked by the brasserie. Szara was certain it hadn't been there when he'd gone into the place. She directed him into the passenger seat and positioned herself directly behind him. If she shot him in the back of the neck, he thought, his dying words would be *why did you go to all this trouble?* Unfortunately, that particular wound didn't allow for last words, and Szara, who had been on battlefields in the civil war that followed the revolution, knew it. All he'd manage was *why – za chto?* what for? – but everyone, all the victims of the purge, said that.

The driver turned on the ignition and they drove away from the square. 'Heshel,' said the woman behind him, 'did it . . . ?'

'Yes, missus,' the driver said.

Szara studied the driver as they wound through the cobbled streets of the city. He knew the type, to be found among the mud lanes in any of the ghettos in Poland or Russia: the body of a gnome, not much over five feet tall, thick lips, prominent nose, small, clever eyes. He wore a tweed worker's cap with a short brim tilted down over one eyebrow, and the collar of his old suit jacket was turned up. The man was ageless, and his expression, cold and humorous at once, Szara understood perfectly. It was the face of the survivor, whatever survival meant that day – invisibility, guile, abasement, brutality – anything at all.

They drove for fifteen minutes, then rolled to a stop in a crooked street where narrow hotels were jammed side by side and women in net stockings smoked lazily in doorways.

Renate Braun climbed out, Heshel waited. 'Come with me,' she said. Szara followed her into the hotel. There was no desk clerk to be seen, the lobby was empty except for a Belgian sailor sitting on the staircase with his head in his hands, a sailor cap balanced on his knee.

The stairway was steep and narrow, the wooden steps dotted with cigarette burns. They walked down a long corridor, then stopped in front of a door with 26 written on it in pencil. Szara noticed a tiny smudge of blue chalk at eye level on the door frame. The woman opened her shoulder bag and withdrew a ring of keys – Szara thought he saw the crosshatched grain of an automatic pistol grip as she snapped the bag closed. The keys were masters, with long shanks for leverage when the fit wasn't precise.

She unlocked the door and pushed it open. The air smelled like overripe fruit cut with ammonia. Khelidze stared at them from the bed, his back resting against the headboard, his trousers and underpants bunched around his knees. His face was spotted with yellow stains and his mouth frozen in the shape of a luxurious yawn. Wound within the sheets was a large, humped mass. A waxy leg had ripped through the sheet; its foot, rigid as if to dance on point, had toenails painted baby pink. Szara could hear a fly buzzing against the windowpane and the sound of bicycle bells in the street.

'You confirm it is the man from the ship?' she said.

'Yes.' This was, he knew, an NKVD killing, a signed NKVD killing. The yellow stains meant hydrocyanic acid used as a spray, a method known to be employed by the Soviet services.

She opened her bag, put the keys inside, and took out a white cotton handkerchief scented with cologne. Holding it over her nose and mouth, she pulled a corner of the sheet free and looked underneath. Szara could see curly blonde hair and part of a ribbon.

The woman dropped the sheet and rubbed her hand against the side of her raincoat. Then she put the handkerchief away and began to go through Khelidze's trouser pockets, tossing the contents onto the end of the bed: coins, rumpled notes of various currencies, a squeezed-out tube of medication, the soft cloth he'd used to polish his glasses, and a Dutch passport.

Next she searched the coat and jacket, hung carefully in a battered armoire, finding a pencil and a small address book that she added to the pile. She took the pencil and poked through the items on the bed, sighed with irritation, and searched in her bag until she found a razor blade with tape along both edges. She peeled off one of the tapes and went to work on the jacket and the coat, slicing open the seams and splitting the pads in the shoulders. This yielded a Soviet passport, which she put in her bag. Taking hold of the cuffs, she removed the trousers and methodically took them apart. When she let out the second cuff, a folded square of paper was revealed. She opened it, then handed it to Szara.

'What is it, please?'

'The printing is Czech. A form of some kind.'

'Yes?'

He studied the paper for a moment. 'I think it is a baggage receipt, from a shipping company. No, for the railway station. In Prague.'

She looked the room over carefully, then walked to the tiny, yellowed sink in the corner and began to wash her hands. 'You will collect the parcel,' she said, drying herself with her handkerchief. 'It is for you.'

They left the room together; she did not bother to lock the door. In the lobby she turned to him and said, 'Of course you'll be leaving Ostend immediately.'

He nodded that he would.

'Your work is appreciated,' she said.

He followed her out of the hotel and watched her get into the Simca. He crossed the narrow street and turned to look back. Heshel was watching him through the window of the car and smiled thinly as their eyes met. *Here is the world*, said the smile, *and here we are in it.*

Arriving in Antwerp at dusk, and adding two hours to local time for Moscow, he called his editor at home. From Nezhenko, who handled foreign assignments, he expected no trouble. This would not normally be the case, given a three-week lapse in communication, but when he was asked to do 'favours' for the *apparat*, someone stopped by the *Pravda* office for a cup of tea. 'That André Aronovich, what fine work he does! He must take endless time and pains in writing his dispatches. Your patience is admirable.' Enough said. And just as well, for Viktor Nezhenko smoked sixty cigarettes every day and had a savage temper; he could, if he chose, make life miserable for his staff.

Szara booked his call from a hotel room, it went through an hour later. Nezhenko's wife answered the phone, her voice bright and shrill with feigned insouciance.

When Nezhenko came to the phone, he offered no patronymic and no greeting, just, 'Where have you been?'

'I'm in Antwerp.'

'Where?'

Szara repeated himself. Something had gone wrong – Nezhenko had not been 'advised' of his assignment.

'So good of you to call,' Nezhenko said.

Szara hunted desperately for water to put out the fire. 'I'm doing a piece on dockworkers up here.'

'Yes? That will be interesting.'

'I'll wire it tomorrow.'

'Send it by mail if you like. Third class.'

'Did Pavel Mikhailovich cover for me?'

'Pavel Mikhailovich isn't here any more.'

Szara was stunned. *He isn't here any more* was code. When heard from friends, family, landladies, it meant that the person had been taken away. And Pavel Mikhailovich was – had been – a decent little man without enemies. But none of Szara's reactions, to ask questions, to show even the most civilized grief, was permissible on a telephone line.

'And people have been asking for you,' Nezhenko added. This too was code, it meant the *apparat* was looking for him.

Szara felt as though he'd walked into a wall. Why were they looking for him? They knew very well where he was and what he was doing – the world's plainest man had not been a mirage, and Renate Braun and her helper were realler yet. 'It's all a misunderstanding,' he said after a moment. 'The right hand doesn't tell the left hand . . .'

'No doubt,' Nezhenko said. Szara could hear him lighting a cigarette.

'I want to go down to Prague after I finish the piece on the dock-workers. There's the reaction to the Anti-Comintern Pact, views on the Sudetenland, all sorts of things. What do you think?'

'What do I think?'

'Yes.'

'Do as you like, André Aronovich. You must please yourself in all things.'

'I'll file on the dockworkers tomorrow,' Szara said.

Nezhenko hung up.

Writing the story of the Belgian dockworkers was like eating sand.

Once upon a time he'd persuaded himself that technical facility was its own reward: a sentence singing hymns to the attainment of coal production norms in the Donets Basin was, nonetheless, a sentence, and could be well rendered. It was the writer's responsibility in a progressive society to inform and uplift the toiling masses – word had, in fact, reached him that the number one toiler himself had an eye for his byline – so when some demon within wanted to write dark fables of an absurd universe, he knew enough to keep that imp well bottled up. To stay alive, Szara had taught himself discretion before the *apparat* had a chance to do the job for him. And if, by chance, an intransigent pen stubbornly produced commissar wolves guarding flocks of worker sheep or Parisian girls in silk underwear, well, then the great characteristic of paper was the ease with which it burned.

And these were, had to be, private fires. The world didn't want to know about your soul, it took you for who you said you were. The workers in the dark little hiring hall by the Antwerp docks were impressed that anybody cared enough to come around and ask them how they felt. 'Stalin is our great hope,' one of them said, and Szara sent his voice around the world.

He sat in yet one more hotel room as the Atlantic fog came curling up the streets and wrote these men into the brutal drama being played out in Europe. He caught the strength in their rounded shoulders and brawlers' hands, the way they quietly took care of one another, the granite decency of them. But for the wives and children who depended on them they would fight in Spain – some of the younger ones in fact were there – would fight in the worker suburbs of Berlin, would yet, families or not, fight from behind the cranes and sheds of their own docks. It was true, and Szara found a way to make it true on the page.

Stalin *was* their great hope. And if Khelidze mocked this with the yawn on his yellow-stained face, that was Szara's private problem. And if the 'small favour' was now a large favour, that, too, was Szara's private problem. And if all that made it hard to write, made writing the story like eating sand, who really could he blame? He could always say no and take the consequences. The Russian proverb had it just right: *You said you were a mushroom, now jump into the basket.*

*

And people have been asking for you.

Nezhenko's phrase rode the cadence of the train over the rails from Antwerp all the way to Paris. Much for the best, he calculated, to rush into their arms and find out what they wanted. He hadn't the courage to stand coolly apart from it all, whatever it was, so he did the next best thing. Checked in with the large *Pravda* bureau in Paris and asked the secretary to book him on the Paris–Prague express for the following day. He looked into her eyes, saw ball bearings, swore he could hear her lift the phone before the door was properly latched.

He stopped back that evening, picked up the ticket and drew both salary and expense funds, then went early to the Gare d'Austerlitz the following day in case they wanted to talk to him there. He did not precisely fear abduction, he was simply more comfortable in an open, public space with crowds of people about. He dawdled over coffee at a café by the departure platform, gazed mindlessly at the sullen Parisian sky above the glass roof on its vast iron fretwork, read *Le Temps*, found himself quoted in the Communist daily, *L'Humanité* – 'as *Pravda* correspondent André Szara has pointed out, bilateral relations between France and the USSR can only proceed once the Czechoslovakian question has been . . .' – and watched the appetizing French women sweep past, their heels clattering on the cement, their animation seemingly inspired by a grave sense of mission.

He had made himself available, but no contact was made. When his train was announced and the engine vented plumes of white steam on the platform, he climbed aboard and found himself alone in a first-class compartment. *Pravda* did not buy whole compartments – only the *apparat* did that. Clearly, something was planned. *Perhaps in Nancy*, he thought.

He was wrong. Spent the afternoon staring through the rain at the low hills of eastern France and watching the names of battlefields glide past on the railway stations. At the Strasbourg border control, just on the other side of the Rhine, a trio of German passport officials, two soldiers and a civilian in streaming black rubber raincoats, entered the compartment. They were cold-eyed and courteous, and his Soviet passport produced no evident reaction. They asked him a question or two, apparently just to hear his voice. Szara's German was that of someone who'd spoken Yiddish as a child, and the civilian, a security type, made clear that he knew Szara was a Jew, a Polish Jew, a Soviet Bolshevik Jew of Polish origin. He probed efficiently through Szara's travelling bag without removing his black gloves, then examined press and travel documents and, when he was done, stamped the passport with a fat swastika in a circle and handed it back politely. Their eyes met for just a moment: this business they had with each other would be seen to in the future, that far they could agree.

But Szara travelled too much to take the hostility of border police to heart and, as they gained speed leaving Stuttgart station, he fell into the rhythm of the tracks and the dense twilight of Germany: smoking factories on the horizon, fields left to the November frost.

He touched the baggage receipt in the inside pocket of his jacket for the tenth time that day; he might have taken yet one more look at the thing, but the sound of the train was suddenly amplified as the door to his compartment swung open.

On first glance, an ordinary businessman of Central Europe in dark overcoat and soft-brimmed hat, carrying a buckled briefcase of the kind that is held under one arm. Then, recognition. This was a man to whom he had been briefly introduced, perhaps a year earlier, at some Moscow function he couldn't recall. His name was Bloch, a lieutenant general of the GRU, military intelligence, and recently, according to rumour, the illegal – clandestine – *rezident* operating GRU and NKVD networks based in Tarragona. Thus a very senior member of the Soviet cadre involved in the Spanish Civil War.

Szara was immediately on his guard; powerful people in Moscow were afraid of this man. It was nothing specific. Those who knew the details didn't tell war stories, but they veered away from his name when it came up in conversation, looked around to see who might be listening, made a certain gesture of the face that meant *stay away*. What little was said about Bloch implied an insatiable appetite for success – an appetite gratified by means of ferocious tyranny. Life for those assigned to work for him was said to be a nightmare.

Yaschyeritsa, they called him behind his back, a kind of lizard. Because he had the look of the basilisk: a sharp triangular face, stiff hair combed back flat from the forehead, thin eyebrows angled steeply towards the inner corners of his eyes, which, long and narrow, were set above hard cheekbones that slanted upwards.

André Szara, like everyone who moved in those circles known as the *nomenklatura*, the elite, was an adroit reader of faces. You had to know who you were dealing with. A Byelorussian? An Armenian? A native Russian? With Jews, it was often difficult because Jewish women had for centuries borne the children of their tormentors and thus carried the genes of many races. God only knew, Szara thought, what brutal band of marauders had forced themselves on Bloch's female ancestor to make him look as he did. Did evil, he wondered, travel in the blood as well?

Bloch nodded a greeting, sat down across from Szara, leaned over and locked the compartment door, then turned off the lamps on the wall around the window. The train was moving slowly through a village, and from the darkened compartment they could see that a local festival was in progress; a bonfire in the public square, cattle wearing garlands, Hitler Youth in shorts holding swastika banners hung lengthwise down long poles, like Roman fasces.

Bloch stared intently at the scene. 'At last,' he said pensively, 'they are back in the Middle Ages.' He turned his attention to Szara. 'Forgive me, comrade journalist, I am General Y. I. Bloch. I don't think we've ever spoken, but I read your work when I have a moment, so I know who you are. Do I need to tell you who I am?'

'No, comrade General. I know you are with the special services.'

Bloch acknowledged Szara's awareness as a compliment: a knowing smile, a brief inclination of the head, *at your service.*

'Tell me,' the general said, 'is it true you've been away from Moscow for a time? Several months?'

'Since late August,' Szara said.

'No easy life – trains and hotel rooms. Slow steamships. But foreign capitals are certainly more amusing than Moscow, so there are compensations. No?'

This was a trap. There was a doctrinal answer, something to do with *building socialism*, but Bloch was no fool and Szara suspected a pious response would embarrass them both. 'It's true,' he said, adding, 'though one gets tired of being the eternal stranger,' just in case.

'Do you hear the Moscow gossip?'

'Very little,' Szara said. A loner, he tended to avoid the Tass and *Pravda* crowd on the circuit of European capitals.

Bloch's face darkened. This has been a troubled autumn for the services, surely you've heard that much.'

'Of course I see the newspapers.'

'There is more, much more. We've had defections, serious ones. In the last few weeks, Colonel Alexander Orlov and Colonel Walter Krivitsky, who is called general in the European press, have left the service and sought refuge in the West. The Krivitsky matter has been made public, also the flight of the operative Reiss. As for Orlov, we'll keep that to ourselves.'

Szara nodded obediently. This had quickly become a very sensitive conversation. Orlov – a cover name within the service, he was in fact Leon Lazarevich Feldbin – and Krivitsky – Samuel Ginsberg – were important men, respectively NKVD and GRU officials of senior status. The Ignace Reiss affair had shocked him when he read about it. Reiss, murdered in Switzerland as he attempted to flee, had been a fervent idealist, a Marxist-Leninist in his bones.

'Friends?' Bloch raised an eyebrow.

'I knew Reiss to say hello to. No more than that.'

'And you? How does it go with you?' Bloch was concerned, almost fatherly. Szara wanted to laugh, had the services been panicked into *kindness?*

'My work is difficult, comrade General, but less difficult than that of many others, and I am content to be what I am.'

Bloch absorbed his answer and nodded to himself. 'So you march along,' he said. 'There are some,' he continued pensively, 'who find themselves deeply disturbed by the arrests, the trials. We cannot deny it.'

Oh cannot we? 'We've always had enemies, within and without. I served in the civil war, from 1918 to 1920, and fought against the Poles. It isn't for me to judge the operations of state security forces.'

Bloch sat back in his seat. 'Very well put,' he said after a time. Then his voice softened, just barely audible above the steady rumble of the train. 'And should it come your turn? Then what?'

Szara could not quite see Bloch's face in the shadow of the seat across from him, the countryside was dark, the light from the corridor dim. 'Then that is how it will be,' Szara said.

'You are a fatalist.'

'What else?' They lingered there a moment too long for Szara. 'I have no family,' he added.

Bloch seemed to nod at that, a gesture of agreement with a point made or a confirmation of something he believed. 'Not married,' he mused. 'I would have guessed otherwise.'

'I am a widower, comrade General. My wife died in the civil war. She was a nurse, in Berdichev.'

'So you are alone,' Bloch said. 'Some men, in such circumstances, might be careless of their lives, since nothing holds them to the world. Unconcerned with consequence, such men rise to an opportunity, sacrifice themselves, perhaps to cure their nation of a great evil. And then we have – why not say it? A hero! Do I have it right? Is this your view?'

A man and a woman – she had just said something that made him laugh – went by in the corridor. Szara waited until they passed. 'I am like everybody else,' he said.

'No,' Bloch said. 'You are not.' He leaned forward, his face taut, concentrated. 'To be a writer, that requires work. Work and sacrifice. And the determination to follow a certain road, wherever it may lead. Remember that, comrade journalist, whatever might happen in the days ahead.'

Szara started to reply, to fend off a version of himself he found grandiose, but Bloch raised a hand for silence. The gesture was casual enough, but it struck Szara dumb. The general stood and unlatched the door, stared at Szara a moment, a look that openly weighed and calculated, then left the compartment abruptly, closing the door firmly behind him and disappearing down the passageway.

Some time later, the train halted at Ulm. The station platform was a lacework of shadows, and raindrops refracted trails of light as they rolled down the compartment window. A figure with a hat and an underarm briefcase hurried across the platform and entered the passenger door of a black Grosser Mercedes – a car often used by Reich officials – which sped away from the railway station and was soon lost in the darkness.

A hero?

No, Szara thought. He knew better. He'd learned that lesson in war.

At the age of twenty-three, in 1920, he had campaigned with Marshal Tukachevsky, writing dispatches and inspirational stories for the home front, much as the writer Babel – a Jew who rode with Cossack cavalry – had served General Budenny. In the midst of the war against Poland, the Soviet forces had been driven back from Warsaw, from the banks of the Vistula, by an army commanded by General Pilsudski and his adviser, the French general Weygand. Szara's squadron, during the retreat, had been set upon by Ukrainian bandits, a remnant of the Petlyura army that had occupied Kiev. Attacked from the ridge of a hillside, and outnumbered, they had fought like men possessed, all of them – cooks, clerks, wagonmasters, and military correspondents. For the previous day they'd come upon the body of a Polish colonel, stripped bare, tied by one foot to a high tree branch, the impaling stake protruding from between his legs. The Ukrainian bands fought both sides, Poles and Russians, and God help anyone they took alive.

From horseback, Szara had ridden down one man, slashed at another with his sabre. In the next instant he and his horse were down in the dust, the horse whinnying in pain and terror, its legs thrashing. Szara rolled frantically away from the animal, then a smiling man walked towards him, a small dagger in his hand. Horses galloped past them, there were shots and screams and pointless shouted commands, but this man, in cap and overcoat, never stopped smiling. Szara crawled on all fours, a horse leapt over him and its rider cursed, but he could gain no ground. The battle that raged around them mattered not to Szara nor, apparently, to his good-humoured pursuer. The smile was meant, he understood, to be reassuring, as though he were a pig in a sty. As the man closed on him he made a cooing sound and Szara came suddenly to his senses, fumbled his revolver loose of its holster, and fired wildly. Nothing happened. The smile broadened. Then Szara took hold of his fear, as though he could squeeze it in his fist, aimed like a marksman on a target range, and shot the man in the eye.

What he remembered later was not that he had fought bravely, he had simply decided that life mattered more than anything else in the world and had contrived to cling to it. In those years he had seen heroes, and how they went about their work, how they did what had to be done, and he knew he was not one of them.

The train was late getting into Prague. A Jewish family had attempted to board at Nürnberg, the last stop on German soil. Jews had been strongly 'encouraged' to emigrate from Germany – not least by a hundred and thirty-five racial decrees, together entitled 'The Law for the Protection of German Blood and German Honour' – to whatever country would accept them. But the situation, Szara knew, was not unlike that under the czar: a bureaucratic spider's web. While you could get Paper A stamped at the local police station, the stamp on Paper B, received from the Economic Ministry, was now out of date and would have to be applied for all over again. Meanwhile, Paper A ran its term and automatically revoked itself.

The Jewish family at Nürnberg simply attempted to board the train, a pointless act of desperation. Thus young children, grandparents, mother and father, scampered in terror all around the station while policemen in leather coats chased them down, shouting and blowing whistles. Meanwhile, the passengers peered curiously from the train windows. Some, excited by the chase, tried to help, calling out, 'There, under the luggage compartment!' or 'She's crossed the tracks!'

Just after midnight it was cold in Prague, there were frost flowers on the paving stones, but the hotel was not far from the station, and Szara was soon settled in his room. He stayed up for hours, smoking, writing notes on the margin of *Le Temps*, studying the luggage ticket he'd been given. He was being drawn into something he did not understand, but he had a strong intuition about what awaited him at the end of it.

This extramarital affair with the services had been simple in the beginning, five or six years earlier, for they'd used him as an intellectual, an agent of influence, and he'd liked it, found it flattering to be trusted. Now he had got in over his head, and he had no doubt it would kill him. They were using him for something important, an official opera-tion of the *apparat* or, and here was the death sentence, the plotting of a cabal within it. He only knew it was very dark and very serious. Soviet generals of military intelligence did not board German trains to chat with writers.

Nonetheless, he refused to blind himself to the possibility of exits. He would die, he thought, but did not want to discover as he died that there had been, after all, a way out. *That is the difference, comrade General, between the hero and the survivor.* The hours of reflection revealed nothing, but did serve to dissipate tension and tire him out. He crawled into bed and slept without dreams.

He woke to a day of light snow and subtle terror in Prague. He saw nothing, felt everything. On the fifth of November, Hitler had made a speech once again declaring the urgency, for Germany, of *Lebensraum*, the acquisition of new territory for German growth and expansion, literally 'room to live.' Like an operatic tenor, singing counterpoint to Hitler's bass, Henlein, the leader of the Sudeten Germans, pleaded publicly in an open letter carried by Czech newspapers the following day for a halt to Czech 'persecution' of German minorities in the Sudetenland, the area bordering southern Germany. On 12 November the countertenor, Reich Interior Minister Wilhelm Frick, said on the radio: 'Race and nationality, blood and soil, are the principles of National Socialist thought, we would be acting in contradiction if we attempted to assimilate a foreign nationality by force.'

This may have sounded warm and comforting in France, but the Sudeten Germans were not a foreign nationality, and neither were the Austrians – not according to German diplomatic definitions. Sudeten German representatives next staged a mass exodus from parliament, informing reporters waiting outside that they had been physically abused by Czech police.

Everybody in Prague knew this game – incidents, provocations, speeches – it meant that the German tank divisions sitting up on the border were coming down. Today? Tomorrow? When?

Soon.

On the surface, there was nothing to see. But what they felt here made itself known in subtle ways: the way people looked at each other, a note in a voice, the unfinished sentence. Szara took the receipt he'd been given in Ostend to the central railway station. The attendant shook his head, this was from a smaller station, and gestured towards the edge of the city.

He took a taxi, but by the time he arrived, the left-luggage room of the outlying station was closed for lunch. He found himself in a strange, silent neighbourhood with signs in Polish and Ukrainian, boarded windows, groups of tieless men with buttoned collars gathered on street corners. He walked along empty streets swept by wind-driven swirls of dust. The women were hidden in black shawls, children held hands and kept close to the buildings. He heard a bell, looked down a steep lane, and saw a Jewish pedlar with a slumped, starved horse, plumes of breath streaming from its nostrils as it attempted to pull a cart up a hill.

Szara found a tiny café; conversation stopped when he walked in. He drank a cup of tea. There was no sugar. He could hear a clock ticking behind a curtained doorway. What was it in this place? A demon lived here. Szara struggled to breathe, his persona flowed away like mist and left a dull and anxious man sitting at a table. The clock behind the curtain chimed three and he walked quickly to the station. The left-luggage clerk limped painfully and wore a blue railway uniform with a war medal pinned on the lapel. He took the receipt silently and, after a moment of study, nodded to himself. He disappeared for a long time, then returned with a leather satchel. Szara asked if a taxi could be called. 'No,' the man said. Szara waited for more, for an explanation, something, but that was it. *No.*

So he walked. For miles, through zigzag streets clogged with Saturday life, where every ancient stone leaned or sagged; past crowds of Orthodox Jews in caftans and curling sidelocks, gossiping in front of tiny synagogues; past Czech housewives in their print dresses, carrying home loaves of black bread and garlic sausages from the street markets; past children and dogs playing football on the cobblestones and old men who leaned their elbows on the windowsills and smoked their pipes and stared at the life in the street below. It was every quarter in every city in Europe in the cold, smoky days of November, but to Szara it was like being trapped in the dream where some terrifying thing was happening but the world ignored it and went blindly about its business.

Reaching the hotel, he trudged upstairs and hurled the satchel onto the bed. Then he collapsed in a chair and closed his eyes in order to concentrate. Certain instincts flared to life: he must write about what he'd felt, must describe the haunting of this place. Done well, he knew, such stories spread, took on a life of their own. The politicians would do what they did, but the readers, the people, would understand, care, be animated by pity to speak out for the Czech republic. How to do it? What to select? Which fact really *spoke*, so that the writer could step aside and allow the story to tell itself. And if his own dispatch did not appear in other countries, it most certainly would run in the Communist party press, in many languages, and more foreign journalists than cared to admit it had a glance at such newspapers. Editorial policy said *anything to keep the peace*, but let the correspondents come here and see it for themselves.

Then the satchel reminded him of its presence. He examined it and realized he'd never seen one like it: the leather was dense, pebbled, the hide of a powerful, unknown animal. It was covered with a thick, fine dust, so he wet his index finger and drew a line through it, revealing a colour that had once been that of bitter chocolate but was now faded by sun and time. Next he saw that the seams were hand-sewn; fine, sturdy work using a thread he suspected was also handmade. The satchel was of the portmanteau style – like a doctor's bag, the two sides opened evenly and were held together by a brass lock. Using a damp towel, he cleaned the lock and found a reddish tracery etched into the metal surface. This was vaguely familiar. Where had he seen it? In a moment it came to him: such work adorned brass bowls and vases made in western and central Asia – India, Afghanistan, Turkestan. He tried to depress the lever on the underside of the device, but it was locked.

The handgrip bore half a label, tied on with string. Peering closely, he was able to make out the date the satchel had been deposited as left luggage: 8 February 1935. He swore softly with amazement. Almost three years.

He put one finger on the lock. It was ingenious, a perfectly circular opening that did not suggest the shape of its key. He probed gently with a match, it seemed to want a round shaft with squared ridges at the very end. Hopefully, he jiggled the match about but of course nothing happened. From another time the locksmith, perhaps an artisan who sat cross-legged in a market stall in some souk, laughed at him. The device he'd fashioned would not yield to a wooden match.

Szara went downstairs to the hotel desk and explained to the young clerk on duty: a lost key, a satchel that couldn't be opened, important papers for a meeting on Monday, what could be done? The clerk nodded sympathetically and spoke soothingly. Not to worry. This happens here every day. A boy was sent off and returned an hour later with a locksmith in tow. In the room the locksmith, a serious man who spoke German and wore a stiff, formal suit, cleared his throat politely. One didn't see this sort of mechanism. But Szara was too impatient to make up answers to unasked questions and simply urged the man to proceed. After a few minutes of meditation, the locksmith reluctantly folded up his leather tool case, put it away, and, reddening slightly, drew a set of finely made burglar's picks from the interior pocket of his jacket. Now the battle between the two technicians commenced.

Not that the Tadzik, the Kirghiz, the craftsman of the Bokhara market – whoever he'd been – didn't resist, he did, but in the event he was no match for the modern Czech and his shining steel picks. With the emphatic *snick* of the truly well-made device the lock opened, and the locksmith stood back and applied an immaculate grey cloth to his sweaty forehead. 'So beautiful a work,' he said, mostly to himself.

So beautiful a bill, as well, but Szara paid it and tipped handsomely besides, for he knew the *apparat* could eventually find out anything, and he might have signed this man's death warrant.

At dusk, André Szara sat in his unlit room with the remnants of a man's life spread out around him.

There wasn't a writer in the world who could resist attributing a melancholy romance to these artefacts, but, he argued to his critical self, that did not diminish their eloquence. For if the satchel itself spoke of Bokhara, Samarkand, or the oasis towns of the Kara Kum desert, its contents said something very different, about a European, a European Russian, who had travelled – served? hidden? died? – in those regions, about the sort of man he was, about pride itself.

The objects laid out on the hotel desk and bureau made up an estate. Some clothing, a few books, a revolver, and the humble tools – thread and needle, digestive tea, well-creased maps – of a man on the run. On the run, for there was equal clarity, equal eloquence, in the items *not* found. There were no photographs, no letters. No address book, no traveller's journal. This had been a man who understood the people he fled from and protected the vulnerability of those who may have loved him.

The clothing had been packed on top, folded loosely but perfectly, as though by someone with a long history of military service, someone to whom the ordered neatness of a footlocker was second nature. It was good clothing, carefully preserved, often mended but terribly worn, its wear the result of repeated washings and long use in hard country. Cotton underdrawers and wool shirts, a thick sailor's sweater darned at the elbows, heavy wool socks with virtually transparent heels.

The service revolver dated from pre-revolutionary days, a Nagant, the double-action officer's model, 7.62mm from a design of 1895. It was well oiled and fully loaded. From certain characteristics, Szara determined that the side arm had had a long and very active life. The lanyard ring at the base of the grip had been removed and the surface filed flat, and the metal at the edges of the sharp angles, barrel opening, cylinder, the trigger itself, was silvery and smooth. A look down the barrel showed it to be immaculate, cleaned not with the usual brick dust – an almost religious (and thereby ruinous) obsession with the peasant infantry of the Great War – but with a scouring brush of British manufacture folded in a square of paper. Not newspaper, for that told of where you had been and when you were there. Plain paper. A careful man.

The books were also from the time before the revolution, the latest printing date 1915; and Szara handled them with reverence for they were no longer to be had. Dobrilov's lovely essays on noble estates, Ivan Krug's *Poems at Harvest*, Gletkhin's tales of travel among the Khivani, Pushkin of course, and a collection by one Churnensky, *Letters from a Distant Village*, which Szara had never heard of. These were companions of journey, books to be read and read again, books for a man who lived in places where books could not be found. Eagerly, Szara paged through them, looking for commentary, for at least an underlined passage, but there was, as he'd expected, not a mark to be found.

Yet the most curious offering of the opened satchel was its odour. Szara could not really pin it down, though he held the sweater to his face and breathed it in. He could identify a hint of mildew, woodsmoke, the sweetish smell of pack animals, and something else, a spice perhaps, cloves or cardamom, that suggested the central Asian marketplace. It had been carried in the satchel for a long time, for its presence touched the books and the clothing and the leather itself. Why? Perhaps to make spoiled food more palatable, perhaps to add an ingredient of civilization to life in general. On this point he could make no decision.

Szara was sufficiently familiar with the practices of intelligence services to know that chronology meant everything. 'May God protect and keep the czar' at the end of a letter meant one thing in 1916, quite another in 1918. With regard to the time of 'the officer,' for Szara discovered himself using that term, the satchel's contents offered an Austrian map of the southern borders of the Caspian Sea dated 1919. The cartography had certainly begun earlier (honorary Bolshevik names were missing), but the printing date allowed Szara to write on a piece of hotel stationery 'alive in 1919'. Checking the luggage label once again, he noted 'tentative terminal date, 8 February 1935'. A curious date, following by two months and some days the assassination of Sergei Kirov at the Smolny Institute in Leningrad, 1 December 1934, which led to the first round of purges under Yagoda.

A terminal date? *Yes*, Szara thought, *this man is dead.*

He simply knew it. And, he felt, much earlier than 1935. Somehow, another hand had recovered the satchel and moved it to the left-luggage room of a remote Prague railway station that winter. Infinite permutations were of course possible, but Szara suspected that a life played out in the southern extremity of the Soviet empire had ended there. The Red Army had suppressed the pashas' risings in 1923. If the officer, perhaps a military adviser to one of the local rulers, had survived those wars, he had not left the region. There was nothing of Europe that had not been packed on some night in, Szara guessed, 1920.

That the satchel itself had survived was a kind of miracle, though presently Szara came upon a rather more concrete possibility – the stitching on the bottom lining. This was not the same hand that had lovingly and expertly crafted the seams. The reattachment had been managed as best it could be done, with waxed thread sewn into a cruciform shape anchoring each corner. So, the officer carried more than books and clothes. Szara remembered what Renate Braun had said in the lobby of Khelidze's hotel: 'It is for you.' Not old maps, books, and clothing certainly, and not a Nagant pistol. What was now 'his' lay beneath the satchel's false bottom in a secret compartment.

Szara called the desk and had a bottle of vodka sent up. He sensed a long, difficult night ahead of him – the city of Prague was bad enough, the officer's doomed attempt to survive history didn't make things any better. He must, Szara reasoned, have been a loyal soldier in the czar's service, thus fugitive after the revolution in 1917. Perhaps he'd fought alongside White Guardist elements in the civil war. Then flight, always southeast, into central Asia, as the Red Army advanced. The history of that place and time was as evil as any Szara knew – Basmatchi, the marauding bandits of the region, Baron Ungarn-Sternberg, a sadist and a madman, General Ma and his Muslim army; rape, murder, pillage, captives thrown into locomotive boilers to die in the steam. He suspected that this man, who carried a civilized little library and carefully darned the elbows of his sweater, had died in some unremembered minor skirmish during those years. There were times when a bullet was the best of all solutions. Szara found himself hoping it had been that way for the officer.

The vodka helped. Szara was humming a song by the time he had his razor out, sawing away at the thick bands of crisscrossed thread. The officer was no fool. Who, Szara wondered, did he think to deceive with this only too evident false bottom contrivance? Perhaps the very densest border patrolman or the most slow-witted customs guard. The NKVD workshops did this sort of thing quite well, leaving only the slimmest margin for secreting documents and disguising the false bottom so that you really could not tell. On the other hand, the officer had likely done what he could, used the only available hiding place and hoped for the best. Yes, Szara understood him now, better and better; the sewn-down corners revealed a sort of determination in the face of hopeless circumstances, a quality Szara admired above all others. Having cut loose the final corner, he had to use a nail file to pry up the leather flap.

What had he hoped to find? Not this. A thick stack of greyish paper, frayed at the edges, covered with a careful pen scrawl of stiff Russian phrases – the poetry of bureaucrats. It was official paper, a bluntly printed letterhead announcing its origin as Bureau of Information, Third Section, Department of State Protection (Okhrannoye Otdyelyenye), Ministry of the Interior, Transcaucasian District, with a street address in Tbilisi – the Georgian city of Tiflis.

A slow, sullen disappointment drifted over Szara's mood. He carried the vodka bottle over to the window and watched as a goods train crawled slowly away from the railway station, its couplings clanking and rattling as the cars jerked into motion. The officer was not a noble colonel or a captain of cavalry but a slow-footed policeman, no doubt a cog in the czar's vast but inefficient secret police gendarmerie, the Okhrana, and this sheaf of misery on the hotel desk apparently represented a succession of cases, a record of *agents provocateurs*, payments to petty informers, and solemn physical descriptions of Social Revolutionary party workers in the early days of the century. He'd seen this kind of report from time to time, soul-destroying stuff it was, humanity seen through a window by the dim glow of a street lamp, sad and mean and obsessed with endless conspiracies. The thought of it made you want to retire to the countryside with a milk cow and a vegetable patch.

Not a military officer, a police officer. Poor man, he had carried this catalogue of small deceits over mountain and across desert, apparently certain of its value once the counterrevolution had succeeded and some surviving spawn of the Romanovs once again sat upon the Throne of All the Russias. In sorrow more than anger Szara soothed his frustrated imagination with two tiltings of the vodka bottle. *A paper creature*, he thought. *A uniform with a man in it.*

He walked back to the desk and adjusted the gooseneck lamp. The organization Messame Dassy (Third Group) had been founded in 1893, of Social Democratic origin and purpose, in political opposition to Meori Dassy (Second Group) – Szara sighed at such grotesque hairsplitting – and made its views known in pamphlets and the newspaper *Kvali (The Furrow)*. Known principals of the organization included N. K. Jordania, K. K. Muridze, G. M. Tseretelli. The informant DUBOK (it meant 'little oak' and had gone on to become the name for a dead-drop of any kind) enrolled and became active in 1898, at age nineteen.

Szara flipped through the stack of pages, his eye falling randomly on summaries of interviews, memoranda, alterations in handwriting as other officers contributed to the record, receipts for informer payments signed with cover names (not code names like DUBOK; one never knew one's code name, that belonged to the Masters of the File), a change to typewriter as the case spanned the years and reports were sent travelling upwards from district to region to central bureau to ministry to Czar Nicholas and perhaps to God Himself.

Szara's temples throbbed.

Serves you right! What in the name of heaven had he expected? Swiss marks? Perhaps he had, deep down. Those exquisitely printed passports to anywhere and everything. *Idiot!* Maybe gold coins? The molten rubies of children's books? Or a single pressed rose, its last dying fragrance only just discernible?

Yes, yes, yes. Any or all of it. His eye fell in misery on the false plate lying on the floor amid a tangle of cut-up thread. He'd learned to sew as a child in Odessa, but this was not the sort of job he could do. How was he to put all this back together again? By employment of the hotel seamstress? *The guest in Room 35 requires the false bottom sewed back on his suitcase – hurry woman, he must cross the Polish frontier tonight!* A victim of betrayed imagination, Szara cursed and mentally called down the *apparat* as though summoning evil spirits. He willed Heshel with his sad little smile or Renate Braun with her purse full of skeleton keys, or any of them, grey shapes or cold-eyed intellectuals, to come and take this inhuman pettifoggery away from him before he hurled it out of the window.

In fact, where were they?

He glanced at the bottom of the door, expecting a slip of paper to come sliding underneath at that very moment, but all he saw was worn carpet. The world suddenly felt very silent to him, and another visit with the vodka did not change that.

In desperation he shoved the paper to one side and replaced it with sheets of hotel stationery from the desk drawer. If, in the final analysis, the officer did not deserve this vodka-driven storm in the emotional latitudes, the anguished people of Prague most assuredly did.

It was midnight when he finished, and his back hurt like a bastard. But he'd got it. The reader would find himself; *his* street, *his* neighbour-hood, *his* nation. And the hysteria, the nightmare, was where it belonged, just below the horizon so you felt it more than saw it. To balance a story on 'the people' he'd have to do one on 'the ministry': quote from Beneš, quote from General Vlasy, something vicious from Henlein, and the slant – since the country had been created a par-liamentary democracy in 1918 and showed no sign of yearning to become a socialist republic – would have to serve Soviet diplomatic interests by fervid anti-Hitlerism. No problem there. He could file on ministries with one eye shut and the pencil in his ear, and it would mean just about that much. Politicians were like talking dogs in a circus: the fact that they existed was uncommonly interesting, but no sane person would actually believe what they said.

Then, as always happened after he wrote something he liked, the room began to shrink. He stuffed some money in his pocket, pulled up his tie, threw on his jacket, and made his escape. He tried walking, but the wind blowing down from Poland was fierce and the air had the smell of winter, so he waved down a taxi and gave the address of the Luxuria, a *nachtlokal* where the cabaret was foul and the audience worse, thus exactly where he belonged in his present frame of mind.

Nor was he disappointed. Sitting alone at a tiny table, a glass of flat champagne at his elbow, he smoked steadily and lost himself in the mindless fog of the place, content beneath the soiled cutout of yellow paper pinned to a velvet curtain that served as the Luxuria's moon – a thin slice, a weary old moon for nights when nothing mattered.

Momo Tsipler and his Wienerwald Companions.

Five of them, including the oldest cellist in captivity, a death-eyed drummer called Rex, and Momo himself, one of those dark celebrities nourished by the shadows east of the Rhine, a Viennese Hungarian in a green dinner-jacket with a voice full of tears that neither he nor anyone else had ever cried.

'*Noch einmal al Abscheid dein Händchen mir gib,*' sang Momo as the cello sobbed. 'Just once again give me your hand to press' – the interior Szara was overjoyed, this horrid syrup was delicious, a wicked joke on itself, an anthem to Viennese love gone wrong. The title of the song was perfect: 'There Are Things We Must All Forget.' The violinist had fluffy white hair that stood out in wings and he smiled like Satan himself as he played.

The Companions of the Wienerwald then took up a kind of 'drunken elephant' theme for the evening's main attraction: the enormous Mottel Motkevich, who staggered into the spotlight to a series of rimshots from the drummer and began his famous one-word routine. At first, his body told the story: I just woke up in the maid's bed with the world's worst hangover and someone pushed me out onto the stage of a nightclub in Prague. What am I doing here? What are *you* doing here?

His flabby face sweated in the purple lights – for twenty years he'd looked like he was going to die next week. Then he shaded his eyes and peered around the room. Slowly, recognition took hold. He knew what sort of swine had come out to the *nachtlokal* tonight, ah yes, he knew them all too well. '*Ja,*' he said, confirming the very worst, his thick lips pressed together with grim disapproval.

He began to nod, confirming his observation: drunkards and perverts, dissolution and depravity. He put his hands on his broad hips and stared out at a Yugoslav colonel accompanied by a well-rouged girl in a shiny feather hat that hugged her head tightly, '*Ja!*' said Mottel Motkevich. There's no doubt about you two. Likewise to a pair of pretty English boys in plus fours, then to a Captain of Industry caught in the act of schnozzling a sort of teenage dairymaid by his side.

Suddenly, a voice from the shadows in the back of the room: 'But Mottel, why not?' Quickly the audience began to shout back at the comedian in a stew of European languages: 'Is it bad?' 'Why shouldn't we?' 'What can be so wrong?'

The fat man recoiled, grasped the velvet curtain with one hand, eyes and mouth widening with new understanding, '*Ja?*' You mean it's really all right after all? To do just every sort of thing we all know about and some we haven't figured out yet?

Now came the audience's great moment, '*Ja!*' they cried out, again and again; even the waiters joined in.

Poor Mottel actually crumpled under the assault. A world he presumed to love, of order and rectitude, had been torn to shreds before his very eyes and now the truth lay bare. With regret, he bade all that fatuous old nonsense adieu, '*Ja, ja,*' he admitted ruefully, so it has always been, so it will always be, so, particularly so, will it be tonight.

Just then something extremely interesting caught his eye, something going on behind the curtain to his right, and, eyes glittering like a love-maddened satyr, he bequeathed his audience one final, drawn-out *jaaa*, then stomped off the stage to applause as the Companions struck up a circus melody and the zebras ran out from behind the curtain, bucking and neighing, pawing their little forehooves in the air.

Naked girls in papier-mâché zebra masks, actually. Prancing and jiggling among the tables, stopping now and again to stick their bottoms out at the customers, then taking off again with a leap. After a few minutes they galloped away into the wings, the Companions swung into a sedate waltz, and the dancers soon reappeared, without masks and wearing gowns, as *Animierdamen* who were to flirt with the customers, sit on their laps, and tickle them into buying champagne by the bottle.

Szara's was heavy-hipped, with hair dyed a lustrous, sinister black. 'Can you guess which zebra was me? I was so very close to you!'

Later he went with her. To a secret room at the top of a cold house where you walked upstairs, then downstairs, across two courtyards where cats lived, finally to climb again, past blind turns and dark passageways, until you came to a low corridor under the roof gables.

'Zebra', he called her; it made things simpler. He doubted he was the originator of the idea, for she seemed quite comfortable with it. She cantered and whinnied and shook her little white tummy – all for him.

His spirit soared, at last he'd found an island of pleasure in his particular sea of troubles. There were those, he knew, who would have found such sport sorrowful and mean, but what furies did they know? What waited for them on the other sides of doors?

The Zebra owned a little radio; it played static, and also a station that stayed on the air all night long, playing scratchy recordings of Schumann and Chopin from somewhere in the darkness of Central Europe, where insomnia had become something of a religion.

To this accompaniment they made great progress. And delighted themselves by feigning shock at having tumbled into such depths where anything at all may be found to swim. 'Ah yes?' cried the Zebra, as though they'd happened on some new and complex amusement, never before attempted in the secret rooms of these cities, as though their daring to play the devil's own games might stay his hand from that which they knew, by whatever obscure prescience, he meant to do to them all.

Warm and exhausted at last, they dozed off in the smoky room while the radio crackled, faded in and out, voices sometimes whispering to them in unknown languages.

The leaders of the Georgian *khvost* of the NKVD usually met for an hour or two on Sunday mornings in Alexei Agayan's apartment on Tverskaya street. Beria himself never came – he was, in some sense, a conspiracy of one – but made his wishes known through Dershani, Agayan, or one of the others. Typically, only the Moscow-based officers attended the meeting, though comrades from the southeast republics stopped by from time to time.

They met in Agayan's kitchen, large, dilapidated, and very warm, on 21 November at eleven-thirty in the morning. Agayan, a short, dark-skinned man with a thick head of curly grey hair and an unruly moustache, wore an old cardigan in keeping with the air of informality. Ismailov, a Russified Turk, and Dzakhalev, an Ossete – the Farsi-speaking tribe of the north Caucasus from whom Stalin's mother was said to be descended – were red-eyed and a little tender from Saturday-night excesses. Terounian, from the city of Yerevan in Armenia, offered a small burlap sack of ripe pears brought to Moscow by his cousin, a locomotive engineer. These were laid out on the table by Stasia, Agayan's young Russian wife, along with bowls of salted and sugared almonds, pine nuts, and a plate of Smyrna raisins. Agayan's wife also served an endless succession of tiny cups of Turkish coffee, *sekerli*, the sweetest variety, throughout the meeting. Dershani, a Georgian, the most important among equals, was also the last to arrive. Such traditions were important to the *khvost* and they observed them scrupulously.

It was altogether a traditional sort of gathering, as though in a coffeehouse in Baku or Tashkent. They sat in their shirt-sleeves and smoked, ate, and drank their coffees and took turns to speak – in Russian, their only common language – with respect for one another and with a sense of ceremony. What was said mattered, that was understood, they would have to stand by it.

Agayan, squinting in the rising smoke of a cigarette held in the centre of his lips, spoke solemnly of comrades disappeared in the purges. The Ukrainian and Polish *zhids*, he admitted, were getting much the worst of it, but many Georgians and Armenians and their allies from all over (some *zhids* of their own, for that matter) had also vanished into the Lubianka and the Lefortovo. Agayan sighed mournfully when he finished his report, all the eulogy many of them would ever have.

'One can only wonder . . .' Dzakhalev said.

Agayan's shrug was eloquent. 'It's what he wants. As for me, I was not asked.' The nameless *he* in these conversations was always Stalin.

'Still,' Dzakhalev said, 'Yassim Ferimovich was a superb officer.'

'And loyal,' Terounian added. At thirty-five, he was by far the youngest man in the room.

Agayan lit a new cigarette from the stub of the old one. 'Nonetheless,' he said.

'You have heard what he said to Yezhov, in the matter of interrogation? "Beat and beat and beat." ' Terounian paused to let the felicity of that phrasing hang in the air, to make sure everyone understood he honoured it. 'Thus anyone will admit anything, will surely name his own mother.'

'Yours too,' Ismailov said.

Dershani raised his right hand a few inches off the table; the gesture meant *enough* and stopped Ismailov dead in his tracks. Dershani had the face of a hawk – sharp beak, glittering, lifeless eyes – thin lips, high forehead, hair that had gone grey when he was young – some said in a single night when he was sentenced to die. But he'd lived. Changed. Into something not quite a man. A specialist at obtaining confessions, a man whose hand was rumoured to have 'actually held the pliers'. Ismailov's tone of voice was clearly not to his taste.

'His thinking is very broad,' Dershani said. 'We are not meant to understand it. We are not meant to comment upon it.' He paused for coffee, to permit the atmosphere in the room to rise to his level, then took a few pine nuts. These are delicious,' he said. 'If you look at our history – the history of our service, I mean – his hand may be seen to have grasped the tiller just at the crucial moment. We began with Dzerzhinsky, a Pole of aristocratic background from Vilna. Catholic by birth, he shows, early in life, a great affection for Jews. He comes to speak perfect Yiddish, his first lover is one Julia Goldman, the sister of his best friend. She dies of tuberculosis, in Switzerland, where he had placed her in a sanatorium, and his sorrow is soothed by a love affair with a comrade called Sabina Feinstein. Eventually he marries a Polish Jewess, from the Warsaw intelligentsia, named Sophie Mushkat. His deputy, the man he depends on, is Unshlikht, also a Polish Jew, also an intellectual, from Mlawa.

When Dzerzhinsky dies, his other deputy, Menzhinsky, takes over. No Jew, Menzhinsky, but an *artiste*. A man who speaks Chinese, Persian, Japanese, in all twelve languages and who, while doing our work in Paris, is a poet one day, a painter the next, and lies around in silk pyjamas, smoking a perfumed cigarette in an ivory holder, the leader of a, a salon. Lenin dies. This young state, troubled, gravely threatened, thrusts itself at our leader, and he agrees to take its burdens upon his shoulders. He seeks only to continue the work of Lenin but, in 1934, the Trotskyite centre begins to gather power. Something must be done. In Lenin's tradition he turns to Yagoda, a Polish Jew from Lodz, a poisoner, who eliminates the writer Gorky through seemingly natural means. But he is too clever, keeps his own counsel, and by 1936 he is no longer the right sort of person for the job. Now what is the answer? Perhaps the dwarf, Yezhov, called familiarly "the blackberry", which his name suggests. But this one is no better than the other – not a Jew this time but a madman, truly, and malicious, like a child of the slum who soaks cats' tails in paraffin and sets them alight.'

Dershani stopped dead, tapping four fingers on the kitchen table. A glance at Agayan's wife, standing at the stove in the far part of the kitchen, brought her swiftly with a fresh little cup of coffee.

'Tell us, Efim Aleksandrovich, what will happen next?' Ismailov thus declared himself suitably chastened, symbolically sought Dershani's pardon for his momentary flippancy.

Dershani closed his eyes politely as he drank off his coffee, smacked his lips politely in appreciation. 'Stasia Marievna, you are a jewel,' he said. She nodded silently to acknowledge the compliment.

'It evolves, it evolves,' Dershani said. 'It is beautiful history, after all, and guided now by genius. But he must move at the proper speed, certain matters must be allowed to play themselves out. And, I tell you in confidence, there are many considerations that may elude our vision. These *zhids* from Poland cannot just be swept away wholesale. Such cleaning, no matter how appropriate, would draw unwelcome attention, might alienate the Jews of America, for instance, who are great idealists and do our special work in their country. Thus Russians and Ukrainians, yes, and even Georgians and Armenians must leave the stage along with the others. This is necessity, historical necessity, a stratagem worthy of Lenin.'

'Then tell us, Efim Aleksandrovich,' said Agayan, not unconsciously echoing Ismailov's phrasing, 'if today we are not in fact privileged to hear the views of our comrade in Tbilisi?' He referred to Lavrenty Pavlovich Beria, presently first secretary of the Georgian Communist party and previously head of the Georgian NKVD. The modest bite in the question suggested that Dershani should perhaps not call his wife a jewel in front of his colleagues.

Dershani took only the smallest step backwards. 'Lavrenty Pavlovich might not disagree with the drift of what I am saying. We both believe, I can say, that we will win this battle – though there are actions which must be taken if we intend to do so. Most important, however, to perceive his, *his*, wishes and to act upon them with all possible measures.'

This opened a door. Agayan tapped his cup on the saucer and his wife brought him a fresh coffee. Dershani had cited *all possible measures*, and form now decreed that Agayan seek to discover what they were. Once described, they had to be undertaken.

Dershani glanced at his watch. Agayan leapt at the possibility. 'Please, Efim Aleksandrovich, do not permit us to detain you if duty calls elsewhere.'

'No, no,' Dershani said dismissively, 'I'm simply wondering what's become of Grigory Petrovich – he was specifically to join us this morning.'

'You refer to Khelidze?' Ismailov asked.

'Yes.'

'I'll call his apartment,' Agayan said, rising quickly, delighted with the interruption. 'His wife will know where he's got to.'

Dzakhalev snickered briefly. 'Not likely,' he said.

Monday morning, striding through a fine, wet mist that made the streets of Prague even greyer than usual, Szara went early to the SovPressBuro, which handled all Soviet dispatches, and filed the story he'd written on Saturday night. It had taken him some twenty-eight tries to get a title that settled properly on the piece. His initial instinct led down a path marked 'Prague, City in—.' He tried 'Peril', 'Sorrow', 'Waiting', 'Despair', and, at last, in fury that it wouldn't work, 'Czechoslovakia'.

At the end of patience the rather literal 'Silence in Prague' took the prize, a title, on reflection, that turned out to be a message from the deep interior where all the work really went on. For those who read with both eyes, the melodramatic heading would imply a subtle alteration of preposition, so that the sharper and truer message would concern silence *about* Prague – not the anguished silence of a city under political siege but the cowardly silence of European statesmen, a silence filled with diplomatic bluster that nobody took seriously, a silence that could be broken only by the sputter of tank ignitions as armoured columns moved to reposition themselves on the borders of Germany.

There was, in fact, another zone of silence on the subject of Prague, to the east of Czechoslovakia, where Stalin's Franco-Russian alliance specified that the USSR would come to the aid of the Czechs if Hitler attacked them, but only after the French did. Thus the USSR had positioned itself to hide behind the promises of a regime in Paris that compromised on every issue and staggered from scandal to catastrophe and back again. Yes, Stalin's Red Army was in bloody disarray from the purges of June '37, but it was sorrowful, Szara thought, that the Czechs would get the bill for that.

And there was, unknown to Szara, some further silence to come.

The dispatch clerk at the bureau near the Jiráskův bridge, a stern, full-breasted matron with mounds of pinned-up grey hair, read 'Silence in Prague' sitting in front of her typewriter. 'Yes, comrade Szara,' she breathed, 'you have told the truth here, this is just the way this city feels.' He accepted the compliment, and more than a little adoration in her eyes, with a deflective mumble. It wouldn't do to let her know just how much such praise meant to him. He saw the story off, then wandered along the streets that ran next to the Vltava and watched the barges moving slowly up the steel-coloured November river.

Szara returned to the press bureau on Tuesday morning, meaning to wire Moscow his intention to travel up to Paris. There was always a story to be found in Paris, and he badly needed to breathe the unhealthy, healing air of that city. What he got instead, as he came through the door, was a pitying stare from the maternal transmission clerk. 'A message for the comrade,' she said, shaking her head in sympathy. She handed him a telegram, in from Moscow an hour earlier:

CANNOT ACCEPT SILENCE/PRAGUE IN PRESENT FORM STOP BY 25
NOVEMBER DEVELOP INFORMATION FOR PROFILE OF DR JULIUS

BAUMANN, SALZBRUNNER 8, BERLIN, SUCCESSFUL INDUSTRIAL-
IST STOP SUBMIT ALL MATERIAL DIRECTLY TO SOVPRESS SUPER-
VISOR BERLIN STOP SIGNED NEZHENKO

He saw that the clerk was waiting for him to explode but he shut his
emotions down at once. He was, he told himself, a big boy, and shifts of
party line were nothing new. His success as a correspondent, and the
considerable freedom he enjoyed, were based equally on ability and a
sensitivity to what could and could not be written at any given moment.
He was annoyed with himself for getting it wrong, but something was
brewing in Moscow, and it was not the moment for indignation, it was
the moment for understanding that political developments excluded
stories on Prague. For the clerk's benefit, he nodded in acceptance:
Soviet journalism worker accepts criticism and forges ahead to build
socialism. Yes, there was an overflowing wastebasket at his feet, and yes,
he yearned to give it a mighty kick that would send it skittering into the
wall, but no, he could not do it. 'Then it's to be Berlin,' he said calmly.
He folded the telegram and slid it into the pocket of his jacket, said
good-bye to the clerk, smiled brightly, and left, closing the door behind
him so softly it made not a sound.

That night he was early for the Berlin express and decided to have a
sandwich and coffee at the railway station buffet. He noticed a group of
men gathered around a radio in one corner of the room and wandered
over to see what was so interesting. It was, as he'd supposed, a political
speech, but not in Czech, in German. Szara recognized the voice
immediately – Adolf Hitler was born to speak on the radio. He was a
brilliant orator to begin with, and somehow the dynamics of wireless
transmission – static, the light hiss of silence – added power to his voice.
Hitler teased his audience, tiptoeing up to a dramatic point, then
hammering it home. The audience, tens of thousands by the sound of
it, cheered itself hoarse, swept by political ecstasy, ready to die then and
there for German honour.

Szara stood at the outer fringe of the group and listened without
expression or reaction, pointedly ignoring an unpleasant glance of
warning from one of the Czechs – Slovakians? Sudeten Germans? –
gathered around the radio. The voice, working towards a conclusion,
was level and sensible to begin with:

*Then the final aim of our whole party is quite clear for all of us. Always I
am concerned only that I do not take any step from which I will have to
retreat, and not to take any step that will harm us.*

I tell you that I always go to the outermost limits of risk, but never beyond. For this you need to have a nose [laughter; Szara could imagine the gesture], a nose to smell out, more or less, 'What can I still do?' Also, in a struggle against an enemy, I do not summon an enemy backed by a fighting force, I do not say 'Fight!' because I want to fight. Instead I say 'I will destroy you' [a swell of voices here, but Hitler spoke through it]. And now, Wisdom, help me. Help me to manoeuvre you into a corner where you cannot fight back. And then you get the blow, right in the heart. That's it!

The crowd roared in triumph and Szara felt his blood chill. As he turned to walk away there was a blur of motion to his right, the side of his head exploded, then he found himself sprawled on the filthy tiles of the restaurant floor. Looking up, he saw a man with a twisted mouth, his upper body coiled like a spring, his right fist drawn back over his left shoulder in order to hit a second time. The man spoke German. 'Jew shit,' he said.

Szara started to get up, but the man took a step towards him so he stayed where he was, on hands and knees. He looked around the restaurant; people were eating soup, blowing on their spoons before sipping it up. On the radio, a commentator's voice sounded measured and serious. The other men around the radio did not look at him, only the man with his fist drawn back – young, ordinary, broad, in a cheap suit and a loud tie. Szara's position seemed to mollify the man, who pulled a chair towards him and sat back down with his friends. He placed a metal salt shaker next to the pepper.

Slowly, Szara climbed to his feet. His ear was on fire, it throbbed and buzzed and he could hear nothing on that side. His vision was a little fuzzy and he blinked to clear it. As he walked away he realized that there were tears in his eyes – *physical, physical,* he told himself – but he was in many kinds of pain and he couldn't sort it out at all.

The Prague-Berlin night express left the central station at 9:03 P.M., due in at Berlin's Bahnhof am Zoo station at 11:51, stopping only at the Aussig border control post on the east bank of the Elbe. Szara now travelled with two bags, his own and the leather satchel. The train was cold and crowded and smoky. Szara shared a compartment with two middle-aged women he took to be sisters and two teenage boys whose windburned faces and khaki shorts suggested they'd been on a weekend mountain-climbing holiday in Czechoslovakia and had stayed on until Tuesday before returning to school in Germany.

Szara had some anxiety about the German customs inspection, but the officer's revolver now lay at the bottom of the Vltava and he doubted that a file written in Russian – something it would be normal for him to have – would cause any difficulty. Border inspections concentrated on guns, explosives, large amounts of currency, and seditious literature – the revolutionary toolkit. Beyond that, the inspectors were not very interested. He was taking, perhaps, a small chance, that a Gestapo officer would be in attendance (not unlikely) and that he would know enough Russian to recognize what he was looking at (very unlikely). In fact, Szara realized he didn't have much of a choice: the file was 'his,' but not his to dispose of. Sooner or later, *they* would want to know what had become of it.

As the train wound through the pine forests of northern Czechoslovakia, Szara's hand rose continually to his ear, slightly red and swollen and warm to the touch. He'd been hit, apparently, with the end of a metal salt shaker enclosed in a fist. As for other damage – heart, spirit, dignity; it had a lot of names – he finally managed to stand off from it and bring himself under control. *No*, he told himself again and again, you *shouldn't* have fought back. The men listening to the radio would've done far worse.

The border control at Aussig was uneventful. The train slowly gained speed, ran briefly beside the Elbe, shallow and still in the late autumn, and soon after passed the brown brick porcelain factories of Dresden, red shadows from the heating kilns flickering on the train windows. The track descended gradually from the high plain of Czechoslovakia to sea-level Germany, to flat fields and small, orderly towns, a stationmaster with a lantern standing on the platform at every village.

The train slowed to a crawl – Szara glanced at his watch, it was a few minutes after ten – then stopped with a loud hiss of decompression. The passengers in his compartment stirred about irritably, said '*Wuss?*' and peered out the windows, but there was nothing to see, only farm fields edged by woodland. Presently, a conductor appeared at the door to the compartment. An old gentleman with a hat a size too large for him, he licked his lips nervously and said, 'Herr Szara?' His eye roamed among the passengers, but there was really only one possible candidate. 'Well?' Szara said. *Now what?*

'Would you be so kind as to accompany me, it's just . . .'

Entirely without menace. Szara considered outrage, then sensed the weight of Teutonic railway bureaucracy standing behind this request, sighed with irritation, and stood up.

'Please, your luggage,' the conductor said.

Szara snatched the handles and followed the man down the corridor to the end of the car. A chief conductor awaited him there. 'I am sorry, Herr Szara, but you must leave the train here.'

Szara stiffened. 'I will not,' he said.

'Please,' said the man nervously.

Szara stared at him for a moment, utterly confounded. There was nothing outside the open door but dark fields. 'I demand an explanation,' he said.

The man peered over Szara's shoulder and Szara turned his head. Two men in suits stood at the end of the corridor. Szara said, 'Am I to walk to Berlin?' He laughed, inviting them to consider the absurdity of the situation, but it sounded false and shrill. The supervisor placed a tentative hand above his elbow; Szara jerked away from him. 'Take your hands off me,' he said.

The conductor was now very formal. 'You must leave.'

He realized he was going to be thrown off if he didn't move, so he took his luggage and descended the iron stairway to the cinderbed on which the rails lay. The conductor leaned out, was handed a red lantern from within, and swung it twice towards the engine. Szara stepped away from the train as it jerked into motion. He watched it gather momentum as it rolled past him – a series of white faces framed by windows – then saw it off into the distance, two red lamps at the back of the guard's van fading slowly, then blackness.

The change was sudden, and complete. Civilization had simply vanished. He felt a light wind against his face, the faint rime of frost on a furrowed field sparkled in the light of the quarter moon, and the silence was punctuated by the sound of a night bird, a high-low call that seemed very far away. He stood quietly for a time, watched the slice of moon that dimmed and sharpened as haze banks drifted across it in a starless sky. Then, from the woodland at the near horizon, a pair of headlights moved very slowly towards a point some fifty yards up the track. He could see strands of ground mist rising into the illumination of the beams.

Ah. With a sigh Szara hefted the two bags and trudged towards the lights, discovering, as his eyes adjusted to the darkness, a narrow country lane that crossed the railway tracks. *General Bloch,* he thought. *Doing tricks with the German rail system.*

The car reached the crossing before he did and rolled gently to a stop. Somehow, he'd missed a signal – this meeting had the distinct feel of an improvised fallback. He was, on balance, relieved. The heart of the *apparat* had skipped a beat but now returned to form and required the parcel from Prague. Well, thank God he had it. As he approached the car, its outline took shape in the ambient glow of the headlamps. It was not the same Grosser Mercedes that had carried General Bloch away from the station at Ulm, but the monarchs of the *apparat* changed cars about as casually as they changed mistresses and tonight had selected something small and anonymous for the *treff*, clandestine meeting, in a German beet field.

The middle-aged sisters in the train compartment that Szara had recently occupied were amused, rather sentimentally amused, at the argument that now began between the two students returning from their mountain-climbing exertions in the Tatra. Sentiment was inspired by the recollection of their own sons; wholesome, Nordic youths quite like these who had, from time to time, gone absolutely mulish over some foolery or other, as boys will, and come nearly to blows over it. The sisters could barely keep from smiling. The dispute began genially enough – a discussion of the quality of Czech matches made for woodcutters and others who needed to make outdoor fires. One of the lads was quite delighted with the brand they'd purchased, the other had reservations. Yes, he'd agree that they struck consistently, even when wet, but they burned for only a few seconds and then went out: with damp kindling, clearly a liability. The other boy was robust in defence. Was his friend blind and senseless? The matches burned for *a long time*. No, they didn't. *Yes*, they did. Just like miniature versions of their papas, weren't they, disputing some point in politics or machinery or dogs.

As the train approached the tiny station at Feldhausen, where the track crosses a bridge and then swings away from the river Elster, a bet of a few groschen was struck and an experiment undertaken. The defender of the matches lit one and held it high while the other boy counted out the seconds. The sisters pretended not to notice, but they'd been drawn inexorably into the argument and silently counted right along.

The first boy was an easy winner and the groschen were duly handed over – offered cheerfully and accepted humbly, the sisters noted with approval. The match had burned for more than thirty-eight seconds, from a point just outside Feldhausen to the other end of the station platform and even a little way out into the countryside. The point was made: those were excellent matches, just the thing for woodsmen, mountain climbers, and any others who might need to light a fire.

As Szara approached the car, the man next to the driver climbed out, held the back door open and said, 'Change of travel plans,' with a smile of regret.

His Russian was elementary but clear, phrased in the slow cadence characteristic of the southeastern reaches of the country, near the Turkish border. 'It won't be so inconvenient.' He was a dark man with a great belly; Szara could make out a whitening moustache and thinning grey hair spread carefully over a bald head. The driver was young – a relative, perhaps even a son of the passenger. For the moment he was bulky and thick, the extra chin just beginning, the hair at the crown of his head growing sparse.

Szara settled himself in the back seat and the car moved forward cautiously through the night mist. 'You tried to contact me in Prague?' he asked.

'Couldn't get your attention, but no matter. Which one do we want?'

Szara handed the satchel over the seat.

'Handsome old thing, isn't it,' said the man, running an appreciative hand over the pebbled hide.

'Yes,' Szara said.

'All here?'

'Except for a pistol. That I dared not take through German border control. It's at the bottom of the river.'

'No matter. It's not pistols we need.'

Szara relaxed. Wondered where and how he'd be put back on his way to Berlin, knew enough about such *treffs* not to bother asking. The Great Hand moved everyone about as it would.

'Must keep to form,' said the man, reaching inside his coat. He brought out a pair of handcuffs and held them out to Szara over the back of the seat. The car entered a farming village, every window dark, thatched-roof stone barns, then they were again among the fields.

Szara's heart pumped hard; he willed his hand not to rise and press against his chest.

'What?' he said.

'Rules, rules,' said the fat man disconsolately. Then, a bit annoyed: 'Always something.' He shook the handcuffs impatiently. 'Come, then . . .'

'For what?' *Za chto?*

'It isn't *for* anything, comrade.' The man made a sucking noise against his tooth. He tossed the handcuffs into Szara's lap. 'Now don't make me irritable.'

Szara held the cuffs in his hand. The metal was unpolished, faintly oily.

'You better do what we say,' the young driver threatened, his voice uncertain, querulous. Clearly he wanted to give orders but was afraid that nobody would obey him.

'Am I arrested?'

'Arrested? *Arrested?*' The fat man had a big laugh. 'He thinks we're arresting him!' The driver tried to laugh like the other man but he didn't have the voice for it.

The fat man pointed a blunt index finger at him and partly closed one eye. 'You put those on now, that's plenty of discussion.'

Szara held his wrist up to the faint moonlight in the back window.

'In back – don't you know anything?' He sighed heavily and shook his head. 'Don't worry, nothing will happen to you. It's just one of those things that has to be done – you're certainly aware, comrade, of the many things we all must do. So, humour me, will you?' He turned back around in his seat, dismissively and peered through the ground mist rising from the road. As he turned, Szara could hear the whisper of his woollen coat against the car upholstery.

Szara clicked the handcuff around his left wrist, then put it behind his back and held the other cuff in his right hand. For a time, the men in the front seat were silent. The road moved uphill into a wood where it was very dark. The fat man leaned forward and peered through the window. 'Take care,' he said. 'We don't want to hit an animal.' Then, without turning around, 'I'm waiting.'

Szara closed the cuff on his right wrist.

The car left the forest and headed down a hill. 'Stop here,' the fat man said. 'Turn on the light.' The driver stared at the dashboard, twisted a button; a windshield wiper scraped across the dry glass. Both men laughed and the driver turned it off. Another button did nothing at all. Then the dome light went on.

The fat man leaned over and rummaged through the open satchel between his feet. He drew out a sheet of paper and squinted at it. 'I'm told you're sly as a snake,' he said to Szara. 'Haven't been hiding anything, have you?'

'No,' Szara said.

'If I have to, I'll make you tell.'

'You have all of it.'

'Don't sound so miserable. You'll have me weeping in a minute.'

Szara said nothing. He shifted in the seat to make his hands more comfortable and looked out the side window at the cloudy silhouette of the moon.

'Well,' the fat man said at last, 'this is just the way life is.' A shrill whine reached them from around a bend in the road and the single light of a motorcycle appeared. It shot past them at great speed, a passenger hanging on to the waist of the driver.

'Crazy fools,' the young man said.

'These Germans love their machines,' the fat man said. 'Drive on.'

They went around the bend where the motorcycle had come from. Szara could see more woodland on the horizon. 'Slowly, now,' said the fat man. He reached over and turned off the dome light, then stared out the side window with great concentration. 'I wonder if it's come time for eyeglasses?'

'Not you,' the driver said. 'It's the mist.'

They drove on, very slowly. A dirt track for farm machines broke away from the road into a field that had been harvested to low stubble. 'Ah,' the fat man said. 'You better back up.' He looked over the seat at Szara as the car reversed. 'Let's see those hands.' Szara twisted around and showed him. 'Not too tight, are they?'

'No.'

'How far?' said the driver.

'Just a little. I'm not pushing this thing if we get stuck in a hole.'

The car inched forward down the dirt path. 'All right,' said the fat man. 'This will do.' He struggled out of the car, walked a few feet, turned his back, and urinated. Still buttoning his fly, he walked to Szara's door and opened it. 'Please,' he said, indicating that Szara should get out. Then, to the driver: 'You stay here and keep the car running.'

Szara shifted himself along the seat, swung his legs out, and, leaning forward in a crouch, managed to stand upright.

'Let's walk a little,' said the fat man, positioning himself just behind Szara and a little to his right.

Szara walked a few paces. As the car idled he could hear that one cylinder was mistimed and fired out of rhythm. 'Very well,' said the fat man. He took a small automatic pistol from the pocket of his coat. 'Is there anything you would like to say? Perhaps a prayer?'

Szara didn't answer.

'Jews have prayers for everything, certainly for this.'

'There's money,' Szara said. 'Money and gold jewellery.'

'In your valise?'

'No. In Russia.'

'Ah,' said the fat man sorrowfully, 'we're not in Russia.' He armed the automatic with a practised hand, the wind gusted suddenly and raised a few strands of stiff hair so that they stood up straight. Carefully, he smoothed them back into place. 'So . . .' he said.

The whine of the motorcycle reached them again, growing quickly in volume. The fat man swore softly in a language Szara didn't know and lowered the pistol by the side of his leg so that it was hidden from the road. Almost on top of them, the cyclist executed a grinding speed shift and swung onto the farm track in a shower of dirt, the light sweeping across Szara and the fat man, whose mouth opened in surprise. From somewhere near the car an urgent voice called out, 'Ismailov?'

The fat man was astonished, for a moment speechless. Then he said, 'What is it? Who are you?'

The muzzle flare was like orange lightning – it turned the fat man into a photographic negative, arms spread like the wings of a bird as a wind swept him into the air while down below a shoe flew away. He landed like a sack and hummed as though he'd hit his thumb with a hammer. Szara threw himself onto the ground. From the car, the young driver cried out for his father amid the flat reports of a pistol fired in the open air.

'Are you hurt?'

Szara looked up. The little gnome called Heshel stood over him, eyes glittering in the moonlight above his hooked nose and knowing smile. His cap was pulled down ridiculously over his ears and a great shawl was wound around his neck and stuffed into his buttoned jacket. Three shotgun shells were thrust between the fingers of his right hand. He broke the barrel and loaded both sides. A voice from near the car said, 'Who's humming?'

'Ismailov.'

'Heshie, please.'

Heshel snapped the shotgun back together and walked towards the fat man. He fired both barrels simultaneously and the humming stopped. He returned to Szara, reached down, thrust a small hand into Szara's armpit, and tugged. 'Come on,' he said, 'you got to get up.'

Szara managed to scramble to his feet. At the car, the second man was hauling the driver out by his ankles. He flopped onto the ground. 'Look,' said the man who had pulled him out. 'It's the son.'

'Ismailov's son?' Heshel asked.

'I think so.'

Heshel walked over and stared down. 'From this you can tell?'

The other man didn't answer.

'Maybe you better start the machine.'

While Heshel retrieved the key and unlocked the handcuffs, the other man took a crank that clamped behind the rider's seat and locked it onto a nut on the side of the engine. He turned it hard a few times and the motorcycle coughed, then sputtered to life. Heshel made a hurry-up motion with his hand, the man climbed on the motorcycle and rode away. As the noise faded, they could hear dogs barking.

Heshel stood silently for a moment and stared at the front seat of the car. 'Look in the boot,' he told Szara. 'Maybe there's a rag.'

*

In Berlin, it was raining and it was going to rain – a slow, sad, persistent business shining black on the bare trees and polishing the soot-coloured roof tiles. Szara stared out a high window, watching umbrellas moving down the street like phantoms. It seemed to him the city's very own, private weather, for Berliners lived deep inside themselves – it could be felt – where they nourished old insults and humiliated ambitions of every sort, all of it locked up within a courtesy like forged metal and an acid wit that never seemed meant to hurt – it just, apparently by accident, left a little bruise.

Late Tuesday night, Heshel had driven Szara to the terminus of a suburban branch line where he'd caught a morning train into Berlin. Once aboard, he'd trudged to the WC and, numb with resignation, forced himself to look in the mirror. But his hair was as it had always been and he'd barked a humourless laugh at his own image. *Still vanity, always, forever, despite everything.* What he'd feared was something he had seen, and more than once, during the civil war and the campaign against Poland: men of all ages, even in their teens, sentenced to die at night, then, the next morning, marched to the wall of a school or post office with hair turned, in the course of one night, a greyish white.

He took a taxi to an address Heshel had given him, a tall, narrow private house on the Nollendorfplatz in the western part of Berlin, not far from the Holländische Taverne, where he'd been told he could take his meals. A silent woman in black silks had answered his knock, shown him to a cot in a gabled attic, and left him alone. He supposed it to be a safe house used by the Renate Braun faction, but the ride in Ismailov's car and a few, apparently final moments in a stubbled wheat field had dislocated him from a normal sense of the world and he was no longer sure precisely what he knew.

Heshel, driving fast and peering through the steering wheel – there were bullet holes in the driver's side of the window and the glass had fractured into frosted lace around each of them – had signalled with his headlights to two cars and another motorcycle racing down the narrow road. So Szara gained at least a notion of the sheer breadth of the operation. Yet Heshel seemed not to know, or care, why Szara was headed into Berlin, and when Szara offered him the satchel he simply laughed. 'Me?' he'd said, heeling the car through a double-S curve in the road, 'I don't take nothing. What's yours is yours.'

What did they want?

To use the material in the satchel that rested between his feet. To discredit the Georgians – Ismailov and Khelidze had only that connection, as far as he knew. And *they* were? Not his friends in the Foreign

Department. Who then? He did not know. He only knew they'd stuck him with the hot potato.

The kids in the Jewish towns of Poland and Russia played the game with a stone. If the count reached fifty and you had it, well, too bad. You might have to eat a morsel of dirt, or horse pie. The forfeit varied but the principle never did. And there was always some tough little bastard like Heshel around to play enforcer.

Heshel was a type he'd always known, what they called in Yiddish a *Luftmensch*. These *Luftmenschen*, it meant men of the air or men without substance, could be seen every morning but the Sabbath, standing around in front of the local synagogue, hands in pockets, waiting for a day's work, an errand, whatever might come their way. They were men who seemed to have no family or village, a restless population of day labourers that moved through eastern Poland, the Ukraine, Byelorussia, all over the Jewish districts, available to whoever had a few kopecks to pay them. The word had a second, ironic, meaning that, like many Yiddish expressions, embellished its literal translation. *Luftmenschen* were also eternal students, lost souls, young people who spent their lives arguing politics in cafés and drifting through the student communities of Europe – gifted, bright, but never truly finding themselves.

Yet Szara knew that he and Heshel were perhaps more similar than he wanted to admit. They were both citizens of a mythical country, a place not here and not there, where national borders expanded and contracted but changed nothing. A world where *everyone* was a *Luftmensch* of one kind or another. The Pale of Settlement, fifteen provinces in southwest Russia (until 1918, when Poland sprang back into national existence) ran from Kovno in the north, almost on the shores of the Baltic, to Odessa and Simferopol in the south, on the Black Sea; from Poltava in the east – historic Russia – to Czestochowa and Warsaw in the west – historic Poland. One had also to include Cracow, Lvov, Ternopol, and such places, part of the Austro-Hungarian empire until 1918. Add to this the towns of other off-and-on countries – Vilna in Lithuania and Jelgava in Latvia – throw in the fact that people thought of themselves as having regional affiliations, believing they lived in Bessarabia, Galicia (named for the Galicia in Spain from which the Jews were expelled in 1492), Kurland, or Volhynia, and what did you have?

You had a political landscape best understood by intelligence services and revolutionary cadres – fertile recruiting either way it went and often enough both and why not?

What can be so bad about a cover name or a *nom de révolution* if your own name never particularly meant anything? The Austro-Hungarian bureaucracy in the nineteenth century gave the Jews the right to call themselves whatever they liked. Most chose German names, thinking to endear themselves to their German-speaking neighbours. These names were often transliterated back into, for example, Polish. Thus some version of the German for *sharer* (and why that? nobody knew) became Szara, the Polish *sz* standing in for the German *s*, which was sounded *sch*. Eventually, with time and politics and migration, it changed again, this time to the Russian ш. And, when Szara was born, his mother wanted to emphasize some quietly cherished claim to a distant relation in France, so named him not the Polish Andrej or the Russian Andrei, but André.

A man invented. A man of the air. Just how would such a man's allegiance be determined? In a land of, at best, shifting political loyalties often well leavened with fumes of Hasidic mysticism, a land where the name Poland was believed by many to be a version of the Hebrew expression *polen*, which meant *Here ye shall remain!*, and was thus taken to be good news direct from heaven.

The czar's Okhrana was recruiting in the Pale as early as 1878, seeking infiltrators – Jews *did* wander, turning up as pedlars, merchants, auction buyers, and what have you, just about anywhere – for their war against Turkey. Thus, when the operatives of the Okhrana and the Bolshevik faction went at each other, after 1903, there were often Jews on both sides: men of both worlds and none – always alien, therefore never suspected of being so.

They tended to show up somewhere with a business in one pocket. Szara's father grew up in Austro-Hungarian Ternopol, where he learned the trade of watchmaker, eventually becoming nearly blind from close work in bad light. As a young man, seeking a better economic climate in which to raise his family, he moved to the town of Kishinev, where he survived the pogrom of 1903, then fled to the city of Odessa, just in time for the pogrom of 1905, which he did not survive. By then, all he could see were grey shadows and was perhaps briefly surprised at just how hard shadows punched and kicked.

His death left Szara and his mother, and an older brother and sister, to get along as best they could. Szara was, in 1905, eight years old. He learned to sew, after a fashion, as did his brother and sister, and they survived. Sewing was a Jewish tradition. It took patience, discipline, and a kind of self-hypnosis, and it provided money sufficient to eat once a day and to heat a house for some of the winter. Later, Szara learned to steal, then, soon after, to sell stolen goods, first in Odessa's Moldavanka market, then on the docks where foreign ships berthed. Odessa was famous for its Jewish thieves – and its visiting sailors. Szara learned to sell stolen goods to sailors, who told him stories, and he grew to like stories more than almost anything else. By 1917, when he was twenty years old and had attended three years of university in Cracow, he was a confirmed writer of stories, one of many who came from Odessa – it had something to do with seaports: strange languages, exotic travellers, night bells in the harbour, waves pounding into foam on the rocks, and always distance, horizon, the line where sky met water, and just beyond your vision people were doing things you couldn't imagine.

By the time he left Cracow he'd been a socialist, a radical socialist, a communist, a Bolshevik, and a revolutionary in all things – whatever one might become to oppose the czar, for that mattered above all else.

After Kishinev, where, as a six-year-old, he'd heard the local citizens beating their whip handles on the cobblestones, preparing their victims for a pogrom, after Odessa, where he'd found his father half buried in a mud street, a pig's tail stuffed in his mouth – *thus we deal with Jews too good to eat pork* – what else?

For the pogroms were the czar's gift to his peasants. There was little else he could give them, so, when they were pressed too hard by misery, when they could no longer bear their fate in the muddy villages and towns at the tattered edges of the empire, they were encouraged to seek out the Christ-killers and kill a few in return. Pogroms were announced by posters, the police paid the printing bills, and the money came from the Interior Ministry, which acted at the czar's direction. A pogrom released tension and, in general, evened things up: a redistribution of wealth, a primitive exercise in population control.

Thus the Pale of Settlement produced a great number of Szaras. Intellectuals, they knew the capitals of Europe and spoke their languages, wrote fiercely and well, and had a great taste and talent for clandestine life. To survive as Jews in a hostile world they'd learned duplicity and disguise: not to show anger, for it made the Jew-baiters angry, even less to show joy, for it made the Jew-baiters even angrier. They concealed success, so they would not be seen to succeed, and learned soon enough how not to be seen at all: how to walk down a street, the wrong street, in the wrong part of town, in broad daylight – invisible. The czar was in much more trouble than he ever understood. And when his time came, the man in charge was one Yakov Yurovsky, a Jew from Tomsk, at the head of a Cheka squad. Yurovsky who, while an émigré in Berlin, had declared himself a Lutheran, though the czar was in no position to appreciate such ironies.

Having lived in a mythical country, a place neither here nor there, these intellectuals from Vilna and Gomel helped to create another and called it the Union of Soviet Socialist Republics. Such a name! It was hardly a union. The Soviets – workers' councils – ruled it for about six weeks; socialism impoverished everybody, and only machine guns kept the republics from turning into nations. But to Szara and the rest it didn't matter. He'd put his life on the line, preferring simply to die at the wrong end of a gun rather than the wrong end of a club, and for twelve years – until 1929, when Stalin finally took over – he lived in a kind of dream world, a mythical country where idealistic, intellectual Jews actually ran things, quite literally a country of the mind. Theories failed, peasants died, the land itself dried up in despair. Still they worked twenty hours a day and swore they had the answer.

It could not last. Who *were* these people, these Poles and Lithuanians, Latvians and Ukrainians, these people with little beards and eyeglasses who spoke French down their big noses and read books? Asked Stalin. And all the little Stalins answered. *We were wondering that very thing, only nobody wanted to say it out loud.*

The steady rain beat down on Berlin; somewhere in the house the landlady's radio played German opera, the curtains hung limp by the window and smelled of the dead air in a disused attic room. Szara put on his belted raincoat and walked through the wet streets until he found a telephone box. He called Dr Julius Baumann and managed to get himself invited to dinner. Baumann sounded suspicious and distant, but Nezhenko's telegram had been specific: the information was wanted by 25 November. There was no Soviet press bureau in Berlin, he'd have to file through the press office at the embassy, and 25 November was the next day. So he'd given Baumann a bit of a push – sometimes finesse was a luxury.

He walked slowly back to the tall house and spent the afternoon with the Okhrana, DUBOK, the Caspian Oil Company, and thirty-year-old *treffs* in the back streets of Tbilisi, Baku, and Batum. They wanted him to be an intelligence officer and so he was. Fearless, heroic, jaw set with determination, he read reports for five hours in an anonymous room while the rain drummed down and he never once dozed off.

The Villa Baumann stood behind a high wall at the edge of the western suburbs, in a neighbourhood where gardeners pruned the shrubbery to sheer walls and flat tabletops and architects dazzled their clients with turrets and gables and gingerbread that made mansions seem colossal dolls' houses. A yank at the rope of a ship's bell by the gate produced a servant, a stubby man with immense red hands and sloping shoulders who wore an emerald green velvet smoking jacket. Mumbling in a dialect Szara could barely understand, he led the way down a path that skirted the Villa Baumann and ended at a servant's cottage at the rear of the property, then tramped off, leaving Szara to knock at the door.

'I take it Manfred showed you the way,' Baumann said dryly. 'Of course this used to be his' – the cottage was small and plain, quite pleasant for a servant – 'but the new regime has effected a more, ah, even-handed approach to domicile, who shall live where.'

Baumann was tall and spare, with thin, colourless lips and the face, ascetic, humourless, of a medieval prince or monastic scholar. His skin was white, as though wind or sun had never touched it. Perhaps fifty, he was hairless from forehead to crown, which drew attention to his eyes, cold and green, the eyes of a man who saw what others did not, yet did not choose to say what he saw. Whatever it was, however, faintly displeased him, that much he showed. To Szara, German Jew meant mostly German, a position of significant hauteur in the Central European scheme of things, a culture wherein precise courtesies, intellectual sophistication, and quiet wealth all blended to create a great distance from Russian Jews and, it was never exactly expressed, most Christians.

Yet Szara liked him. Even as the object of that jellyfish stare down a long, fine, princely nose – *who are you?* – even so.

They were four for dinner: Herr Doktor and Frau Baumann, a young woman introduced as Fräulein Haecht, and Szara. They ate in the kitchen – there was no dining room – at a rickety table covered by a dazzling white damask cloth embroidered with blue and silver thread. The porcelain service showed Indian princes and thick-lipped, gold-earringed princesses boating on a mountain lake, coloured tomato red and glossy black with gold filigree on the rims. At one point, the tines of Szara's fork scraped across the scene and Frau Baumann closed her eyes to shut out the sound. She was a busy little pudding of a woman. A princess with a dowry? Szara thought so.

They ate poached salmon fillets and a rice and mushroom mixture in a jellied ring. 'My old shop still serves me,' Frau Baumann explained, the unspoken *of course* perfectly audible. 'During the hours of closing, you understand, Herr Szara, at the door in the alley. But they still do it. And they do cook the most lovely things and I am enough the domestic to reheat them.'

'A small premium is entailed,' Baumann added. He had a deep, hollow voice that would have been appropriate for the delivery of sermons.

'Naturally,' Frau Baumann admitted, 'but our cook . . .'

'A rare patriot,' said Baumann. 'And a memorable exit. One would never have supposed that Hertha was capable of giving a speech.'

'We were so good to her,' said Frau Baumann.

Szara sensed the onset of an emotional flood and rushed to cut it off. 'But you are doing so very well, I haven't eaten like this . . .'

'You are not wrong,' said Baumann quietly. 'There are bad moments, too many, and one misses friends. That more than anything. But we, my family, came to Germany over three hundred years ago, before there was even such a thing as Germany, and we have lived here, in good times and bad, ever since. We are German, is what it amounts to, and proud to be. That we proved in peace and war. So, *these people* can make life difficult for us, Jews and others also, but they cannot break our spirit.'

'Just so,' Szara said. Did they believe it? Perhaps Frau Doktor did. Had they ever seen a spirit broken? 'Your decision to stay on is, if I may say it, courageous.'

Baumann laughed by blowing air through his nose, his mouth deformed by irony. 'Actually, we haven't the choice. You see before you the Gesellschaft Baumann, declared a strategically necessary enterprise.'

Szara's interest showed. Baumann waved off dinnertime discussion of such matters. 'You shall come and see us tomorrow. The grand tour.'

'Thank you,' Szara said. There went filing on time. 'The editors at *Pravda* have asked for material that could become a story. Would it be wise for a Jew to have attention called to him in that way? In a Soviet publication?'

Baumann thought for a moment. 'You are frank, Herr Szara, and it is appreciated. Perhaps you'll allow me to postpone my answer until tomorrow.'

Why am I here? 'Of course, I understand perfectly.'

Frau Baumann was breathless. 'We must stay, you see, Herr Szara. And our position is difficult enough as it is. One hears frightful things, one sees things, on the street—'

Baumann cut his wife off. 'Herr Szara has kindly consented to do as we wish.'

Szara realized why he liked Baumann – he was drawn to bravery.

'Surely, Herr Szara, a little more rice and mushroom ring.'

This from his left, Fräulein Haecht, obviously invited to balance the table. At first, in the little whirlpool of turmoil that surrounds the entry of a guest, her presence had floated by him; a handshake, a polite greeting. Obviously she was nobody to be interested in, a young woman with downcast eyes whose role it was to sit in the fourth chair and offer him rice and mushroom ring. Hair drawn back in a maiden's bun, wearing a horrid sort of blue wool dress with long sleeves – somehow shapeless and stiff at once – with a tiny lace collar tight at the throat, she was the perennial niece or cousin, invisible.

But now he saw that she had eyes, large and soft and brown, liquid, and intense. He knew her inquiring look to be a device, worked out, practised at length in front of a dressing table mirror and meant to be the single instant of the evening she would claim for herself.

Said Frau Baumann: 'Oh yes, please do.'

He reached for the platter, held delicately in a small hand with bitten nails, set it beside him, and served himself food he didn't want. When he looked up she was gone, back into cover. It was the sort of skin, olive toned, that didn't exactly colour, yet he thought he saw a shadow darken above the lace collar.

'. . . just the other day . . . the British newspapers . . . simply cannot continue . . . friends in Holland.' Frau Baumann was well launched into an emotional appraisal of the German political situation. Meanwhile, Szara thought, *How old are you? Twenty-five?* He couldn't remember her name.

'Mmm!' he said, nodding vigorously at his hostess. How true that was.

'And one does hear such excellent news of Russia, of how it is being built by the workers. War would be such a waste.'

'Mm.' He smiled with enthusiasm. 'The workers . . .'

Finished eating, the Fräulein folded her little hands in her lap and stared at her plate.

'It cannot be permitted to happen, not again,' said the Herr Doktor. 'I believe that support for the present regime in the senior civil service and the army is not at all firm, *that man* does not necessarily speak for all of Germany, yet the European press seems blind to the possibility that—'

'And now,' the Frau Doktor cried out and clapped her hands, 'there is crème Bavarienne!'

The girl stood up quickly and assisted in clearing the table and making coffee while the Herr Doktor rumbled on. The blue dress descended to midcalf; white ribbed stockings rose to meet it. Szara could see her lace-up shoes had got wet in the evening rain.

'The situation in Austria is also difficult, very complex. If not handled with delicacy, there could be instability . . .'

By a cupboard in the far corner of the kitchen, Frau Baumann laughed theatrically to cover embarrassment. 'Why no, my dearest Marta, the willow pattern for our guest!'

Marta.

'. . . there must be rapprochement and there must be peace. We are neighbours, all of us here, there is no denying it. The Poles, the Czechs, the Serbs, they wish only peace. Can the Western democracies be blind to this? Yet they give in at every opportunity.' He shook his head in sorrow. 'Hitler marched into the Rhineland in 1936, and the French sat behind their Maginot Line and did nothing. Why? We cannot understand it. A single, determined advance by a French company of infantry – that's all it would have taken. Yet it didn't happen. I believe – no, frankly, I know – that our generals were astounded. Hitler told them how it would be, and then it was as he said, and then suddenly they began to believe in miracles.'

'And now this terrible politics must be put aside, Herr Szara,' said Frau Baumann, 'for it is time to be naughty.' The Bavarian cream, a velvety mocha pond quivering in a soup plate, appeared before him.

As the evening wore on, with cognac served in the cramped parlour, Dr Julius Baumann became reflective and nostalgic. Recalled his student days at Tübingen, where the Jewish student societies had taken enthusiastically to beer-drinking and fencing, in the fashion of the times. 'I became a fine swordsman. Can you imagine such a thing, Herr Szara? But we were obsessed with honour, and so we practised until we could barely stand up, but at least one could then answer an insult by challenging the offender to a match, as all the other students did. I was tall, so our president – he is now in Argentina, living God only knows how – prevailed on me to take up the sabre. This I declined. I most certainly did not want one of these!' He drew the traditional sabre scar down his cheek. 'No, I wore the padded vest and the full mask – not the one that bares the cheek – and practised the art of the épée. Lunge! Guard. Lunge! Guard. One winter's day I scored two touches on the mighty Kiko Bettendorf himself, who went to the Olympic games the following year! Ach, those were wonderful days.'

Baumann told also of how he'd studied, often from midnight to dawn, to maintain the family honour and to prepare himself to accept the responsibility that would be passed down to him by his father, who owned the Baumann Ironworks. Graduating with a degree in metallurgical engineering, he'd gone on to convert the family business, once his father retired, to a wire mill. 'I believed that German industry had to specialize in order to compete, and so I took up that challenge.'

He had always seen his life in terms of challenge, Szara realized. First at Tübingen, then as an artillery lieutenant fighting on the western front, wounded near Ypres and decorated for bravery, next in the conversion of the Baumann business, then survival during the frightful inflations of the Weimar period – 'We paid our workers with potatoes;

my chief engineer and I drove trucks to Holland to buy them!' – and now he found himself meeting the challenge of remaining in Germany when so many, 150,000 of the Jewish population of 500,000, had abandoned everything and started all over as immigrants in distant lands. 'So many of our friends gone away,' he said sorrowfully. 'We are so isolated now.'

Frau Baumann sat attentively silent during the discourse, her smile, in time, becoming a bit frozen – *Julius, my dearest husband, how I love and honour you but how you do go on.*

But Szara heard what she did not. He listened with great care and studied every gesture, every tone of voice. And a certain profile emerged, like secret writing when blank paper is treated with chemicals:

A courageous and independent man, a man of position and influence, and a patriot, suddenly finds himself bitterly opposed to his government in a time of political crisis; a man whose business, whatever it really was, has been officially designated *a strategically necessary enterprise*, who now declares himself, to a semi-official representative of his nation's avowed enemy, to be *so isolated.*

This added up to only one thing, Szara knew, and the rather dubious assignment telegram from Nezhenko began to make sense. What he'd written off as a manifestation of some new, hopelessly convoluted political line being pursued in Moscow now told another story. The moment of revelation would come, he was virtually certain, during his 'grand tour' of the Baumann wire mill.

The dance of departure began at ten o'clock precisely, as Frau Baumann accepted with courteous despair the inevitability of Szara's return to his lodgings and instructed her husband to walk Fräulein Haecht back to her family's house. Ah but no – Szara fought back – Herr Doktor must in no way discommode himself, this was an obligation he insisted on assuming. What? No, it was unthinkable, they could not let him do that. Why not? Of course they must allow him to do that very thing. No, yes, no, yes, it went on while the girl sat quietly and stared at her knees as they fought over her. Szara finally prevailed – becoming emotional and Russian in the process. To dine so splendidly, then drive one's host out into the night? Never! What he needed was a good long walk to punctuate the pleasure of the meal. This proved to be an unanswerable attack and carried the day. Arrangements to meet the following morning were duly made, and Szara and Fräulein Haecht were ceremoniously walked to the gate and waved out into the night.

The night made over into something very different.

Sometime after dusk the rain of the afternoon had turned to snow –

soft, feathery stuff, night-time snow, that floated down slowly from a low, windless sky. They were startled, it simply wasn't the same city, they laughed in amazement. The snow crunched beneath their shoes, covered tree branches and rooftops and hedges, changed the streets into white meadows or into silvered crystal where street lamps broke the shadow. Suddenly the night was immensely silent, immensely private; the snow clung to their hair and made their breaths into mist, surrounded them, muffled the world, cleaned it, buried it.

He had no idea where she lived and she never suggested one street or another, so they simply wandered. Walking together made it easy to talk, easy to confide, easy to say whatever came to you, because the silence and the snow made careful words seem empty. In such a moment one couldn't be hurt, the storm promised that among other things.

Some of what she said surprised him. For instance, she was not, as he'd thought, a cousin or a niece. She was the daughter of Baumann's chief engineer and longtime friend. Szara had wondered why she'd remained in Germany but this was simply answered: she was not Jewish. Thus her father would, she explained, almost certainly become the Aryan owner of the business – new laws decreed that – but he had already arranged for Baumann's interest to be secretly protected until such time as events restored them all to sanity. Was her father, then, a progressive? A man of the left? No, not at all. Simply a man of great decency. And her mother? Distant and dreamy, lived in her own world, who could blame her these days? She was Austrian, Catholic, from the South Tyrol down near Italy; perhaps the family on that side had been, some time in the past, Italian. She looked, she thought, a little Italian. What did he think?

Yes, he thought so. That pleased her; she liked being so black-haired and olive-skinned in a nation that fancied itself frightfully Nordic and blond. She belonged to the Italian side of Germany, perhaps, where romance had more to do with Puccini than Wagner, where romance meant sentiment and delicacy, not fiery Valhalla. Such private thoughts – she hoped he didn't mind her rambling.

No, no he didn't.

She knew who he was, of course. When Frau Baumann had asked her to make a fourth for dinner she hadn't let on, but she'd read some of his stories when they were translated into German. She very much wanted to meet the person who wrote those words, yet she'd been certain that she never would, that the dinner would be called off, that something would go wrong at the last minute. Generally she wasn't lucky that way. It was people who didn't care much who were lucky, she thought.

She was twenty-eight, though she knew she seemed younger. The Baumanns had known her as a little girl and for them she had never grown up, but she had, after all, one did. One wound up working for pfennigs helping the art director of a little magazine. Wretched things they printed now, but it was that or shut the doors. Not like him. Yes, she had a little envy, how he went the world over and wrote of the people he found and told their stories.

She took his hand – leather glove in leather glove down some deserted street where a crust of snow glittered on a wall. He wanted, now and then, to cry out that he was forty years old and scarred so badly he could not feel that snow melted or changed back to rain, but of course he didn't. He knew every bad thing about the Szaras of the world, their belted raincoats and reputations, and their need to plunder innocence in girls like this. For, twenty-eight or lying, she was innocent.

They walked endlessly, miles in the snow, and when he thought he recognized the name of a street near the house where he was staying, he told her. She looked at him for the first time in a long while, her face lit up by walking in the night, wisps of hair escaped from the dreadful bun, and took off her glove, so he took his off, and they froze in order to touch. She told him he mustn't worry, her parents thought that she was staying with a girlfriend. Later they kissed, dry and cold, and he felt a taut back beneath the damp wool of her coat.

In his room, she was suddenly subdued, almost shy. Perhaps it was the room itself, he thought. Perhaps to her it seemed mean and anonymous, not the surroundings she would have imagined for him. Understanding, he smiled and shrugged – *yes, it's how my life is lived, I don't apologize* – hung up their coats, put the wet shoes by the hissing radiator. The room was dark, lit only by a small lamp, and they sat on the edge of the bed and talked in low voices and, in time, recaptured some part of the nameless grace they had discovered in the falling snow. He took her hands and said that their lives were different, very different. He'd be leaving Berlin almost immediately, was never in one place for very long, might not come back for a long time. Soon, even writing to someone in Germany might be difficult for somebody like him. It *was* a magic night, yes, he would never forget it, but they'd stolen it from a twilight world, and soon it would be dark. He meant . . . He would walk her home now. It might be better. She shook her head stubbornly, not meeting his eyes, and held his hands tightly. In the silence they could hear the snow falling outside. She said, 'Is there a place I may undress?'

'Only down the hall.'

She nodded, let go of his hands, and walked a little way off from the bed. He turned away. He heard her undoing buttons, the sliding of wool over silk as she pulled her dress over her head, and silk on silk as she took off her slip. He heard her roll down her white stockings, the shift of weight from foot to foot, the sound of her unhooking her brassiere, the sound of her lowering her underpants and stepping out of them. Then he couldn't keep his eyes away. She undid her hair and it hung loose about her face, crimped where she'd pinned it up. She was narrow-waisted, with pale, full breasts that rose and fell as she breathed, broad hips, and strong legs. Unconsciously, he sighed. She stood awkwardly in the centre of the room, olive skin half-toned in the low light, the tilt of her head uncertain, almost challenging. Was she desirable?

He stood and turned back the covers and she padded past him, heavy-footed on the bare wooden boards, and slid herself in carefully, staring at the ceiling as he undressed. He got in next to her, lying on his side, head propped on his hand. She turned towards him and started to tell him something, but he had guessed and stopped her from saying it. When, almost speculatively, he touched her nipples with his flattened palm, she drew a sharp breath through closed teeth and squeezed her eyes shut, and if he'd not been who he was, had not done everything he'd done, he would have been stupid and asked her if it hurt.

He was too excited to be as clever as he wanted to be; it was the nature of her, generosity and hunger mixed, heat and warmth at once, the swollen and smooth places, pale colours and dark, the catch of discovery in her breathing, and the way she abandoned not innocence – he'd been wrong; she had never been innocent – but modesty, the way she crossed her barriers.

'Lift up a little,' he said.

For a time he was afraid to move, her hands trembling against his back, then, when he did, he was in anguish when it ended. A little later she got out of bed to go down the hall, not bothering to put anything on, a pretty wobble in the way she walked, *I know you're watching.*

When she returned, she took the cigarette away from him and stubbed it out in the ashtray. So many things she had thought about for such a long time.

Thursday morning was cold and windy under dirty skies of shattered grey cloud. The streets to the factory district, at the northern reaches of the city, were banked by soot-stained hills of snow. Szara's taxi was driven by a meat-coloured giant with crossed swastika flags bound to his sun visor with ribbon, and, as they drove through the Neukolln district, where miles of factories mixed with workers' flats, he hummed beer songs and chattered on about the virtues of the New Germany.

The Baumann wire mill proved hard to find. High, brown brick walls, name announced by a small, faded sign, as though anybody who mattered should know where it was. Szara was amused by the driver, whose face twisted with near-sighted effort as he looked for the entry gate.

A business-day Baumann awaited him in a cluttered office that looked out on the production lines. Szara found him edgy, overactive, eyes everywhere at once, and not at all stylish in a green V-neck sweater worn beneath a sober suit to keep out the chill of the factory. The narrative of the tour was delivered in a shout that was barely audible above the noise of the machinery.

Szara was a little dazed by it all. He'd arrived still in a lover's state of being, sensual, high strung, and the roaring hearth fires and clattering belt drives pounded at his temples. Steel was really the last thing in the world he wanted to think about.

One bad moment: he was introduced to Herr Haecht, a dour man in a smock, distracted from tally sheets on a clipboard when Baumann yelled an introduction. Szara managed a smile and a limp handshake.

Chicken sandwiches and scalding coffee were served in the office. When Baumann slammed the glass-panelled door, the racket of the place diminished sufficiently that a conversation could be held in almost normal tones.

'What do you think of it?' said Baumann, eager for his visitor to be impressed.

Szara did his best. 'So many workers . . .'

'One hundred and eight.'

'And truly on a grand scale.'

'In my father's day, may he rest in peace, no more than a workshop. What he didn't make wasn't worth mentioning – ornamental fence palings, frying pans, toy soldiers.' Szara followed Baumann's eyes to a portrait on the wall, a stern man with a tiny moustache. 'And everything by hand, work you don't see any more.'

'I can only imagine.'

'One naturally cannot compare systems,' Baumann said diplomatically. 'Even our largest mills are not so grand as the Soviet steel works at Magnitogorsk. Ten thousand men, it's said. Extraordinary.'

'Each nation has its own approach,' Szara said.

'Of course here we specialize. We are all *nichtrostend*.'

'Pardon?'

'One says it best in English – austenitic. What is known as stainless steel.'

'Ah.'

'When you finish your sandwich, the best is yet to come.' Baumann smiled conspiratorially.

The best was reached by way of two massive doors guarded by an elderly man seated on a kitchen chair.

'Ernest is our most senior man,' Baumann said. 'From my father's time.' Ernest nodded respectfully.

They stood in a large room where a few workers were busy at two production lines. It was much quieter and colder than the other part of the factory. 'No forging here,' Baumann explained, grinning at the chill overtaking Szara. 'Here we make swage wire only.'

Szara nodded, drew a pencil and a notebook from his pocket. Baumann spelled the word for him. 'It's a die process, steel bars forced through a swage, a grooved block, under enormous pressure, which produces a cold-worked wire.'

Baumann took him closer to one of the production lines. From a table he selected a brief length of wire. 'See? Go ahead, take it.' Szara held it in his hand. 'That's 302 you've got there – just about the best there is. Resists atmosphere, doesn't corrode, much stronger than wire made from molten steel, this is. Won't melt until around twenty-five hundred degrees Fahrenheit, and its tensile strength is greater than that of annealed wire by a factor of approximately one third. Hardness can be figured at two hundred and forty on the Brinnell scale as opposed to eighty-five. Quite a difference all round, you'll agree.'

'Oh yes.'

'And it won't stretch – that's the really crucial thing.'

'What is it for?'

'We ship it to the Rheinmetall company as multiple strands twisted into cable, which increases its strength by a considerable factor but it remains flexible, to pass under or around various barriers, yet extremely responsive, even at great length. That's what you need in control cable.'

'Control cable?'

'Yes, for aircraft. For instance, the pilot sets his flaps by controls in his cockpit, but it's Baumann swage wire that actually makes the flaps go down. Also the high-speed rudder on the tail, and the ailerons on the wings. These are warplanes! They must bank and dip, dive suddenly. Response is everything, and response depends on the finest control cables.'

'So you are very much a factor in Luftwaffe rearmament.'

'In our own speciality, one could say pre-eminent. Our contract with

Rheinmetall, which instals control cable on all heavy bombers, the Dornier 17, the Heinkel 111, and the Junkers 86, is exclusive.'

'All the swage wire.'

'That's true. A third production line is contemplated here. Something around four hundred and eighty feet per aircraft – well, it's quite a heavy demand.'

Szara hesitated. They were on the brink now; it was like sensing the tension of a diver at the instant preceding a leap into empty air. Baumann remained supremely energetic, expansive, a businessman proud of what he'd accomplished. Did he understand what was about to happen? He had to. He had almost certainly contrived this meeting, so he knew what he was doing. 'It's quite a story,' Szara said, stepping back from the edge. 'Any journalist would be delighted, of course. But can it be told?' *A door*, he thought. *Will you walk through it?*

'In the newspaper?' Baumann was puzzled.

'Yes.'

'I hardly think so.' He laughed good-naturedly.

Amen. 'My editor in Moscow misinformed me. I'm normally not so dense.'

Baumann clucked. 'Not so, Herr Szara, you are not anything like dense. Of Soviet citizens who might turn up in Germany, outside diplomatic staffs or trade missions, your presence is quite unremarkable. Surely not liked by the Nazis, but not unusual.'

Szara was a little stung at this. *So you know about clandestine life, do you?* 'Well, one could hardly expect your monthly production figures to be published in trade magazines.'

'Unlikely.'

'It would be considerable.'

'Yes it would. In October, for example, we shipped to Rheinmetall approximately sixteen thousand eight hundred feet of 302 swage wire.'

Divide by four hundred and eighty, Szara calculated, and you have the monthly bomber production of the Reich. Though tanks would be of great interest, no number could so well inform Soviet military planners of German strategic intentions and capabilities.

Szara jotted down the number as though he were making notes for a feature story – *our motto has always been excellence, Baumann claims.* 'Substantial,' he said, tapping his pencil against the number on the page. 'Your efforts must surely be appreciated.'

'In certain ministries, that's true.'

But not in others. Szara put the notebook and pencil in his pocket. 'We journalists don't often meet with such candour.'

'There are times when candour is called for.'

'Perhaps we'll be meeting again,' Szara said.

Baumann nodded his assent, a stiff little bow: a man of dignity and culture had made a decision, taken honour into account, determined that greater considerations prevailed.

They went back to the office and chatted for a time. Szara restated his gratitude for a delightful evening. Baumann was gracious, saw him to his taxi when it arrived, smiled, shook hands, wished him safe journey home.

The taxi rattled along past brown factory walls. Szara closed his eyes. She stood at the centre of the room, olive skin in half tones, pale breasts that rose and fell as she breathed. *Marta Haecht*, he thought.

Fate rules our lives. So the Slavs seemed to believe, and Szara had lived among them long enough to see the sense of the way they thought. One simply had to admire the fine hand of destiny, how it wove a life, tied desire to betrayal, ambition to envy, added idealism, love, false gods, missed trains, then pulled sharply on the threads, and behold! – there a human danced and struggled.

Here, he thought, was that exquisite deployment of fate known as *the coincidence*.

A man goes to Germany and is offered, simultaneously, both salvation for his aching soul and a guarantee of life itself. Amazing. What should such a man believe? For he can see that a clandestine affiliation with Dr Baumann and his magic wire will make him so appetizing a fellow to the special services that they will keep him alive if the devil himself tries to snatch his ankle. As for his soul, well, he'd been having rather a bad time with it lately. A man whose friends are vanishing every day must learn to nuzzle death in order to keep his sanity – didn't a kind of affection always take root in proximity? This is a man in trouble. A man who sits in a park in Ostend, offered, at least, a possibility of salvation, then stands and walks away in order to keep a timely appointment with those he has every reason to believe mean to abduct him – this man must need a reason to live. And if the reason to live is in Berlin? Tightly locked to the very means that will ensure survival?

Oh, a glorious coincidence.

In a vast and shifting universe, where stars glitter and die in endless night, one may choose to accept coincidence of every sort. Szara did.

There remained, amid such speculation, one gravely material difficulty, the Okhrana document, and the need to satisfy what he now believed to be a second group of masters – Renate Braun, General Bloch – within the intelligence *apparat*. For the Baumann assignment came, he was almost positive, from his traditional, longtime friends in the

NKVD – the Foreign Department crowd, Abramov and others, some known, some forever in shadow.

Now, to stay alive, he would have to become an intelligence officer: an NKVD of one.

On the morning of 26 November, Szara filed as instructed at the Soviet embassy in Berlin. Not a dispatch, but the development of information that Nezhenko's telegram had specified: Baumann's age and demeanour, his wife, how they lived, the factory, the proud history. Not a word about swage wire, only 'plays a crucial part in German rearmament production.'

And there had been only three for dinner. Marta Haecht he would not give them.

Had the *apparat* known what it was getting, Szara reasoned, they'd have sent real officers. No, this was somebody who'd been informed of a potential opportunity in Berlin, somebody who'd told his assistant, *Oh send Szara up there*, figuring he'd let them know if he came across something useful. That was the nature of the intelligence landscape as he understood it: in a world of perpetual night, a thousand signals flickered in the darkness, some would change the world, others were meaningless, or even dangerous. Not even an organization the size of the NKVD could examine all, so now and then it called on a knowledge-able friend.

The people at the embassy had been told to expect him, they took his report without comment. Then they informed him he was to return to Moscow. On the Soviet merchant vessel *Kolstroi*, departing Rostock, on the Bay of Pomerania, at five in the afternoon on 30 November. That was four days away. *Recall to Moscow*. Szara had to fight for equilib-rium. The phrase sometimes meant arrest; the request to return was polite enough, but once they had you back in the country . . . *No*. Not him, and not now. He could anticipate some fairly uncomfortable interrogations. By 'friends' who would show up at his apartment bringing vodka and food – that was, at least, the usual method: *so glad to have you back, you must tell us everything about your trip.*

You really must.

He calmed himself down, decided not to think about it, and left the embassy with a pocket full of money and a determined heart, the twin pillars of espionage.

Were they watching him? The Foreign Department group? The Renate Braun group? He assumed they were – they'd certainly, thank God, been with him on the journey from Prague to Berlin. A lot of them.

He knew just enough, he thought, to lose a surveillance. Three hours it took – museums, train stations, department stores, taxis, trams, and restaurants with back doors. At last arriving, alone as far as he could tell, at an antique shop. Here he bought a painting, oil on canvas, dated 1909, in a heavy gilt frame. By one Professor Ebendorfer, the proprietor rather haughtily informed him, of the University of Heidelberg. A four-by-three-foot rectangle, the painting was executed in the Romantic style: a Greek youth, a shepherd, sat cross-legged at the foot of a broken column and played his pipe whilst his flock grazed nearby, a rich blue sky was studded with fleecy clouds, snow-capped mountains rose in the distance. *Huldigung der Naxos*, it was called – *Homage to Naxos* – and Professor Ebendorfer had signed it artfully in the lower right corner, on a laurel bush beset by a nibbling ram.

Back in the room at the narrow house, Szara went seriously to work, as he should have done all along.

And since he was not looking for anything in particular, simply performing a mechanical task that left his mind in a rather listless, neutral state, he eventually found everything. He immediately wished he hadn't. It was poison he found: the knowledge that kills. But there it was. He'd meant only to leave the original dossier, which would not pass a Russian border inspection, in Berlin, and carry with him to Moscow a condensed document, in a personal shorthand, of facts and circumstances. Using a cipher of contemporary dates and meaningless cities for the ones in the dossier, he believed he could get it past the NKVD border guards as 'journalist's notes'. These guards were not at all the NKVD types who worked in foreign political affairs – they were thorough, uncorruptible, and dull. He could handle them.

The job he set himself was like adding columns of figures – but it was this very exercise in brainless transposition that raised the answer above the horizon. Szara was accustomed to writer's thinking: the flash of insight or the revealing perspective produced by the persistent mind. Copying, he'd thought, was idiot's work. So now he learned a lesson.

To organize the effort he began at the beginning and proceeded, in a table of events, week by week, month by month. Without really meaning to, he'd fashioned what intelligence officers called a chron, short for chronology. For in that discipline *what* and *who* were of great interest, but it was often *when* that produced usable information.

Before the revolution, Bolshevik contact with the Okhrana was common enough. Between revolutionaries and government special services there is almost always a relationship, sometimes covert, sometimes not. It might be said that they spend so very much time thinking and scheming about each other that it becomes their inevitable destiny to meet, and both write such connections off to intelligence-gathering. The illusion of virginity is thereby maintained.

But DUBOK far exceeded the bounds of normalcy in this relationship, bought his safety with his comrades' lives, and was nurtured by the Okhrana like the most tender sprout imaginable. For him they duplicated the grim reality of the revolutionary experience but took care to buffer it, to draw its teeth. He went, like all the underground operatives, to jail and, like many others, escaped. But duration told the tale. They put him in Bailov prison, in Baku (he spent his time learning German), but had him out four months later. Exile, too, he had to experience, but it was to Solvychegodsk they sent him, in the north of European Russia, and not to Siberia. And he 'escaped' after only four months. Lucky, this DUBOK. Two years later he was 'caught' again, then sent back to finish his term in Solvychegodsk but tired of it after six months: long enough to hear what other exiles had to say, long enough to maintain his credibility as a Bolshevik operative, then, a man on a string, home again.

DUBOK, it became clear, was a criminal, was possessed of a criminal mind. His method never varied: he softened those around him by saying what they wanted to hear – he had a superb instinct for what that might be – then sacrificed them as necessary. He exploited weakness, emasculated strength, and never hesitated to indulge his own substantial cowardice. The Okhrana officer, Szara came to realize, manipulated DUBOK effortlessly because of a lifetime spent in the company of criminals. He understood them, understood them so well that he'd come to feel a sort of sorrowful affection for them. With time he developed the instincts of a priest: evil existed; the task was to work productively within its confines.

The officer, if one read between the lines, was profoundly interested in DUBOK's effect on Bolshevik intellectuals. These men and women were often brilliant, knew science, languages, poetry, philosophy. DUBOK, for them, was a kind of symbol, a beloved creature from the lower depths, an enlightened thug, and their comradeship with him confirmed them as members of a newly reordered society. A political scientist, a philosopher, an economist, a poet, could only make revolution if they shared their destiny with a criminal. He was the official representative of *the real world*. Thus they advanced his standing at every opportunity. And DUBOK knew it. And DUBOK loathed them for it. Understanding condescension with every bone in his body, taking revenge at his leisure, proving that equality was in their minds, not his, as he obliterated them.

Now Szara had known from the beginning he had in his hands a Georgian and, when his perfectly capable mind finally bothered to do arithmetic, a Georgian at least fifty-five years old with a history of revolutionary work in Tbilisi and Baku. It could have been any one of a number of candidates, including the leaders of the Georgian *khvost*, but, as Szara worked laboriously through the dossier, these were eliminated by DUBOK himself. For the benefit of the Okhrana, DUBOK had written out a description of his friend Ordjonikidze. Eighteen months later he mentioned the Armenian terrorist Ter Petrossian, seen taking part in a bank 'expropriation' in Baku; referred, a few pages later, to the good-natured Abel Yenukidze; and spoke harshly against his hated enemy, Mdivani. In May of 1913, he was pressed to organize a situation in which the revolutionary Beria might be compromised, but DUBOK never quite managed to do more than talk about that.

After a day and a half, André Szara could no longer avoid the truth: this was Koba himself, Iosif Vissarionovich Dzhugashvili, son of a savage, drunken cobbler from Gori, the sublime leader Stalin. For eleven years, from 1906 to 1917, he had been the Okhrana's pet pig, snouting up the most rare and delicious truffles that the underground so thoughtlessly hid from its enemies.

This room, Szara thought, staring out at the grey sky over Berlin, *too much happens in it* He rose from the desk, stretched to ease his back, lit a cigarette, walked to the window. The lady in silks was rustling about downstairs, doing whatever mysterious things she did all day. Below, on the pavement, an old man was holding the leash of a grizzled Alsatian dog while it sprayed the base of a street lamp.

Szara spent part of Sunday morning removing a soiled sheet of cotton cloth that sealed the back of *Huldigung der Naxos*, then distributing the sheets of the Okhrana dossier across the back of the painting itself, securing them with brown cord tied off to the heads of tiny nails he pounded in with a tack hammer. The cotton cloth he refitted with great care, the bent nails installed by the original framer repositioned in the dents and rust tracks they'd formed over the years. The weight of the heavy gilded frame concealed the presence of the paper, he thought, and *a hundred years from now, some art restorer . . .*

On Monday he was, for the first time, on stage as a German, speaking with slow deliberation, purging the Yiddish lilt from his accent, hoping to pass for a mildly unusual individual born somewhere far away from Berlin. He found that if he combed his hair straight back off his forehead, tied his tie very tight, and carried his chin in a position that, to him, felt particularly high, the disguise was credible. He took the name Grawenske, suggesting distant Slavic or Wendish origins, not at all uncommon in Germany.

He telephoned the office of an auctioneer and was given the name of a warehouse that specialized in the storage of fine art ('Humidity is your enemy!' the man told him). Herr Grawenske appeared there at eleven promptly, explained that he was joining the accounting staff of a small Austrian chemical company in Chile, muttered about his wife's sister who would be occupying his residence, and left Professor Ebendorfer's masterpiece in their care, to be crated, then stored. He paid for two years, a surprisingly reasonable amount of money, gave a fictitious address in Berlin, and was handed a receipt. The remainder of the officer's effects, and the fine satchel, were distributed to shops that supported charity missions.

Marta Haecht had given him the phone number at the little magazine where she 'helped out the art director'. Szara tried to call several times, chilled to the bone as the flat Berlin dusk settled down on the city. The first time, she'd gone on an errand to the printers. The second time, somebody giggled and said they didn't know where she'd got to. On the third try, close to quitting time, she came to the phone.

'I'm leaving tomorrow,' he said. 'May I see you tonight?'

'There is a dinner. My parents' wedding anniversary.'

'Then late.'

She hesitated. 'I'll be returning home . . .'

What? Then he understood there were people near the telephone. 'Home from a restaurant?'

'No, it isn't that.'

'Home to sleep.'

'It would be better.'

'What time is the dinner over?'

'One can't rush away. I hope you'll understand. It is a, it is an occasion, festive . . .'

'Oh.'

'Do you have to go away tomorrow?'

'It can't be helped.'

'Then I don't see how . . .'

'I'll wait for you. Maybe there's a way.'

'I'll try.'

Just after eleven the doorbell rang. Szara raced downstairs, hurried past the landlady's door – opened the width of an eye – and let her in. In the little room, she took off her coat. An aura of the cold night clung to her skin, he could feel it. She was wearing a midnight blue party dress, taffeta, with ruffles. The back was all tiny hooks and eyes. 'Be careful,' she said as he fumbled. 'I mustn't stay too long. Here it is not done to leave a party.'

'What did you tell them?'

'That a friend was going away.'

It was not a magic night. They made love, but the tension in her did not break. Afterwards she was sad. 'Maybe I shouldn't have come. Sweeter to have a memory of the snow.' With the tips of his fingers he pushed the hair back off her forehead. 'I'll never see you again,' she said. She bit her lip to keep from crying.

He walked her home, almost to the door. They kissed good-bye, dry and cold, and there was nothing to say.

In the late November of 1937, the Soviet merchant vessel *Kolstroi* shipped anchor in the port of Rostock, moved slowly up the Warne-münde inlet into Lübeck bay and, swinging north into the Baltic and setting a north-by-easterly course to skirt the Sasenitz peninsula and pass south of the Danish isle of Bornholm, made for Leningrad harbour, some eight hundred and forty nautical miles away.

The *Kolstroi*, heavily laden with machine tools, truck tyres, and bar aluminium loaded at the French port of Boulogne, docked at Rostock only to complete its complement of eleven passengers bound for Leningrad. Moving up the Warnemünde in gathering darkness, the *Kolstroi* sounded its foghorn continually, joining a chorus of in- and outbound freighters as it reached Lübeck bay, where the Baltic fogbanks rolled in towards shore in the stiff northerly winds. André Szara and the other passengers were not allowed the freedom of the deck until the ship was beyond the German territorial limit. When Szara did seek the air, after the close quarters of the ship's lounge where they were fed supper, there was little visibility, nothing of the lights on the German coast, only black water heaving in November swells and a building gale that drove iced salt spray onto the metal plates of the deck, where it froze into a lead-coloured glaze. He bore it as long as he could, staring into the fog whipping past the ship's lights, unable to see land.

The *Kolstroi* was Soviet territory; he'd bowed under the vast weight of it before they ever sailed, his possessions spread out on a table under the cold eyes of a security officer. *The journalist Szara* meant nothing to this one, *Homo Staliens*, a clock disguised as a human. He was thankful he had disposed of the Okhrana dossier before he left Berlin – memory itself was frightening in the atmosphere aboard the freighter.

The passengers were a mixed group. There were three English

university students, with creamy skins and bright eyes, terribly earnest young men on a dream voyage to what they believed to be their spiritual homeland. There was one middle-aged trade representative, suffering from an illness – attempted escape, Szara thought – who was dragged on board by NKVD operatives. The tips of his shoes scraped the wooden gangplank as they carried him onto the ship – obviously he had been drugged senseless. He was not the only passenger going home to die. They were a strange brotherhood, silent, self-contained, having abandoned themselves to a fate they deemed inevitable; the man who'd been dragged on board proved the futility of flight. They rarely slept, greedy for their remaining hours of introspection, pacing about the deck when they could stand the cold, their lips moving as they rehearsed imagined conversations with their interrogators.

Mostly they avoided one another. A conversation with a tainted diplomat or scientist would be reported by the attentive security men and, how was one to know, might be made evidence in the cases against them, telling evidence, uncovered only in the last hours of the journey home – *we thought you were clean until we saw you talking to Petrov* – and dangerously sweet to the NKVD appetite for the fatal irony.

Szara spoke to one of them, Kuscinas, in younger days an officer in the Lettish rifle brigades that supported Lenin when he overthrew the Kerensky government, now an old man with a shaved head and a face like a skull. Yet there was still great strength in Kuscinas; his eyes glittered from deep in their sockets, and his voice was strong enough to hear above the gale. As the *Kolstroi* rose and crashed into the heavy seas off the Gulf of Riga, on the second day of the voyage, Szara found shelter under a stairway where they could smoke cigarettes and shield themselves from the bitter wind. Kuscinas never said exactly what he did, simply waved his hand when Szara asked, meaning that such things didn't matter. As for what was about to happen to him, he seemed to be beyond caring. 'For my wife I'm sorry, but that's all. Foolish woman, and stubborn. Unfortunately she loves me and this will break her heart, but there's nothing to be done about it. My sons they've turned into snakes, all the better for them now, I think, and my daughter married some idiot who pretends to run a factory in Kursk. They'll find a way to disown me, if they haven't done it already. I'm sure they will sign anything put before them. My wife, though . . .'

'She'll have to go to friends,' Szara said.

The old man grimaced. 'Friends,' he said.

The *Kolstroi*'s steel plates creaked as the ship pitched particularly high, then slammed down into the trough, sending aloft a huge explosion of white spray. 'And fuck you too,' Kuscinas said to the Baltic.

Szara steadied himself against the iron wall and closed his eyes for a moment.

'You're not going to give it up, are you?'

He flicked his cigarette away. 'No,' he said, 'I'm a sailor.'

'Will they arrest you?'

'Perhaps. I don't think so.'

'You have the right friends, then.'

Szara nodded that he did.

'Lucky. Or maybe not,' Kuscinas said. 'By the time you get to Moscow they may be the wrong friends. These days you can't predict.' For a time he was silent, eyes inward, seeing some part of his life. 'You're like me, I suppose. One of the faithful ones, do what has to be done, don't ask to see the sense of it. Discipline above all.' He shook his head sorrowfully. 'And in the end, when it's our turn, and somebody else is doing what has to be done, somebody else who doesn't ask to see the sense of it, the discipline of the executioner, then all we can say is *za chto?* – why? What for?' Kuscinas laughed. 'A sorry little question,' he said. 'For myself, I don't mean to ask it.'

That night, Szara couldn't sleep. He lay in his bunk and smoked, the man across from him mumbling restlessly in his dreams. Szara knew the history of that question, *Za chto?* Rumour attributed its initial use to the Old Bolshevik Yacov Lifschutz, a deputy people's commissar. His final word. Szara remembered him as a little man with wild eyebrows, the obligatory goatee, and a twinkling glance. Shuffling down the tile corridor in the basement of the Lubianka – you got it on the way, nobody ever reached the end of that corridor – he stopped for a moment and turned to his executioner, an officer he happened to have known in childhood, and said, '*Za chto?*'

Along with the purge, the word spread everywhere; it was scrawled on the walls of cells, carved in the wooden benches of the Stolypin wagons that hauled prisoners away, scratched into planks in transit camps. Almost always the first words spoken to the police who came in the night, then again the first words of a man or a woman entering a crowded cell. 'But why? Why?'

We are all alike, Szara thought. We don't offer excuses or alibis, we don't fight with the police, we don't for compassion, we don't even plead. We don't fear death; we always counted on it – in the revolution, the civil war. All we ask, rational men that we are, is to see the sense of the thing, its meaning. Then we'll go. Just an explanation. Too much to ask?

Yes.

The savagery of the purge, Szara knew, gave them every reason to believe there was, must be, a reason. When a certain NKVD officer was taken away, his wife wept. So she was accused of resisting arrest. Such events, common, daily, implied a scheme, an underlying plan. They wanted only to be let in on it – certainly their own deaths bought them the right to an answer – and then they'd simply let the rest of it happen. What was one more trickle of blood on a stone floor to those who'd seen it flow in streams across the dusty streets of a nation? The only insult was ignorance, a thing they'd never tolerated, a thing they couldn't bear now.

In time, the cult of *Za chto* began to evolve a theory. Particularly with the events of June 1937, when the only remaining alternative to the rule of the dictator was ripped to shreds. That June came the turn of the Red Army and, when the smoke cleared, it was seen to be headless, though still walking around. Marshal Tukachevsky, acknowledged as Russia's greatest soldier, was joined in his disappearance by two of four remaining marshals, fourteen of sixteen military commanders, eight of eight admirals, sixty of sixty-seven corps commanders, on and on and on. All eleven vice-commissars of defence, seventy-five of the eighty members of the Supreme Military Soviet. All of this, they reasoned – the shootings, the icebound mining camps, an army virtually destroyed by its own country – could have only one intention: Stalin simply sought to remove any potential opposition to his own rule. That was the way of tyrants: first eliminate enemies, then friends. This was an exercise in consolidation. On a rather grand scale, ultimately counted in millions – but what was Russia if not a grand scale?

What was Russia, if not a place where one could say, down through the centuries, times and men are evil, and so we bleed. This, for some, concluded the matter. The Old Bolsheviks, the Chekists, the officer corps of the Red Army – these people *were* the revolution but now had to be sacrificed so that the Great Leader could stand unthreatened and supreme. Russia's back was broken, her spirit drained, but at least for most the question had been answered and they could get on with the trivial business of execution with acceptance and understanding. A final gesture on behalf of the party.

But they were wrong, it wasn't quite that simple.

There were some who understood that, not many, only a few, and soon enough they died and, in time, so did their executioners, and, later, theirs.

The following day, Szara did not see Kuscinas. Then, when the *Kolstroi* steamed up the Gulf of Finland, the first ice of the season pinging against the hull, the lights of the fortress at Kronstadt twinkling in the darkness, the security men and sailors began a frantic search, combing the ship, but Kuscinas had gone, and they could not find him.

8 Rue
Delesseux

The OPAL Network – 1938 – Brussels/Paris/Berlin

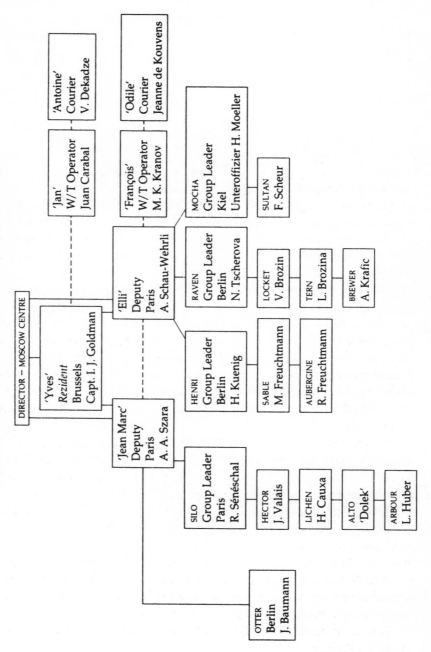

'André Aronovich! Over here!'

An urgent female voice, cutting through the uproar of a densely packed crowd in the living room of an apartment in the Mochovaya district. Szara peered through the smoke and saw a hand waving at him. 'Pardon,' he said. 'So sorry. Excuse me.' He chose an indirect route towards the hand and voice, swinging wide to avoid the dangerous elbows of those who had managed to break through to the buffet. Moscow was ravaged by shortages of nearly everything, but here there was black Servuga, grilled lamb, pirozhki, salted peas, stacks of warm blini, and platters of smoked salmon. What you had, then, was desperation: a roomful of *apparatchiks*, mandarins of agriculture and road planning, timber and foreign policy, as well as the security services, trying to feed themselves for the week to come. More than one pocket was stuffed with meat, smoked fish, even butter – whatever one could swipe.

For an instant, Szara caught sight of a vaguely familiar face that appeared over the shoulder of a naval officer, then vanished in the crowd. A sophisticated woman, lightly made up, with simple but stylishly managed hair and dangling silver earrings.

He figured it out just about the time they found each other: a curiously altered Renate Braun, wearing a full blouse of lime-coloured silk and the modestly coquettish smile one saw in films of cocktail parties. 'Heavens, what a crowd!' she said, brushing his cheek with hers – a dear friend one simply doesn't see often enough. Last seen slicing up a dead man's trouser cuffs with a razor blade in an Ostend whorehouse, here was an entirely different version of the woman.

'You must meet Mr Herbert Hull,' she gushed, speaking in German-accented English.

Now Szara noticed that she had in tow a tall, sandy-haired man with a weather-beaten face and wildly overgrown eyebrows. He was perhaps in his late forties and, from his casual, loose-jointed posture, evidently American. He was smoking, with difficulty, a poorly rolled *makhorka* cigarette, a self-conscious attempt to be part of the local scenery, Szara thought. 'Herb Hull,' he said. He had a powerful grip and sought something in Szara's eyes when they shook hands.

'Herb has been so anxious to meet you,' Renate Braun said.

'We all know André Szara,' Hull said. 'I'm a great fan of your work, Mr Szara.'

'Oh but you must call him André.'

'Yes. Please.'

Szara's English was at best uncertain. He was going to sound awful, hesitant and somehow importunate – an impression often created when Slavs spoke English. He already felt a hatefully ingratiating smile creeping over his face.

'Herb's an editor with a new American magazine. A very important undertaking. You'll know him, of course, from when he was with the *Nation* and the *New Republic*.'

'Ah yes.' Szara knew the names, prayed he wouldn't be questioned about specific articles. The anxious smile grew. 'Of course. Importantly.'

Szara saw Renate Braun wince, but plunged ahead. 'You are liking Russia?'

'Never the same place two days in a row, things go wrong, but there's a strength in the people that's irresistible.'

'Ach!' – mock horror from Renate Braun – 'he knows us too well.'

Hull smiled and shrugged. 'Trying to learn, at any rate. That's what we need. Firsthand knowledge, a feel for the real Russia.'

'I am certain that André can help you with that, Herb. Positive.'

'Yes?' Szara said.

'Why not?' Hull's eyebrows rose. 'After all, I'm an editor, you're a writer. For a new magazine, well, a Russian writer speaking about the USSR would be a change, change for the better I'm inclined to think. No?'

'Ah, but my English.'

'No problem, André. We'd be happy to do the translation, or it could be done here. Won't be perfect, but we'll guarantee to preserve the sense of it.'

'I am honoured,' Szara said. He was. The thought of appearing in a respected journal before an American audience, not the usual *Daily Worker* crowd, was immensely pleasing. Ilya Ehrenburg, *Pravda*'s number one correspondent, had done it, occupying the journalistic territory in the Spanish Civil War so effectively that Szara was virtually restricted to other parts of Europe.

Hull let the offer sink in, then went on. 'Renate tells me you're working on a historical piece that might be right up our alley. I won't kid you, running something like that would get us the attention we need. And we'll pay for it. Won't be Hollywood, of course, but I think you'll find us competitive in the New York market.'

Renate Braun seemed quite excited by the prospect. 'We've even discussed a title, André Aronovich.'

Szara stared at her. What was she talking about?

'Just discussed,' Hull broke in. He knew what a certain look on a writer's face meant. 'Working title is all it is, but I can tell you it caught my attention.'

'Title?'

Renate Braun said, 'The piece must be exciting – our plan fulfilment norms won't do, I suspect. It must have . . .' She looked at Hull for the word.

'Intrigue?'

'Yes. That's it. Intrigue! A story of Russia's revolutionary past, its secret history. We aren't completely sure what it is you're working on – you writers keep close with ideas – but we thought perhaps something on the order of "The Okhrana's Mysterious Man".' She turned to Hull. 'Yes? It's good English?'

'Yes indeed. Good enough to put on the cover, I'd say.'

Szara repeated the title in Russian. Renate Braun nodded vigorously. 'Your English is better than you think, André Aronovich.'

'Of course,' Hull said, 'you can always use a pen name if you like, I'm not unaware how easy it is to get into trouble these days. We'd rather have your name, of course, but we'll protect your identity if that makes you more comfortable.'

Szara just stared. How much did this man know? Did he have any idea what happened to people who played such games? Was he brave? Stupid? Both?

'Well, André, would you consider it?' Hull asked, eyes keen, head tilted inquiringly to one side, gauging his quarry.

'How could he not?' Renate Braun said. 'Such an opportunity!'

Szara walked for a long time that night. His tiny apartment in Volnitzky Alley wasn't far from the house where the party had been given, so he circled the centre of the city, crossing the icebound river, a lone, January figure in fur hat and overcoat. He kept an eye out for *bezprizorniye*, bands of children orphaned by the purge who attacked and robbed solitary walkers of their money and clothing – you might just as easily freeze to death if your head wasn't bashed in – but it was evidently too cold for hunting.

Sooner or later, he thought *things fall into place and, often as not, you'd rather they hadn't.* Now the long leash in Prague and Berlin made sense. They were letting him have his time with the dossier, counting on the fact that he'd stick his curious writer's nose into the business. Seen externally, a well-known journalist had sniffed out a big story which, in the normal way of things, he'd tell the world. They'd protected him when the Georgian *khvost* operatives had him taken off the train, then left him free to work.

And now they were rather casually asking him to commit suicide.

Was it too much to ask? That one life should be sacrificed so that hundreds, perhaps thousands, might survive? All he need do was practise his natural trade. Who was the Okhrana's mysterious man? Well, we know a few small details. A, B, C, and D. A new and provocative enigma from enigmatic Russia. Perhaps, someday, we'll learn his real identity. Yours truly, André Szara. (Please omit flowers.)

Or, oh yes, the pen name. *Boris Ivanov has served in the Soviet diplomatic corps.* That would surely throw the NKVD off the scent. For perhaps a month. Or maybe a year. Not much longer.

Still, it would certainly communicate a point of view:

We know what you did and we can prove it, now stop killing us or we'll finish you. Blackmail. Plain old-fashioned politics. Ancient as time.

He admired the plan, though he felt more than a little chagrin over his apparently boundless capacity for self-deception. Certain things now made sense. On the train to Prague, General Bloch had told him, albeit obliquely, just what they had in mind for him. Szara had triumphantly misunderstood him, of course, taking delicately phrased information to be some sort of pompous philosophy, a homily.

With some difficulty Szara won back from his memory the general's statements: 'Some men, in such circumstances, might be careless of their lives. Such men rise to an opportunity. And then we have a hero!' In an empty street coated with grey ice, Szara laughed out loud. Bloch had said something about Szara's attitude towards himself after pointing out, dexterously enough, that he had neither wife nor children. What else? Oh yes. 'To be a writer requires work and sacrifice, to follow any road wherever it may lead.'

Yes. Well. Now one knew where it led. Just as one knew in 1917 when one was twenty and what did death matter. From the beginning, in the park in Ostend, Szara had sensed his fate. He'd dodged a time or two, yet here it was, back again. The Szara that Bloch found on the train was, like his revolutionary brethren, a man who had no business being alive, a man who had evaded the inevitable just long enough.

Suddenly, the walls of his irony collapsed and real anguish struck his heart. He stopped cold, his face twisted with pain and anger; a sob rose to the base of his throat and stuck there – he had to bite his lip to keep from howling the dreaded question directly at God and the streets of Moscow:

Why now?

Because *now* everything was different. Bloch had met a certain kind of man on the train to Prague but *now* he was not that man. He was instead that man who presses his face against the skin of a woman to inhale such fragrance as makes him want to cry out with joy. He was that man who spins between tenderness and raging lust like a helpless top, who wakes up on fire every morning, who spends his hours thinking of only one thing – yet how brilliantly he thinks of it!

He recovered. Regained himself, breathed deeply, resumed walking. The wall inside him must not be breached: it kept in, it kept out. He had to have it to survive.

He realized that the frost had stolen the feeling from his face and he turned towards home, walking quickly. Later he scalded his mouth with tea while sitting in his overcoat and fur hat at the table his wife, only a few months before she died, had insisted he put by the kitchen window. It had been a lovely table, an absurdly ornamental cherrywood thing with heavy, scrollworked legs. Using it in the kitchen they'd ruined it, of course. Now it was a place to watch the white dawn come up over the chimneys of Moscow, thin smoke standing motionless in the dead, frozen air.

Szara's interrogation – a form of debriefing for those cooperating with the special services – was the province of his official 'friend' in Moscow, Abramov. Nonetheless, an interrogation. And the fact that it was supervised by a friend made it, as the *apparat* intended, worse not better – a system that turned friends into hostages held against the subject's honesty. If you lied, and your interrogator believed it, and then they caught you lying, you were both finished: de facto conspirators. Maybe you didn't care to save your own miserable life, but perhaps you'd think twice about murdering a friend.

Szara lied.

Sergei Abramov lived in the higher reaches of the NKVD Foreign Department, a confidant of the godlings Shpigelglas and Sloutsky if not officially their equal. He would arrive at Szara's apartment every day at about eleven with egg sandwiches wrapped in newspaper, a paper sack of tea, sometimes vodka, occasionally little almond cakes with a sticky coating of honey that had you licking your fingers while you answered questions. He was a thickset, bulky man, handsome in his bulk, in a much-worn blue pinstripe suit, the jacket buttoned across his belly over a rippling vest with a gold watch chain stretched from pocket to pocket. Abramov had sharp eyes that caught the light, a broken nose, a black homburg that he never removed, and a full black beard that gave him the air of a successful operatic baritone – an artist used to getting his own way and certain to create havoc if he didn't. He would sit on a kitchen chair with his knees apart, place a cigarette between his lips, light it with a long, wooden match, then half close his eyes as he listened to you, apparently on the verge of sleep. Often he made a small noise, a grunt that might mean all sorts of things: sympathy – *what a time you've had of it* — or disbelief, perhaps an acknowledgment that what you said was true, perhaps the groan of a man too often deceived. It was in fact a stratagem, meant nothing, and Szara knew it.

Abramov spoke in a low, hoarse rumble, a voice rich with sorrow at having found all humankind to be the most absurd collection of liars and rogues. Posing a question, his face was filled with gloom. Like a teacher who knows his hopeless pupils will offer only wrong answers, Abramov was an interrogator whose subjects never told the truth. The method was ingenious. Szara understood and admired it but nevertheless felt the powerful undertow it created: he found himself wanting to please Abramov, to offer such resoundingly honest statements that the man's sour view of the world would be swept away by idealism reborn.

Alert to Abramov's dangerous gift, the ability to stimulate the essential human desire to please, Szara laid out his defences with care. To begin with, resistance. Later, a strategic submission, giving up everything but that which mattered most: Marta Haecht and all the signposts that pointed to her existence. Thus Szara's description of dinner at the Villa Baumann was laden with detail while the cast of characters was decreased by one. On visiting the wire mill he encountered the chief engineer, called Haecht, the man who might become the nominal owner of the company. A technician, Szara said, not anybody they could work with. Abramov grunted at that but did not pursue it.

Bloch and Renate Braun he assigned to the second, the confessional, stage, thus restricting the initial part of the interrogation to writing the dockworkers' story in Antwerp, an uneventful journey to Prague, conditions in that city, and his rejected dispatch on the potential abandonment of Czechoslovakia. Baumann's revelation on the manufacture of swage wire he reported in perfect detail and was rewarded by a series of appreciative grunts. This ground was then covered a second time – Abramov's probing was artful, ingenious, a series of mirrors revealing every possible surface of the exchange. As for Khelidze, Szara described the conversations aboard the *Nicaea*, omitting their final confrontation in Ostend.

Until Monday of the second week, when Abramov began to show signs of restlessness. Interrogations always revealed something, something even better than a little orgy with a nightclub *animateur*. So? Where was it? Had he at last met a true saint? Szara caved in, warned elliptically that he now needed to say things that could not be said in a Moscow apartment. Abramov nodded sorrowfully, a physician coming at last upon the feared diagnosis, and touched his lips with his index finger. 'You've done well today, André Aronovich,' he said for the benefit of the listeners. 'Let us adjourn to the Metropol for a change of scenery.'

But, crunching through the fresh snow on Kusnetzki Most, they passed the Hotel Metropol and its popular café – where *apparat* operatives were in abundance – and entered instead a grimy hole-in-the-wall on a side street. Abramov ordered *viesni*, parfaits, which were served in chipped, greyish coffee cups but swam in fresh cream.

Szara told stage two: the corpse in the hotel, the receipt, the satchel, General Bloch, the dossier, and the American magazine editor. Abramov was a study in acute discomfort. Every word of Szara's took him deeper into the affair and he knew it – his face knotted with pain, the encouraging grunts became groans of horror, he signalled for more *viesni*, swore in Yiddish, drummed his thick fingers on the tabletop. When Szara finally wound down he sighed. 'André Aronovich, what have you done?'

Szara shrugged. How was he to have known that his orders did not come from Abramov or his associates? The second group based their play on that very assumption.

'I absolve you,' Abramov rumbled. 'But I am the least of your problems. I doubt the Georgians will shoot you in Moscow, but it would be wise to watch what you eat here, and stay away from high windows. It's a commonplace of ours; anyone can commit a murder, but suicide requires an artist. They have such artists. However, the fact that they've left you alone this long means they're scheming. This too they do very expertly. After all, they are our Sicilians, these southerners, and their feuds end only one way. Apparently, they have their own plans for the Okhrana material, and have not informed the Great Leader or his official toads; thus you remain alive. Of course, if you were to publish such an article . . .'

'Then what shall be done?'

Abramov rumbled.

'Nothing?'

Abramov thought for a moment, spooned the last of his *viesni* from the coffee cup. 'This *khvost* business is a little more complicated than meets the eye. Yes, things *have* happened, but. Instance: two years ago, at the trial of Lev Rosenfeld and Grigory Radomilsky – "Kamenev" and "Zinoviev" – the prosecutor Vyshinsky, in his summation to the judges, said an odd thing, something that sticks in the mind. He called them "men without a fatherland". He would claim that he meant they'd betrayed, as Trotskyites, their country. But we've heard that kind of thing before, and we know what it means, just as it's said very openly in Germany, not so quietly in Poland, and has been said in all sorts of places for a very long time.

'Still, if somebody simply yearned to believe Vyshinsky, and such people exist, let them consider the case of the diplomat Rosengolts. They played with him like a cat with a mouse: released him from all official positions and let him stew for many weeks. He knew what was coming, for a certainty, but the *apparat* let it fester so that every day became a hundred hours long. This was hardest on his wife, a happy sort of person, not worldly, not so educated, from a typical *shtetl* somewhere in the Pale. Over a period of months, the waiting destroyed her, and when the NKVD searched Rosengolts after they finally got around to arresting him, they found she'd written out a charm against misfortune, the Sixty-eighth and Ninety-first psalms, secreted it within a piece of dry bread, wrapped it in a cloth, then sewed it into his pocket.

'At the trial, Vyshinsky made much humour of this pathetic little piece of paper. He read the psalms, such as, "For He shall deliver thee from the snare of the hunter: and from the noisome pestilence. He shall defend thee under His wings and thou shalt be safe under His feathers: His faithfulness and truth shall be thy shield and buckler. Thou shalt not be afraid for any terror by night: nor for the arrow that flieth by day." You see what she'd done. Vyshinsky spoke these words in a tone of savage contempt, then asked Rosengolts how the paper had got into his pocket. He admitted his wife put it there and told him it was for good luck. Vyshinsky pressed him on the point, mentioning "good luck" again and again, until the spectators in the court-room were roaring with laughter and Vyshinsky turned and winked at them.

'Very well, you'll say, the case is made. The purge is really a pogrom. But is it? Is this really true? Maybe not. The Section for Extraordinary Matters is headed by I. I. Shapiro – so if Jews are being purged, the purge is, often, guided by Jews. Now we come to the people who've involved you in their operation. General Bloch is a Jew, granted, though I should mention he is in military intelligence, the GRU, and not the NKVD – a fact you might keep in mind. Renate Braun is a German, likely from one of the Protestant sects, and she has nothing to do with the NKVD. She is a *spez* – a foreign specialist – employed by Mezhdunarodnaya Kniga, the State Publishing House, where she works on the publication of German texts to be smuggled into Germany. That clearly associates her with the Comintern.

'What I'm saying is this: consider the intelligence services as an ocean. Now consider the currents that might be found in it, some running one way, some another, side by side for a time, then diverging. So new? Nothing's new. It would be so at U.S. Steel or the British telephone company. In work there is competition, alliance, betrayal. Unhappily, when an intelligence *apparat* plays these games, they are equipped with very sharp tools, vast and practical experience, and the level of play can be frightful. A journalist, any normal citizen, will simply be eaten alive. What do we have here? A political battle between nationalist interests? Or a pogrom? They're not the same thing.

'If a pogrom, a very quiet one. Of course Stalin cannot afford, politically, to estrange the Jews of the world because we have many friends among them. You know the old saying: *they join the ideology.* And now, with the birth of a hideous monster in Germany, they are mad to take action, any action, against fascism. This is, you understand, a useful circumstance for people in my profession. One can ask favours. Is Stalin capable of running a secret pogrom? Yes. And he would have to do it that way in the present political climate. Therefore, it's not so easy to pin down.

'Meanwhile, you. Drawn into an operation you cannot survive, yet I take it you wish to do so. You seem different, I might add. Changed. Not quite the cynical bastard I've known all these years. Why is that? All right, you had a close call; the Turk, Ismailov, almost did your business. Is that it? You looked death in the face and became a new man? Can happen, André Aronovich, but one sees that rarely, sometimes in a grave illness, where a man may ask a favour of his God, but less often in wet affairs. Still, it happened. I'm your friend. I don't ask why. I say what's to be done for poor André Aronovich?

'Now it would be normal to hand Baumann on to one of our operators in Germany – a thousand ways he can be run, even under present Jewish restrictions. He has a love affair, sees a dentist, goes to *shul*, takes a walk in the country and fills a dead-drop or visits his father's grave. Believe me, we can service him.

'On the other hand, we might make a case that he's skittish, nervous, not really committed, which in turn implies special needs in the selection of a case officer. What, in fact, are his motives? I might make a point of asking that question. Is he out to hurt Hitler? Or does he wish to feather a nest if things get worse in Germany? To aid the working classes? To get rich? *Mice*, we say of spies; the *m* stands for money, the *i* for ideology, the *c* for coercion, and the *e* for egotism. Which is it with Baumann? Or is there, we must ask, a fifth letter?

'Prove to me he's not the toy of the Abwehr, or worse, the Referat VI C of the Reichsicherheitshauptamt, the Main Security Office under that insufferable prick Heydrich. Referat VI C is Gestapo counter-espionage both within and outside German borders, Walter Schellenberg's little shop, and Schellenberg is perfectly capable of this sort of dangle – he'll get hold of one end of the thread and pull so slowly and sweetly that you'll see an entire network unravel. Years of work wasted! And, in Moscow, careers destroyed. So I'm suspicious. My job depends on it. I'll surely point out that Szara can't be expected to know whether this is any good or it's the RSHA offering a temptation. What do we know? That a third secretary had a piece of paper slipped in his overcoat pocket while it was in the cloakroom of the opera house and he was suffering through three hours of Wagner. That a journalist had a dinner and heard a proposal and saw a piece of wire. What's that? That's nothing. We Russians have always favoured the *agent provocateur*, our intelligence history is crowded with them, and the Cheka learned the trick the hard way – from the Okhrana. Azeff, Malinovsky, maybe you-know-who himself. So, naturally, we fear it above all things for we know how well it works, how well it tickles our great vulnerability – intelligence officers are like men in love, they want to believe.

'What's the answer? What to do? Abramov is brilliant! *Let Szara do the work*, he says. Make him truly *nash*, our very own. He's been a journalist who does his patriotic duty and, from time to time, undertakes special work; now he'll be one of us, and now and then he'll write something. Kolt'sev, the editor of *Pravda*, is finished – sorry to tell you that, André Aronovich – and Nezhenko, the foreign editor, is no problem. We'll hook Szara up with one of the networks in Western Europe and let him play spymaster.'

Abramov settled back in his chair, put a cigarette in his mouth, and lit it with a long wooden match.

'Do you mean they won't find me in Europe?'

'They'll find you in *hell*. No, that's not what I mean. *We* become your protection, not this *khvost* and not that, the service itself. Your status will be adjusted and narrowly made known. I see Dershani every day, his office is down the hall from mine; we're both citizens of the USSR, we work in the same profession, and we don't shoot each other. I'll let him know, obliquely, that you're doing important work for us. So, hands off. That's an implicit promise from me, by the way, that you're going to be a good boy and not go off involving yourself in conspiracies and pranks. Understood?'

He did understand. Suddenly he stood on the threshold of a new life. One where he'd have to follow orders, trade freedom for survival, and live in a completely different way. Yes, he'd seen this opening after receiving information from Baumann, and quite smug he'd been about it. But the reality tasted awful, and Abramov laughed at his evident discomfort.

'This is a web you climbed into all by yourself, my friend; now don't go cursing the spider.'

'And shall I write for the American magazine?'

'After *I* have protected you? Well, that would be gratitude, wouldn't it. No good deed goes unpunished, Abramov, so here's a knife in the back for you. André Aronovich, you are forty years of age, perhaps it's time you grew up. Ask yourself: why have these people chosen me to do their dirty work? What will it accomplish? If the game is entirely successful and Soso – Joe – hurls himself out a Kremlin window, what is gained? Who takes over? Are you expecting some sort of Russian George Washington to appear? Are you? Look in your heart. No, forget your heart, look in your mind! Do you want to make Adolf Hitler happy? Why do you think anything will happen? Molotov will say "more imperialist lies" and the world will yawn, all except for one journalist, floating face down in a swamp somewhere so that nobody can see what a noble and superior smile he wore when he died.'

Szara felt miserable.

Abramov sighed. 'For the moment,' he said kindly, 'why not just do what everybody else in the world does. Try to get along, do the best you can, hope for a little happiness.' Abramov leaned across the table and patted him reassuringly on the cheek. 'Go to work, André Aronovich. Be a mensch.'

March 1938.

Winter would not go. At night the air froze and the stars did not shimmer, but stood as cold, steady lights in the distance. In the wind, the eyes ran, then tears turned to ice. Indoors it was not much better – when Szara woke in the morning his breath was a white plume against the dark blanket.

It was warmer in Central Europe: Hitler marched into Austria, France and Britain protested, crowds cheered in the Vienna streets, Jews were dragged from hiding, humiliated, and beaten. Sometimes they died from the beatings, sometimes from the humiliation. In Moscow, a new trial: Piatakov, Radek (Sobelsohn), Krestinsky, Yagoda, and Bukharin. Accused of conspiring with Nazi intelligence agents, accused of entering into secret agreements with the German government. The final sentence of Vyshinsky's summation had remained constant for three years: 'Shoot the mad dogs!' And they did.

Szara dragged himself through his days and drank all the vodka he could find, craving anaesthesia that eluded him; only the body went numb. He wanted to call Berlin but it was impossible – no words could leave Moscow. Slowly, the images of the attic room in the narrow house, too often summoned, lost reality. They were now too perfect, like mirages of water in the desert. Angry, lonely, he decided to make love to any woman who came along, but when he met women the signal system went awry and nothing happened.

At Abramov's direction, he attended a series of training schools – an endless repetition of dead-drops, codes and ciphers, forgery, and the construction of false identities. It was all about paper, he realized, a world of paper. Identity cards, passports, embassy cables, maps of defensive positions, order-of-battle reports. A mirror image of a former life, when he'd also lived amid paper.

Sometimes he wrote for Nezhenko; Abramov insisted on that. Stories about progress, always progress; life was getting better and better. What did such drudgery do to the secret spirit that he imagined lived deep within him? Curiously, nothing. For an hour or two it did what it had to do, then returned to its hiding place. He tried a version of 'The Okhrana's Mystery Man' and surprised himself, it positively *blazed*. He burned it.

He did see friends from time to time, those who remained, but no honest thing could be said and the accumulated caution and reserve strangled affection. Still, they met. Sometimes, finding themselves alone and unobserved, they spoke of what they'd seen and heard. Horror stories; separations, disappearances, failures of nerve. The light had gone out, it seemed, the very notion of heroism excised, the world now filled with soft, bruised, frightened people scheming over a few lumps of coal or a spoonful of sugar. You caught fear from friends, like a malady, and they caught it from you, and nobody suggested a cure.

Abramov was a rock, and Szara clung to him like a drowning man. They would sit in a warm office in Dzerzhinsky Square and the officer would teach him what he had to know. The principles of the work couldn't be spelled out precisely, you had to listen to anecdotes until you had an intuitive feel for what was effective and what wasn't. They discussed cities – some operations in Germany were run from neighbouring countries, which meant cities like Geneva, Paris, Luxembourg, Amsterdam, Brussels. Prague was no longer a possibility. Warsaw was extremely dangerous; the Polish services were powerful and deft, had an astute understanding of Soviet operational habits. Brussels was best – espionage, as long as it wasn't aimed at the Belgian government, wasn't even illegal.

Sometimes Abramov took him to meet people; these were momentary, casual occasions, a handshake, a few minutes of conversation. He had the impression of individuals who instantly knew who you were, what you were. He met Dershani in his office: a plain desk, filing cabinets, a dead flower in a glass. The man himself was exceptionally polite; the thin lips smiled. 'I'm very pleased to meet you,' he said. Szara thought about that later. The face was memorable – like looking at a hawk, it was the quality of the eyes that held your attention, suggested a world where they had seen things you hadn't.

He kept busy in the daytime, but the nights were not good. When the icy March show rattled on the window he'd bury himself in blankets and clothing and sometimes his dead wife would visit him, and he would talk to her. Out loud. Talk to an empty room, in a certain quiet, definite language they had devised, a language meant to exclude the world from the fortress of sanity they had built to protect themselves.

They had been married – some might say 'married' – by a Red Army major in 1918. 'Be as one with the new order' was the way he'd blessed the union. Three years later she was dead, and they'd often been separated during that period by the exigencies of civil war. Working as a nurse in the Byelorussian town of Berdichev, she'd written him every day – notes scrawled on newsprint or scraps of paper – then sent a packet through when the postal system functioned. Byelorussia and the Ukraine were then, as always, the storm centres of madness. During the civil war, Berdichev was taken fourteen times, by Petlyura's army, by Denikin's, by Bolshevik units, by Galician irregulars, Polish infantry, Tutnik's bands, Maroussia's rebels, the anarchists under the insane Nestor Makhno – whose cavalry favoured Jewish prayer shawls as saddlecloths – and by what the writer Grossman referred to as 'nobody's Ninth Regiment'. Eventually, somebody had killed her, exactly who or where or under what circumstance he'd never learned.

Despite the long separations, there had been an iron bond between them, as though they were twins. There was nothing he feared to tell her, and nothing she did not understand. In the Moscow nights that March he needed her desperately. It was insane to speak out loud in the empty little apartment – he feared the neighbours, denunciation, so he used his softest voice – but he could not stop doing it. He asked her what to do. She told him to live a day at a time, and to be kind. Somehow this eased his heart and he could fall asleep.

There was one event that month which was to mean a great deal to him later, though at the time it had no special significance. It seemed just one more manifestation of the Great Inexplicable that lay at the heart of Russia, something you had to get used to if you meant to hang on to your sanity in that place. Nezhenko invited him to a semi-official evening at the Café Sport on Tverskaya street. This was principally a gathering of Moscow's foreign community, so there was plenty of food and plenty to drink. At the height of the evening, conversation was quieted by somebody banging a spoon on a glass, then a well-known actor rose to present a recitation. Szara knew him slightly, Poziny, a barrel-chested man with a deeply lined face who played character roles in the Moscow Art Theatre – Szara had seen him do a splendid Uncle Vanya that had brought the audience to its feet for the curtain call.

To cries of Oop-la! a grinning Poziny was hoisted atop a table by the wall. He cleared his throat, gathered the audience to him, then announced he would recite a work by Aleksandr Blok, written in the early days of the Revolution, called *The Scythians*. The Scythians, he explained for the benefit of foreign guests, were the earliest Russian tribe, one of the world's most ancient peoples, known for intricate goldworking and exemplary horsemanship, who inhabited a region north of the Black Sea. While Poziny introduced the poem, several young men and women distributed translations in French, English, and German so that the guests could read along.

Poziny held nothing back. From the first line on, his powerful voice burned with conviction:

> *There are millions of you; of us,*
> *swarms and swarms and swarms.*
>
> *Try and battle against us.*
> *Yes, we are Scythians; yes, Asiatics,*
> *With slanting, greedy eyes.*
> *. . . Oh, old world*
>
> *Russia is a Sphinx. In joy and grief,*
> *And pouring with black blood,*
> *She peers, peers, peers at thee,*
> *With hatred and with love.*

Yes, love, as only our blood can love,
You have forgotten there can be such love
That burns and destroys.

Come to our side. From the horrors of war
Come to our peaceful arms;
Before it is too late, sheathe the old sword.
Comrades, let us be brothers.

And if not, we have nothing to lose.
We, too, can be perfidious if we choose;
And down all time you will be cursed
By the sick humanity of an age to come.

Before comely Europe
Into our thickets and forests we'll disperse,
And then we shall turn upon you
Our ugly Asiatic face.

But we ourselves henceforth shall be no shield of yours,
We ourselves henceforth will enter no battle.
We shall look on with our narrow eyes
When your deadly battles rage.

Nor shall we stir when the ferocious Hun
Rifles the pockets of the dead,
Burns down cities, drives herds into churches,
And roasts the flesh of the white brothers.

This is the last time – bethink thee, old world! –
To the fraternal feast of toil and peace,
The last time – to the bright, fraternal feast
The barbarian lyre now summons thee.

There were several very long seconds of silence; only Poziny's graceful inclination of the head summoned applause that resolved the tension in the room. Everyone there knew what the poem meant, in the early days of the revolution and in March of 1938. Or thought they knew.

The Austrian chemical engineer H. J. Brandt arrived in Copenhagen on the Baltic ferry *Krøn Lindblad* from Tallinn, Estonia, on 4 April, 1938.

The school teacher E. Roberts, from Edinburgh, took the Copenhagen-Amsterdam train, arriving at Amsterdam's Central Station in the early evening of 6 April.

The naturalized Belgian citizen Stefan Leib, of Czechoslovakian origin, got off the Amsterdam train at Brussels towards noon on 7 April, going immediately to the shop called Cartes de la Monde – maps of the world; antique, old, and new – he owned in the rue de Juyssens, in the winding back streets of the old business district.

A serious man, Monsieur Leib, in his early thirties, quiet, somewhat scholarly in his tweed jacket and flannels, and notably industrious. He could be found, most nights, in the small office at the rear of the store at a large oak desk piled high with old maps – perhaps the Netherlands of the seventeenth century, decorated with curly-haired cherubs puffing clouds of wind from the cardinal points of the compass – as well as utilitarian road maps of the Low Countries, France, and Germany; tidal charts, Michelin and Baedeker guides, or the latest rendering of Abyssinia (important if you had followed the fortunes of Italian expeditionary forces), Tanganyika, or French Equatorial Africa. Whatever you might want in cartography, Monsieur Leib's shop was almost sure to have it.

On the evening of 12 April, those with an eye for moderately prominent journalists might have spotted Monsieur Leib out for dinner with A. A. Szara, recently assigned to the Paris bureau of *Pravda*. Spotted, that is, if one happened to visit a very dark and out-of-the-way Chinese restaurant, of dubious reputation, in the Asian district of Brussels.

In the end, Abramov and his associates had not made a choice of cities or networks for Dr Baumann's case officer. Life and circumstance intervened and chose for them. Even the multiple European networks of the Rote Kapelle – the Red Orchestra, as the German security services had nicknamed them – were not immune to the daily vicissitudes and tragedies that the rest of the world had to confront. In this instance, a deputy officer of the Paris-based OPAL network, work name Guillaume, was late for a clandestine meeting established in Lyon – one of his group leaders from Berlin was coming in by train under a cover identity – and drove recklessly to avoid having to wait for a fallback meeting three days later. His Renault sedan failed to make a curve on the N6 just outside Mâcon and spun sideways into a roadside plane tree. Guillaume was thrown clear and died the next day in the hospital in Mâcon.

Captain I. J. Goldman, *rezident* of OPAL under the painstakingly crafted cover of Stefan Leib, was brought back to Moscow by a circuitous route – 'using passports like straw,' grumbled one of the 'cobblers' who manufactured or altered identity papers at the NKVD Foreign Department – for lengthy consultations. Goldman, son of a Marxist lawyer from Bucharest, had volunteered for recruitment in 1934 and was, following productive service in Spain, something of a rising star.

Like all *residents*, he hated personnel problems. He accepted the complicated burdens of secrecy, a religion whose rituals demanded vast expenditures of time, money, and ingenuity, and the occasional defeat managed by the police and counter-espionage forces that opposed him, but natural disasters, like road accidents or wireless telegraph breakdowns, seemed especially cruel punishments from heaven. When a clandestine operator like Guillaume met an accidental death, the first thing the police did was to inform, or try to, a notional family that didn't exist. Had Goldman himself not contacted hospitals, police, and mortuaries in the region, Guillaume might have been determined a defector or runaway, thereby causing immense dislocation as the entire system was hurriedly restructured to protect itself.

Next, Goldman had to assure himself, and his directorate in Moscow, that the accident *was* an accident, an investigation complicated by the need to operate secretly and from a distance. Goldman, burning a cover identity that had cost thousands of roubles to construct, hired a lawyer in Mâcon to make that determination. Finally, by the time he arrived in Moscow, he was able to defend himself against all accusations save one: his supervision had been lax to the degree that one of his staff drove in an undisciplined manner. On this point he criticized himself before his superiors, then described countermeasures – lectures, display of the autopsy report obtained by the Mâconnais lawyer – that would be undertaken to eliminate such events in the future. Behind their stone faces, the men and women who directed OPAL laughed at his discomfort: they knew life, love affairs, bizarre sexual aberrations, lost keys, gambling, petty jealousies; all the absurd human horseshit that network *residents* had to deal with. They'd learned to improvise, now it was his turn.

When they were done scowling, they gave him a choice: elevate the Paris group leader to Guillaume's position or accept a new deputy. This was no choice at all, group leaders were infamously difficult to replace. On their ability to stroke and soothe, wheedle, nag, or threaten, everything depended. He could, on the other hand, accept a new deputy, the journalist Szara, an amateur 'who had done a few things with fair success'.

Goldman would have preferred experienced help, perhaps transferred from what he believed to be less crucial networks, for OPAL ran some fourteen agents in France and Germany and would now service a fifteenth (Baumann, officially designated OTTER), but the purges had eaten down into the *apparat* from the top and operationally sophisticated staff simply wasn't available. It was arranged for him to meet with Szara, who would work with a co-deputy in OPAL but would essentially be on his own in Paris while Goldman, as 'illegal' *rezident*, worked in protective isolation in Brussels. In the end he put a good face on it and indicated he was pleased with the arrangement. Somewhere, operating deep within the committee underbrush, there was a big, important rat who wanted Szara in Paris – Goldman could smell him.

Then too, for Goldman, it was best to be cooperative; his rising star was lately a little obscured, through no fault of his own, by a dark cloud on the horizon. His training class, the Brotherhood Front of 1934 – in fact a fractious crowd recruited from every lost corner of the Balkans – was not turning out as senior *apparat* people thought it would. A distressing number of the 'brothers' had left home; some defected, harbouring far less fraternal affection than their Russian family had supposed. The undisputed leader of the class, a Bulgarian, had vanished from Barcelona and resurfaced in Paris, where he'd become entangled in émigré politics and got himself arrested by French internal security officers in July of '37. A Serbian had disappeared back into the mountains of his homeland after a very complex exfiltration from a Spanish prison – a dreadful instance of ingratitude, though it was the NKVD that had shopped him to Franco's military intelligence in the first place, expedient neutralization after he resisted an order to purge POUM members in his guerrilla unit. And a Hungarian from Esztergom, worthless to the *apparat* from day one, had also fled to Paris where, hiding out in a Montmartre hotel, he'd apparently been murdered by a merchant seaman. What had *he* been involved in? Nobody knew.

Given that chamber of horrors, Goldman would be saying *yes sir* to senior officers for the foreseeable future. Privately, he had grave misgivings about André Szara. The journalist seemed both arrogant and insecure – a normal enough combination but potentially lethal under the stresses of clandestine work. Goldman was familiar with Szara's writing, he thought it sometimes powerful, almost always informative. But Goldman had been in the business just long enough to fear the creative personality. He'd developed a taste for blunt, stolid types, unemotional, who worked day and night without coming down with fevers, men and women who didn't nurse grudges, who preferred verification to intuition, were endlessly dependable and there when you needed them, could think on their feet in a crisis, *recognized* a crisis when one developed, and had the sense to ask you what to do when they weren't sure. Careers were made with such people. Not with the André Szaras of the world. But he was stuck, in no position to argue, and so he'd do the best he could.

Over the ghastly chop suey in Brussels, Goldman told him, '*Be* a journalist!'

What?

'Well, you are one, of course, very good, yes, but you must now make a special effort to live the life, and to be seen to live the life, one would expect of such a person. Go about, seek out your colleagues, haunt the right cafés. No slinking around, is what I mean. Of course you'll see the necessity of it, yes?'

Goldman made him mad, pointing this out. It was true that he'd habitually avoided journalists' haunts and parties and gone off on his own. For one thing, it didn't pay to be too friendly with Western Europeans – the lead diva of the Moscow Opera had been sent to the camps for dancing at a party with the Japanese ambassador. For another, he forever had to accomplish some special little task for the *apparat*. Such things took time, care, patience. And you didn't want colleagues around when you did it. *So, General Vlasy, the tread problem on the new R-20 tank turns out to be no problem at all, eh?* and all that sort of thing, certainly *not* with some knowing fellow journalist suppressing a cackle in the background.

Szara never really did respond to Goldman's direction. He looked at the grey noodles on his plate for a moment, then went on with the conversation. Inside he was broiling. Wasn't he unhappy enough about mortgaging his soul to Abramov and secretly abandoning his profession? Apparently not. They now laid upon his heart a heaping tablespoon of Russian irony, directing him to act more like what he no longer was. All this from some snotty little Roumanian who thought he spoke idiomatic Russian, was very much his junior in age, and looked like (and probably acted like) some kind of rodent. Small eyes that glittered, ears a little too big, features set close together. Like a smart mouse. Maybe too smart. Who the hell did he think he was?

Back in Paris the following day, however, he kept his opinions to himself. 'You've met Yves,' said his fellow deputy, using Goldman's work name. 'What do you think?'

Szara pretended to ponder the question. He did not want to commit himself, but neither did he want to seem like a spineless idiot – he was going to have to work closely with this woman. She was the sort of individual who, in the setting of a business office, might well be known

as *a bit of a terror*. Abramov had warned him about her: work name –
Elli, real name – Annique Schau-Wehrli, reputation – lioness. In person
she turned out to be fiftyish, short, stout, with a thrust-out bosom like a
pouter pigeon and glasses on a chain around her neck. She wore a built-
up shoe on one foot and walked with a cane, having been born with one
leg shorter than the other. Szara found himself drawn to her – she was
magnetic, perceptive, and also rather pretty, with a rosy complexion,
light, curly hair, a screen siren's long eyelashes, and omniscient eyes lit
by a brisk, cheerful hatred.

She was an ardent, blistering Marxist, a former pillar of the Swiss
Communist party from a wealthy bourgeois (and long ago rejected)
family in Lucerne. She had a tongue like a sword, spoke six languages,
and feared absolutely nothing. In Paris, she worked as office manager
and resident saint for a League of Nations satellite office, the International Law Institute, which issued oceans of studies attempting to
encourage the countries of the world to normalize and standardize their
legal codes. Wasn't the theft of a female ancestor's soul in Nyasaland
much the same, when all was said and done, as a stock swindle in
Sweden?

'Well?' she repeated. 'Don't tell me you have no opinion of the man. I
won't believe you.'

They were in her living room, a typical Parisian concoction of rich
red draperies, silk pillows, naked gold women holding ebony-shaded
lamps above their heads, and little things – ashtrays, onyx inkwells,
ivory boxes, Gallé bottles, and porcelain bull terriers – on every shelf
and table. Szara kept his elbows jammed well against his sides.

'Young,' he said.

'Younger than you.'

'Yes.'

'Brilliant, my dear comrade.'

'Glib.'

'Boof!' she said, a Gallic explosion of incredulous air. 'But how can
you be like this? Measured any way you like, brilliant. Against the
norm? Genius. Recall the Russian operative who went to London last
year, pockets just stuffed with British pounds. He is there two days,
ventures from his hotel for the first time. Persuaded by Soviet propaganda, he actually believes that the English working classes are so poor
they wear paper shoes. He suddenly spies a shop window full of leather
shoes, not at all expensive. *Ah-ha*, says he, my lucky day, and buys ten
pairs. Then, at another store, *look, they too have shoes today!* He thinks
his dear departed mother is sending down gifts from heaven. Again, ten
pairs. And so on, until the poor soul had over a hundred pairs of shoes,

no money for party work, and the MI5 surveillance team is practically rolling on the pavement. Just wait and see what some of our people can do, then you'll change your tune.'

Szara pretended to be slightly abashed. He was the new boy in the office, he had to make a decent impression, but he'd known Goldman's type before: a genius all right, a genius for self-advancement. 'I suppose you're right,' he said amiably.

Friday, the last week in April, in a warm, gentle rain that shone on the spring leaves of the boulevard trees, Szara booked a telephone call to Marta Haecht's magazine office in Berlin.

Twenty minutes later he cancelled it.

The gospel according to Abramov: 'Look, you can never be sure what they know about you, just as they can never be sure what we know about them. In times of peace, the services do two things in particular, they watch and they wait. This is a war of invisibility, fought with invisible weapons: information, numbers, wireless telegraph trans-missions, social acquaintance, political influence, entrée to certain circles, knowledge of industrial production or infantry morale. So, show me an infantry morale. You can't. It's intangible.

'Counter-intelligence operations are the most invisible of all. The people who run them don't want to neutralize their opponents – not right away. Some boss is screaming *stop it! stop it!* and his operatives are pleading *no. We want to see what they do.* For you it means this: you have to assume you have typhoid, you're infectious, and anyone you meet or know gets the disease. Whether this meeting is innocent or not, they must fall under suspicion if a third party is watching. You wonder why we recruit friends, family, lovers? We might as well – they're going to be considered guilty anyhow.'

The seed Abramov planted in Moscow grew a frightful garden in Paris. It grew in Szara's imagination, where it took the form of a voice: a quiet, resourceful voice, cultured, sure of itself, German-speaking. It was the voice of presumed surveillance, and when Szara contemplated something foolish, like a telephone call to Germany, it spoke to him. *28 April 16:25.* SZARA (the flat, official format would be similar to DUBOK's file and Szara imagined the German officer to be not unlike the author of the Okhrana dossier) *telephones* MARTA HAECHT *at Berlin 45.633; conversation recorded and currently under analysis for code or Aesopian language.*

Aesopian language suggested reality with symbolism or implication. Are you still studying French? I sent you a card from Paris – did you receive it? I'm writing a story about the workers who built the Gare du

Nord. I don't know where the time goes, I have to finish the piece by noon on the fourth of May.

It fooled nobody.

Even if *the voice* did not yet speak, Szara feared discovery. By 1938, Germany had been converted into a counter-espionage state. Every patriotic German took it as his or her duty to inform the authorities of any suspicious behaviour, denunciation had become a national mania – *strangers visited them, a curious sound from their basement, a printing press?*

Of course he considered using the network for communication. This would either evade all suspicion or end in absolute tragedy. A lover's choice, *nyet?* Passion or death. They had described to him the details of what the Gestapo actually did, *kaschumbo*, whips soaked in pails of water. The idea of exposing her to that . . .

He worked.

The Parisian spring flared to life – one hot morning and all the women were dressed in yellow and green, on the café terraces people laughed at nothing in particular, aromas drifted through the open doors of bistros where the owner's briard flopped by the cash register, a paw over its nose, dreaming fitfully of stock bones and cheese rinds.

The OPAL network was run from a three-storey building near the quais of the canal Saint-Martin and the canal del l'Ourcq, at the tattered edge of the nineteenth arrondissement where the streets around the Porte de Pantin turned to narrow roads leading into the villages of Pantin and Bobigny. A pulsating, sleepless *quartier*, home to the city's slaughterhouses as well as the stylish restaurants of the avenue Jean-Jaurès, where partygoing swells often ventured at dawn to eat fillet of beef baked in honey and avoid the tourists and taxi drivers down at Les Halles. Paris put things out there she wasn't sure whether she wanted or not – the Hippodrome where they held bicycle races and boxing matches, an infamous *maison close* where elaborate exhibitions could be arranged. In spring and fall, fog rose from the canal in the evening, the blue neon sign of the Hôtel du Nord glowed mysteriously, slaughterhouse workers and bargemen drank *marc* in the cafés. In short, a *quartier* that worked all night long and asked no questions, a place where the indefatigable snooping of the average Parisian wasn't particularly welcome.

The house at 8, rue Delesseux was crumbling brown brick like the rest of the neighbourhood, dirty and dark and smelling like a *pissoir*. But it could be entered through a street-level door, through a rear entrance to the *tabac* that occupied its tiny commercial space, or through an alley strewn with rags and broken glass that ran at an angle to the rue des Ardennes. It was handy to barges, a cemetery, a park, nameless village lanes, a sports arena, restaurants crowded with people – just about every sort of place that operatives liked to use.

The top floor of the house provided living and working space for the OPAL encipherer and wireless telegraph operator, work name François, true name M. K. Kranov, an 'illegal' with Danish passport, suspected to hold NKVD officer rank and, likely, the *apparat* spy reporting secretly to Moscow on the activities and personnel of the network.

On the second floor lived 'Odile,' Jeanne de Kouvens, the network's courier who serviced both Goldman in Brussels and the networks in Germany, the latter a twice-monthly run into Berlin under the pretext of caring for a non-existent mother Odile was Belgian, a tough nineteen-year-old with two children and a philandering husband, not a bit beautiful but violently sexy, her hair cut in a short, mannish cap – the street kid look – her cleft chin, swollen upper lip, tip-tilted nose, and indomitable eyes tossing a challenge at any man in the immediate vicinity. Her husband, a working-class fop with bushy, fin de siècle muttonchop whiskers, ran a portable merry-go-round that circulated through the neighbourhood squares of Paris. The *tabac* on the ground floor was served by Odile's brother, twenty years older than she, who had been wounded at Ypres and walked with the aid of two canes. He spent his days and nights on a stool behind the counter, selling Gitanes and Gauloises, Métro tickets and postage stamps, lottery chances, pencils, commemorative key rings, and more, an astonishing assortment of stuff, to a steady trickle of customers who created camouflage for operatives entering and leaving the house.

The Moscow Directorate had shuffled assignments to make life a little easier for Szara, putting Schau-Wehrli in charge of the three German networks, HENRI, MOCHA, and RAVEN, which left him with SILO, assigned to attack elements of the German community in Paris, and Dr Julius Baumann.

Spring died early that year, soft rains came and went, the sky turned its fierce French blue only rarely, a mean little wind arrived at dusk and blew papers around the cobbled streets. The end of April was generally admitted to be *triste*, only the surrealists like such unhappy weather, then summer came before anybody was really ready for it. The rising temperature seemed to drive the politicians further from sanity than usual.

Nobody could agree about anything: the Socialists had blocked a rearmament programme in March, then the Foreign Office claimed the

French commitment to Czechoslovakia to be 'indisputable and sacred'. One senator pleaded for pacifism in the morning, called for preservation of the national honour in the afternoon, then sued the newspaper that described him as ambivalent. Meanwhile, senior civil servants demanded things of their mistresses that caused them to raise their eyebrows when they had their girlfriends in for coffee. Nobody was comfortable: the rich found their sheets scratchy and carelessly ironed, the poor thought their *frites* tasted of fish oil.

On the top floor of the house at 8, rue Delesseux, the afternoons grew hot as the sun beat on the roof; the dusty window shades were never raised, no air stirred, and Kranov worked at a large table with his shirt off. He was a small, sullen man with curly hair and Slavic features who seemed, to Szara, to do nothing but work. All OPAL transmissions, incoming and outgoing, were based on one-time pads, encrypted into five-digit numerical groups, then transformed – using a changing mathematical key and 'false' addition ($5 + 0 = 0$) – by a second encryption. Brief, pro forma transmissions were fleshed out with null groups to avoid the type of message that had always been the cryptanalyst's point of attack. From Egyptian times to the present, the phrase used to break codes never varied: *nothing new to report today*.

Szara usually slipped into the house at night. In Kranov's transmitting room a blanket was nailed across the window, a tiny lamp used for illumination. Swirls of cigarette smoke hung in the air. Kranov's fingers jittered on the telegraph key, the dots and dashes flowing through the ether to a code clerk on Dzerzhinsky Square in Moscow:

91464 22571 83840 75819 11501

On other frequencies, a French captain in the Naval Intelligence section at Sfax, on the Tunisian coast, requested Paris to approve additional funds for Informant 22, the third secretary of the Czechoslovakia embassy in Vienna reported on private meetings held by the Sudeten leader Henlein with German diplomats in the spa town of Karlsbad, the Polish service in Warsaw asked an operative in Sofia to ascertain the whereabouts of the priest JOSEF. All nightlong the W/T operators *played their pianos*, not only for the Rote Kapelle, but in a hundred orchestras performing for scores of espionage *Konzertmeisters* from a dozen countries. Szara could hear it. Kranov let him put the earphones on and turn the dial. It was a theatre of sound, pitched treble or bass, quick-fingered or deliberate, an order to liquidate an informer or a request for the local weather forecast. Sometimes crackling with the static of an electrical storm in the Dolomites or the Carpathians, sometimes clear as a crystal chime, the nightlong symphony of numbers flew through the darkened heavens.

If there was no *critical/immediate* signal, Kranov broke out Moscow's transmissions after he woke from a few hours' sleep. Szara fancied it a kind of critical daylight that inevitably followed the coded mysteries of the night. Slowly, as May turned to June, and the sweat soaked through Kranov's undershirt in the morning heat, Szara began to gain a sharper appreciation of the interplay between OPAL and its masters, the simply phrased requests for information and the terse responses now resolved to a dialogue from which the mood of the Directorate could be read.

Moscow was restless. It had been so from the beginning. Abramov, sacrificing information in the hope of enforcing discipline, had let Szara know just exactly what he would be dealing with. Emphatically *not* Nezhenko – or any editor. Both Abramov and his *khvost* rival Dershani sat on the OPAL Directorate, as did Lyuba Kurova, a brilliant student in neuropathology in the years before the revolution, a ruthless Chekist in Lenin's terror campaign, now, in her forties, a friend of Poskrebyshev, Stalin's personal secretary; also Boris Grund, an *apparatchik*, an experienced technician, and a majority voter in every instance, and Vitaly Mezhin, at thirty-six years of age quite young for the work, a member of the generation of 'little Stalins' who crept into the power vacuum created by the purge, as the Big Stalin intended them to do. 'If you wilfully disobey an order,' Abramov said, 'this is who you disobey.'

Szara now saw that Dr Baumann made them uncomfortable: (1) He was a Jew in Germany, his future gravely insecure. (2) His motives were unknown. (3) His product was crucial. Szara could imagine them, seated at a table covered with a green baize cloth, flimsies of decrypted signals arranged at every place, smoking nervously at their stubby Troika cigarettes, speaking so very carefully, conscious of nuance in themselves and others, groping towards a protective consensus.

Swage wire figures for January, February, March, and April received, projections from orders on hand for May. Case officer asked to obtain listing of company personnel, especially in accounting office. Characterize: age, political affiliation, cultural level. They clearly wanted Baumann to get to work finding his own replacement. It was up to Szara to find some sort of honey to make him swallow that pill.

Of course they wanted more than that – Dershani in particular thought Baumann ought to be pumped dry, the quicker the better. He must know other subcontractors – who were they? Could they be approached? If so, how? What were their vulnerabilities? Then too – Mezhin now took his turn, you didn't want to be a wilting flower in this crowd – what of his association with senior officers of Rheinmetall? Might there not be something for them in that? Boris Grund thought this line productive. And what was Baumann paying for austenitic steel? Grund said his pals downstairs in the Economic Section were starving for such information, maybe we should toss them a bone.

Kurova didn't like the dead-drop. They'd got the Baumanns to buy a dog, a year-old schnauzer they named Ludwig, so that Baumann could be out on the street at night and use a stone wall near his house as a letter-box. This brought Odile, in a maid's uniform, into the neighbourhood two or three times a month to drop off mail and collect a response. A bent nail in a telephone pole was used as a signal: head turned up told Baumann to collect, head turned down confirmed that his deposit had been picked up. All according to standard form and practice, Kurova acknowledged. But Germans were naturally curious, they stared out their windows, and they had an insatiable appetite for detail. *Why does Dr Baumann reach behind the stone in Herr Bleiwert's wall? Look how poor little Ludwig wants only to play.* Kurova just didn't like it. Both operatives were too much in the open.

Dershani agreed. What about a restaurant, something in the industrial neighbourhood where the wire mill was located?

Abramov thought not. As a Jew, Baumann's activities were limited – he couldn't just go to a restaurant. This would be noticed.

The factory, then, Mezhin offered. Best of all, could they reach the engineer Haecht, who would, according to Szara, be nominally in control of the business as new anti-Jewish statutes were promulgated. They looked in their dossiers. They had a blurry photograph of Haecht, taken by an officer from the Berlin embassy. University records. Exemplar of handwriting. Inventory of family: wife Ilse, son Albert a pharmaceutical salesman, daughter Hedwig married to an engineer in Dortmund, daughter Marta an assistant art editor at a literary magazine.

Literary magazine? Perhaps a friend of ours, Dershani wondered idly.

Perhaps, Kurova admitted, but nice German girls don't go to factories.

Slow and easy, Abramov counselled, we don't want to create a panic.

This is no time for caution, Dershani said.

That was true.

Baumann's product *was* crucial. They had other sources of information on the German aircraft industry, but none that determined the numbers quite so exactly. The Directorate that handled the product coming in from Burgess and Philby and others in Great Britain confirmed the OPAL Directorate's hypotheses, as did sources in the French services. The German industrial machine was building a nightmare.

Baumann had shipped 14,842 feet of swage wire in October; this meant a monthly bomber production rate of 31 planes. From there they could project, using range and load factors already in their possession. The German bomber force as constituted in a theoretical month – May of 1939, for instance – would be able to fly 720 sorties in a single day against European targets and deliver 945 tons of bombs, causing a projected 50 casualties per ton – a total of almost 50,000 casualties in a twenty-four-hour period. A million casualties every three weeks.

And the USSR, Great Britain, and France were in absolute harmony on one basic assumption: *the bomber would always get through.* Yes, anti-aircraft fire and fighter planes would take their toll, but simply could not cause sufficient damage to bring the numbers down.

The Russians, using their British spies, had followed with interest developments in British strategic thinking in the last month of 1937. The RAF experts had urged building up the British aircraft industry to deliver heavy bombers to match the German numbers, ultimately to create a counterweight of terror: you destroy our cities, we'll destroy yours. But the cabinet had overruled them. Said Sir Thomas Inskip: 'The role of our air force is not an early knockout blow . . . but to prevent the Germans from knocking us out.' This was not the usual thinking, but the cabinet, in the end, had determined the defensive system a better option, and British industry began to build fighters instead of bombers.

In Germany, also, a strategic decision was made, though this one rested on Hitler's power. When the Reich marched into the Rhineland in 1936 and opposition did not materialize, the German General Staff lost credibility. Hitler was right. It was proven. Soon thereafter, he turned his attention to Hermann Göring's Luftwaffe. Where, Hitler wanted to know, are my aeroplanes? Göring felt the pressure, and took steps to protect himself. Germany stopped production of four-engined bombers, the Dornier Do-19 and the Junkers Su-89. Those planes could operate at greater distances, in England or the USSR, and stay longer over target, as well as extend the air cover provided to U-boat packs beset by sub chasers or destroyers, but they were not going to be built. Driven by Hitler's impatience, Göring directed the aircraft industry to build twin-engined bombers. 'The Fuhrer,' Göring said, 'does not ask me *what kind* of bombers I have. He simply wants to know *how many.*' The comment was believed to be private.

It wasn't.

And that was the point. The Moscow Directorate had to know what Göring said, and what the British cabinet thought, and had to do whatever, *whatever*, had to be done in order to know. In the same complex of buildings where the OPAL Directorate met, other groups laboured to keep Germany and Great Britain from finding out what Stalin said, or what the Politburo thought. That work, though, was none of their business. Their business was *a million casualties every three weeks.* With a threat of that dimension, how carefully could Dr Julius Baumann be treated? They had to, as Dershani counselled, take their chances, and if the man went slack with terror or rigid with fury it was Szara's job to handle him. If Szara couldn't do it, they'd find somebody who could. They were not in a position to be gentle with spies, even less with case officers.

'Then we are agreed,' Kurova said. There were stern nods of assent around the table.

That night, the W/T operator in Dzerzhinsky Square settled in on his frequency at 1:33 A.M., Moscow time, as scheduled for that date. He discovered a neighbour, some plodding fool out there somewhere, sending five-digit groups as though he had all eternity to get the job done. The operator swore softly with irritation, caressed his dial until he found a private little band of silent air, then began a long signal to his nameless, faceless, yet very familiar colleague in Paris. *Paris,* he thought, *a city I'll never see.* But that was fate. So, instead, he put a bit of his soul into the telegraphy, flying ghostlike across the sleeping continent along with his secret numbers.

Goldman had said, '*Be* a journalist!' so Szara did what he asked, but he didn't like it. He found a large, gloomy room on the rue du Cherche-Midi (literally, the street that looked for the sun, which it rarely found), midway between brawling Montparnasse and fashionably arty Saint-Germain; coming out of his doorway he turned right to buy a chicken, left to buy a shirt. He drank wine and ate oysters at the Dôme, a noisy barnyard of artists and artistes, the people who came to look at them, predators scenting the money of the people who came to look at them. *petits-bourgeois* celebrating their anniversaries and saying 'Ah!' when the food came to the table, and – he only grew aware of them with time – a surprisingly large number of reasonably appealing and attractively dressed people of whom one couldn't say more than that they ate at the Dôme. Simply Parisians.

Szara attended the occasional session of the Senate, dropped in at the trial of this week's murderer, browsed the women in bookstores, and showed up at certain *salons.* Where journalists were, there was André Szara. He passed through the *Pravda* office from time to time, collected a phone message or two, and if with some frequency he disappeared completely from sight for a day or two, well, so did many people in

Paris. Szara was running an espionage network, God only knew what the rest of them were doing.

On the days when Ilya Ehrenburg wasn't in town, André Szara was the pre-eminent Soviet journalist in Paris. The city's hostesses made this clear to him – 'It's terribly late, I know, but could you come? We'd so love to have you!' He went, and Ehrenburg was never there. Szara had been called in as a last-minute substitute, *the* Soviet Journalist in the room, along with the Tragic Ballerina, the Rich American Clod, the Knave of Attorneys, the Sexually Peculiar Aristocrat, the Cynical Politician, and all the rest – like a pack of tarot cards, Szara thought. He much preferred relaxed social evenings at friends' apartments, spontaneous gatherings rich with combative exchanges on politics, art, and life, at the Malrauxs' on the rue du Bac, sometimes at André Gide's place on the rue Vaneau, occasionally at Ehrenburg's apartment on the rue Cotentin.

He was jealous of Ehrenburg, who occupied a position above him in the literary and social order of things, and when they did meet, Ehrenburg's kindness and courtesy towards him only made it worse. Not the least of the problem was Ehrenburg's writing itself – not so much the diction, but the sharp eye for a detail that told a story. Reporting from the civil war in Spain, Ehrenburg had described the different reactions of dogs and cats to bombing attacks: dogs sought safety by getting as close to their masters as they could, while cats went out the window and as far from humans as possible. Ehrenburg knew how to capture the reader's emotions better than he did, and now that he'd effectively left the competition, such good Ehrenburg stuff as he saw in print depressed him. There were rumours that Ehrenburg did favours for the *apparat*, but if he did, Szara had no evidence of it; and suspected that Ehrenburg's contacts were up in the Central Committee, well beyond his own reach.

One Thursday night in May, Szara dropped around to Ehrenburg's apartment to discover André Gide, under full throttle in a lengthy discourse on some point of literary philosophy. To drive home his point, Gide picked up a dog biscuit from a plate on the kitchen table and used it to draw lines in the air. Ehrenburg's dog, a terrier-spaniel mix called Bouzou, studied the progress of the biscuit for a time, then rose in the air and snapped it neatly out of Gide's fingers. Unperturbed, Gide picked up another biscuit and continued the lecture. Bouzou, equally unperturbed, did it again. A girl sitting near Szara leaned over and whispered, '*C'est drôle, n'est-ce pas?*'

Oh yes. Very funny.

Upstaged by Ehrenburg's dog, he thought, and immediately hated himself for thinking such things. *Ingrate! Listen to what Gide is saying, how mankind thrashes amid life's futility; how his tragi-comic destiny is, may be described as, has always been, will always be . . . some French word I don't know. Ah, but everybody is smiling wisely and nodding, so it's evidently a stunning insight.*

Such evenings. Wine and oysters. Frosted cakes. Aromatic women who leaned close to say some almost intimate little thing and brushed one's shoulder. The old Szara would have been lighthearted with ecstasy. Not all was roses, of course. The city was famous for its artful, petty humiliations – had not Balzac fashioned a career from such social warfare? – and Szara knew himself to be the sort of individual who took it to heart, who let it get into his bloodstream where it created malicious antibodies. Nonetheless, he told himself, he was lucky. Two thirds of the Russian writers were gone in the purges, yet here he was in Paris. That all the world should have no more problems than the envy of a fellow journalist and the obligation to do a bit of nightwork!

He looked at his watch. Stood, smiled genially, and turned to go. 'The witching hour, and the mysterious Szara leaves us,' said a voice.

He turned and made a helpless gesture. 'An early day tomorrow,' he said. 'A scene observed at dawn.'

A chorus of good nights and at least one disbelieving snicker accompanied him out the door.

He strolled a few blocks towards the edge of the seventh arrondissement, idling, crossing and recrossing a boulevard, then flagged a cab from the line at the Duroc Métro and sped to the Gare Saint-Lazare. Here he rushed through the station – *late for a train* – then found another taxi at the rue de Rome exit and gave his destination as the Gare d'Austerlitz. 'No hurry,' he said to the driver. 'There's something extra for you if we just wander a bit.' A novel instruction, but heeded, and as the cab meandered eastward Szara slumped lazily in the back seat, a posture that allowed him to watch the street behind him in the driver's rearview mirror. He changed cabs again at the Austerlitz station, then paid off the new driver on the boulevard de la Gare and crossed the Seine, now at the eastern edge of Paris where the railway tracks ran southeast between the Gare de Lyon and the wine *comerçants'* warehouses in the Bercy district. He had become, in the course of these clandestine exercises, what he thought of as *the other Szara*, a midnight self, a figure in a raincoat on a bridge above the Bercy marshalling yards, avoiding the yellow flare of a street lamp. *And here*, he thought, *Monsieur Gide, Monsieur Ehrenburg, Master Bouzou, we have quite another sort of antidote to the futility of existence.* A goods train chugged slowly under the bridge, the white steam from its engine spilling over the rampart as it passed beneath him. He liked the burned smell of the railway yards, the distant crash of couplings, the bright steel maze of rails that merged and parted and merged again, the hiss of decompression from an idling locomotive. He glanced at his watch, one-twenty, strolled casually – a reflective man thinking things over – to the end of the bridge. Reached the street just as a boxy Renault puttered to a stop. The passenger door opened and he swung smoothly into the front seat, the car accelerating onto the empty boulevard as he closed the door. It was well timed, he thought, quite artistic in its own way.

'*Et bonsoir, mon cher,*' said the driver cheerfully. He was the SILO group leader, Robert Sénéschal, the very perfection of the young, French, communist lawyer. Like so many French men, he seemed theatrically suited to his role in life – the spiky hair, acerbic smile, pigskin gloves, and upturned raincoat collar would have quite pleased a film director. Szara was drawn to him. Sénéschal's charm, his throwaway courage, reminded him of his own style ten years earlier: committed, self-assured, amused by the melodrama of clandestine life yet scrupulously meeting its demands.

Szara reached into the glove compartment and withdrew a thick manila envelope. He unwound the string and riffled through a sheaf of paper, squinting in order to make out the writing in the glow of the boulevard street lamps. He held up a page with twelve words on it, enormous letters fashioned in a torturous scrawl. Slowly, he tried to decipher the German. 'Can you make any sense of this?'

'A letter from the sister, it seems.'

'He steals a bit of everything.'

'Yes. Poor ALTO. He takes whatever feels important to him.'

'What is *Kra . . . Krai . . .*'

'*Kraft,* I think. *Kraft durch Freude.* "Strength through Joy", the Nazi recreation clubs for workers.'

'What's it to do with anything?'

'I managed to work my way through all of it. The sister in Lübeck is taking a cruise to Lisbon on one of the chartered liners they have, it's only costing a few reichsmarks, how she looks forward to it after the demands of her job. ALTO offers as well the telephone numbers of procurement specialists in the attaché's office.'

'That they'll like. As for the letter . . .'

'I'm just the postman,' Sénéschal said. He turned into the traffic *ronde-point* at the place Nation. Even though the May night was chilly, the terraces of the brasseries were crowded, people drinking and eating and talking, a white blur of faces and amber lights as the Renault swept past. Sénéschal moved up on the bumper of a rattletrap market truck in front of him, preventing an aggressive Citroën from cutting in. 'So much for you,' he said triumphantly.

ALTO was a sixteen-year-old boy known as Dolek, a Slovak nickname. His mother, whom Sénéschal had secretly observed and termed 'ravishing', lived with a German major who worked in the office of the military attaché. They'd begun their love affair when the major was stationed in Bratislava and stayed together when he was transferred to Paris. The child of a previous love affair, Dolek suffered from a disease of the nervous system: his speech was slurred and difficult to understand, and he hobbled along with one arm folded against his chest while his head rested on his collarbone. His mother and her lover, intoxicated by the physical perfection of their own bodies, were sickened by his condition and ashamed of him, and kept him out of sight as much as they could. They treated him as though he were retarded and did not understand what they said about him. But he was not retarded, he understood everything, and eventually a desperate anger drove him to seek revenge. Left alone in the apartment, he copied out, as best he could and with immense effort, the papers the major brought home and left in a desk drawer. He made no distinctions – thus the letter from the sister – if the major treated the paper as private, Dolek copied it. Some months after the move to Paris he'd been locked in the apartment while his mother and the major spent a weekend at a country house. He'd got the door open and dragged himself to Communist party headquarters, where a young nurse, busy making banners for a workers' march, had listened sympathetically to his story. Word of the situation had then reached Sénéschal, who'd visited the boy while the mother and her lover were at work.

Szara sighed and stuffed the paper back in the envelope. The Renault turned up a dark side street and he could see into an apartment with open drapes, lit in such a way as to make the room seem suffused with golden light. 'Are you still taking Huber to Normandy?' he asked.

'That's the plan,' Sénéschal said. 'To make love, and eat apples in cream.'

Szara reached into an inside pocket and handed a wad of fifty-franc notes across the gearshift. 'Go to a nice restaurant,' he said.

Sénéschal took the packet. 'I thank you,' he said lightly.

'We want you to know you're appreciated.' Szara paused. 'I don't suppose you actually have much feeling for her.'

'It's *curieux*, if you want the truth. The fat little Nazi maiden squirming away . . . one closes one's eyes with passion.'

Szara smiled. Sénéschal clearly didn't mind all that much, yet there was a melancholy note of martyrdom in his voice, *that the world should come to this.* 'The broad masses stand and applaud as you build socialism.'

Sénéschal laughed and Szara was gratified that the joke worked. Being funny was easily the most difficult trick of all in a foreign language, sometimes the French just stared at him in palpable confusion – what *did* this man mean?

Lötte Huber was a chubby German woman employed as a clerk at the German Trade Mission. Working with his lawyer friend Valais, who helped various German enterprises with residence permits and the infinite complexities of French bureaucracy, Sénéschal had 'met' Huber by sitting next to her and a girlfriend at the theatre. During the intermission the four of them got to talking, then went out for drinks after the play. Sénéschal had presented himself as a young man of wealthy and aristocratic family, seduced the clerk, eventually proposed marriage. To his fury, his unseen 'parents' categorically rejected the match. He then estranged himself from his family, abandoning the vast inheritance that awaited him, sacrificing all for his darling Lötte. He determined, once the dust settled, to make his own way in life, supposedly obtaining employment as a minor functionary in the French Foreign Office. But they could only, he told her, afford to get married if he were able to advance himself, which he would certainly do if she would supply helpful information about German Trade Mission business and personnel. In love, she told him all sorts of things, more than she could have understood, for the Gestapo intelligence service, the SD, used jobs at the Mission as cover for operatives – individuals seen to have contacts well beyond the scope of commercial affairs.

When this information was added to what Valais supplied – new arrivals needing *cartes de sejour* – the *apparat* was able to track German intelligence officers with considerable efficiency, leading to knowledge of French traitors, operations run against third countries, and insights into German objectives both in France and several other countries in Europe. Sénéschal had more than earned his weekend in Normandy.

The money was not at all a bribe – Sénéschal was motivated by idealism – but rather recognition that a group leader simply hadn't the time to earn much of a living for himself.

Sénéschal rolled down the window of the Renault and lit a cigarette. Szara closed the envelope and checked the signs on corner buildings to see what street they were on – anywhere but the neighbourhood of the rue Delesseux base would serve his purposes. Sénéschal was essentially the cut-out; the people he worked with did not know of Szara's existence, and he himself knew Szara only as 'Jean Marc', had no idea of his true name, where he lived or the location of radios or safe houses.

Meetings were arranged at different sites every time, with fallbacks in case one party or the other failed to show up. If the network were closed down. Sénéschal would appear three times at various places, nobody would be there to meet him, and that would be the end of it. The *apparat* could, of course, find him again if they wanted to.

Preparing to disengage, Szara asked, 'Anything you want or need?'

Sénéschal shook his head. He seemed to Szara, at that instant, a man perfectly content, doing what he wished to do without reservations, even though he could not safely share this side of his life with anyone. There were moments when Szara suspected that many idealists drawn to communism were at heart people with an appetite for clandestine life.

Szara said, 'The LICHEN situation remains as before?' LICHEN was a prostitute, a dark, striking woman of Basque origin who had fled north from the civil war in Spain. The intention was to use LICHEN to entice low-level German staff into compromising situations, but she had yet to produce anything beyond free sexual entertainment for a few Nazi chauffeurs.

'It does. Madame has the clap and will not work.'

'Is she seeing a doctor?'

'Being paid to. Whether she actually does it or not I don't know. Whores do things their own way. The occasional dose gets them vertical for a while, and she really doesn't seem to mind.'

'Anything else?'

'A message for you was left at my law office. It's in with the reports.'

'For me?'

'It says Jean Marc on the envelope.'

This was unusual, but Szara did not intend to go burrowing for the message in front of Sénéschal. They drove in silence for a time, up the deserted boulevard Beaumarchais past the huge wedding cake of a building that housed the Winter Circus. Sénéschal flipped his cigarette out the window and yawned. The light changed to red and the Renault rolled to a stop beside an empty taxi. Szara handed over a small slip of paper with the location, time, and date of the next meeting. 'Enjoy your weekend,' he said, jumped out of the Renault, and slid neatly into the back of the taxicab, slightly startling the driver. 'Turn right,' he said as the light went green, then watched as Sénéschal's car disappeared up the boulevard.

It was a little after three in the morning when Szara slipped into the rue Delesseux house and climbed to the third floor. Kranov was done with his W/T chores for the evening and Szara had the room to himself. First he found the envelope with Jean Marc printed across the front. Inside was a mimeographed square of paper with a drawing of a bearded man in Roman armour, a six-point star on his shield and a dagger held before him. The ticket entitled the bearer to Seat 46 in the basement theatre at the Rue Muret Synagogue at seven-thirty in the evening of the eighteenth day of the month of Iyyar, in the year 5698, for the annual Lag b'Omer play performed by the synagogue youth group. The address was deep in the Marais, the Jewish *auartier* of Paris. For those who might need a date according to the Julian calendar, a rather grudging 18 May was written in a lower corner.

Szara tucked it in a pocket – really, what would they think of next. A communication travelling upwards from a network operative to a deputy was something he'd never heard of, and he rather thought that Abramov would go a little pale if he found out about it, but he was becoming, over time, quite hardened to exotic manifestations, and he had no intention of permitting himself to brood about this one. He had a ticket to a synagogue youth play, so he'd go to a synagogue youth play.

A thin sheet of paper bearing decrypts from the previous night's Moscow traffic awaited his attention, and this he did find disturbing. The problem wasn't with the SILO net – some of the answers to the Directorate's questions were probably in the manila envelope he'd picked up from Sénéschal – but the transmission that concerned OTTER, Dr Baumann, worried him. Moscow wanted him squeezed. Hard. And right away. There was no misreading their intention, even in the dead, attenuated language of decoded cables. At first glance, it seemed as though they wanted to turn Baumann Milling into what the Russians called an *espionage centre* – why else show such a profound interest in personnel? Because, if you thought about it a moment, they expected a conflagration. Soviet intelligence officers were not queasy types. Disaster only made them colder – that he'd seen for himself. The Foreign Department of the NKVD – now called the First Chief Directorate – had a hundred windows on Germany. What did they see coming? Whatever it was, they didn't believe that Baumann would survive it.

With some effort he recaptured his mind and forced himself to go to work, emptying the manila envelope on the table. Valais's list of German applications for residence permits presented no problems, he simply recopied it. Sénéschal's material from ARBOUR, Lötte Huber, was brief and to the point, the lawyer had essentially synthesized what he got and in effect done Szara's job for him: the German Trade Mission was probing the French markets for bauxite (which meant aluminium, which meant airframes), phosphorus, (flares, artillery shells, tracer bullets), cadmium (which meant nothing at all to him), and assorted domestic products, notably coffee and chocolate. From ALTO, Dolek, he would pass on the revised telephone directory of the attaché's office but would eliminate the major's letter from his sister in Lübeck. For himself, he informed the Directorate that he'd met with the SILO group leader, disbursed funds, and learned that LICHEN was not functioning due to illness.

Next he tore up the SILO originals, burned them in a ceramic ashtray, then walked down the hall and flushed the ashes down the toilet. Almost anyone who came in contact with the espionage world was told the story of the beginner operative who'd been instructed to either burn his papers or tear them into bits and flush them down the toilet. An anxious sort, he'd become confused, crumpled up a large wad of paper and dropped it in the toilet, then put a match to it and watched, aghast, as the flames set the toilet seat on fire.

Back in the W/T office, the big alarm clock by Kranov's work area said it was four-fifteen in the morning. Szara sat at the table and lit a cigarette; the darkened window hid any change of light, but he could hear a bird start up outside. He thought of the hundreds of operatives all across Europe who had finished with their nightwork, as he had, and now fell prey to the same predawn malaise: useless white energy, a nagging sense of some nameless thing left undone, a mind that refused to disengage. Sleep was out of the question.

He squared up the pad of flimsy paper and began to doodle. The memory of Dolek's handwriting, the enormous letters painfully carved into the paper with successive jerks of the pencil, would not leave his mind. Nor would the substance of the letter, especially the Strength through Joy cruise. His imagination wandered, picturing the sort of German worker who would sail off for Lisbon.

Dearest Schätzchen – Little Treasure – he wrote. *I wish to invite you on a special outing arranged by my Kraft durch Freude club.*

He went on a bit with it, mawkish, blustering, then signed it *Hans.* Changed that to *Hansi.* Then tried *Your Sweet Hansi.* No, too much. Just *Hansi* would do.

What would Marta do if she got such a letter? At first she'd think it was a practical joke, tasteless, upsetting. But what if he crafted it in such a way that he made it clear, to her, who was writing? Odile could drop it in a letter-box in Hamburg, that would bypass the postal inspectors who processed all foreign mail. He could address it to her personally and sign with a meaningful alias. She could sail to Lisbon on such a cruise. He had to consider it carefully, a lot could go wrong.

But, in principle, why not?

The evening of 18 May was cool and cloudy, but the basement of the Rue Muret Synagogue was warm enough for the women in the audience to produce scented handkerchiefs from their shiny leather handbags. It was not, Szara discovered, an extremely Orthodox synagogue, nor was it quite as poor as it first seemed. Buried deep in the gloom of a twisting little street in the Marais, the building seemed to sag in every possible direction, its roofline jagged as though scribbled on paper. But the basement was packed with well-dressed men and women, probably parents of the children in the play, their relatives and friends. The women seemed more French than Jewish, and though Szara had taken the precaution of buying a yarmulke (let the Moscow Directorate reimburse him for *that*), there were one or two men in the audience with uncovered heads. Certain cars parked outside, half on the narrow pavement, indicated to Szara by their licence plates that some members of the congregation were now doing well enough to live just outside Paris, but retained a loyalty to the old synagogue on the rue Muret, a street that retained a distinct flavour, and aroma, of its medieval origins.

Szara expected to recognize the occupant of Seat 47 or 45, but the place to his right was more than filled by a bulky matron in diamond rings while to his left, on the aisle, sat a dark, teenage girl in a print dress. He had arrived early, been handed a playbill, and waited patiently for contact. But nobody showed up. Eventually, two droopy curtains creaked apart to reveal ten-year-old Pierre Berger, in cardboard armour, as Bar Kochba, the Jewish rebel of Judea in A.D. 132, in the act of recruiting his friend Lazar for service against the legions of the Emperor Hadrian.

BAR KOCHBA (pointing at the roof): Look, Lazar! There, in the east. There it is!
LAZAR: What do you see, Simon Bar Kochba?
BAR KOCHBA: I see a star. Brighter than all others. A star out of Jacob.
LAZAR: As in the Torah? 'A star out of Jacob, a sceptre out of Israel'?
BAR KOCHBA: Yes, Lazar. Can you see it? It means we shall free ourselves from the tyrant, Hadrian.
LAZAR: Always you dream! How can we do this?
BAR KOCHBA: By our faith, by our wisdom, and by the strength of our right hand. And you, Lazar, shall be my first recruit, but you must pass a test of strength.
LAZAR: A test?
BAR KOCHBA: Yes. Do you see that cedar tree over there? You must

tear it from the earth to prove you are strong enough to join our rebellion.

As Lazar strode across the stage to a paper cedar pinned to a clothes tree, a grandmother's aside was stilled by a loud 'Shhh!' Lazar, a stocky, red-cheeked – the makeup artist had been a little overenthusiastic with the rouge – child in a dark blue tunic, huffed and puffed as he struggled with the clothes tree. Finally, he lifted it high, shook it at Bar Kochba, and laid it carefully on its side.

The play, *A Star out of Jacob*, proceeded as Szara, from his own days at the *cheders* in Kishinev and Odessa, knew it had to. A curious holiday, Lag b'Omer, commemorating a host of events all across the span of Jewish tradition and celebrated in a variety of ways. It was sometimes the Scholars' Festival, recalling the death of Rabbi Akiva's students in an epidemic, or the celebration of the first day of the fall of Manna as described in the Book of Exodus. It was a day when the three-year-old children of Orthodox Jews got their first haircuts or a day of weddings. But in Szara's memory of eastern Poland, it was particularly the day that Jewish children played with weapons. Toy bows and arrows long ago, then, during his own childhood, wooden guns. Szara perfectly remembered the Lag b'Omer rifle that he and his father had carved from the fallen branch of an elm tree. Szara and his friends had chased each other through the mud alleys of their neighbourhoods, street fighting, peering around corners and going 'Krah, krah' as they fired, a fairly accurate approximation by kids who had heard the real thing.

These children were different, he mused, more sophisticated, miniature Parisians with Parisian names: Pierre Berger, Moïse Franckel, Yves Nachmann, and, standing out sharply from all the others, the stunning Nina Perlemère, as Hannah, inspiring the Bar Kochba rebels when they are reluctant to creep through the underground passages of Jerusalem to attack the legionnaires, sweeping her cardboard sword into the sky and slaying Szara entirely with her courage.

HANNAH: Let there be no despair. First we will pray, then we will do what we must.

This one, pretty as she was, was the warrior: her lines rang out and produced a scattering of spontaneous applause, causing a Roman centurion in the wings to peer around the curtain through blue-framed eyeglasses. There was a slight disturbance to Szara's left as the dark girl in the print dress moved up the aisle and was replaced by General Yadomir Bloch. He reached over and took Szara's left hand in his right for a moment, then whispered, 'Sorry I'm late, we'll talk after the play.' This produced a loud 'Shh!' from the row behind them.

Through the dark streets of the Marais, Bloch led him to a Polish restaurant on the second floor of a building propped up by ancient wooden beams braced against the pavement. The tiny room was lit by candles, not for atmosphere but – Szara could smell the paraffin they were using for the stove – because there was no electricity in the building. Squinting at the menu written in chalk on the wall, they ordered a half bottle of Polish vodka, bowls of tschav – sorrel soup – a plate of radishes, bread, butter, and coffee.

'The little girl who played Hannah,' Bloch said, shaking his head in admiration. 'There was one like that in Vilna when I was a boy, eleven years old and she drew every eye. You didn't mind coming to the play?'

'Oh no. It brought back the past. Lag b'Omer, playing guns.'

'Perfect, yes, I intended it so. Soviet Man this, Soviet Man that, but we mustn't forget who we are.'

'I don't think I ever forget, comrade General.'

Bloch tore a strip of crust from the brown loaf, trailed it through his soup, leaned over his bowl to eat it. 'No? Good,' he said. 'Too many do. A little hint of pride in one's heritage and somebody screams *bourgeois nationalism! Take the Zionist away!*' Having finished the bread, he wiped his mouth with a small cloth napkin, then began an expedition through his pockets, finally retrieving a folded page torn from a journal, which he opened carefully. 'You know Birobidzhan?'

'Yes.' Szara smiled grimly. 'The Jewish homeland in Siberia – or so they insisted. Lenin's version of Palestine, to keep the Zionists in Russia. I believe some thousands of people actually went there, poor souls.'

'They did. A sad place, surely, but effective propaganda. Here, for instance, is a German Jew writing on the subject: "The Jews have gone into the Siberian forests. If you ask them about Palestine, they laugh. The Palestine dream will have long receded into history when in Birobidzhan there will be motorcars, railways and steamers, huge factories belching forth their smoke. . . . These settlers are founding a home in the taigas of Siberia not only for themselves but for millions of their people . . . Next year in Jerusalem? What is Jerusalem to the Jewish proletarian? Next year in Birobidzhan!" '

Szara raised his glass in a mock Seder toast and drank off the vodka. Bloch folded his paper back up and put it in his pocket. 'It would be funnier if people didn't believe it,' Bloch said.

Szara shrugged. 'Bundists, communists, socialists left and right, three kinds of Zionists, and mostly, when all is said and done, people in the shtetls of the Pale who say *do nothing, wait for the Messiah*. We may not own anything to speak of, but we are wealthy when it comes to opinions.'

'So, you must have one too.'

Szara thought for a moment. 'For centuries we have run around Europe like scared mice, maybe it's time to at least consider a hole in the wall, especially lately, as the cat population seems to be on the rise.'

Bloch seemed satisfied. 'I see. Now, to a tender subject. You have, one is told, a splendid opportunity to write something for an American magazine, but nothing appears. Perhaps others counsel you not to do it. Maybe somebody like Abramov, a man you admire – a man I admire, come to that – convinces you that it's not really worth it. He takes you under his protection, he solves your problems with the Georgians, he makes life possible. If it's that, well, you've made a decision and, really, what can I do about it? On the other hand, maybe there's something you need, maybe I can be of assistance. Or not. It's for you to say. At worst, a little play from the synagogue youth group and a plate of nice tschav – not a wasted evening at any rate.'

'Comrade General, may one ask a frank question?'

'Of course.'

'What, actually, is the nature of your business?'

'That's a good question, I'll try to answer it. The truth is I'm in several businesses. Like you, like all of us, I was in the paradise business. We got rid of the czar and his pogroms to make a place where Jews, where everyone, could live like human beings and not like slaves and beasts – that's one definition of paradise and not a bad one. This paradise, we soon saw, needed a few willing souls to serve as guardians. Isn't that always the way with paradise? So I offered my humble services. Thus my second business, one could say, became the GRU, the military intelligence business. In this choice I was guided by the example of Trotsky, who became a soldier when he had to and did pretty well at it. And yet, even so, paradise slipped away. Because now we have a new pogrom, run, like so many in history, by a shrewd peasant who understands hatred, who knows its true value and how to use it.

'There is a trick, André Aronovich, played on us through the centuries and now played again: the Jew is accused of being cunning, by someone a thousand times more cunning than any Jew has ever been. So, sorrowfully, this problem has become my third business, and now I'm taking you out to theatre and dinner in a businesslike sort of way and trying to interest you in becoming an associate. What do I offer my associates? A chance to save a few Jewish lives, never a commodity with much value, but then Jews have always found their way to such enterprises – they deal in cheap stuff: old rags, scrap metal, bones and gristle, whatever, like themselves, people don't really want. And that's all, frankly, that I can offer you. Is it dangerous? Oh yes. Could you die? It's likely. Will your heroism be known to history? Very doubtful. Now, have I successfully persuaded you to throw everything you value in life away and follow this peculiar, ugly man over the nearest horizon to some dreadful fate?'

General Bloch threw his head back and laughed – it was unfettered, infectious. Szara joined in, was then unable to stop. People at other tables turned to look at them, smiling nervously, a little frightened to be trapped in a tiny Polish restaurant with a pair of madmen. Neither of them could have explained it. They had, somehow, in this strange, hidden, broken building, caught the tail of absurdity, and the thrash of it made them laugh. 'God forgive me,' Bloch said, wiping his eyes with his hand, 'for enjoying such a life as much as I do.'

A good laugh. A successful laugh. For it prevented Szara from actually having to answer Bloch's question, from saying *no* immediately. Later they walked to the Métro together. Bloch kept coming back to the play. Oh the little girl who played the part of Hannah, what was her name? Perlemère? Yes, he was sure Szara had it right, a few months on the front lines and already he had the operative's trained memory. Perlemère, mother-of-pearl, like Perlmutter in German. Where did Jews get these names? But, under any name at all, wasn't she a treasure.

Weren't they all.

Even those in Russia. Not so quick and clever as these children, perhaps, but bright and eager, little optimists, knock them down and they bounce. Szara surely knew them: the sons and daughters of the Jews in the universities, in the state bureaus and the diplomatic corps, yes, even in the security services.

Those children. The ones who no longer had homes or parents. The ones who ate from garbage cans in the darkness.

Long after Bloch left him, Szara continued the conversation with himself.

A writer once again, Szara sat at his kitchen table at noon; through the open window he could smell lunch being cooked in the other apartments on the courtyard. When it was served, he could hear the sounds of knives and forks on porcelain and the solemn lilt of conversation that always accompanied the midday meal.

He would write the story.

Then he would have to disappear. For, under NKVD scrutiny, a nom de plume would not protect him for long.

So, where did one disappear to these days? America. Shanghai? Zanzibar? Mexico?

No, America.

You met people in Moscow now and then who'd gone off to America – the ones who had come back to Russia. That little fellow who'd worked in a tie factory. What was his name? At some party somewhere they'd been introduced. Szara remembered a face soured by despair. 'Hat in hand,' he'd said. 'Always hat in hand.'

Szara was haunted by that image, and now it coloured his vision of the future. He saw himself with Marta Haecht, they were hand in hand like fugitives in a storybook. The mad run from Paris at midnight, the steamship boarded at Le Havre. Ten days in steerage, the Statue of Liberty, Ellis Island. New York! Vast confusion, adrift in a sea of hopes and dreams, the sidewalks jammed with his fellow adventurers, everybody could be a millionaire if they tried. The pennies scraped together for the new suit, the offices, editors, lunches, encouragements, high hopes, then, ultimately . . . a janitor.

A janitor with an alias. A *nom de mop*. A cartoon capitalist with a cigar loomed up before him: 'You, Cohen, you call this floor clean? Lookit here! And here!' Hat in hand, always hat in hand. The obsequious immigrant, smiling and smiling, the sweat running from his armpits.

But what would he do in Shanghai? Or Zanzibar? Where, in fact, *was* Zanzibar? Or did it exist only in pirate movies?

On the table before him sat a secondhand Underwood, bought at a junk shop, some vanished novelist's golden calf, no doubt. Poor thing, it would have to be left on a street corner somewhere; it too would have to run away once it wrote forbidden words in its own, very identifiable handwriting. Szara stabbed idly at the keyboard with his index fingers, writing in Polish, putting in accents with a sharp pencil.

To the musical clatter of lunchtime in the courtyard, André Szara wrote a magazine story. *Who was the Okhrana's mysterious man? Certain documents are said to exist . . . revolutionary times in Baku . . . intrigue . . . rumours that won't die . . . perhaps high in the Soviet government today . . . tradition of the agent provocateur, Roman Malinovsky who rose to be head of the Bolshevik party in the Russian Duma was known to have been an Okhrana agent and so was the engineer Azeff, who actually led the Battle Organization of the Socialist Revolutionary party and personally organized the bomb assassination of the minister of the interior, Plehve, in 1904 . . . banished to Siberia . . . records said to have been burned in 1917, but did they get them all? Will we ever know for certain . . . secrets have a way . . . once the identity is known . . . that the course of history will once again be altered, perhaps violently, by the Okhrana's mysterious man.*

In personal code, Szara had the address in a little book. He found an envelope and typed across the front Mr Herbert Hull, Editor, and the rest of it. The following morning would be time enough to put it in the mail. One always liked to let these articles settle a bit, to see later on, with fresh eyes, what might need changing.

That evening he took a long walk. If nothing else, he owed himself some serious thinking. Perhaps he was letting fate decide, but, if he was, it did. Paris chose that night to be rather a movie of itself. An old man was playing a concertina and a few aristocrats were dancing in the street – the French were tight as fiddle strings until they decided to let loose, and then they could be delightfully mad. Or, perhaps, it was a day for some special little ritual – they arrived frequently and Szara never knew exactly what was going on – when everybody was expected to do the same thing: eat a particular cake, buy a prescribed bouquet, join open-air dancing on the boulevards. Some street corner toughs; wide jackets, black shirts, white ties, their shoulders hunched a certain way, beckoned him over, then stood him a Belgian beer at a corner bar. A girl with blonde hair flowing like the wind floated by him and said some deliriously indecipherable thing. It made him want the girl in Berlin – to live such a night unshared was a tragedy. It stayed light forever, a flight of little birds took off from the steeple of a church and fled northwards past the red-stained clouds in a fading sky. So lovely it hurt. He walked past the Santé prison, looked up at the windows, wondered who might be watching this same sky, could taste the freedom in his own life. He stopped for a sausage in a small French loaf, bought from an old lady in a windowed booth. The old lady gave him a look, she knew life, she had him figured out, she knew he'd do the right thing.

Odile returned from her courier run on 12 June. The product generated by the Berlin networks, as well as OTTER material from Dr Baumann, was photographed on microfilm in the basement of a Berlin butcher shop; the spool was then sewn into the shoulder pad of Odile's suit jacket for the German border crossing and the train ride back to Paris. By the morning of 13 June the film had been developed, and Szara, working at the rue Delesseux house, had an answer to his carefully phrased – *peripheral data,* he'd been told to call it, as though nobody really cared – request for identification of Baumann Milling office workers and sketches of their personalities. Baumann's response was brusque:

FINAL PRODUCTION FOR MAY WAS 17715. WE PROJECT JUNE AT 20588 BASED ON ORDERS AT HAND. THE OTHER DATA YOU REQUEST IS NOT PER OUR AGREEMENT. OTTER.

Szara was not pleased by this rejection but neither was he surprised. A week earlier, he'd made a day trip to Brussels and conferred with Goldman, a discussion that had prepared him for what the *rezident* suspected might happen, and set up his return message. This he wrote on a sheet of paper that would find its way to Baumann on Odile's next trip to Berlin:

WE HAVE RECEIVED YOUR MAY/JUNE FIGURES AND ARE AP-PRECIATIVE AS ALWAYS. ALL HERE ARE CONCERNED FOR YOUR CONTINUED HEALTH AND WELL-BEING. THE ANNOTATED LIST IS NEEDED TO ASSURE YOUR SECURITY AND WE URGE YOU STRONG-LY TO COMPLY WITH OUR REQUEST FOR THIS INFORMATION. WE CAN PROTECT YOU ONLY IF YOU GIVE US THE MEANS TO DO SO. JEAN MARC.

Untrue, but persuasive. As Goldman put it, 'Telling somebody that you're protecting him is just about the surest way to help him see that he's threatened.' Szara looked up from his plate of noodles and asked if it in fact were not the case that Baumann was in peril. Goldman shrugged. 'Who isn't?'

Szara took another piece of paper and wrote a report to Goldman, which would then be retransmitted to Moscow. He assumed that Goldman would, in the particular way he chose to put things, protect himself, Szara, and Baumann, in that order. The message to Goldman went to Kranov for encryption and telegraphy late that night.

Szara checked his calendar, made a note of Odile's 19 June courier run, Moscow's incoming transmission, and his next meeting with Sénéschal – that afternoon, as it happened. He squashed out a cigarette, lit another. Ran his fingers through his hair. Shook his head to clear it. Times, dates, numbers, codes, schedules, and somebody might die if you made a mistake.

New piece of paper.

He'd acquired from the Lisbon port authority the expected arrival date, 10 July, of a Strength through Joy cruise from Hamburg. Figuring from Odile's 19 June courier mission, he saw that Marta could just make it if there was room on the boat. For an hour he worked on the letter. It had to be sincere; she had great respect for honesty of a certain kind, yet he knew he mustn't gush. She would hate that. He tried to be casual, *let's enjoy ourselves*, and romantic, *I do need to be with you*, at the same time. Difficult. Suddenly he sat bolt upright. How on earth could he find a German stamp in Paris? He would have to ask Odile to buy one when she got off the train in Berlin. Should he confide in her? No, better not. He was the deputy director of the net, and this was simply another form of communication with an agent. Even love had become espionage, he thought, or was it just the times he lived in? That aside, when was his meeting with Sénéschal? Where was it? He had it written down somewhere. Where? Good God.

4:20 P.M. The racetrack at Auteuil. By the rail, facing the entrance to Section D. A well-conceived location for a *treff* – shifting crowds, anonymous faces – except if it was raining, which it was. Szara saw immediately that he and Sénéschal would wind up standing together, isolated, in the view of thousands of people with sense enough to move into the shelter of the grandstand.

Such tradecraft, he thought, whistling loudly to catch Sénéschal's attention as he emerged from the entry gate. Silently they climbed to the last row of the grandstand as a few horses splattered mud on each other at the far turn of the oval track. '*Allez* you shithead,' said a dispirited old man in an aisle seat.

Szara was by nature acutely aware of shifts in mood, and he sensed Sénéschal's discomfort right away. The lawyer's tousled hair was soaked, a damp cigarette hung from his lips – nobody liked getting wet, but there was more to it than that. His face was pale and tense, as though something had broken through his insouciant defences and drained his optimism.

For a time they watched galloping horses, a primitive loudspeaker system crackled and popped, the muffled voice of an excited Frenchman could just barely be made out as he called the race.

'A difficult weekend with Fräulein?' Szara asked, not unsympathetically. He had a hunch that the romantic trip to Normandy had gone wrong.

A Gallic shrug, then, 'No. Not so bad. She gives herself like a woman in love – anything at all to please since nothing between lovers can be wrong. If she feels I'm not sufficiently passionate she gets up to tricks. You're a man, Jean Marc, you know.'

'It can't always be easy,' Szara said. 'Humans aren't made of steel, and that includes communists.'

Sénéschal watched eight new horses being led out into the rain.

'Shall we give you a little breathing space? Perhaps a notional journey, something to do with the Foreign Office. The crisis in Greece.'

'Is there one?'

'Usually.'

Sénéschal grunted, not terribly interested. 'She wants to get married. Immediately.'

'I can't believe you didn't use a . . .'

'No. It's not that. She thinks she's to be dismissed from her position, sent back to Germany in disgrace. Last weekend, after we'd done with all the little shrieks and gasps, there were tears. Floods. She turned bright red and puffed up. It rained like a bastard up there. All weekend the stuff ran down the windows. She bawled, I tried to comfort her but she was inconsolable. Now, she says, only marriage can keep her in France, with me. As for my job at the Foreign Office and the information she's provided, well, too bad. We will live on love, she says.'

'Did she explain?'

'She gabbled like a goose. What I can make of it is that her boss, Herr Stollenbauer, is under severe pressure. Lötte spent all last week running around Paris in taxis – and she claims she's frightened of Parisian cab drivers – because no Mission cars were available. She says she hunted through every fancy shop in the city, Fauchon, Vigneau, Rollet, the finest *traiteurs* you see, in search of what she calls Rote Grütze. Do you know what that is? Because I don't.'

'A sort of sweetened sauce. Made of red berries,' Szara said.

'Also, they're trying to rent a house, somewhere just outside Paris. In Suresnes or Maisons-Laffitte, places like that. According to her they're more than willing to pay, but French *propriétaires* take their time, want papers signed, bank guarantees, first this, then that. It's ceremonial, drives the Germans crazy; they just want to wave money about and get what they want. They think the French are venal – they aren't wrong but they don't understand how French people worry about their properties. From her stories I gathered, more or less, that this is what's going on. And the worse it gets, the more Stollenbauer feels the pressure, the more he shouts at her. She isn't used to that, so now the answer is to get married, she'll stay in France, and I suppose tell Stollenbauer off into the bargain.'

'*Somebody's* coming to Paris.'

'*Évidemment.*'

'Somebody with an aide to call up and say, "Oh yes, and make sure the man's Rote Grütze sauce is available when he eats his pfann-kuchen." '

'Shall one go to the forest and pick red berries?'

To Szara's horror, Sénéschal was not at all sarcastic. 'Not to worry,' he said sternly. Sénéschal was clearly in the process of wilting. He was physically brave, Szara knew that for a fact, but the prospect of daily married life with Huber had unnerved him. Szara spoke with authority: 'It's the Frenchwoman of your dreams you'll marry, my friend, and not the Fräulein. Consider that an order.'

The new information was provocative. Szara's old instincts – the journalist happening on a story – were sharply aroused. Suddenly the horses churning through the mud seemed triumphant, images of victory: their nostrils flaring, flanks shining with kicked-up spray. The business with the Rote Grütze sauce was curious, but the search for a safe house, that was truly *interesting*. Trade Missions didn't acquire safe houses. That was embassy business, a job undertaken by resident intelligence officers. But the embassy was being circumvented, which meant a big secret, and a big secret meant a big fish, and guess who happened to be standing there with a net. *Cameras*, he thought, *just every kind of camera*.

He made a decision. 'Huber won't be fired,' he said. 'It's to be quite the opposite. Stollenbauer will be crawling at her feet. And as for you, your only problem will be a woman in triumph, a star of stage, screen, and radio, a princess. Demanding, I think, but not something you can't deal with.'

Fully mobilized, Szara's web of contacts had an answer within days.

An Alsatian *traiteur* was located; a smiling Lötte Huber left his shop trailed by a taxi driver struggling under the weight of two cases of Rote Grütze sauce in special crocks of the Alsatian's own design. He was also prepared to offer weisswurst, jaegerwurst, freshly cured sauerkraut subtly flavoured with juniper berries because – and here the rosy-cheeked *traiteur* leaned over the counter and spoke an exquisitely polite German – 'a man who favours Rote Grütze will always, *always*, madame, want a hint of juniper in his sauerkraut. This is an appetite for piquancy. And this is an appetite we understand.'

Schau-Wehrli dismissed the house dilemma with an imperious Swiss flick of the hand. Her progressive friends and colleagues at the International Law Institute were sounded out and a suitable property was soon located. It was in Puteaux, a step or two from the city border, a dignified, working-class neighbourhood near the Citroën loading docks on the southwestern curve of the Seine: everywhere a grim, sooty brown, but boxes of flowers stood sentry at all the parlour windows, and the single step up to each doorway was swept before eight every morning. At the far edge of the district sat a three-storey, gabled brick residence – the home of a doctor now deceased and the subject of an interminable lawsuit – with a high wall covered in ivy and a massive set of doors bound in ironwork. A bit of a horror, but the ivied wall turned out to hide a large, formal garden. Sheets were removed from the furniture, a crew of maids brought in to freshen up. Terracotta pots were placed by the entryway and filled to overflowing with fiery geraniums.

Stollenbauer was, as Szara had predicted, magically relieved of much of his burden. The pending visit still made him nervous, much could go wrong, but at least he now felt he *had some support.* From chubby little Lötte Huber no less! Had he not always said that someday her light would shine? Had he not always sensed the hidden talent and initiative in this woman? She'd been so clever in finding the house – where his pompous assistants had shouted guttural French into the phone, cunning Lötte had taken the feminine approach, spending her very own weekend time wandering about various neighbourhoods and inquiring of women in the marketplace if they knew of something to rent, not too much legal foolishness required.

Meanwhile, Szara arrayed his forces and played his own office politics. Oh, Goldman was *informed,* he had to be, but the cable was a masterpiece of its genre – *Trade Mission apparently expecting important visitor sometime in near future,* item eight of seventeen items, not a chance under heaven that such a phrase would bring the greedy *rezident* swooping down from Brussels to snaffle up the credit.

Using a copy of the house key, Szara and Sénéschal had a look around for themselves one evening. Szara would have dearly loved to record the proceedings, but it would simply have been too dangerous, requiring a hidden operative running a wire recorder. Then too, important visitors usually had security men in attendance, people with a horror of unexplained ridges under carpets, miscellaneous wires, even fresh paint.

Instead they approached a birdlike little lady, the widow of an artillery corporal, who lived on the top floor of the house across the street and whose parlour window looked out over the garden. *A troublesome affair,* they told her; *a wayward wife, a government minister, the greatest discretion.* They showed her very official-looking identity documents with diagonal red stripes and handed over a crisp envelope stuffed with francs. She nodded grimly, perhaps an old lady but a little more a woman of the world than they might suppose. They were welcome to her window; it was a change to have something going on in this dull old street. And did they wish to hear a thing or two about the butcher's wife?

Stollenbauer summoned Lötte Huber to his office, sat her down on a spindly little chair, rested his long fingers lightly on her knee, and told her, in strictest confidence, that their visitor was an associate of Heydrich himself.

Sénéschal had walked Lötte Huber through the 'discovery' of the safe house and the Rote Grütze sauce and counselled how these successes should be explained. And what thanks did he get? The young woman's new sense of pride and achievement made her shut up like a clam. Under Szara's tutelage, he applied pressure every way he could. Told her *the big job* was now open at the Foreign Office – would he get it, or would his sworn enemy? Only she could help him now.

He took her to dinner at Fouquet's, fed her triangles of toast covered thickly with goose liver pâté and a bottle of Pomerol. The wine made her cute, funny, and romantic, but not talkative. Finally they fought. What use, she wanted to know, had the French Foreign Office for information that an associate of Heydrich's was coming to town for an important meeting? That was *the very sort of thing* that interested them, he said. The big cheese in his office was secretly a great admirer of Hitler and could be counted on to help, quietly, if any more problems developed with the meeting. But he had to be told exactly what was going on. No, she said, stop, you begin to sound like a spy. That made Sénéschal pale and Szara even paler when the conversation was reported. 'Apologize,' Szara said. 'Tell her you were overwrought and' – he reached into a pocket and came forth with francs – 'buy her jewellery.'

Szara accepted the inevitable. They weren't going to get the meeting date or the names of the other participants, surveillance was their only other option. He could not risk pressing Huber too hard and losing her as a source. It was the first time a wisp of regret floated across his view of the operation – it was not to be the last.

They drove to Puteaux in Sénéschal's car, parked in the narrow street, and watched the house – a surveillance technique that lasted exactly one hour and twelve minutes, perhaps a record for brevity. Children stared, young women pretended not to notice, an angry streetsweeper scraped the hubcap with his twig broom, and a drunk demanded money. *Discomfort* did not begin to describe how it felt; it just wasn't a neighbourhood where you could do something like that.

Odile returned from her courier run to Berlin on 22 June (Baumann wouldn't budge), so she, Sénéschal, and Szara took turns sitting in the old lady's parlour. The wisp of regret had by now become a smoky haze that refused to dissipate. Goldman had the people to do this kind of work; Szara had to improvise with available resources. As for surveillance from the apartment, the principle was one thing, the reality another. The building, cold stone to the eye, was alive, full of inquisitive neighbours you couldn't avoid on the stairs. Szara squared his shoulders and scowled – *I am a policeman* – and left the old lady to deal with the inevitable tongue-wagging.

For her part, she seemed to be enjoying the attention. What she did not enjoy, however, was their company. They were, well, *there.* If somebody read a newspaper, it rattled; if she wanted to clean the carpet, they had to lift their feet. Odile finally saved the situation, discovering that the old lady had a passion for the card game called bezique, a form of pinochle. So the surveillance evolved into a more or less permanent card party, all three watchers contriving to play just badly enough to lose a few francs.

The smoky haze of regret thickened to a fog. What point in having Sénéschal or Odile watch the house if Szara could not be reached when something finally happened – this was *his* operation. But the rules emphatically excluded contact with an agent-operator at his home or, God forbid, at the communications base. Thus he found a rooming house in Suresnes with a telephone on the wall in the corridor, gave the landlady a month's rent and an alias, and there, when he wasn't on duty in Puteaux, he stayed, waiting for Sénéschal or Odile to use the telephone in a café just down the street from the old lady's building.

Waiting.

The great curse of espionage: Father Time in lead boots, the skeleton cobwebbed to the telephone – any and all of the images applied. If you were lucky and good an opportunity presented itself. And then you waited.

July came. Paris broiled in the sun, you could smell the butcher shops half a block away. Szara sat sweating in a soiled little room, not a breath of air stirred through the window; he read trashy French novels, stared out at the street. *I dared to enter the world of spies,* he thought, *and wound up like the classic lonely-pensioner-alone-in-a-room of a Gogol story.* There was a woman who lived just down the hall, fortyish, dyed blonde, and fleshy. Fleshy the first week, sumptuous the second, Rubenesque thereafter. She too seemed to be waiting for something or other, though Szara couldn't imagine what.

Actually he could imagine, and did. Her presence in the hallway was announced by a trail of scent called Cri de la Nuit, cheap, crude, sweet, which drove his imagination to absurd excesses. As did her bitter mouth, set in a permanent sneer that said to the world, and especially to him, 'Well?'

Before he could answer, the phone rang.

'Can you come to dinner?' Odile said. Heart pounding, Szara found a cranky old taxi at the Suresnes Maine and reached the Puteaux house in minutes. Odile was standing well back from the window, looking through a pair of opera glasses. With a little grin of triumph she handed them over. 'Second floor,' she said. 'To the left of the entryway.'

By the time he focused, they weren't where she said they were, but had moved to the top floor, two colourless men in dark suits seen dimly through the gauze curtain shielding the window. They vanished, then reappeared for a moment when they parted the drapes in an adjoining room. 'A security check,' he said.

'Yes,' Odile said. 'Their car is parked well down the street.'

'What model?'

'Not sure.'

'Big?'

'Oh yes,' she said. 'And shiny.'

Szara felt his blood race.

The following afternoon, 8 July, they were back. This time it was Szara on duty. He'd moved the bezique table in front of the window and, having begged the old lady's pardon, removed his shirt, appearing in sleeveless undershirt, a cigarette stuck in his lips, a hand of playing cards held before him, a sullen expression on his face. This time a heavy man with a bow tie accompanied the other two and from the open gateway stared up at Szara, who stared right back. *A living Brassai*, he thought, *Card Player in Puteaux* – he lacked only a bandanna tied around his neck. The man in the bow tie broke off the staring contest, then slowly closed the door that concealed the garden from the street.

9 July was the day.

At 2:00 P.M. sharp, two glossy black Panhards pulled up at the gate. One of the security men left the first car and opened the gate as his partner drove off. The second car was aligned in such a way that Szara could identify the driver as the man with the bow tie. He also caught a glimpse of the passenger, who sat directly behind the driver and glanced out the window just before the Panhard swung through the gateway and the security man pushed the doors shut. The passenger was in his early forties, Szara guessed. The angle of sight, from above, could be misleading, but Szara took him to be short and bulky. He had thick black hair sharply parted, a swarthy, deeply lined face, and small dark eyes. For the occasion he wore a double-breasted suit, a shirt with a stiff high collar, a grey silk tie. *Gestapo*, Szara thought, dressed up like a diplomat, but the face read policeman and criminal at once, with a conviction of

337

power that Szara had seen in certain German faces, especially – no matter how they preached the Nordic ideal – the dark men who ruled the nation. Important, Szara realized. The single glance out the window had asked the question *Am I pleased?*

'Ten of clubs,' said the old lady.

Fifteen minutes later, a grey Peugeot coasted to a stop in front of the house. A hawk-faced man got out on the side away from Szara and the car immediately left. The man looked about him for a moment, made certain of his tie, then pressed the doorbell set into the portal of the gateway.

Dershani.

Sénéschal knocked twice, then entered the apartment. 'Christ, the heat,' he said. He collapsed in an armchair, set a Leica down carefully among the framed photographs on a rickety table. His suit was hopelessly rumpled, black circles at the armpits, a grey shadow of newsprint ink darkening the front of his shirt. He had spent the last two hours lying on sheets of newspaper in a lead-lined gutter at the foot of the sloped roof. The building's scrollwork provided a convenient portal for photography.

Sénéschal wiped his face with a handkerchief. 'I took all the automobiles,' he said. 'The security man who worked the door – several of him. Tried for the second man, but not much there I'm afraid, perhaps a one-quarter profile, and he was moving. As for the face in the back seat of the Panhard, I managed two exposures, but I doubt anything will show up.'

Szara nodded silently.

'Well? What do you think?'

Szara gestured with his eyes towards the old lady, waiting not quite patiently to resume the card game. 'Too early to know much of anything. We'll wait for them to use the garden,' he said.

'What if it rains?'

Szara looked up at the sky, a mottled grey in the Paris humidity. 'Not before tonight,' he said.

They appeared just before five – *a break in the negotiation.* Odile had arrived at her usual time, Szara now used her opera glasses and stood well back from the window.

The man he took to be a German intelligence officer was short and heavy, as he'd supposed. Magnification revealed a thin white scar crossing his left eyebrow, a street fighter's badge of honour. The two men stood at the garden entrance for a moment, open French doors behind them. The German spoke a few words, Dershani nodded, and they walked together into the garden. They were the image of diplomacy, strolling pensively with hands clasped behind their backs, continuing a very deliberate conversation, choosing their words with great care. Szara studied their lips through the opera glasses but could not, to his surprise, determine if they were speaking German or Russian. Once they laughed. Szara fancied he could hear it, faintly, carried on the heated air of the late afternoon amid the sound of sparrows chirping in the trees of the garden.

They made a single circuit on the gravel path, stopping once while the German pointed at an apple tree, then returned to the house, each beckoning the other to enter first. Dershani laughed, clapping the German on the shoulder, and went in ahead of him.

At 7:20, Dershani left the house. He turned up the street in the direction his car had gone and disappeared from view. A few minutes later, the security man opened the gate and, after the car had passed through, closed it again. He climbed in beside the driver and the Panhard sped away. In the garden, the setting sun made long shadows on the dry grass, the birds sang, nothing moved in the still summer air.

'*Tiens,*' said the old lady. 'Will the government fall tomorrow?'

Sénéschal was grave. 'No, madame, I can in confidence inform you that, thanks to your great kindness and patience, the government will stand.'

'Oh, too bad,' she said.

Odile left first, to walk to the Neuilly Métro stop. Sénéschal disappeared into the old lady's closet and emerged a few minutes later smelling faintly of mothballs. He handed Szara a spool of film. Szara thanked the old lady, told her they might be back the following day, gave her a fresh packet of money, and went out into the humid dusk.

Sénéschal's car was parked several blocks away. They walked through streets deserted by the onset of the dinner hour; smells of frying onions and potatoes drifted through the open windows.

'Do we try again tomorrow?' Sénéschal asked.

Szara thought it over. 'I sense that they've done what they came together to do.'

'Can't be certain.'

'No. I'll contact you at your office, if you don't mind.'

'Not at all.'

'I should say, officially, that gratitude is expressed – charming the way they put these things. Personally, thank you for everything, and I'm sorry your shirt is ruined.'

Sénéschal inspected the front of his shirt. 'No. My little friend is a wonder. No matter what I get into she knows a way to take care of it. Nothing is to be thrown out, it can always last "a bit longer". '

'Is she aware of your, ah, love affair?'

'They always know, Jean Marc, but it's part of life here. It's what all those sad little café songs are about.'

'You are in love, then.'

'Oh that word. Perhaps, or perhaps not. She is my consolation, however, always that, and doesn't she ever know it. *L'amour* covers quite some territory, especially in Paris.'

'I expect it does.'

'Have you a friend?'

'Yes. Or I should say "perhaps". '

'She's good to you?'

'Good for me.'

'*Et alors!*'

Szara laughed.

'Beautiful too, I'd wager.'

'You would win, eventually, but it's not the sort of dazzle that catches the eye right away. There's just something about her.'

They reached the car; the smell of overheated upholstery rushed out when Sénéschal opened the door. 'Come have a beer,' he said. 'There's plenty of time for your vanishing act.'

'Thank you,' Szara said.

Sénéschal turned the ignition, the Renault came reluctantly to life as he fiddled expertly with the choke. 'This whore drinks petrol,' he said sourly, racing the engine.

They wandered through the twisting streets of Puteaux, crossed the Seine on the pont de Suresnes – the tied-up barges had pots of flowers and laundry drying on lines – then the Bois de Boulogne appeared on their left, a few couples out strolling, men with jackets over their arms, an organ grinder. Sénéschal stopped by an ice cream seller. 'What kind?'

'Chocolate.'

'A double?'

'Of course. Here's a few francs.'

'Keep it.'

'I insist.'

Sénéschal waved the money away and bought the cones. When he got back in the car he drove slowly through the Bois, steering with one hand. 'Watch, now I really will ruin the shirt.'

Szara's double cone was a masterpiece – he ate the ice cream and looked at the girls in their summer dresses.

But what he'd seen that afternoon did not leave him. His mind was flying around like a moth in a lamp. He didn't understand what he'd witnessed, didn't know what it meant or what, if anything, to do about it. He'd seen something he wasn't supposed to see, that much he did know. Maybe it meant nothing – intelligence services talked to each other when it was in the interest of both to do so, and Paris was a good, neutral place to do it.

'If you've the time, we'll find ourselves a brasserie,' Sénéschal said.

'Good idea. Is there a place you go?' Szara wanted the company.

Sénéschal looked at him oddly. Szara realized his error, they couldn't go to a place where Sénéschal was known. 'We'll just pick one that looks good,' he said. 'In this city you can't go too far wrong.'

They'd drifted into the fifteenth arrondissement, headed east on the boulevard Lefebvre. 'We're in the right place out here,' Sénéschal said. 'They have great big ones where the whole family shows up – kids, dogs. A night like this' – the Renault idled roughly at a red light; a fat man in suspenders was picking through books at a stall – 'the terraces will be . . .' The Panhard rolled to a gentle stop on Sénéschal's side of the car.

Seen from a window in the old lady's apartment, he'd been a colourless man in a suit. Now, looking through the Panhard's passenger window, he was much realer than that. He was young, not yet thirty, and very bright and crisp. His hair was combed just so, swept up into a stiff pompadour above his white forehead. 'Please,' he said in measured French, 'may we speak a moment?' He smiled. *What merry eyes*, Szara thought. For a moment he was unable to breathe.

Sénéschal turned to him for help, his knuckles white on the steering wheel.

'Please? Yes?' said the man.

The driver was older, his face a silhouette in the lights of the boulevard shops. 'Don't be so fucking polite,' he grumbled in German. He turned and looked at Sénéschal. It was the face of a German worker, blunt and stolid, with hair shaved above the ears. He was smoking a cigar, the tip reddened as he inhaled.

The light went green. A horn beeped behind them. 'Drive away,' Szara said. Sénéschal popped the clutch and the car stalled. Swearing under his breath, he twisted the ignition key and fumbled with the choke. The driver of the Panhard laughed, his partner continued to smile. *Like a clown in a nightmare*, Szara thought.

The engine caught and the Renault roared away from the light. Sénéschal cut into an angled street, took a narrow cobbled alley between high walls at full speed – the car bouncing and shimmying – tried to turn sharply back into the boulevard traffic, but the light had changed again and he had nowhere to go. The Panhard rolled up beside them. 'Whew,' said the smiling man. 'What a bumping!'

'Look,' the driver said in French, holding his cigar between thumb and forefinger, 'don't make us chase you around all night . . .'

Traffic started to move and Sénéschal forced his way between two cars. The Panhard tried to follow, but the driver of a little Fiat cut them off with a spiteful glare.

'Tell me what to do,' Sénéschal said.

Szara tried to think of something, as though he knew. 'Stay with the traffic,' he said. Sénéschal nodded vigorously, he would follow Szara's plan meticulously. He settled the Renault into traffic, which now began to thin out noticeably as they approached the eastern border of the city. At the next light, Szara leaned over in order to look in the rearview mirror. The Panhard was two cars back in the adjoining lane. The passenger saw what he was doing, stuck his arm out the window and waved. When the light changed, Sénéschal stamped the gas pedal against the floorboards, swerved around the car in front, changed lanes, turned off the headlights, and shot across the oncoming traffic into a side street.

Szara twisted around, but the Panhard was not to be seen. Sénéschal began to make lefts and rights, tearing through the darkness of deserted side streets while Szara watched for the Panhard. 'Any idea where we are?' he said.

'The thirteenth.'

A shabby neighbourhood, unlit; peeling wooden shutters protected the shopfronts. Up ahead, a broad boulevard appeared and Sénéschal pulled over and left the car idling as they both lit cigarettes. Szara's hands were trembling. 'The passenger was at the safe house,' Sénéschal said. 'You have his photograph. But the other one, with the cigar, where did he come from?'

'I never saw him.'

'Nazis,' Sénéschal said. 'Did you *see* them?'

'Yes.'

'What did they want?'

'To talk, they said.'

'Oh yes! I believe it!' He exhaled angrily and shook his head. 'Shit.'

'Their time will come,' Szara said.

'Did you hear him? That cunt? "Please, may we speak a moment."' Sénéschal made the man sound effeminate and mincing.

'That was a good idea, cutting across.'

Sénéschal shrugged. 'I just did it.' He flicked his cigarette out the window and eased the Renault into first gear, turning the headlights back on. He swung left onto the deserted boulevard. 'A bad neighbourhood,' he said. 'Nobody comes here at night.'

They drove for five minutes, Szara spotted a Métro station on the corner. 'Expect a contact by telephone. After that, our meetings will be as usual.'

'I'll be waiting,' Sénéschal said, voice mean and edgy. The brush with the Germans had frightened him. Now he was angry.

The car stopped in midblock and Szara got out and closed the door behind him. He thrust his hands in his pockets, squeezing the roll of film to make sure of it, and walked quickly towards the Métro entrance. He reached the grillwork arch above the stairway, saw it was the Tolbiac station, stopped dead as a metallic explosion echoed off the buildings followed by the sound of shattered glass raining on the pavement. He stared at the noise. Two blocks away the Renault was bent around the front of a car that had ploughed into the driver's door. The passenger door was jammed open and something was lying in the street a few feet away from it. Szara started to run. Two men got out of the black car that had struck the Renault. One of them held his head and sat on the ground. The other ran to the thing in the street and bent over it. Szara stopped dead and found the shadows next to a building. Lights began to go on, heads appeared in windows. The glow of the street lamps was reflected in the liquid running into the street from the two cars, and the smell of petrol reached him. The man who had been bending over the thing in the street squatted for a moment, seemed to be searching for something, then rose abruptly and kicked savagely at whatever it was that was lying there. People began to come out of their doorways, talking excitedly to each other. The man by the Renault now turned, took the other man under one arm and hauled him to his feet, pulling him forward, at last getting him to stumble along quickly. They disappeared up a side street across the boulevard.

Walking quickly towards the cars, Szara found himself amid a small crowd of people. The Panhard's windscreen was starred on the right side, and the driver's door on the Renault had been mashed halfway across the front seat by the impact. Sénéschal lay face down near the Renault's sprung passenger door, his jacket up over his head, shirttail pulled halfway out of his trousers. A group of men stood around him, one bent down for a closer look, lifted the jacket, then straightened up, eyes shut in order not to see what he'd seen. He waved a dismissive hand across his body and said, 'Don't look.' Another man said, 'Did you see him *kick* him?' The voice was quivering. 'He kicked a dead man. He did. I saw it.'

TRANSMISSION 11 JULY 1938 22:30 HOURS

TO JEAN MARC: DIRECTORATE JOINS YOU IN REGRET FOR LOSS OF
COMRADE SILO. INQUIRY TO BE UNDERTAKEN BY YVES WITH
ASSISTANCE OF ELLI, A REPORT TO BE MADE TO DIRECTORATE
SOONEST OF CIRCUMSTANCES PERTINENT TO THIS INCIDENT
WITH SPECIAL REGARD TO PREVIOUS ACCIDENT INVOLVING
FORMER DEPUTY. ESSENTIAL TO DETERMINE EXACT CIRCUM-
STANCES OF BOTH THESE INCIDENTS WITH REGARD TO THEIR
POSSIBLE INTENTIONAL ORIGIN. THE REMOTEST POSSIBILITY TO
BE CONSIDERED. ALL OPAL PERSONNEL TO BE ON HIGHEST ALERT
FOR HOSTILE ACTION AGAINST THE NETWORK.

THERE IS GRAVE CONCERN FOR THE CONTINUITY OF THE ARBOUR
PRODUCT. SINCE HECTOR WAS PRESENT WHEN INITIAL CONTACT
MADE BETWEEN ARBOUR AND SILO, AND HECTOR HAS BEEN
PRESENTED AS THE FRIEND OF SILO, CAN HECTOR FIND MEANS
TO OPERATE AS SILO'S REPLACEMENT IN THIS RELATIONSHIP?
HECTOR TO SHOW CONCERN AS FAMILY FRIEND AND PROVIDE
COMFORT AS HE IS ABLE. IT IS SUGGESTED THAT SILO'S FUNERAL
IS THE LOGICAL SETTING FOR CONTACT BETWEEN HECTOR AND
ARBOUR. ALTERNATIVELY, IF SILO'S TRUE POLITICAL AFFILIA-
TION IS REVEALED, CAN PRESSURE BE BROUGHT TO BEAR ON
ARBOUR? WILL ARBOUR COOPERATE IN THIS CONTEXT? RESPOND
BY 14 JULY.

OTTER MUST BE PRESSED TO EXPAND HIS REPORTING. RECOM-
MEND NEW MEASURES TO BE TAKEN WITHIN 48 HOURS.

ACCOUNT NO. 414–223–8/74 AT BANQUE SUISSE DE GENEVE TO BE
CLOSED. NEW ACCOUNT NO. 609–846 DX 12 AT CREDIT LEMANS
OPERATIVE AS OF 15 JULY IN NAME COMPAGNIE ROMAILLES WITH
CREDIT OF 50,000 FRENCH FRANCS. 10,000 FRANCS TO BE TAKEN
BY COURIER TO YVES. DIRECTOR

Sitting in the hot, dirty room where Kranov transmitted and decoded,
Szara tossed the message aside. The frantic endgame attempted by the
Directorate, their shrill tone, and the certainty of failure he found
faintly depressing. He perfectly remembered the André Szara who
would have been enraged by the Directorate's calculating attitude, a
man who, not so very long ago, believed passionately that the only
unforgivable human sin was a cold heart. Now he was not that man. He
understood what they wanted, understood them for wanting it, and

knew the result: Lötte Huber was lost. Sénéschal's friend Valais, HECTOR, also a lawyer formerly active in the French Communist party, had been with Sénéschal the night they'd 'met' Huber and her friend at the theatre, and had been brought on stage as a confidant – *Lötte, he's so worried and upset, you must help him* – to move the operation along. But Huber would never accept him as a lover; this was *analyst's* thinking, a scheme created at a great distance from events and in breathtaking ignorance of the personalities involved. Valais was a ponderous, contemplative man, a fair-skinned Norman lacking entirely Sénéschal's Mediterranean intensity and charm.

And blackmail was absurd. Huber would go to pieces, bring the French police down on their heads. Moscow was clearly rattled: losing first the operative Szara had replaced, in a car accident outside Mâcon, and now Sénéschal in what had been presented to them as a second car accident, a hit-and-run tragedy.

For Szara had not told them otherwise.

A pawn in *khvost* politics had become an active participant.

Was he to inform the Directorate, and thus Dershani, of photographs taken in a Puteaux garden? A secret meeting of senior Soviet and German intelligence officers, perhaps of diplomatic importance, not so secret after all. Penetrated. Photographed. Maybe the Directorate knew of Dershani's contact with the Nazi service.

Maybe it didn't.

The Germans certainly wanted to keep the contact secret – they'd murdered Sénéschal on that basis. So what would the NKVD have in store for him? He chose not to find that out, instead undertook a damage control programme to protect himself, informing Schau-Wehrli that, according to Huber's final report to Sénéschal, the grand meeting had not yet taken place, and cabling both Goldman and Moscow to that effect.

Odile, of course, presented a very different problem and he'd had to approach her directly. He'd got her off by herself and placed his life in her hands: there will be an investigation; you must not tell the Brussels *rezident*, or anybody, what you were doing on the days leading up to 9 July. He'd watched her, a tough Belgian girl from the mining towns, raw, nineteen, and loyal to the death once she got it straightened out what was what. She'd thought it over for quite some time. Her face, usually flip and sexy and moody all at once, was closed, immobile, he couldn't read it. Finally, she'd agreed. She trusted him, instinctively, and perhaps she feared it was already too late to tell the truth. She also knew, from growing up within Communist party politics, that conspiracy was bread-and-butter to them all: you chose a side and lived with the result.

The photographs had turned out to be adequate. He'd had them developed by randomly choosing a little shop, assuming the technician would make no particular sense of the subjects. Picking them up in midafternoon, he'd found an empty booth in a deserted café and spent an hour turning them over in his hands, cloudy black and white impressions shot from above, eleven prints paid for with a life. The crisp, young security man opening a gate. Head and shoulders of a man at the wheel of a car. Car window with a faint blur behind it. Dershani and the Gestapo officer in a garden, the German speaking tentatively, left hand turned up to emphasize a point. There was no photograph of the man with the cigar who drove the Panhard, Sénéschal had not managed to record his own murderer.

Now, what to do with them. He'd thought about that for a long time, then decided that if Bloch didn't contact him he'd pass them to Abramov whenever an opportunity presented itself. Not officially, not through the system, friend to friend. Until then, he'd hide them in his apartment.

As he thought about the photographs, the blacked-out room began to feel claustrophobic. A few feet away, facing the opposite wall, Kranov worked like a machine. The rhythmic tapping of his wireless key grated across Szara's nerves, so he filed the Moscow cable in a metal box and left the house, walking out into the still night air and heading towards the canals. The slaughterhouse workers were hard at it on the loading docks of the abattoirs, hefting bloody beef quarters on their shoulders, then swinging them in to butchers who waited in the backs of their trucks. They cursed and laughed as they worked, wiping the sweat from their eyes, brushing the flies off their spattered aprons. In a brightly lit café, a blind man played the violin and a whore danced on a table while the raucous crowd teased him with lurid descriptions of what he was missing, and he smiled and played in such a way as to let them know he saw more than they did. Szara walked on the cobbled pathway by the canal, then stood for a time and watched the reflections of the neon signs, bending and bowing with the motion of the black water.

To Sénéschal, dead because of his, Szara's, ignorance and inexperience, he could only give a place in his heart. He wondered if he'd ever learn how the Germans had managed it – the discovery of the surveillance, the tracking of the Renault while remaining invisible. Technically, they were simply more adept than he was – only the chance decision to use the Tolbiac Métro had saved his life – thus Sénéschal was gone, and he was the one left to stare into the dead waters of the canal and think about life. His sentence was to understand that, and to remember it. To remember also, forever, the driver of the Panhard, a dim shape seen at a distance, barely the form of a man, then the savage kick, a spasm of useless rage. *Sudden, without warning*; like the blow that had knocked him to the floor of a railway station buffet in Prague. He watched the wavering signs in the water, red and blue, recalled what Sénéschal had said about his girlfriend, the one who threw nothing away, the one for whom anything could be made to last a little longer.

8 July.

He took the night train to Lisbon.

Sat up in coach class, saving money, anticipating the cost of lovers' feasts: iced prawns with mayonnaise, the wine called Barca Velha, cool from the cellar of the *taberna*. Then too, he did not want to sleep. Somewhere out on the ocean, he imagined, Marta Haecht was also awake. Avoiding the ghastly end-of-voyage parties she would be standing at the rail, watching for a landfall glow in the distance, only dimly aware of the Strength through Joy revellers braying Nazi songs in the ship's ballroom. In her purse she would have the letter, carefully folded, something to laugh about in Portugal.

Nothing so good for a lover as a train ride through the length of the night, the endless click of the rails, the engine sometimes visible in the moonlight as it worked its way around a long curve. All night long he summoned memories – *Is there a place I may undress?* The train pounded through the vineyards of Gascony at dawn. He stood in the alcove at the end of the car, watched the rails glitter as they swept below the coupling, smelled the burnt cinder in the air. It was cold in the foothills of the Pyrénées; the scent of pine resin sharpened as the sun climbed the slopes. Falangist Guardia in leather hats checked the passports at the Hendaye border crossing, then they were in Franco's Spain all day long. They passed a burned-out tank, a raw lumber gallows standing at the edge of a town.

The haze shimmered in the hills north of Lisbon. The city itself was numb, exhausted in the faded summer light of evening. The carriage horses at the station barely bothered to flick their tails. Szara found a hotel called the Mirador, with Moorish turrets and balconies, and took a room above a courtyard where a fountain gushed rusty water over broken tiles and heavy roses lay sodden in the heat. He put his toothbrush in a glass, then went out for a long walk, eventually buying a pair of linen trousers, a thin white shirt, and a panama hat. He changed in the store and a Spanish couple asked directions of him on the way back to the hotel.

He spotted a Russian émigré newspaper at a kiosk, then spent the night reading to the whirr of cicadas and the splashing of the cracked fountain. *Stalin the Murderer! Prince Cheyalevsky Presents a Cheque to the Orphans' league. Mme Tsoutskaya Opens Milliner's Shop.* At dawn, he forced the ancient shutters closed, but he could not sleep. He had not asked Goldman's permission to leave Paris – he doubted it would have been granted; Sénéschal's death had everybody on edge – nor had he told Schau-Wehrli where he was going. Nobody knew where he was, and such freedom made it impossible to sleep. He wasn't seriously missing, not yet. He gave himself a week for that; then they'd panic, start calling the morgue and the hospitals.

Walking back to the hotel, he'd happened on a family of Jews: ashen faces, downcast eyes, dragging what remained of their possessions down the hill towards the docks. From Poland, he suspected. They'd come a long way, and now they were headed – where? South America? Or the United States?

Would *she* go? Yes, eventually she would. Not at first, not right away – one didn't just walk away from one's life. But later, after they'd made love, really made love, then she would go with him. He could see her: head propped on hand, sweat between her breasts, brown eyes liquid and intense; could hear the cicadas, the shutter creaking in the evening breeze.

He had money. Barely enough, but enough. They'd go to the American consulate and request visitors' visas. Then they would vanish. What else was America but that, the land of the vanished.

At ten the next morning he watched the docking of the liner *Hermann Krieg* – a Nazi martyr, no doubt. A crowd of German workers streamed down the gangplank, grinning at the brutal white sun they'd come to worship. The men leered at the dark Portuguese women in their black shawls, the wives took a firm grip on their husbands' arms.

Marta Haecht was nowhere to be seen.

That summer, the heat spared nobody.

And while London gardens wilted and Parisian dogs slept under café tables. New York positively steamed, ANOTHER SCORCHER, the *Daily Mirror* howled, while the *New York Times* said 'Temperatures Are Expected to Reach 98° Today.' It was impossible to sleep at night. Some people gathered on tenement stoops and spoke in low voices; others sat in the darkness, listened to Benny Goodman's band on the radio, and drank gallons of iced tea.

It was bad during the week, but the August heatwave seemed to save its truly hellish excesses for the weekends. You could take the subway to

Coney Island or the long trolley ride to Jones Beach, but you could hardly see the sand for the bodies much less find a spot to spread out your towel. The ocean itself seemed warm and sticky, and a sunburn made everything worse.

About the best you could hope for on the weekends was to own a little house in the country somewhere or, almost as good, to have an invitation to stay with somebody who did. Thus Herb Hull, senior editor at the magazine trying to make space for itself between the *Nation* and the *New Republic*, was elated to receive a Tuesday morning telephone call from Elizabeth May, asking him to come down with them on Friday night to their place in Bucks County. Jack May ran one of the Schubert box offices in the West Forties theater district, Elizabeth was a social worker at a Lower East Side settlement house. They were not Hull's close friends, but neither were they simply acquaintances. It was instead something in between, a sort of casual intimacy New Yorkers often fell into.

After the usual misadventures – a traffic jam in the Holland Tunnel, an overheating problem in the Mays' '32 Ford outside Somerville, New Jersey – they reached a sturdy little fieldstone house at the edge of a small pond. The house was typical: small bedrooms reached by a staircase with a squeaky step, battered furniture, bookcase full of murder mysteries left by former guests, and a bed in the guest room that smelled of mildew. Not far from Philadelphia, Bucks County had summer homes and artists' studios up every dirt road. Writers, painters, playwrights, editors, and literary agents tended to cluster there, as did people who worked at a great range of occupations but whose evenings were committed to books and plays and Carnegie Hall. They arrived on Friday night, unloaded the weekend groceries (corn, tomatoes, and strawberries would be bought at roadside stands), ate sandwiches, and went to bed early. Saturday morning was spent fussing at projects that never got done – you just weren't enjoying the country if you didn't 'fix' something – then the rest of the weekend drifted idly by in talking and drinking and reading in all their combinations. At Saturday night parties you'd see the same people you saw in Manhattan during the week.

Herb Hull was delighted to spend the weekend with the Mays. They were very bright and well read, the rye and bourbon flowed freely, and Elizabeth was a fine cook, known for corn fritters and Brunswick stew. That's what they had for dinner on Saturday night. Then they decided to skip the usual party, instead sat around, sipping drinks while Jack played Ellington records on the Victrola.

The Mays were charter subscribers to Hull's magazine and avid supporters of the causes it embraced. Not Party people but enlightened and progressive, fairly staunch for Roosevelt though they had voted for Debs in '32. The conversation all across Bucks County that night was politics, and the Mays' living room was no exception. In unison, the three lamented the isolationists, who wanted no part of 'that mess in Europe', and the German–American Bund, which supported them, de facto encouragement to Hitler. Sorrowfully, they agreed that there was no saving the Sudetenland; Hitler would snap it up as he had Austria. There would eventually be war, but America would stay out. That was shameful, cowardly, ultimately frightening. What had become of American idealism? Had the grinding poverty of the Depression gutted the national values? Was the country really going to be run by Westbrook Pegler and Father Coughlin? Did the American people hate Russia so much they were going to let Hitler have his way in Europe?

'That's the crux of it,' Jack May said angrily, shaking his head in frustration.

Hull agreed. It was all pretty sad stuff: Henry Ford and his anti-Semite pals, plenty of people down in Washington who didn't want to get involved in Europe, the hate groups claiming that Roosevelt was 'Rosenfeld', a Bolshevik Jew. 'But you know,' Hull said, 'Stalin isn't exactly helping matters. Some of the statements out of Moscow are pretty wishy-washy, and he's got Litvinov, the foreign minister, running all over Europe trying to play the same sort of diplomacy game as England and France. That won't stop Hitler, he understands the difference between treaties and tanks.'

'Ah for Christ sakes,' Jack May said. 'You know the situation in Russia. Stalin's got two hundred million peasants to feed. What's he supposed to do?'

'Herb, weren't you there this year?' Elizabeth asked.

'Last winter.'

'What was it like?'

'Oh, secret and strange – you get the sense of people listening behind the drapes. Poor. Just not enough to go around. Passionate for ideas and literature. A writer there is truly important, not just a barking dog on a leash. If I had to put it in two words, I guess one would be *inconvenient*. Why I don't know, but everything, and I do mean everything, is just so damn difficult. But the other word would have to be something like *exhilarating*. They're really trying to make it all work, and you can definitely feel that, like something in the air.'

Jack May looked at his wife, a mock-quizzical expression on his face. 'Did he have a good time?'

Elizabeth laughed.

'It was fascinating, that I can't deny.'

'And Stalin? What do they think about him?' she asked.

May took Hull's glass from the coffee table and splashed some bourbon over a fresh ice cube. Hull took a sip while May turned the record over. 'They certainly watch what they say. You never know who's listening. But at the same time they're Slavs, not Anglo-Saxons, and they want to open their heart to you if you're a friend. So you do hear stories.'

'Gossip?' May said. 'Or the real thing?'

'Funny, they don't gossip, not truly, not the way we do. They're instinctively restrained about love affairs and such. As for "the real thing", yes, sometimes. I met one fellow who's got a story about how Stalin was secretly in cahoots with the Okhrana. Pretty good story, actually – lively, factual. I think we'll run it around Christmas.'

'Oh, that old red herring,' Elizabeth scoffed. 'That's been around for years.'

Hull chuckled. 'Well, there you have the magazine business. It'll make the Stalinists mad as hell, but they won't cancel their subscriptions, they'll just write letters. Then the socialists and the Trotskyites will write back, madder yet. We'll sell some newsstand copies in the Village. In the long run it's just dialogue, open forum, everyone gets to take their turn at bat.'

'But is this person actually in a position to know something like that?' Elizabeth was slightly wide-eyed at the possibility.

Hull thought for a time. 'Maybe. Maybe not. We'll acknowledge, implicitly, that we really don't know. "Who can say what goes on behind the walls of the Kremlin?" Not quite so obvious as that, but in that general direction.'

'What are you? *Time* magazine?' May was getting ready to argue.

Hull shrugged it off. 'I wish we had the Luces' money. But I'll tell you something, though it's never to leave this room. We're all of us, *Time* included, in the same boat. The editorial slant is different – is it ever – but we're nothing without the readership, and we've just got to come up with something juicy once in a while. But don't be alarmed, the rest of the issue will be as usual – plenty of polemic, snarling capitalists and courageous workers, a Christmas cry for justice. I think you'll like it.'

'Sounds pretty damn cynical to me,' May grumbled.

Elizabeth rushed in. 'Oh poo! Just think about the stuff they put on stage where you work. You're just being critical, Jack, admit it.'

May smiled ruefully. 'Democracy in action,' he said. 'Makes everybody mad.'

*

It certainly made somebody mad.

On the night of 14 September the editorial offices of Hull's magazine were burned, and 'Who Was the Okhrana's Mysterious Man?' went up with all the other paper, or was presumed to have, because all they ever found were grey mounds of wet ash that went into the East River along with the chairs and desks and typewriters and, in the event, the magazine itself.

It was certainly no accident – the petrol can was left right there on the floor of the editor-in-chief's office, where the arson investigators found it when they picked through what remained of the ceiling. Some of the newspaper beatmen asked the Fire lieutenant who'd done it, but all he gave them was an eloquent Irish smile: these little commie outfits, how the hell was anybody going to know what went on, maybe a rival, maybe they didn't pay the printer, the list was too long.

At first, the magazine's board of directors thought they intended to go forward bravely, but wisdom ultimately prevailed. The venture had already eaten one trust fund and ruined a marriage, maybe they'd best leave the field to the competition. Herb Hull was on the street for exactly three weeks, then signed on with a glossy, general readership magazine, a big one. His new job was to go up against *Collier's* and the *Saturday Evening Post*, which meant getting to know a whole new crowd of writers, but Hull, God help him, liked writers and soon enough he had the stories coming – 'Amelia Earhart, Is She Still Alive?' – and life for him was back to normal. He had a pretty good idea of why the magazine office burned up but he kept it to himself – martyrdom was not in his stars – though he did sometimes play a little game with four or five names he could have jotted down if he'd wanted to.

André Szara found out a few days later. Standing at a zinc bar in the rue du Cherche-Midi, drinking his morning coffee, he thumbed through one of the official newspapers of the French left and read about the fire, obviously set, said its American correspondent, by J. Edgar Hoover's FBI or its fascist stooges, as part of their hate campaign against the progressive and peace-loving workers of all nations.

Szara felt little enough on reading it, simply a sense of recognition. He turned the event over in his mind for a time, staring out at the street. The purge was slowly dying out, like a fire that has consumed everything in its path and at last consumes itself: one week earlier, Goldman had quietly informed him during a meeting in Brussels that Yezhov was on the way out. What had actually happened? The NKVD had surely learned of the article and prevented its publication. But just as surely

Stalin had been told – or seen the article himself, since they had likely stolen it before they started the fire. Had he been influenced? Jogged just enough in a certain way at a certain time so that ending the purge now seemed preferable to continuing it? Or was it simply coincidence, a confluence of events? Or was there yet more to the story than he knew? There was an excellent possibility that he had not been the only one set in motion against the purge; intelligence operations simply did not work that way – one brave man against the world. The expectation of failure was too high in any individual case for the skilful operator not to have several attacks going at once.

Finally, he couldn't be sure of anything. *Perhaps this morning I have actually been victorious*, he thought. He could not imagine a greater absence of drums and trumpets. And he did not care. Since Sénéschal's death and his return from Lisbon he found he didn't particularly care about anything, and he found also that this made life, or his life anyhow, much simpler. He finished the coffee, left a few coins on the bar, and headed off to a press conference with the Swedish ambassador, first putting up his umbrella, for it had begun to rain.

The Iron
Exchange

10 October 1938.

André Szara, as long as he lived, remembered that day as a painting.

A curious painting. Quite literal, in the style of the 1880s yet touched by an incongruity, something askew, that suggested the surrealism of a later period. The subject was a long, empty beach near the Danish city of Aarhus on the coast of Jutland; the time was late afternoon, beneath the mackerel sky of the Scandinavian autumn, rows of white scud shifting slowly towards a pale wash horizon. To the east lay an expanse of flat, dark water, then a cloud bank obscuring the island of Samsoe. Small waves lapped at the shore; pebbly, dark sand with a meandering tideline marked by a refuse of broken shells. Gulls fed at the water's edge, and on the dunes that rose behind the beach the stiff grass swayed in the offshore breeze. A common, timeless seascape caught at a common, timeless moment.

But the figures in the scene were alien to it. Sergei Abramov, in his dark blue suit and vest with watch chain, his black homburg and black beard and black umbrella – just there the painting had gone wrong. This was a city man who belonged to city places – restaurants, theatres – and his presence on the beach somehow denied nature. No less his companion, the journalist A. A. Szara, in a rumpled raincoat with a French newspaper rolled up in one pocket.

The final touch, which perfected the incongruity, was the stack of eleven photographs that Abramov held, studying them as people do, placing the topmost at the back when he was done with it, proceeding in turn until it reappeared, then starting over.

Could the artist have caught Abramov's mood? Only a very good artist, Szara felt, could have managed it. There was too much there. Drawn deep inside himself, impervious to the screaming gulls, to the gust of wind that toyed with his beard, Abramov wore the expression of a man whose brutal opinion of humankind has, once again, been confirmed. But, in the cocked eyebrow, in the tug of a smile at one corner of the mouth, there was evidence that he expected no less, that he was a man so often betrayed that such events now seemed to him little more than an inconvenience. Very deliberately he squared the stack of photographs, resettled them in an envelope, and slid them into the inside pocket of his jacket. 'Of course,' he said to Szara.

Szara's expression showed that he didn't understand.

'Of course it happened, of course it was Dershani who made it happen, of course the proof comes too late.' He smiled grimly and shrugged, his way of saying *udari sudbi*, the blows of fate, wasn't this exactly the way of the world. 'And the negatives?'

'Burned.'

'Sensible.'

'Will you burn these as well?'

Abramov thought a moment. 'No,' he said. 'No, I shall confront him.'

'What will he do?'

'Dershani? Smile. We will smile at each other: brothers, enemies, conspirators, fellow wolves. When we've got that over with, he'll inquire how I came to have such photographs.'

'And you'll tell him?'

Abramov shook his head. 'I will tell him some rich, transparent lie. Which he will acknowledge with one of his predatory stares. I'll stare back, though he'll know that's a bluff, and that will be that. Then, later, as if from nowhere, something may happen to me. Or it may not. Something may happen to Dershani instead – political fortune is a tide like any other. In any event, the photographs prove he was clumsy enough to get caught, perhaps a margin of vulnerability that will keep me alive a little longer. Or, perhaps, not.'

'I didn't know,' Szara apologized. 'I thought we'd caught him at it.'

'At what?'

'Collaboration.'

Abramov smiled gently at Szara's innocence. 'Such a meeting can be explained a thousand ways. For instance, one could say that Herr Joseph Uhlrich has now been brought under Soviet control.'

'You know him.'

'Oh yes, it's a small world. The SS Obersturmbannführer, to give him his proper rank, the equivalent of a lieutenant colonel in Russia, is an old friend. A brave, fighting street communist in his youth, then a Brown Shirt thug, eventually a spy for Hitler's faction, the Black Shirts, against Ernst Röhm. He took part in the Brown Shirt executions of 1934 and is now one of Heydrich's assistants in the Sicherheitsdienst, SD,

Gestapo foreign intelligence. He works in the Unterabteilung sub-division that concerns itself with Soviet intelligence services. Perhaps Dershani has been brought under the control of the SD rather than the other way around.'

'Uhlrich had the security, the Germans planned the meeting, Der-shani was essentially alone and unguarded. To me, it seemed a cour-teous welcome for a traitor.'

Abramov shrugged. 'I will find out.' He put his back to the wind, lit a cigarette, and put the extinguished match in his pocket. 'But, even so, doing something about it may be impossible. Dershani is now chairman of the OPAL Directorate. Abramov is demoted to simple membership. He may be demoted further, even much further – you understand – and Yezhov is no longer Dershani's superior. That position now belongs to the Georgian Beria, so the Georgian *khvost* is victorious. And they are cleaning house. A writers' conspiracy has been uncovered; Babel, too friendly with Yezhov's wife, has disappeared, and so has Kolt'sev. *Pravda* will soon have a new editor. Then there were others, many others: writers, poets, dramatists, as well as Yezhov's associates, every single one of them, seventy at last count.'

'And Yezhov?'

Abramov nodded. 'Ah yes, Yezhov himself. Well, I may inform you that Comrade Yezhov turned out to be a British spy. Imagine that! But, poor man, perhaps he was not fully aware of what he was doing.' Abramov closed one eye and tapped his temple with an index finger.

'Nicolai Ivanovich evidently went mad. For late one night an ambu-lance appeared at his apartment block, then two attendants, sturdy fellows, were seen to remove him in a straitjacket. He was taken to the Serbsy Psychiatric Institute and, regrettably, left alone in a cell, where he contrived to hang himself from the barred window by ingeniously fashioning his underpants into a noose. This would have required an extraordinary feat of acrobatics, and "the bloody dwarf" was never known as much of an athlete, but, who knows, perhaps madness lent him unimagined physical prowess. We all like to think so, at any rate.'

'I was told that Yezhov was in decline,' Szara said, 'but not this.'

'*Decline* could describe it, I suppose. Meanwhile, *bratets'* – the affectionate term meant 'little brother' – 'now more than ever, you better keep your nose clean. I don't know what actually happened to your agent SILO in Paris, but here I see these photographs and they tell me you've been meddling with Germans, and so to put two and two together doesn't take a genius.'

'But it was—'

'Don't tell me,' Abramov interrupted. 'I don't want to know. Just understand that, once again, it's a good time for Jews to be invisible, even in Paris. Beria is no *shabbos goy* – you know, a friend of the Orthodox Jews who turns the lights on and off on the sabbath so the prohibition against work is observed. Far from it. His most recent experience involved a man you may have known, Grisha Kaminsky, formerly people's commissar for health. He came forward at the February Plenum and made a most interesting speech, claiming that Beria once worked for the Transcaucasian Muslims, the Mussavat nationalists, at a time when the British controlled them during the intervention at Baku, just after the revolution. According to Kaminsky's speech, Beria was operating a Mussavatist counter-intelligence network, and that made *him* a British spy. Needless to say, Kaminsky disappeared into thin air after the Plenum. So, you'll understand I'm in no hurry to run to Beria with a story, even an illustrated story, that his *khvost* pal Dershani is in contact with the fascist enemy.'

Abramov paused to let it all sink in, and the two men stood silently on the beach for a time.

In Szara's understanding, the ascendency of Beria, despite Kaminsky's near suicidal attack, confirmed what Bloch had said five months earlier: the purge, grinding, deliberate, somehow both efficient and random at once, was in effect a pogrom. He doubted that Abramov, as strong and as smart as he was, would survive it. And if Yezhov's allies were murdered, Abramov's friends would be treated no differently when the time came. 'Perhaps, Sergei Jakobovich,' he said hesitantly, 'you ought to consider your personal safety. From Denmark, for instance, one can go virtually anywhere.'

'Me? Run? No, never. So far I'm just demoted, and I've absorbed that like a good ghetto *zhid* – eyes cast down, quiet as a mouse, no trouble from me, Gospodin, sir. No, what saves me is that with Hitler in the Sudetenland, Germany gains three and a half million people – all but seven hundred thousand of them ethnic Germans – easily four army divisions, the way we think, plus industrial capacity, raw materials, food, you name it. This adds up to one more big, strategic headache for Russia and, when all is said and done, that's my business, and I've been in that business since 1917 – it's what I know how to do. So they'll want to keep me around, at least for the time being.'

'And me too, they'll want to keep around.'

'Oh very definitely you. After all, you operate an important mine for us – without you and your brethren the Directorate can produce nothing. We manufacture precision tools, at least we try to, but where would we be without iron ore? Which brings me to what I came here to talk about, I didn't drag myself to some beach in Denmark just to get a pocketful of dirty pictures.

'The background is this: Hitler has the Sudetenland, we know he's going for all of Czechoslovakia, we think he wants more, a lot more. If the OTTER material was significant, it's now crucial, and the Directorate is going to have its way with this man whether he likes it or not. To that end, we've determined to send you to Berlin. This is dangerous, but necessary. Either you can talk OTTER into a more, ah, generous frame of mind or we're really going to put the screws on. In other words, patience now exhausted. Understood?'

'Yes.'

'Also, we want you to deliver money to the RAVEN network, to RAVEN herself. Take a good look at her; you're going to be asked for your views when you return to Paris. The Directorate has faith in Schau-Wehrli, please don't misunderstand, but we'd like a second opinion.'

'Will Goldman supply passports for the trip?'

'What passports? Don't be such a noodle. You go as yourself, writing for *Pravda*, on whatever takes your fancy. Goldman will discuss with you the approach to OTTER and to RAVEN, and you'll work with him on questionnaires – we want you to guide OTTER into very particular and specific areas. Questions?'

'One.'

'Only one?'

'Why were you sent all this way? The "third country" meeting is usually reserved for special circumstances – you taught me that – and I haven't heard anything, anything official that is, that couldn't have been communicated by wireless. Am I missing something?'

Abramov inhaled deeply and acknowledged the impact of the question with a sigh that meant *look how smart he's getting*. 'Briefly, they're not so sure about you. You haven't made headway with OTTER, you lost an agent – even if that wasn't your fault, the Directorate doesn't excuse bad luck – and your one great triumph, which I now have in my pocket, is unknown to them. To be blunt, your credit is poor. So they wanted me to have a look at you, and make a decision about whether or not you should continue.'

'And if not?'

'That's not the decision, so don't be too curious. Now I used a car to get here, but I want you to leave first. You've got about a half-hour walk back into Aarhus, so you'll forgive me if I pass you on the road like I never saw you. Last word: again I remind you to be very careful in Berlin. Your status as a correspondent protects you, but don't go finding out how far. When you contact agents, follow procedure to the letter. As for all the chaos in Moscow, don't let it get you down. No situation is as hopeless as it appears, André Aronovich – remember the old saying: nobody ever found a cat skeleton in a tree.'

They said good-bye and Szara struggled up the soft sand to the top of the dunes. Looking back, the sense of the scene as a painting returned to him. Sergei Abramov, umbrella hooked on one forearm, hands thrust in pockets, stared out to sea. The autumn seascape surrounded him – crying gulls, incoming waves, the rustling beach grass, and pale-wash sky – but he was alien to it. Or, rather, it was alien to him, as though the idea of the painting was that the solitary figure on the shore was no longer part of life on earth.

27 October 1938.

Such visions did not leave him.

A fragment of bureaucratic language, *date of expiry*, the sort of phrase one saw on passports, visas, permits of every kind, became his private symbol for what was essentially a nameless feeling. *Europe is dying*, he thought. The most commonplace *good-bye* had an undertone of *farewell*. It was in the songs, in the faces in the streets, in the wild changes of mood – absurd gaiety one moment, desolation the next – he saw in friends and in himself.

The dining car on the Nord Express to Berlin was nearly deserted, the vibrations of stemware and china at the empty tables far too loud without the normal babble of conversation. An elderly waiter stood half asleep at his station, napkin draped over one arm, as Szara forced himself to eat a lukewarm veal chop. When the train approached the border, an officious porter came through the car lowering the window shades, presumably denying Szara and one other couple a view of French military fortifications.

And the passport control in Germany was worse than usual. Nothing he could exactly put his finger on, the process was the same. Perhaps there were more police, their side arms more noticeable. Or perhaps it was in the way they moved about, bumping into things, their voices a little louder, their intonations not so polite, something almost exultant in their manner. Or it might have been the men in suits, sublimely casual, who hardly bothered to look at his documents.

Or was he, he asked himself, merely losing his nerve? There had been no horrid Chinese food in Brussels this time. He'd spent hours in the back office of Stefan Leib's cartography shop, where Goldman had inflicted on him a series of exhausting, repetitious briefings that often lasted well past midnight. This was a different Goldman, leaning over a cluttered desk in the glow of a single lamp, voice tense and strained, breath sharp with alcohol, slashing pencil lines across a street map of Berlin or explaining, in sickening detail, the circumstances in which Dr Baumann now found himself.

The situation for German Jews had deteriorated, but far worse was the form the deterioration took. There was something hideously measured about it, like a drum, as some new decree appeared every month, each one a little worse than the last, each one inspiring, and clearly meant to inspire, its victims with a terrifying sense of orchestration. Whatever ruled their destiny simply refused to be placated. No matter how precisely and punctually they conformed to the minutiae of its rules, it grew angrier and more demanding. The more they fed it, the hungrier it got.

In April of 1938 only forty thousand Jewish firms remained in Germany; all others had passed to Aryan ownership, sometimes for a nominal fee, sometimes for nothing. Those businesses that remained under Jewish control either brought in foreign currency, which Germany desperately needed to buy war materials or, like Baumann Milling, were directly connected to rearmament efforts. In June, Jews had to provide an inventory of everything they owned, with the exception of personal and household goods.

In July, a glimmer of hope, a conference on Jewish emigration held at the French spa town of Évian, where representatives of the world's nations met to consider the problem. But they refused to take in the German Jews. The United States would accept only twenty-eight thousand, in severely restricted categories. Australia did not wish to import 'a racial problem'. South and Central American countries wanted only farmers, not traders or intellectuals. France had already accepted too many refugees. Britain claimed not to have space available, and immigration to British-controlled Palestine was sharply curtailed to a few hundred certificates a month since Arab riots and ambushes – beginning in 1936 – had created political difficulties for those who favoured letting Jews into the country. In addition, British access to oil in the Middle East was based on the maintenance of good relations with the Arab sheikdoms, and they were in general opposed to Jewish settlement in Palestine. Of all the nations convened at Évian, only Holland and Denmark would accept Jewish refugees who could leave Germany. By the end of the conference, most German Jews understood they were trapped.

The decrees did not stop. On 23 July, all Jews were required to apply for special identification cards. On 17 August it was ordered that Jews with German given names would have to change them – male Jews now to be known as Israel, females to be called Sarah. On 5 October, Jews were forced to hand in their passports. These would be returned, they were told, with an entry identifying the holder as a Jew.

As the train sped through the Rhine valley towards Düsseldorf, Szara raised the window shade and watched the little clusters of village lights go by. He consciously tried to free his mind of Goldman's briefing and to concentrate on the likelihood of seeing Marta Haecht during his time in Berlin. But even in his imagination she lived in the shadow of her city, a very different Marta from the one he had believed was rushing to meet him in Lisbon. Perhaps she was nothing at all like his construction of her. Was it possible that she existed only in a fantasy world he'd built for himself? It did not matter, he realized, letting his head rest against the cold glass of the window. Whatever she might be, he ached for her presence, and this need was the single warmth that survived from the time when he'd believed the whole world lived for desire. Otherwise, there was only ice.

The journalist Szara got off the train at Potsdam station a few minutes after three in the morning, woke a taxi driver, and was taken to the Adlon, where all Russian journalists and trade delegations stayed. The hotel, musty and creaky and splendidly comfortable, was on Pariser Platz at the foot of the grandiose avenue Unter den Linden, next to the British embassy and three doors down from the Russian embassy. Trailing a sleepy porter down the long hall to his room, Szara heard exuberant, shouted Russian and the crash of a lamp. *Home at last*, he thought. The old man carrying his bag just shook his head sorrowfully at the uproar.

In the morning he saw them, groping towards coffee in the elegant dining room. Tass correspondents, officially, a range of types – from the broad-shouldered, fair-haired, and pale-eyed to the small, intense ones with glasses and beards and rumpled hair. Nobody he knew, or so he thought, until Vainshtok materialized at his table with a dish of stewed figs. 'So, now Szara arrives. Big news must be on the way.' Vainshtok, son of a timber merchant from Kiev, was infamously abrasive. He had wildly unfocused eyes behind round spectacles and a lip permanently curled with contempt. 'Anyhow, welcome to Berlin.'

'Hello, Vainshtok,' he said.

'So pleased you have chosen to honour us. I have to file on *everything*, up half the night. Now you're here maybe I get a break now and then.'

Szara gestured inquisitively towards the Tass reporters scattered about the dining room.

'Them? Ha!' said Vainshtok. 'They don't actually write anything. You and me, Szara, we have to do the work.'

After breakfast he tried to phone Marta Haecht. He learned she'd left the magazine two months earlier. He tried her home. Nobody answered.

The day before he left Paris, Kranov had handed him a personal message from Brussels:

THE WORK HAS BEEN COMPLETED FOR YOUR ASSIGNMENT. HAVE A SAFE AND PRODUCTIVE JOURNEY. REZIDENT.

In Berlin, on the night of 28 October, André Szara understood what that message truly meant. Of those who undertook *the work*, he knew only one, Odile, whose 26 October dead-drop deposit for OTTER had warned of *a visit from a friend* who would arrive *at night*. The greatest part of the preparation, however, had been managed by nameless, faceless operatives – presumably stationed in Berlin, though he could not be certain of that. Perhaps some of the Tass reporters seen stumbling towards their morning coffee at the Adlon, perhaps a team brought in from Budapest; he was not to know. Once again, the unseen hand.

But the André Szara moving towards a clandestine meeting in Gestapo territory was more than grateful for it. He entered the Grunewald neighbourhood in the gathering dusk, leaving the Ringbahn tram stop with a few other men carrying briefcases and indistinguishable from them. Most of the residents of the Grunewald came and went by car, many of them chauffeured. But the evening return from business was as much cover as the operatives had been able to devise, and Szara was thankful for even that minimal camouflage.

The Baumann villa faced Salzbrunner street, but he was going in the back way. Thus he walked briskly up Charlottenbrunner, slowed to let one last returning businessman find his way home, crossed a narrow lane, then counted steps until he saw a rock turned earth side up. Here he entered a well-groomed pine wood – at the blind spot the operatives had discovered, away from the view of nearby houses – found the path that was supposed to be there, and followed it to the foot of a stucco wall that enclosed the villa adjoining the Baumann property.

Now he waited. The Berlin weather was cold and damp, the woods dark, and time slowed to a crawl, but they'd hidden him here to accommodate an early entry into the neighbourhood, at dusk, and now kept him on ice to await the magic hour of nine o'clock, when the servant couple who occupied the main residence on the Baumann property were known to go to sleep – or at least turn off their lights. At ten minutes after nine he set out, feeling his way along the wall and counting steps until, just where they said it would be, he found a foothold that an operative had dug into the stucco facing. He put his left foot into the small niche, drove his weight upwards, and grabbed the tiled cap of the wall. He'd been told to wear rubber-soled shoes, and the traction helped him as he scrabbled his feet against the smooth surface. It wasn't graceful, but he eventually lay flat on the corner formed by the wall he'd climbed and that which divided the two properties.

Looking down to his left, he saw a woman in a flowered robe reading in a chair by the window. To his right, the servants' cottage had its blinds drawn. Just below, a garden shed stood against the wall – he cautiously lowered himself to its shingle roof, which gave unpleasantly under the strain but held until he hopped off. From the cottage came the high-pitched barking of a small dog – that would be Ludwig, the *apparat* mechanism for moving Baumann out into the neighbourhood at night – which was almost immediately calmed. Staying out of sight of the villa itself, he found the back door of the cottage and knocked lightly three times – not a signal, but a style recommended by Goldman as 'informal' and 'neighbourly'. The door opened quickly and Dr Baumann let him in.

The operatives had got him safely inside. Somebody, shivering in the Berlin mist at dawn, had dug a piece out of the wall with a clasp knife – or however it had been done, by twelve-year-olds for all he knew – anyhow, he was in. He had been manoeuvred, like a weapon, into a position where his light, his intellect, influence, craft, whatever it was, could shine.

They'd done their job. Pity he couldn't do his.

Oh, he tried. Goldman had said, 'You must control this man. You can be courteous, if you like, or lovable. Threats sometimes work. Be solemn, patriotic, or just phenomenally boring – this too has been done – but you must control him.' Szara couldn't.

Dr Julius Baumann was grey. The brutal, ceaseless pressure orchestrated by the Reich bureaucracies was proceeding quite successfully in his case. His face was ruined by tension and lack of sleep; he had become thin, stooped, old. 'You cannot know what it's like here.' This he said again and again, and Szara could find no way through it. 'Can we help you?' he asked. 'Do you need anything?' Baumann just shook his head, somehow closed off behind a wall that no such offer could breach.

'Be positive,' Goldman had said. 'You represent strength. Make him feel the power you stand for, let him know it supports him.'

Szara tried: 'There's little we can't do, you know. Your account with us is virtually unlimited, but you must draw on it.'

'What is there to want?' Baumann said angrily. 'What they've taken from me you cannot give back. Nobody can do that.'

'The regime is weakening. Perhaps you can't see it, but we can. There's reason to hope, reason to hang on.'

'Yes,' Baumann said, the man who will agree to anything because he finds the argument itself tiresome. 'We try,' he added. *But we do not succeed*, his eyes said.

Frau Baumann had changed in a different way. She was now more hausfrau than Frau Doktor. If in fact it was her pretensions – the desire for social prominence and the need to condescend – that had driven a nation of fifty million people into a blind fury she had certainly been cured of all that. Now she fussed and fiddled, her hands never still. She had reduced her existence to a series of small, household crises, turned fear into exasperation with domestic life; thimbles, brooms, potatoes. Perhaps it was her version of the world in which the common German housewife lived, perhaps she hoped that by joining the enemy she could keep – they would allow her to keep – what remained of her life. When she left the room, Baumann followed her with his eyes. 'You see?' he whispered to Szara, as though something needed to be proved.

Szara nodded sorrowfully; he understood. 'And work?' he asked. 'The business? What's it like there? How do they feel about you, your employees. Still faithful? Or do most of them follow the party line?'

'They look out for themselves. Everybody does, now.'

'No kindness? Not one good soul?'

Perhaps Baumann wavered for an instant, then realized what came next – just who is that good soul – and said, 'It doesn't matter what they think.'

Szara sighed. 'You refuse to help us. Or yourself.'

Something flickered in Baumann's eyes – a strange kind of sympathy? Then it was gone. 'Please,' he said, 'you must not ask too much of me. I am less brave every day. Going to the stone wall for the message is an agony, you understand? I make myself do it. I—'

The telephone rang.

Baumann was paralysed. He stared through the doorway into the kitchen while the phone rang again and again. Finally Frau Baumann picked up the receiver. 'Yes?' she said. Then: 'Yes.' She listened for a time, started to exclaim, was evidently cut off by the person at the other end of the line. 'Can you wait a moment?' she asked. They heard her set the receiver down carefully on a wooden shelf. When she entered the living room she was holding both hands lightly to the sides of her face.

'Julius, darling, do we have money in the house?' She spoke calmly, as though drawing on a reserve of inner strength, but her hands were trembling and her cheeks were flushed.

'Who is it?'

'This is Natalya. Calling on the telephone to say that she must return to Poland. Tonight.'

'Why would she . . . ?'

'It has been ordered, Julius. The police are there and she is to be put on a train after midnight. They are being very polite about it, she says, and are willing to bring her here on the way to the station.'

Baumann did not react; he stared.

'Julius?' Frau Baumann said. 'Natalya is waiting to see if we can help her.'

'In the drawer,' Baumann said. He turned to Szara. 'Natalya is her cousin. She came here from Lublin six years ago.'

'There isn't very much in the drawer,' Frau Baumann said.

Szara took a thick handful of reichsmarks out of his pocket. 'Give her this,' he said, handing it to Baumann.

Frau Baumann returned to the telephone. 'Yes, it's all right. When are you coming?' She paused for the answer. 'Good, then we'll see you. I'm sure it will be straightened out. Don't forget your sweaters, Polish hotels . . . Yes . . . I know . . . Twenty minutes.' She hung up the phone and returned to the living room. 'All the Jewish immigrants from Poland must leave Germany,' she said. 'They are being deported.'

'*Deported?*' Baumann said.

His wife nodded. 'To a place called Zbąszyń.'

'Deported,' Baumann said. 'A sixty-three-year-old woman, deported. What in God's name will she do in Poland?' He stood up abruptly, then walked to a bookcase by the window, took a large book down and thumbed through the pages. 'What is it called?'

'Zbąszyń.'

Baumann moved the atlas under a lamp and squinted at the page. 'Warsaw I could understand,' he said. 'I can't find it.' He looked up at his wife. 'Did she think to call ahead for a room at least?'

Szara stood. 'I'll have to be going,' he said. 'The police will . . .'

Baumann looked up from the book.

'I think you should get out,' Szara said. 'This must involve thousands of people. Tens of thousands. Next they'll find someplace to send you, it's possible.'

'But we're not Polish,' Frau Baumann said. 'We're German.'

'Well get you out,' Szara said. 'To France or Holland.'

Baumann seemed dubious.

'Don't answer now. Just think about it. I'll have you contacted and well meet again in a few days.' He put his raincoat on. 'Will you consider it?'

'I'm not sure,' Baumann said, evidently confused.

'We'll at least discuss it,' Szara said and, looking at his watch, headed for the door.

Outside, the still air was cold and wet. A rickety ladder got him to the roof of the shed; from there he mounted the wall, hung by his hands to decrease the distance, then dropped the few feet to the ground. His exfiltration time was 10:08, but the forced exit had made him early, so he waited in the woods as he'd done before. In the silence of the Grunewald neighbourhood, he heard what he took to be the brief visit of the cousin: opening and closing car doors, an idling engine, muffled voices, doors again, then a car driving away. That was all.

29 October.

Szara decided that calling Marta Haecht on the telephone was a bad idea; a conversation necessarily awkward, difficult. Instead he wrote, on a sheet of Adlon stationery, 'I've returned to Berlin on assignment from my paper. I would like, more than I can say in this letter, to be with you for whatever time we can have. Of course I'll understand if your life has changed, and it would be better not to meet. In any case your friend, André.'

He spent a listless day, trying not to think about the Baumanns. There was no Directorate plan to take them out of Germany, and he had no authorization to make such an offer, but Szara didn't care. *Enough is enough*, he thought.

The following morning, Szara had an answer to his letter, in the form of a telephone message taken at the Adlon desk.

An address, an office number, a date, a time. From Fräulein H.

31 October.

Szara stood by the open window and stared out into the Bischofstrasse, shiny with rain in midafternoon, wet brown and yellow leaves plastered to the pavements. The damp air felt good to him. He heard Marta's heavy tread as she moved across the room, then felt her warm skin against his back as she hid behind him. 'Please don't stand there,' she whispered. 'The whole world will see there's a naked man in here.'

'What will you give me?'

'Ah, I will give you that for which you dare not ask, yet want beyond all things.'

'Name it.'

'A cup of tea.'

They walked away from the window together and he sat at a table covered with an Indian cloth and watched as she made tea.

The room was a loft on the top floor of an office building, with large windows and a high ceiling that made it the perfect studio for an artist. *Benno Ault.* So the name read on a directory in the great, echoing marble lobby below, vestige of a lost grandeur. *Herr Benno Ault, Room 709.* And he was? According to Marta, 'a university friend. Dear, sweet, lost.' An artist who now lived elsewhere and rented her his studio as an apartment. His presence remained. Tacked to the walls – painted an industrial beige many years before, now water-stained and flaking – was what Szara took to be the oeuvre of Benno Ault. Dear, sweet, and lost he may well have been but also, from the look of the thing, mad as a hatter. The unframed canvases writhed with colour, garish yellows and greens. These were portraits of the shipwrecked and the damned, pink faces howled from every wall as saffron oceans pulled them under and they clawed at the air with grotesque hands.

She brought him tea in a steaming mug, standing by his chair and spooning in sugar until he told her to stop, the curve of her hip pressed against his side. 'It's sweet the way you like?' she said, innocent as dawn.

'Just exactly,' he said.

'Good,' she said firmly and arranged herself in a nearby armchair, a huge velvet orphan that had seen better times. She spread a napkin across her bare tummy – a pun on decorum, as though she were a Goya nude minding her manners. When she sipped her tea she closed her eyes, then wiggled her toes with pleasure. The background for this performance was provided by a giant radio with a station band lit up bright amber, which had played Schubert lieder since the moment he'd walked in the door. Now she conducted, waving a stern index finger back and forth. 'Am I,' she said suddenly, 'as you remember?'

'Am I?' he said.

'Actually, you are quite different.'

'You also.'

'It's the world,' she said. 'But I don't care. Your letter was sweet – a little forlorn. Did you mean it? Or was it just to make things easy? Either way it's all right, I'm just curious.'

'I meant it.'

'I thought so. But then I thought; after an hour, we'll see.'

'The hour's over. The letter stands.'

'Soon I must go back to work. Shall I see you again? Or will we wait another year?'

'Tomorrow.'

'I haven't said I would.'

'Will you?'

'Yes.'

She had answered his knock at the door in a short silk robe tied loosely at the waist – just purchased; the scent of new clothing lingered on it beneath her perfume – hair worn loose and brushed out, red lipstick freshly applied. A woman of the world now, looking forward to an assignation in the middle of the day. Seeing her like that, framed in the doorway, stunned him. It was too good to be true. When she lifted her face to him and closed her eyes he felt like a man suddenly and unexpectedly warmed by sunlight. He actually, for an instant as they embraced, felt her mouth smile with pleasure. But after that everything – being led by the hand to a sofa, pillows kicked off, robe flung away – happened too quickly. What he had imagined would be artful and seductive wasn't like that at all. It wasn't really like them. Two other people, then, very hungry, urgent, selfish people. They laughed about it later, but things were different and they knew it.

At one point she'd raised her head from the sofa and whispered delicately next to his ear. The words were familiar enough, a lover's request, but they had shocked him – because they were German words and the sound of them unlocked something inside him, something cold and strong and almost violent. Whatever it was, she felt it. She liked it. This was a very dangerous place to go, he sensed, but they went there just the same.

He had wondered, later on, drinking tea, how much she understood of what had happened. Was this *eternal woman*, accepting, absorbing? Or had she, for a moment, become his companion in decadence, playing her part in some mildly evil version of a lovers' game? He couldn't ask. She seemed happy, making jokes, wiggling her toes, content with herself and the afternoon.

Then she got dressed. This too was different. By degrees she became a working woman, a typical Berliner: the ingenuous, vaguely Bohemian Marta, adoring of Russian journalists, was no more. Garter belt, stockings, a crisp shirt with a rounded collar, a rusty tweed, mid-calf-length suit, then a small, stylish hat with a feather – the perfect disguise, ruined at the last when she made a little-girl brat face at him: what they called here *Schnauze*, literally snout, a way of telling the world to go to hell. She gave him a cool cheek to kiss on the way out – not to ruin the lipstick – and rumpled his hair.

He stayed for a time after she left, drinking tea, watching out of the window as a cloud of starlings swerved away through the rainy sky. The radio programme changed, to what he guessed was Beethoven – something dark and thoughtful at any rate. The city drew him into its mood; he found it almost impossible to resist, became autumnal and meditative, asked questions that really could not be answered. Marta Haecht, for instance: had she, he wondered, become so newly sophisticated at the hands of other lovers? Certainly, that was it. Who, he wondered. That was, in his experience of such things, always a surprise. *Him?*

With a Russian girl he would have known all. Every private thought would have been bashed about between them, plenty of tears to wash it all down with, then forgiveness, tenderness, and wild – likely drunken – love-making to paste everything back together again. Poles and Russians knew how hidden feelings poisoned life; in the end the vodka was just a catalyst.

But she wasn't Russian or Polish, she was German, like this damned sorrowful music. The reality of that had come home to him when they were on the sofa. What was *that?* The Eastern conqueror takes the Teutonic princess? Whatever it was, it was no game.

Restless now, wishing that Marta hadn't gone back to work, Szara walked around the room as he got dressed, confronted by Ault's maniacal paintings. *Strange people,* he thought. *They make a virtue of anguish.* Nonetheless, he began counting the hours until he'd see her again and tried to shake off the sense of oppression gathering in his heart.

Perhaps it was the influence of the building itself. Dating from the early days of the century, its long hallways, set in tiny octagonal black and white tiles, echoed with every footstep and lived in perpetual dusk, a greyish light that spilled from frosted glass door panels numbered in Gothic script. Called Die Eisenbourse Haus, the Iron Exchange Building, it had certainly been some builder's cherished dream. There was no Iron Exchange, not that Szara knew about. Had one been planned, perhaps somewhere nearby? Only its adjunct had been built, in any case, seven storeys of elaborate brickwork with the name in gold script on the glass above the entryway. The lift would have been installed later, he thought. It was enormous, an anthill intended as home to every sort of respectable commerce. But the builder had raised it in the wrong place. Bischofstrasse was across the river Spree from the better part of Berlin, reached by the Kaiser Wilhelm bridge, on the edge of the ancient Jewish quarter. Had a commercial district once been planned here? The builder evidently thought so, locating just west of the Judenstrasse, across from Neue Markt, between Pandawer and Steinweg streets.

But it had not turned out that way. The building stood as a grand edifice among tenements and dreary shops, and its lobby directory told the story: piano teachers, theatrical agents, a private detective, a club for sailing instruction and a club for lonely hearts, an astrologer, an inventor, and Grömmelink the cut-rate denture man.

Szara rang for the lift, which wheezed ponderously to the top floor. The metal door slid open, then a soiled white glove slowly drew the gate aside. The operator was an old man with lank hair parted in the middle and swept back behind his ears, fine, almost transparent skin, and a face lined by tragedy. He was called Albert, according to Marta, who thought him an original, rather amusing, the ruling troll of the Castle Perilous, her moat-keeper. Szara, however, was not amused by Albert, who stared at him with sullen and intense dislike as he got on the elevator, then sniffed loudly as he slammed the gate. *I smell a Jew*, that meant. On the wall above the control handle were taped two curling photographs of serious young men in Landwehr uniform. Sons dead in the war? Szara thought so. As the floors bumped slowly past, Szara repressed a shiver. He never would have imagined Marta Haecht living in such a place.

But then there were all sorts of new things about Marta. Wandering about in the apartment, he'd found a wooden rack holding a further collection of Ault's paintings – these evidently not worthy of display. Idly curious, he'd looked through them, come upon a pink nude standing pensively, almost self-consciously, amid frantic swirls of green and yellow. Something familiar piqued his interest, then he realized he knew the model, knew her in that very pose. All sorts of things new about Marta.

The elevator came to a stop. Albert opened the gate, then the exterior door. 'Lobby,' he said harshly. 'Now you get out.'

Back in his room at the Adlon he closed the heavy drapes to shut out the dusk, locked the door, and lost himself in ciphering. Using the German railway timetable Goldman had handed him – a very unremarkable find if he were searched – he converted his plaintext into numerical groups. In his statement to the Directorate he'd been extremely cautious, in fact deceptive: the broken man in the Grunewald, described as he was, would set off alarms and excursions all over Dzerzhinsky Square. Dr Baumann was not under anyone's control, including his own, and Szara could only imagine what the Directorate might order done if they found that out, especially the Directorate as led by Dershani.

The report described an agent under stress yet operating efficiently. Stubborn, self-motivating, a prominent and successful businessman after all, thus not just somebody that could be ordered about. Szara strengthened the deception by implying, faintly, that the Directorate should soften its instinct for bureaucratic domination and acknowledge that it was dealing with a man to whom independence, even as a Jew in Germany, was instinctive, habitual. Baumann had to believe he was in control, Szara suggested, and to perceive the *apparat* as a kind of servant.

But if Baumann was steadfast, Szara continued, the situation as he found it in Germany was extremely unstable. He described the telephone call from the cousin forced to return to Poland, noted the disbursement of emergency funds, then went on to suggest that OTTER ought to be offered exfiltration – *if the time should ever come* – followed by resettlement in a European city. Against that day, Baumann Milling ought to hire a new employee, as designated by the case officer, who would remain in deep cover until activated. Szara closed with the statement that he would be remaining in Berlin for at least seven days, and requested local operative support in arranging a second meeting.

He grouped his numbers, did his false addition, counted letters in the timetable a second time, just to be sure. Garbled transmissions drove Moscow wild – *What's a murn? And why does he ask for raisins?* – and he urgently needed to have their trust and good faith if they were going to accept his analysis of the situation.

He walked the half block to the embassy, a place the journalist Szara would be expected to visit, found his contact, a second secretary named Varin, and delivered the cable. Then he disappeared into the Berlin night.

He had, oh, a little company, he thought. Nothing too serious. Nothing he couldn't deal with.

Said Goldman: 'There are two situations which, if I were you, would be of concern: (a) You find yourself truly blanketed – perhaps a moving box: one in front, one behind, two at three o'clock and nine o'clock, go down an alley and the whole apparatus shifts with you. Or maybe it's people in parked cars on an empty street, women in doorways. All that sort of thing, they're simply not going to let you out of their sight. Either they insist on knowing who you really are and where you're going, or they're trying to panic you, to see what you do. You'll break it off, of course. Go back to the hotel, use your telephone contact, the 4088 number. There'll be no answer, but one ring will do the job.

'Or, (b) you ought to be alarmed if there's absolutely no sign of surveillance. A Soviet journalist in Berlin must, *must*, be of interest at some level of the counter-intelligence bureaux. The normal situation would be periodic, one or two men, probably detectives who'll look like what they are. They'll follow at a medium distance. Ideally, don't go showing them a lot of tradecraft – if you're too slick it will provoke their curiosity. If you can't dispose of them with a casual manoeuvre or two, give it up and try again later. A normal approach for the Germans would be to tag along at night, leave you free in the daytime. But if it's – what? the Sahara, then be careful. It may mean they're really operating – that is, they've put someone really good on you, and he, or she for that matter, is better than you are. In that case, see the second secretary at the embassy and we'll get you some help.'

Very well, he thought. This time the little genius in Brussels knew what he was talking about. *Out for a stroll*, Szara lit a cigarette on the Kanonierstrasse, standing in front of the vast gloomy facade of the Deutsche Bank, then, *stranger in your city*, he peered about him as though he were slightly at sea. The other man lighting a cigarette, about forty metres behind him, visible only as a hat and an overcoat, was company.

Not a good night for company. With ten thousand reichsmarks wadded up in his pockets he was headed towards the Reichshallen theatre for a meeting with Nadia Tscherova, actress, émigrée, RAVEN, and group leader of the RAVEN network. Tscherova would be available to him backstage – not at the grandiose Reichshallen but at a small repertory theatre in a narrow lane called Rosenhain Passage – after 10:40. Szara refused to hurry, wandering along, waiting until he reached Kraussenstrasse before making a move to verify the surveillance. If he didn't make the *treff* tonight, Tscherova would be available to him for three nights following. Run by Schau-Wehrli with a very firm hand, RAVEN was known to follow orders, so Szara relaxed, taking in the sights, a man with no particular place to go and all the time in the world to get there.

About Tscherova he was curious. Schau-Wehrli handled her with fine Swiss contempt, referring to her as *stukach*, snitch, the lowest rank of Soviet agents, who simply traded information for money. Goldman's view differed. He used the word *vliyaniya*, fellow traveller. This term was traditionally reserved for agents of influence, often self-recruited believers in the Soviet dream: typically academics, civil servants, artists of all sorts, and the occasional forward-looking businessman. In the sense that Tscherova moved in the upper levels of Nazi society, he supposed she was *vliyaniya*, yet she was paid, as were the brother and sister Brozin and Brozina and the Czech balletmaster Anton Krafic, the remainder of the RAVEN network. As for the highest-level agents, the *proniknoveniya* – penetration specialists serving under direct, virtually military discipline – Szara was not allowed anywhere near them, though he suspected Schau-Wehrli's MOCHA group might fall under that classification, and Goldman was rumoured to be running, personally, an asset buried in the very heart of the Gestapo.

Of course the system varied with the national point of view. Low-level agents for the French were called *dupeurs*, deceivers, and principally reported on the military institutions of various countries. *Moutons*, sheep, went after industrial intelligence while *baladeurs*, strolling players, took on freelance assignments. The French equivalent of the *proniknoveniya*, highly controlled and highly placed, was the *agent fixe*, while the *trafiquant*, like Tscherova, handled a net of sub-agents.

At the corner of Kraussenstrasse Szara paused, studied the street signs, then hurried across the intersection, not running exactly, but managing in such a way that two speeding Daimlers went whizzing past his back. A tobacconist's shop window, briefly inspected, revealed his company peering anxiously from the other side of the street, then crossing behind him. Szara quickened his pace slightly, then trotted up the steps of the Hotel Kempinski, passed through the elegant lobby, then seated himself at a table in the hotel bar. This was sophisticated Berlin; a study in glossy black and white surfaces with chrome highlights, palm trees, a man in a white dinner-jacket playing romantic songs on a white piano, a scattering of well-dressed people, and the soothing, melodic hum of conversation. He ordered a schnapps, leaned back in a leather chair, and focused his attention on a woman who was alone at a nearby table – rather ageless, not unattractive, very much minding her own business; which was a tall drink with a miniature candy cane hung on the side of the glass.

Ten minutes later, company arrived. Sweaty, moon-faced, anxious; an overworked detective who'd evidently parked himself on a chair in the lobby, then got nervous being out of contact with his assignment. He stood at the bar, ordered a beer, counted out pocket change to pay for it. Szara felt sorry for him.

Meanwhile, the woman he'd picked out made steady progress with her drink. Szara walked over to her and, presenting his back to the detective, leaned over and asked her what time it was. She said, politely enough, that she didn't know, but thought it was getting on towards ten. Szara laughed, stood up, turned halfway back towards his table, thought better of it, looked at his watch, said something like 'I'm afraid my watch has stopped' in a low voice, smiled conspiratorially, then returned to his chair. Fifteen minutes later, she left. Szara checked his watch, gave her five minutes to get wherever she was going, then threw a bill on the table and departed. Out in the lobby, he hurried into an elevator just before the door closed and asked to be let off at the fourth floor. He walked purposefully down the hall, heard the door close behind him, then found a stairway and returned to the lobby. The detective was sitting in a chair, watching the elevator door like a hawk, waiting for Szara to return from his assignation. Szara left the hotel through a side entrance, made certain he had no further company, then hailed a cab.

Rosenhain Passage was medieval, a crooked lane surfaced with broken stone. Half-timbered buildings, the plaster grey with age, slanted backwards as they rose, and a cold smell of drains hung in the dead air. What had happened here? He heard water trickling from unmended pipes, all shutters were closed tight, the street was lifeless, inert. There were no people. In the middle of all this stood Das Schmuckkästchen – the Jewel Box – theatre, as though a city cultural commission had been told to *do something about Rosenhain Passage* and here was their solution, a way of brightening things up. A hand-painted banner hung from the handle of an old-fashioned coach horn announcing the performance of *The Captain's Dilemma* by Hans-Peter Mütchler.

Midway down an alley next to the theatre, a door had been propped open with a pressing iron. Szara shoved it out of the way with his foot, let the door close gently until the lock snapped. Behind a thick curtain he could hear a play in progress, a man and a woman exchanging domestic insults in the declamatory style reserved for historical drama – *listen carefully, this was written a long time ago.* The insults were supposed to be amusing, the thrust of the voice told you that, and someone in the theatre did laugh once, but Szara could feel the almost palpable discomfort – the shifting and coughing, the unvoiced sigh – of an audience subjected to a witless and boring evening.

As Goldman had promised, there wasn't a soul to be seen where he entered. He peered through the darkness, found a row of doors, and tapped lightly at the one marked C.

'Yes? Come in.'

He found himself in a small dressing room: mirrors, costumes, clutter. A woman with a book in her hand, place held with an index finger, was sitting upright on a chaise longue, her face taut and anxious. Goldman had shown him a photograph. An actress. But the reality left him staring. Perhaps it was Berlin, the grotesque weight of the place, its heavy air, thickly made people, the brutal density of its life, but the woman seemed to him almost transparent, someone who might float away at any moment.

She put her head to one side and studied him clinically. 'You're different,' she said in Russian. Her voice was hoarse, and even in two words he could hear contempt.

'Different?'

'They usually send me a sort of boar. With bristles.' She was tall and slight, had turned up the cuffs of a thick sweater to reveal delicate wrists. Her eyes were enormous, a blue so pale and fragile it reminded him of blindness, and her hair, worn long and loose, was the colour of an almond shell. It was very fine hair, the kind that stirred with the slightest motion. Also she had been drinking; he could smell wine. 'Sit down,' she said softly, changing moods.

He sat in a thronelike armchair, clearly a stage prop. 'Are you in the play?' She was wearing slacks and strapped shoes with low heels, the outfit didn't go with the old-fashioned bluster he could hear from the stage.

'Done for the night.' Her voice easily suggested quotation marks when she added, 'Beatrice, a maid.' She shrugged, a dismissive Russian gesture. 'It's my rotten German. Sometimes I play a foreigner, but mostly it's maids. In little maid costumes. Everybody likes little maid costumes. When I bend over you can almost see my ass. But not quite.'

'What play is it?'

'What? You don't know *The Captain's Dilemma?* I thought everybody did.'

'No. Sorry.'

'Mütchler suits the current taste – that is, Goebbels's taste. He's said to consider it quite excellent. The captain returns to his home ten years after a shipwreck; he finds his wife living beyond her means, a slave to foolish fashion, beset by sycophants and usurers. He, on the other hand, is a typical *Volk*: sturdy, forthright, honest, a simple man from Rostock with the pleasures of a simple man. Simple pleasures, you see – we play him as a turnip. So now we have *conflict*, and a kind of drawing room comedy, with all sorts of amusing character parts: hypocrites, fops, oily Jews.'

'And the dilemma?'

'The dilemma is why the playwright wasn't strangled at birth.'

Szara laughed.

'What are you? A writer? I mean beside the other thing.'

'How do you know I'm the other thing?'

'Cruel times for Nadia if you're not.'

'And why a writer?'

'Oh, I know writers. I have them in my family, or used to. Do you want some wine? Be careful – it's a test.'

'Just a little.'

'You fail.' She reached behind a screen, poured wine into a water glass, and handed it to him, then retrieved her own glass, hidden behind a leg of the chaise longue. '*Nazhdrov'ya.*'

'*Nazhdrov'ya.*'

'Phooey.' She wrinkled her nose at the glass. 'Your pretty little niece, who is no doubt dying to be an actress – tell her it all rests on a tolerance for atrocious white wine.'

'You are from Moscow?' he asked.

'No, Piter, St Petersburg. So sorry, I mean Leningrad. An old, old family. Tscherova is my married name.'

'And Tscherov? He's in Berlin?'

'Pfft,' she said, casting her eyes up at the ceiling and springing four fingers from beneath her thumb, flicking Tscherov's soul up to heaven. 'November 1917.'

'Difficult times,' he said in sympathy.

'A Menshevik, a nice man. Married me when I was sixteen and didn't I give him a hellish time of it. The last eight months of his life, too. Poor Tscherov.' Her eyes shone for a moment and she looked away.

'At least you survived.'

'We all did. Aristocrats and artists in my family, all crazy as bats; revolution was the very thing for us. I have a brother in your business. Or I should say had. He seems to have vanished. Sascha.' She laughed at his memory, a harsh cackle, then put her fingers to her mouth, as though it were a drunken sound and embarrassed her. 'Sorry. Colonel Alexander Vonets – did you know him?'

'No.'

'Too bad. Charming bastard. Ah, the elegant Vonets family – but see what they've come to now. Miserable *stukachi*, dealing in filthy Nazi gossip. "Oh, but my dear General, how absolutely fasss-cinating!" ' She snickered at her own performance, then leaned towards him. 'You know what they say in Paris, that a woman attending a soirée needs only two words of French to be thought an elegant conversationalist? *Formidable* and *fantastique*. Well, it's the same here. You look up at them – you sit down if they're squatty little things; the eyes simply must look up at them – and they talk and talk, and you say – in German of course – *formidable!* after one sentence and *fantastique!* after the next. "Brilliant woman!" they say later.'

'So it's all nothing more than conversation.'

She studied him for a moment. 'You are very rude,' she said.

'Forgive me. It's just curiosity. I don't care what you do.'

'Well, as I'm certain you know, this wasn't my idea.'

'No?'

'Hardly. When they discovered I'd escaped from Russia and was in Berlin, they sent some *people*, not like you, around.' She shrugged, remembering the moment. 'Offered a choice between death and money, I chose money.'

Szara nodded in sympathy.

'We go to . . . parties, my little troupe and I. Parties of a sort, you know. We're considered a terrific amount of fun. People drink. Lose their inhibitions. Shall you hear it all?'

'Of course not.'

She smiled. 'It isn't so bad as you think. I avoid the worst of it, but my associates, well. Not that I'm innocent, you understand. I've known a couple of them better man I should have.' She paused. Looked at him critically, closed one eye. 'You must be a writer – so serious. Everything *means* something, but for us . . . In the theatre, you know, we're like naughty children, like brothers and sisters playing behind the shed. So these things don't mean so much, it's a way to forget yourself, that's all. One night you're this person and the next night you're that person, so that sometimes you're no person at all. This profession . . . it deforms the heart. Perhaps. I don't know.'

She was lost for a moment, sitting on the edge of the chaise, weight borne by elbows on knees, glass held in both hands. 'As for the Nazis, well, they're really more like pigs than humans, if you think about it. The men – and the women – just like pigs, they even squeal like pigs. It's no insult to say this, it's literal. It isn't their "*Schweine!*" that I'm talking about but real pigs: pink, overweight, quite intelligent if you know anything about them, certainly smarter than dogs, but very appetitious, there the common wisdom has it just right. They do want what they want, and lots of it, and right away, and then, when they get it, they're happy. Blissful.'

'I thought you said the man who came to see you was like a boar.'

'I did say that, didn't I. I'm sure there's a difference, though. You just have to be much smarter than me to see it.'

From the stage Szara could hear the ringing tones of a soliloquy, a kind of triumphant anger shot through with blistering rectitude. Then a pause, then desultory applause, then the creak of an unoiled mechanism closing the curtain. This was followed by a heavy tread in the hallway, a man's gruff voice, '*Scheiss!*' and the emphatic slam of a door.

'There,' said Tscherova, switching into German, 'that's the captain now. A simple *Volk*.'

Szara reached into his pockets and withdrew the thick wads of reichsmarks. She nodded, took them from him, stood, and stuffed the pockets of a long wool coat hanging on a peg.

Szara now assumed their conversation to be perfectly audible to the 'captain' next door. 'You'll take care of your, ah, health. I really hope you will.'

'Oh yes.'

He stood in order to leave; in the small room they were a little closer together than strangers would normally have been. 'It's better,' he said quietly, 'not to find out how it would be. Yes?'

She smiled impishly, amused that the proximity affected him. 'You *are* different, you are. And you mustn't be too concerned.' Her slim hand brushed the waistband of her slacks, then held up a tiny vial of yellow liquid. Her eyebrow lifted, *see how clever?* 'End of story,' she said. 'Curtain.' Then she hid it behind her back, as though it didn't exist. She bent towards him, kissed him lightly on the mouth – very warm and very brief – and whispered good-bye, in Russian, next to his ear.

Szara walked east from the theatre, away from the Adlon, unconsciously following procedure. Balked by the Neu-Kölln Canal, he veered south to Gertraudten Bridge, lit a cigarette, watched orange peels and scrapwood drifting past on the black water. It was colder, the lamp lights had pale haloes as mist drifted off the canal.

The Directorate never knew their agents in person; Szara now saw the reason for that. Tscherova's vulnerability would not leave his mind. Caught between the Gestapo and the NKVD, between Germany and Russia, she lived by her wits, by looking as she did, by clever talk. But she would have to drink the yellow liquid eventually, maybe soon, and the idea of so much life – all the emotional weather that blew across her heart – winding up as a formless shape collapsed in a corner tormented him. Could a woman be too beautiful to die? Moscow wouldn't like his answer to that. Was he a little bit in love with her? What if he was. Was all her capering about, the way she worked on him with her eyes, meant to draw him to her? He was sure of it. How could that be wrong?

She'd have to drink the liquid because agents didn't survive. The result of all the elaborate defences, secrecy and codes and clandestine methods of every sort, was time gained, only that, against a known destiny. Things went wrong. Things always, eventually, went wrong. The world was unpredictable, inconsistent, volatile, ultimately a madhouse of bizarre events. Agents got caught. Almost always. You replaced them. That's what the *apparat* expected you to do: reorganize the chaos, mend the damage, and go on. There were ways in which he accepted that, but when women entered the equation he failed. His need was to protect women, not to sacrifice them, and he could not, would not, change. An ancient instinct, to stand between women and danger, sapped his will to run operations the way they had to be run and made him a bad intelligence officer – it was just that simple. And the worst part of it was that the yellow liquid wasn't part of some spy kit – the NKVD didn't believe in such things. No, Tscherova had obtained the liquid herself, because she knew what happened to agents just as well as he did and she wanted to have it over and done with when the time came. The idea made him ill, the world couldn't go on that way.

But they had a Jew up on the end of Brüderstrasse, where Szara turned north, a pack of drunken Hitlerjugend in their fancy uniforms, teenagers, forcing some poor soul on hands and knees to drink the black water in a gutter, and they were shouting and laughing and singing and having a tremendously good time at it.

Szara faded into a doorway. For a moment he thought he was having a stroke – his vision swam and a terrible force hammered against his temples like a fist. Steadying himself against a wall, he realized it wasn't a stroke, it was rage, and he fought to subdue it. For a moment he went mad, shutting his eyes against the pounding blood and pleading with God for a machine gun, a hand grenade, a pistol, any weapon at all – but this prayer was not immediately answered. Later he discovered a small chip missing from a front tooth.

Some time after midnight, having crept away into the darkness, walking through deserted streets towards his hotel, he made the inevitable connection: Tscherova, by what she did, could help to destroy these people, these youths with their Jewish toy. She could weaken them in ways they did not understand, she was more than a machine gun or a pistol, a far deadlier weapon than any he'd wished for. The knowledge tore at him, on top of what he'd seen, and there were tears on his face that he wiped off with the sleeve of his raincoat.

The following afternoon, he told Marta Haecht what he'd seen. Instinctively she reached for him, but when her hands flew to touch him he no more than allowed it, unwilling to reject an act of love, but equally unwilling to be comforted.

This was pain he meant to keep.

To maintain his cover, he had to write something.

'Nothing political,' Goldman had warned. 'Let Tass file on diplomatic developments; you find yourself something meaningless, filler. Just pretend that some ambitious editor has taken it into his head that *Pravda's* view on Germany needs the Szara touch. Even with all the bad blood and political hostility, life goes on. A bad job but you're making the best of it; you want to lead the Reich press office to believe that, a little of their fine Teutonic contempt is the very thing for you. For the moment, let them sneer.'

Midmorning, in the dining room at the Adlon, Szara submitted himself to the tender mercies of Vainshtok. The little man ran his fingers through his hair and studied his list of possible stories. 'A Szara needs help from a Vainshtok?' he said. 'I knew the world was turning upside down, Armageddon expected any day now, but this!'

'What have you got?' Szara said. He caught the attention of a passing waiter: 'A Linzer torte for my friend, plenty of schlag on it.'

Vainshtok's eyebrows shot up. 'You're in trouble. That I can tell. My mama always warned me, "Darling son, when they put the whipped cream on the Linzer torte, watch out." What is it, André Aronovich? Have you fallen from favour at last? Got a girlfriend who's giving you a hard time? Getting older?'

'I can't stand Berlin, Vainshtok. I can't think in this place.'

'Oy, he can't stand Berlin. Last year they sent me to Madagascar. I ate, I believe I actually ate, a lizard. Did you hear the china breaking, Szara, wherever you were? Eleven generations of Vainshtok rabbis were going wild up in heaven, breaking God's kosher plates, "*Gott im Himmel!* Little Asher Moisevich is eating a lizard!" Ah, here's something, how about weather?'

'What about it?'

'It's happening every day.'

'And?'

'Well, it's not especially cold, and it's not especially hot. But more than likely such a story won't stir up the Reichsministries. On the other hand, it might. "What do you mean, *normal?* Our German weather is clean and pure, like no other weather anywhere!"'

Szara sighed. He hadn't the strength to fight back.

'All right, all right,' Vainshtok said as his treat arrived, swimming in cream. 'You're going to make me cry. Take Frau Kummel, up in Lübeck. Actually she's called Mutter Kummel, Mother Kummel. It's a story you can write, and it gets you out of Berlin for the day.'

'Mutter Kummel?'

'I'll write down the address for you. Yesterday she turned a hundred years old. Born the first of November, 1838. Imagine all the exciting things she's seen – she may even remember some of them. 1838?

Schleswig-Holstein still belonged to the Danes, Lübeck was part of the independent state of Mecklenburg. Germany – of course you'll have to say *Germany as we know it today* – didn't exist. You're to be envied, Szara. What a thrilling time that was, and Mutter Kummel somehow lived through every minute of it.'

He took the train that afternoon, a grim ride up through the flatlands of the Lüneberg Plain, through marshy fields where gusts of wind flattened the reeds under a hard, grey sky. He avoided Hamburg by taking the line that went through Schwerin, and outside a little village not far from the sea he spotted a traffic sign by a tight curve in the road: *Drive carefully! Sharp curve! Jews 75 miles an hour!*

Mutter Kummel lived with her eighty-one-year-old daughter in a gingerbread house in the centre of Lübeck. 'Another reporter, dear mother,' said the daughter when Szara knocked at the door. The house smelled of vinegar, and the heat of the place made him sweat as he scribbled in his notebook. Mutter Kummel remembered quite a bit about Lübeck: where the old butcher shop used to be, the day the rope parted and the tumbling church bell broke through the belfry floor and squashed a deacon. What Nezhenko would make of all this Szara could only imagine, let alone some coal miner in the Donbas, wrapping his lunch potato in the newspaper. But he worked at it and did the job as best he could. Towards the end of the interview the old lady leaned forward, her placid face crowned by a bun of white hair, and told him how *die Juden* were no longer to be found in Lübeck – yet one more change she'd witnessed in her many years in the town. Polite people when one met them in the street, it had to be admitted, but she wasn't sorry to see them go. 'Those Jews,' she confided, 'for too long they've stolen our souls.' Szara must have looked inquisitive. 'Oh yes, young man. It's what they did, and we here in Lübeck knew about it,' she said slyly. Szara, for a moment, was tempted to ask her to explain – for he sensed she'd worked it out – the mechanics of such a thing: how it was actually accomplished, where the Jews hid the stolen souls and what they did with them. But he didn't. He thanked the ladies and took the train back to Berlin and an evening with Marta Haecht, the promise of which had kept him more or less sane for another day.

Later on, he would have reason to remember that afternoon.

Later on, when everything had changed, he would wonder what might have happened if he'd missed the Berlin train, if he'd had to spend the night in Lübeck. But he knew himself, knew that he would have found some way to be with Marta Haecht that night. He considered himself a student of destiny, perhaps even a *connoisseur* – that obnoxious word – of its tricks and turns: how it hunted, how it fed.

He would see himself on the train to Berlin, a man who'd beaten his way across a lifeless afternoon by banking thoughts of the evening. And though the browns and greys of the German November flowed past the train window he was not there to see them; he was lost in anticipation, lost in lover's greed. In fact, he would ask himself, what *didn't* he want? He certainly wanted her, wanted her in the ways of a Victorian novel kept in a night table drawer – what magnificent fantasies he made for himself on that train! But that wasn't all. He wanted affection; kindness, refuge. He wanted to spend the night with his lover. He wanted to play. The game of temptations and surrenders, cunning noes and yesses. And then he wanted to talk – to talk in the darkness where he could say anything he liked, then he wanted to sleep, all wrapped and twined around her in a well-warmed bed. He even wanted breakfast. Something delicious.

And what he wanted, he got.

In its very own diabolical way, destiny delivered every last wish. Only it added a little something extra, a little something he didn't expect, buried it right in the midst of all his pleasures where he'd be sure to find it.

The Iron Exchange Building was even stranger at night: the long tile hallways in shadow, the frosted glass doors opaque and secretive, the silence broken only by an agonizing piano lesson in progress on the floor below and the echo of his footsteps.

But in low light the studio of the painter Benno Ault was agreeably softened. The shrieks and torments pinned to the wall faded to sighs, and Marta Haecht, at centre stage, appeared in short silk robe and Parisian scent, slid gracefully into his arms, and gave him every reason to hope that his thoughts on the train had not been idle fantasies.

They had their Victorian novel – in feeling if not in form – and wound up sprawled together across the sofa, for a moment stunned senseless. Then Marta turned the lamp off and they lay peacefully in the darkness for a time, sticky, sore, thoroughly pleased with themselves and the very best of friends. 'What was that you said?' she asked idly. 'Was it Russian?'

'Yes.'

'I wasn't sure, perhaps it was Polish.'

'No, Russian. Very much so.'

'Was it a sweet thing to say?'

'No, a rough thing. Common. A command.'

'Ah, a command. And I obeyed?' She was smiling in the darkness.

'You did. Somehow you understood.'

'And that you liked.'

'Couldn't you tell?'

'Yes. Of course.' She thought for a time. 'We are so different,' she mused.

'Not really.'

'You mustn't say that. Such a difference is a, a pleasure for me.'

'Oh. Day and night, then.'

She put a hand on his chest. 'Don't,' she said.

They were still for a while. He looked up at the large window, illuminated by the pale night sky of a city. A few snowflakes drifted against the glass and melted into droplets. 'It's snowing,' he said.

She turned halfway around to look. 'It's a sign,' she said.

'You mean the night we met, back again.'

'Yes, just so. I can still see you in Dr Baumann's kitchen, making small talk. You hadn't even noticed me. But I knew everything that would happen.'

'Did you truly?'

She nodded yes. 'I knew you would take me off somewhere, a hotel, a room. I thought, *a man like you can always have a woman like me*. It struck me, that thought, I was so surprised at myself. Because I was so *good*. I'd always known boys who wanted me, at the university and so forth, but *I* was such a little *Mädchen*, I wouldn't. I'd blush and push them away – they were so earnest! And then – this thing always happens when you aren't expecting it – the Baumanns, the stuffy old Baumanns, invited me to their house.' She laughed. 'I didn't want to go. My father made me.'

'But you said you knew who I was, that you wanted to meet me.'

'I know I said that. I lied. I meant to flatter you.'

'Ach!' He pretended to be wounded.

'But no, you should be flattered by such a lie, because the moment I saw you I wanted everything, to be made to do everything. Your dark shirt, your dark hair, the way you looked into me – it was so . . . Russian – I can't describe it. Something about you, not polite, not at all polite the way Germans are, but strong, intense.' She smoothed his hair back above his ear; the gesture seemed to last a long time and he could feel the heat of her hand.

'Isn't that what Germans always think of Russians, when they don't hate them?'

'It's true. Some hate, and are hateful. But for the rest of us it's complicated. We are all tied up inside ourselves, almost embarrassed at

being in the world. It's our German culture I think, and we see Russians
– Jews, Slavs, all the people in the East – as passionate and romantic,
their feelings out for all to see, and deep in our hearts we're envious of
them because we sense that they *feel*, whereas we just think about
everything, think and think and think.'

'What about Dr Baumann? Passionate and romantic?'

'Oh, not him.' She laughed at the idea.

'But he's a Jew.'

'Yes of course he is. But here they're more like us than anything else,
all tight and cold, self-conscious. That's the problem here in Germany;
the Jews have become German, consider themselves German, just as
good as any German; and there are many Germans who feel it is a
presumption. They don't like it. Then, after the revolution in 1917 we
had here in Berlin the Russian and Polish Jews, and they are really quite
different from us – perhaps rude is the word, not cultured. Mostly they
stay off by themselves, but when one sees them, for instance when they
are on the trolley car and it is crowded, they stare, and one can smell
the onions they eat.'

'The Jews from Poland have been sent back.'

'Yes, I know this and it's sad for them. But there were some who
wanted to go back, and Poland would not let them in, and there are
people who said why must this be always Germany's problem? So now
they all have to go back, and for them I feel sad.'

'And Dr Baumann? Where can he go?'

'Why should he go anywhere? For most Jews it's terrible, a tragedy,
they lose everything, but for him it's not like that. The Dr Baumanns of
the world always find a way to get along.'

'Is this something your father tells you?'

'No. Something I know from my own eyes.'

'You see him?'

'Socially? Of course not. But I work for a man called Herr Hanau, a
man from the little town of Greifswald, up on the Baltic. Herr Hanau
has a small shipping company, one big ship and three little ones, and to
receive consideration for government contracts he has moved his
business to Berlin, and here I am his assistant. So, some weeks ago, we
were awarded a small shipment of machine tools that goes up to
Sweden, a great victory for us, and Herr Hanau invited me to lunch at
the Kaiserhof, to celebrate. And there, large as life, is Dr Baumann,
eating a cutlet and drinking Rhine wine. Life cannot be so bad for him
after all.'

Puzzled, Szara stared at the window, watched the snowflakes drifting
slowly downwards on the still air. 'How could he do that?' he asked.

'Can a Jew, like Dr Baumann, walk into one of the better hotels in Berlin and just have lunch?'

'I think not. These waiters have a sense of propriety, alone he would not have been served or there might have been a scene. But he was with his protector, you see, and so everything just went along in the normal way.'

'Protector?'

'Naturally. Though my father stands ready to help him, to take over the ownership of the mill, Dr Baumann remains in charge. Baumann Milling does defence work, as you may have guessed, and so Dr Baumann is protected.'

'By whom?'

'It seemed strange to me, these two men having lunch. Dr Baumann and some very tall, reedy fellow, almost bald, with little wisps of blond hair. An aristocrat, I thought, that's what they look like: late thirties, no chin, and that hesitant little smile, as though somebody were about to break a priceless vase and they're afraid they'll let on that they're brokenhearted.'

Szara shifted his weight on the couch. 'I hope you don't describe me to anyone,' he said with mock horror.

She clucked. 'I don't tell secrets, *Liebchen*.'

'Who do you suppose he was?'

'I asked Herr Hanau. "Don't meddle," says he. "That's Von Polanyi from the Foreign Office, a clever fellow but not someone for you to know." '

'He sounds Hungarian.'

He felt her shrug. 'During the Austro-Hungarian time the noble families moved around, we have all sorts in Germany. In any event, don't be too concerned for Herr Doktor Julius Baumann, for it turns out he's rather comfortably situated.'

Szara was silent for a long time.

'Are you asleep?'

'No, dreaming.'

'Of me?'

He moved closer to her.

'Give me your hand,' she said.

And in the morning, when the light woke them up, after the Victorian novel, the affection, the honest talk in darkness, and, well, some condition of absence that at least imitated sleep, Marta Haecht tied the little silk robe at her waist and stood before the stove and made blini, thin ones like French crêpes, then spread them with strawberry jam from Berlin's finest store, folded them carefully, and served them on pretty plates and Szara realized, just about then, that had he been able to taste anything at all they would have been, as he'd imagined on the train to Berlin, delicious.

5 November.

A telephone message at the Adlon desk requested that he stop by the press office at the embassy. On the Unter den Linden, in a light, dry snowfall that blew about like dust, thousands of black-shirted Nazi party members were marching towards the Brandenburg Gate. They sang in deep voices, roared out their chants, and threw their arms into the air in fascist salutes. Amid the sea of black there were banners denouncing the Comintern and the Soviet Union, and the men marched by slamming their boots against the pavement; Szara could actually feel the rhythm of it trembling beneath his feet. He pulled his raincoat around him and pretended to ignore the marchers. This was what most Berliners did – glanced at the singing men, then hurried on about their business – and Szara followed their example.

The embassy was extremely busy. People were rushing about here and there, clerks ran by with armloads of files, and the tension could be easily felt. Varin, the second secretary, was waiting for him in the press office, rather pointedly not watching the parade below his window. He was a small, serious man, determined, and not inclined towards conversation. He handed over an envelope; Szara could feel the waxy paper of the folded flimsy inside. A radio was playing in the press office and when the news forecast came on at noon, all talk stopped. 'They have a big mess over at Zbąszyń,' Varin said when the commentator had finished. 'Fifteen thousand Polish Jews penned up in barbed wire at the border. Germany's thrown them out, but Poland won't let them in. There's not enough water, hardly any shelter, and it's getting colder. Everybody's waiting to see who gives in first.'

'Maybe I should go up there,' said the journalist Szara.

Varin closed his eyes for an instant and just barely moved his head to indicate that he should do no such thing.

'Is that what the parade is all about?'

Varin shrugged, indifferent. 'They like to march, so let them. It's the weather – they always feel spirited when the winter comes.'

Szara stood to go.

'Watch yourself,' said Varin quietly.

For just a moment, Szara had been tempted to lay his troubles at Varin's door, but it was a temptation instantly dismissed. Still, as he walked back to the Adlon, the word *Funkspiele* drummed relentlessly in his consciousness. Playback, it meant, when a wireless was used. In general, the operation of a doubled agent. There might have been an innocent explanation for Baumann meeting with someone from the Foreign Office, but Szara didn't think so. The Directorate had been restless with Baumann from the very beginning; now he understood that they'd been right. People like Abramov had spent most of their lives in clandestine work – against the Okhrana before 1917, against the world after that. One developed sharpened instincts; on certain nights the animals are reluctant to approach the waterhole.

Suddenly there wasn't a choice, he had to be an intelligence officer like it or not. If Baumann was under German control, all the traditional questions bobbed up to the surface: From the beginning? Or caught then turned? How accomplished? By coercion, clearly. Not money, not ego, and not, God forbid, ideology. A frightened Jew was appropriate to their purposes. Which were? Deceptive. In what way deceptive, towards what end? If the swage wire figures were high, that meant they wanted to scare the USSR into thinking they had more bombers than they did, a tactic of political warfare, the same method that had proved fatal for Czechoslovakia. If they were low, it was an attempt to lull the USSR into false strategic assumptions. And that meant war.

At the Adlon he knocked, harder than he meant to, at Vainshtok's door. The little man was in shirtsleeves, a cloud of cigarette smoke hung in the air, and a sheet of paper protruded from a typewriter on the desk. 'Szara? It better be important. You scared the shit out of my muse.'

'May I come in?'

Vainshtok beckoned him inside and closed the door. 'Don't knock like that, will you? Call from the lobby. These days, a knock on the door . . .'

'Thank you for the Mutter Kummel story.'

'Don't mention it. I thought you needed all the excitement you could get.'

'Do you know anything about the Reich Foreign Office?'

Vainshtok sighed. He went over to an open briefcase, dug around inside for a time, and emerged with a thin, mimeographed telephone directory. 'Oh the forbidden things we have here in the Adlon. I expect the Gestapo will set fire to it any day now. That'll be something to see – a hundred firemen, all wearing eyeglasses.' He cackled at the idea. 'What do you want to know?'

'Do you find a man called Von Polanyi?'

It took only a moment. 'Von Polanyi, Herbert K.L. Amt 9.'

'What is it?'

'I don't know. But then, that in itself is informative.'

'How so?'

'When you don't know, chances are they don't want you to know. So, they're not the people who keep track of the Bulgarian bean harvest.'

Back in his room, Szara drew the blinds, set out pencils and paper, propped up the railway timetable against the back of the desk, spread the code flimsy out under the lamp, and decrypted it.

TRANSMISSION 5 NOVEMBER 1938 04:30 HOURS

TO: JEAN MARC

A SECOND MEETING WITH OTTER IS APPROVED. FOR 10 NOVEM-
BER, 01:15 HOURS, AT 8 KLEINERSTRASSE, WITTENAU. YOU WILL
BE TRANSPORTED TO THE TOWN OF WITTENAU, APPROXIMATELY
30 MINUTES FROM BERLIN, BY CAR. AT 12:40 HOURS BE AT THE
KOLN FISCHMARKT, AT INTERSECTION OF FISCHERSTRASSE AND
MUHLENDAMM, ASSIGNED TO COVER STORY OF FISH MARKET
VISITED BY TOURISTS AT NIGHT. A MAN IN A TARTAN SCARF
WILL APPROACH YOU. THE PAROL WILL BE: CAN YOU TELL ME
WHAT TIME IT IS? THE COUNTERSIGN WILL BE: I'M SORRY. MY
WATCH STOPPED ON THURSDAY.

8 KLEINERSTRASSE IS AN OLD WOODEN BUILDING FACING
NORTH, AT THE EASTERN END OF THE STREET BORDERING
PRINZALLEE. A SIGN ABOVE THE DOOR IDENTIFIES IT AS BETH
MIDRESH, A SYNAGOGUE. APPROACH SUBJECT THROUGH DOOR
AT THE END OF THE LEFT-HAND AISLE. YOU ARE TO SPEND NO
MORE THAN THIRTY MINUTES WITH SUBJECT, THEN RETURN TO
BERLIN BY CAR, HAVING ARRANGED MEETING WITH DRIVER.

NO OFFER OF FUTURE EXFILTRATION OR RESETTLEMENT IS TO BE
MADE.

DIRECTOR

7 November.

He arrived at the loft just after nine, a little out of breath, his face cold from the night air, carrying a bottle of expensive wine wrapped in paper. A different mood for Marta: hair carefully pinned up, red Bakelite earrings with lipstick to match, tight sweater and skirt. She gave him a leather case holding a pair of gold cuff links set with tiny citrines, a faded lemon colour. His shirt had buttons, so she brought one of her own out of a bureau to show him what they looked like; he found them almost impossible to attach and fumbled grimly till she came to the rescue, grinning at his efforts. They drank the wine and ate biscuits from a box with a paper doily in it. He turned the radio to a different station – light Viennese froth that drew a sneer from

Marta – but he'd come to associate the serious German composers with the mood of the city and he didn't want that in his sanctuary. They talked, aimless and comfortable; she picked candied cherries off the tops of the biscuits and put them in an ashtray. They would eat supper later, after they made love. But tonight they were in no hurry.

It had become, in just a few days, a love affair with rules of its own, a life of its own, a life that radiated from a bulbous old green sofa at its centre, an affair with ups and downs, rough moments smoothed over, and unimportant, courteous lies. Something between adults. Marta, a working woman, a sophisticated Berliner with a life of her own, accepted him for what she thought he was: a Soviet journalist who travelled constantly, a man to whom she was deeply, sexually, attracted, a man she'd encountered in the last days of girlhood who now loved her as a woman.

It was too bad they couldn't go out to restaurants or concerts, but the present reality was uncertain in that way and they agreed without discussion not to put themselves in a situation where unpleasantness might occur – life was too short for turmoil, it was best to float with the tide. Szara did not mention the Aesopic letter or the trip to Lisbon. He doubted she knew he'd written it. If she did, she'd also decided it would not bear discussion. They had negotiated a treaty, and now they lived by it.

The radio played 'Barcarole' from *The Tales of Hoffman*. She sat on his lap. 'This is pretty,' she said. 'Two lovers on a boat, drifting along a canal.' He slipped a hand under her sweater; she closed her eyes, leaned her head on his shoulder and smiled. The song ended and an announcer, rattling a paper into the microphone, stated that a special bulletin from Dr Joseph Goebbels would follow. 'Oh, that hideous man!' Marta said.

Goebbels's delivery was professional, but the nasal whine of his personality was more than evident. As he read, from an editorial that would appear the following day in the *Völkischer Beobachter*, a kind of choked-off rage thickened his voice. This news, the tone implied, was well beyond shouting. Ernst Vom Rath, third secretary at the German embassy in Paris, had been shot and gravely wounded by a seventeen-year-old Polish Jew named Hershl Grynszpan, a student whose parents had been deported from Germany to Poland, then held at the frontier town of Zbąszyń. Goebbels's point was clear: we try to help these people, by sending them away from a nation where they aren't wanted to a place where they will be more at home, and look what they do – they shoot German diplomats. And just how long shall we Germans be expected to put up with such outrages? The bulletin ended, a Strauss waltz followed. 'This world,' said Marta sadly, closing her eyes again and wriggling to get comfortable. 'We must be tender to one another,' she added, placing her warm hand over his.

10 November.

A German dearly loves his fish. Making a show of being a journalist, Szara jotted down impressions on a pocket notepad. *Herring and whitebait,* he wrote. *Flounder and haddock.* After midnight, the stalls of the Koln Fischmarkt began to fill with the day's catch trucked in from the coast: glistening grey and pink eels on chipped ice, baskets of whelks and oysters trailing seaweed, crayfish floating in a lead tank filled with cloudy brine. The sawdust underfoot was wet with blood and seawater, and the air, even in the cold November night, was rank – *the iodine smell of tidal pools,* Szara wrote, *barrels of cast-off fishheads. Stray cats.* There were plenty of people around; vendors shouted snappy fish jokes at their customers – a bit of psychology: lively talk implied fresh seafood. Some local swells and their girlfriends, faces bright with drinking, were waltzing around with half a dripping mackerel. There was even a bewildered British tourist, asking questions in slow, loud English, puzzled that he couldn't get an answer.

The operative was precisely on time, a heavy man with eyebrows grown together and red cheeks, hair sheared off in a military cut. After the parol was completed, they walked silently to the car, a black Humboldt parked a little way down the Muhlendamm. The operative was an expert driver, and cautious, squaring blocks and ceaselessly crossing back over his own tracks to make sure they weren't followed. They worked their way west through the Grunewald and eventually turned north on the near bank of the Havel, following a succession of little roads to avoid police on the main highways. 'I'm told to warn you there's some kind of trouble brewing,' the driver said.

'What kind of trouble?'

'*Aktionen.* Actions against the Jews. A monitoring unit at the embassy distributed a teleprinter message just as I was leaving; it was from Müller's office to all Gestapo headquarters. The timing was specified as "at very short notice". You'll probably get in and out without difficulties – but don't dawdle.'

'The *treff* takes place in a synagogue.'

'I know where it takes place. The point is, there won't be anyone around, and it's best for your contact, who comes from the east without going into the city. We got him in for Friday night services and he just didn't leave.'

The car slowed as they came to the outskirts of Wittenau. The street swung away from the Havel, and the sheds and low buildings of small industrial shops appeared on both sides. The driver pulled over and turned off the engine. The night was still, the air smelling faintly of coal smoke. The *apparat* had a genius, Szara thought, for finding such places; dead zones, night-time deserts on the edges of cities.

'This is Prinzallee,' said the driver. 'Up ahead of you, about fifty paces, is the start of Kleinerstrasse. Your synagogue is on the corner. What time do you have?'

'Eight minutes after one.'

'It will take you only a minute to walk.'

Szara fidgeted in the front seat. A bird started up nearby, otherwise the silence was oppressive. 'Does anybody live here?' he asked.

'No more. It was a ghetto thirty years ago, then it turned into factories. Only the synagogue is left, and a few tenements with old Jews living in them – most of the young ones got out after '33.'

Szara kept looking at his watch.

'All right,' said the driver. 'Don't close the car door – it's a noise everybody knows. And please keep it short.'

Szara climbed out. The bulb had been removed from the roof light, so the interior of the car remained dark. He walked close to a board fence on a dirt pathway that muffled his footsteps, but the night was so quiet he became conscious of his own breathing.

The synagogue was very old, a two-storey wood frame structure with a sloping roof, built perhaps a century earlier for use as a workshop, possibly a carpentry workshop since it stood against the low shed of a neighbouring lumberyard.

A sign in Hebrew above the door said Beth Midresh, which meant House of Worship. That told Szara that it was being used by immigrant Jews from Poland and Russia – all synagogues in the Pale were identified that way. In France they used the name of the street, while the wealthy Jews of Germany often named their synagogues after a leader in the community – the Adler synagogue, for instance. Those were grand and glorious temples, nothing like what he approached. Seen in the light of a waning moon, the synagogue on Prinzallee might have stood in Cracow or Lodz, seemed to come from another time and place.

The impression held. The front door was unlocked, but the frame was warped and Szara had to pull hard to get it open. The interior took him back to Kishinev – the smell of sweat and urine in stale air, as though the windows were never opened. Behind the altar, above the double-doored ark that held the scrolls of the Torah, was a tiny lamp, the eternal light, and he could just make out two narrow aisles between rows of wooden chairs of several different styles. He took the aisle on the left and walked towards the front, the boards creaking softly under his feet. The door to one side of the altar was ajar; he gave it a gentle push and it swung open to reveal a man sitting slumped at a bare table. The room was narrow, perhaps serving at one time as a rabbi's study — there were empty book shelves built up one wall.

'Dr Baumann,' he said.

Baumann looked up at him; his collapsed posture didn't change. 'Yes,' he said in a low voice.

There was a chair directly across the table from Baumann's and Szara sat down. 'You're not sick, are you?'

'Tired,' Baumann said. He meant the word in both senses: exhausted, and tired of life.

'We have to discuss a few things, quickly, and then we can leave. You have a way to get safely home?'

'Yes. It isn't a problem.'

Perhaps he had a driver waiting or was driving his own car, Szara didn't know. 'We want to find out, first of all, if you've come under pressure from any of the Reichsministries. I don't mean having to hand in your passport, or any of the laws passed against the Jews in general, I mean you in particular. In other words, have you been singled out in any way, any way at all?'

Szara thought he saw the probe hit home. The room was dark, and the reaction was very brief, not much more than a pause, but it was there. Then Baumann shook his head impatiently, as though Szara was wasting his time with such foolish notions: this was not a question he wished to discuss. Instead, he leaned forward and whispered urgently: 'I'm going to accept your offer. Your offer to leave here, for my wife and I. The dog too, if it can be managed.'

'Of course,' Szara said.

'Soon. Maybe right away.'

'I have to ask . . .'

'We want to go to Amsterdam. It shouldn't be too hard; our friends say that the Dutch are letting us in, no questions asked. So the only difficulty is getting out of Germany. We'll take a suitcase and the little dog, nothing else, they can have it all, everything.'

'One thing we'll need to—' Szara stopped cold and leaned his head to one side.

Baumann sat up straight as though he'd been shocked. 'My God,' he said.

'Is it singing?'

Baumann nodded.

395

Szara instinctively looked at his watch. 'At one-thirty in the morning?'

'When they sing like that,' Baumann said, then paused, his voice fading into silence as he concentrated on the sound.

Szara remembered the parade on the Unter den Linden. These were the same voices, deep and vibrant. Both of them sat still as the sound grew louder, then Baumann stood suddenly. 'They must not see us.' The beginning of panic was in his voice.

'Would we be better off out in the street?'

'They're coming here. *Here.*'

Szara stood. He remembered the road into Wittenau – there was nothing there. By now the words of the song were plainly audible; it was something they sang in the Rathskellers as they drank their beer: *Wenn's Judenblut vom Messer spritzt / Dann geht's nochmal so gut, dann geht's nochmal so gut.* When Jewish blood squirts under the knives / Then all is well, then all is well. Baumann turned away from the door and the two men stared at each other, both frightened, uncertain what to do and, suddenly, perfect equals.

'Hide.' Baumann spoke the word in a broken whisper, the voice of a terrified child.

Szara fought for control of himself. He had been through pogroms before – in Kishinev and Odessa. They always attacked the synagogue. 'We're getting out,' he said. It was an order. Whatever else happened, he wasn't going to end his life in dumb shock like an animal that knows it's going to die. He walked quickly out of the narrow room and had taken two steps back up the aisle when one of the dark windows flanking the entry door suddenly brightened; a golden shadow flickered against it for a moment, then the glass came showering in on the floor. The men outside sent up a great cheer and, simultaneously, Baumann screamed. Szara spun and clapped his hand over the man's mouth; he felt saliva on his palm but held on tight until Baumann made a gesture that he could control himself. Behind them, the other window exploded. Szara leaned close to Baumann. 'A stairway,' he whispered. 'There must be a stairway.'

'Behind the curtain.'

They ran up three steps onto the altar. Szara heard the stubborn door squeak at the other end of the building just as Baumann threw the curtain aside and they disappeared behind the ark. There was no banister on the stairs, just steps braced against the wall. He raced up, Baumann behind him, and tried the door. On the other side of the curtain he could hear chairs being kicked around and the other windows being broken to a chorus of laughter and cheers, 'Jews come out!' roared a drunken voice. Szara tore the door open with one hand and reached back for Baumann's sleeve with the other, pulling him into the upstairs room, then turning and kicking the door shut. The second storey was unused – a pile of drapes, cobwebbed corners, broken chairs, the smell of old wood . . . and something else. Burning. He turned to look at Baumann; his mouth was wide open, gasping for air, and his hand was pressed against the middle of his chest. 'No!' Szara said. Baumann looked at him strangely, then sank to his knees. Szara ran to the closest window, but there were torches below and dim shapes moving across the alley side of the synagogue. He crossed the room to a second window and saw that the upper storey was just above the roof of the lumberyard shed. It was a very old window, tiny panes of glass in wooden strips, and had not been opened for years. He strained at it for a moment, then drew his foot back and kicked out the glass and the bracing, kicking again and again, savagely, even though he felt the fabric of his trousers rip and saw blood droplets suddenly appear in the thick dust on the sill. When the opening was sufficiently wide, he ran to Baumann and took him under the armpits. 'Get up,' he said. 'Get up.'

There were tears on Baumann's face. He did not move.

Szara began dragging him across the floor until, at last, Baumann started crawling. Szara spoke to him like a child: 'Yes, that's it.' Somewhere close by he heard the splintering sound of a door being ripped off its hinges and he glanced, horrified, towards the stairway, then realized the noise came from below, that they were after the scrolls of the Torah in the ark. The smell of burning was getting stronger; a curl of smoke worked through the floorboards in one corner. He leaned Baumann against the wall below the window and spoke by his ear: 'Go ahead, I'll help you, it isn't far and then we'll be safe.' Baumann mumbled something – Szara couldn't understand what he said but it meant he wanted to be left to die. Infuriated, Szara pushed him aside and worked his way through the jagged circle of broken glass and wood, tumbling forward onto his hands on the tarred gravel surface of the roof of the lumberyard shed. He scrambled to his feet and reached back through the opening, getting a grip on the lapels of Baumann's jacket and hauling him forward. When Baumann's weight began to tilt over the sill, he thrust out his hands instinctively and the two of them fell together.

Szara lay stunned for a moment. Falling backwards and taking Baumann's weight had knocked the wind out of him. Then he began to breathe again and, in the cold air, became aware of a wet sock. He struggled away from Baumann and sat up to look at his ankle. Blood was welling steadily from a slash down his shin. He pressed the wound together for a moment, then remembered about silhouettes and threw himself on his stomach. Baumann's breathing distracted him – loud and hoarse, like sighing. He moved the man's hand, which lay flaccid against his chest, and felt for a heartbeat. What he found was a shock – a beating of such force and speed it frightened him. 'How is it?' he asked.

'My God in heaven,' Baumann said.

'We're going to be all right,' Szara said. 'I'll buy you a dinner in Amsterdam.'

Baumann smiled weakly, the wind blowing strands of his hair around, one side of his face pressed against the black surface of the roof, and nodded yes, that's what they would do.

Szara began to think about the operative and the car, then decided to try to get a look from the edge of the roof. Very carefully he moved forward, scraping his cheek against the surface, staying as flat as possible, gaining an inch at a time until he could just see over the end of the shed. He could not get a view of the path by the board fence where he'd left the car – the angle was wrong. But he was high enough to look out over part of Wittenau, the Havel, and an ancient stone bridge that crossed the river. His eyes were beginning to water from the smoke – the fire was taking hold; the old wood snapped and exploded as it caught – but what there was to see, he saw: a group of men with torches shifting restlessly in a knot at the centre of the bridge, an instant of motion in the darkness. Then there was a scream that carried perfectly on the night air, a white churning in the water at the foot of the bridge pier, a strangled cry for help, the yellow arc of a torch hurled into the water, then laughter and cheering as the men on the bridge headed back into Wittenau. Some of them began to sing.

As the fire swept up the front of the synagogue it illuminated the shed, and Szara scrambled backwards, afraid of being seen. Burning embers were all over the roof, producing, for the moment, only an oily black smoke from the tar surface. He realized it was only a matter of time before the shed, and the lumberyard, went up in flames. Just before he retreated, he saw fiery shapes flying into the street from the direction of the synagogue door – long dowels on either side of thick, yellow parchment. The Nazis, not content to burn down the synagogue, were making a special, private bonfire of the Torah scrolls from the ark, first stripping off the ceremonial satin covers. *Now they'll have to be buried*, Szara thought. He wondered how he remembered that but it was true, it was the law: a burnt Torah had to be buried in the graveyard, like a dead person, there was a ceremony for it. It was part of growing up in the Pale of Settlement, knowing such lore – rituals for raped women and all sorts of useful knowledge – for these things had happened many times before.

It was another thirty minutes before they got away. After watching the fire for a time, the mob had gone off in search of further amusement. Szara and Baumann stayed where they were, lying flat to conceal themselves, brushing embers off their clothing with the sleeves of their jackets. From where they lay they could see the dancing orange shadows of other fires against the night sky, could hear the showers of falling glass, occasional shouts or cries, but no sirens. The lumberyard caught first – that was bad because of the burning creosote – and then the shed, an afterthought. Szara and Baumann worked their way backwards off the roof, dropping to the ground on the side away from the street. They circled behind the synagogue, now collapsed into itself around a column of fire that roared like a wind, and made a dash for the Humboldt.

They saw only one person, standing alone in the darkness: a town policeman, wearing the traditional high helmet with polished brasswork and short visor – something like the old-fashioned spiked *Pickelhaube* of the 1914 war – with a strap pulled up ferociously tight just under the chin. By the light of the flames Szara saw his face and was struck by a kind of anguish in it. Not sorrow for Jews or synagogues – it wasn't that. It had more to do with a life dedicated to perfect order, where no crime should ever go unpunished – a murder or a piece of paper tossed in the street, it was all the same to this face. Yet tonight the policeman had certainly seen arson – and perhaps murder, if he'd looked in the direction of the river – and had done nothing about it because he had been told to do nothing about it. Evidently, he had not really known what to do, so had stationed himself across the street from the fire, on the night when the firemen never came, and there he stood, rigid, anguished, in some sense ruined and aware of it.

The car was empty, the passenger door ajar as it had been left.

It would make, Szara thought, at least a hiding place, and he directed Baumann to lie flat on the floor below the back seat while he would do the same in front. As they entered the car, the operative materialized, gliding towards them from some shadow he'd used as cover while the mob roamed the streets. Not a mob, in fact, the operative told Szara later. Party men, some uniformed SS, an organized attack directed by the German state.

It was not the burning and the chaos that upset the operative, he was reasonably used to burning and chaos; it was Dr Julius Baumann,

OTTER, an agent he was not supposed to know about, much less see, least of all to have in a car along with his case officer. This shattered unbreakable rules of every variety and set the man's face dancing with bureaucratic horror. He did the best he could under the circumstances: secreted Baumann in the boot, first prying back a section of the metal jamb to make an air passage. Szara quietly protested as he slid into the front seat. 'Be glad I'm doing that much,' said the operative.

'He may have had a heart attack,' Szara said.

The operative shrugged. 'He will be cared for.'

They drove a little way back towards Berlin, crossed the Havel on a narrow, deserted bridge, then turned north, swinging around Wittenau and moving east, through the back of the Berlin suburbs. It was artful navigation, evidently from memory, a slow but steady progress through the winding lanes of Hermsdorf, Lubans, Blankenfelde and Nieder-schonhausen, where villas and workshops faded into farmland or forest. It was almost four in the morning when they reached Pankow. And here the operative took a complicated route that brought them to the *Bahnhof.* He disappeared into the station for a few minutes and used the public telephone in the waiting room. Then east again, Weissensee and eventually Lichtenburg, where they drove through a very aristocratic part of town, swerving suddenly into the parklike courtyard of a private hospital, the gate closing automatically behind them. The operative opened the boot and helped Baumann into the hospital. He would receive medical attention, the operative explained to Szara, but they'd decided to hide him there whether he needed it or not.

Heinrich Müller's teleprinter message had ordered, along with attacks on synagogues and Jewish businesses throughout Germany, the arrest of twenty to thirty thousand Jews: 'Wealthy Jews in particular are to be selected.' This meant money, which the Nazis especially liked. So, said the operative as they pulled away from the hospital, they needed to put OTTER somewhere he wouldn't be found, else he would be taken to Buchenwald or Dachau, stripped of all assets, and eventually deported.

As they turned back towards Berlin, they drove through streets that sparkled with shattered glass – Szara later learned that fifty per cent of the annual plate glass production of Belgium, the manufacturing centre for German glass, had been smashed. At times the traffic police, after checking their Russian identity papers, would steer them politely around the damage. And here and there they saw things: Jewish men and boys crawling around in the street or capering in the town pond, cheered on by hooting SS troopers and local Nazis. Szara knew them well enough; schoolyard bullies, beerhall fat boys, unpleasant little men with insulted faces, the same trash you would find in any town in Russia, or indeed anywhere at all.

The operative was no Jew. From his accent Szara guessed he might have origins in Byelorussia, where pogroms had been a way of life for centuries, but the events of 10 November had enraged him. And he swore. His thick hands gripped the wheel in fury and his face was red as a beet and he simply never stopped swearing. Long, foul, vicious Russian curses, the language of a land where the persecutors had always, somehow, remained just beyond the reach of the persecuted, which left you bad words and little else. Eventually, as a grey dawn lightened Berlin and ash drifted gently down on the immaculate streets, they reached the Adlon, where Szara was instructed to use a servants' entrance and a back stairway.

By then the operative had said it all, virtually without repeating himself, having covered Hitler, Himmler, Göring, and Heydrich, Nazis, Germans one and all, their wives and children, their grandparents and forebears back to the Teutonic tribes, their weisswurst and kartoffel, dachshunds and schnauzers, pigs and geese, and the very earth upon which Germany stood: urged to sow its fucking self with salt and burn fallow for eternity.

11 November.

By dusk the weather had turned bitter cold and it was like ice in Benno Ault's studio. There was little heat in the Iron Exchange Building at night; the owners maintained a certain commercial fiction, pretending that their tenants, like normal business people, hurried home after dark to the warmth of home and family. But Szara suspected that the blind piano tuner, the astrologer, in fact many of the resident shadows, both worked and lived in their offices.

Marta Haecht was asleep in the bed fitted into an alcove at one end of the studio, warm beneath a mound of feather quilts that rose and fell with her steady breathing. A dreamless sleep, he suspected. Untroubled. When he'd arrived, just after dusk, the street cleaners were still at it in the Bischofstrasse; he could hear them sweeping up the broken glass and dumping it in metal garbage cans.

A blanket pulled over his shoulders, he sat on the green sofa, smoked cigarettes, and stared out of the tall window. His ankle burned beneath the handkerchief he'd tied over the gash, but that wasn't what kept him awake. It was a coldness that had nothing to do with the building. He'd seen it that morning, in his room at the Adlon, when he'd looked in the mirror. His face seemed white and featureless, almost dead, the expression of a man who no longer concerns himself with what the world might see when it looked at him. Marta's breathing changed, the quilt stirred, then everything was again peaceful. *A healthy animal*, he thought. She'd been only briefly disturbed by the events of what they called Kristallnacht. Night of glass. A clever name, like the Night of the Long Knives, when Roehm and his Brown Shirts were murdered in 1934. Not just knives – those were for brawling sailors and thieves – but *long* knives. A mythic dimension. 'This is Goebbels's work,' she'd said, shaking her head at the sorry brutality of bad elements. Then she'd closed the door on it, coaxing him to her, twining herself around him, refusing to consider the possibility of the poison reaching either of them.

But it was Tscherova, the actress, who occupied his thoughts. The second secretary, Varin, and the nameless operative. The war they fought. He'd been contacted at the Adlon and told in no uncertain terms to get out of Germany and go back to Paris. His train left in the morning and he would be on it. He looked at his watch. After 2:30. It *was* the morning – in seven hours he'd be gone. He'd not told Marta Haecht, not yet, he didn't know why. He wouldn't be able to explain convincingly, but that was only part of it. He wished to keep her in his mind a certain way, without tears or, worse, dry-eyed and cool. He treasured the memory of her as she'd been – the girl who thought that deep down she was perhaps Italian, Mediterranean, softer and finer than the stiff, northern people she lived among. The girl in the falling snow.

He stood and walked to the window. By the light of the street lamps he could see a boarded-up shop window down Bischofstrasse; yesterday a toy shop, evidently a Jewish toy shop. In a nearby doorway he caught a momentary pinpoint of red. A cigarette. Was this for him? Some poor bastard freezing through a long night of surveillance? An SD operative? Or somebody from Von Polanyi's *Amt* 9, perhaps. Making sure their secret communication line into Dzerzhinsky Square came to no harm so that Moscow continued to believe whatever Berlin wanted it to believe. Or was it a Russian down there – or a German described as *nash* – some operative sent to make sure nothing happened to him on Berlin territory – *let him screw her, he leaves in the morning*.

Or was it just a man smoking a cigarette in a doorway.

'Can't you sleep?' She was propped on one elbow, hair thick and wild. 'Come and keep warm,' she pouted, folding back the quilts as an invitation.

'In a minute,' he said. He didn't want to be warm, to fold himself around her sweetly curved back; he didn't want to make love. He wanted to think. Like the self-absorbed man he knew he was, he wanted to stay cold and think. He remembered a nursemaid in a little park in Ostend. *Come escape with me.* Marta flopped over on one side and grumbled as she pulled up the bedding. Soon her breathing changed to the rhythm of sleep.

He didn't want her to know he was leaving – it was better simply to disappear. He saw a scrap of paper she used for a marker in the book she was reading – Saint-Exupéry, of all things; no, that was right – and retrieved a pen from the pocket of his jacket. *Dearest love,* he wrote, *I had to go away this morning.* Then he signed it *André.* He doubted he'd see her again, not while the war between Moscow and Berlin went on. He'd caught himself earlier in the evening in the midst of a certain kind of speculation: *Her boss, Herr Hanau, owns ships. What cargoes do they carry and where do they go?* No, he told himself; he wasn't going to let it come to that. Hard enough to report the truth about Baumann to Goldman or Abramov and keep her name out of it. Really very difficult, but he would find a way. Whether they loved each other or not they were lovers, and he was damned if he'd see her sucked into this brutal business.

'What are you writing?'

'Something to remember,' he said, and put the scrap of paper back in her book, hiding his hands behind a vase of flowers on the table. 'I thought you'd gone back to sleep,' he added.

'I fooled you,' she said.

11 November.

Strasbourg.

It was well after eleven A.M. – the official minute of the armistice of the 1914 war, the eleventh hour of the eleventh day of the eleventh month – when Szara's train crossed the border but the train's engineer was French, thus not a man to permit clocks to interfere with honour. Many of the passengers on the train got off when notified by the conductors that a three-minute observance would be held on French soil. Szara left with them, stood beneath a rich blue sky in a fresh breeze, held his hand against his heart and meant it. A few kilometres of trees and fields, yet another world: the smell of frying butter, the sound of sputtering car engines, the look in women's eyes; France. Mentally, he was down on his knees at the foot of a wind-whipped Tricolor and kissing the earth. It was as though the passage across the border had severed a tangled knot in his heart and he could breathe again.

By the time he pushed open the shutters in his musty apartment and welcomed himself back to his courtyard – busy, loud, and smelly as always – Germany seemed like a land of apparitions, a dream, a play. It made no logical sense – truly he believed that people were people – but his instinctive sense of the world told a very different story. He leaned on the windowsill, closed his eyes, and let Paris wash over him.

The *apparat* did not leave him to his pleasures for long – an hour later Odile was at his door to tell him he was expected at Stefan Leib's shop in Brussels that same night. Dutifully he took the train up to Belgium. Goldman shook his hand, welcomed him back like a hero, locked the door, and pulled down the shades.

If they'd given him a little room to breathe, things might have turned out differently; he would have shaped and crafted a functional deception and told them the part of the truth they needed to know: they had a compromised agent in Berlin. Not necessarily – Baumann and Von Polanyi could, at the Kaiserhof, have been discussing the price of pears, or Amt 9 might be the section of the Foreign Office that ordered clothes hangers from wire manufacturers.

But as a rule what you got in the intelligence business was a protruding corner, almost never the whole picture. That nearly always had to be inferred. But it was enough of a corner and Szara knew it. Von Polanyi was an intelligence officer; Herr Hanau seemed to have said so, Vainshtok had more or less confirmed it, and that was certainly more than enough to set the dogs running. Other sources would be tapped – you had the corner, somebody else had the top of the frame, a file already held the name of the artist, a local critic would be sent in to steal the dried paint off the palette. Result: full portrait with provenance. *Funkspiele.* Playback.

He had quite a bit, actually. For instance, the Germans were playing Dr Baumann in a very effective way. They didn't have him sneaking around dead-drops at midnight or playing host to journalists who climbed over his garden wall; they took him for an excellent lunch at the best hotel. Really, there was a lot Szara could have told them, more than enough. From there, they could have either declared Baumann innocent or turned the game back around on the Germans.

But he would not give them Marta Haecht, he would not compromise himself, he would not permit them to own him that completely. And if you were going to report pillow talk, because that's exactly what they called it and that's exactly what it was, you had to put a name and address to the head on the pillow.

So Szara lied. A lie of omission – the hard kind to discover. And in a way Goldman abetted the lie. With the death of Sénéschal, one of the Paris networks wasn't all that productive, because there was no realistic way to regain control of Lötte Huber, and she'd been the star of the show. This had the effect of expanding Baumann's importance to the stature of the OPAL network itself, and Goldman as *rezident* was neither more nor less important than the network he ran. There was competition anywhere you cared to look; hundreds of networks spread out all over Europe, Asia, and America, every one of them run by an officer of the GRU or the NKVD who wanted success, promotion, the usual prizes. So Goldman wanted to hear everything – especially everything good for Goldman.

Szara described Baumann truthfully: grey, suddenly old, under frightful tension.

'It could not be otherwise,' Goldman said sympathetically.

'He almost died at the second meeting,' Szara pointed out.

'Do you know that for a fact?'

'No. It was my impression.'

'Ah.'

This information produced from Goldman a reminiscence of Spain. Some poor soul infiltrated into the Falange in 1936, when the Republican side still had a chance to win the war. 'He too was grey,' Goldman mused. 'He too suffered. The pressure of living a double life consumed him – the Bulgarian case officer watched it happen – and he died in Paris a year later.' Of what? Nobody was really sure. But Goldman and others believed it was the strain and constant danger of duplicity that finished him. And Baumann was not *proniknoveniya*, an agent in the heart of the enemy camp, as the man in Spain had been. 'I appreciate the problem, really I do,' Goldman said. 'Just servicing a drop is enough to make some men quake with terror. From one personality to the next, courage is eternally a variable, but it is our job, André Aronovich, to make them heroes, to give them heart.'

Thus Goldman.

An attitude sharply confirmed when Szara offered warm news of Tscherova. 'She is for the cause,' Szara said. 'I know she was coerced, originally – induced and threatened and paid and what you like. Things have changed, however. An émigrée from Russia she may be, but she is no émigrée from human decency. And the Nazis themselves, by being as they are, have made us a gift of her soul.'

'What did she look like, exactly?' Goldman asked.

But Szara wasn't falling for that. 'Tall and thin. Plain – for an actress. I suppose the greasepaint and the stage lighting might make her attractive to an audience, but up close it's another story.'

'Does she play the romantic lead?'

'No. Maids.'

'Aside from the work, do you suppose she's promiscuous?'

'I don't believe so, she's not really the type. She claims to have had a lover or two in Berlin, but I believe most of that has actually been done by her associates. She is constantly around it, and she is no saint, but neither is she the devil she pretends to be. If I were you, I'd direct Schau-Wehrli to handle her carefully and to make sure nothing happens to her. She's valuable, and certainly worth protection, whatever it takes.'

Goldman nodded appreciatively. He seemed, Szara thought, more and more like Stefan Leib as time went by: hair a little too long, corduroy jacket shapeless and faded, the introverted cartographer, absentminded, surrounded by his tattered old maps. 'And Germany?' he asked.

'In a word?'

'If you like.'

'An abomination.'

Goldman's mask slipped briefly and Szara had a momentary view of the man beneath it. 'We shall settle with them this time, and in a way they will not forget,' he said softly. 'The world will yet thank God for Joseph Stalin.'

With Kristallnacht, a kind of shiver passed through Paris. The French had their own problems: communists and the Comintern, the fascist Croix de Feu, conspiracy and political actions among the various émigré groups, strikes and riots, bank failures and scandals – all against a deafening drumbeat from the Senate and the ministries. Stripped of all the rhetoric, it came out *trouble in Germany and Russia, now what?* They'd not really got over the Great War – there was a political sophism afoot that the French did not die well, that they loved life a little more than they should. But in the 1914 war they had died anyhow, and in great numbers. And for what? Because now, twenty years later, the trouble was back, three hundred miles east of Paris.

Troubles from the east were nothing new. Napoleon's experiment in Russia hadn't gone at all well, and with the defeat at Waterloo in 1815, Russian squadrons, among them the Preobajansky Guard, had occupied Paris. But the French were never quite as defeated as you thought they were; the Russians had, in time, gone home, bearing with them various French maladies of which two proved ultimately to be chronic: unquenchable appetites for champagne and liberty, the latter eventually leading to the Decembrist uprising of 1825 – the first in a series of revolutions ending in 1917.

But the present trouble from the east was German trouble, and the French could think of nothing worse. Burned in 1870 and scorched in 1914, they prayed it would go away. Hitler was such a *cul*, with his little moustache and his little strut; nobody wanted to take him seriously. But

Kristallnacht was serious, broken glass and broken heads, and French-men knew in their stomachs what that meant no matter what the politicians said. They had tried to manoeuvre diplomatically with Stalin, figuring that with an alliance on either side of Hitler they could crush the shitty little weasel between them. But, manoeuvring with Stalin . . . You thought you had it all agreed and then something always just seemed to go wrong.

The days grew shorter and darker but the bistros did not grow brighter – not this year they didn't. The fog swirled along the rue du Cherche-Midi and Szara sometimes went home with the carefree girls from the cafés, but it never made him all that happy. He thought it would, each time – oh, that strawberry blonde hair and those freckles – but only the usual things happened. He missed being in love – definitely he missed that – but winter 1938 didn't seem to be the season for it. So he told himself.

Life ground on.

Baumann reported obediently, milling more swage wire every month as the bombers rolled out of the Reich factories.

Or maybe didn't.

Or maybe did even more than Moscow knew.

The lawyer Valais, HECTOR, picked up a new agent, a mercenary Bavarian corporal called Gettig who assisted one of the German military attachés. Odile's husband ran off with a little Irish girl who worked in a milliner's sewing room. Kranov now wore a thick sweater in the cold upstairs room on the rue Delesseux and stolidly punched away at the W/T key: the eternal Russian peasant in the technological age. To Szara he became a symbol, as the journalist for the first time saw OPAL clearly for what it was: a bureaucratic institution in the business of stealing and transmitting information. It was Kranov who handed Szara the decoded flimsy announcing the accession of Lavrenti Beria to the chairmanship of the NKVD. The official triumph of the Georgian *khvosi* meant little to Szara at the time; it was simply one more manifestation of a bloody darkness that had settled on the world. When Beria cleaned the last of the Old Bolsheviks out of high positions in the intelligence *apparat*, the purge ended.

In the middle of December they came at him again – this time from a different angle, and this time they meant it.

A stiff, creamy envelope addressed to him, by hand, at the *Pravda* bureau, the sort of thing journalists sometimes got. *Le Cercle Rénaissance invites you* . . . A square of clear cellophane slipped from within the card and floated to the floor at his feet. He didn't bite the first time so they tried him again – just before Christmas when nobody in Paris has enough invitations – and this time somebody took a Mont Blanc pen and wrote *Won't you please come?* below the incised lettering.

It meant the barber and it meant the dry cleaner and it meant a white shirt laundered to the consistency of teak – expensive indignities to which he submitted in the vain, vain hope that the invitation was precisely what it said it was. He checked the organization, the Renaissance Club; it did exist, and it was extremely exclusive. One of the excluded, a guest at a gallery opening, shot an eyebrow when he heard the name and said, 'You are very fortunate to be asked there,' with sincere and visible loathing in his expression.

The address was in Neuilly, home to some of the oldest and quietest money in France. The street, once the frantic taxi driver managed to find it, was a single row of elegant three-storey houses protected by wrought-iron palings, discreetly obscured by massed garden foliage – even in December – and bathed in a satin light by Victorian street lamps. The other side of the street was occupied by a private park, to which residents received a key, and beyond that lay the Seine.

A steward collected Szara's dripping umbrella and showed him up three flights of stairs to a small library. A waiter appeared and set down an ivory tray bearing a Cinzano apéritif and a dish of nuts. Abandoned to a great hush broken only by an occasional mysterious creak, Szara wandered along the shelves, sampling here and there. The collection was exclusively concerned with railways, and it was beautifully kept; almost all the books had been rebound. Some were privately printed, many were illustrated, with captioned sepia prints and daguerreotypes:

On the platform at Ebenfurth, Stationmaster Hofmann waits to flag through the Vienna-Budapest mail.

Flatcars loaded with timber cross a high trestle in the mountains of Bosnia.

The 7:03 from Geneva passes beneath the rue Lamartine overpass.

'So pleased you've come,' said a voice from the doorway. He was rather ageless, perhaps in the last years of his fifties, with faded steel-coloured hair brushed very flat against the sides of his head. Tall and politely stooped, he was wearing a formal dinner jacket and a bow tie that had gone slightly askew. He'd evidently walked a short distance through the rain without coat or umbrella and was patting his face with a folded handkerchief. 'I'm Joseph de Montfried,' he said. He articulated the name carefully, sounding the hard *t* and separating the two syllables, the latter lightly emphasized, as though it were a difficult name and often mispronounced. Szara was amused – a cultured Frenchman would as likely have got the Baron de Rothschild's name wrong. This family too had a baron, Szara knew, but he believed that was the father, or the uncle.

'Do you like the collection?' said with sincerity, as though it mattered whether Szara liked it or not.

'It's yours?'

'Part of mine. Most of it's at home, up the street, and I keep some in the country. But the club has been indulgent with me, and I've spared them walls of leatherbound Racine that nobody's ever read.' He laughed self-consciously. 'What've you got there?' Szara turned the book's spine towards him. 'Karl Borns, yes. A perfect madman. Borns, had his funeral cortege on the Zürich local. The local!' He laughed again. 'Please,' he said, indicating that Szara should sit down at one end of a couch. De Montfried took a club chair.

'We'll have supper right here, if you don't mind. Do you?'

'Of course not.'

'Good. Sandwiches and something to drink. I've got to meet my wife for some beastly charity thing at ten – my days of eating two dinners are long over, I'm afraid.'

Szara did mind. Going upstairs, he'd caught a glimpse of a silk-walled dining room and a glittering array of china and crystal. All that money invested at the barber and the dry cleaner and now sandwiches. He tried to smile like a man who gets all the elaborate dinners he cares to have.

'Shall we stay in French?' de Montfried asked. 'I can try to get along in Russian, but I'm afraid I'll say awful things.'

'You speak Russian?'

'Grew up speaking French *en famille* and Russian to the servants. My father and uncle built much of the Russian railway system, then came the revolution and the civil war and most of it was destroyed. Very entrepreneurial place – at one time anyhow. How's it go? "Sugar by Brodsky, Tea by Vysotsky, Revolution by Trotsky." I suppose it's aimed at Jews, but it's reasonably faithful to what happened. Oh well.' He pressed a button on the wall and a waiter appeared almost instantly. De Montfried ordered sandwiches and wine, mentioning only the year, '27. The waiter nodded and closed the door behind him.

They chatted for a time. De Montfried found out quite a bit about him, the way a certain kind of aristocrat seemed able to do without appearing to pry. The trick of it, Szara thought, lay in the sincerity of the voice and the eyes – *I am so very interested in you.* The man seemed to find everything he said fascinating or amusing or cleverly put. Soon enough he found himself trying to make it so.

There was no need for Szara to find out who de Montfried was. He knew the basic outline: a titled Jewish family, with branches in London, Paris, and Switzerland. Enormously wealthy, appropriately charitable, exceptionally private, and virtually without scandal. Old enough so that the money, like game, was well cured. Szara caught himself seeking something Jewish in the man, but there was nothing, in the features or the voice, that he could identify; the only notable characteristics were the narrow head and small ears that aristocrats had come to share with their hunting dogs.

The sandwiches were, Szara had to admit, extremely good. Open-faced, sliced duck or smoked salmon, with little pots of flavoured mayonnaise and cornichons to make them interesting. The wine, according to its white and gold label, was a *prémier cru* Beaune called Château de Montfried – it was easily the best thing Szara had ever tasted.

'We've my father to thank for this,' de Montfried said of the wine, holding it up against the light. 'After we were tossed out of Russia he took an interest in the vineyards, more or less retired down there. For him, there was something rather biblical in it: *work thy vines.* I don't know if it actually says that anywhere, but he seemed to think it did.' De Montfried was hesitantly sorrowful; the world would not, he understood, be much moved by small tragedies in his sort of family.

'It is extraordinary,' Szara said.

De Montfried leaned towards him slightly, signalling a shift in the conversation. 'You are recommended to me, Monsieur Szara, by an acquaintance who is called Bloch.'

'Yes?'

De Montfried paused, but Szara had no further comment. He reached into the inside pocket of his dinner jacket, withdrew an official-looking document with stamps and signatures at the bottom, and handed it to Szara. 'Do you know what this is?'

The paper was in English, Szara started to puzzle through it.

'It's an emigration certificate for British Palestine,' de Montfried said. 'Or Eretz Israel – a name I prefer. It's valuable, it's rare, hard to come by, and it's what I want to talk to you about.' He hesitated, then continued. 'Please be good enough to stop this discussion, now, if you feel I'm exceeding a boundary of any kind. Once we go further, I'm going to have to ask you to be discreet.'

'I understand,' Szara said.

'No hesitation? It would be understandable, certainly, if you felt there were just too many complications in listening to what I have to say.'

Szara waited.

'According to Monsieur Bloch, you were witness to the events in Berlin last month. He seems to feel that you might, on that basis, be willing to provide assistance for a project in which I take a great interest.'

'What project is that?'

'May I pour you a little more wine?'

Szara extended his glass.

'I hope you'll forgive me if I work up to a substantive description in my own way. I don't want to bore you, and I don't want you to think me a hopeless naïf – it's just that I've had experience of conversations about the Jewish return to Palestine and, well, it can be difficult, even unpleasant, as any political discussion is likely to be. Polite people avoid certain topics, experience shows the wisdom in that. Like one's dreams or medical condition – it's just better to find something else to talk about. Unfortunately, the world is now acting in such a way as to eliminate that courtesy, among many others, so I can only ask your forbearance.'

Szara's smile was sad and knowing, with the sort of compassion that has been earned from daily life. He was that listener who can be told anything without fear of criticism because he has heard and seen worse than whatever you might contrive to say. He withdrew a packet of Gitanes, lit one, and exhaled. *I cannot be offended*, said the gesture.

'At the beginning of the Great War, in 1914, Great Britain found itself fighting in the Middle East against Turkey. The Jews in Palestine were caught up in the Turkish war effort – taxed into poverty, drafted into the Turkish armies. A certain group of Jews, in the town of Zichron Yaakov, not far from Haifa, believed that Great Britain ought to win the war in the Middle East, but what could they do? Well, for a small, determined group of people arrayed against a major power there is only one traditional answer, other than prayer, and that is espionage. Thus a botanist named Aaron Aaronson, his sister Sarah, an assistant called Avshalom Feinberg, and several others formed a network they called NILI – it's taken from a phrase in the Book of Samuel, an acronym of the Hebrew initials for *The Eternal One of Israel will not prove false.* The conspiracy was based at the Atlit Experimental Station and was facilitated by Aaron Aaronson's position as chief of the locust control unit – he could show up anywhere, for instance at Turkish military positions, without provoking suspicion. Meanwhile Sarah Aaronson, who was ravishing, became a fixture at parties attended by high-ranking Turkish officers. The British at first were suspicious – the Aaronsons did not ask for money – but eventually, in 1917, NILI product was accepted by British officers stationed on ships anchored off Palestine. There were – it's a typical problem, I understand – communications difficulties, and Avshalom Feinberg set out across the Sinai desert to make contact with the British. He was ambushed by Arab raiders and murdered near Rafah, in the Gaza strip. Local legend has it that he was buried in the sand at the edge of the town and a palm tree grew up from his bones, seeded by dates he carried in his pockets. Then the spy ring was uncovered—too many people knew about it – and Sarah Aaronson was arrested by the Turks and tortured for four days. At that point she tricked her captors into letting her use the washroom, unsupervised, where she had secreted a revolver, and took her own life. All the other members of the network were captured by the Turks, tortured and executed, except for Aaron Aaronson, who survived the war only to die in a plane crash in the English Channel in 1919.

'Of course the Arabs fought on the side of the British as well – they too wished an end to Turkish occupation – and their revolt was led by skilled British military intelligence officers, such as T. E. Lawrence and Richard Meinertzhagen. The Arabs believed they were fighting for independence, but it did not quite turn out that way. When the smoke cleared, when Allenby took Jerusalem, the British ruled Mandate Palestine and the French held Syria and the Lebanon.

'But the NILI network was not the only effort made on Britain's behalf by the Jews. Far more important, in its ultimate effect, was the contribution of Dr Chaim Weizmann. Weizmann is well known as a Zionist, he is an articulate and persuasive man, but he is also known, by people who have an interest in the area, as a biochemist. While teaching and doing research at the University of Manchester, he discovered a method of producing synthetic acetone by a process of natural fermentation. As Great Britain's war against Germany intensified, they discovered themselves running out of acetone, which is the solvent that must be used in the manufacture of cordite, a crucial explosive in artillery shells and bullets. In 1916 Weizmann was summoned before Winston Churchill, at that time first lord of the Admiralty. Churchill said, "Well, Dr Weizmann, we need thirty thousand tons of acetone. Can you make it?" Weizmann did not rest until he'd done it, ultimately taking over many of Britain's large whisky distilleries until production plants could be built.

'Did Weizmann's action produce the Balfour Declaration? It did not hurt, certainly. In 1917 Balfour, as foreign secretary, promised that the British government would "use their best endeavours to facilitate the

establishment in Palestine of a national home for the Jewish people".
The League of Nations and other countries supported that position. It
would be pleasant to think Weizmann had a hand in that, but the
British are a wonderfully practical people, and what they wanted at that
moment was America's entry into the war against the Germans, and it
was felt that Lord Balfour's declaration would mobilize American
Jewish opinion in that direction. But Weizmann played his part.'

De Montfried paused, refilled Szara's glass, then his own. 'By now,
Monsieur Szara, you likely see where this is headed.'

'Yes and no,' Szara said. 'And the story isn't over.'

'That's true, it continues. But this much can be said: the survival of
Jewish Palestine depends on the attitude of the British, and from that
perspective, the Chamberlain government has been a disaster.'

'The Czechs would certainly agree.'

'No doubt. When Chamberlain, after giving in to Hitler in September, asked why Great Britain should risk war for the sake of what
he called "a far-away country of which we know very little and whose
language we don't understand", people who share my views were
horrified. If he perceived the Czechs in that way, what does he think
about the Jews?'

'You see Munich as a moral failure, then.'

De Montfried teetered on the edge of indignation, then asked quietly,
'Don't you?'

He wasn't precisely angry, Szara thought. Simply, momentarily,
balked. And he wasn't used to that. His life was ordered to keep him
clear of uncertainties of any kind, and Szara had, rather experimentally,
said something unexpected. To de Montfried it was like being served
cold coffee for breakfast – it wasn't wrong, it was unthinkable.

'Yes, I do,' Szara said at last. 'But one ought to wonder out loud what
Chamberlain was hearing from the other end of the conference table –
from the generals, and the discreet gentlemen in dark suits. But then,
after they made their case, he had the choice to believe them or not. And
then to act. I can theorize that what he heard concerned what might
happen to England's cities, particularly London, if they started a war
with Germany – bombers and bomb tonnage and what happened in
Guernica when it was bombed. People get hurt in war.'

'People get hurt in peace,' de Montfried said. 'In Palestine, since 1920,
Arab mobs have murdered hundreds of Jewish settlers, and the British
Mandate police haven't always shown much interest in stopping them.'

'Great Britain runs on oil, which the Arabs have and it doesn't.'

'That's true, Monsieur Szara, but it's not the whole story. Like
Lawrence, many officials in the British Foreign Service idealize the

Arabs – the fierce and terrible purity of the desert and all that sort of thing. Whereas with the Jews, well, all you get is a bunch of Jews.'

Szara laughed appreciatively and de Montfried softened. 'For a moment,' he said, 'I was afraid we were very far apart in the way we see these things.'

'No. I don't think so. But your Château de Montfried gives one an elevated view of existence, so I'm afraid you're going to have to be very direct with me.'

Szara waited to see what that might produce. De Montfried thought for a time, then said, 'The Arabs have made it clear they don't want Jewish settlement in the Middle East. Some are more hostile than others – several of the diplomats, in person, are more than decent in their understanding of our difficulties and not insensible to what we have to offer. The German migration brought to Palestine a storehouse of technical information: medicine, engineering, horticulture; and they are people for whom the sharing of knowledge is instinctive, second nature. But Rashid Ali in Iraq is a creature of the Nazis and so is the mufti of Jerusalem. They've chosen the German side; other Arabs may join them if they don't get what they want. England is in a difficult position: how to retain the good will of the Arab nations without alienating America and other liberal countries. So they've adopted, on the subject of the Jewish question, a regime of conferences and more conferences. Instead of actually doing something, they have taken refuge in deciding what to do. I'll grant it's a legitimate diplomatic manoeuvre, one way to simply avoid trouble: thus the Peel Report and the Woodhead Commission and the Évian Conference, and next we're to have, in February, the St James's Conference, after which a White Paper will be issued. Meanwhile, Kristallnacht . . .'

'That was not a conference,' Szara said.

'Hitler spoke to the world: Jews may not live in Germany any longer, this is what we intend to do to them. A hundred dead, thousands beaten, tens of thousands locked up in the Dachau and Buchenwald camps. The German and Austrian Jews certainly understood; they're fighting to get out any way they can. But the problem is, they can't just get out, they have to go somewhere, and there is nowhere for them to go. I happen to have a rather accurate forecast of the White Paper that's going to be written after the St James's Conference. You, ah, journalists will understand how one comes upon such things.'

'One is never entirely without friends. One had better not be, at any rate.'

'Just so. We hear that emigration to Mandate Palestine is going to be limited to fifteen thousand Jews a year for five years, then it stops dead.

At the moment, there are still three hundred thousand Jews in Germany, another sixty-five thousand remain in Austria, and only fifteen thousand of them can get into Palestine. And, if this thing were somehow to spread to Poland – and the way Hitler talks about Poland is the way he used to talk about the Sudetenland – then what? That's three million three hundred thousand more.'

'What is being done?'

De Montfried leaned back in his chair and stared. His eyes were dark, difficult to read, but Szara sensed a conflict between mistrust – the natural, healthy sort – and the need to confide.

'Beginnings,' he said finally. 'From all points on the political compass, the established groups have been fighting this battle for years – the labour people in the Histadrut, Vladimir Jabotinsky's New Zionists and the organization they call Betar. David Ben-Gurion and the Jewish Agency. And others, many others, are doing what they can. It is a political effort – letters written, favours called in, donations given, resolutions passed. It all creates a kind of presence. Also, in Palestine there is the Haganah, a fighting force, and its information bureau, known as Sherut Yediot, generally called Shai, its first initial. But it is all they can do to keep the Jews of *Palestine* alive.

'Then, just lately, there is something more. As you know, emigration to Palestine is called by the name Aliyah. The word has the sense of *return*. The British entry certificates permit a few thousand people a year into the country, and there is a Jewish organization to administer the details – travel, reception, and so on. But there exists within that group, in its shadow, another. There are only ten of them at the moment, nine men and a very young woman, who call themselves the Mossad Aliyah Bet, that is, the Institute for Aliyah B – the letter indicates illegal, as opposed to legal, emigration. This group is now in the process of leasing ships – whatever derelict hulk can be found in the ports of southern Europe – and they intend to bring Jews out of danger and effect clandestine landings on the coast of Palestine.'

'Will they succeed?'

'They will try. And I am in sympathy with them. A moment comes and if you wish to look upon yourself as human you must take some kind of action. Otherwise, you can read the newspapers and congratulate yourself on your good fortune. Weizmann, however, makes an interesting point. After Kristallnacht he said to Anthony Eden that the fire in the German synagogues may easily spread to Westminster Abbey. So the self-congratulatory souls may one day have their own moment of reckoning, we shall see.'

'And you. Monsieur de Montfried, what is it that you do?'

'I invite you to the Renaissance Club of Neuilly, among other things. I somehow happen to meet Monsieur Bloch. I have a few friends, here and there; we try to spend money wisely, in the right places. When I can, I tell important people those things I believe they ought to know.'

'A group of friends. It has, perhaps, a name?'

'No.'

'Truly?'

'The less official the better, is what we think. One can be without structure of any kind and still be of enormous help.'

'What kind of help, Monsieur de Montfried?'

'There are two areas in which we have a very special interest. The first is simple: legitimate emigration certificates above and beyond the publicly stated number allowed by the British foreign office. Each one represents several lives saved, because they can be used by families. The second area is not simple, but can be of far greater impact. Shall we call it a demonstration? As good a word as any. A demonstration that groups sympathetic to Jewish settlement in Palestine are a source of assistance that the British cannot ignore. It's a way of buying influence – as NILI did, as Weizmann did, by serving the interests of the governing nation. It's what, finally, the British understand. Quid pro quo. The White Paper will be debated in Parliament, where there are those who want to help us; we'd like to make it easier for them. The only way to accomplish that is with concrete acts, something definite they can point to. Not in public. Nothing happens in public. But in the halls, in the cloakrooms, the gentlemen's clubs, the country houses – that's where the serious business is done. That's where we must be represented.'

'Can the emigration certificates be produced privately?'

'Forged, you mean.'

'Yes.'

'Of course it's tried, and if one can be proud of forgers, Jewish forgers are among the best, though they have been known to go off on their own and produce the occasional Rembrandt.

'Unfortunately, the British have a tendency to count. And their colonial bureaucracy is efficient. The weakness in the system is that the civil servants in their passport offices are underpaid, a situation that leads only one place. Bribes have been offered, and accepted. Also discovered. The same situation is present in many embassies: Argentine, Liberian, Guatemalan – Jews are turning up as citizens of virtually everywhere. There are also instances where passport officers just give in to compassion when confronted with the unbearable condition of certain applicants – the horrors of this thing simply multiply the more you look at it. But forgery and bribery and whatever else occurs to you do not begin to create the numbers we need. What we have in mind is quite different, a private arrangement that produces real certificates.'

'Difficult. And sensitive.'

De Montfried smiled. 'Monsieur Bloch has great faith in you.'

'Theoretically, in what way would a Soviet journalist involve himself in such matters?'

'Who can say? It's been my experience of life that one does not try to control influential people. One can only present one's case and hope for the best. If on reflection you find yourself in agreement with what has been said here this evening, you'll find a way, I suspect, to bring your abilities to bear on the situation. I myself don't know the solution, so I seek people out and pose the problem. But if I could believe that you would go home tonight and think about these matters I would be frankly overjoyed.'

Gently, and by mutual agreement, the conversation was allowed to drift off into pleasantries and, just in time for de Montfried to attend his 'beastly charity thing,' they parted. Outside the little library, a club member with a bright red face and white hair greeted de Montfried effusively, pretending to pull an engineer's whistle cord and making the French sound for *toot, toot*. De Montfried laughed heartily, the most amiable fellow imaginable. 'We've known each other forever,' he said to Szara. They shook hands in the downstairs hall and the steward returned Szara's umbrella, which had apparently been dried with a cloth.

January 1939.

08942 57661 44898

And so on, which turned out to mean *S novym godom* and *S novym schastyem* – happy new year and the best to you all – cold and formal wishes from the Great Father Stalin. During his week in Berlin, Szara had found himself in the neighbourhood of the storage building that held the painting with the DUBOK dossier secreted behind the canvas. It had seemed to him remote, and very much beside the point. *This is a lesson about time*, he thought. With the surge of German power into Austria and Czechoslovakia, Russia assumed the role of counterweight, and if Stalin had been vulnerable when he decimated the military and intelligence services, he wasn't now. Hitler was driving the world to his door. Stalin's murders were achieved in basements; Hitler's work was photographed for the newspapers. Russia was weak, full of starving peasants. Germany built superb locomotives. The Okhrana dossier had best remain where it was.

*

In early January, Szara suddenly ran a terrible fever. He lay amid soaked sheets; saw, when he closed his eyes, the splashing in the moonlit river Havel and heard, again and again, the scream for mercy. It was not delirium, it was a sickened memory that refused to heal. He saw Marta Haecht dancing in the yard of a thatched-roof cottage in some Ukrainian ghetto village. He saw the eyes of people who had stared at him in Berlin, a long tile hall, the broken face of a Wittenau policeman, the room in the narrow house. It had no name, this sickness; that was its secret, he thought; it fed deep, where words and ideas didn't reach.

He tried the writer's time-honoured cure: writing. Unshaven, in wrinkled pyjamas, he spent a few mornings at it, producing journalistic short stories in pursuit of the German character. Brutal, nasty stuff. He attacked hypocrisy, cruelty, fulminous envy, an obsessive sense of having been wronged, grievously, and misunderstood, eternally. Rereading, he was both horrified and pleased, recalled Lenin's wondrously sly dictum that 'paper will stand for anything you write on it', and thought for a moment he might actually seek publication. But it was not, he came to realize, the blow he needed to strike. All it would do was make them angry. And they already were that, most of the time. It was not something he'd accused them of, yet in some ways he saw it as their dominant characteristic – he had no idea why, not really. One morning, as a fall of thick, wet snowflakes silenced the city, he tore the stories up.

Schau-Wehrli was his January angel, crisscrossed the icy streets of Paris and made his *treffs* with Valais, paid the concierge to bring him bowls of thick, amber soup, and sat on the edge of his bed when she had a spare moment. He came to understand, eventually; that the possibility of feverish babbling made them nervous – they didn't want him in the hospital. Nobody quite said anything about it, but a doctor from the medical faculty at the Sorbonne, a sympathizer, suddenly made house calls to a man with a bad fever. A professor with a grand beard, peering down at him from the heights of professional achievement to say 'Rest and keep warm and drink plenty of hot tea.'

When Schau-Wehrli stopped by they'd gossip – like himself, she really had no one to talk to. After the meeting in the Berlin theatre, she told him, Tscherova had apparently redoubled her efforts, joining the rather lively circles of young, Nazi party intellectuals and thus manoeuvring her sub-agents into extremely productive relationships. 'What did you do to her?' Schau-Wehrli would ask, teasing him as a great lover. He would smile weakly. 'Really nothing. She is just so . . . so Russian,' he would say. 'A little sympathy, a kind word, and a flower suddenly blooms.'

*

The fever broke after ten days and slowly Szara began to work again. In the last week of January, Abramov ordered a third-country meeting to pursue certain details regarding a reorganization of the OPAL network. This time it was to be in Switzerland, near the town of Sion, a couple of hours up the Rhone valley from Geneva, on the night of 7 February. The transmission took its time coming in and Kranov was annoyed. 'They've changed W/T operators again,' he said, lighting a cigarette and sitting back in his chair. 'Slow as mud, this new one.'

Goldman wired the following day, ordering – as he had when Szara had gone to Berlin – a piggyback courier delivery. Sixty thousand French francs were to be taken to Lausanne on the day after his meeting with Abramov and passed, using a complicated identification/parol procedure, to an unnamed individual. This was a lot of money, and it caused a problem. Couriers were limited to a certain level of funds; after that Moscow, evidently in fear of temptation, dictated the presence of a second courier, specifically a diplomatic or intelligence officer and not just a network agent like Odile.

So Maltsaev told him, anyhow.

Szara was eating dinner at his neighbourhood bistro, *Le Temps* folded in half and propped up against the mustard pot, when a man materialized across the table and introduced himself. 'Get in touch with Ilya Goldman,' he said by way of establishing his bona fides. 'He'll confirm who I am – we were in Madrid together. At the embassy.' He was now in Paris, he continued, on temporary assignment from Belgrade, where he'd been political officer for a year or so.

Szara immediately disliked him. Maltsaev was a dark, balding young man with a bad skin and a sour disposition, a man much given to sinister affectations, a man who spoke always as though he were saying only a small fraction of what he actually knew. He wore tinted eyeglasses and a voluminous black overcoat of excellent quality.

Maltsaev made it clear that he found courier work boring and very much beneath him – the order to accompany Szara to Switzerland offended him in any number of ways. 'These little czars in Moscow,' he said with a sneer, 'throw roubles around as though the world were ending tomorrow.' He had a pretty good idea what went on in Lausanne, he confided, typical of the deskbound comrades to try and solve the problem with money. Typical also that some unseen controller in the Dzerzhinsky Square *apparat* was using the occasion to make Maltsaev's life miserable, screwing him with some witless assignment that could be handled by any numskull operative. 'Another enemy,' he grumbled. Somebody jealous of his promotions or his assignment in

Paris. 'But next we'll see if he gets away with it. Maybe not, eh?' He pointed at Szara's plate. 'What's that?'

'Andouillette,' Szara said.

'What is it? A sausage? What's in it?'

'You won't want it if I tell you,' Szara said.

'Probably the chef's mistress,' Maltsaev said with a laugh. 'Order me a steak. Cooked. No blood or back it goes.' His eyes were animated behind the tinted lenses, flicking around the room, staring at the other customers. Then he leaned confidentially towards Szara. 'Who is this Abramov you're going to see?' He looked triumphant and pleased with himself – *surprised I know that?*

'Boss. One of them, anyhow.'

'A big shot?'

'He sits on one Directorate, certainly. Perhaps others, I don't know.'

'Old friend, I'll bet. The way things go these days, you don't last long without a protector, right?'

Szara shrugged. 'Everybody's got their own story – mine's not like that. It's all business with Abramov.'

'Is it.'

'Yes.'

'Hey!' Maltsaev called as a waiter went past and ignored him.

It snowed on the night of the sixth, and by the time Szara and Maltsaev left the Gare de Lyon on the seventh of February the fields and villages of France were still and white. *The nineteenth century*, Szara thought with longing: a pair of frost-coated dray horses pulling a cart along a road, a girl in a stocking cap skating on a pond near Melun. The sky was dense and swollen; sometimes a flight of crows circled over the snow-covered fields. But for the presence of Maltsaev, it would have been a time for dreaming. The frozen world outside the train window was unmoving, cold and peaceful, smoke from farmhouse chimneys the only sign of human life.

Following the rules, they had booked the compartment for themselves, so they were alone. Szara kept a hand or a foot in permanent contact with the small travelling case that held the sixty thousand francs, each packet of hundred-franc notes bound by a strip of paper with Cyrillic initials on it. But even though they were alone, Maltsaev spoke obliquely: *your friend in Sion, the man in Brussels.* A glutton's appetite for gossip, Szara thought. Who do you know? How do the loyalties work? What's the real story? Maltsaev was the classic opportunist, probing for whatever you might have that he could use. Szara parried him on every point, but felt that eventually the sheer weight of the attack might wear him down. To escape, he feigned drowsiness. Maltsaev sneered with delight: 'Going to dreamland with our dear gold on your lap?'

They'd left at dawn, and it was again dark when they reached Geneva. They walked three blocks from the railway station and found the Opel Olympia that had been left in front of a commercial travellers' hotel, the ignition key taped to the base of the steering wheel column. Szara drove. Maltsaev sat beside him, smoking his cardboard-tipped Belomor cigarettes, a road map spread across his lap. They circled the north shore of Lake Leman on good roads in intermittent light snow, then, after Villeneuve, began to climb over the mountain passes.

Here the weather cleared and there was a bright, sharp moon, its light sparkling on the ice crystal in the banked snow at the sides of the road. Sometimes, on the curves, they could see down into the valleys spread out below: clusters of stone villages, ice rivers, empty roads. The sense of deep silence and distance at last reached Maltsaev, who ceased talking and stared out of the window. By ten o'clock they had descended to Martigny and turned north on the narrow plain by the Rhone, here an overgrown mountain stream. There was hardpack snow on the roads and Szara drove carefully but steadily, encountering only one or two cars along the way.

Sion was dark, no lights anywhere, and they had to hunt for a time until they found the gravel road that went up the mountainside. Five minutes later the grade flattened out and they rolled to a stop in front of an old hotel, tyres crunching on newly fallen snow. The hotel – a carved sign above the arched doorway said Hôtel du Vaz – was timber and stucco capped by a steep slate roof hung with icicles. It stood high above the road, at the edge of a shimmering white meadow that sloped gently towards the edge of an evergreen forest. The ground-floor shutters were closed; behind them was a faint glow, perhaps a single lamp in what Szara presumed to be a reception area in the lobby. When he turned off the ignition and climbed out of the Opel, he could hear the sound of the wind at the corner of the building. There were no other cars to be seen; perhaps it was a summer hotel, he thought, where people came in order to walk in the mountains.

Maltsaev got out of the car and closed the door carefully. From an upper window, Szara heard Abramov's voice. 'André Aronovich?'

'Yes,' Szara called. 'Come down and let us in. It's freezing.'

'Who is with you?'

Looking up, Szara saw one shutter partly opened. Before he could respond, Maltsaev whispered, 'Don't say my name.'

Szara stared at him, not understanding. 'Answer him,' Maltsaev said urgently, gripping him hard at the elbow. Abramov must have seen the gesture, Szara thought. Because a moment later they heard the sound, eerily loud in the still, cold air, of a heavy man descending an exterior staircase, perhaps at the back of the hotel. A man in a hurry.

Maltsaev, coat flapping, started to run, and Szara, not knowing what else to do, followed. They were immediately slowed when they moved around the side of the hotel because here the snow was deeper, up to their knees, which made running almost impossible. Maltsaev swore as he stumbled forward. They heard a shout from the trees and to their left. Then it was repeated, urgently. A threat, Szara realized, spoken in Russian.

They came around the corner at the back of the hotel and stopped. Abramov, in a dark suit and homburg hat, was trying to run across the snow-covered meadow. It was absurd, almost comic. He struggled and floundered and slipped, went down on one hand, rose, lifted his knees high for a few steps, fell again, then lurched forward as he tried to reach the edge of the forest, leaving behind him a broken, white path. The homburg suddenly tilted to one side and Abramov grabbed it frantic-ally, instinctively, and held the brim tightly as he ran, as though, late for work, he were running to catch a tram in a city street.

The marksmen in the forest almost let him reach the trees. The first shot staggered him but he kept on a little, only slower, then the second shot brought him down. The reports echoed off the side of the mountain, then faded into silence. Maltsaev walked into the meadow, Szara followed, moving along the broken path. It was slippery and difficult, and soon they were breathing hard. Just before they reached him, Abramov managed to turn on his side. His hat had rolled away and there was snow caught in his beard. Maltsaev stood silently and tried to catch his breath. Szara knelt down. He could see that Abramov had bled into the snow. His eyes were closed, then they flickered open for a moment, perhaps he saw Szara. He made a single sound, a guttural sigh, 'Ach,' of exhaustion and irritation, of dismissal, and then he was gone.

The Renaissance
Club

At the Brasserie Heininger, at the far corner table where you could see everyone and everyone could see you, seated below the scrupulously preserved bullet hole in the vast and golden mirror, André Szara worked hard at being charming and tried to quiet a certain interior voice that told him to shut up and go home.

A newcomer to the crowd of regulars at the corner table, and so the centre of attention, he proposed a toast: 'I would like us to drink to the love . . . to the hopeless loves . . . of our childhood days.' Was there a split second of hesitation – my God, is he going to weep? – before the chorus of approval? But then he didn't weep; his fingers combed a longish strand of black hair off his forehead and he smiled a vulnerable smile. Then everyone realized how very right the toast was, how very right *he* was, the emotional Russian long after midnight, in his grey tie and soft maroon shirt, not exactly drunk, just intimate and daring.

That he was. Beneath the tablecloth, his hand rested warmly on the thigh of Lady Angela Hope, a pillar of the Paris night and a woman he'd been specifically told to avoid. With his other hand, he drank Roederer Cristal from a gold-rimmed champagne flute which, thanks to the attentions of a clairvoyant waiter, turned out to be perfectly full every time he went to pick it up. He smiled, he laughed, he said amusing things, and everyone thought he was wonderful, everyone: Voyschin-kowsky, 'the Lion of the Bourse'; Ginger Pudakis, the English wife of the Chicago meat-packing king; the Polish Countess K—, who, when properly intrigued, made ingenious gardens for her friends; the terrible Roddy Fitzware, *mad, bad, and dangerous to know*. In fact the whole pack of them, ten at last count, hung on his every word. Was his manner perhaps just a shade more Slavic than it really needed to be? Perhaps. But he did not care. He smoked and drank like an affable demon, said, 'For a drunkard the sea is only knee deep!' and other proverbial Russianisms as they came to him, and generally made a grand and endearing fool of himself.

Yet – he was more Slavic than they knew – the interior voice refused to be still. *Stop*, it said. *This is not in your best interest; you will suffer, you will regret it, they will catch you.* He ignored it. Not that it was wrong, in fact he knew it was right, but still he ignored it.

Voyschinkowsky, inspired by the toast, was telling a story: 'It was my father who took me to the Gypsy camp. Imagine, to go out so late at night, and to such a place! I could not have been more than twelve years old, but when she began to dance . . .' Lady Angela's leg pressed closer under the table, a hand appeared through the smoky air, and a stream of pale Cristal fizzed into his glass. What other wine, someone had said of champagne, can you hear?

Like Lady Angela Hope, the Brasserie Heininger was notorious. In the spring of '37 it had been the site of, as the Parisians put it, '*une affaire bizarre*': the main dining room had been sprayed with tommy guns, the Bulgarian maître d' had been assassinated in the ladies' WC, and a mysterious waiter called Nick had disappeared soon after. Such violently Balkan goings-on had made the place madly popular; the most desirable table directly beneath the golden mirror with a single bullet hole; in fact the only mirror that survived the incident. Otherwise, it was just one more brasserie, where moustached waiters hurried among the red plush banquettes with platters of crayfish and grilled sausage, a taste of *fin-de-siècle* devilry while outside the February snow drifted down into the streets of Paris and cabmen tried to keep warm.

As for Lady Angela Hope, she was notorious among two very different sets: the late-night crowd of aristocrats and parvenus, of every nationality and none at all, that haunted certain brasseries and night-clubs, as well as another, more obscure perhaps, which followed her career with equal, or possibly keener, interest. Her name had been raised in one of Goldman's earliest briefings, taken from a file folder kept in a safe in the Stefan Leib shop in Brussels. Both Szara's predecessor and Annique Schau-Wehrli had been 'probed' by Lady Angela, who was 'known to have informal connections with British intelligence stations in Paris.' She was, as promised, fortyish, sexy, rich, foul-mouthed, promiscuous, and, in general, thoroughly accessible; an indefatigable guest and hostess who knew 'everybody'. 'You will meet her certainly,' said Goldman primly, 'but she has entirely the wrong friends. Stay away.'

But then, Goldman.

*

Szara smiled to himself. Too bad Goldman couldn't see him now, the forbidden Lady Angela snugly by his side. Well, he thought, this is fate. This had to happen, and so now it is happening. Yes, there may have been some kind of alternative, but the one person in his life who really understood alternatives, knew where they hid and how to find them, was gone.

That was Abramov, of course. And on 7 February, in a meadow behind the Hôtel du Vaz in Sion, Abramov had resigned from the service. Exactly how that came to happen Szara didn't know, but he'd managed to unwind events to a point where he had a pretty good idea of what had gone on.

Abramov, he suspected, had attempted to influence Dershani by use of the photographs taken in the garden of the house at Puteaux. It hadn't worked. Realizing his days were numbered, he'd at last taken Szara's advice offered on the beach at Aarhus and planned one final operation: his own disappearance. He'd arranged the meeting at the Hôtel du Vaz in Sion (owned, Szara was told that night, by a front corporation operated by the NKVD Foreign Department), which gave him a legitimate reason to leave Moscow. He'd then created a notional agent in Lausanne who needed sixty thousand *French* francs. This made Goldman in Brussels a logical source and Szara's scheduled trip to Sion a convenient method of delivery. The money was meant to give Abramov a running start in a new life; the operation was dovetailed and simple, but it hadn't worked.

Why? Szara could see two possibilities: Kranov, already thought to spy on the OPAL network for the Directorate, might have alerted security units when an untrained and uncertain hand operated the wireless key in Moscow. Every operator had a characteristic signature, and Kranov, trained to be sensitive to change of any kind, had probably reacted to Abramov's rather awkward keying of his own message.

To Szara, however, Goldman was the more interesting possibility. Network gossip suggested the *rezident* had previously had a hand in a special operation, something well outside the usual scope of OPAL's activities, in which a young woman was kidnapped from a rooming house in Paris. And when Szara described to Schau-Wehrli the operatives he'd met later that night at the Hôtel du Vaz – especially the one who used the work name Dodin, a huge man, short and thick, with the red hands and face of a butcher – she had reacted. In the next instant she was all unknowing, but he'd felt a shadow touch her, he was sure of it.

Through Kranov or Goldman – or both – the special section of the Foreign Department had become involved, dispatched Maltsaev to Paris to keep watch on Szara as he went to meet Abramov and to find out if he was an accomplice, or even a fellow fugitive. Szara realized that his instinctive distaste for Maltsaev's personality had provoked him into a blank and businesslike response to the man's offensive needling, and that in turn had quite probably saved his life.

They'd buried Abramov at the edge of the meadow, under the snow-laden boughs of a fir tree, chipping at the frozen ground with shovels and sweating in the cold moonlight. There were four of them besides Maltsaev; they took off their overcoats and worked in baggy, woollen suits, swearing as they dug, their Swiss hunting rifles propped against a tree. They spread snow over the dirt and returned to the empty hotel, building a fire in the fireplace downstairs, sitting in handmade pine chairs and smoking Maltsaev's Belomors, talking among themselves. Szara was part of every activity, taking his turn with the shovel, struggling with Abramov's weight as they put him in the ground. He had no choice; he became a temporary member of the unit. They talked about what they could buy in Geneva before they went back to Kiev, they talked about other operations; something in Lithuania, something in Sweden, though they were oblique with a stranger in their midst. The only ceremony for Abramov was Szara's silent prayer, and he made very sure his lips did not move as he said it. Yet, even at that moment, in the dark meadow, he planned further memorials.

Early in the morning, standing on the platform of the railway station in Geneva and waiting for the Paris train, Maltsaev was blunt: 'The usual way in these affairs is to send the accomplice along on the same journey, innocent or not doesn't matter. But, for the moment, some-body considers you worth keeping alive. Personally I don't agree – you are a traitor in your heart – but I just do what they tell me. That's a good lesson for you, Szara, come to think of it. Being smart maybe isn't so smart as you think – you see where it got Abramov. I blame it on the parents, they should have made him study the violin like all the rest of them.' The train pulled in. Maltsaev, after a contemptuous bow and a sweep of the hand towards the compartment door, turned and walked away.

Staring at Voyschinkowsky across the table, pretending to listen as the man told a story about his childhood, Szara for the first time under-stood the chain of events that had led to the night of 7 February. It had started with Lötte Huber's romance with Sénéschal and from there moved, seemingly driven by fate, to its conclusion. *Inevitable*, he thought. The champagne was cunning; the opposite of vodka in that it didn't numb, it revealed. One could say, he realized, that a Nazi official's appetite for red berry sauce had two years later led to the death of a Russian intelligence officer in a Swiss meadow. He shook his head to make such thoughts go away. *Remember*, he told himself silently, *this must be done with a cold heart.*

Voyschinkowsky paused to take a long sip of champagne. 'The Lion of the Bourse' was in his early sixties, with a long, mournful face marked by the chronically red-rimmed eyes and dark pouches of the lifelong insomniac. He was reputed to be one of the richest men in Paris. 'I wonder whatever became of her?' he said. He had a thick Hungarian accent and a heavy, hoarse voice that seemed to come from the bottom of a well.

'But Bibi,' Ginger Pudakis said, 'did you make love?'

'I was twelve years old, my dear.'

'Then what?'

One side of Voyschinkowsky's mouth twisted briefly into a tart grin. 'I looked at her breasts.'

'Finis?'

'Let me tell you, from one who has lived a, a rich and varied cosmopolitan life, there was never again a moment like it.'

'Oh Bibi,' she breathed. 'Too sad!'

Lady Angela whispered in Szara's ear, 'Say something clever, can you?'

'Not sad. Bittersweet,' he said. 'Not at all the same thing. I think it is a perfect story.'

'Hear, hear,' said Roddy Fitzware.

They went on to a nightclub to watch Apache dancing. A young dancer, her skirt bunched up around her waist, slid across the polished floor into the audience and accidentally drove a spike heel into Szara's ankle. He winced, saw a momentary horror on her face amid the black and violet makeup, then her partner, in the traditional sailor's shirt, whisked her away. *Now I am wounded in the line of duty*, he thought, *and should receive a medal, but there is no nation to award it.* He was very drunk and laughed out loud at the thought.

'Were you stabbed?' Lady Angela asked quietly, evidently amused.

'A little. It's nothing.'

'What a very, very nice man you are.'

'Hah.'

'It's true. Next week, you're to have supper with me, tête-à-tête. Can you?'

'I shall be honoured, dear lady.'

'Mysterious things may happen.'

'The very thing I live for.'

'I expect you do.'
'You're right. Will there be a violinist?'
'Good God no!'
'Then I'll come.'

The dinner was at Fouquet's, in a private room with dark green curtains. Gold-painted cherubs grinned from the corners of the ceiling. There were two wines, and langoustines with artichokes and turbot. Lady Angela Hope was in red, a long, shimmering silk sheath, and her upswept hair, a colour something like highly polished brass, was held in place by two diamond butterflies. He thought her presentation ingenious: glamorous, seductive, and absolutely untouchable – the culmination of the private dinner was . . . that one would have dined privately.

'What *am* I to do with my little place in Scotland? You must advise me,' she said.

'Could anything be wrong?'

'Could anything be wrong – could anything be right! This dreadful man, a Mr *MacConnachie* if you will, writes that the northwest cornice has *entirely* deteriorated, and . . .'

Szara was, in a way, disappointed. He was curious, and the street imp from Odessa in him would have liked the conquest of a titled English lady in a private room at Fouquet's. But he'd understood from the beginning that the evening was for business and not for love. While they dawdled over coffee, there was a discreet knock on the doorframe to one side of the curtain. Lady Angela playfully splayed her fingers at the centre of her chest. 'Why, whoever can that be?'

'Your husband,' Szara said acidly.

She suppressed a giggle. 'Bastard,' she said in English. Her upper-class tone made a poem of the word and he noted that it was absolutely the most honestly affectionate thing she had ever said, or likely ever would say, to him. Underneath it all, he thought her splendid.

Roger Fitzware slipped between the curtains. Something in the way he moved meant he was no longer the slightly effeminate and terribly amusing Roddy that the Brasserie Heininger crowd so adored. Short and quite handsome, with thick reddish-brown hair swept across a noble forehead, he was wearing a dinner jacket and smoking a little cigar. 'Am I *de trop?*' he said.

Szara stood and they shook hands. 'Pleased to see you,' he said in English.

'Mm,' Fitzware said.

'Do join us, dear boy,' Lady Angela said.

'Shall I have them bring a chair?' Fitzware said, just to be polite.

'I think not,' said Lady Angela. She came around the table and kissed Szara on the cheek. 'A very, very nice man,' she said. 'You must ring me up – very soon,' she called as she vanished through the curtain.

Fitzware ordered Biscuit cognac and for a time they chatted about nothing in particular. Szara, a student of technique, found considerable professional satisfaction in watching Fitzware work; intelligence people, no matter their national origin, always had a great deal in common, like people who collected stamps or worked in banks. But the approach, when it came, was no surprise, since it turned out to be the same one favoured by the Russian services, one that created an acceptable motive and solicited betrayal in the same breath.

Fitzware conducted the conversation like a maestro:

The concierge situation in Paris – and here he was quite amusing: his apartment house groaned beneath the heel of a ferocious tyrant, *un vrai dragon* in her eighties with a will of iron – led gracefully to *the political situation in Paris* – here Fitzware implicitly acknowledged the concerns of his guest by citing, with a grim expression, the slogan chalked on walls and bridges, *Vaut mieux Hitler que Blum*, a fascist preference for the Nazis over Léon Blum, the Jewish socialist who'd led the government a year earlier. Then it was time for *the political situation in France*, followed closely by *the political situation in Europe*. Now the table was set and it only remained for dinner to be served.

'Do you think there can be peace?' Fitzware asked. He lit a small cigar and offered Szara one. Szara declined and lit a Gitane.

'Of course,' Szara said. 'If people of good will are determined to work together.'

And that was that.

Fitzware had hoisted a signal flag of inquiry, and Szara had responded. Fitzware took a moment to swirl his cognac and exhale a long, satisfied plume of cigar smoke. Szara let him exult a little in his victory; for somebody in their line of work, recruitment was the great, perhaps the only, victory. Now it was settled, they would *work together for peace*. As who wouldn't? They both knew, as surely as the sun rose in the morning, that there would be war, but that was entirely beside the point.

'We're terribly at sea, you know, we British,' said Fitzware, following the script. 'I fear we haven't a clue to the Soviet Union's intentions regarding Poland – or the Baltics, or Turkey. The situation is complex, a powder keg ready to go up. Wouldn't it be dreadful if the armies of Europe marched over a simple misunderstanding?'

'It must be avoided,' Szara agreed. 'At all cost. You'd think we would have come to understand, in 1914, the price of ignorance.'

'Sorrowfully, the world doesn't learn.'

'No, you're right. It seems we are destined to repeat our mistakes.'

'Unless, of course, we have the knowledge, the information, that permits us to work these things out between diplomats – in the League of Nations, for instance.'

'Ideally, it is the answer.'

'Well,' said Fitzware, brightening, 'I believe there's still a chance, don't you?'

'I do,' Szara said. 'To me personally, the critical information at this time would concern developments in Germany. Would you agree with that?'

Fitzware did not respond immediately; simply stared as though hypnotized. He'd led himself some way down a false trail, assuming that Szara's information concerned Soviet operations – intelligence; political or otherwise. Now he had to shift to a completely different area. Quickly, it dawned on him that what he was being offered was, on balance, even better than he'd realized. Offers of Soviet secrets were, in many cases, provocations or dangles – attempts to involve a rival service in deluding itself or revealing its own resources. One had to wear fire-proof gloves in such cases. Offers of *German* secrets, on the other hand, coming from a Russian, would very likely be hard currency. Fitzware cleared his throat. 'Emphatically,' he said.

'To me, the key to a peaceful solution of the current difficulties would be a mutual knowledge of armaments, particularly combat aircraft. What would be your view on that?'

In Fitzware's eyes Szara glimpsed the momentary light of elation, as though an inner voice cried out, *I'd dance naked on me fookin' birthday cake!* In fact, Fitzware permitted himself a civilized grunt. 'Hm, well, yes, of course I agree.'

'With discretion, Mr Fitzware, it's entirely possible.'

An unspoken question answered: Fitzware was not in communication with the USSR, was not being drawn into the occluded maze of diplomatic initiatives achieved by intelligence means. He was in communication with André Szara, a Soviet journalist operating on his own. That was the meaning of the word *discretion*. Fitzware considered carefully; matters had reached a delicate point. 'Your terms,' he said.

'I have great anxiety on the question of Palestine, particularly with the St James's Conference in session.'

At this, Fitzware's triumphant mood slightly deflated. Szara could not have raised a more difficult issue. 'There *are* easier areas in which we might work,' he said.

Szara nodded, leaving Fitzware to tread water.

'Can you be specific?' Fitzware said at last.

'Certificates of Emigration.'

'Real ones?'

'Yes.'

'Above the legal limit, of course.'

'Of course.'

'And in return?'

'Determination of the Reich's monthly bomber production. Based on the total manufacture of the cold-process swage wire that operates certain non-electronic aircraft controls.'

'My board of directors will want to know the reason you say "total".'

'*My* board of directors believes this to be the case. It is, whatever else one might say, Mr Fitzware, a very good, a very *effective*, board of directors.'

Fitzware sighed in agreement. 'Don't suppose, dear boy, you'd consider taking something simple, like money.'

'No.'

'Another cognac, then.'

'With pleasure.'

'We have a good deal of work yet to do, and I can't promise anything. All the usual, you understand,' Fitzware said, pressing the button on the wall that summoned a waiter.

'I understand perfectly,' Szara said. He paused to finish his cognac. 'But you must understand that time is very important to us. People are dying, Great Britain needs friends, we must make it all work out somehow. If you will save lives for us, we will save lives for you. Surely that's world peace, or damn close to it.'

'Close enough,' Fitzware said.

In the violent, changeable weather of early March, Szara and Fitzware got down to serious negotiation. 'Call it what you like,' Szara was later to tell de Montfried, 'but what it was was pushcart haggling.' Fitzware played all the traditional melodies: it was his board of directors that wanted something for nothing; the mandarins in Whitehall were a pack of blind fools; he, Fitzware, was entirely on Szara's side, but making headway through the bureaucratic underbrush was unspeakably frustrating.

Much of the negotiating was done at the Brasserie Heininger. Fitzware sat with Lady Angela Hope and Voyschinkowsky and the whole crowd. Sometimes Szara joined them, other times he took one of his café girls out for dinner. He would meet Fitzware in the men's WC, where they would whisper urgently back and forth, or they would go out on the pavement for a breath of fresh air. Once or twice they talked in a corner at the social evenings held in various apartments. Over the course of it, Szara realized that being a Jew made bargaining difficult. Fitzware was eternally proper, but there were moments when Szara thought he caught a whiff of the classical attitude: why are you people so difficult, so greedy, so stubborn?

And of course Fitzware's board of directors tried to do to him what his own Directorate had done to Dr Julius Baumann. Who are we really dealing with? they wanted to know. We need to have a sense of the process; where is the information coming from? More, give us more! (And why are *you people* so greedy?)

But Szara was like a rock. He smiled at Fitzware tolerantly, knowingly, as the Englishman went fishing for deeper information, a smile that said, *We're in the same business, my friend.* Finally, Szara made a telling point: this negotiation is nothing, he admitted ruefully to Fitzware, compared to dealings with the French, who had their own Jewish communities in Beirut and Damascus. That seemed to work. Nothing, in love and business, quite like a rival to stimulate desire.

They struck a deal and shook hands.

Baumann's figures, from 1 January 1937 to February 1939, brought an initial payment of five hundred Certificates of Emigration – up from Fitzware's offer of two hundred, down from Szara's demand for seven hundred. One hundred and seventy-five certificates a month would be provided as the information was exchanged thereafter. The White Paper would produce seventy-five thousand legal entries through 1944, fifteen thousand a year, one thousand two hundred and fifty a month. Szara's delivery of intelligence from Germany would increase that number by a factor of fourteen per cent. *Thus the mathematics of Jewish lives*, he thought.

He told himself again and again that the operation had to be run with a cold heart, told himself to accept a small victory, told himself whatever he could think of, yet he could not avoid the knowledge that his visits to the corner *tabac* seemed much more frequent, his ashtrays overflowed, he took more empty bottles to the garbage can in the courtyard, his bistro bills rose sharply, and he ate aspirin and splashed gallons of cold water on his eyes in the morning.

There was too much to think about: for one, unseen Soviet counter-intelligence work that was meant to keep people like him from doing exactly what he was doing; for another, the potential for blackmail come the day when Fitzware wanted a view of Soviet operations in Paris and threatened to denounce him if he refused to cooperate; for a third, the strong possibility that Baumann's information was in fact supplied by the Reich Foreign Office intelligence unit and would in time poison the British estimate of German armaments. What, he wondered, were they hearing on the subject from other sources? He was to find that out, sooner than he thought.

During this period, Szara found consolation in the most unlikely places. March, he discovered, was good spying weather. Something about the fierce skies full of racing clouds or the spring rains blowing slantwise past his window gave him courage – in a climate of turbulence one could put aside thoughts of consequences. The political parties of the left and the right were to be seen daily on the boulevards, bellowing their slogans, waving their banners, and the newspapers were frantic, with thick black headlines every morning. The Parisians had a certain facial expression: lips compressed, head canted a little to one side, eyebrows raised: It meant *where does all this lead?* and implied *no place very good.* In Paris that spring of 1939, one saw it hourly.

De Montfried, meanwhile, had appointed himself official agent runner. He was no Abramov and no Bloch, but he had long experience as a commercial trader and believed he understood intuitively how any business agent should be handled. This assumption produced, in the hushed railway library of the Renaissance Club, some extraordinary moments. De Montfried offering money – 'Please don't be eccentric about this, it is only the means to an end' – which Szara did not care to take. De Montfried in the guise of a Jewish mother, pressing smoked fish sandwiches on a man who could barely stand to look at a cup of coffee. De Montfried handed a stack of five hundred Certificates of Emigration, clearing his throat, playing the stoic with tears of pleasure in his eyes. None of this mattered. The days of Abramov and Bloch were over; Szara had been running OPAL operations for too long not to run his own when the time came. That included making sure he didn't know too much about details that did not directly concern him.

But de Montfried said just enough so that Szara's imagination managed the rest. He could see them, perhaps an eye surgeon from Leipzig with his family or a tottering, old rabbi from Berlin's Hasid community, could see them boarding a steamer, watching the coastline of Germany disappear over the horizon. Life for them would be difficult, more than difficult, in Palestine. What the Nazi Brown Shirts had started the Arab raiding bands might yet finish; but it was at least a chance, and that was better than despair.

The British operatives provided all the usual paraphernalia: a code name, CURATE, an emergency meeting signal – the same 'wrong number' telephone call the Russians sometimes used – and a contact to be known by the work name Evans. This was a rail-thin gentleman in his sixties, from his bearing almost certainly a former military officer, quite possibly of colonial service, who dressed in chalk-stripe blue suits, carried a furled umbrella, cultivated a natty little white moustache, and stood straight as a stick. Contacts were made in the afternoon, in the grand cinemas of the Champs-Élysées neighbourhood: silent exchanges of two folded copies of *Le Temps* placed on an empty seat between Szara and the British contact.

Silent but for, on one occasion, a single sentence, spoken by Evans across the empty seat and suitably muffled by the clatter of a crowd of Busby Berkeley tap dancers on the screen: 'Our friend wants you to know that your numbers have been confirmed, and that he is grateful.' He was not to hear Evans speak again.

Confirmed?

That meant Baumann was telling the truth; his information had been authenticated by other sources reporting to the British services. And that meant, what? That Dr Baumann was betraying a German *Funk-spiele* operation, all by himself and just because? That Marta Haecht's boss had been mistaken: it wasn't Von Polanyi having lunch with Baumann at the Kaiserhof? Szara could have gone on and on; there were whole operas of possibilities to be drawn from Fitzware's message. But there was no time for it.

Szara had to hurry back to his apartment, hide a hundred and seventy-five certificates under the carpet until they could be delivered to de Montfried that evening, make a five P.M. meeting in the third arrondissement, the Marais, then head out to the place d'Italie for a *treff* with Valais, the new group leader of the SILO network, a little after seven.

The meeting in the Marais took place in a tiny hotel, at an oilcloth-covered table in a darkened room. A week earlier, Szara had been offered his very own emigration certificate to Palestine. 'It's a back door out of Europe,' de Montfried had said. 'The time may come when you'll have no other choice.' Szara had politely but firmly declined. There was no doubt a reason he did this, but it wasn't one he wanted to name. What he did ask of de Montfried was a second identity, a good one, with a valid passport that would take him over any border he cared to cross. His intention was not flight. Rather, like any efficient predator, he simply sought to extend his range. De Montfried, his favours refused again and again, was eager to oblige. 'Our cobbler,' he'd said, using the slang expression for forger, 'is the best in Europe. And I'll arrange to have him paid, you're not even to discuss it.'

The cobbler was nameless; a fat, oily man with thinning curls brushed back from a receding hairline. In a soiled white shirt buttoned at the sleeves, he moved slowly around the room, speaking French in an accent Szara could place only generally, somewhere in Central Europe. 'You've brought a photograph?' he said. Szara handed over four passport pictures taken in a photo studio. The cobbler chuckled, chose one, and handed the rest back. 'Myself, I don't keep records – for that you'll have to see the cops.'

He held a French passport between thick forefinger and thumb. 'This, *this*, you don't see every day.' He sat down and flattened the passport out on the table and began removing its photograph by rubbing on chemical solvent with a piece of sponge. When he was done he handed the damp picture to Szara. 'Jean Bonotte,' he said. The man looking back at him was vain, with humorous dark eyes that caught the light and a devil's beard that ran from sideburn tight along the jawline and then swept up to join the moustache, the sort of beard kept closely pruned, trimmed daily with scissors. 'Looks smart, no?'

'He does.'

'Not so smart as he thought.'

'Italian?'

The cobbler shrugged eloquently. 'Born Marseille. Could mean anything. A French citizen, though. That's important. Coming from down there you can always say you're Italian, or Corsican, or Lebanese. It's whatever you say, down there.'

'Why is it so good?'

'Because it's real. Because Monsieur Bonotte will not come to the attention of the Spanish Guardia just about the time you get off the ferry in Algeciras. Because Monsieur Bonotte will not again come to anyone's attention, excepting Satan, but the police don't know anything about it. He's legally alive. This document is legally alive. You understand?'

'And he's dead.'

'Very. What's the sense to talk, but you can have confidence he has left us and will not be dug up by some French farmer. That's why I say it's so good.'

The cobbler took the photo back, lit the corner with a match, and watched the blue-green flame consume the paper before he dropped it in a saucer. 'Born in 1902. Makes him thirty-seven. Okay with you? The less I have to change the better.'

'What do you think?' Szara asked.

The cobbler drew his head back a little, evidently farsighted, and looked him over. 'Sure. Why not? Life's hard sometimes and we show it in the face.'

'Then leave it as it is.'

The cobbler began to glue Szara's photo to the paper. When he was done, he waddled over to a bureau and returned with a stamper, a franking machine that pressed paper into raised letters. 'The real thing,' he said proudly. He placed the device at a precise angle to the photo, then slid a scrap of cardboard atop the part of the page already incised. He pressed hard for a few seconds, then released the device. 'This prevents falsification,' he said with only the slightest hint of a smile. He returned the franking device to the bureau and brought back a rubber stamp and a pad, a pen, and a small bottle of green ink. 'Government ink,' he said. 'Free for them. Expensive for me.' He concentrated himself, then stamped the side of the page firmly. 'I'm renewing it for you,' he said. He dipped the pen into the ink and signed the space provided in the rubber-stamped legend. 'Prefect Cormier himself,' he said. He applied a blotter to the signature, then looked at it critically and blew on the ink to make sure it was dry. He handed the passport to Szara. 'Now you're a French citizen, if you aren't already.'

Szara looked through the pages of the passport. It was well used, with several recorded entries into France and visits to Tangier, Oran, Istanbul, Bucharest, Sofia, and Athens. The home address was in the rue Paradis in Marseille. He checked the new date of expiry, March of 1942.

'When the time comes to renew again, just walk into any police station in France and tell them you've been living abroad. A French embassy in a foreign country is even better. You know the man who sent you to me?'

'No,' Szara said. De Montfried wouldn't, he knew, make such a contact directly.

'Just as well,' the cobbler said. 'You're a gentleman, I'd say. You're happy?'

'Yes.'

'Use it in good health,' said the cobbler. 'Me I'd go and pick up a *carte d'identité* – say you lost it – and a health card and all the rest of it, but that's up to you. And don't put your hand in your pocket, it's all taken care of.'

It was after six when he left the hotel. The St-Paul Métro platform was packed solid. When the train rolled in, he had to force his way on, jamming himself against the back of a young woman who might have been, from the way she was dressed, a clerk or a secretary. She said something unpleasant that he didn't quite catch as the train pulled away, but he got a good strong breath of the sausage she'd eaten for lunch. He could see the place on her neck where her face powder stopped. 'Sorry,' he muttered. She said something in slang he didn't understand. When the crowd surged on at the Hôtel-de-Ville station he was pressed against her even harder; her stiff, curly hair rubbing against his nose. 'Soon we'll be married,' he said, trying to make light of the situation. She was not amused and pointedly ignored him.

After a change of trains he reached his stop, Sèvres-Babylone, and went trotting up the rue du Cherche-Midi towards his apartment. No matter how hard he might be pressed, he could not meet with Valais while a second passport was in his pocket. The concierge said good evening through her little window as he rushed towards his entryway in the dark courtyard. He pounded up three flights of stairs, jiggled the lock open with his key, tucked the Bonotte passport under the carpet with the certificates, then took off downstairs. The concierge raised an eyebrow as he hurried past – very little bothered or surprised her, but in general she did not approve of haste.

Back to the Sèvres Métro, dodging housewives returning from the markets and hurdling a dog leash stretched between an aristocratic gentleman and his Italian greyhound squatting at the kerb.

The Métro was even worse as the hour of seven approached. Valais was forbidden to wait more than ten minutes for him; if he were any later they'd have to try for the fallback meeting the following day. The first train that stopped revealed an impenetrable wall of dark coats when the door opened, but he managed to force his way onto the next. After a change at Montparnasse, with almost no time to make sure he wasn't being followed, he left the station a minute after seven, ran around the first corner, them went tearing back the way he'd come. It was primitive, but the best he could manage under the pressure of time.

With thirty seconds to spare, he entered a women's clothing shop – long racks of cheap dresses and a dense cloud of perfume – just off the place d'Italie. The shop was owned by Valais's girlfriend, a short, buxom woman with a hennaed permanent wave and crimson lipstick. What Valais, a contemplative, pipe-smoking lawyer, and she saw in each other he couldn't imagine. She was a few years older than Valais and hard as nails. Szara was breathless as he strode towards the back of the store. The curtain at the entrance of the dressing room hung open, and a woman in a slip was thrashing her way into a pea green dress that was tangled about her head and shoulders.

Valais was waiting in a small workroom where alterations were done.

When Szara entered he was about to leave, his overcoat buttoned and his gloves on. He looked up from his watch, clenched his pipe in his teeth, and shook hands. Szara collapsed in a chair in front of a sewing machine and put his feet up on the treadle.

Valais launched into a long, determined, cautiously phrased description of his activity over the past ten days. Szara pretended to pay attention, his mind returning to what Evans had said in the cinema that afternoon, then found himself thinking about the woman he'd stood with on the Métro. Had she pressed back against him? No, he thought not. 'And then there is LICHEN,' Valais said, waiting for Szara to respond.

Who the hell is LICHEN? Szara experienced a horrible moment of dead memory. At last it came: the young Basque prostitute Hélène Cauxa, virtually inactive the past two years but collecting a monthly stipend nonetheless. 'What's she done now?' Szara asked.

Valais put a black briefcase on the sewing machine stand. 'She, ah, met a German gentleman in the bar of a certain hotel where she sometimes has a drink. He proposed an arrangement, she agreed. They went off to a cheaper hotel, nearby, where she sometimes entertains clients. He forgot his briefcase. She brought it to me.'

Szara opened the briefcase: it was stuffed with a package of pamphlet-size booklets, perhaps two hundred of them, bound with string. Clipped to the cover of the one on top was a slip of paper with the word WEISS printed in pencil. He worked one of the booklets loose and opened it. On the left-hand side of the page were German phrases, on the right the same phrases in Polish:

> *Where is the mayor (head) of the village?*
> *Tell me the name of the chief of police.*
> *Is there good water in this well?*
> *Did soldiers come through here today?*
> *Hands up or I'll shoot!*
> *Surrender!*

'She demanded additional money,' Valais said.

Szara's hand automatically went to his pocket. Valais told him how much and Szara counted it out, telling himself he'd surely remember later how much it was and forgetting almost instantly. 'WEISS must be the name of the operation,' he said to Valais. The word meant white.

'The invasion of Poland,' Valais said. He made a sucking noise, and a cloud of pipe smoke drifted to the ceiling of the dress shop. From the front of the store, Szara heard the ring of the cash register. Had the woman in the slip bought the pea green dress?

'Yes,' he said. 'These are intended for Wehrmacht officers who will be transferred from attaché duty in Paris, a few of them anyhow, back to their units in Germany before the attack. Then some for the Abwehr, military intelligence. Still, seems quite a few. Maybe he was on his way to other cities after Paris.'

'More Polish sorrow,' Valais said. 'And it puts Hitler on the frontier of the Soviet Union.'

'If he's successful,' Szara said. 'Don't underestimate the Poles. And France and England have guaranteed the Polish border. If the Germans aren't careful they're going to take on the whole world again, just like 1914.'

'They are confident,' Valais said. 'They have an unshakable faith in themselves.' He smoked his pipe for a time. 'Have you read Sallust? The Roman historian? He speaks of the Germanic tribes with awe. The Finns, he says, in winter find a hollow log to sleep in, but the Germans simply lay down naked in the snow.' He shook his head at the thought. 'I am, perhaps you don't know, a reserve officer. In an artillery unit.'

Szara lit a cigarette and swore silently in Polish – *psia krew*, dogs' blood. Now everything was going straight to hell.

Back on the Métro with the briefcase. Running up the stairs on the rue du Cherche-Midi. Looking in the mirror and combing his hair back with his fingers, he discovered a white streak of plaster dust on the shoulder of his raincoat – he'd rubbed up against a wall somewhere. He brushed at it, then gave up, put the briefcase in the back of his cupboard, and went out the door. Raced halfway down the stairs, reversed himself, and climbed back up. Re-entered his apartment, snatched the pile of emigration certificates from under the carpet, put them in his own briefcase, and went out a second time.

The streets were crowded: couples going out for dinner, people coming home from work. The wind was ferocious, swirling up dust and papers. People held their hats on and grimaced; waves of chalk-coloured cloud were speeding across the night sky. He'd take the Métro to Concorde, then change to the Neuilly line. From there it was a half-hour walk at least if he couldn't find a taxi. It would certainly rain. His umbrella was in the cupboard. He'd arrive at the Cercle Rénaissance late, looking like a drowned rat, with a white streak on his shoulder. He held tightly to the briefcase with its hundred and seventy-five certificates inside. Had she pressed back against him? A little?

*

When Szara entered the library de Montfried was reading a newspaper. He looked up, his face flushed with anger. 'He's going into Poland,' he said. 'Do you know what that will mean?'

'I think so.' Uninvited, Szara sat down. De Montfried closed the paper emphatically and took off his reading glasses. His eyes seemed the colour of mud in the half light of the small room.

'All this ranting and raving about the *poor, suffering* German minority in Danzig – that's what it means.'

'Yes.'

'My God, the Jews in Poland are living in the ninth century. Do you know? They're . . . when the Hasid hear of the possible invasion they dance to show their joy – the worse it gets, the more they are certain that Messiah is coming. Meanwhile, it's already started, the Poles themselves have started it. No pogroms just yet but beatings and knifings – the gangs are running free in Warsaw.' He glared angrily at Szara. His face was twisted with pain but, at the same moment, he was an important man who had the right to demand explanations.

'I was born in Poland,' Szara said. 'I know what it's like.'

'But why is he alive, this man, this Adolf Hitler? Why is he permitted to live?' He folded the newspaper and put it down on a small marquetry table. The club's dinner hour was approaching and Szara could smell roasting beef.

'I don't know.'

'Can nothing be done?'

Szara was silent.

'An organization like yours, its capacities, resources for such things . . . I don't understand.'

Szara opened his briefcase and passed the stack of certificates to de Montfried, who held them in his hands and stared at them vacantly. 'I have another engagement,' Szara said, as gently as he could.

De Montfried shook his head to clear it. 'Forgive me,' he said. 'What I feel is like an illness. It will not leave me.'

'I know,' Szara said, rising to leave.

Back to the rue du Cherche-Midi. Briefcases exchanged. Szara headed out into the windy night and slowly made his way to the rue Delesseux house. The Directorate, he thought, would want physical possession of the pamphlets, would have a special courier bring them to Moscow. Still, he believed it was best to transmit the contents and the WEISS code name as soon as possible. He began to switch from Métro line to Métro line, now following procedures closely; rue Delesseux was not to be approached by a direct route. At the La Chapelle station there was fighting. Perhaps communists and fascists, it was hard to tell. A crowd of workingmen in caps, all mixed together, three or four of them down on the floor with blood on their faces, two holding a third against a wall while a fourth worked on him. The motor-man didn't stop. The train rolled slowly through the station with white faces staring from the windows. They could hear the shouts and curses over the sound of the train, and one man was hurled against the side of the moving carriage and bounced hard, the shock felt by the passengers as he hit – several people gasped or cried out when it happened. Then the train returned to the darkness of the tunnel.

Schau-Wehrli was at work in the rue Delesseux. Szara handed her a pamphlet and stood quietly while she looked it over. 'Yes,' she said reflectively, 'everything points to it now. My commissary people in Berlin, who work for the German railway system, say the same thing. They've heard about requests for a traffic analysis on the lines that go to the Polish border. That means troop trains.'

'When?'

'Nobody knows.'

'Is it a bluff?'

'No, I think not. It most certainly was with the Czechs, but not now. The Reich industrial production is meeting quotas, the war machinery is just about in place.'

'And what will we do?'

'Stalin alone knows that,' Schau-Wehrli said. 'And he doesn't tell me.'

It was well after midnight when Szara finally got home. He'd never managed to eat anything, but hunger was long gone, replaced by cigarettes and adrenaline. Now he just felt cold and grimy and used up. There was a large tin bathtub in the kitchen, and he turned on the hot water tap to see what might be left. Yes, there was one good thing in the world that night, a bath, and he would have it. He stripped off his clothes and threw them on a chair, poured himself a glass of red wine, and turned the radio dial until he found some American jazz. When the tub was ready he climbed in and settled back, drank a little wine, rested the glass on the broad part of the rim, and closed his eyes.

Poor de Montfried, he thought. All that money, yet he could do little, at least that was the way he saw it. The man had virtually humiliated him in the library, had been so angry that the certificates, bought at a cost he could not imagine, seemed a small and insufficient gesture. Oh the rich. Would any of the café girls still be about? No, that was hopeless. There was one he could telephone – full of understanding, that one, she loved what she called *adventures of the night*. No, he thought, sleep. The music ended and a man began to announce the news. Szara reached for the dial, his arm dripping water on the kitchen floor, but the radio was just a little too far. So he had to hear that the miners were on strike in Lille, that the minister of finance had denied all allegations, that the little girl missing in the Vosges had been found, that Madrid continued to hold out, factions fighting each other in the besieged city. Stalin had issued an important political statement, referring to the current crisis as 'the Second Imperialistic War'. He stated he would 'not allow Soviet Russia to be drawn into conflicts by warmongers who are accustomed to having others pull their chestnuts out of the fire', and attacked those nations who wanted 'to arouse Soviet anger against Germany, to poison the atmosphere, and to provoke a conflict with Germany without visible reason'.

Then the music returned, saxophones and trumpets from a dance hall on Long Island. Szara rested his head against the tub and closed his eyes. Stalin claimed that England and France were plotting against him, manoeuvring him to fight Hitler while they waited to pounce on a weakened winner. Perhaps they were. Aristocrats ran those countries, intellectuals and ministers of state, graduates of the best universities. Stalin and Hitler were scum from the gutters of Europe who'd managed to float to the top. Well, one way or another, there would be war. And he would be killed. Marta Haecht as well. The Baumanns, Kranov, the operative who'd driven him away from Wittenau on Kristallnacht, Valais, Schau-Wehrli, Goldman, Nadia Tscherova. All of them. The bath was cooling much too fast. He pulled the plug and let some of it gurgle out, then added more hot water and lay back in the steam.

In London, on the fourth floor at 54 Broadway – supposedly the headquarters of the Minimaz Fire Extinguisher Company – MI6 officers analysed the CURATE product, packaged it alongside information from a variety of other sources, then shipped it off to intelligence consumers in quiet little offices all over town. It travelled by car and bicycle, by messenger and pneumatic tube, sometimes down long, damp corridors, sometimes to panelled rooms warmed by log fires. The product came recommended. Confirming data on German swage wire manufacture was independently available, and German bomber production numbers were further supported by factory orders, in Britain itself, for non-interference technology that protected aviation spark plugs, and by engineers and businessmen who had legitimate associations with German industry. The material arrived, for example, at the Industrial Intelligence Centre, which played the key role in analysing Germany's ability to fight a war. The centre had become quite important and was connected to the Joint Planning subcommittee, the Joint Intelligence subcommittee, the Economic Pressure on Germany subcommittee, and the Air Targets committee.

The CURATE story also floated upwards, sometimes unofficially, into the precincts of Whitehall and the Foreign Office, and from there it wandered even further. There was always somebody else who really ought to hear about it; knowledge was power, and people liked to be known to have secret information because it made them seem important: *secret*, but not secret from them. Simultaneously, in a very different part of the civil service, the bureaux that dealt in colonial affairs had been stirred up like hornets' nests when the espionage types had come poaching on their territory. British Mandate Palestine was their domain and – love the Arabs or love the Jews or hate them all – the brawl over legitimate Certificates of Emigration had been bloody and fierce. And it was discussed.

So people knew about it, this CURATE, a Russian in Paris feeding the odd morsel to the British lion in return for a subtle shift of the paw. And some of the people who knew about it were, privately, rather indignant. To begin with, their hearts' passion lay elsewhere. From the time of their undergraduate days at Cambridge they'd thrown in their lot with the idealists, the progressives, the men of conscience and good will at the Kremlin. Precisely who did the work it would be difficult to say – Anthony Blunt or Guy Burgess, Donald MacLean or H. A. R. Philby, or others unknown; they all traded on the information exchanges of the intelligence and diplomatic bureaucracies – but one or more of them thought it worthwhile to let somebody know, and so they did. Spoken over supper at a private club or left in a dead-drop in a cemetery wall, the code name CURATE and the very general outline of what it meant began to move east.

It did not move alone – many other facts and all sorts of gossip needed to be passed along – and it did not move with great speed; alarms were not raised. But it did, in time, reach Moscow and, a little later, the proper office in the appropriate department. It fell among cautious people, survivors of the purge who lived in a dangerous, undersea twilight of predators and their prey, people who moved carefully and with circumspection, people who knew better than to catch a fish that might be too big for their nets – that way one might wind up at the bottom of the ocean; it had happened. In the beginning, they contented themselves with pure research, with trying to find out who it was, where it was, and why it was. Action would follow at the appropriate time and in the appropriate way. It has been said that counter-intelligence people are by nature voyeurs. They like to watch what goes on because when the moment finally comes to rush out of the shadows and kick down the doors, the fun is really over, the files are taken away, the wheels begin to grind, and then it's time to start all over again.

One morning in early May the Paris newspapers soberly reported a change of Soviet foreign ministers: M. M. Litvinov replaced by V. M. Molotov.

Some went on to read the article beneath the headline; many did not. These were the redemptive hours of spring – Paris was leafy and soft and full of girls, life would go on forever, the morning light danced on the coffeecup and the bud vase, and sun streaming into a room turned it into a Flemish painting. Russian diplomats came and went. Who, really, cared?

André Szara, true to his eternally divided self, did both: read on and didn't care. He judged the story rather incomplete, but that was nothing new. M. M. Litvinov was in fact Maxim Maximovich Wallach, a pudgy, Jewish, indoor gentleman of the old school, a thorough intellectual, myopic and bookish. How on earth had he lasted as long as he had? V. M. Molotov, in fact Vyacheslav Mikhaylovich Skryabin, had changed his name for a rather different reason. As Djugashvili became Stalin, Man of Steel, so Skryabin became Molotov, the Hammer. *So*, thought Szara, *between them they'll make a sword*.

Szara's flip commentary turned out to be just the truth, but he had a lot to think about that day. He contemplated a good deal of rushing about here and there, and he was no less receptive to spring breezes than any other man or woman in Paris, so the weight of the news didn't quite reach him – he didn't hear the final piece of a complex machine snap into its housing. He heard the birds singing, the neighbour flapping her bedding before she hung it over the windowsill to air, the scissors grinder ringing his bell out on the rue du Cherche-Midi – but that was all.

Adolf Hitler heard it, certainly, but then he had very sharp ears. He was later to say 'Litvinov's dismissal was decisive. It came to me like a cannon shot, like a sign that the attitude of Moscow towards the Western powers had changed.'

The French intelligence services heard it, though probably not so loud as a cannon shot, reporting on 7 May that unless great diplomatic effort was exerted by England and France, Germany and the USSR would sign a treaty of non-aggression by the end of the summer.

*

Szara was summoned to Brussels on the tenth of May.

'We're going to have to make an arrangement with Hitler,' Goldman said with sorrow and distaste. 'It's Stalin's own damn fault – the purges have weakened the military to a point where we simply cannot fight and expect to win. Not now. So time is going to have to be bought, and the only way to buy it is with a treaty.'

'Good God,' Szara said.

'Can't be helped.'

'Stalin and Hitler.'

'The European communist parties aren't going to be happy, our friends in America aren't going to like it, but the moment has come for them to learn a little realpolitik. The hand-wringers and the crybabies will go off in a great huff. Them we'll have to kiss good-bye. And good riddance. The ones who decide to remain faithful will be true friends, people who can be depended on to see things the way we see them, so maybe all is for the best. We've been sweating and bleeding since 1917 to build a socialist state; we can't let it all go down the river in the service of starry-eyed idealism. The factories, the mines, and the collective farms; those are the reality – and to protect that investment we'll make a deal with the devil himself.'

'We're evidently to do just that.'

'Can't be helped. Most of the intelligence services have already got it figured out, the public will know by the summer, July or August. That gives us a few weeks to do the work.'

'Not much time.'

'It's what we have, so we'll manage. First, and most important, the networks themselves. Don't waste your time on the mercenaries, work with the believers. You're letting them in on the secret life at the top, where strategic decisions are made. The Nazis will never be anybody's friends, and not ours either, but we need time to arm for the confrontation and this is the way to buy it. Anybody who doesn't accept this line – I am to be informed. Is that understood?'

'Yes.'

'With our German informants nothing changes. In war we fight our enemies, in peace we fight our friends. So now we'll have a form of peace, but operations continue as before. We want, now more than ever, to know what goes on with the Germans – their thinking, their planning, their capacities, and their military dispositions. Times are perilous and unstable, André Aronovich, and that is when networks must operate at their maximum capability.'

'If we have a, a misfortune. If somebody gets caught, what does that do?'

'God forbid. But I don't expect Referat VI C will send everybody home to tend their rose gardens, so neither will we. The way to handle what you call "a misfortune" is to make sure it doesn't happen. Does that answer your question?'

Szara made a wry face.

'Second, get busy with your personal connections. Oh-me oh-my the world is a terrible place, whatever is to be done? However *shall* we find peace? There must be a compromise, someone must be willing to budge an inch and let the other fellow see he means no harm. Only the USSR is strong enough to do that. Let the British and the French rattle their swords and wheel their cannons about; we mean to relieve the pressure on Hitler's eastern border, we mean to sign trade agreements and cultural exchanges – let the folk dancers fight this out between them – we mean to find a way we can all live together in a world where not everything is as we'd wish it to be. No more mobilizations! No more 1914!'

'Hurrah!'

'Don't be clever. If you don't believe it, nobody else will. So find a way.'

'And the Poles?'

'Too stubborn to live, as usual and as always. They'll stand on their honour and make pretty speeches and wake up one morning speaking German. There is nothing to be done for the Poles. They've chosen to go their own way. Good, now let them.'

'Should they give up Danzig?'

'Give up your *sister*. We sit here in this little shop and we happen to know that once the German bombers get busy, Warsaw will turn into a blazing hell. That's the reality. Now, for number three, pick up your ingenious pen and go to work. Try one of those intellectual French journals guaranteed to give you a headache and start shaping the dialogue. If there were some way to co-opt the argument itself – you know, by stating the initial questions – life would be perfect. To that we can't aspire – every writer under the sun is going to have a say on this, but at least you can give them a nudge. As in: what must world socialism do to survive? Must we all die, or is there an alternative? Is diplomacy truly exhausted? Could the bloodbath in Spain have been avoided if everybody had been a little more willing to negotiate?

'You'll be crucified by the doctrinaire Marxists, of course, but so what. The important thing is to get the discussion rolling by claiming some territory. There's bound to be somebody who'll rush to defend you – there always is, no matter what you say. And if, no, *when* people come up to you at parties and tell you that Lenin's spinning in his display case, you'll have the right answers: remember, the USSR is the hope of progressive mankind and the only ongoing remedy to fascism. But it must survive. Stalin is a genius, and this pact will be a work of genius, a diplomatic side step to avoid the crippling blow. And the minute the pact becomes public, that's what I want to read under your byline, without hauling you all the way up to Belgium. Is everything clear?'

'Oh yes,' Szara said. 'England and France want war to satisfy their imperialist aspirations, Russia stands alone in seeking peace. Subtext, with a wink and a poke in the ribs, that sly old fox from the Caucasus is doing what he has to in order to gain time. We'll settle with Hitler when *we're* ready. Is that about it?'

'Exactly. You're not alone in this, of course. All the Soviet writers will take a hand – they'll likely have a play onstage in Moscow in ninety days. Your participation was directly ordered, by the way: "You've got Szara over there, put him to work!" is exactly how it was said. It's a broad effort now – they've brought Molotov in to negotiate with Ribbentrop, the German foreign minister, in case you wondered about that. We can't be sending a chubby little Jewish man off to deal with the Nazis, you agree?'

'Realpolitik, as you said.'

'That is the word. By the way, I suggest you pack a bag and keep it by the door. If the situation evolves the way we think it might, there's a possibility you may be travelling on short notice.'

'On OPAL business?'

'No, no. As the journalist Szara, the voice of Russia speaking out from foreign lands. You really ought to treat yourself to a grand dinner, André Aronovich, I see great professional advancement in your future.'

The Molotov appointment – on the surface no more than a piece of diplomatic business during a time when there was more than an ample supply of it – induced in Paris, and evidently in other European capitals, a change of chemistry.

André Szara found himself doing things he didn't quite understand but felt compelled to do anyhow. As Goldman had suggested, he prepared to travel on a moment's notice. Climbed up on a chair, took his suitcase down from the top of the armoire, blew some of the dust off it, and decided he needed something else. His twelve-year-old suitcase, its pebbled surface a soiled ochre colour with a maroon stripe, had seen hard service in his *Pravda* days. It was nicked and scratched and faded and made him look, he thought, like a refugee. All it needed was the knotted rope around the middle. So he went off to the luggage stores, but he didn't really like what he found – either too fashionable or too flimsy.

He passed a custom leathergoods shop one day in the seventh arrondissement – saddles and riding boots in the window – and, on the spur of the moment, went inside. The owner was a Hungarian, a no-nonsense craftsman in a smock, his hands hard and knotted from years of cutting and stitching leather. Szara explained what he wanted, a kind of portmanteau like a doctor's bag, an old-fashioned but enduring form, made of long-wearing leather. The Hungarian nodded, produced some samples, and quoted an astonishing price. Szara agreed none-theless. He hadn't wanted an *object* so badly for a long while. Oh, and one last thing: from time to time he carried confidential business papers, and what with the sort of people one finds working in hotels these days . . . The Hungarian was entirely understanding and indicated that Szara was not the only customer to express such concerns. The traditional false bottom was as old as the hills, true, but when properly crafted it remained effective. A second panel would be fashioned to fit precisely on the bottom; papers could be safely stored between the two layers. 'It is, sir, naturally safest if you were to have it sewn in place. Not so much for light-fingered hotel staff, you understand, for the bag will be provided with an excellent lock, but more a matter of, one might say, frontiers.' The delicate word hung in the air for a moment, then Szara made a deposit and promised to return in June.

A week later he decided that if he was to travel, he didn't want to leave the Jean Bonotte passport in his apartment. Robberies were rare but they did occur, especially when people went away for an extended period. And from time to time the NKVD might send a couple of technicians around, just to see whatever there was to see. So he opened an account in the Bonotte name, using the passport for identification, at a Banque du Nord office on the boulevard Haussmann, then rented a safe deposit box for the passport itself. Three days later he returned, on a perfect June morning, and put an envelope holding twelve thousand francs on top of the passport. *What are you doing?* he asked himself. But he really didn't know; he only knew he was uncomfortable, in some not very definable way, like a dog that howls on the eve of a tragedy. Something, somewhere, was warning him. His ancestry, perhaps. Six hundred years of Jewish life in Poland, of omens, signs, portents, instincts. His very existence proved him to be the child of generations that had survived when others didn't, perhaps born to know when the blood was going to run. *Hide money*, something told him. *Arm yourself,* said the same voice, a few nights later. But that, for the moment, he did not do.

A strange month, that June. Everything happened. Schau-Wehrli was contacted by a group of Czech émigrés who lived in the town of Saint-Denis, in the so-called Red Belt north of Paris. They were communists who'd fled when Hitler took over the remainder of Czechoslovakia in March, and the contact with OPAL was made through the clandestine apparatus of the French Communist party. The group was receiving intelligence by means of secret writing on the backs of bank envelopes, which contained receipts for funds mailed to Prague and Brno for the support of relatives. They were using an invisible ink concocted in a university chemistry laboratory. Like the classics, lemon juice and urine, application of a hot iron brought up the message. The information itself was voluminous, ranging from Wehrmacht order of battle, numbers and strengths of German units, to financial data, apparently stolen by the same bank employees who prepared the envelopes, as well as industrial information – almost all the renowned Czech machine shops were now at work on Reich war production.

This group required a great deal of attention. There were eight of them, all related by blood or marriage, and though motivated by a passionate loathing of the Nazis, they perceived their contribution as a business and knew exactly what this kind of information was worth. Three of the Saint-Denis members had intelligence experience and had created a network in Czechoslovakia, after Hitler took the Sudetenland, with the goal of supporting themselves and their families when they resettled in France. The two bank employees were the daughters of sisters, first cousins, and their husbands worked at acquiring information through friendships maintained at men's sports clubs. Such an in-place network, already functioning efficiently, was almost too good to be true, thus the Directorate in Moscow was simultaneously greedy for the product and wary of Referat VI C counter-intelligence deception. This ambivalence created a vast flow of cable traffic and exceptional demands on the time of the deputy director, Schau-Wehrli, so that Goldman eventually ordered the RAVEN network transferred to Szara's care.

He nodded gravely when given the new assignment, but the idea of working with Nadia Tscherova did not displease him. Not at all.

At the rue Delesseux he read his way through the RAVEN file, which included Tscherova's most recent reports in their original format: an aristocratic literary Russian printed in tiny letters, on strips of film that had been carried over the border in Odile's shoulder pads, then developed in an attic darkroom. Previous reports had been retyped, verbatim, and filed in sequence.

Szara read with pure astonishment. After the tense aridity of Dr

Baumann and the lawyer's precision of Valais, it was like a night at the theatre. What an eye she had! Penetrating, malicious, ironic, as though Balzac were reborn as a Russian émigrée in 1939 Berlin. Read serially, RAVEN's reports worked as a novel of social commentary. Her life was made up of small roles in bad plays, intimate dinners, lively parties, and country house weekends in the Bavarian forest, with boar-hunting by day and bed-hopping by night.

Szara had tender feelings for this woman, even though he suspected she was a specialist in the provocation of tender feelings, and he would have expected himself to read of her never-quite-consummated *liaisons intimes* with a leaden heart. But it just wasn't so. She'd told him the truth that night in her dressing room: she protected herself from the worst of it and was unmoved by what went on around her. This casual invulnerability was everywhere in her reports, and Szara found himself, above all else, amused. She had something of a man's mind in such matters, and she characterized her fumbling, half-drunken, would-be lovers and their complicated *requests* with a delicate brutality that made him laugh out loud. By God, he thought, she was no better than he was.

Nor did she spare her sub-agents. Lara Brozina she described as writing 'a kind of ghastly, melancholy verse that Germans of a certain level adore.' Brozina's brother, Viktor Brozin, an actor in radio plays, was said to have 'the head of a lion, the heart of a parakeet'. And of the balletmaster Anton Krafic she wrote that he was 'sentenced every morning to live another day'. Szara could positively see them – the languid Krafic, the leonine Brozin, the *terribly* sensitive Brozina – amusing frauds making steady progress along the shady underside of Nazi society.

And Tscherova did not spare the details. During a weekend in a castle near the town of Traunstein, she entered a bathroom after midnight 'to discover B. [that meant BREWER, Krafic] drinking champagne in the bathtub with SS Hauptsturmführer Bruckmann, who was wearing a cloche hat with a veil and carmine lipstick'. What in heaven's name, Szara wondered, had the Directorate made of *this*?

Referring to the file of outgoing reports he discovered the answer: Schau-Wehrli had reprocessed the material to make it palatable. Thus her dispatch covering RAVEN's description of the jolly bath said only that 'BREWER reports that SS Hauptsturmführer BRUCKMANN has recently been with his regiment on divisional manoeuvres in marshy, swamplike terrain near the Masurian Lakes in East Prussia.' Another pointer, Szara noted, towards the invasion of Poland, where such conditions might be encountered.

A rich, rewarding file.

He worked his way through the last of it on the afternoon of the summer solstice, *the day the sun is said to pause,* he thought. Pleasing, that idea. Something Russian about it. As though the universe stopped for a moment to reflect, took a day off from work. One could sense it, time slowing down: the weather light and sunny, rather aimless, a bird twittering away on a neighbouring balcony, Kranov coding at his desk, humming a Russian melody, the little bell on the door of the ground-floor *tabac* tinkling as a customer entered.

Then the warning buzzer went off beside Kranov's table – a danger signal operated from beneath the counter in the *tabac.* This was followed, a moment later, by a knock on the door at the bottom of the stairs, a door shielded by a curtain on the back wall of the shop.

Szara had absolutely no idea what to do, neither did Kranov. They both froze, sat dead still like two hares caught in a winter field. They were literally surrounded by incrimination – files, flimsies, stolen documents, and the wireless telegraph itself, with its aerial run cleverly up the unused chimney by way of the attic. There was no getting rid of anything. They could have run down the stairs and rushed out the back door, or jumped the three storeys and broken their ankles, but they did neither. It was three-thirty on a bright summer afternoon and not a wisp of darkness to cover their escape.

So they sat there and presently heard a second knock, perhaps a bit more insistent than the first. Szara, not knowing what else to do, walked down the stairs and answered it. To find two Frenchmen waiting politely at the door. They were Frenchmen of a certain class, wore tan summerweight suits of a conservative cut, crisp shirts, silk ties not terribly in fashion but not terribly out. The brims of their hats were turned down at precisely the same angle. Szara found himself thinking in Russian, *My God, the hats are here.* The two men had a particular coloration that a Frenchman of the better sort will assume after lunch, a faint, rose-tinted blush on the cheeks which informs the knowledgeable that the beef was good and the wine not too bad. They introduced themselves and presented cards. They were, they said, fire inspectors. They would just have a brief look around, if it wasn't terribly inconvenient.

Fire inspectors they were not.

But Szara had to go along with the game, so he invited them in. By the time they'd climbed to the third floor, Kranov had pulled the blanket off the window and flung it over the wireless, turning it into a curious dark hump on an old table from which a wire ran up the corner of the wall and disappeared into the attic through a ragged hole in the ceiling. Kranov himself was either in a closet or under the bed in Odile's apartment on the second floor – one of those truly inspired hiding places found amid panic – but in the event he was unseen. The Frenchmen didn't look, they didn't strip the blanket off the wireless, and they didn't even bother to enter Odile's apartment. One of them said, 'So much paper in a room like this. You must be careful with your cigarettes. Perhaps a bucket of sand ought to be placed in the corner.'

They touched the brims of their hats with their forefingers and departed. Szara, his shirt soaked at the armpits, collapsed in a chair. Somewhere on the floor below he heard a bump and a curse as Kranov extricated himself from whatever cranny he'd jammed himself into. A *comedy*, Szara said to himself, *a comedy*. He pressed his palms against his temples.

Kranov, swearing under his breath, threw the blanket into a corner and flashed Goldman a disaster signal. For the next two hours messages flew back and forth, Kranov's pencil scratching out columns of figures as he encoded responses to Goldman's precise questions. Somewhere, Szara was certain, the French had a receiver and were taking note of all the numbers crackling through the summer air.

By the end of the exchange Szara realized that the game was not actually over, the network was not blown. Not quite. They had, evidently, been warned, probably by the Deuxième Bureau – diplomatic and military intelligence – using agents of the Paris Préfecture of police or the Direction de la Surveillance du Territoire, the DST, the French equivalent of the American FBI. The warning came in two parts:

We know what you're doing, went the first.

This was no great surprise, when Szara had a moment to think about it. The French police had always insisted, since Fouché served Napoleon, on knowing exactly what went on in their country, and most particularly in their capital. Whether they actually did anything about what they knew was treated as a very different matter – here political decisions might be involved – but they were scrupulously careful in keeping track of what went on, neighbourhood by neighbourhood, village by village. So their knowledge of the existence of OPAL was, finally, no great surprise.

From their point of view it did not hurt them that the Russians spied on Germany, the traditional enemy of France. They may have received, at a very high level, compensation for allowing OPAL a free hand, compensation in the form of refined intelligence product. Always, there were arrangements that did not meet the eye.

But the second part of the warning was quite serious: if you truly mean to become an ally of Germany, we may decide that your days here are numbered, since such an alliance might damage French interests, and that will not be permitted to happen. So here, gentlemen, are a pair of fire inspectors, and we send them to you in a most courteous and considerate fashion, which is to say before anything actually starts burning.

We're sure you'll understand.

In July, the OTTER operation ended. They would hear from Dr Baumann no more. So that month's exchange of information for emigration certificates was the last. Szara signalled de Montfried for a meeting, he responded immediately.

De Montfried was driven in from his country house, a château near Tours. He was wearing a cream-coloured suit, a pale blue shirt, and a little bow tie. He carefully placed his straw hat on the marquetry table in the library, folded his hands, and looked expectantly at Szara. When told the operation was over, he covered his face with his hands, as though in great fatigue. They sat for some time without speaking. Outside it was oppressively quiet; a long, empty, summer afternoon.

Szara felt sorry for de Montfried but could find no words of consolation. What was there to say? The man had discovered himself to be rather less powerful than he'd thought. Yet, Szara realized, how little would change for him. He would present the same image to the world, would live beautifully, move easily in the upper realms of French society; the haughty Cercle Rénaissance would still be the place where a library of railway books was maintained for his pleasure. Certainly he was to be envied. He had simply found, and rather late in life, the limits of his power. Perceiving himself to be a wealthy and important man, de Montfried had attempted to exert influence on political events and, based on Szara's understanding of this world, had succeeded. He simply did not understand how well they'd done. He simply did not understand that he'd imposed himself on a world where the word *victory* was hardly to be heard.

Together, he and Szara had been responsible for the distribution of one thousand three hundred and seventy-five Certificates of Emigration to Mandate Palestine. As these covered individuals and their families, and were so precious that marriages and adoptions were arranged, sometimes overnight, the number of salvaged lives was perhaps three thousand. What, Szara wondered, could he say? *You bloody fool, you want to save the world – now you know what it takes to save three thousand lives!* No, he could not say that. And had he said it he would have been wrong. The true price of those lives was yet to be paid and would turn out to be higher, for Szara and others, than either of them could have realized at that moment.

De Montfried dropped his hands heavily to the arms of his chair and sat back, his face collapsed with failure. 'Then it's finished,' he said.

'Yes,' Szara said.

'Can anything be done? Anything at all?'

'No.'

Szara had certainly thought about it – *thought* wasn't really the word; his mind had spun endless scenarios, reached desperately for a solution, any solution at all. But to no avail.

It was Szara's opinion that Evans had told him the truth that afternoon in the cinema: the British services *were* able to confirm the figures from other sources. That meant he could not simply lie, offer numbers that would appear to be logical. They would know. Not at first – for a month or two it might be managed, and a month or two meant another three hundred and fifty certificates, at least seven hundred lives. Seven hundred lives were worth a lie – in Szara's calculus they certainly were. But it was worse than that.

When he'd first gone to the British, he'd believed his figures to be false, part of a German counter-intelligence attack. It had not mattered, then. But the world had shifted beneath his feet; Germany would take Poland, and Russia would agree to a treaty that left Britain and France isolated. False figures delivered now might deform the British armament effort in unforeseen ways, false figures could well help the Nazis, false figures could cost thousands of lives, tens of thousands, once the Luftwaffe bombers flew. So those seven hundred lives were lost.

'Have you told them?' de Montfried asked.

'Not yet.'

'Why not?'

'On the possibility that you and I, sitting here, might invent something, discover something, find another way. On the possibility that you have not been forthcoming with me and that you have resources I don't know about, perhaps information of some kind that can be substituted.'

De Montfried shook his head.

They sat in silence.

'What will you tell them?' de Montfried said at last.

'That there has been an interruption at the source, that we wish to continue until a new method can be worked out.'

'And will they accept that?'

'They will not.'

'Not even for one month?'

'Not even that.' He paused for a moment. 'I know it's difficult to understand, but it's like not having money. Lenin said that grain was "the currency of currencies". That was in 1917. For us, it might now be said that information is the currency of currencies.'

'But surely you know other things, things of interest.'

'For the people I deal with directly, that might very well work. But we are asking for something I'm certain they – MI6 – had to fight for, and only the magnitude of what we were offering made it possible for them to win that battle. I don't think they'll go back to war for other material I might offer. I'm sure they won't. Otherwise, believe me, I would try it.'

Slowly, de Montfried gathered himself to face the inevitable. 'It is very hard for me to admit to failure, but that is what's happened, we've failed.'

'We've stopped, yes.'

De Montfried withdrew a leather case and a fountain pen from the inside pocket of his jacket, unscrewed the top of the pen, and began to write a series of telephone numbers on the back of a business card. 'One of these will find me,' he said. 'I am almost never out of touch with my office – that's the number you've been using – but I've included several other numbers, places where I'm to be found. Otherwise we'll leave it as it's been, simply say *Monsieur B. is calling.* I'll leave instructions for the call to be put through to me directly. Day or night, any time. Whatever I have is at your disposal should you need it.'

Szara put the card in his pocket. 'One can never be sure what might happen. One has to hope for the best.'

De Montfried nodded sadly.

Szara stood and offered his hand. 'Good-bye,' he said.

'Yes,' de Montfried said, rising to shake hands. 'Good luck.'

'Thank you,' Szara said.

The card joined the money and the Jean Bonotte passport that afternoon.

The OTTER operation had ended suddenly and badly.

Odile must have activated an emergency signal available in Berlin, because Goldman called a special meeting, to take place just after she got off the train. Szara and Schau-Wehrli were summoned to a place called Arion, in Belgium, an iron mining town just over the Luxembourg border a few kilometres north of the French city of Longwy. It was hot and dirty in Arion. Coal smoke from the mills drifted through the soot-blackened streets, the sunset was a dark, sullen orange, and the night air was dead still. The meeting was held in a worker's tenement near the centre of town, the home of a party operative, a miner asked to spend the night with relatives. They sat in the cramped parlour with the shutters closed amid the smells of sweaty clothes and boiled food.

Odile was shaken – her face an unnatural white – but determined. She had got off a local train from the German border only a few minutes before they arrived. Goldman was there with another man Szara did not know, a short, heavy Russian in middle age, with wavy fair hair and extremely thick glasses that distorted his eyes. At first Szara thought he might be asthmatic: his breath rasped audibly in the little room. After they'd settled down, Szara noticed that the man was staring at him. Szara met his glance but the man did not look away. He put an oval cigarette between his lips, creased the head of a wooden match with his thumbnail, and lit the cigarette from the flare. Only then did he turn to face Odile. As he shook the match out, Szara saw that he wore a large gold watch on his wrist.

By the time Szara and Schau-Wehrli arrived, Odile had told her story to Goldman and the other man and produced Baumann's message. Goldman handed it to Szara. 'Have a look,' he said.

Szara took the slip of paper, read quickly over the production numbers, then discovered a terse sentence scrawled along the bottom of the sheet: *You should be aware that rumours of a rapprochement between Germany and the USSR have angered members of the diplomatic and military class.*

'What is your opinion?' Goldman asked.

'My opinion,' Szara said. 'It seems he's trying to supply additional information. We've been after him for months to do that. Do such rumours exist?'

'Perhaps. In the class of people he refers to, they could easily be more than rumours,' Goldman said. 'But how would Baumann know such things? Who is he talking to?'

Szara said he didn't know.

Goldman turned to Odile. 'Please tell us again what happened.'

'I always clear the drop early in the morning,' Odile said, 'when the maids go to work in the neighbourhood. I went to the wall by the little wood, made certain I was not observed, reached over the wall and felt around until I found the loose rock, then withdrew the paper and put it in the pocket of my raincoat. There was no message from the network, so I was next going to the telephone pole to acknowledge reception by turning the bent nail. I went about ten steps when a woman came out of the woods. She was approximately fifty years old, wearing a house-dress, and extremely agitated and nervous. "He has been taken," she said to me in German. I pretended not to understand what it was all about. "He is in a camp, in Sachsenhausen," she said, "and his friends can't help him." I stared at her and started to hurry away. "Tell them they must help him," she called after me. I walked very fast. She came a few steps after me, then stopped and went back into the woods. I did not see her do this, but I looked over my shoulder a few seconds later and she was gone. I heard a dog barking, a little dog, from the woods somewhere. I made my way to the Ringbahn station at Hohenzollern-Damm, went into the public toilet, and hid the message in my shoulder pad. I was out of Berlin on a local train about one hour later. I saw nobody unusual on the train, had no other experience out of the ordinary.'

'Friends?' Schau-Wehrli said. 'His *friends* can't help? Did she mean the Jewish community? Lawyers, people like that?'

'Or work associates,' Szara mused. 'People at the German companies he deals with.'

'The point is,' Goldman said, 'has he been arrested as a Jew? Or a spy?'

'If they caught him spying, they would have taken her as well, Schau-Wehrli said. 'And the Gestapo would have him – that means Columbia House, not Sachsenhausen.'

'Perhaps,' Goldman said. 'It's hard to know.'

'Can he be helped?' Szara asked.

'That's a question for the Directorate, but yes, it has been done before. For the time being, the Berlin operatives are going to try and contact him in the camp and let him know we're aware of what's happened and that we're going to get him out. We're trying to help him to resist interrogation. Do you think he can?'

Szara sensed that Baumann's life hung on his answer: 'If anyone can, he will. He's a strong man, psychologically. His physical condition is another matter. If the interrogation is extreme, he may die on them.'

Goldman nodded at the answer. 'At your meeting in Berlin, was anything said that can help explain either his message, the "members of the diplomatic and military classes" business, or his wife's reference to "friends"? Are those, perhaps, the same people?'

'They could be,' Szara lied. 'I can't say.'

'Is that your answer?' the man in the glasses asked.

Szara faced him. The eyes behind the thick lenses were watery and lifeless. 'My answer is no. Nothing was said that would explain either of those statements.'

Travelling back to Paris on a succession of local trains they had to sit in separate compartments. That gave Szara time to think while the sombre towns of northeastern France rolled past the window.

He felt old. It was the business with Nadia Tscherova again, only worse. He was tormented by what had happened to Baumann, and by his own part in the man's destruction, yet what he had seen on Kristallnacht went a long way towards justifying what they had done together. A sacrifice of war. A machine gun position left to delay an enemy's progress down a road while the rear guard retreats. All very well, he thought, until you're the machine gunner. In his not so secret heart he thought it might be for the best if Baumann were to die. Peacefully. A death of mercy. But his instinct told him that would not happen. Baumann was frightened, exhausted, beaten down and humiliated, but also strong. A hard soul lived in that old grey man.

Of course the Russian-German treaty explained it all. From the beginning, Von Polanyi's intelligence unit in the German Foreign Office had fathered Baumann's approach to the Soviet *apparat:* a communications channel had been opened up. Baumann's production figures were probably being traded for information coming back the other way, but moving along an entirely different path. At this very moment, he speculated, some Russian in Leningrad was being told to have no further contact with a certain Finnish ferry captain. That's how things were done, agreements made and kept. *We will keep you informed,* they'd said to somebody in 1937, *of our bomber production.* Secretly, by intelligence means, because neither our countries, nor our leaders, Hitler and Stalin, may be seen by the world to accept each other's existence. We are officially mortal enemies, yet it is to our mutual advantage to have certain understandings. Thus, Szara realized, Baumann's numbers were confirmed by the British because he was *not* being run by Nazi counter-intelligence, Schellenberg's office in the Referat VI C.

In another month the pact between Hitler and Stalin would be revealed to the world. Thus they'd shut down the Baumann operation because they no longer needed to communicate in this way. Henceforth such figures would travel by telex from foreign office to foreign office. Meanwhile somebody – *not* Von Polanyi, based on what Frau Baumann had said to Odile – had decided to throw Baumann into Sachsenhausen. Their way of saying thank you, evidently.

No, Szara told himself, you may not think that way. Germans do things for reasons. It was more likely their way of saying *now get out of Germany, Jew.* And here's a little taste of something unpleasant to help you remember to keep your mouth shut.

Maybe, Szara told himself. Just maybe. Something in Goldman's statement about Sachsenhausen had been hopeful, as though Baumann's extrication could be achieved and he knew it.

Oh, but that clever little bastard was smart! He'd sniffed all around the truth. Which was that the 'friends' and the 'diplomats' were one and

the same and that 'you' meant Szara and nobody else. What had
Baumann actually intended? That would bear thinking about, but
there was a nugget to be mined somewhere in those formal words,
something he wanted to give to Szara – a present to his case officer.
Why? Because he knew Szara, and, despite endless orders and urgent
requests for more information – requests unheeded, orders ignored –
Szara had not abandoned him or threatened him. Now he said: Please
help me, and I'll help you.

Meanwhile that other one, with the glasses, who was he?

Oh Russia, he said to himself, what strange humans you grow.

And now he had to follow Goldman's orders, given a month ago in
Brussels and repeated as he left Arion: *write something*. Now he had to
go home and do it. Of all the things in the world he didn't want to do,
that was near the top of the list. *In these turbulent days, people of good
will ought to be asking themselves certain difficult questions. Close the
window, shut out the noise of the crowds marching in the streets, and face
the issue squarely and without emotion: What can be the future of
socialism in today's world? How shall it best survive?*

At somebody's intellectual soirée he'd met an editor. What was his
name? A proud little rooster crowing on his own little dunghill of a
magazine. 'Come and see me, André Aronovich,' the man had crooned.
Now aren't you, Szara thought at the time, just the most clever fellow to
address me by my patronymic, you oily little bore. Ah, but look here,
here's fate with a swift kick in the backside – the rooster was going to
get what he wanted, a fat scoop of corn tossed into his yard. Would
Szara perhaps get paid? Hah! A meagre lunch maybe – 'I always order
the daily special here, André Aronovich, I recommend it.' Do you? Well,
myself I think I'll have the peacock in gold sauce.

He'd better get it done, he thought. He'd collected his portmanteau
from the Hungarian in the seventh arrondissement and expected to get
his travel orders any day. Where, he wondered, would they send him.

He woke as in a dream. For a moment he wasn't anywhere at all, adrift
in no place he knew but, as in a dream, it did not matter, there was
nothing to fear. He lay on top of his raincoat in the loft of a barn, the
smell of the hay beneath him sweet, freshly cut. High above him was a
barn roof, silvery and soft with age, early light just barely glowing
between the cracks where the boards had separated. Sitting up, he faced
a broad, open window – it was what they used, standing on their
wagons, to pitch forkfuls of hay into the loft. He crawled across the hay
in order to look out and saw that it was just after dawn: a shaft of
sunlight lay across a cut field, strands of ground mist rising through it.

Beside a narrow road of packed, sandy soil stood a great oak; its leaves rattled softly in the little wind that always comes with first light.

There were three men on the road. Men from a dream. They wore black shoes and black leggings and long black coats and black hats with broad brims. They were bearded, and long sidelocks curled from beneath the brims of their hats. Hasidim, he thought, on their way to *shul*. Their faces were white as chalk. One of them turned and looked at him, a look without curiosity or challenge; it took note of a man watching from the window of a barn, then it turned away, back towards the road. They made no sound as they walked, and then, like black and white ghosts in a dream, they vanished.

Poland.

His mind came to life very slowly. The previous day, when he tried to recall it, had broken into fragments, blurred images of travel. He had flown to an airfield near Warsaw on an eight-seater plane that bumped across a ridged tar surface after it landed. There was deep forest on three sides of the airfield, and he'd wondered if this were the main field that served the city. All day he'd never really known exactly where he was. There was a taxi. A train. No, two trains. A ride in a wagon on a hot day. A dog who growled deep in his throat yet wagged his tail at the same moment. A pedlar met on a road. The slow apprehension that he would not arrive anywhere in particular any time soon, that he was where he was, that travellers slept in barns. An old woman, a kerchief tied around her seamed face, said that he was welcome. Then there was a mouse, a moon, the slow, swimming dreams of sleep in an unknown place.

He leaned against the worn barnwood and watched the day break. There was still a quarter moon, white against the blue-black morning sky. A band of storm clouds moved east, edges stained red by the rising sun. Here and there light broke through the clouds, a pine wood appeared on the horizon, a rye field took colour, a sharp green, as he watched. This ghostly, shifting light, wet smell of morning earth, crows calling as they flew low along the curve of a field, he could remember. He had once lived in this part of the world, a long time ago, and sometimes they had ventured beyond the winding streets of Kishinev and he'd witnessed such mornings, when he was a little boy who woke up long before anyone else did in order not to miss any of the miracles. He could see himself, kneeling on a bed in front of a window, a blanket around his shoulders. He could see the sun climbing a hill on a morning in late summer.

'Hey up there, *pan*, are you asleep still?'

He leaned out the window and peered down to find the old woman looking up at him from the yard. She stood, with the aid of a stick, like a small, sturdy pyramid, wearing sweaters and jackets on top, broad skirts below. Her dogs, a big brown one and a little black and white one, stood by her side and stared up at him as well. 'Come along to the house,' she called up to him. 'I'll give you coffee.'

She hobbled away without waiting for an answer, the dogs romping around her, sniffing the bushes, lifting a leg, pressing the earth with their extended forepaws to have a morning stretch.

On the way to the farmhouse, Szara saw that she'd left two large, wooden buckets by the well and, like any tramp worth his salt, he knew she wanted him to bring the water in. First he took off his Paris shirt, worked the squeaky pump handle, and splashed himself with surges of icy water from the spout. He shivered in the early morning air and rubbed himself dry with the shirt, then put it back on and combed his wet hair back with his fingers. When he rinsed his mouth, the cold water made his teeth ache. Next he filled the buckets and staggered into the kitchen, absolutely determined not to slop water on the floor. The farmhouse was an old drystone building with a low ceiling, a tile stove with a large crucifix on the wall above it, and glass windows. The smell of the coffee was strong in the close air of the kitchen.

She brought it to him in a china cup – the saucer was apparently no more – that must have been a hundred years old. 'Thank you, *matrushka*,' he said, taking a sip. 'The coffee is very good.'

'I always have it. Every morning,' she said proudly. 'Except when the wars come. Then you can't get it for any money. Not around here, you can't.'

'Where am I, exactly?'

'Where are you? Why you're in Podalki, that's where!' She cackled and shook her head at such a question, made her way to the stove, and, using her skirt as a potholder, withdrew a pan of bread from the oven. This she placed by the side of his coffee, went off to the pantry and returned with a bowl of white cheese covered with a cloth. She put a knife and a plate before him, then stood by the stove while he ate. He wanted to ask her to sit with him, but he knew that such a request would offend her sense of propriety. She would eat when he was done.

He sawed off the heel of the loaf and covered the steaming slab with white cheese. 'Oh, this is very good,' he said.

'You must be on your way to the city,' she said. 'To Czestochowa.'

'I'm on my way to Lvov.'

'Lvov!'

'That's right.'

'Blessed Mother, Lvov. You're a long way from there,' she said with awe at the distance he contemplated travelling. 'That's a Ukrainian place, you know,' she told him.

'Yes. I know.'

'They say it's in Poland, but I don't think so, myself. You'll want to watch your money, over there.'

'Have you been there, *matrushka?*'

'Me?' She laughed at the idea. 'No,' she said. 'People from Podalki don't go there.'

When he was done with the breakfast he put a few zlotys under the rim of the plate. Back in the barn loft he spread his map out on the hay, but the village of Podalki wasn't to be found. One of the Tass men from Paris who'd been on the plane with him had a much more detailed map, but they'd become separated at the railway station in Warsaw. He found Czestochowa easily enough. If that was the next town of any size, he'd crossed the river Warta the day before. The man driving the cart had called it something else, and it was just a wide expanse of water, sluggish and shallow at summer's end. The man in the wagon had driven up a tiny path, and Szara was taken across the river by an old Jewish ferryman with a patch over one eye. He had a wooden raft and pulley system, hauling on a rope until they were on the other bank. The ferryman told him that the little road would, if he were patient and lucky, eventually take him to Cracow. 'From there you can go anywhere at all, if you want,' the man had said, pocketing the tiny fare with a shrug that questioned why anybody bothered going anywhere at all.

Szara folded the map, returned it to his satchel, put his soft felt hat on, and slung his jacket over his shoulder. When he came out of the barn, the old lady and her dogs were taking the cow out to pasture. He thanked her again, she wished him a safe journey, made the sign of the cross to protect him on his way, and he headed down the narrow, sandy road in the direction of Podalki village.

Twenty minutes later he was there. It wasn't much. A few log houses scattered on both sides of a dirt street, a man with shaven head and cavalry moustache, sleeves rolled up on the hot day, thumbs hooked in braces as he lounged in the doorway of what Szara took to be the Podalki store. There was a tiny, Jewish ghetto on the other side of the village: women in wigs, a Hasid, yarmulke pinned to his hair, chopping wood in the little yard of his house, pale children with curly sidelocks who watched him, cleverly, without actually staring, as he went past. Then Podalki was no more, and he was alone again on the broad Polish steppe, amid endless fields that ran to the forest on the horizon.

He walked and walked, the sun grew hotter, the valise heavier; he started to sweat. The fields on either side of the narrow road were alive;

insects buzzed and whirred, the black, moist earth had a certain smell to it, rotting and growing, sweet and rank at once. Sometimes a clump of white birch stood by a small stream, the delicate leaves flickering in the slightest breeze. From this perspective, his life in the city looked frantic and absurd. The intensity of his work, the grating, fretful anxiety of it, seemed utterly artificial. How strange to care so deeply about such nonsense – codes and papers, packages exchanged in cinemas, who had lunch with who at a hotel in Berlin. It was madness. They spun around like the blindfolded It in a children's game. In early August someone had broken into a dry cleaning plant on the outskirts of Paris and stolen the uniforms of the Polish military attaché's staff. A great hubbub ensued: meetings, wireless messages, questions without answers, answers without questions.

But that was nothing compared to what came next: on the twenty-third of August the Hitler/Stalin pact was announced. Oh and hadn't there been just every sort of hell to pay! Weeping and moaning and gnashing of teeth. It had been just as Goldman had predicted – the idealists wringing their hands and beating their breasts. Some people were quite literally stunned – walked about the streets of Paris and were heard to make doleful and solemn declarations: 'I have determined to break with the party.' There were even suicides. What, Szara wondered, had they thought they were playing at? Philosophy?

He heard the creak of cart wheels behind him and the clop of hooves. A wagon driven by a young boy overtook him, a vast load of hay mounded in the bed. Szara moved to one side of the road to let it pass, stepping between furrows at the edge of a field. 'Good morning, *pan*,' said the boy as the cart drew up beside him. Szara returned the greeting. The smell of the old horse was strong in the heat of the day. 'A pretty morning we have,' said the boy. 'Would you care to ride a way?' The wagon didn't actually stop, but Szara hauled himself up and perched on the wooden rim next to the driver. The horse slowed perceptibly. 'Ah, Gniady, now you mustn't be like that,' said the boy, clucking at the horse and flapping the reins. They rode for a time in silence; then a tiny track, two ruts wide, opened up between fields and the boy chucked the left rein to turn the horse. Szara thanked the boy and dismounted. Walking once again, he thought. *Now there's the job for me.* Sometimes he saw men and women at work in the fields. The harvest was only just beginning, but now and then the flash of a scythe would catch the light. The women worked with skirts tucked up, their bare legs white against the wheat or rye stalks.

Somebody, Szara realized, was going to be very annoyed with him for dropping out of sight like this, but that was just too bad. Let them go to hell and rage at the devils. He was tired of their threats – he had rejoined reality, as it happened, and they would have to get along in their dream world as best they could. Above him, the sky spread out to heaven, the morning blue growing pale and hazy as the day wore on. Well to the south there rose a low, dark shape, a distant mountain range, with white cloud building slowly above it, a thunderstorm for the humid evening to come. *This* was what existed: the steppe, the enormous sky, the wheat, the packed sand of the little road. For a moment he was part of it, simply a fact of nature, no more, no less. He didn't even know what day it was. He'd left Paris on the thirtieth of August, though he'd thought of it as the twenty-ninth, since it was three o'clock in the morning, still 'last night', when he'd taken a taxi to Le Bourget airport. The long day of meandering through eastern Poland had been, in fact, the thirtieth. That made it the very end of summertime.

Summer would actually continue, he realized, for a long while yet, well into September, when the harvest would occupy almost everybody in the countryside, when people would sleep in the fields in order to start work at first light. At night they'd sit around and talk in low voices, they'd even have a small fire once a field was cleared, and couples would go off into the shadows to make love. Still, for him, the summer had just about run its course. He had a schoolboy's sense of time, and the end of August was the end of liberty, just as it had been in childhood, just as, he supposed, it always would be. Strange, he thought, that he found himself once again free as the summer ended. 31 August 1939 – that was the official date. He reckoned once again and made sure. Yes, that was it. By tomorrow he'd likely be 'himself' again, the official himself, the journalist André Szara, riding on trains, writing things down, doing what everyone expected of him.

But for the moment he was a lone traveller on the tiny road to Czestochowa, enjoying a perfect freedom on the last day of summer.

He reached Czestochowa by late afternoon, thanks to a ride in an ancient lorry delivering cucumbers to the markets in the city. A tram ride took him to the railway station and he bought a ticket to Cracow, where he could get another train to Lvov. 'We call it the midnight train to Lvov,' said the dignified ticket seller. 'We also say, however, that dawn in the city of Lvov is very beautiful.' Szara smiled with appreciation at the characteristically Polish bite of the description. The cities were a hundred and eighty miles apart. That meant the train from Cracow was not expected to leave on time, that the locomotive was very slow, or both.

At the restaurant across the street from the station he prepared for the journey, eating cold beet soup, rye bread with sweet butter, a piece of boiled beef accompanied by fresh red horseradish that made tears inevitable, and several glasses of tea. He was sore from sleeping in a hayloft and from miles of walking and was covered with a fine, powdery dust from the road, but the dinner was curative, and he dozed in the first-class compartment until the 6:40 for Cracow chugged away from the station a little after eight. In the gathering dusk of the Czestochowa countryside he saw a lightning storm, great, white bolts of it, three and four in a row, on the southern horizon. Two hours later they were in Cracow.

He had long ago been a student at the university, but he elected to remain at the station until the 'midnight train to Lvov' actually departed. The ticket seller in Czestochowa had told him the truth – the train was very late leaving; some of the people who joined him in the compartment arrived after two in the morning. He watched the night streets of Cracow go by under flaring gas lamps, the Zydowski cemetery, the railway bridge across the Vistula, and then he dozed once more until the muttered comments of his fellow travellers woke him up. The train was barely moving on what seemed to be a branch track, people in the compartment were trying to peer out the window, and then, suddenly, they lurched to a halt. Such a stop was apparently quite unusual. One or two groans of fury were heard, others attempted to solve the mystery by lowering the window and squinting into the darkness outside. A man in a railway uniform came down the track carrying a lantern, passengers called out to him, asked him what the problem was, but he ignored them all. The compartment was dark; Szara lit a cigarette, sat back against the worn plush fabric of the seat, and set himself to wait. Other passengers followed his example. Newspaper crackled as a sandwich was unwrapped, a young couple spoke confidentially in low voices. From the third-class car, a violin started up. Some minutes later a troop train went past, moving very slowly. Soldiers could be seen hanging out the windows and standing packed in the aisles, some dangling their feet from open doorways. Szara could see the glow of their cigarettes. 'They go north,' said the young woman across from him. 'Away from the border. Perhaps the crisis with Hitler has been settled.'

A man sitting next to her lit a match and pointed to the front page of the evening newspaper. 'Shooting in Danzig,' he said. 'You see? I would have to say they're headed up there.'

The conductor came down the passageway, opened the door of the compartment, and said, 'Ladies and gentlemen, I fear I must ask you to get off the train. Please.'

This statement was greeted with general indignation. 'Yes, yes,' the conductor sympathized, 'but what's to be done? I'd tell you the problem if I knew, I'm sure it will all be fixed quickly.' He had a drooping moustache and rather doleful eyes that gave him the look of a spaniel. He went off to the next compartment and the young man called after him, 'Do we take our baggage?'

'Why no,' the conductor said. 'Or maybe yes. I'm not sure. I leave it up to you, good ladies and gentlemen.'

Szara took his valise down from the rack above the window and helped the other passengers with their luggage. 'I tell you . . .' the man with the newspaper said forcefully, but then seemed not to have anything to tell. Slowly the train emptied and the passengers half-slipped, half-jumped, down a grassy embankment and stood about on the edge of a field of weeds. 'Now what?' Szara said to the man with the newspaper.

'I'm sure I don't know,' he said. Then he bowed slightly and extended his hand. 'Goletzky,' he said. 'I'm in soap.'

'Szara. Journalist.'

'Ah, well. Here's someone who'll know what's going on.'

'Not at all,' Szara said.

'Do you write for the Cracow papers?'

'No,' Szara said. 'I've been in Paris the last few months.'

'You're a lucky fellow, then. I count myself fortunate if I get to Warsaw once a year. Mostly I call on the southern provinces – perfumed soaps for the gentry, the old-fashioned yellow bar for the farmer, Dr Grudzen's special formula for young ladies. There isn't much I don't offer.'

'What do you suppose they're going to do with us?' Szara asked. He glanced at his watch. 'It's well after four.' He looked to the east and saw a faint glow on the horizon, then he yawned.

Up the track, the engine released a long hiss of steam, then the slow march of pistons could be heard as it moved off. A cry went up from the assembled passengers: 'Oh no! It's leaving!' Some people started to climb aboard the coaches; then everybody realized that the train was standing still, only the locomotive was moving away.

'Well, that's very nice I must say,' said Goletzky angrily. 'Now they've uncoupled the engine and left us sitting here in the darkness between Cracow and Lord only knows where!'

The passengers began to realize that nothing was going to happen very quickly, and sat gloomily on their suitcases to wait for someone in the railway system to remember them. Fifteen minutes later their locomotive reappeared – they had the conductor's word that it was theirs – now pulling the troop train in the opposite direction. The engineer waved his cap: a gesture taken variously as cruelty, compassion, or an arcane signal known only to railwaymen; and the soldiers were singing, their voices strong in the early morning air. The troop train's original locomotive appeared last, ignominiously towed backwards. 'So,' Goletzky commented, 'it's army manoeuvres that have got us stranded.'

Szara didn't like what he saw, but he didn't know why. He wrote the feeling off to the sort of pointless irritation that comes with fatigue. Some of the passengers returned to their seats in the coaches. The conductor made no very great attempt to stop them. 'Really, ladies and gentlemen,' he said sadly, shaking his head at the anarchy of it all. Others remained outdoors, trying to make a holiday of it. Somebody got a fire going and the garlicky aroma of roasting sausage filled the air. Another group gathered about the violin player. Still others could be seen wandering into the fields, some in search of privacy, others taking the opportunity to observe the countryside.

The drone of an aeroplane caught everyone's attention. It was flying somewhere above them in the darkness, circling perhaps. Then the noise of its engine grew suddenly stronger, a drawn-out mechanical whine that climbed the musical scale and grew louder in the same instant. 'It's going to crash,' said the young woman from Szara's compartment, her voice shrill with fear, her face lifted anxiously towards the sky. She crossed herself as her lips moved. Goletzky and Szara both stood at the same instant, as though drawn to their feet by an invisible force. Somebody screamed. Goletzky said, 'Shall we run?' Then it was too late to run – the noise swelled to an overwhelming shriek that froze the passengers in place. The plane materialized from the darkness for only a fraction of a second. Szara saw swastikas on its wings. Something made him flinch away, then the bomb exploded.

The blast wave took him off his feet – for an instant he was adrift in the air – then threw him into the embankment. He felt the force of impact shift the teeth and bones on one side of his face and his hearing stopped, replaced by a hissing silence. When he opened his eyes they didn't work: the right half of the world was higher than the left, as though a photograph had been cut in two and pasted back together with the halves misaligned. This terrified him, and he was frantically blinking his eyes, trying to make his vision come right, when bits and pieces of things began to rain down on him and he instinctively protected his head with his forearm. Then something moved inside his face and his vision cleared. He forced himself to sit up, searching his clothing, frightened of what he might find but compelled to look. He found only dirt, bits of fabric and leaves, and a stain on the lapel of his jacket. Nearby, Goletzky sat with his head in his hands. At the bottom of the embankment the conductor lay still, face down in the earth. His feet were bare and a red line ran down one heel. Szara looked for the young woman but could not see her anywhere. An older woman he did not recognize – hair wild, tears streaming from her eyes, dress half blown away – was screaming at the sky. From the way her mouth worked and the sickened anger on her face Szara could tell she was screaming, but he could not hear any sound at all.

He was taken first to a hospital in the city of Tarnów. There he sat in a corridor while the nursing sisters cared for the injured. By then, most of his hearing had returned. By then his valise had miraculously reappeared, brought down the corridor by a soldier asking if anyone knew who it belonged to. By then he had heard that Germany had attacked Poland sometime after four in the morning. Polish soldiers, the Germans claimed, had overrun a German radio station at Gleiwitz, killed some German soldiers, and broadcast an inflammatory statement. This was no more than a classic staged provocation, he believed. And now he knew what had become of the Polish uniforms stolen in Paris. When his turn finally came, he was seen by a doctor, told he'd possibly had a concussion. If he became nauseated he was to seek medical assistance. Otherwise, he was free to continue his journey.

But that was not quite the truth. Outside the examining room a young lieutenant politely informed him that certain authorities in Nowy Sacz wished to speak with him. Was he under arrest? Not at all, the lieutenant said. It was only that someone at the hospital had notified the army staff that a Soviet journalist had been injured in the attack on the Cracow-Lvov line. Now a certain Colonel Vyborg earnestly wished to discuss certain matters with him at the Nowy Sacz headquarters. The young lieutenant had the honour of escorting him there. Szara knew it was pointless to resist, and the lieutenant led him to an aged but functional Czechoslovakian motor car and had him safely in Nowy Sacz an hour later.

Lieutenant Colonel Anton Vyborg, despite his Scandinavian surname, seemed a vestige of the old-fashioned Polish nobility. Szara fancied the name might date from the medieval wars between Poland and Sweden, when, as in all wars, families found themselves living on the wrong side of the lines. Whatever the story, there was something of the Baltic knight in Vyborg; he was tall and lean and thin-lipped, in his forties Szara thought, with webbed lines at the corners of his narrow eyes and pale hair cut short and stiff in the cavalry officer style. Like a cavalry officer, he wore high boots of supple leather and jodhpur-cut uniform trousers. Unlike a cavalry officer, however, his uniform jacket was hung over the back of his chair, his collar was unbuttoned and tie pulled down, and his sleeves were folded back. When Szara entered his office he was smoking a cigar, and a large metal ashtray held the stubs of many others. He had a handshake like steel, and looked hard at Szara with very cold blue eyes when they introduced themselves. Then, having made a rapid and intuitive judgment of some kind, he grew courtly, sent his orderly scurrying for coffee and rolls, and presented what was likely, Szara thought, the genial half of a sharply two-sided personality.

While he waited for his orderly to return, Colonel Vyborg smoked contentedly and stared into space, apparently at peace with the world. He was alone in this, however, since officers were rushing past the open door with armloads of files, telephones were jangling continuously, and the sense of the place was frantic motion, just barely below the level of panic. At one point, a young officer stuck his head in the door and said, 'Obidza' – which could only have been the name of a small town. Colonel Vyborg made the merest gesture of acknowledgment, a polite, almost ironic inclination of the head, and the man wheeled and trotted off. Szara heard him somewhere down the hall, 'Obidza,' telling some-one else the news. Vyborg blew a long stream of cigar smoke into the air, rose abruptly, walked to the window, and stared down into the courtyard. The office – obviously temporary; the sign on the door read Tax Assessor – was in the Nowy Sacz city hall, an imposing monstrosity dating from the days of the Austro-Hungarian Empire, when Galicia had been a province of Austria. Vyborg stared onto the courtyard for a long time. 'Now we burn files,' he said.

He looked meaningfully at Szara and cocked an eyebrow, but did not seem to want to hear what a journalist might think about such events. He settled himself back at the desk and said, 'I think perhaps we ought to start our discussion without the coffee – nothing is really going to go smoothly today, and that includes my orderly's trip to the bakery. Do you mind?'

'Not at all,' Szara said.

'Now a Soviet journalist, if he's survived the last two years, can be no fool. You certainly know who you're talking to.'

Szara had assumed from the beginning that Vyborg was the director or the deputy of a military intelligence unit. 'An, ah, information bureau,' he said.

'Yes. That's right. You're legally a neutral, Mr Szara, since last week, 23 August. As a Soviet citizen you are officially neither a friend nor an enemy of Poland, so I'm going to offer you an accommodation of mutual interest. For our part, we'd like to know what you're doing here. Your papers are all in order, we assume you've been assigned a specific task. We'd like to know what's of such interest that *Pravda* would send you here a week after the USSR has signed a treaty that's going to turn out to be this country's obituary. In return, I'll make certain that you are provided with transportation out of this region – we're forty miles north of the border, by the way – and will in general make sure you get to Lvov, if that's where you want to go.

'That's the offer. You can certainly refuse to accept it. The Germans' promise of non-aggression no doubt extends to you personally, and you may feel you want to take them up on it. If so, you needn't move very far, you may stay right herein Nowy Sacz – in two or three days they'll come to you. Or even sooner. On the other hand, you may want to leave right away. In that case I'll have my aide drive you to the railway station – or as close to it as the crowd will permit. Thousands of people are milling around down there, trying to get out any way at all, and the trains don't seem to be running. Still, you can take your chances if you like. So, how shall it be?'

'Seems a fair offer,' Szara said.

'You'll tell me, then, the nature of your assignment in Lvov.'

'They want to know something of the daily life of national minorities in eastern Poland: Byelorussians, Ukrainians, Jews, Lithuanians.'

'*Persecuted* national minorities, you mean. In a former Russian province.'

'The assignment, Colonel Vyborg, is not that. I'd like to point out that I was asked to make this journey some weeks before any pact was announced between the USSR and Germany. They did not, in other words, send me into the middle of a war to write a story about the lives of tailors and farmers. I don't really know what my editors had in mind – they send me somewhere and I do what I'm told to do. Maybe they didn't have very much in mind at all.'

'Jolly anarchic old Russia – the right hand never knows what the left hand is doing. Something like that?'

'What can't be said about Russia? Everything is true, eventually.'

'You are, in fact, a Pole.'

'A Jewish family from Poland, in Russia since I was a teenager.'

'Then I'll revise my statement – a typical Pole.'

'Some would say not.'

'Some certainly would. But others would answer them by saying horseshit.'

Vyborg drummed his fingers on the table. A studious-looking man in an exceptionally rumpled uniform, a sort of shambling professor with spectacles, appeared in the doorway and stood there hesitantly, eventually clearing his throat. 'Anton, excuse me, but they are in Obidza.'

'So I'm told,' Vyborg said.

'Well then, shall we . . .'

'Pack up our cipher machines and go? Yes, I suppose. I've asked Olensko to organize it. Tell him to begin, will you?'

'With you commanding?'

'I'll find you in Cracow. First I'm going to take our Russian war correspondent to see the front.'

'Russian war correspondent?' The man was amazed. 'So soon?' He stared at Szara without comprehension. 'Will they print a dispatch from this war?' the man finally asked, disbelief in his voice. 'Fifty German divisions attack Poland? My, my, no. Perhaps "Some German units bravely defend their borders thirty miles inside Poland." '

Vyborg laughed bitterly by way of agreement. 'Who knows,' he said with resignation, 'it may give old Kinto something to think about.' The word he used for Stalin meant a kind of singing bandit, a merry figure from Georgian folklore. Szara grinned at the remark. 'You see?' Vyborg said triumphantly. 'He's on our side.'

Speeding southwest in an open military command car, Szara and Vyborg sat grimly in the back seat. Vyborg's driver was a big sergeant with close-cropped hair, a lion tamer's moustache, and a veinous, lumpy nose that was almost purple. He swore under his breath without pause, swinging the big car around obstacles, bouncing through the fields when necessary, hewing a path through the wheat stalks. The road was a nightmare. Refugees walked north, their possessions on their backs or in little carts. Some drove their farm animals before them or led them on a rope halter. Four people carried a sick man in a bed. Meanwhile, Polish military units – marching infantry, horse-drawn artillery and ammunition wagons – attempted to move south. The car passed a burnt-out wagon with two horses dead in the traces. 'Stukas,' Vyborg said coldly. 'A terror weapon.'

'I know,' Szara said.

They were climbing steadily on the rutted dirt road that worked its way through the hills that led to the Polish side of the Carpathian mountains. The air was cooler, the rolling countryside softening as the daylight began to fade. Szara's head ached horribly; the bouncing of the hard-sprung car was torture. He'd not survived the bomb attack as well as he'd thought. His mouth tasted like brass, and he felt as though a path of tiny pins had been pushed into the skin along one side of his face. The car turned west, into a sunset coloured blood red by smoke and haze, the sort of sky seen in late summer when the forests burn. Their road followed the path of a river, the Dunajec, according to Colonel Vyborg.

'We still hold the west bank,' he said. 'Or we did when we left Nowy Sacz.' He produced a large pocket watch and gazed at it. 'Perhaps no longer,' he mused. 'We haven't much hope militarily. Perhaps diplomatically something can be done, even now. We face a million and a half Germans, and tanks and planes, with perhaps two thirds that number – and we haven't any air force to speak of. Brave pilots, yes, but the planes . . .'

'Can you hold?'

'We must. The French and the British may come to help – they've at least declared war. Time is what we need. And, whatever else happens, the story must be told. When people are ground into the dirt that is always what they say, isn't it, that "the story must be told".'

'I'll do what I can,' Szara said softly. In the people on the road he saw sometimes sorrow, or fear, or anger, but mainly they seemed to him numb, lost, and in their eyes he could find only perplexity and exhaustion beyond feeling. He had no immunity to these refugees. His eyes held each one as the car wove among them, then went on to the next, and then the next.

'An effort,' Vyborg said. 'It's all I ask of you.' He was silent while they passed a priest giving last rites by the side of the road. 'More likely, though, it will wind up with my getting us both killed. And for what. Russia will not be sorry to see the last of Poland.'

'Was a treaty possible?'

'Not really. As one of our leaders put it, "With the Germans we risk losing our freedom, with the Russians we shall lose our soul." Still, it may be in the Politburo's interest for attention to be called to what the Germans are doing. It's not impossible.'

When Szara heard the drone of the aeroplane he clenched his fists. Vyborg's eyes searched the sky and he leaned forward and put a hand on the sergeant's shoulder. 'Slow down. Sergeant,' he said. 'If he sees a staff car he'll attack.'

The Stuka came out of a sun-broken cloud, and Szara's heart began to beat hard as he heard the accelerating whine of the engine. 'Stop,' Vyborg said. The driver jammed on the brakes. They leaped out of the car and ran for the ditch by the side of the road. Szara pressed himself into the earth as the plane closed. *God save me*, he thought. The noise of the dive swelled to a scream, he heard horses neighing with terror, shouts, screams, chattering machine guns, a whipcrack above his head, then the ground rocked as the bomb went off. When the sound of the engine had disappeared into the distance he sat up. There were red ridges across his palms where his fingernails had pressed into his hands. Vyborg swore. He was picking broken cigars out of his breast pocket. On the road a woman had gone mad; people were running after her into a field, yelling for her to stop.

At dusk the column of refugees thinned, then stopped altogether. The land was deserted. They sped through a village. Some of the houses had been burned; others stood with doors wide open. A dog barked at them frantically as they drove by. Szara opened the valise, took out a small notebook, and began to write things down. The driver swung around a bomb crater and cursed it loudly. 'Quiet!' Vyborg commanded. Szara appreciated the gesture, but it didn't really matter. *Germans bomb civilians*, he wrote. No, they would not publish that. *Poles suffer after government refuses compromise.* He scribbled over the words quickly, afraid Vyborg could see what he was writing. *A new kind of war in Poland as Luftwaffe attacks non-military targets.*

No.

It was hopeless. The futility of the journey made him sad. Typical, somehow. Killed on Polish soil while making a useless gesture – an obituary that told the truth. Suddenly he knew exactly who Vyborg was: a Polish character from the pages of Balzac. Szara stole a glance at him. He'd lit the broken stump of a cigar and was pretending to be lost in thought as his writer wrote and they travelled to the lines. Yes, the defiant romantic. Pure courage, cold to the dangers of whatever passion took the present moment for its own. Such men – and the women were worse – had destroyed Poland often enough. And saved it. Either could be true, depending on the year you chose. And the great secret, Szara thought, and Balzac had never tumbled to it, was that the Polish Jews were just as bad – in their faith they were unmovable, no matter what form faith took: Hasidism, Zionism, communism. They were all on fire, and that they shared with the Poles, that they had in common.

And you?

Not me, Szara answered himself.

The driver braked suddenly and squeezed to the right on the narrow road. A convoy of three horse-drawn ambulances was making slow progress in the other direction. 'Getting close to it now,' Vyborg said.

The car made its way up a wooded mountainside. Szara could smell the sap, the aroma sharp and sweet after the long heat of the day. The night air was cooling quickly, a wall of dark pines rose on either side of the road. They had very little light to drive by, the headlamps of the car had been taped down to slits. The sergeant squinted into the darkness and braked hard when, with a sudden twist or turn, the road simply disappeared. Nonetheless, their progress was observed. On two occasions a Wehrmacht artillery observer spotted the light moving on a mountain road and tried his luck: a low, sighing buzz, a flash in the forest, a muted *crump* sound, then the muffled boom of the German gun bouncing among the hills. 'Missed,' Vyborg said tartly as the echo faded away.

Once again, he was awake at dawn.

Wrapped in a blanket on the dirt floor of a ruined shepherd's hut, kerosene splashed on his neck, wrists, and ankles against the lice. From the hut, an artillery observer's position in support of the battalion holding the west bank of the Dunajec, they could see a narrow valley between the water and the wooded hillside, a village broken and burned by German shelling, a section of the river, the wooden pilings that had served as stanchions for a blown bridge, and two concrete pillboxes built to defend the crossing. The observer was no more than eighteen, a junior lieutenant who'd been mobilized only three days earlier and still wore the suit he'd had on in an insurance office in Cracow. He'd managed to scrounge an officer's cap and wore officer's insignia on the shoulders of a very dirty white shirt – his jacket neatly folded in a corner of the little room.

The lieutenant was called Mierczek. Tall and fair and serious, he was somebody's good son, an altar boy no doubt, and now a soldier. A little overawed at first by the presence of a colonel and a war correspondent, he'd made them as comfortable as he could. A harassed infantry major had greeted them the night before and brought them up to the post. Szara had described him in his notebook as *1914 war vintage or earlier; ferocious, bright red face; complaining he hasn't sufficient ammunition, field guns, etc. He gave us bread and lard and tea and a piece of a dense kind of currant cake his wife had baked for him before he left for the front. He wears a complicated – Masonic? noble? – ring. Not happy to see us. 'There's no knowing what will happen. You will have to take your chances as best you can.' They are facing elements of the XVIII Corps of the Wehrmacht Fourteenth Army under Generaloberst List. Advances from northern Slovakia have already been made through the Jablunkov and Dukla passes. Some German units advanced more than fifteen miles the first day. We may, no matter what happens here, be cut off. A delightful prospect. Polish air force bombed on the ground in the first hours of the war, according to Colonel V.*

The tiny river valley in the Carpathians was exquisite at dawn. Streaky red sky, mist banks drifting against the mountainside, soft light on the slate blue river. But no birds. The birds had gone. Instead, a deep silence and the low, steady rumble of distant gunnery. Mierczek stared for a long time through a missing section of roof at the back of the hut, searching the sky for clouds, praying silently for rain. But Hitler's timing had been perfect: the German harvest was in – the population would not suffer deprivation because farmhands were suddenly called to serve in the army. The infamous Polish roads, which would turn to mud of a diabolical consistency once the autumn rains began, were dry; and the rivers, the nation's only natural defence positions, were low and sluggish.

The German attack started at 05:00. Szara and Vyborg both looked at their watches as the first shells landed in the village. Mierczek cranked his field telephone and made contact with the Polish counter-battery at the edge of the forest above the town. Gazing through binoculars, he located the muzzle flashes at a point in the wood on the other side of the river, then consulted a hand-drawn map with coordinates pencilled on it. 'Good morning, Captain, sir,' Mierczek said stiffly into the telephone. Szara heard the earpiece crackle with static as a voice shouted into it. 'They're in L for Lodz twenty-four, sir,' Mierczek responded. He continued to stare through the binoculars, then consulted his map again. 'To the southeast of the grid, I think. Sir.' Vyborg passed his binoculars to Szara. Now he could see the village in sharp focus. A fountain of dirt rose into the air. Then a housefront fell into the little street, a cloud of dust and smoke rolling out behind it. A few small flames danced along a broken beam. He swung the binoculars to the river, then to the German side. But he could see very little happening there.

The Polish field guns began to fire, the explosions leaving dirty brown smoke drifting through the treetops. Now Szara saw an orange tongue of flame in the German-occupied woods. 'Two points left,' Mierczek said into the phone. They waited but nothing happened. Mierczek repeated his instructions. Szara could hear an angry voice amid the static. Mierczek held the phone against his chest for a moment and said confidentially, 'Some of our shells do not explode.' As the Polish guns resumed firing, Szara saw the orange flash again, but this time in a different place. Mierczek reported this. Two men in dark shirts with their sleeves rolled up went running from house to house in the village. They disappeared for a time, then emerged from a back door with a grey shape on a stretcher.

It was getting harder and harder for Szara to see anything; the pall of smoke thickened until solid objects faded into shapes and shadows. The flashes from the German artillery seemed to change position – there simply, he decided, couldn't be that many of them in the forest. Then a

Polish machine gun opened up from one of the pillboxes. Szara moved the binoculars towards the far bank of the river and saw hundreds of grey shapes, men running low, come out of the woods and dive flat on the ground. Polish rifle fire began to rattle from the houses in the village. A Polish ammunition dump was hit by a shell; the sound of the blast was ragged, a huge billowing cloud swirled upward, brilliant white stars trailing smoke arched over the river. Mierczek never stopped reporting, but the Polish counterfire seemed ineffective. Finally Colonel Vyborg spoke up. 'I believe. Lieutenant, you're trying to pinpoint a tank battery. It seems they've cut passages into the woods for the tanks to move around.'

'I think you're right, sir,' Mierczek said. In the midst of communicating this information his face tensed, but he carried his report through to the end. Then he unconsciously held his lower lip between his teeth and closed his eyes for an instant. 'The battery's been hit,' he said. Szara traversed the Polish woods but could see little through the smoke. Vyborg was staring out the low, uneven rectangle cut into the logs that served as a window. 'Give me the binoculars,' he said to Szara. He watched for a few seconds, then said, 'Pioneers,' and handed the binoculars back to Szara. German troops were in the river, shielded by the wooden stanchions where the bridge had stood, firing machine pistols at the portals of the pillboxes. The German Pioneer closest to the Polish side was shirtless, his body pink against the grey water. He swam suddenly from behind a stanchion with a rope held in his teeth. He took long, powerful strokes, then he let go of the rope, which floated away from him when he turned on his back and moved downstream with the current. Behind him, soldiers hauled themselves along the rope as far as the stanchion he'd just left. Some of them floated away also but were replaced by others.

'Hello? Captain? Hello?' Mierczek called into the phone. He cranked the handle and tried again. Szara could no longer hear the static. 'I think the line has been severed,' Mierczek said. He took a pair of electrician's pliers from a khaki bag, moved quickly to the low doorway, and disappeared. His job was, Szara knew, to follow the line until he found the break, repair it, and return. Szara saw a flash of the white shirt to his left, towards the battery, then it vanished into the dense smoke hanging amid the trees.

Szara swept his binoculars to the village. Most of the houses were now on fire. He saw a man run from one of them towards the woods, but the man fell on his knees and pitched forward after a few steps. Back on the river, the Pioneers had gained two more stanchions, and crowds of Germans were firing from the ones they held. The fire was returned.

White chip marks appeared magically in the old, tarred wood and sometimes a German trooper fell backwards, but he was immediately replaced by another man working his way along the line. A little way down the river there were flashes from the front rank of trees and, concentrating hard, Szara could see a long barrel silhouetted against the trunk of a shattered pine tree. He could just make out a curved bulk below the barrel. Yes, he thought, Vyborg had been right, it was a tank. A group of Polish infantrymen moved out of the forest below him, three of them carrying a machine gun and ammunition belts. They were trying to take up a position with a field of fire that would enfilade the stanchions. They ran bent over, rushing forward, one of them lost his helmet, but then all three made it to a depression in the sand between the edge of the water and a grove of alder trees. He could see the muzzle flash of the machine gun. Swept the binoculars to the stanchion and saw panic as several of the Germans fell away from the pilings. He felt a rush of elation, wanted to shout encouragement to the Polish machine gunners. But by the time he had again located their position, only one man was firing the gun and, as Szara watched, he let it go, covered his face with his hands, and slumped backwards. Slowly, he got himself turned over and began to crawl for the edge of the woods.

The field telephone came suddenly to life, static popping from the earpiece. Vyborg grabbed it and said, 'This is your observer position.' A voice could be heard yelling on the other end. Then Vyborg said, 'I don't know where he is. But he repaired the line and until he returns I will direct your fire. Is there an officer there?' Szara heard the negative. 'Very well. Corporal, you're in charge then. There are tanks in the woods to your north, at the edge of the forest. Can you fire a single round, short? Even in the river will work.' There was a reply, then Vyborg stared at the map Mierczek had left behind. 'Very well, Corporal,' he said. 'My advice is quadrant M28.' Szara moved the binoculars to see the impact of the ranging fire Vyborg had directed but was distracted by a group of Germans who had reached the west bank of the river and were running into the woods. 'They're across,' he said to Vyborg. Vyborg said, 'You're too short, come up a couple of degrees.'

Szara glanced at the doorway, wondering where Mierczek was, then realized he was not going to return. Szara could now see muzzle flashes from positions in and above the village as Polish troopers fired at the Germans who had established a flank attack in the woods. Five Panzer tanks moved out of the woods onto the sandy shore of the river, rumbling forward to the edge of the water and forming an angle that allowed them to fire directly into the Polish forces in the village. Szara's binoculars found the Polish machine gunner who'd tried to crawl away from the beach. He lay still in the sand. 'Corporal?' Vyborg said into the phone.

By late afternoon, they were near the town of Laskowa, not far from the river Tososina – uncertain where to go next, possibly cut off by Wehrmacht encirclement, but, narrowly, alive.

They had escaped from the scene of the German bridgehead over the Dunajec – a matter of minutes. Colonel Vyborg had taken the precaution of leaving the staff car, with the sergeant to guard it, up the road from the village. Had it been in the village itself they would now be captured or, more likely, dead. As Polish resistance had worn down, the German infantry had negotiated the river on wooden rafts, isolated the remaining Poles in a few positions at the far end of the village, and demanded surrender. The Poles, from the look of it, had refused. Vyborg had watched the beginning of the final attack through his binoculars, then, unwilling to witness the end, had carefully restored them to their leather case and deliberately pressed both snaps shut. Working their way through the hillside brush they had come under fire several times, German rounds singing away through the branches, but the forest itself had protected them from the German marksmen.

For a time, the road crossing the Carpathian foothills was clear, then they came upon the remnants of a retreating Polish regiment driven back from the border: exhausted soldiers, faces and uniforms grey with dust, wagonloads of bandaged, silent men, walking wounded leaning on their rifles or helped by friends, officers who gave no orders. It was, for Szara and evidently for Vyborg as well, worse than the battle at the Dunajec. There they had seen courage in the face of superior force; this was the defeat of a nation's army. A group of peasants harvesting wheat in a field stopped working, took their caps off, and watched silently as the troops walked past.

For a time, the sergeant drove slowly, at the pace of the regiment. Then, around noon, the forward units were engaged. According to a lieutenant questioned by Vyborg, a German corps that had fought its way across one of the Carpathian passes from northern Slovakia had now turned east – with extraordinary, unheard-of speed; a completely motorized force that moved in trucks and tanks – to close the pocket and cut off Polish forces attempting to retreat along the road. When the mortar and machine gun exchanges started up and the regiment began to organize its resistance, Vyborg directed the sergeant to take a tiny cart track – two wagon ruts in the dirt – that cut through a wheat field.

Thus they spent the day. 'We will get you to a telegraph or a telephone somewhere,' Vyborg said, his mind very much on Szara's presumptive dispatch to *Pravda*. But the tiny path wound its way among the hills, in no hurry to get anywhere, over numberless little streams that watered farm cattle, past the occasional peasant settlement deep in the Polish countryside, far, far away from telegraph wires or much of anything. Deeper and deeper, Szara thought, into the fourteenth century – a land of high-sided hay carts with enormous wooden wheels hewed by axes, farm women in aprons, the rooty smells of dry September earth flavoured with pig manure, sweet hay, and woodsmoke. 'See what we have lost,' Vyborg said.

They stopped in midafternoon at a dusty farmyard and bought bread and sausage and freshly brewed beer from a frightened peasant who called them '*pan*', sir, with every other breath. A man with the fear of armies running in his very blood – getting him to take money almost required force. *Just go*, said his eyes while he smiled obsequiously. *Just go*. Leave me my wife and daughters – you already have my sons – spare my life, we've always given you whatever you asked. Take it. Note that I'm a humble, stupid man of no interest. Then go away.

They stopped in a wood to eat. The sergeant drove the car far enough in so that German spotter aircraft would not see it. When the engine was turned off a deep silence descended, broken only by the low, three-note song of a single bird. The forest reminded Szara of a cathedral; they sat beneath tall oak trees that filtered and darkened the light until it was like the cool shadow of a church. One worshipped simply by being there. But it seemed to do Vyborg more harm than good; his mood grew darker by the moment, and the sergeant finished his bread and sausage and took his canteen of beer over to the car, folded the bonnet back, and began to tinker with the engine. 'He disapproves,' Vyborg said. 'And shows it in his own way.' But for courtesy, Szara would have joined him. He knew this black depth that lived in the Polish soul and feared it – the descent to a private hell where nothing could ever be fixed, or better, or made right often ended badly. He'd seen it. He noticed that the flap on Vyborg's holster was unbuttoned. An innocuous detail, but this was not the sort of officer who would be casual about such things. He knew that if Vyborg determined his honour lay in the single shot fired in a forest there was nothing he could say or do to stop it. 'You cannot take this on yourself, Colonel,' Szara finally said to break the silence.

Vyborg was slow to answer. Considered not bothering to say anything at all, finally said, 'Who else, then?'

'Politicians. Not least, Adolf Hitler.'

Vyborg stared at him in disbelief, wondering if perhaps he'd adopted the most hopeless fool in the world to tell his nation's story. 'Sir,' he said, 'do you believe that what you saw forcing the Dunajec was the Nazi party? What have I missed? If there was a lot of drunken singing and pissing on lamp posts I somehow didn't see it. What I saw was Deutschland, Poland's eternal enemy. I saw Germans. "C'mon fellows, there's a job to be done here and we're the ones to do it, so let's get busy." I saw the Wehrmacht, and I would have been, any officer worth his salt would have been, proud to command it. Do you believe that a bunch of shitbag little grocers and naughty schoolboys, led by Himmler the chicken farmer and Ribbentrop the wine salesman, would have overcome a Polish battalion? Do you?'

'No. Of course not.'

'Well then.'

Vyborg had raised his voice. The sergeant, sleeves rolled up to his elbows, working at the engine of the car, began whistling. 'And,' Vyborg went on, now in control of himself, 'I do take this on myself. Is there somewhere, in some filing cabinet in Warsaw, a report signed A. S. Vyborg, lieutenant colonel, that says the Stuka divebomber may be expected to do such and such? That says the Wehrmacht is able to cover fifteen miles of countryside a day, using tanks and motorized infantry? There is not. We are going to lose this war, we are going to be subjugated, and the fault lies with diplomacy – you're not entirely wrong – but it also lies with me and my colleagues. When a country is conquered, or subdued by political means, the secret services are always to blame – they, who are supposedly allowed to do *anything*, should have done *something*. In political life it is the cruellest equation there is, but we accept it. If we do not accept it we cannot continue with the work.'

He paused, drank the remaining beer in his canteen, and wiped his lips delicately with his fingers. The sergeant had stopped whistling, and the three-note bird had started to sing again, low and mournful. Vyborg settled his back against a tree trunk and closed his eyes. He was very pale, Szara realized, tired, perhaps exhausted. The strength of his personality was deceptive. The lost light of the forest muted the colour of his uniform – now it seemed heavy wool fabric, cut by a tailor, not a uniform at all, and his side arm became a bulky nuisance on a belt. The colonel forced himself to return from wherever he'd been, leaned forward, searched his breast pocket for a cigar, and showed a brief anger when he couldn't find any. When he spoke again his voice was quiet and resolved. 'Every profession defines its own failures, my friend. The doctor's patient does not recover, the merchant closes his shop, the politician leaves office, the intelligence officer sees his country dominated. Surely, on the level you've lived in Russia, you know that. You've had, so to speak, at least contacts with your own services.'

'Rarely,' Szara said. 'To my knowledge, at any rate. You're referring not to the secret police – of course one sees them every day in some form or another – but to those who concern themselves with international issues.'

'Exactly. Well, I'll tell you something, you've missed a historic era, a phenomenon. We know the Soviet services, we oppose them after all so we had better know them, and what most of us feel, alongside the appropriate patriotic wrath, is perhaps just a little bit of envy. Seen together it is a curious group: Theodor Maly – the former Hungarian army chaplain, Eitingon, Slutsky, Artuzov, Trilisser, General Shtern, Abramov, General Berzin, Ursula Kuczynski – called Sonya, that bastard Bloch, all the Latvians and Poles and Jews and what have you – they are, or perhaps one ought to say, in most cases, *were*, the very best that ever did this work. I don't speak to their morals, their personal lives, or their devotion to a cause in which I do not believe, no, one really can't see them in that light. But in the business of espionage there have never been any better, possibly won't ever be. I suppose it could be considered a pity; all of them slaughtered to some strange, enigmatic purpose known only to Stalin, at least a pity you never came to experience their particular personalities.'

'You've met them?'

'Not in the flesh, no. They are paper men who live in file folders, but perhaps it is, for them, their truest manifestation. What, after all, is there to see? A little fellow with glasses reading a newspaper in a café. An overweight Jewish gentleman choosing a tie, charming the sales clerk. A man in shirtsleeves and suspenders, berated by his wife for some small domestic stupidity.' Vyborg laughed at the thought of it, his gallery of rogues muddling through their daily lives. 'Ah, but on paper, well, that's another story. Here an ambassador is compromised, there a powerful émigré group simply disintegrates, plans for an ingenious ciphering machine are copied and no one knows it has happened. An incident in Brussels, a disappearance in Prague – one must surmise that a fine hand is at work. As the stage magician says: now you see it, now you don't. Ah, but dear ladies and gentlemen you must forgive me, I cannot tell you how the trick is done.'

The sound of an approaching aircraft made Vyborg glance up through the trees. For a time, while the plane wandered invisible somewhere in the clouds above the forest, neither of them spoke. At last, it faded away into the distance. Vyborg stood and brushed himself off. 'One thing we certainly do know: it isn't one of ours.' Szara stood up. Vyborg glanced back up at the sky. 'We'd better be moving,' he said, 'or one of these clever Wehrmacht pincer manoeuvres is going to close around us and we'll wind up as prisoners. In the last war the officer class respected the gentleman's code, but this time around I'm not so certain.'

They drove on, the countryside shimmering a thousand shades of green and gold in the haze of the waning afternoon. Three wagons came towards them and the sergeant, at Vyborg's direction, pulled over to let them use the twin ruts of the path. Polish Jews, men, women, and children, eyes downcast for the occasion of passing army officers, headed east, away from the advancing Germans. When the car was again in motion, Szara said to Vyborg, 'No gentleman's code for them, evidently.'

'I fear not. If we are to be occupied by German forces, I am afraid our Jews will suffer. Those who just passed us believe that, and I have to agree. They, however, are headed east. Will Russia have them?'

'Russia does what it has to do,' Szara said. 'Life won't be good for them there, but most of them will survive. Stalin will find some use for them in the end.'

'In the camps?'

'Perhaps in labour battalions. They won't be allowed to settle down and live their lives.'

'Don't you love your adopted land, Mr Szara?'

'It doesn't love me, Colonel, and in an affair of any sort that tends to make life uncomfortable.'

'But you could go away, yet you don't.'

'Who hasn't thought of it? And I'm just as human as the rest of them. But something about this part of the world makes it hard to leave. It's not to be explained in the ordinary ways, and poetic yearnings for the sky and the earth seem awfully meagre when the Chekists come around. Yet one stays. One decides to leave, puts it off a week, then something happens, so then it's Thursday for certain, but on Thursday it can't be done, then suddenly it's Monday but the trains aren't running. So you wait for March, and some new decree gives you hope, then spring comes in April and your heart is suddenly strong enough for anything. Or so you think.' He shrugged, then said, 'You wake up one morning; you're too old to change, too old to start again. Then the woman in your bed snuggles up because her feet are cold and you realize you're not that old, and after that you start to wonder what shattering horror or peculiar pleasure the rest of the day might bring, and by God your heart has grown Russian and you didn't even notice.'

Vyborg smiled. 'I should read your writing,' he said. 'But what kind of a Russian speaks this way yet lives in Paris? Or do I have it wrong?'

'No. You have it right. And all I can say in my defence is, what poet doesn't praise the love that loves from afar?'

Vyborg laughed, first politely, then for real as the notion tickled him. 'What a shame,' he said, 'that we're about to lose this beautiful, heartbreaking country of ours. If that weren't the case, Mr Szara, I assure you I would recruit you to the very corner of hell simply for the pleasure of your company.'

That night he lay on a blanket beside the car and tried to will himself to sleep. That was the medicine he needed – for exhaustion, sore spirit, for survival – but when it came, for a few minutes at a time, it wasn't the kind that healed. An area around his right temple throbbed insistently, seemed swollen and tender, and he feared something far worse than he'd imagined had gone wrong inside him. The night was starless and cool. They'd driven and driven, managing only a few miles an hour over the wagon ruts, then given it up just at the last moment of dusk.

Leaving the oak forest, they'd suddenly entered a seemingly endless wheat field that ran uninterrupted for miles. There were no villages, no people at all, only ripe wheat that rustled and whispered in the steady evening wind. The last jerrycan of fuel had been poured in the gas tank; somehow they would have to find more. Szara had frightening dreams – the genial irony that had sustained their morale during the day disappeared in darkness – and when he did manage to sleep he was pursued and could not run. The ground beneath him was hard as stone, but turning on his other side made his head swim with pain and forced him back to his original position. Long before dawn he awakened to the roll of thunder, then saw on the horizon that it was not thunder: a pulsing, orange glow stained the eastern edge of the night sky. For a few minutes he was the only one awake; rested his head on his arm and watched what he knew to be a burning city under artillery barrage.

When the sergeant and the colonel awoke, they too watched the horizon. For a long time nobody spoke, then the sergeant took both canteens and went off to try and find water. They'd had nothing to eat or drink since afternoon of the previous day, and thirst was becoming something it was hard not to think about. Vyborg lit a match and tried to study the map, not at all sure where they were.

'Could it be that Cracow is on fire?' Szara asked.

Vyborg shook his head that he didn't know and lit another match. 'Our little wagon track is not on the map,' he said. 'But I've estimated we'll hit the north-south rail line at a switching station somewhere north and east of here.'

Szara took the last crushed Gitane from a battered pack. He had two more in his valise, rolled up in a clean shirt. He thought about changing clothes. He had sweated and dried out many times and was everywhere coated with a fine, powdery dust that made him feel itchy and grimy. Too much Parisian luxury, he thought. Baths and cigarettes and coffee and cold, sweet water when you turned on the tap. From his perspective of the moment it seemed a dream of a lost world. France had declared war, according to the colonel, and so had England. Were the German bombers flying over their cities? Perhaps Paris was an orange glow in the sky. Vyborg looked at his watch. 'There must not be water anywhere near,' he said. Szara sat against the tyre of the staff car and smoked his cigarette.

An hour later the sergeant had not returned, and dawn was well advanced. Colonel Vyborg had twice walked a little way up the path – with no results. Finally he seemed to make a decision, opened the boot and took out an automatic rifle. He detached the magazine from its housing forward of the trigger guard and inspected the cartridges, then snapped it back into place and handed the weapon to Szara. From the markings it was a Model ZH 29 made in Brno, Czechoslovakia, a long, heavy weapon, not quite clumsy; the hand grip just behind the barrel was protected by a ribbed metal alloy so the shooter didn't blister his fingers when the gun fired automatically. Vyborg said, 'There are twenty-five rounds, and one in the chamber. The setting is for single shots, but you can move the lever behind the magazine to automatic.' He reached over and worked the bolt. 'I've armed it,' he said. He drew his weapon, a short-barrelled automatic, from its holster, and inspected it as he had the Czech rifle. 'Best we stay a few yards apart but side by side – a field is a bad place for walking about with armed weapons.'

For a time they moved along the path, the colonel stopping every now and then and calling out softly. But there was no answer. The track curved upwards around a low hill and, as the sun came above the horizon, they found the sergeant on the other side, some three hundred yards away from the car, at a place where the wheat stalks had been crushed and broken. His throat had been cut. He lay stretched on his stomach, eyes wide open, a look of fierce worry settled on his face. A handful of dirt was frozen in each fist. Vyborg knelt and brushed the flies away. The sergeant's boots were gone, his pockets were turned out, and, when Vyborg reached inside his uniform jacket, a shoulder holster worn just below the armpit was empty. There was no sign of the canteens. For a time, Szara and Vyborg remained as they were: Szara standing, the rifle heavy in his hands, Vyborg kneeling by the body, which had bled out into the earth. The silence was unbroken – only the distant rumble and the sound of the wheat stalks brushing against each other. Vyborg muttered an obscenity under his breath and went to take a religious medal from around the sergeant's neck, but if he'd worn one it had also been stolen. At last the colonel rose, the pistol held loosely in his hand. He kicked at the ground experimentally with the toe of his boot, but it was hard and dry as rock. 'We have no shovel,' he said at last. He turned and walked away. When Szara caught up with him he said, 'This always starts here when there's war.' His voice was bitter, disgusted and cold. 'It's the peasants,' he said. 'They've decided to look out for themselves.'

'How did they know we were here?'

'They know,' Vyborg said.

By full daylight they could see columns of black smoke where the city was burning and the sound of the barrage had grown more distinct, could be heard to crackle like wet wood in a fire. Vyborg drove, Szara sat beside him. They did not speak for a long time. Szara watched the needle on the petrol gauge, quivering just below the midpoint on the dial. Now, when they encountered a rise or a low hill, Vyborg stopped the car just below the top, took his binoculars, and climbed the rest of the way. Szara stood guard, rifle in hand, back protected by the metal side of the car. On the fourth or fifth scouting expedition, Vyborg appeared just below the brow of a hill and waved for Szara to join him. When he got there Vyborg said. 'They're on the other side. Go slowly, stay as close to the ground as you can, and do not speak; make gestures if you have to. People notice motion, and they hear human sounds.' The sun was blazing. Szara crawled on his elbows and his knees, breathing dust, the rifle cradled across his arms. Sweat beaded in droplets at his hairline and ran down the sides of his face.

When they crested the hill, Vyborg handed him the binoculars, though he could see the valley very well without them. They'd reached the railway switching station – as Vyborg had predicted – which lay by a dirt road at the foot of a long gentle grade. A single set of rails curved to the west, coming together by the switching station with a double-track north-south axis. A switchman's hut and a set of long iron levers housed in a wooden framework stood to one side of two laybys, lengths of track where one train could be held while another used the right-of-way.

The little valley, mostly weeds and scrub trees, was alive with Wehrmacht grey. The hut and the switching apparatus had been protected by a sandbagged machine gun position; a number of Wehrmacht railway officers, identifiable by shoulder patches when he used the binoculars, were milling about with green flags in hand. From the position of the long row of goods wagons parked on the western track, Szara inferred that the troop train had arrived directly from the German side of the border. There was further evidence of this. Across the wooden boards of one of the wagons was a legend printed with chalk: *Wir fahren nach Polen um Juden zu versohlen,* We are riding to Poland to beat up the Jews. Insignia indicated that he was witnessing the arrival of elements of the Seventeenth Infantry Division; about a thousand of them had already formed up while hundreds more continued to jump down from the open doors of the goods wagons.

With the binoculars, details of faces were very clear to Szara. He saw them through a smoky haze that lay over the valley, with foreground weeds cutting across his field of vision and with the eerie detachment of observation at long range – mouths move yet no sound is heard – but he could see who they were. Farm-boys and idlers and mechanics, street toughs and clerks, factory workers and students – an army of young faces, dark and fair, some laughing, some anxious, some full of bravado, some silent and withdrawn, some handsome and some ugly, others entirely unremarkable – an army like all others. A group of officers, generally in their thirties and forties (as the troopers were in their teens and twenties), stood to one side and smoked and talked quietly in little groups while the inevitable confusion of a military force on the move was sorted out by the NCOs, the sergeants and corporals.

Szara observed this particular group with interest. They were all of a type: big, strong, competent, full of easy authority but without swagger. They were, he knew, the soul of an army, supervisors and foremen rather than executives, and upon their abilities would ultimately rest defeat or victory. They worked with their units almost casually, sometimes taking a stray by a handful of uniform and heading it where it belonged, usually without any comment at all, simply pointing it in the direction it ought to go and giving it a bit of a shove to get it moving.

From a group of cattle trucks farther down the track, the division's horses were being led to the staging area. They were great, muscular beasts, bred for army life on the horse farms of East Prussia. They would pull the divisional artillery, the provisioning and ammunition wagons, and some of the better ones would be ridden by officers: the German army, like most other European armies, moved by horsepower. There would be a few open staff cars, like the one Szara and the colonel were using, for senior officers and the medical staff, but it was horses who did all the heavy work, four thousand of them for each division of ten

thousand soldiers. The spearhead of the German offensive was armoured – divisions of tanks and trucks, and their speed had so far entirely
outmanoeuvred the Polish defence – but the units moving up now
would hold the territory that the fast-moving armoured groups had
captured.

Szara shifted his binoculars up the road that led north, where several
companies were already on the move. It was no parade, they were
walking not marching, weapons casually slung – as always the giants
carried rifles while small, lean men lugged tripod machine guns and
mortar tubes – in a formation that was ragged but functional. The
machine was, for the moment, running in low gear. Szara saw that a
field gun had tipped over into a ditch, the horses tangled up in their
reins and skittering about to get their balance – the accident had
evidently just happened. The situation was quickly put right: a sergeant
shouted orders, several troopers soothed the horses, others freed the
reins, a group organized itself to lift the gun back onto the road. It took
only a moment, many willing hands – *heave!* – and the job was done,
the advance continued.

Vyborg touched him on the shoulder to get his attention and made a
hand motion indicating they'd spied long enough. Szara slithered
backwards for a time, then they rose and walked towards the car.
Vyborg spoke in an undertone – even though they were well away
from the Germans, something of their presence remained. 'That,' he
said, 'was the road to Cracow. Our reckoning was, after all, correct. But,
as you can see, the road is presently in use.'

'What can we do?'

'Swing around behind or try to sneak through at night.'

'Are we cut off, then?'

'Yes. For the time being. What was your impression of the Wehrmacht?'

They reached the car; Vyborg started the engine and slowly backed
down the track until a curve took them out of the direct sightline of the
hill they'd climbed. 'My impression,' Szara said after Vyborg had
backed the car into the wheat and turned it off, 'is that I do not want
to go to war with Germany.'

'You may have no choice,' Vyborg said.

'You believe Hitler will attack Russia?'

'Eventually, yes. He won't be able to resist. Farmlands, oil, iron ore;
everything a German loves. By the way, did you take note of the horses?'

'Handsome,' Szara said.

'Useless.'

'I'm no judge, but they seemed healthy. Big and strong.'

'Too big. The Russians have tough little horses called *panje,* they can live on weeds. These big German beasts will disappear in the Russian mud – that's what happened to Napoleon, among other things. They're strong enough, powerful, but too heavy. And just try and feed them.'

'Hitler knows all about Napoleon, I'd imagine.'

'He'll think he's better. Napoleon came out of Russia with a few hundred men. The rest remained as fertilizer. Hundreds of thousands of them.'

'Yes, I know. What the Russians call General Winter finally got them.'

'Not really. Mostly it just wore them down, then finished the job. What got them was spotted fever. Which is to say, lice. Russia defends herself in ways that nobody else really thinks about. The peasant has lived with these lice all his life, he's immune. The Central European, that is the German, is not. Far be it from me to intrude on old Kinto's information *apparat,* but if Hitler starts making hostile noises, somebody ought to go and have a look at what sort of salves and preventatives the German pharmaceutical houses are turning out. That could, in the long run, matter a great deal. Of course, why on earth would I be telling you such things? It will hardly do for *Pravda.* Still, if you do get out of here alive, and should you chance to meet one of the operatives you've never known, there's a little something to whisper in his ear.'

The night was exquisite, starlight a luminous silver wash across the black of the heavens. Szara lay on his back and watched it, hands clasped to make a pillow beneath his head, simultaneously dazzled by the universe and desperate for water. It was now almost too painful to talk; his voice had gone thick and hoarse. Just after dark they had crept once more to their point of vantage, sensing, like thirsty animals, that somewhere near the switchman's hut there was a stream or a well. But a new train idled on the western track and, by the light of several roaring bonfires, units organized themselves and moved off north on the road to Cracow.

At midnight they made a decision: abandoned the car and worked their way south through the countryside, carrying weapons, canteens, and hand baggage. The first two hours were agony, groping and stumbling through thick brush that bordered the wheat field, halting dead still at every miscellaneous sound of the night. What helped them, finally, was a German railway patrol; a locomotive, its light a sharp, yellow cone that illuminated the track, moved cautiously south pushing a flatcar manned by soldiers with machine pistols. Following the light, they walked for another hour, saw the silhouette they wanted, then simply waited until the engine disappeared over the horizon.

The tiny railway station had a water tower. They twisted open a valve at the bottom and took turns drinking greedily from the stream sluicing onto the ground. It was foul water, bad-smelling and stale, and Szara could taste dirt and rotting wood and God knew what else, but he lapped at it avidly, drinking from cupped hands, not caring that the stream soaked his shirt and trousers. A man and a woman came out of a little cottage that backed up to the station; he was likely a sort of stationmaster, flagman, switchman, or whatever else might be required.

Vyborg greeted the couple politely and told the man he would require new clothing, whatever might be available. The woman went off and returned with a faded shirt and trousers, broken-down shoes, a thin jacket, and a cap. Vyborg took a wallet from his jacket and offered the man a sheaf of zloty notes. The man looked stubbornly at his feet, but the woman stepped forward and accepted the money silently. 'What will become of us now?' the man asked.

'One can only wait and see,' Vyborg said. He bundled up the clothing, took charge of the rifle and the canteens, and said, 'I will take these off and bury them.' The man found him a coal shovel, and Vyborg vanished into the dark fields away from the track.

'To bury fine boots like those . . .' said the woman.

'Best forget them,' Szara told her. 'The Germans know what they are and who wears them.'

'Yes, but still,' said the woman.

'It's bad to see such a thing,' the man said sharply, angry that the woman saw only fine boots. 'To see a Polish officer bury his uniform.'

'Is there a train?' Szara asked.

'Perhaps in a few days,' the man said. 'From here one goes to Cracow, or south to Zakopane, in the mountains. In normal times every Tuesday, just at four in the afternoon.'

They stood together awkwardly for a time, then a workman came out of the field and stepped across the track. 'It's done,' Vyborg said.

There was no train. Szara and Vyborg determined to go east, on a road that ran well to the south of the railway station, skirting the Slovakian border, winding its way through the river valleys of the Carpathians. They joined an endless column of refugees, on foot, in carts drawn by farm horses, in the occasional car. German units were posted at the crossroads, but the soldiers did not interfere with the migration; they seemed bored, disinterested, slouching against stone walls or bridge abutments, smoking, watching without expression as the river of humanity flowed past their eyes. No papers were demanded, no one was called out of line or searched. Szara noticed what he took to be other soldiers in the column who, like Vyborg, had shed their uniforms and obtained civilian clothing. Among the refugees there were various points of view about the German attitude, ranging from attributions of benevolence – 'The Fritzes want to win our confidence' – to pragmatism – 'The less Poles in Poland, the happier for them. Now we'll be Russia's problem.' The road east became a city: babies were born and old people died, friends were made and lost, money was earned, spent, stolen. An old Jew with a white beard down to his waist and a sack of pots and pans clanking on his back confided to Szara, 'This is my fourth time along this road. In 1905 we went west to escape the pogroms, in 1916 east, running away from the Germans, then in 1920, west, with the Bolsheviks chasing us. So, here we are again. I don't worry no more – it'll sort itself out.'

It took them six days to reach the small city of Krosno, some eighty miles east of the Cracow-Zakopane line. There, Szara saw with amazement that the Polish flag still hung proudly above the entrance to the railway station. Somehow, they'd managed to outdistance the German advance. Had the Wehrmacht permitted the column of refugees to enter Polish-held territory in order to overload supply and transport systems? He could think of no other reason, but that seemed to him dubious at best. Vyborg left Szara at the station and went off to look for an intelligence unit and a wireless telegraph among the forces manning the Krosno defences. Szara thought he'd seen him for the last time, but two hours later he reappeared, still looking like a dignified, rather finely made workman in his cap and jacket. They stood together by a beam supporting the wooden roof of the terminal, restless crowds of exhausted and desperate people shifting endlessly around them. The noise was overwhelming: people shouting and arguing, children screaming, a public address system babbling indecipherable nonsense. They had to raise their voices in order to make themselves heard. 'At last,' Vyborg said, 'I was able to reach my superiors.'

'Do they know what's going on?'

'To a point. As far as you're concerned, Lvov is not currently under attack, but that is a situation which may change quickly. As for me, my unit was known to have reached Cracow, but there they vanished. Communication is very bad – several Polish divisions are cut off, mostly trying to break out and fight their way to Warsaw. The capital will be defended and is expected to hold. Personally I give it a month at most, probably less. I'm afraid there isn't much hope for us. We do have miracles in this country, even military ones from time to time, but the feeling is that there's not much that can be done. We've appealed to the world for help, naturally. As for me, I have a new assignment.'

'Outside the country?'

Vyborg's thin-lipped mouth smiled tightly for a moment. 'I can tell you nothing. You may wish me well, though, if you like.'

'I do, Colonel.'

'I would ask you, Mr Szara, to write about what you've seen, if you can find a way to do that. That we were brave, that we stood up to them, that we did not surrender. And I would say that the next best thing, for us, if you can't do that, is silence. I refer to your assignment from *Pravda*. Stories about our national minorities have already appeared in London and Paris, even in America. Perhaps you will decline to add your voice to the baying chorus.'

'I'll find a way.'

'I can only ask. That's all that officers of defeated armies can do, appeal to conscience, but I ask you anyhow. Perhaps you still feel yourself, at heart, a Pole. People of this nation are far-flung, but they often think of us, it would not be inappropriate for you to join them. Meanwhile, as to practical matters, I'm told that a train for Lvov will be pulling in here within the hour. I'd like to think that you'll be on it – you have your work cut out for you, I can see – but at least that way I'll have kept my part of the bargain, albeit by an unexpected route.'

'Journalists are very good at forcing their way onto trains, Colonel.'

'Perhaps we'll meet again,' Vyborg said.

'I would hope so.'

Vyborg's handshake was strong. 'Good luck,' he said, and slipped away into the milling crowd of refugees.

Szara did get on the train, though not actually inside it. He worked his way to the side of a coach, then moved laterally until he came to the extended iron stair. There was a passenger already in residence on the lowest step, but Szara waited until the train jerked into motion, then forced his way up and squeezed in beside him. His fellow traveller was a dark, angry man clutching a wicker hamper in both arms and, using his shoulder, he attempted to push Szara off the train – the step belonged to him, it was his place in the scheme of things.

But Szara availed himself of a time-honoured method and took a firm grip on the man's lapel with his free hand so that the harder the man pushed, the more likely he was to leave the train if Szara fell off. The train never managed to pick up any speed; there were people hanging out the windows, lying flat on the roof, and balancing on the couplings between cars, and the engine seemed barely capable of moving the weight forward. For a long time the two of them glared at each other, the man pushing, Szara hanging on to him, their faces separated only by inches. Then, at last, the pushing and pulling stopped and both men leaned against the bodies occupying the step above theirs. The train made the eighty miles to Lvov in six agonizing hours, and if the station at Krosno had been a hell of struggling crowds, Lvov was worse.

Attempting to cross the platform, Szara literally had to fight. The heat of the crowd was suffocating, and he shoved bodies out of his way, tripped over a crate of chickens and fell flat on the cement floor, then struggled desperately among a forest of legs in order to rise before he was trampled to death. Someone punched him in the back, hard – he never saw who did it, he simply felt the blow. Once he got to the waiting room, he fell in with a determined phalanx using their combined weight to move towards the doors. They'd almost got there when a crowd of frantic, terrified people came sweeping back against them. Szara's feet left the ground, and he was afraid his ribs might break from the pressure; he flailed out with one hand, hit something wet that produced an angry yelp, and with enormous effort got his feet back on the floor.

Somewhere, only barely touching the edge of his consciousness, was a drone, but he made no attempt to connect it with anything in the real world, it was simply there. He moved sideways for a few seconds, then some mysterious countercurrent picked him up and sent him sprawling through the doors of the station – he kept his balance only by jamming one hand against the cement beneath him, gasping at the air as he came free of the crowd.

He found himself not in the main square of Lvov, but at a side street entrance to the railway station. People were running and shouting, he had no idea why. Several carts had been abandoned by their drivers, and the horses were galloping wildly up the cobbled street to get away from whatever it was, loose vegetables and burlap sacks flying off the wagons behind them. The air was full of tiny, white feathers, from where he did not know, but they filled the street like a blizzard. The drone grew insistent and he looked up. For a moment he was hypnotized. Somewhere, in some file in the house on the rue Delesseux, was a silhouette, as seen from below, identified in a careful Cyrillic script as the Heinkel-111; and what he saw above him was a perfect match of the darkened outline among the pages of what he now realized was the Baumann file. This was one of the bombers controlled by the swage wire manufactured on the outskirts of Berlin. There was a second flight approaching, at least a half-dozen of them in the clouds above the city, and he remembered, if not precise facts and figures, at least the certain conclusion: they were known to produce the virtual annihilation of every stick and stone and living thing once they released their bombs. As the planes flew in slow formation, a series of black, oblong cylinders floated away beneath them and tumbled, in a crooked line, towards the earth.

The first explosion – he felt it in his feet and heard it in the distance – startled him, then several more followed, each time growing louder. He ran. Blindly and without purpose, in panic, then tripped and fell at the base of a doorway. He lashed out at the door, which swung open, and he crawled frantically into a room. He smelled sawdust and shellac, spotted a large, rough-hewn work table, and rolled beneath it. Only then did he discover he was not alone – there was a face close to his, a man with a scraggly beard, half glasses, and a stub of pencil wedged between his temple and the hem of his cap. The man's eyes were enormous and white, blind with terror. Szara squeezed himself into a ball as a shattering roar rocked the table above him, perhaps he howled, perhaps the man curled up next to him did – he no longer had any idea who he was or where he was, the world exploded inside his head and he forced his eyes shut until he saw brilliant colours in the darkness. The floor bucked and sang with the next explosion and Szara tried to claw his way through it into the safe earth below. Then there was another, and then another, receding, and, finally, a silence that rang in his ears before he realized what it meant.

'Is it over?' the man said in Yiddish.

The air was thick with smoke and dust; they both coughed. Szara's throat felt as though it had caught fire. 'Yes,' Szara said. 'They've gone.' Together, and very slowly, they crawled from beneath the table. Szara saw that he was in a carpentry shop, and the man with the half glasses was apparently the carpenter. The windows were gone, Szara had to look for a long time before he discovered tiny sparkles of glass embedded in the back wall. But he could find no other damage. What had dissolved the windows had also slammed the door, and the carpenter had to pull hard before it sprang open.

Cautiously, they looked out into the street. To their left was a gap where a house had been – only a pile of board and brick remained – and the house next to it was on fire, black smoke boiling out of the upper windows. Somebody nearby shouted, 'Help' – perhaps a woman's voice. The carpenter said '*Mein Gott*' and pressed his face between his hands.

At the opposite end of the street from the burning house a vast crater had been torn open. They walked over to it and peered down; a broken pipe gushed water from a ragged end. 'Help,' said the voice again. It came from a shop directly across from the hole in the street. 'It's Madame Kulska,' said the carpenter. The door of the shop had disappeared and the interior, a dressmaker's workroom, had been swirled by a typhoon, bits and pieces of material were everywhere. 'Who's there?' said the voice. 'Nachman,' said the carpenter. 'I'm under here,' said the voice. *Under here* was covered by a jumbled layer of fallen bricks. Szara and the carpenter quickly cleared the rubble away, revealing the dusty back of a huge armoire and a small woman pinned beneath it. Szara took one corner, the carpenter the other. '*Ein, zwei, drei*,' said the man, and together they raised the cabinet until it fell back into the smashed brick wall, the door swinging open to reveal a row of dresses, of various shapes and colours, suspended from wooden hangers.

'Give me your hand, Mr Nachman,' said the woman. They both helped her to sit upright. Szara could see no blood. The woman looked curiously at her hand, then wiggled the fingers. 'Are you hurt?' the carpenter said. 'No,' said the woman, her voice faint and giddy with astonishment. 'No. I don't think so. What happened?'

He heard the sound of a bell clanging. Leaving the carpenter with the woman, Szara went to the door. A fire engine had driven up to the burning building, and firemen were uncoiling a hose connected to a tank of water on the back. Szara wandered out of the shop and down the street. Two men hurried by, carrying an injured boy on a stretcher improvised from a quilt. Szara's heart sickened. What was the point of dropping bombs on this neighbourhood? To murder? Simply that? A man on a ladder was helping a young woman out of a window from which smoke drifted in a pale mist. She was weeping, hysterical. A crowd of neighbours, gathered at the foot of the ladder, tried to call out soothing words.

The next street was intact. So was the one after that. A man ran up to him and said, 'There are eight people dead at the railway station.' Szara said, 'It's terrible. Terrible.' Then the man ran off to tell somebody else. Another fire engine drove past. The driver was a rabbi with a bloody handkerchief tied around his forehead; sitting next to him a small boy conscientiously rang a bell by pulling on a rope. Szara sank to the cobblestones. Looking down, he saw that his hand still clutched the valise. He had to use his free hand to pry the fingers open. People wandered by, dazed, in shock. Szara put the valise between his feet and held his head in his hands. *This is not human*, he thought, *to do this is not human.*

But there was something else in his mind, a ghost of a thought caught up among everything he felt. The city of Lvov had been bombed by a flight of Heinkel-111s. People had been killed, houses blown up, and there were fires that had to be put out and wounded who had to be treated.

But the city was still there. It had not been reduced to a mound of smoking ashes, not at all. He suddenly understood that a dark shape he'd seen half buried in a neighbouring alley was a bomb that had failed to explode. Others had fallen in the streets, between houses, in courtyards and parks, while some had destroyed rooftops but left the occupants of the building miraculously unharmed. Slowly, a realization worked its way into his consciousness. He could not believe it, at first, so he spoke the words out loud. 'My God,' he said. 'They were wrong.'

Poste
Restante

In the dappled, aqueous dusk of the hydrotherapy room, the journalist Vainshtok cleaned his spectacles with a soiled handkerchief. He screwed up his eyes and wrinkled the bridge of his nose, producing the ferocious scowl of the intellectual momentarily separated from his glasses. '*Chornaya grayáz,*' he said with contempt, squinting through each lens in turn. 'That's all it was.' The slang phrase was peculiar to journalists – literally it meant grey mud – and described a form of propaganda intended to obscure an issue and cover up reality. ' "The *pathetic* state of Poland's national minorities",' Vainshtok quoted himself with a sneer. 'Boo-hoo.'

'Why?' Szara asked.

Vainshtok settled the spectacles back on his nose and thought a moment. 'Well, whatever the reason, they certainly did want it – they gave me the front page, and a fat byline.'

They were six miles from Lvov, at the Krynica-Zdroj, one of the more elegant spas in Poland, where the privileged had gathered to have their exhausted livers, their pernicious lumbago, and their chronic melancholia cured by immersions and spritzes, dousings and ingestions, of the smelly sulphurous waters that bubbled up from deep within the earth. And if simultaneously they chanced to do a little business, to find a husband or a wife, to consummate a love affair, well so much the better. Currently the spa's clientele was limited to a handful of Soviet journalists and a horde of foreign diplomats and their families who'd fled east from the fighting in Warsaw. 'As to why they wanted it, really why,' Vainshtok went on, 'that seems fairly obvious.' He inclined his head and gave one of his wild eyebrows a conspiratorial twitch.

Szara almost laughed. Vainshtok was one of those people who are forever impervious to their physical presence, but he looked, at that moment, extraordinarily strange. His skin shaded green by the rainy-day gloom of the basement pool, he wriggled in discomfort on the skeleton of a garden chair – the cushions had disappeared, along with the white-smocked attendants who'd laid them out every morning – and wore, the strap crushing a hand-painted tie, a shoulder holster with the grip of an automatic protruding from it. On the wall behind him, the foam green tile gave way to a Neptune riding a sea horse in ultramarine and ochre. 'It is certainly not the truth,' he said. 'Those starving Ukrainians and sorely persecuted Byelorussians groaning under the heel of Polish tyranny are, in fact, as we sit in this godforsaken grotto, attacking army units as they try to set up defensive positions in the marshland. What you have are the same old Ukrainian outlaw bands behaving in the same old ways, yet Moscow requires a sympathetic view. So, what do they want with it? You tell me.'

'They're preparing an action against the Poles.'

'What else?'

Szara stared into the pool. It was green and still. At either end stood imposing water machines, nickel-plated monsters with circular gauges and ceramic control knobs, their rubber hose-works strung limply from iron wheels. He imagined a long line of naked, bearded aristocrats awaiting treatment – there was something nineteenth century, and slightly sinister, about the apparatus, as though it were meant to frighten madmen back to sanity.

'Meanwhile,' Vainshtok said, 'the highly regarded André Szara goes off on a tour of the battlefields of southern Poland, misses his chance to write the big national minorities story, and in general causes great consternation.'

Szara grinned at Vainshtok's needling. 'Consternation, you say. Such a word. Why not *alarms and excursions*, as the English put it. In fact, with all this chaos, I doubt anybody even noticed.'

'They noticed.'

A certain tone in Vainshtok's voice caught Szara's attention. 'Did they?'

'Yes.'

Again the note, this time a monosyllable. Not at all typical of Vainshtok. Szara hesitated, then leaned forward, a man about to ask frank and difficult, possibly dangerous, questions.

'Oh, you know how they are,' Vainshtok said hurriedly. 'Just any little thing and they turn bright red and throw a few somersaults, like the king's ministers in a children's book.' He laughed a little.

'Someone here?'

The question was dismissed with a shrug and a frown. 'Three Jews meet in heaven, the first one says—'

'Vainshtok . . .'

' "The day I died, the whole city of Pinsk-M—" '

'Who asked?'

Vainshtok sighed and nodded to himself. 'Who. The usual who.'

Szara waited.

'I didn't ask him his name. He already knew mine, as he no doubt also knew the length of my *schvontz* and the midwife who took me from my mother. Who indeed! A Cossack in a topcoat. With the eyes of a dead carp. Look, André Aronovich, you're supposed to show up in Lvov. Then you don't. You think nobody's going to notice? So they come around looking for you. What am I supposed to say? Szara? He's my best pal, tells me *everything*, he just stopped off in Cracow to buy rolls, don't worry about him. I mean, it was almost funny – if it wasn't like it was it would be funny. Mind you, it was the same day the Germans finally broke into Lvov: buildings on fire, people weeping in the streets, tanks in the marketplace, that fucking swastika flying over the town hall, a few diehards sniping from the windows. And suddenly some, some *apparat* type appears from nowhere and all he wants to know is where's Szara. I almost said, "Pardon me, you're standing in my war," but I didn't, you know I didn't. I crawled on my belly until he went away. What do you want? Remorse? Tears? I don't really know anything about you, not really. So I told him nothing. It just took some time to get it said.'

Szara sat back in the garden chair. 'Don't worry about it,' he said. 'And I was in the city that day. I saw the same things you did.'

'Then you know.' Vainshtok said. He took off his glasses and looked at them, then put them back on. 'All I want is to stay alive. So I'm a coward, so now what.'

He could see that Vainshtok's hands were shaking. He took out a cigarette and silently offered it, then lit a match and held it while Vainshtok inhaled. 'Have the Germans been out here?' he asked.

Vainshtok blew smoke through his nose. 'Only a captain. The day after they took the city he came around. A couple of the ambassadors went out to meet him, they all put their heads together, then he came in and drank a cup of tea in the lobby. A diplomatic crisis was averted, as the old saying goes, and the SS never showed up. Myself, I didn't take any chances.' He patted the automatic affectionately. 'Somehow I get the feeling that in certain situations the Non-Aggression Pact doesn't quite cover somebody who looks like me. "Oops! Sorry. Was that a *Russian* Jew? Oh, too bad." '

'Where'd you get it?'

'You met Tomasz? The caretaker? Big white eyebrows, big belly, big smile – like a Polish Santa Claus?'

'When I arrived. He told me where you were.'

'Tomasz will get you, for a small fee, whatever you want.' Vainshtok took the pistol out of the holster and handed it to Szara. It was a blued-steel Steyr automatic, an Austrian weapon, compact and heavy in his hand.

'You get to play with it for three minutes,' Vainshtok said. 'But you have to give me five marbles and a piece of candy.'

Szara handed it back. 'Is there anything to eat in this place?'

Vainshtok looked at his watch. 'In an hour or so they serve boiled beets. Then, at dinnertime, they serve them again. On the other hand, the china is extremely beautiful, and they're actually very good beets.'

Szara slept on a wicker couch on the sunporch. The hotel was jammed with people and he was lucky to find anything at all to sleep on. At a right angle to the couch, a Spanish consular official had claimed the porch swing for a bed, while a Danish commercial attaché, one of the last to arrive from Warsaw, curled up on the floor next to a rack of croquet sets. The three of them had managed a conversation in French, talking in low voices after midnight, cigarettes glowing in the dark, in general trying to sort out rumours – the prime topic of conversation at the spa. Elements of the Polish army were said to have withdrawn to the Pripet marshes with the idea of holding out for six months while French and British expeditionary forces were organized to come to Poland's defence. A Norwegian diplomat was believed to have been interned. This was curious because Norway had declared neutrality, but perhaps the Germans intended the 'mistake' as a warning. Or perhaps it hadn't happened at all. The United States, the Dane was certain, had declared neutrality. A special train would be organized to remove diplomats from Poland. But many diplomats from Warsaw, having taken refuge in the town of Krzemieniec, in western Poland, had been casualties of a heavy bombing attack by the Luftwaffe. The Polish government had fled to Roumania. Warsaw had surrendered; Warsaw still held; Warsaw had been so obliterated by bombing that there was nothing left *to* surrender. The League of Nations would intervene. Szara faded away without realizing it; the quiet voices on the porch and a light patter of rain lulled him to sleep.

It was a particularly golden dawn that woke him. The distant forest was alive with light. How hard summer died here, he thought. It made him wonder what day it was. The seventeenth of September, he guessed, making what sense he could of the jumble of days and nights he'd wandered through. The lawns and gravelled paths sparkled with last night's raindrops as the sun came up and it was, but for a faint buzz of static somewhere in the hotel, immensely quiet. A rooster began to crow; perhaps a village lay on the other side of the forest. He looked at his watch – a few minutes after five. The Spaniard on the porch swing was lying on his back, coat spread over him like a blanket and pulled decorously up to his chin. Beneath a lavish moustache his mouth was slightly open, and his breath hissed in and out daintily as he slept. Szara caught, for just a moment, the barest hint of coffee in the air. Was it possible? Just wishful thinking. No, he did smell it. He wrestled free of the jacket tangled about him and sat upright – *oh, bones* – checking to make sure the valise was under the couch where he'd put it the night before. His beard itched. Today he would find some way to heat up a pot of water and have a shave.

Some campaigner he'd turned out to be. Not any more. He was a creature of hotels now. Someone was making coffee – he was sure of it. He stood and stretched, then walked into the lobby. Anarchy. Bodies everywhere. A woman with two chins was snoring in a chair, a Vuitton suitcase tied securely to her finger with a shoelace. What did she have in there? he wondered. The silver service from some embassy? Polish hams? Wads of zlotys? Little good they'd do her now; the Germans no doubt had occupation scrip already printed and ready to spend. He moved towards the staircase and lost the scent, then backtracked into the dining room. Cautiously, he pushed open one of the swinging doors to the kitchen. Only a cat sleeping on a stove. The static was louder, however, and the coffee was close. At one end of the kitchen, another swinging door opened onto a small pantry and two women looked up quickly, startled at his sudden appearance. They were hotel maids, he guessed, pretty girls with tilted noses and cleft chins, one dark, the other fair, both wearing heavy cotton skirts and blouses, their hands red from scrubbing floors. A zinc coffeepot stood on a small parlour stove wedged into one corner, and an old-fashioned radio with a curved body sat on a shelf and played symphonic music amid the static. The maids were drinking coffee from the hotel's demi-tasse cups. After Szara said good morning he pleaded for coffee. 'Just tell me how much,' he said. 'I would be happy to pay.'

The blonde girl coloured and looked down at her shoes. The dark one found him a tiny cup and filled it with coffee, adding a shapeless chunk of sugar from a paper sack. She offered him a piece of twig to use as a stirrer, explaining. 'They have locked up the spoons somewhere. And of course there is nothing to pay. We share with you.'

'You are kind,' he said. The coffee was sharp and hot and strong.

'There is only a little left,' the dark girl said. 'You won't tell, will you?'

'Never. It's our secret.' He drew an X over his heart with one finger and she smiled.

The symphonic music faded away, replaced by a voice speaking Russian: 'Good morning, this is the world news service of Radio Moscow.'

Szara looked at his watch. It was exactly five-thirty, that made it seven-thirty Moscow time. The announcer's voice was low and smooth and reasonable – one need not concern oneself too much with the news it broadcast; somewhere in the Kremlin all was being carefully seen to. There was a reference to a communiqué, to a meeting of the Central Committee, then the news that some forty divisions of the Red Army had entered Poland along a five-hundred-mile front. In general they had been welcomed, there was no fighting to speak of, little resistance was expected. Foreign Minister Molotov had announced that 'events rising from the Polish-German war have revealed the internal insolvency and obvious impotence of the Polish state'. There was great concern that some 'unexpected contingency' could 'create a menace to the Soviet Union'. Molotov had gone on to say that the Soviet government 'could not remain indifferent to the fate of its blood brothers, the Ukrainians and Byelorussians inhabiting Poland'. The announcer continued for some time; the phrasing was careful, precise. All had been thought out. War and instability in a neighbouring state posed certain dangers; the army was simply moving up to a point where the occupation of contested territory would insulate Soviet citizens from fighting and civil disorders. The announcer went on to give other foreign news, local news, and the temperature – forty-eight degrees – in Moscow.

Later that morning word came from Lvov that the Germans were preparing to leave the city. A great wave of excitement and relief swept over the population of the Krynica-Zdroj, and it was determined that a column would be formed – Ukrainian bands continued their offensive; several travellers were known to have disappeared – to make the journey into town. A light but steady rain was deemed to be of no importance; the spa had an ample supply of black umbrellas and these were distributed by the smiling caretaker, Tomasz. The diplomatic corps made every effort to appear at its best – men shaved and powdered, women pinned up their hair, formal suits were dug out of trunks and suitcases. The procession was led by Tomasz, wearing an elegant little hat with an Alpine brush in the band, and the commercial counsellor of the Belgian embassy in Warsaw, carrying a broomstick with a white linen table napkin mounted at one end, a flag of neutrality.

It was a long line of men and women beneath bobbing black

umbrellas that advanced down the sandy road to Lvov. The fields were bright green and the smell of black earth and mown hay was sharp and sweet in the rainy air. The spirit of the group was supremely optimistic. Prevailing views were concentrated on the possibility of a diplomatic resolution of the Polish crisis as well as on cigarettes, coffee, soap, perhaps even roast chicken or cream cake; whatever might be had in newly liberated Lvov.

Szara marched near the end of the column. The people around him were of various opinions about the Soviet advance, news of which had spread like wildfire. Most thought it good news: Stalin informing Hitler that, despite their expedient pact, enough was enough. It was felt that a period of intense diplomacy would now take place and, no matter the final result of the German invasion, they could go home. To Szara there was something infinitely Polish about the scene, these people in their dark and formal clothing marching along a narrow road in the rain beneath a forest of umbrellas. Towards the end of the six-mile walk, some of the diplomats were tiring, and it was determined that every-body should sing – 'The Marseillaise' as it turned out, the one song they all knew. True, it was the national anthem of a recently declared belligerent, but they were advancing under a white flag, and for raising the spirits on a rainy day there simply wasn't anything better. Vainshtok and Szara marched together; the former, his shoulder holster aban-doned for the journey, thrust his clenched fist into the air and sang like a little fury in a high, wavering voice.

Szara didn't sing. He was too busy thinking. Trying to sort a series of images in his mind that might, if he found the organizing principle, come together to form a single, sharp picture. Beria's ascension, Abramov's murder, the suicide of Kuscinas, the Okhrana dossier, Baumann's arrest: it all ended with forty Russian divisions marching into Poland. *Stalin did this*, he thought. Stalin did what? Szara had no name for it. And that made him angry. Wasn't he smart enough to understand what had been done? *Maybe not.*

What he did know was that he had been part of it, witness to it, though mostly by accident. He didn't like coincidence, life had taught him to be suspicious of it, but he was able to recall moment after moment when he'd seen and heard, when he'd known – often from the periphery but known nonetheless – what was going on. *Why me, then?* he demanded of himself. The answer hurt: *because nobody took you very seriously. Because you were seen to be a kind of educated fool. Because you were useful in a minor but not very important way, you were permitted to see things and to find out about things in the same way a lady's maid is*

ALAN FURST

permitted to know about a love affair: whatever she may think about it doesn't matter.

What he needed, Szara thought, was to talk it out. To say the words out loud. But the one person he could trust, General Bloch, had disappeared from his life. Dead? In flight? He didn't know.

' "*Aux armes, citoyens!*" ' Beside him, Vainshtok sang passionately to the cloudy Polish heavens.

No, Szara thought. *Let him be.*

In the city, people stood soberly in the square that faced the ruined station and watched in silence as the Wehrmacht marched west, back towards Germany. It was so quiet that the sound of boots and horses' hooves on the cobblestones, the creak of leather and the jangle of equipment, sounded unnaturally loud as the companies moved past. Some of the infantrymen glanced at the crowd as they went by, their faces showing little more than impersonal curiosity. The diplomats stood under their umbrellas alongside the Poles and watched the procession. To Szara they seemed a little lost. There was nobody to call on, nobody to whom a note could be handed; for the moment they had been deprived of their natural element.

The normal progress of the withdrawal was broken only by a single, strange interlude in the grey order of march: the Germans had stolen a circus. They were taking it away with them. Its wagons, decorated with curlicues and flourishes in brilliant gold on a dark red field, bore the legend Circus Goldenstein, and the reins were held by unsmiling Wehrmacht drivers, who looked slightly absurd managing the plumed and feathered horses. Szara wondered what had become of the clowns and the acrobats. They were nowhere to be seen, only the animals were in evidence. Behind the bars of a horse-drawn cage Szara saw a sleepy tiger, its chin sunk on its forepaws, its green-slit eyes half closed as it rolled past the crowd lining the street.

Towards evening, the diplomats walked back down the sandy road to the spa. Two days later, a Russian tank column rolled into the city.

Behind the tanks came the civil administration: the NKVD, the political commissars, and their clerks. The clerks had lists. They included the membership of all political parties, especially the socialists – Polish, Ukrainian, Byelorussian, and Jewish. The clerks also had the names of trade union members, civil servants, policemen, forestry workers, engineers, lawyers, university students, peasants with more than a few animals, refugees from other countries, landowners, teachers,

508

commercial traders, and scores of other categories, particularly those, like stamp dealers and collectors, who habitually had correspondence with people outside the country. So the clerks knew who they wanted the day they arrived and immediately set to work to find the rest, seizing all civil, tax, educational, and commercial records. Individuals whose names appeared on the lists, and their families, were to be deported to the Soviet Union in trains, eventually to be put to work in forced labour battalions. Factories were to be disassembled and sent east to the industrial centres of the USSR, stores stripped of their inventories, farms of their livestock.

Special units of the NKVD Foreign Department arrived as well, some of them turning up at the spa, their black Pobedas spattered with mud up to the door handles. The diplomats were to be sorted out and sent on their way home as soon as the western half of Poland conceded victory to Germany. 'Be calm,' the operatives said. 'Warsaw will surrender any day now, the Poles can't hold out much longer.' The Russians were soft-spoken and reassuring. Most of the diplomats were relieved. A registration table was set up in the dining room with two polite men in civilian clothes sitting behind it.

Szara and Vainshtok waited until five o'clock before they joined the line. Vainshtok was philosophical. 'Back to dear old Berlin.' He sighed. 'And dear old Dr Goebbels's press conferences. How I've lived without them I don't know. But, at least, there'll be something for dinner besides beets.'

Vainshtok was skinny and hollow-chested, with thin, hairy arms and legs. He reminded Szara of a spider. 'Do you really care so much what you eat?' Szara asked. The line moved forward a pace. 'You certainly don't get fat.'

'Terror,' Vainshtok explained. 'That's what keeps me thin. I eat plenty, but I burn it up.'

The man in front of them, a minor Hungarian noble of some sort, stepped up to the table, stood at rigid attention, and, announcing his name and title, presented his diplomatic credentials. Szara got a good look at the two operatives at the table. One was young and alert and very efficient. He had a ledger open in front of him and copied out the information from documents and passports. The other seemed rather more an observer, in attendance only in case of some special circumstance beyond the expertise of his partner. The observer was a short, heavy man, middle-aged, with wavy fair hair and extremely thick glasses. As his junior questioned the Hungarian in diplomatic French – 'May I ask, sir, how you managed to find your way to this area?' – he put an oval cigarette in the centre of his lips, creased the head of a wooden match with his thumbnail, and lit the cigarette from the flare.

Where? Szara asked himself.

The Hungarian's French was primitive. 'Left Warsaw on late train. Night in eight September . . .'

Where?

The observer glanced at Szara, but seemed to take no special notice of him.

'Stopping in Lublin . . .' said the Hungarian.

'I don't feel well,' Szara said confidentially. 'You go ahead.' He turned and walked out of the dining room. Manoeuvred his way through the crowded lobby, excusing himself as he bumped into people, and took the passageway that led to the hydrotherapy pool and the treatment areas in the basement. The spiral staircase was made of thin metal, and his footsteps clattered and echoed in the stairwell as he descended. He took the first exit, walking quickly through a maze of long tile halls, trying doors as he went. At last one opened. This was a water room of some sort; the ceiling, floor, and walls were set with pale green tiles, hoses hung from brass fittings, and a canvas screen shielded a row of metal tables. The screen had a series of rubber-rimmed apertures in it – for arthritic ankles to be sprayed with sulphurous water? He hiked himself up onto a metal table, took a deep breath, tried to calm down.

Where, he now realized, was in some lost Belgian mining town the night that Odile was debriefed after she got off the train from Germany. The observer was the man with the gold watch; Szara remembered him lighting a cigarette off a match flare, remembered him asking a single question: 'Is that your answer?' Some such thing. Intimidation. A cold, watery stare.

And so? So he'd turned up at the Krynica-Zdroj, sitting behind a table with a ledger on it. So? That's probably what he did with his life. Szara resisted a shiver. The little room was clammy, its air much too still, a cavern buried in the earth. What was wrong with him, running away like a frightened child? Was that all it took to panic him, two operatives sitting at a table? Now he'd have to go back upstairs and join the line; they'd seen him leave, perhaps it would make them suspicious. *See how you incriminate yourself!* No, there was nothing to fear. What could they do, surrounded by a crowd of diplomats. He hopped off the table and left the room. Now, which hallway led where?

He wandered a little distance towards where he thought the exit was, stopped dead when he heard footsteps on the staircase. Who was this? A normal, deliberate descent. Then Vainshtok, nasal and querulous: 'André Aronovich? André Aronovich!'

Vainshtok, from the sound of it, was walking down the corridor at right angles to where he stood. 'I'm over here,' Szara said.

Coming around the corner, Vainshtok signalled with his eyes and a nod of the head that someone was behind him, but Szara could see no one. 'I've come to say good-bye,' he said, then reached out suddenly and took Szara in his arms, a powerful hug in the Russian style. Szara was startled, found himself pulled hard against Vainshtok's chest, then tried to return the embrace, but Vainshtok backed away. Two men turned the corner into the hallway, then waited politely for farewells to be said. 'So,' Vainshtok said, 'let those who can, do what they must, eh?' He winked. Szara felt the bulging weight between his side and the waistband of his trousers and understood everything. Vainshtok saw the expression on his face and raised his eyebrows like a comedian. 'You know, Szara, you're not such a snob after all. You'll come and see me when you get to Moscow?'

'Not Berlin?'

'Nah. Enough!'

'Lucky for you.'

'That's it.' His eyes glistened.

He turned abruptly and walked away. When he reached the end of the corridor, he turned towards the staircase, followed by one of the men. A moment later Szara heard them climbing the stairs. As the other man came to join him, Szara saw that it was Maltsaev, dark and balding, wearing tinted eyeglasses and the same voluminous overcoat wrapped about him, his hands thrust deep in the pockets. He nodded at Szara with evident satisfaction. 'The wandering troubadour – at last!' he said merrily.

Szara looked puzzled.

'You've given Moscow fits,' Maltsaev explained. 'One moment you're landing at Warsaw airfield, the next, nothing, air.'

'A detour,' Szara said. 'I was, how shall I put it, *escorted* by Polish military intelligence. They picked me up at a hospital in Tarnow, after a bombing on the rail line, and drove me to Nowy Sacz. Then we couldn't get through the German lines. Eventually, I managed to cling to the platform of a train that was going to Lvov. Once I got there, a policeman sent me out here to the spa, with the diplomats.'

Maltsaev nodded sympathetically. 'Well, everything's going to be fine now. I'm up here on some liaison assignment with the Ukrainian *apparat*, but they wired me in Belgrade to keep an eye out for the missing Szara. I'm afraid you'll have to go into the city and tell some idiot colonel the whole saga, but that shouldn't trouble you too much.'

'No, I don't mind,' he said.

'Your friend Vainshtok's going back to Moscow. Probably you won't have to. I would imagine you'd prefer to stay in Paris.'

'If I can, I'd like to, yes.'

'Lucky. Or favoured. Someday you'll tell me your secret.'

Szara laughed.

Maltsaev's mood changed, he lowered his voice. 'Look, you didn't mind, I hope, the last time we spoke, at the station in Geneva . . .'

Szara remembered perfectly, a remark about Abramov: *his parents should have made him study the violin like all the rest of them.* 'I understand completely,' he said. 'A difficult time.'

'We're none of us made of iron. What happened with Abramov, well, we only wanted to talk with him. We were certainly prepared to do more, but it would never have come to that if he hadn't tried to run. We couldn't, you understand these things, we couldn't let him disappear. As it was, I got a thorough roasting for the whole business. Any hope of getting out of the embassy in Belgrade – there it went. Anyhow, what I said at the station . . . I hadn't slept, and I knew I was in trouble, maybe a lot of trouble. But I shouldn't have taken it out on you.'

Szara held up a hand. 'Please. I don't hold a grudge.'

Maltsaev seemed relieved. 'Can we go back upstairs? Maybe get you a decent dinner in Lvov before you have to see the colonel? I'd rather not try the Polish roads in the dark if I don't have to. Driving through the Ukraine was bad enough, especially with Soviet armour on the roads.'

'Let's go.'

'It smells awful down here.' Maltsaev wrinkled his nose like a kid.

'Sulphur. Just like in hell.'

Maltsaev snorted with amusement. 'Is *that* how they cure you! Sinner, cease your drinking and depravity or here's how it will be.'

They walked together along the corridor towards the stairway. 'Your friends are waiting for us?' Szara asked.

'Fortunately, no. Those guys make me nervous.'

They came to the spiral staircase. 'Is there a sub-basement?' Maltsaev asked, peering down.

'Yes. There's a pool in it, and the springs are there somewhere.'

'Just every little thing you'd want. Ah, the life of the idle rich.' He gestured for Szara to precede him up the steps.

'Please,' said Szara, standing back.

'I insist,' Maltsaev said, a parody of aristocratic courtesy.

They both hesitated. To Szara, a long moment. He waited for Maltsaev to climb the stairs but the man stood there, smiling politely; apparently he had all the time in the world. Szara took the gun out and shot him.

He expected a huge, ringing explosion in the confined space of the stairwell but it did not happen that way. The weapon snapped, something fizzed – it was as though he sensed the path of the bullet – and he could smell burned air.

Maltsaev was furious. 'Oh you didn't,' he said. He started to take one hand out of his pocket but Szara reached over and grasped him by the wrist. He was curiously weak; Szara held him easily. Maltsaev bit his lip and scowled with discomfort. Szara shot him again and he sat down abruptly, his weight falling back against an iron rung of the stairway. He died a few seconds later. By then he just looked melancholy.

Szara stared at the weapon. It was the blued-steel Steyr that Vainshtok had carried. Why had he given it up? Why had he not defended himself? Szara found the safety device, then put the automatic in the side pocket of his jacket. He listened hard, but there was no running, no commotion above him. The shots had not been heard. Perhaps the powder load in the bullet was minimal; he really didn't understand. He pulled Maltsaev's hand free of his pocket and went looking for the weapon he knew was there, but he didn't find it. Nor could he find it anywhere else. That meant Maltsaev's crew, perhaps the same one that had finished Abramov, was nearby. Maltsaev wasn't a murderer, Szara reminded himself, he was an arranger of murders. Szara found a car key in an inside pocket and a set of identity papers. Running his hands down the overcoat, he discovered a flap sewn into the sleeve that held a sword and shield NKVD pin in a soft pigskin bag with a drawstring. There was also a wallet packed with roubles, zlotys, and reichsmarks. Szara put everything in his own pockets. Next he grabbed Maltsaev's ankles and pulled. It was difficult, he had to use all his strength, but once he got the body moving, the smooth wool overcoat slid easily across the floor. It took at least two minutes to drag Maltsaev down the hall and into the unlocked room, and the trip left a long maroon streak on the tile. The lock on the door was simple enough, it worked on a lever. Szara thumbed it down and pulled the door closed until he heard it click.

At the foot of the iron stairway he paused, retrieved both ejected cartridges, then climbed, shoes in one hand, gun in the other; but there was no one waiting for him on the landing and he dropped the weapon into his pocket and hopped on one foot to put his shoes back on. The lobby was as he'd left it; people milling about, affable confusion, a line working its way up to the table. 'Well,' said the Spanish official who'd shared the sunporch with him, 'your friend has finally made it out of here. It's given us all hope.'

'He's known to be clever – and lucky,' Szara said, clearly a bit envious.

The Spaniard sighed. 'I'll be going back to Warsaw eventually. As you know, Germany is exceptionally sympathetic to our neutrality. Perhaps it won't be too long.'

'I hope not,' Szara said. 'Such disorder helps nothing.'

'How true.'

'Perhaps we'll dine together this evening.'

The Spaniard inclined his head, an informal bow of acceptance.

Szara used a wall mirror to assure himself that the observer was still at the table, then avoided his line of vision by taking a back door, walking behind the kitchen area where the two young Polish women were preparing beets over a wooden tub, saving every last peeling in a metal pan. They both smiled at him as he went past, even the shy one. He entered the sunporch by a side door and looked out through the screen. There were two black Pobedas parked in the gravel semicircle. One was coated with road dust and grime, the other spattered with mud and clay. Recalling what Maltsaev had said about Soviet armour on the roads, he decided to try the latter. He picked up his valise, took a deep breath, and walked off the sunporch onto the lawn. He nodded to a few diplomats strolling along the paths, then slid into the front seat of the muddy Pobeda as though it were the most natural thing in the world for him to do.

The car's interior smelled strongly: of pomade, sweat, cigarettes, vodka, mildewed upholstery, and petrol. He put Maltsaev's key into the ignition and turned it, the starter motor whined, died, whined on a higher note, produced a single firing of the engine, sank to a whisper, suddenly fired twice, and at last brought the engine to sputtering life. He wrestled with the gear-lever – mounted on the steering column – until it went into one of the gears. Through the streaked panel window on his left he could see the diplomats staring at him: who was he to simply climb into a car, valise in hand, and drive away? One of them started to walk towards him. Szara lifted the clutch pedal – the car lurched forward a foot and stalled. The diplomat, a handsome, dignified man with grey wings of hair that rested on his ears, had raised an interrogatory index finger – *oh, just a moment*. Szara turned the ignition key again and the starter motor whined up and down the musical scale as it had before. When the engine at last fired he blinked the sweat out of his eyes. '*Un moment, s'il vous plaît*,' the diplomat called out, only a few feet away. Szara gave him a tight smile and a shrug. The gears meshed and the car rolled forward, crunching over the gravel. Szara looked in the rearview mirror. The diplomat was standing with hands on hips, the caricature of a man offended by simply unspeakable rudeness.

There wasn't a road sign left in Poland – Vyborg's colleagues had seen to that – only a maze of dirt tracks that ran off every which way. But he had walked the route to Lvov and that was the one direction he knew he had to avoid. Maltsaev's assistants could well be waiting for him there, by the side of the road, just conveniently out of sight of the diplomatic corps at the spa.

There was a much-used map of eastern Poland on the floor of the car, and the sun, at six-twenty on an afternoon in late September, was low in the sky. That was west. Szara kept the sun on his left side and headed north, managing some ten miles before dusk overtook him. Then he backed off what he believed to be a main road onto a smaller road and turned off the engine. Next he took a careful inventory: he had plenty of money, no water, no food, the best part of a tank of petrol, six rounds in the Steyr. It was, he now saw, an MI2, thus a Steyr-Hahn – Steyr-with-hammer – stamped 08 on the left-hand surface of the slide, which had something to do with the absorption of the Austrian army into the German army after 1938, a mechanical retooling. Exactly what this was he could not remember; a rue Delesseux circular unread, who cared about guns? He also had three sets of identity papers: his own, Maltsaev's, and the Jean Bonotte passport in the false bottom of the valise, bound with a rubber band to a packet of French francs and a card with telephone numbers written on it. In the boot of the Pobeda was a full can of petrol and a blanket.

Enough to start a new life. Many had started with less.

'The wind and the stars.' Whose line was that? He didn't remember. But it perfectly described the night. He sat on the blanket at the foot of an ancient linden tree – the road was lined with them, creating an avenue that no doubt wound its way to some grand Polish estate up the road. The night grew chilly, but if he pulled his jacket tight he stayed warm enough.

He had thought he'd sleep in the car, but the smell of it sickened him. Not that he wasn't used to what he took to be its various elements. Nothing new about vodka or cigarettes, his own sweat was no better than anyone else's, and all Russian cars reeked of petrol and damp upholstery. Something else. To do with what they'd used the Pobeda for, perhaps a lingering scent of the taken, the captured. Or maybe it was the smell of executioners. Russian folklore had it that murder left its trace: the vertical line at the side of the mouth, the mark of the killer. Might it not change the way a man smelled?

A former Szara would have turned such light on himself, but not now. He had done what he had to do. 'Let those who can, do what they must.' Thus Vainshtok had saved his life. Because he would not, or could not, use the weapon himself? No, that was absurd. Szara refused to believe it. There was some other reason, and he had to face the possibility that he might never find out what it was.

There was a great deal he didn't understand. Why, for instance, had they sent Maltsaev after him? Because he'd disappeared from view for several days? Had they found out what he'd done in Paris with the British? No, that was impossible. Of all the world's secret services it was the British the Soviets truly feared. Their counter-intelligence array – Scotland Yard, MI5 – was extremely efficient; Comintern agents trying to enter Great Britain under false identities were time and again discovered, for the British maintained and used their files to great effect. As for MI6, it was, in its way, a particularly cold-blooded and predatory organization. A consequence of the British national character, with its appetite for both education and adventure, a nasty combination when manifested in an intelligence service. Szara could not imagine the problem lay in that direction. Fitzware, for all his peculiarities of style, was a serious, a scrupulous officer. The courier, then, Evans. No. It was something else, something in Russia, something to do with Abramov, Bloch, the Jewish *khvost*. Perhaps Beria or his friends just decided one morning that he'd lived long enough. But André Szara had made his own decision, at some point, that he would not be one of those who went meekly into captivity, carving *za chto* into the stone of a cellar wall. Now a single act, the pulling of a trigger, had freed him. Now – a Jew, a Pole, a Russian – he had no country at all.

'The wind and the stars.' Strange how he couldn't stop thinking it. He wondered how long he might live. Probably only a little while longer. Just after dark a car had rumbled down the road he'd left. Then, an hour later, another. Was it them? They would certainly be looking for him. And they'd never stop until they found him; that was the rule of the game and everybody understood it. Ah but if this were to be his last night on earth how he would treasure it. A little breeze blowing steady across the Polish farmland, the grand sky – that immense and perfect and glittering mystery. There were frogs croaking in the darkness, life all around him. He didn't have much of a plan, only to try and get across the Lithuanian border to the north. After that he'd see. Possibly Sweden, or Denmark. So far he'd stolen seven hours of existence; every hour was a victory, and he had no intention of going to sleep.

Szara was later to put it this way:

'If ever the hand of God guided my path it was when, from the twentieth to the twenty-third of September, 1939, I drove from southern Poland to Kovno, Lithuania, in a stolen NKVD car. Clearly there was a tragedy taking place in Poland; I saw the signs of it, I walked in its tracks, and I fear that it may have contributed to my escape, for it absorbed the energies of all Soviet security forces. Finally I do not know for certain, and I can only say that I survived. This was, equally, an accident of geography. Had I been thirty miles to the west, NKVD officers or political commissars serving on the front line surely would have arrested me. I believe they knew who I was, what I had done, and had a description of the car I was driving. In the same way, had I been thirty miles to the east, I would have been arrested by the NKVD of the Soviet Ukraine or murdered by the Ukrainian bands, who were then very active. But I was in the middle, in an area behind the lines but not yet secured by the *apparat*. Those who may have experience of a zone in which Soviet troops are manoeuvring, not fighting, will know what I mean. I moved among lost units hampered by poor communications, amidst confusion and error and inefficiency, and it was as though I were invisible.'

Well yes, true as far as it went, but not the whole story by any means. He was able, for instance, to choose an identity suitable to the moment. Confronted by a Soviet patrol at dawn on the twenty-second, he produced Maltsaev's NKVD badge, and the officer waved him ahead and cursed his troopers when they didn't get out of the road quickly enough. But in a *shtetl* village in the middle of nowhere, he became Szara the Polish Jew, was given a bench in the study house to sleep on, and fed by the rabbi's wife. Meanwhile, the remarkable fact of the Pobeda was ignored by the villagers. He drove it into a muddy, unfenced yard full of chickens and there it sat, safe and invisible from the road, while he slept. Later, when it suited his purpose, he presented himself as André Szara, Soviet journalist, and, later still, Jean Bonotte of Marseille, a French citizen.

It took him some twenty hours to negotiate almost three hundred miles to a point just short of the border with Lithuania. The first night, moved by some obscure but very powerful instinct – 'the hand of God'? – he drove away from his refuge at midnight and continued on the same road, north he hoped, for some six hours. He feared he would be unable to cross the many rivers that lay across his path but, as it turned out, the Poles had not blown the bridges. So the Pobeda rattled over the loose boards of the narrow structures spanning first the Berezina, then the

Belaja. Just beyond the former he came to a cobbled road, heading east and west, flanked by birch trees. He knew, just for that moment, precisely where he was, for those cobblestones had been laid by the Emperor Napoleon's Corsicans in 1812, a solid foundation for wheeled guns and ammunition carts, and it led off in the direction of Moscow. Szara drove across it, heading due north.

Somewhere near Chelm, just before dawn, his path was blocked by a train of cattle trucks standing idle at a crossing. Uniformed NKVD soldiers were guarding the train, and in the darkness he could just make out the barrel of a machine gun, mounted on top of a goods wagon, as it swung to cover the Pobeda. One of the sentries unslung his rifle and walked over to ask him who he was and what he was doing there. Szara was about to reach for the badge, then didn't. Something told him to leave it where it was. Just a Pole, he said. His wife had gone into labour and he was off to fetch the midwife. The soldier stared. Szara could hear voices inside the cattle trucks, speaking Polish, pleading for water. Without further conversation, Szara put the car in reverse and backed up, his heart pounding, while the soldier watched him but did nothing – a potential problem was simply removing itself. When he was out of sight of the train, he rested his head on the steering wheel for a time, then turned the car around, backtracked a few miles, picked a road at random, and, an hour later, after several turnings, drove over the tracks at a deserted crossing.

Passing a farm early in the morning, he heard the drawn-out lowing of unmilked cattle and the frantic barking of deserted dogs left at the end of their chains. At another level crossing there was a wooden cattlegate blocking the road and when he got out to open it he saw something yellow on the ground and bent down to see what it was: it turned out to be a scrap of paper bound to a small stone with yellow wool, perhaps unravelled from a shawl. Unwinding the wool, he found a note: *Please tell Franciszka Kodowicz that Krysia and Wladzia have been taken away in a train. Thank you.* The wind blew at the piece of paper in his hand. He stood by the car for a long time, then carefully wrapped the paper around the stone and rebound it with the yellow wool, placing it back on the ground where it had landed when the girls had thrown it from the moving train. He was, he noted dispassionately, now beyond vows or resolutions. He slid into the front seat of the car, holding his breath as the musky scent of pomade and sweat assaulted him, forced the gear lever down, and drove north. That was his resolution, that was his vow: to exist.

On the third night, having swung west to avoid the market town of Grodno, he saw from the map that he'd entered the country of the

Pripet marshes. He suspected the Russian line of advance had not yet reached the area, its northern flank held up for some reason, for he could find no evidence of an occupying force. He stopped the car and waited for morning, telling himself to remain awake and alert. He woke, again and again, when his chin hit his chest, finally fading away altogether into the blank sleep of exhaustion. The next time he came to it was daybreak, and he saw that he was surrounded by marshland that ran to the low horizon, a plain of swaying reeds and long reaches of flat water coloured by a grey, windswept sky. The land was ancient, desolate, its vast silence punctuated by the distant cries of waterfowl.

He walked around for a time, trying to get his bearings, washing his face and hands in the chill, dark water of the marsh. He searched the sky but there was no sun – he had no idea where he was, or which way was north. And he didn't care. That was the worst part, he truly did not care. His resolve had flowed away like sand on the outgoing tide. He sat on the running board of the Pobeda, slumped against the door, and stared out over the grey ponds and blowing reeds. He had somehow come to the end of his journey, the future he'd held out to himself no more than a trick of the illusionist, the self-deluded survivor. Against the vast background of the deserted land he saw his insignificance only too clearly – a vain, petty man, envious and scheming, an opportunist, a fraud. Why should such a man remain alive? *Get in the car*, he told himself. But the wilful interior voice sickened him – all it knew was greed, all it did was want. Even here, at the end of the world, it sang its little song, and any gesture, no matter how absurd, would satisfy it. But the only act he could imagine called for removing the Steyr from beneath the driver's seat of the car and relieving the earth of an unneeded presence – at least an act of grace. Did he have the courage to do it? Surprisingly, he did. What had he done with his life – other than seek a transient peace between the legs of women. He had, in order to live another day, and then another, served the people who now did what they did and who would, he knew for a certainty, do what they would do. And to put a good finish on the history of his particular life, the time and place were perfect: *ironically, he was only a few miles from the safety of the Lithuanian border.* He looked at his watch, it was sixteen minutes after nine. The sky shifted across his vision, a hundred shades of grey, drifting and rolling like battlesmoke blown by a wind off the sea.

What saved him – for he was very, very close to it – was a vision. Of this he was not to write; it was not germane, and there may have been other reasons. Well down the long, straight road ahead of him appeared the silhouette of a hunter; a man stepped out of the reeds, a shotgun, the barrel broken safely from the stock, riding his forearm. A spaniel followed, stood at the side of the hunter and shook a fine spray of marshwater from its coat. Then the man walked across the road, the dog trotting ahead, and both vanished.

Then, almost the next thing he knew, he was driving. Through a great labyrinth of roads and paths that could have led anywhere or nowhere. Sometimes, with tears in his eyes, he drove into a blur, but never lifted his foot from the accelerator. He drove, fiercely, angrily, towards the wind. Took any road on which the churning skies hurried towards him, their speed heightened by the rush of the car in the opposite direction. He passed, and barely noticed, an empty guard tower, barbed wire strung away in both directions, a wire gate hanging crazily on one hinge as though brushed aside by a giant. At last he saw an old man by the side of the road, poking listlessly at a garden patch with a primitive hoe. Szara stamped on the brake. 'Where in God's name am I?' he called out.

'*Vas?*' said the man.

Szara tried again and got the same answer. They stared at each other, deadlocked, Szara angry, the old man more confused than frightened and saying finally, with politely controlled irritation, 'What is the matter with you, sir, that you shout so?' The man was speaking German, Szara finally realized, the common second language in that country. He let out a single cry of absurd laughter, slammed the car into gear, and roared on into Lithuania.

He arrived in Kovno a fugitive. And stayed to become a refugee.

Two cities anchored the northern and southern extremes of the Pale of Settlement, Kovno and Odessa. Szara, who had grown up in the latter, soon came to understand the former. These were border cities, Odessa on the Black Sea across from Istanbul, Kovno at the conjunction of Russia, Poland, and Lithuania, and border cities lived by a particular set of instincts: they knew, for instance, when war was coming, because when there was war they were not spared. They knew the people who showed up before the wars. Immigrants, refugees, whatever you called them, they had a way of arriving just ahead of the armies and were taken to be an omen of difficult times, as migrating birds portend winter.

But Kovno's long and complicated history had marked its citizens with the very characteristics that enabled them to survive it. Actually, by the time Szara arrived in the city known in his childhood as Kovno, it was called by the Lithuanian name Kaunas. Its nearby neighbour, however, remained Wilno, since it had been declared Polish territory, rather than Vilna, the Russian name before 1917. The Lithuanians themselves preferred Vilnius, but at that particular moment this alternative was running a poor third.

The people of Kovno, now Kaunas, were obviously multilingual. Szara had spoken German, Polish, and Yiddish in the city before he ever slept there. They were also virtually immune to politics, not strange for a city that has known Teutonic Knights and Bolshevik lawyers and everything in between. And they were, in their own quiet way, deeply obstinate. In all things but particularly in matters of nationality. The Lithuanians knew they were home, the Poles knew what they stood on was Polish soil no matter what anybody said, the Jews had been there for hundreds of years, faring about as well as they did anywhere, while the better part of the German population looked west, with longing hearts and the occasional song, to the Fatherland.

Nonetheless, obstinate though the citizens of Kovno might have been, it seemed, in the autumn of 1939, that quite a considerable number of them were intent on being somewhere else.

Szara rented a third of a room in a boardinghouse, actually a boarding apartment, at the top of seven flights of stairs, sharing with two Polish Jews, cameramen in the Polish film industry who'd fled Warsaw by riding cross country on a motorcycle. One of the men worked nights as a sweeper at the railway station, and Szara had his bed until he arrived home at six-thirty in the morning. That got Szara up early. After breakfast he haunted the steamship offices, willing to leave from any of the Baltic ports – Liepāja, Riga, Tallinn – but there were simply too many people with the same idea. Ships and ferries to Denmark – his first choice – in fact to anywhere on earth, were booked well into 1940. Cabins, deck space, every available inch. Undaunted, he took a train up to Liepāja and tried to bribe his way onto a Norwegian timber freighter, but only a precipitate exit from a waterfront café saved him from arrest. And the incident was witnessed – there were two vaguely familiar faces at the same café, seen perhaps at the steamship offices. No matter where he went or what he tried it was the same story.

Even at the thieves' market, where the Pobeda caused low whistles of appreciation but very little financial interest. Sublime realists, Kovno's thieves – where could one drive? South was occupied Poland, north the Baltic, east the USSR. To the west, the port of Memel had been snaffled up by the Reich in March, Königsberg was German, now Danzig as well. Szara took what was offered for the Pobeda and fled. Trust the NKVD, he thought, to have eyes and ears at the Kovno thieves' market.

Attempts at currency conversion got him precisely nowhere. He couldn't sell his zlotys; German marks were being introduced in Poland and nobody was going there anyhow. The roubles weren't even supposed to be outside the USSR – those he burned. The French francs, by far the greatest part of his little treasury, would have moved very briskly on the kerbside foreign exchange markets, but he refused to part with them; they could be used anywhere and everybody else wanted them for the same reason he did.

The first few days in Kovno Szara was extremely cautious; he knew the Soviet intelligence *apparat* in Lithuania to be well established and aggressive. But, in time, he abandoned the principles of clandestine practice and became one more nameless soul whose principal occupation was waiting. He sat in the parks and watched the chess games with all the other refugees as the leaves turned gold in the slow onset of autumn. He frequented the cheapest cafés, dawdled endlessly over coffees, and soon people began to nod good morning: he was part of their day, always at the table in the corner.

He made one friend, an unlikely one, a gentleman known as Mr Wiggins, who was to be found at the Thomas Cook steamship and travel office. Mr Wiggins came from the pages of Kipling; he had a waxed moustache, parted his hair in the middle, and wore an old-fashioned collar, formal, uncomfortable, and reassuring. He was, in his way, a terribly decent man who served the Thomas Cook company with conviction and chose to see, in the refugee flood that swept through his office from dawn to dusk, not the flotsam of Europe but a stream of clients. Szara seemed to be one of his favourites. 'I am so sorry,' he'd say, very real regret in his voice. 'No cancellations today. But you will try tomorrow, I hope. One can't ever tell. People do change their minds, that's one thing I have learned in this business.'

Mr Wiggins, and everyone else, knew that war was coming to Lithuania – or, if not war, at least occupation. The country had been freed of Russian rule in 1918 – of Lenin's dictum 'Two steps forward and one step back', this had been a step back – and had got rather to enjoy being a free nation. But its days were numbered and nothing could be done about it. Szara, as always encountering familiar faces, bought the local and foreign newspapers early in the morning and took them back to his lair, in the common kitchen of the apartment, for intensive study, sharing the bad news with his fellow boarders as they drank thin, warmed-up coffee and tried not to say anything compromising.

The future became clearer as the days passed: a great shifting of population was to take place in Estonia and Latvia and simultaneously in Germany. Slavs east, Germans west, it was just about that simple. The Germans, more than a hundred thousand of them, were to be taken aboard Baltic passenger steamers and shipped back to Germany, whence their great-great-grandfathers had migrated hundreds of years earlier.

Meanwhile, various Slavic nationalities resident in Germany were headed east to join their long-lost brothers in the Soviet Union. This shuffling of populations was intended to re-establish the racial purity of Germany and to relieve the pressure on German settlers in Eastern Europe. They suffered horribly, according to Goebbels, because they retained their language and customs and dress in the midst of alien cultures and nobody liked them, being principally envious of their success. *One could call them blond Jews*, Szara thought.

But the fact of the migration hung over the breakfast table like a pall: if the Germans were leaving the Baltic states, who was coming?

There was only one candidate nation, and it wasn't France. To Szara, schooled in a certain way of thinking since 1937, it had even a deeper resonance: if the division of Poland was one of the secret protocols in the Hitler–Stalin pact, what were the others? 'Terribly sorry,' said Mr Wiggins. 'There simply isn't a thing.'

Like all refugees, Szara had too much time to think. He sat on a park bench and smoked a cigarette while the leaves drifted down. He had supposed, in escaping from Poland, that either death or glory awaited him, and so he'd taken his chances. With Maltsaev murdered he really had nothing to lose. But he had never for a moment imagined it might end up as a penurious life spent in dim cafés and shabby apartments, waiting for the Red Army to reach the gates of the city. He thought of trying to put a call through to de Montfried, to ask for help, but what kind of help could he offer? Money? More money that wouldn't buy what Szara needed? Some of the prosperous Jews in Kovno were spending literally fortunes to buy their way out before the Russians arrived, and there were stories going around that some of them wound up losing everything, forbidden to board steamers by cold-eyed pursers with armed seamen at their side. Other rumours – and Szara knew at least one of them to be true – told of desperate refugees putting to sea in rowboats, sometimes guided by self-proclaimed smugglers, never to be seen again. Drowned? Murdered? Who knew. But the confirming postal card never arrived in Kovno and friends and accomplices could draw only one conclusion from that.

In the end, Szara realized that the trap opened in only one direction and he determined to try it.

'From Hamburg? Copenhagen from Hamburg, you say?' Mr Wiggins, for just an instant, permitted himself to be startled. Then he cleared his throat, once again the traveller's perfect servant. 'No trouble at all, I'd think. Plenty of room. First-class cabin, if you like. Shall I book?'

*

It should have worked.

There were, of course, improvisations, as there had to be, but he managed those well enough and, in the end, it wasn't his fault that it didn't work. Fortunes of war, one might say.

He began with the hospitals. Wiggins helped him – the wealthy members of the German community went here, those of lesser means went there. Szara went there. A sad, brown brick structure, according to the name a Lutheran institution, in an innocuous neighbourhood away from the centre of the city. In a day or two of watching he'd determined how the hospital worked. In need of coffee or something stronger, the doctors, in accordance with their standing, patronized the Vienna, a dignified restaurant and pastry shop. The orderlies, janitors, clerks, and the occasional nurse used a nearby rathskeller for the same purposes. Szara chose the rathskeller. The hospital's day shift ended at four in the afternoon, so the productive time at the rathskeller ran for an hour or two after that. He spent three days there during the busy hours, just watching, and he spotted the loners. On day four he picked his man: sulky, homely, no longer young, with large ears and slicked-back hair, always one of the last to leave, not in a hurry to go home to a family. Szara bought him a beer and struck up a conversation. The man was a native Lithuanian, but he could speak German. Szara found out quickly why he drank alone: there was something a little evil about this man, something he covered up by use of a sneering, suggestive tone that implied there was something a little evil about everybody. Asked just what it was that *he* did, Szara admitted he was a dealer in paper. He bought and sold paper, he said, adding a sly glance to show the man what a smart fellow he thought he was.

The orderly, as he turned out to be, understood immediately. He knew about such matters. He even winked. This one, Szara guessed, had seen the inside of a jail, perhaps for a long time, perhaps for something very unpleasant.

And what kind of paper was the gentleman buying these days?

German paper.

Why?

Who could say. A client wanted German paper. Not from Germany, mind you, and not from Lithuania. Paper from Poland or Hungary would do. Yugoslavia was even better.

The orderly knew just the man. Old Kringen.

Szara ordered another round, the best they had, and a discussion of money ensued. A bit of bargaining. Szara pretended to be shocked, leaned on the price, didn't gain an inch, looked grumpy, and gave in. Would old Kringen, he wanted to know, get much older?

No. He was finished, but he was taking his time about it, didn't seem to be in much of a hurry.

Szara could understand, but his client couldn't afford any, ah, embarrassment.

The orderly snickered, a horrible sound. Old Kringen wasn't going anywhere. And lying where he was he didn't need his passport, which was kept in the hospital records office. The orderly had a friend, however, and the friend would see him right. It was going to cost a little more, though.

Szara gave in on the price a second time.

And a third, visiting the rathskeller two days later. But he had what he needed. Old Kringen was a Siebenbürger, from the Siebenbürgen – Seven Hills – district of Roumania, an area long colonized by German settlers. Szara had no idea why he'd come to Kovno, perhaps to take advantage of the emigration offer in neighbouring Latvia, perhaps for other reasons. He was much older than Szara, from his photo a grumpy, hard-headed fellow, his occupation listed as swine breeder. Szara bought what he needed and, in search of privacy, found a hotel room in the tenement district that could be rented by the hour. He eradicated the birth date with lemon juice, wrote in an appropriate year for himself, smeared the page with fine dust to coat the damage to the paper, and changed the photograph, signing something illegible across the corner. Then he held it up to the light.

The new Kringen.

He had disposed of the Maltsaev papers while still in Poland; now it was the turn of the Szara papers. The walls of the tiny room were thin, and various groans and shouts to either side of him indicated that Friday night was in Kovno much as it was everywhere else. There was a woman – he imagined her as an immensely fat woman – with an enormous laugh on the other side of the wall. Something went thud and she shrieked with mirth, making whooping noises and pausing, he guessed, only to wipe her eyes. To such accompaniment, André Szara died. He sat on a straw mattress with a soiled sheet spread over it, his only light a candle, and scratched at whatever was biting his ankle. He'd borrowed a coffee cup from his afternoon café and used it as a fireplace, ripping a page at a time from his passport, setting the corner aflame, and watching the entry and exit stamps disappear as the paper curled and blackened. The red cover resisted – he had to tear it into strips and light match after match – but finally it too was dropped, its flame blue and yellow, into the cup of ashes. Farewell. He wondered at such soreness of heart, but there was no denying what he felt. It was as though André

Szara, his raincoat and smile and a clever thing to say, had ceased to exist. *Troublesome bastard just the same*, Szara thought, stirred the ashes with his finger and poured them out the window into a courtyard full of cats.

A small canal ran through that part of Kovno. The NKVD badge sank like a stone. So did the Steyr.

The dock in Riga was packed with Germans – their baggage, their docks, their dogs, and a band to play while it all marched up the gangplank. German newsreel cameramen were much in evidence, Szara kept his face averted. By a curious tribal magic he could not divine, the crowds had organized themselves into castes – the prominent and the wealthy in front, pipe-smoking farmers next, and workmen and other assorted types to the rear. Everybody seemed content with the arrangement.

His papers had received only the most cursory check – who in God's name would want to sneak under the tent of this circus? In fact, though it did not occur to Szara, the NKVD took full advantage of the Baltic migration to infiltrate agents into Germany: such returns to the homeland had always suggested interesting possibilities to intelligence services.

Szara was fully prepared for exposure. Any determined Gestapo officer would spot the crudely altered passport, and five minutes of interrogation was all it would require for the certain knowledge that he was an imposter. He planned to admit it, long before they ever went to work on him. The Jean Bonotte passport was sewn into his jacket, the French francs hidden in the false bottom of the valise, just where a type like Bonotte, a man from Marseille, no doubt a Corsican, no doubt a criminal type, would hide them. Germany and France were legally at war, though it had not yet come to any serious fighting. Mostly talk. German diplomacy was continuing, an attempt to smooth things over with the British and the French – why should the world be set on fire over a bunch of Poles? Szara expected he would, if discovered, be interned as a citizen of France. At worst a war spent in excruciating boredom in a camp somewhere, at best exchanged for a German citizen who happened to be on the wrong side of the line when the first cannon was fired. On the bright side, a German internment camp was probably the last place in the world the NKVD would think to look for André Szara.

Still, he did not wish to be caught. He was no German, not even a Roumanian swine-breeding German from the Seven Hills, and he did not wish to be beaten up by this crowd. There was a deep and patient anger in them. For the newsreel cameras they were glad to be 'going home', but among themselves they promised that they would soon enough be 'going back', At which time, evidently, certain scores would be definitively settled. And worst of all, he knew, if they had cause to single him out and concentrate on his features, they were not above having a look to see if he were a Jew. No, he did not wish to be caught, and he had determined to avoid direct contact in every possible way.

To this end he played the part of a man ruined by sorrow, a victim of anti-German hostility. Practised saying a single sentence in the sort of *Volksdeutsch* accent common to a man like Kringen: 'They took . . . everything.' He had to use it almost immediately. A burly fellow, standing next to him on the dock, wanted to strike up a conversation and offered a greeting. Szara stared at him, as though he were intruding on a world of private anguish, and delivered his line. It worked. As Szara watched, the man's expression went from surprise to pained sympathy, then tightened with anger. Szara bit his lip; he could not say any more without losing control. He turned his face away, and the man laid a great paw of a hand on his shoulder, the honest human warmth of the gesture very nearly shaming him into real tears.

A bright day. A calm sea.

Life aboard the passenger steamer was tightly organized. There were numerous officials in attendance but they seemed to Szara benign, meant to ease the transition of the emigrants into German life. He was processed – a matter of saying yes and no – given a temporary identity card, and told to report to the proper authorities wherever he settled and permanent residence documents would be provided at that time. Had he any notion of where he wished to live? Family in Germany? Friends? Szara hid behind his catastrophe. 'Don't worry, old fellow, you're in good hands now,' said one official.

The public address system was constantly at work: a schnauzer discovered in the crew quarters, an uplifting message of welcome from Dr Goebbels, the Winterhilfe charity was stationed at a table on the afterdeck, those with last names beginning A to M should report to the dining room for midday dinner promptly at one P.M., N to Z at two-thirty. To promote the appetite, a songfest would begin in fifteen minutes on the foredeck, led by the well-known contralto Irmtrud Von something from the Munich State Opera Company and the well-known countertenor SS Untersturmführer Gerhard something else of the Bavarian Soldiers' Chorus, two inspirational artists who had volunteered to accompany the voyage and join their fellow *Volk* in singing some of the grand old songs.

For one ghastly moment Szara thought he might have to sing, but saw to his relief that a sufficient number of people remained at the perimeter so that he could safely avoid it. He stood for the rousing performance of 'Deutschland über Alles' that began the programme, watched the breasts of the contralto swell mightily with patriotism, then moved to the railing and became part of the small audience.

Almost all the passengers took part, and they were deeply affected by the singing; there were unashamed tears on the cheeks of both the men and the women and a kind of joyous agony on their faces as they raised their voices together. The mass rendition of 'Silent Night' – Christmas carols were familiar to all – was extraordinary, sung with great and tender feeling as the ship rumbled through the flat Baltic waters.

Szara maintained his cover, nodding in time and seeming to mumble the old words to himself, but his internal reaction to the performance was something very nearly approaching terror. It was the instinctive and passionate unity of the singers that frightened him; the sheer depth of it was overwhelming. You couldn't, he thought, find three Jews in the world who would agree on what it meant to be Jewish, yet there were apparently fifty million of these people who knew exactly what it meant to be German, though many of those on deck had never set foot in Germany.

Something was wrong, what was it? Obviously they suffered injustice without end – that certain look was plain on their faces. They swayed and sang, seemingly hypnotized, held hands – many wept – and together formed a wall of common emotion, a wall of nostalgia, regret, self-pity, sentimentality, resentment, hatred, ferocity. The words bounced around inside him, none of them right, none of them wrong, none of them mattered. What he did know for certain at that moment was that they were poisoned with themselves. And it was the rest of the world that would suffer for it.

He avoided lunch, knowing it would be impossible to escape conversation over a table laden with food. A short, fleshy woman, with the tiny eyes of pure malice, sought him out – he could tell she'd been watching him – and silently presented a generous wedge of *Bundt* cake in a napkin. The group had understood him, accepted him; he was damaged goods, to be left alone yet not neglected. She turned and walked away, leaving him to eat his cake in peace, while he suppressed a violent shiver that seemed to come from the very centre of his being.

As the sun set, the voice on the public address system grew suddenly whispery with reverence and awe. A fortuitous change of plans: the ship would be met at Hamburg by a train of first-class coaches, all passengers would proceed to Berlin, there to be addressed by the Führer himself. Please do not be concerned for the friends and family who will come to the dock to meet you, there will be plenty of room for everybody. Heil Hitler!

And if Szara had a passing notion that he could slip away in the confusion of landing and find his way to the Copenhagen ferry, the reality of the arrival, two days later, put a firm lid on such nonsense. A wall of cheering Germans stood to either side of the disembarking passengers, an aisle of welcome, as effective as barbed wire, that lined the way to the railway station.

So he went to Berlin.

To Szara, the city seemed dark and solemn. Stiff. Brooding. Whatever he scented in the streets was worse, much worse, than Kristallnacht in November of '38. Now the nation was at risk; this business was no longer some political manoeuvre of the Nazi party. France and England had declared war – the gall, the presumption of them! – and the people had coalesced in the face of such an astonishing development. That civilized nations – the British at any rate, not the unbathed French – would side with the Poles and the Jews and the other Slavic trash was simply beyond comprehension, but it was a fact of life and it had to be faced. They were equal to it.

At the Potsdam terminal a fleet of buses waited to transport the returning *Volksdeutsch* to the Olympic Stadium, where a crowd of seventy-five thousand people awaited their arrival. A special section towards the front was reserved for the Baltic emigrants, and Adolf Hitler would address them later in the evening. Szara had no intention of going anywhere near the place; security measures would be intensive wherever a national leader was expected and in this instance would include the Gestapo, Berlin plainclothes detectives, identity checks – an imposter's nightmare. Though his thin cover had worked on the docks of Latvia, it would never stand up under that level of scrutiny.

But there was an accursed absence of confusion as the buses were boarded; the *Volksdeutsch* were infuriatingly patient and malleable, organizing themselves into neat lines – who, Szara tried to remember, had called the Germans *carnivorous sheep?* – and when he tried to disappear between two buses a young woman wearing an armband chased him down and courteously headed him back in the proper direction. In desperation he doubled over, his free hand clutching his belly, and ran groaning back into the station. *That* they understood and they let him go. He found a different exit, now simply a traveller with a valise. He spotted a sign for the number 24 tram, the Dahlem line, that would take him to Lehrter Bahnhof, where he could catch the late train to Hamburg. Things were looking up.

But it was not to be. He walked about on the streets near the station for a half-hour or so, giving the busloads of *Volksdeutsch* time to depart, then re-entered Potsdam station. But he saw a uniformed policeman and a Gestapo functionary checking identification at every gate that led to the tramways and realized that without the protective coloration of the emigrants he was in some difficulty. He stood out, he could sense it. Who was this rather aristocratic looking man in soiled clothing and a soft felt hat worn low over the eyes? Why did he carry a fine leather valise?

Resisting the urge to panic, he walked away from the station and found himself in even worse trouble. Now he was alone, on deserted streets.

The Berlin he'd known a year earlier still had its people of the night, those who liked darkness and the pleasures it implied. But no longer. The city was desolate, people stayed home, went to bed early; Hitler had chased decadence indoors. Szara knew he had to get off the streets. He felt it was a matter of minutes.

He walked quickly west, to the Leipzigerplatz, where he knew there was a public telephone. He'd memorized several telephone numbers, in case he lost the valise, and the receiver was in his hand before he realized he had no German coins. He'd obtained reichsmarks from Poles who'd fled into Lithuania, enough to buy a ticket on the Copenhagen steamer, but he'd not foreseen the need to use a telephone. *Not like this, not for such a stupid miscalculation,* he pleaded silently. He saw a taxicab and waved it down. The driver was offended, declared himself 'no travelling change purse', but Szara bought two ten-reichsmark coins for fifty reichsmarks and the driver's attitude turned instantly to grave decency. 'Can you wait?' Szara asked him, thumbing through his remaining bills. The driver nodded politely. Anything for a gentleman.

The telephone rang for what seemed like a long time, then, unexpectedly, a man answered. Szara mentioned a name. The man's voice was terribly languid and world-weary. 'Oh, she's not *here*,' he said. Then: 'I suppose you'll want the number.' Szara said he did, fumbling in his pocket for a pencil and a matchbox. The man gave him the number and Szara hung up. Out of the corner of his eye he saw the driver scowling at his watch. There was a police car on the other side of the Leipzigerplatz. 'Another minute,' he called out. The driver noticed his odd German and stared. Szara dialled the new number and a maid answered. Szara asked for 'Madame Nadia Tscherova.' Relief flooded over him when he heard her voice.

'I find myself in Berlin,' he said. 'Would it be terribly inconvenient . . . ?'

'What? Who is it?'

'A backstage friend. Remember? The terrible play? I brought you . . . a present.'

'My God.'

'May I come and see you?'

'Well,' she said.

'Please.'

'I suppose.'

'Perhaps you'll tell me where.'

'How can you not know?'

'The fact is I don't.'

'Oh. Well, it's a villa. Facing the Tiergarten, just at the edge of Charlottenburg, on Schillerstrasse. The third from the end of the street. There's a . . . I'll have the coach lamps put on. When will you come?'

'I have a taxi waiting for me.'

'Soon then,' she said and hung up.

He got into the cab and gave the driver directions. 'What part of Germany do you come from?' asked the driver.

'From Italy,' Szara said. 'From the Tyrol. Actually, we rarely speak German.'

'So you're Italian.'

'Yes.'

'For an Italian you don't speak so badly.'

'*Grazie.*'

The driver laughed and pulled away as the police car began to circle slowly around the Leipzigerplatz.

'Dearest!' She cried out in Russian. This was a different Nadia – affected, brittle. She threw an arm around his shoulders – her other hand held a glass – drew him close, and kissed him full on the lips. The kiss tasted like wine. ' "What ingenious devil has cast you on my doorstep?" ' she said. The maid who'd shown him in curtseyed, her starched uniform rustling, and left the room.

'And go iron yourself,' Tscherova muttered to her back as she drew the tall door closed.

'What sort of devil?' Szara asked.

'It's from Kostennikov. *The Merchant's Bride.* Act Three.'

Szara raised an eyebrow.

'Come upstairs,' she said.

He followed her through rooms of oiled walnut furniture and

towering emerald draperies, then up a curving marble staircase with gilded banisters. 'Well you've certainly—'

'Shut up,' she whispered urgently. 'They listen.'

'The servants?'

'Yes.'

Sweeping up the stairs in ice-coloured silk shirt and trousers, voluminous lounging pyjamas, she called out, 'Last one up is a monkey!'

'Aren't you making it awfully obvious?' he said quietly.

She snorted and danced up the last few steps. Her gold slippers had pompoms on them and the soles slapped against the marble. She paused for a sip of wine, then took his hand and towed him into a bedroom, kicking the door shut behind them. A fire burned in a marble fireplace, the wallpaper was deep blue with white snowdrops, the cover on the huge bed was the same blue and white, and the carpet was thick, pale blue wool.

'Oh, Seryozha,' she said, her voice full of woe. A borzoi crept guiltily off a blue and white settee and slunk over to the fireplace, settling down on his side with the mournful sigh of the dispossessed and a single swish of his feathery tail. Then he yawned, opened his long, graceful jaws to the limit, and snapped them shut with a brief whine. *What settee?*

'Won't they suspect I'm your lover?' Szara asked.

'Let them.'

Szara looked confused.

'I can have all the lovers, and generally strange guests, that I want. What I can't have is spies.'

'They know Russian?'

'Who knows what they know? From my émigré friends they expect Russian, shouting and laughter. Anything political or confidential, keep your voice down or play the Victrola.'

'All this. It's yours?'

'I will tell you everything, my dear, but first things first. Forgive me, but I do not know your name. That's going to become awkward. Would you like me to make something up?'

'André,' he said. 'In the French spelling.'

'Good. Now I must ask you, André in the French spelling, if you have any idea what you smell like.'

'I'm sorry.'

'I've been through hard times in Russia: little rooms, long winters, everybody terrified, and no privacy. I'm no shrinking violet, believe me, but . . .'

She opened a door with a full mirror on it and gestured towards the clawfoot tub within. 'I lack nothing. You will find a sponge, bath salts, lavender soap or almond, facecloth, back-brush, shampoo from Paris. You may give yourself a facial, if you like, or powder yourself like a cruller from the Viennese bakery. Yes? You're not insulted?'

'A long journey,' he said, walking into the bathroom.

He undressed, horrified at the condition of his clothing. In the scented air of the bathroom his own condition became, by contrast, all too evident. Still, when he looked in the mirror, he could see that he'd survived. A day's growth of beard – was one side of his face still slightly swollen from the dive-bombing? – hair quite long, newly grey here, and here, and here, eyes yellowish with fatigue. Not old. Yet. And very lean and sharp, determined.

He ran the steaming water into the tub and climbed in. The heat woke up various nicks and scrapes and bruises he'd acquired in his travels and he grimaced. It felt as though he had a hundred places that hurt, each in a different way. He watched the water darken, added a handful of crystals from a jar and stirred them about. 'That's the spirit!' she called through the open door, smelling the bath salts. She hummed to herself, opened a bottle of wine – he heard the squeak of the cork being drawn – and put a record on the Victrola. Italian opera, sunny and sweet: *on market day, peasants gather in the village square.*

'I like this for a bath, don't you?' she said from the bedroom.

'Yes. Just right.'

She sang along for a few bars, her voice, lightly hoarse, hunting shamelessly for the proper notes.

'May I have a cigarette?'

A moment later her hand snaked around the door with a lit cigarette. He took it gratefully. 'Smoking in the bath,' she said. 'You are truly Russian.'

The borzoi came padding in and lapped enthusiastically at the bath-water.

'Seryozha!' she said.

With his index finger Szara rubbed the dog between the eyes. The borzoi raised its head and stared at him, soapy water running from its wet muzzle. 'Go away, Seryozha,' he said. Surprisingly, the dog actually turned and left.

'Yes, good dog,' he heard her say.

'When I'm done – I don't have anything clean, I'm afraid.'

'I'll get you one of the general's bathrobes. Not the old rag he actually wears. His daughter gave him one for his birthday – it's still in the box. Red satin. You'll look like Cary Grant.'

'Is he your lover?'

'Cary Grant? I thought we'd been discreet.'

He waited.

'No. Not really. Nobody is my lover. When the general and I are together the world thinks otherwise, but we don't fool ourselves or each other. It takes some explaining, but I can't imagine you're going anywhere else tonight, so there's time. But for one thing I can't wait. You really have to tell me why you came here. If you are going to ask me to do all sorts of wretched things, I might as well hear about it and have it done with.' She turned the record over. There was a certain resignation in her voice, he thought, like a woman who dreads a squabble with the butcher but knows it can't be avoided.

'The truth?'

'Yes. Why not?'

'I've . . . Well, what have I done? I haven't defected. I guess I've run away.'

'Not really. You have?'

'Yes.'

She was silent for a moment, thinking it over. 'Run away to Berlin? Is, uh, that where one generally goes?'

'It was a rat's maze. I ran down the open passage.'

'Well, if you say so.' She sounded dubious.

He put his cigarette out in the bathwater, rested the butt on the edge of the tub, then pulled the plug and watched the grey water swirl above the drain. 'I'm going to have to fill up the tub again,' he said.

'I'll bring you a glass of wine if you like. And you can tell me about your travels. If it's allowed, that is.'

'Anything's allowed now,' he said. He burst out laughing.

'What?'

'Really nothing.' He laughed again. It was as though a genie had escaped.

It was well past midnight when they tiptoed down the stairs to the kitchen, a narrow room with a lofty ceiling and porcelain worn dark on its curves by years of scrubbing. They made absurdly tall sandwiches of cheese and pickles and butter and stole back across the Baluchi carpets like thieves. Szara caught a glimpse of himself in a mirror: shaved, hair combed, wearing a red satin bathrobe with a shawl collar, a giant sandwich teetering on a plate – it was as though in headlong flight he'd stumbled through a secret door and landed in heaven.

Back in Nadia's sanctuary, they settled on the carpet close to the dying fire while Seryozha rested on crossed forepaws and waited alertly for his share of the kill. Szara watched her tear into the sandwich, a serious Russian eater, her hair falling around her face as she leaned over the plate. He simply could not stop looking at her. She apparently ignored it, was perhaps used to it – after all, the job of an actress was to be looked at – still, he did not want to seem a goggling, teenage dolt and tried to be subtle, but that was a hopeless tactic and he knew it. *This is God's work,* he thought: drifting hair the colour of an almond shell and the fragile blue of her eyes, the lines and planes and light in her. There weren't words, he realized. Only the feeling inside him and the impulse to make sure, again and again, that he saw what he saw. Suddenly, she looked up and stared back at him, blank-eyed, jaw muscles working away as she chewed, until he sensed that she'd composed her expression into a reasonable imitation of his own. He turned away. 'Yes?' she said, raising an eyebrow.

'It's nothing.'

She poured wine into his glass.

'Do we expect the general home at any moment?' he asked. 'Do I hide in a closet?'

'The general is in Poland,' she said. 'And if he were here you would not have to hide. Krafic comes to see me with his boyfriends. Lara Brozina and her brother. You know them, in what we'll call a different setting. Others also. A little Russian colony, you see: émigré intellectuals, free thinkers, batty painters, and what-have-you. The general refers to us as "an antidote to Frau Lumplich".'

'Who is she?'

'A character he made up. "Madame Lump", one would say in Russian.'

'An enlightened general. An enlightened German general.'

'They exist,' she said. She brushed crumbs from her hands and held a bite of sandwich out to Seryozha, who arched his neck forward and took it daintily between his small front teeth for a moment, then inhaled it. She rose and brought over a framed photograph from the night table next to her bed. 'General Walter Boden,' she said.

A man in his late sixties, Szara thought. Fleshless, ascetic face below a bald head, deep care lines, mouth a single brief line. Yet the look in his eyes told a slightly different story. At some point, in a life that left his face like stone, something had amused him. Permanently.

'Extraordinary,' Szara said.

'It pleases me you see that,' she said with feeling.

'When I put this picture together with what you've told me, I would have to guess that this is not a man well loved by the Nazis.'

'No. They know how he feels about them; in the general's world, the notion of *beneath contempt* is taken quite literally. He is rich, however. Very, very rich. They do respect that. And his position with the General

Staff is not unimportant, though he speaks of it as "the maid's room in the lion's den". His friends include the old aristocracy, the Metternichs and Bismarcks, princes and counts, the Prussian landholders. Hitler hates them, foams at the mouth because he can't get at them; they occupy two powerful fortresses in Germany, the army and the foreign ministry.'

'Fortresses. Will they hold under siege?'

'We shall see.'

You don't, Szara reminded himself, *have to think about such things any more*. 'Is there another log for the fire?' he asked. The embers were dark red.

'No. Not until the morning. One is a prisoner of servants, in some ways.'

'A long way from Rosenhain Passage, though, and that awful theatre.'

She nodded that it was. He stared at her, forced himself to look away. She yawned, took a foot out of her slipper, and propped it inside her opposite knee. 'How did you meet?' Szara said.

'At a reception. We went to dinner a few times. Talked into the night – he speaks passable Russian, you yourself know what that feels like, especially when you have no country to go home to. A strange romance. I waited for the inevitable offer, *a relaxing weekend in the country*, but it never came. One night at a restaurant he simply said "Nadia, my girl, generals and actresses are nothing new in Berlin. A cliché of the nightclubs. But come along to my house, even so, and see how you like it." I did. And in this room I asked, "Whose bedroom is this?" for I'd already seen his, and everything was obviously new. "I believe it is yours, if you like," he said. I had expected anything but this, and I was speechless. That strip of Persian carpet, the one by your hand? He'd meant it for Seryozha. Suddenly I started to cry – inside, I didn't want him to see. And that was the end of the discussion. I came to live here and it was a kind of salvation; I stopped doing all those other things, seeing those vile people. Now this is my life. When he wants to see me, I'm here. I sit across from him at dinner, we converse, my job is to be exactly who I am. Any affectation, to become what I imagine he might want, would break his heart. We have a life together, we go – what is the phrase? – we go out in society. To his friends. Sometimes to the country, to grand estates. In Germany, civilized life continues in such places, much as it does in the basements of Moscow. But no matter where we go, I am always at his shoulder. I take his arm. Now I could – and of course I would, nothing would be easier – make the world believe that he was a sublime lover. A few small signals and the tongues begin to wag. If he desired that, it would be little enough to ask. But he does not. He does not care what people think of him. I'm not here for his vanity, for his reputation. I'm here because it gives him pleasure to have me here.'

Her face was flushed; she drank the last of the wine in her glass. When she met his eyes he saw anger and sorrow, and all the courage and defiance she could possibly summon. Not that it was overwhelming, it wasn't, but for her it was everything she possessed. 'And God damn you if you've come here to make me work again. No matter *what* you've said. For I won't. Won't betray this man in the way you want. I'll go where even your power does not reach. And we both know where that is.'

Szara took a deep breath and let the air between them cool a little. Then he said, 'I've told only the truth' – he looked at his watch – 'since ten-thirty last night. Almost six hours. The way things are for me lately, I have a right to be proud of even that.'

She lowered her eyes. He stood, the carpet soft beneath his bare feet, and walked to a mirrored cabinet with glasses and a silver ice bucket on it. He opened the door and found a bottle of Saint-Estèphe, took a corkscrew and worked it open, then filled both their glasses. She had meanwhile found a newspaper, was bunching up wads of it and feeding it to the fire. 'It looks warm, anyhow,' she said.

'I was wondering,' he said, 'what had become of the people in Paris in all this. Because if you'd let them know about an intimacy with a senior staff officer they would have been – inquisitive. To say the least.'

'And something terrible would have happened. Because even if I'd tried to conceal everything, I don't trust my little friends in Berlin. They've had to improvise their lives for too long – not all humans are made stronger by that.'

'Very few.'

'Well, for me there is only one escape, and I was prepared to take it. I'd made my peace with the idea. In the beginning, when I stole away from Russia and came to live in Berlin, these people approached me. Threatened me. But I gave them very little, only bits of gossip and what they could read in the newspapers if they wanted. Then they played a second card. Your brother Sascha is in a camp, they said, where he deserves to be. But he's as comfortable as he can be under the circumstances; he works as a clerk in a heated room. If you want his situation to continue, you must be productive. It's up to you.'

'And you did what you had to do.'

'Yes. I did. In exile, I cared very little what I made of my life because I discovered I wasn't touched by it. Perhaps Russia has something to do with that – to be sensitive yet not at all delicate, a curious strength, or weakness, or whatever you want to call it. But then I met this man, and suddenly it was as though I'd woken from a long sleep. Every small thing now mattered – the weather, the way a vase stood on a table, meeting someone and wanting them to like me. I had built walls – now they crumbled. And this I knew I could not survive. Not for long. I could no longer do what I'd done for the people who came around with money, and once they began to press I knew there would be only one way out. So I hadn't, as I saw it then, very long to live. Yet each day was vivid, and I trembled with life. They say it is the only gift, and now I came to understand that with all my heart. I never cried so hard, and never laughed so much, as I did in those weeks. Perhaps it was a form of prayer, because what came next was a miracle, I know of no other word to describe it.

'It was in early August. A man came to see me. Not here. At the theatre, in the same way you did. Clearly he knew nothing of the general. A dreadful man, this one. Fair, wavy hair, thick glasses, a vile little chunk of a thing with no mercy anywhere in him. None. And what he mostly wanted to talk about was you. Something had gone wrong, something extremely serious, for nothing has happened since. No money, no demands, no couriers, nothing.'

She twisted the glass about in her hands, watching the light of the burning newspaper reflected in the red surface of the wine. 'I've no idea what happened,' she said. 'I only know it saved my life. And that you seemed to be the cause of it.'

He woke up in a kind of heaven. He had no idea how he'd happened to wind up on her bed but there he was, his face against the soft coverlet, his side a little sore from sleeping on the knot in the twisted belt of the bathrobe. He was in heaven, he decided, because it smelled exactly the way heaven, or his heaven at any rate, ought to smell: the perfume she wore – which reminded him of cinnamon – and scented soap, as well as wine, cigarette smoke, the ashes of a dead fire, and the sweetish odour of a well-washed borzoi. He could, he thought, detect Nadia herself, sweet in a different, a human way. For a time he simply lay there, suspended in a perfect darkness, and inhaled. When he felt himself slipping back into unconsciousness, he forced his eyes open. A knitted quilt was tossed carelessly on the settee – so that's where she'd slept. His suit – apparently the maids had cleaned it – hung from a hanger on the knob of the bathroom door, and the rest of his clothing was piled neatly on a dresser. Miraculously clean and dry.

He struggled to sit up. Returning from the dead, it felt like. All those nights in Poland, lying on the ground on a blanket; followed by restless hours on a thin mattress in the Kovno apartment, people around him awake, coughing, talking in low voices. Now he hurt for every minute of it. He unhooked the white shutter that covered the lower half of the window and pushed it aside. An autumn garden. Surrounded by high walls. Dead leaves had drifted across the paths and mounded at the foot of a hedge. Nadia sat at a weathered iron table – she was reading, he could not see her face – one hand dangling above the wolfhound stretched out at her side. *Am I in Russia?* Wrapped in a long black coat and a red wool scarf she was lost in her book. The wind lifted her autumn-coloured hair, leaves spun down from the trees and rattled along the garden paths; the sky was at war, broken towers of grey cloud, blown and battered, swept past a pale sun. Certainly it would rain. His heart ached for her.

Later he sat in a garden chair across from her and saw that she was reading Babel's *Red Cavalry*. The wind was cool and damp and he pulled his jacket tightly about him.

For a long time they did not say anything.

And she did not look away, did not deny him her eyes: *if this is what you wish*, she seemed to say, *I will pose for you*. She touched nothing, changed nothing, and did not defend herself. The wind blew her hair across her face, Seryozha sighed, the light shifted as the clouds crossed the sun, she never moved. Then he began to understand that he'd misread her. This stillness was not simply poise – what he saw in her eyes was precisely what was in his own. Could she be that deluded? To want somebody so lost and useless? Was she blind?

No.

From the moment he'd walked through the door of the dressing room he had been in love with her. That it might be the same for her had never occurred to him, simply had not crossed his mind. But maybe it worked that way – women always knew, men never did. Or maybe not, maybe it all worked some other way. He didn't really care. Now he understood that everything had changed. And now he understood what, just exactly what, he had been offered.

Sad, he thought, that he couldn't take it. They were castaways, both of them, marooned together on an exotic island – as it happened, the garden of a Florentine villa on the Schillerstrasse. But somewhere beyond the high walls a military band was playing a march and, he thought, the general will soon return from the wars. Only for a moment did he imagine a love affair in flight: the unspeakable hotel rooms, the secret police, the predators. No. She belonged in his imagination, not in his life. A memory. Met in the wrong way, in the wrong place, in the wrong year, in times when love wasn't possible. One remembers, and that's all. Something else that didn't happen in those days.

'When will you leave?' she said. 'Today?'

'Tomorrow.'

Just for an instant he was clairvoyant: he could watch the question as it took shape in her mind. She leaned across the table until she was very close, he could see that her lips were dry from the wind, a red mark on the line of her jaw – suddenly she was out of perspective, too near to be beautiful. And when she spoke it was a voice he didn't know, so soft he could barely hear what she said. 'Why did this happen?'

'I don't know,' he said. 'I don't.'

She pressed her lips together and nodded a little. She agreed. There was no answer.

'There isn't anything we have to do, you know,' he said.

Her face changed, gracefully but completely, until he was confronted by the single great inquisitive look of his life. 'No?'

He had never in his life been the lover he was with her.

They waited for nightfall – only the first in a series of common consents that flowed to meet the occasion. Szara could not safely go out in the street, and Nadia knew it, so there was no point in raising the issue. They simply passed a rather nineteenth-century sort of day; they read, they talked, they cut clusters of autumn berries from a shrub to make a table decoration, avoided the servants, played with the dog, touched only accidentally and only now and then, and neither of them let on how it affected them. If living in the days of war demanded a love affair measured in hours and not in months, they discovered that a love affair was something that could be compressed in just that way.

They could have looked, from any of the windows in the front of the three-storey villa, out on the Tiergarten and observed that day's life in Berlin: strollers and idlers, officers and couples, old men reading newspapers on a park bench. But they declined to do so. The private world suited them. They did not, however, build sand castles, did not pretend the present was anything other than what it was, and they tried to talk about the future. Difficult, though. Szara's plans focused vaguely on Denmark; from there he would extemporize. He had no idea how he might be able to earn a living; his writing languages, Russian and Polish, would not serve him very well anywhere he could think of. Émigré intellectuals lived in penury – sometimes the little journal paid, sometimes it didn't. The former aristocrats gave parties, everyone ate as much as they could. But even that tenuous existence was denied him – he was a fugitive, and the émigré communities were the first places they would look for him. Of course he could not go back to Paris, much too dangerous. Sad, because to be there with her . . .

Sad, because even to know him put her in danger. This he did not say. But she knew it anyhow. She'd seen enough of Soviet life to apprehend vulnerability in every one of its known forms. So she understood that one did what one had to do. This realpolitik was very alchemical stuff. It started with politicians and their intellectuals, all this doing what had to be done, but it had a tendency to migrate, and the next time you looked it was in bed with you.

Still, they agreed, one had to hope. Humans survived the most awful catastrophes: walked away from the inferno with singed hair, missed the train that went over the cliff. Both felt they might just be owed a little luck from whatever divine agency kept those books. There were still places on earth where one could get irredeemably lost, it only took finding one. And how exactly did one go about herding sheep? Could it be all that difficult?

In the end, they refused to let the future ruin their day, which made them heroes of a low order but heroes nonetheless. And they had the past to fall back on, realizing almost immediately that the sorts of lives they'd led created, if they did nothing else, long and luxuriant anecdotes. They discovered that they had, on several occasions, been within minutes of meeting each other, in Moscow, in Leningrad. Had been in the same apartments, known some of the same people; their trails through the snowy forest crossed and recrossed. What would have happened had they met? Everything? Nothing? Certainly something, they decided.

They weren't very hungry, as the day wore on towards evening, and just after dark they toyed with a light supper. Their conversation was somewhat forced, slightly tense, in the dining room with a ticking grandfather clock that made every silence ring with melodrama. Nadia said, 'If it weren't for the general's feelings, I'd have poured soup in that monster long ago.'

They retired early. He, for form's sake, to a guest room, she to her blue and white sanctuary. When the noise in the kitchen subsided and the house grew quiet, Szara climbed the marble staircase.

They lit a fire, turned out the lights, played the Victrola, drank wine.

She surprised him. The way she moved through the daily world, fine boned, on air, made her seem insubstantial – one could hold her only cautiously. But it wasn't so. With a dancer's pointed toe she kicked the bottoms of her silk pyjamas fully across the room, then melted out of the top and posed for him. She was full and lovely and curved, with smooth, taut skin coloured by firelight. For a moment, he simply looked at her. He'd supposed their joined spirits might float to some unimagined romantic height, but now he fell on her like a wolf and she yelped like a teenager.

And what a good time they had.

Much later, when they simply hadn't the strength to go on any longer, they fell sound asleep, still pressed together, the sheets tangled around their legs, drifting away in the midst of the most charming and vile conversation.

It was not yet dawn when they woke up. He reached for her, she flexed with pleasure, slowly, like stretching, and sighed. He watched her from cover, a pale shape in the darkness, eyes closed, mouth open, breasts rising and falling. Suddenly he understood that sometimes there was no reaching the end of desire, no satisfying it. They simply would not, he realized, ever quite get enough of each other. Nonetheless, he thought, they could hope for the best. They could try. They could make a beginning.

He could have crawled out of bed at dawn and set out into the cold world, but he didn't. They stole another day, and this time they didn't wait for nightfall. They disappeared in the middle of the afternoon. At eight in the evening a servant set out a tureen of soup at the long table in the dining room with the ticking grandfather clock. But nobody showed up. And at eight-thirty she took it away.

He left in the middle of the following day. A taxi was called. They stood in the vestibule together until it came. 'Please don't cry,' he said.

'I won't,' she promised, tears running everywhere.

The taxi honked twice and he left.

The Gestapo had him an hour later. He never even got out of Berlin.

To his credit, he sensed it. He did not enter the Lehrter Bahnhof immediately but walked the streets for a while, trying to calm himself down – simply another traveller, a little bored, a little harassed, a man who had to take the train up to Hamburg on some prosaic and vastly uninteresting errand.

But the passport control people at the staircase that led down to the platform didn't care what he looked like. A Berlin policeman took the Kringen identity papers and compared them to a typewritten list, looked over Szara's shoulder, made a gesture of the eyes and a motion of the head, and two men in suits closed in on either side of him. Very correct they were: 'Can you come with us for a moment, please?' Only willpower and raw pride kept him from collapsing to his knees, and he felt the sweat break out at the roots of his hair. One of the men relieved him of his valise, the other frisked him, then they marched him, to the great interest of the passing crowd, towards the station police post. He wobbled once and one of the detectives caught him by the arm. They took him down a long corridor and through an unmarked door where a uniformed SS officer was sitting behind a desk, a file open in front of him. Reading upside down, Szara could see a long list of names and descriptive paragraphs on a yellow sheet of teletype paper. 'Stand at attention,' the man said coldly.

Szara did as he was told. The officer concentrated on the Kringen identity documents and left him to stew, the standard procedure. 'Herr Kringen?' he said at last.

'Yes.'

'Yes, *sir.*'

'Yes, sir.'

'What did you use to obliterate the birthdate? Lemon? Oxalic acid? Not *urine* – I hope for your sake I haven't touched your piss.'

'Lemon, sir,' Szara said.

The officer nodded. He tapped the Kringen name with the eraser at the end of a pencil. 'The actual Herr Kringen went into the Lutheran hospital to have a bunion removed from his foot. And while this poor man lay in a hospital bed, some little sneak made off with his papers. Was that you?'

'No, sir. It wasn't me. I bought the passport from an orderly at the hospital.'

The officer nodded. 'And you are?'

'My name is Bonotte, Jean Bonotte. I am of French nationality. My passport is hidden in the flap of my jacket.'

'Give it to me.'

Szara got his jacket off and with shaking hands tried to rip the seam open. It took a long time but the heavy thread finally gave. He placed the passport on the desk and put his jacket back on, the torn flap of lining hanging ludicrously down the back of his leg. Behind him, one of the detectives snickered. The officer picked up the telephone and requested a number. He turned the pages of the Bonotte passport with the pencil eraser. While he waited for his call to go through he said, 'What reason have you for your visit to Germany? A mad impulse?' The detective laughed.

'I fled Poland, but could not find a way out of Lithuania.'

'So you obtained Kringen's passport and came out with the *Volksdeutsch* from Riga?'

'Yes, sir.'

'Well, aren't you clever?' said the officer, looking at Szara carefully for the first time and meaning what he said.

They drove him to Columbia House, Gestapo headquarters in Berlin, and locked him in an isolation cell. Small but clean, a cot and a bucket, a heavily grilled window nine feet up and a light bulb in the ceiling. They weren't entirely sure what they had, he guessed, not the sort of poor fish at whom they screamed, *Spy! You will be executed!* but, just maybe, the real thing, and that had to be handled at length and in a very different way. Perhaps with delicacy, perhaps not. If the decision was 'not,' the next step was no secret. Szara could hear the screaming from distant parts of the building, and it sickened him and weakened his will to resist, as it was intended to.

Abramov, with evident distaste, had covered this possibility during the time of his training: nobody resists torture, don't try. Tell them what you have to, it's our job to keep you from knowing too much. There are two goals you must try to accomplish: one, the less you say in the first forty-eight hours the better – that gives us time – but in any event, feed them the least important material you can. You are just a low-level opportunist forced to work for the government – contemptible, but not important. And two, try to signal us that you've been caught. That's crucial. We can protect a network from damage, close down everything you touched, and rescue your associates while we work through channels to get you free or at least to keep you from harm. The signals will change based on circumstance: a technical variation in wireless telegraphy or simply vanishing from our sight while working in hostile territory. But there will certainly be a signal established and an appropriate way to deliver it. Remember, in this organization there is always a chance, we can do almost anything. 'If you are taken,' Abramov had said, 'you must cling to hope as a sailor cast into the sea clings to a spar.'

Szara closed his eyes and rested his head against the cold cement wall. *No, Sergei Jakobovich* – he addressed Abramov's departed soul – *not this time.* Hope, despair – all such fancies were now entirely beside the point. He'd at last made the error that could not be overcome. Had not sufficiently understood the capability, the magnitude, of the German security machine – not until he'd seen the long sheet of yellow teletype paper with the name KRINGEN in the left-hand column. The identity that had been purchased in Paris would not hold up, not once they went to work on it, it wouldn't. When he worked his way back through the last two years of his life – Khelidze, Renate Braun, Bloch, Abramov, the OPAL network, then de Montfried and the British, finally the assignment in eastern Poland – he saw himself as a man willing to do almost anything in order to stay alive. He'd not done badly, had lasted a long time compared to the others – the intellectuals. Old Bolsheviks, Jews, foreign communists. Had outlived almost all of them, twisted and turned, lied and schemed, survived.

But it was not meant to be, and this he faced.

He suspected that what he'd almost done to himself in the Pripet marsh, the day he'd crossed into Lithuania, had been a shadow of the future – somehow he'd sensed that he was living out his last few days. But he had slightly misread the omen; he wasn't done with life, that wasn't it. Life was done with him. And in his deepest heart, he wondered if he hadn't come to Berlin knowing that he would find a way to Tscherova, an unconscious appeal to fate to let him passionately love a woman once more before he left the earth. If so, his wish had been granted, and now it was time to accept the inevitable cost of the bargain. He marvelled at the coldness of his heart. The time of dreams and delusions was ended; he saw the world, and himself, in perfect clarity. Certain obligations remained – to protect Tscherova, principally – but there were others, and he would now plan how to sacrifice himself in the most effective way. How late, he thought, strength comes to some people.

The interrogator was called Hartmann. An SS Obersturmbannführer, a major, a well-fed man with a placid face and small, carefully groomed hands, who addressed him politely. Hartmann was nothing more, Szara realized, than the intake valve of an information machine. He existed to acquire facts – perhaps a lawyer, or some functionary in a judicial system, before being called to his present duty by the Nazi party. He did not process the information. That happened elsewhere, far above him in the hierarchy, where an administrative panel, a directorate, made decisions.

To begin with, Hartmann pointed out that if they were straight-forward with each other, all would turn out for the best. He implied, without actually saying it, that his job was best done if Szara did not have to be taken to the cellars; they were, together, men who could proceed with their obligations – Szara's to confess, Hartmann's to certify the quality of that confession – while remaining innocent of such measures. That sort of thing was for another sort of person.

Szara did not resist. He cooperated. By the afternoon of the first day he had to admit he was not Jean Bonotte. Hartmann had provided paper and pencil and asked him to write a biography, beginning with his childhood in Marseille – names and places, schools and teachers. 'I cannot write such a biography because I did not grow up there,' Szara said. 'And I am not named Jean Bonotte.'

'This passport is a forgery, then,' Hartmann said.

'Yes, Herr Obersturmbann-führer, it is.'

'Then will you tell me your true name? And your nationality, if it is not French?'

'I will,' Szara said. 'My real name is André Aronovich Szara. As for my nationality, I was born a Polish Jew when Poland was a province of Russia. By 1918 I was living in Odessa, and so remained a citizen of the Soviet Union, eventually becoming a journalist for the newspaper *Pravda*.'

Hartmann was puzzled. 'Is it a newspaper that sent you to Berlin? With false identity? I wonder if you could clarify this.'

'I can. I obtained the false identity myself, and the newspaper has known nothing of me since I left Poland.'

Hartmann paused. Szara sensed discomfort. The interrogator took refuge in the notes he'd made to himself to guide him in the interview, but they were all wrong now. His Frenchman, trapped on the wrong side of the lines, had disappeared. In his place stood a Russian, a rather prominent one he suspected, captured while in flight from the USSR, Germany's nominal ally. Hartmann cleared his throat, for him a gesture of irritation. He had to question his competence to work in such areas. All sorts of intimidating issues suddenly made themselves felt; the prisoner's culpability under German law, possible extradition, others he could not even imagine. All of them grave, difficult, complex, and ultimately to be resolved in a political, not a legal, context. This was obviously not going to be a case he would be allowed to pursue; he could put himself in a good light only by presenting to his superiors the most precise information. Hartmann took up his pen and turned to a fresh page in his writing tablet. 'Slowly and clearly,' he said, 'and beginning with your surname, you will please spell.'

It rained hard that night, for Szara a blessing. It reminded him that there was a world outside his cell, and the steady splash on the high, grilled window muted, if it could not quite obliterate, the sounds of a Gestapo prison. His plan was successfully launched; Hartmann had ended the interview with the utmost correctness. Szara suspected they would not see each other again, and in the event this turned out to be the case.

Szara's strategy of revelation without defiance had proceeded from one basic assumption: he could not be sure he would withstand what was euphemistically known as intensive interrogation. He feared he would first give up the existence of the OPAL network, and that would lead inexorably to the exposure of Nadia Tscherova. He had to avoid the cellars in Berlin and then, if it came to that, the cellars in Moscow.

The conventions of the German character first specified efficiency – thus they'd arrested him. A crucial component of that efficiency, however, was thoroughness, and this he perceived to be his possible ally. Now that they knew who he was, he expected they would want from him all they could get, essentially political intelligence. Who did he know? What were they like? How, precisely, was the political line of *Pravda* determined? What personalities were at play? For his part, he meant to make use of what he called the Scheherazade defence: as long as he intrigued them with stories, they would not execute him or send him back to Russia. In the normal interrogation process, where every statement raised questions, a cooperative subject might continue the discussion for a period of months. Szara's hope lay in the fact that Germany was at war, and in war it was given that unpredictable things happened, including catastrophes of all sorts – invasions, raids, bomb- ings, mass escapes, even negotiations and peace. Any or all of it might be to his advantage. And if they should reach the end of the line with him and determine to ship him back to Russia, he then had one last move to make: he could contrive to take his life by attempted escape, from the Germans or the Russians, whoever gave him the barest edge of an opportunity.

It wasn't much of a plan, he knew, but in his circumstances it was all he had. It might have worked. He was never to find out, because there was one convention of the German character he'd neglected to include in the equation.

They came for him after midnight, when the sounds of the Gestapo interrogations were impossible not to hear and sleep was out of the question. First there was the clang of a gate, then approaching footsteps in the corridor. Szara gripped the frame of the cot with all the strength in his hands, but the footsteps halted outside his cell and the door burst open. Two SS troopers stood in the spill of strong light, recruiting poster SS, tall and fair and sallow in their black uniforms. Then it was '*Raus!*' and all that, toothy grins, the silent sharing of the great joke that only they understood. Holding his beltless trousers up with his hands, he hurried along the corridor as best he could, shuffling because they'd taken his shoelaces as well. His mind had gone numb, yet his senses seemed to operate independently: the troopers smelled like a gymna- sium, a man in an isolation cell moaned as though in a dream. They went down several flights of stairs, at last arriving in a brightly lit office filled with desks, the walls covered with beautifully drawn charts and lists.

A little gnome of a man waited for him at a railing; in his hands a wet hat dripped onto the linoleum. Eyes down, Szara thought he saw an edge of pyjama bottom peeking out from one leg of the man's trousers. 'Ah,' said the man in a soft voice. 'It's Herr Szara.'

'You'll have to sign for him,' said the taller of the two SS.

'It's what I do,' said the man, almost to himself.

Papers were produced and laid on a desk. The gnome carefully unscrewed the cap of a silver fountain pen. He began to scratch a well-flourished signature at the bottom of each page. 'Have we all his things?' he asked as he wrote.

The SS man pointed to the door, where Szara's valise stood to one side with several envelopes stacked on top of it. When the last signature was executed, the gnome said, 'Come along, then.' Szara held the envelopes under one arm, picked up the valise, and used his free hand to hold his trousers up. 'Do you have an umbrella we can use?' the gnome asked the SS trooper.

'A thousand apologies, *mein Herr*, it's something we don't have.'

The gnome sighed with resignation. 'Good night, then. Heil Hitler. Thank you for your kind assistance.'

In the floodlit courtyard stood a small green Opel, its bonnet steaming in the rain. The man opened the door and Szara climbed in and leaned back against the leather seat. Water sluiced down the windscreen and blurred the floodlights to golden rivers. The little man slid behind the wheel, turned on the ignition, said, 'Excuse me,' and, leaning across Szara, retrieved a Luger automatic pistol from the glove compartment. 'Your forbearance,' he said formally, 'in not punching me will be appreciated. And please don't jump out of the car – I haven't run since childhood. Well, to tell you the truth, I didn't run then either.'

'May I ask where we're going?' Szara opened the envelopes, put his belt on and laced up his shoes.

'You certainly may,' said the gnome, peering through the rain, 'but it wouldn't mean anything even if I told you.' Uncertainly, he steered the Opel across the broad courtyard, flipped a leather card case open and showed it to a guard, then drove ahead when the iron gate swung open. There was a sudden shout behind them.

'What are they yelling about?'

'To turn on the windscreen wipers.'

'Yes, well,' the gnome grumbled, turning on the wipers, 'wake a man up at midnight and what do you expect.' The Opel turned the corner from Prinz-Albrechtstrasse to Saarlandstrasse. 'So,' he said. 'You're the man who worked in Paris. You know what we Germans say, don't you. "God lives in France." Someday I would like to go.'

'I'm sure you will,' Szara said. 'I really must insist on asking you where we are going.' He didn't care if the man shot him. His fingers rested lightly on the door handle.

'We're going to a place near Altenburg. There. Now the secret's out.'

'What's there?'

'You ask entirely too many questions, if you'll permit me. Perhaps it's done in France – it isn't here. I can only say that I'm sure everything will be explained. It always is. After all, you're not handcuffed, and you've just left the worst place you could possibly be – now doesn't that tell you something? You're being rescued, so be a gentleman, sit quietly, and think up some entertaining stories about Paris. We'll be driving for a few hours.'

They drove, according to the road signs, south, through Leipzig, in the general direction of Prague. Eventually the car entered a network of small roads, the engine whining as they climbed. At the top of a hill, the Opel entered the courtyard of a small inn surrounded by woods. A single light could be seen, illuminating a yellow room at the apex of the steeply slanted roof.

The man who opened the door of the yellow room was not someone he'd met before, of that Szara was certain. Yet there was something strangely familiar about him. He was a tall, reedy fellow in his late thirties, balding, a few wisps of fragile blond hair combed neatly to one side. He was chinless, unfortunately so, with a hesitant, almost apologetic little smile that suggested ancient family and rigid breeding – as though a guest had just broken a terribly valuable vase while the host, fearing only that he would be seen to be discourteously brokenhearted, smiled anxiously and swore it was nothing. 'Please come in,' the man said. The voice was intelligent and strong, entirely at odds with his physical presence. He extended his hand to Szara and said, 'I am Herbert Von Polanyi.'

Now Szara understood, at least, his curious sense of recognition: Marta Haecht, describing Dr Julius Baumann's luncheon companion at the Hotel Kaiserhof, had drawn a perfect verbal portrait of him. Szara evidently stared. Von Polanyi canted his head a little to one side and said, 'You don't know who I am, of course.' The statement was not entirely sure of itself – a tribute, Szara guessed, to the NKVD's reputation for omniscience.

'No,' Szara said. 'I don't. But I am greatly in your debt, whoever you are, for getting me out of that very bad place. Apparently, you must know who I am.'

'Well yes, I do know who you are. You are the Soviet journalist Szara, André Szara. Connected, formerly connected I think, with a certain Soviet organization in Paris.' Von Polanyi gazed at him for a moment. 'Strange to meet you in person. You can't imagine how I studied you, trying to learn your character, trying to predict what you, and your directors, would do in certain situations. Sometimes I worried you would succeed, other times I was terrified you might fail. The time one spends! But of course you know that. We were connected through Dr Julius Baumann; I was his case officer, as were you. Two sides of the same game.'

Szara nodded, taking it all in as though for the first time.

'You didn't know?'

'No.'

Von Polanyi's face glowed with triumph. 'It is nothing.' He brushed victory away with a sweep of his hand. 'Come in, for God's sake. Let's be comfortable – there's coffee waiting.'

It was a spacious room with a few pieces of sturdy old furniture. Two small couches stood perpendicular to the window, facing each other over a coffee table. Von Polanyi, slightly awkward and storklike, arranged himself on one of the couches. He was dressed for the country, in wool trousers and flannel blazer with a broad, quiet tie. A coffee service was laid out on the table, and Von Polanyi performed the various rituals with pleasure, fussing with sugar lumps and warm milk. 'This is something of an occasion,' he said. 'It's rare for two people like us to meet. But, here we are. You are physically well, I hope.' His face showed real concern. 'They didn't – do anything to you, did they?'

'No. They were very correct.'

'It isn't always so.' Von Polanyi looked away, a man who knew more than was good for him.

'May I ask,' Szara said, 'what has become of Dr Baumann and his wife?'

Von Polanyi nodded his approval of the question; that had to be cleared up immediately. 'Dr Baumann was, against the wishes of the Foreign Ministry which, ah, sponsored his relationship with the USSR, imprisoned in Sachsenhausen camp. Certain individuals insisted on this and we were unable to stop it. There he spent two months before we found a way to intercede. He was mistreated, but he survived. Physically and, I am certain, psychologically. You would find him today much the same as he was. He and his wife were expelled from Germany, having forfeited their possessions, including the Baumann Milling works, now owned by his former chief engineer. The Baumanns are at least safe and have established themselves in Amsterdam. As by now you are aware, all the information Dr Baumann passed on to you was controlled by an office in the Foreign Ministry. It was, however, and I will discuss this further in a moment, correct information. To the centimetre. So, in the end, you were not fooled. Did you suspect?'

Szara answered thoughtfully: 'Russians, Herr Von Polanyi, suspect everyone, always, doubly so in the espionage business. I can say Baumann's bona fides were permanently in question, but never seriously challenged.'

'Well then, it only means we did our job properly. Of course, he had no choice but to cooperate. Originally, we were able to offer him continued ownership of the business. Later, after Czechoslovakia was taken, the Nazi party gained confidence – the world's armies did not march, the American Neutrality Act was an inspiration – and the issue became life itself. I am not a sentimentalist, Herr Szara, but coercion on that level is disagreeable and in the end, I suspect, leads to betrayal, though Baumann, according to you, did keep his end of the bargain.'

'He did,' Szara said. *Unless,* he thought, *you count his hint in the final transmission and Frau Baumann's approach to Odile.*

'An honourable man. On the subject of Jews the Nazis are like mad dogs. They will not be reasonable, and such blindness may ultimately destroy us all. I believe that could actually happen.'

This was treason, pure and simple. Szara felt his guard drop a notch.

'On the same subject, I must say it's fortunate for you that you admitted your real identity – though not, I imagine, your vocation. When the information was disseminated to the various intelligence bureaux we took immediate steps to secure your release. We're a small office at the Foreign Ministry, simply a group of educated German gentlemen, but we have the right to read everything. I believed that the Gestapo might use you against us, and that is the reason we agreed to spend various favours and obligations in order to have you released. In bureaucratic currency, it was quite costly.'

'But there's more to it than that,' Szara said.

'Yes. There is. A great deal more. I hope you'll indulge me and let me come at this in my own particular way.' Von Polanyi glanced at his watch. 'You're to be taken across the border, but we have some few hours to ourselves. I've wanted to tell a certain story for a very long time, and what remains of this night may well be the only chance I'll ever have to tell it. So, do I have your permission to continue?'

'Yes, of course,' Szara said. 'I want to hear it.'

'While the coffee's still warm . . .' Von Polanyi said, filling Szara's cup, then his own. He settled back and made himself comfortable on the couch. The room, Szara realized, was very nearly a stage set, and not by accident. The light was low and confidential; in the woods outside the window there was only darkness and silence and the steady drip of the rain. The man in the green Opel had driven away; the sense of privacy was complete.

'This is,' Von Polanyi said, 'the story of a love affair. A love affair carried on at a distance, over a long period of time – six years, to date, and it continues – a love affair with roots in the personalities of two very different nations, a love affair in which you and I have both been intimately involved, a love affair, as it happens, between two powerful men. The reference is clear?'

'I would think so.'

'Love affair is a dramatic term, isn't it, but what else could one call a relationship based on a deep and sympathetic understanding, a shared passion for certain ideals, a common view of the human race? Love affair describes it. Especially when you include such elements as secrecy. There's always that in a love affair. Maybe one of the lovers is promised to somebody else, or it could be that the family doesn't approve. Or maybe it doesn't matter *why* – the two lovers want to meet but everything is in their way; they're misunderstood, even hated, and all they want to do is unite, to become as one. It's all so unfair.'

Von Polanyi paused, took a pack of Gitanes from a wooden box on the coffee table, and offered one to Szara. The same kind he'd smoked when he'd visited Dr Baumann, naturally. After he'd lit Szara's cigarette with a silver lighter, Von Polanyi continued. 'Now if we are writing a play, the logical ending for such a love affair is doom. But, if we leave the theatre and enter the world of politics, the doom may be for the world and not the lovers. Imagine that Shakespeare rewrote the final act of *Romeo and Juliet*: now the lovers poison the wells of Verona and, in the final scene, they're all alone and living happily ever after.

'Well,' Von Polanyi said, 'I suppose that's the end of my literary career. Because the reality, I'm afraid, is not so amusing. The lovers, of course, are Joseph Stalin and Adolf Hitler. In August, their secret love affair ended with the announcement of an engagement – the Non-Aggression Pact – and a lavish engagement present: Poland. And this is merely the engagement. One may well ask what splendours are planned for the wedding itself!

'But that's the future. For tonight, in the few hours we have, I want to talk about the past. But where to begin? Because this passion, this romance, does not confine itself to the lovers, it starts in the villages where they live and it starts a long time ago. Germany has always needed what Russia has: her oil, iron ore, rare metals and grain. And Russia has always needed what Germany has: our science and technology, our skills, the simple ability to get something done. A German sees a job that needs doing, he thinks a minute, rolls up his sleeves, spits on his hands, and – it's done! When we try to go it alone, alas, when we exclude the world outside our borders, things don't go so well. An example: our latest campaign is to get our people to eat rye bread, from grain we can grow ourselves, and to that end the Ministry of Propaganda is claiming that white bread weakened our soldiers in the 1914 war. Of course no one believes it.

'Now two countries like this, and practically next-door neighbours to boot – is it not a match that cries out to be made? It's been tried before, but somehow it never seems to take. Catherine the Great imported Germans by the wagonload; they helped, but nothing really changed. A more recent example: in 1917, the German General Staff put old Lenin on an armoured train and thus destroyed imperial Russia. Yet even so, the minute the world settled down, in 1922, they were at it again with the Treaty of Rapallo. Now we had the two most despised states in Europe rushing into each other's arms – if nobody else will love me, surely this ugly old thing will!

'Poor Rapallo. Another *treaty*, another date to torment the student suffering over his history text. But this marriage is a little more interesting if you look under the covers. The German War Ministry forms a development company called GEFO and funds it with seventy-five million gold reichsmarks. This allows the Junkers company to build three hundred fighter aircraft at a Russian town called Fili, just outside Moscow. Germany receives two hundred and forty of them, the USSR gets sixty and the technology. Next comes a joint stock company called Bersol – by now our poor, suffering student is surely reeling. Perhaps reeling in fact, since Bersol undertakes the manufacture of poison gas at Trotsk, in the province of Samara. In 1925, in Tambov province, near the town of Lipetsk, the Lipetsk Private Flying School comes into existence. Rather nebulous, though known today as the Luftwaffe. By September of 1926, Russian freighters deliver three hundred thousand shells plus gunpowder and fuses to Germany, disguised as pig iron and aluminium. Can the poor student stand any more of this? Once you add the fact that the Heavy Vehicle Experimental and Test Station near the town of Kazan is in fact a site for Krupp and Daimler and Rheinmetall to build light tractors – tanks is a better description – probably not. It's all so tiresome, unless of course the student goes to school in Prague. This goes on for twelve years. Germany rebuilds its forces; the two armies participate in exchanges of military officers, establishing facilities in both Berlin and Moscow. And that's just the secret part of Rapallo. In full view of the world, the Russian wheat and ore boats travel west, the German technicians pack their little black bags and head east.

'When Hitler came to power, though, in 1933, all had to end. Here was Germany's evil face, and the idealistic Soviet Union and its friends the wide world over had to be seen to turn away from it. Pity, because everything had been going so well.

'Any diplomat would say that such a moment, if nothing else can be done, is a time to keep a dialogue alive, but Hitler and Stalin shared a special and characteristic trait: they both believed that language was God's gift to liars, words existed only to manipulate those who thought otherwise. Both these men had risen from the gutters of Europe – here I am partial to a Russian saying: power is like a high, steep cliff, only eagles and reptiles may ascend to it – and they believed diplomacy to be the tool of those who had historically kept them down, the intelligentsia, professors, Jews, all such people. But then, a problem: how could any sort of communication be achieved? Solution: only by deeds, by gestures, by irrevocable actions that made one's intentions plain and clear. They certainly didn't invent this method. Since the first days of the newspaper, nations have communicated in this way – on the third page, on the second page, on the first page. We must admit, though, that Hitler and Stalin used the method with some particular flair.

'In 1933, Stalin wasn't quite sure what he was dealing with in Berlin. He'd read translations of Hitler's speeches, maybe even his book, but, as I've said, what did that mean? Then, in 1934, something even Stalin could understand. The Night of the Long Knives. Hitler had a rival, Ernst Röhm, who led the Brown Shirts. What did he do about it? Murdered them. All the important ones, and all in one night. And so much for rivals. Well, Stalin felt, apparently, the first stirrings of romantic passion, because by December of that year he answered in kind. The assassination of Kirov was organized, and Stalin's political rivals were eliminated in a purge that continued into 1936.

'Then it was Hitler's turn. In 1936 he marched into the Rhineland. He took *territory*. Once again, Stalin sat up and took notice. Found a way to express a kind of approval: the show trial of Kamenev and Zinoviev. That they were Jews is less important than Vyshinsky's *statement*, at the trial, that they were Jews. Here we see Stalin beginning to come to grips with his real problem, which was very simply this: the twelve years of Rapallo had taught both countries that they could cooperate; now, how was that cooperation to be reinstated? Because, with Hitler in power, those two countries could rule the world if they worked together. They were, like lovers, made whole each by the other, and thus invincibly strong.

'But Stalin had a difficult problem, the fact that communism had traditionally been a religion of idealists. On one side of him was Tukhachevsky, Trotsky's protégé, and the most powerful figure in the Red Army. Tukhachevsky was young, handsome, brilliant, and courageous, proven in battle, beloved by his officers. At a show trial, he would have made mincemeat of an oily little opportunist like Vyshinsky and Stalin knew it. Now he needed help, and help was at hand. You'll recall the officer exchanges that went on during the Rapallo period? Letters, orders, communications of various sorts, still existed in German files. At Stalin's behest, certainly through NKVD intermediaries of the most trusted sort, Reinhard Heydrich and the Gestapo SD intelligence service found Tukhachevsky's communications and remade them into forgeries proving that Tukhachevsky and four other Soviet marshals – two of them Jews! – had conspired with Hitler to overthrow the government of the USSR in a coup d'état. Exit the marshals and most of the leadership of the Red Army. What did the world, the *knowledgeable* world, civil servants and journalists, think of this? That the conspiracy was born in Germany, a brilliant manoeuvre by the intelligence services to weaken the military leadership of the USSR. Certainly, except for Stalin at the bottom of it, it could seem that way.

'That left Stalin with one final, but very grave, difficulty: the intelligence services themselves, the real levers of his power. The NKVD and the GRU were staffed by thousands of Old Bolsheviks and foreign communists, many of them Jews, every last one of them an ideologue. These people were concentrated in crucial positions – including the Foreign Departments of both services – and handled the most secret and sophisticated tasks. These were the people who'd bled in the revolution, these were the people who believed that whatever else might be wrong with the Soviet Union, at least it stood against Hitler's bullyboys and Jew baiters. Rapprochement with Germany under Nazi rule? Unthinkable.

'But, as I suspect you know, a man in love will do almost anything, and Stalin craved Hitler as ally, accomplice, and friend. Perhaps he thought, *There is one man in the world, and only one, with whom I could have a complete understanding, but here are all these stiff-necked romantics in my way. Will no one rid me of these meddlesome* – well, one can't say *priests*, but it isn't so far from true. And there was, there almost always is, someone at hand to take him up on it. On one level, the purge of 1936 to 1938 was seen as an elimination of those who knew too much, those who knew where the bodies were buried, the final act of a criminal securing his crime. To those with an inside view, however, it seemed principally a war for power in the intelligence services: the so-called Ukrainian *khvost*; Jews and Poles and Latvians versus the Georgian *khvost*, mostly those from Transcaucasia; Georgians, Armenians, Turks, with a few Jewish allies thrown in to muddy the issue. In fact, it was an extended pogrom, led by Beria, and when it was done the stage was set for a public consummation of the love affair.

'Hitler certainly knew what was going on, because Kristallnacht, the world's first real taste of what Germany had in mind for the Jews of Europe, was then allowed to take place, in late 1938. The former operatives of the NKVD would have assassinated him then and there, but they were either dead or working at the bottom of some gold mine in Siberia and soon to be. Stalin, eternally shrewd, left a few show pieces alive, to forestall the accusation that he'd done exactly what he did do – Lazar Kaganovich for instance, Maxim Litvinov for instance, some of the operatives in the European networks for instance, and a few prominent journalists, for instance Ilya Ehrenburg, for instance André Szara.'

Von Polanyi paused – perhaps he expected Szara to sputter and curse – and in a rather studied way chose that moment to discover that he wanted more coffee. Szara found himself dispassionate, nodding in polite affirmation, *yes, it could have been like that*, but he'd learned more about his own situation in that moment than he had about Joseph Stalin. He felt no anger at all. His mind was now ruled, he saw, by the suspended judgment of the intelligence officer. What he'd once pretended to be he had, by necessity, become, for his principal reaction to Von Polanyi's revelation was *perhaps*. It could be true. But, more to the point, why was he being told this? What role was Von Polanyi assigning him?

There had to be one. Von Polanyi had known about him for a long time, as far back as 1937, when he'd come to Berlin to recruit Dr Baumann – when the NKVD had agreed, far above his head, to receive strategic information by means of a clandestine network. Unwittingly, Szara had been an operative of the Reich Foreign Ministry's intelligence service – 'a small office . . . simply a group of educated German gentlemen' – and he had no very good reason to believe that Von Polanyi wanted the relationship to end. 'As far as I can tell,' Szara said carefully, 'everything you say is true. Can anything be done about it?'

'Not immediately,' Von Polanyi said. 'Tonight, the centre of Europe runs on a line down the middle of Poland, and I believe the intention is to forge a Russo-German empire on either side of it. For Germany there is Western Europe: France, Scandinavia, the Low Countries, Great

Britain; Spain and Portugal will come along when they see how things are, Italy remains a junior partner. Stalin will expect to acquire a substantial part of the Balkans, Lithuania, Latvia, Estonia, Turkey, Iran, and India – eventually a common border with a Japanese empire in the Pacific. The United States is to be isolated, slowly squeezed to death or invaded by a thousand divisions. Both Hitler and Stalin prefer political conquest to actual war, so the former alternative is the more likely.'

'For me,' Szara said, 'a world in which I could not live. But you are a German, Herr Von Polanyi, a German patriot. Is it possible you dislike the present leader so deeply that you would damage your country in order to destroy him?'

'I am a German, most certainly a German patriot. From that perspective, I will tell you that the damage has already been done, and a world has been created in which I refuse to live. If Germany loses this war it will be devastating, almost the worst thing that could happen but not the very worst. The very worst would be for Adolf Hitler and Joseph Stalin, and the people around them, to win such a war. That I cannot permit.'

Von Polanyi's arrogance was stunning; Szara forced himself to look puzzled and a little lost. 'You have something particular in mind, then.'

'At this moment, I frankly don't know what to do, not specifically. I do know, however, that a structure needs to be established, a structure with which Hitler's power may be damaged, perhaps destroyed, when the opportunity presents itself. Why would I want to create such a structure? I can only say: who will if I won't? I don't want to bore you with a history of the Von Polanyi family – in a sense you already know it. An old family, hundreds of years old. Never peaceful. A war family, if you like, but always honourable. Obsessed with honour. So, always, we die young. We also breed young, however, so the line continues despite the inevitabilities of such a heritage. For me, honour lies in the sort of action I am proposing. I am not unaware that this thorn in the German character is despised by some, but I think you can find a way to see the use of it.'

'Of course,' Szara said. 'But my own situation . . .' He didn't know where to begin.

Von Polanyi leaned forward. 'To do what I have in mind, Herr Szara, I need a man outside Germany, a man not only in a neutral country but in a neutral state of being. A man without affiliation, a man not obligated to any particular state or political creed, a man who understands the value of information, a man who can direct this information where it will do the most good – which is to say the most harm – and a

557

man who can achieve that sort of liaison skilfully, in such a way that the source remains protected. Thus a man with the technical ability to support an act inspired by ethics, honour, call it by any name you like. Briefly put, I need a man who can do good and not get caught at it.'

So I am described, Szara thought, and a strange conspiracy is proposed: a Polish Jew and a German aristocrat shall work together to push Adolf Hitler over the edge of some yet unseen cliff. The presumption of the idea! That two rather ordinary men in an inn near Altenburg would even dare to dream of opposing a state of the magnitude of Nazi Germany, with its Gestapo, its Abwehr, SS divisions, Panzer tanks and Luftwaffe. Yet it was possible and Szara knew it – the power of intelligence was such that two ordinary men in an inn near Altenburg could destroy a nation if they used it properly.

'You are attracted to the idea,' Von Polanyi said, an edge of excitement in his voice.

'Yes,' Szara said. 'Perhaps it could be done. But I am officially a traitor to the Soviet Union, a network operative in flight, so my time on earth is very limited. Weeks, probably. Nothing can change that.'

'Herr Szara.' Von Polanyi's feelings were clearly hurt. 'Please try to think better of me than that. We have a friend in the SD who is, covertly, a friend of the NKVD. With your permission, we are going to have you leave this troubled world tonight, one of the many who did not survive Gestapo interrogation. You may, if all goes smoothly, read your own obituary should the Russians choose to proceed in that way. But you must not betray us, must not spring alive with your name at the foot of a newspaper column. Can you give me your word that it will be so – forever?'

'You have my word,' Szara said. 'But it cannot be that simple.'

'*Auf!*' Von Polanyi said in despair. 'Of course it isn't. Nothing is. You will live in mortal fear of chance recognition. But I do believe that a certain inertia will help to keep you safe. A Soviet officer will think a long time before insisting that an enemy declared dead by the NKVD is in fact still with us. To discredit the leadership of his own organization is something he will not do easily. Better to convince himself that he's seen a ghost, and that Moscow remains infallible.'

'They'll want proof.'

'The proof is that they've discovered the event by clandestine means, and that when a feeler is extended at some remote level – "Seen our man Szara anywhere?" – we'll deny we ever heard of you. Then they'll believe it. The real danger to you is gossip – a group of émigrés, for example, chattering about a Russian-speaking Frenchman who sneaks off to eat blini when he thinks no one's looking. You have a French passport, according to the Gestapo teletype. They describe it as "valid". Use it. Be that Frenchman. But you must alter your appearance as best you can and live the life of a Frenchman – a Frenchman who best not return to France, a Jew from Marseille, mixed up in who knows what unsavoury affair. Grow yourself a vulgar little moustache, grease your hair, gain weight. You won't fool the French; they'll know you're a fraud the minute you speak a word. But with luck they'll take you for nothing more than a creature of the gutter – just not their gutter. Put it about that you lived in Cairo and sold the wrong stocks to the chief of police. There is a bustling world at the margins of society; I'm sure you know it. It hides all sorts of people, it may possibly hide you. Well, what do you think?'

Szara didn't answer right away. He stared at his hands and finally said, 'Maybe.'

'The best deception is the one we ourselves believe in, and that is always the sort of deception that saves our lives,' Von Polanyi said, a bit of the philosopher's gleam in his eye. 'Survive, Herr Szara. I think it's your gift in this life. Trust in the fact that most people are never very sure of themselves – "Oh but you do remind me of him," they'll say. You must, however, become the legend you create for yourself, and you may not take vacations from it. For you, perhaps a little job of some sort might make all the difference – something not quite legitimate.'

Szara turned and looked out the window, but nothing had changed; a starless night, the steady rhythm of rain in a forest. Finally he said, 'How would we communicate?'

Von Polanyi let the silence rest for a moment; it meant they had reached an understanding, the sort that does not require words. Then he went through the procedures: a postal card to a certain drapery shop, a *poste restante* return address, then contact. His tone was casual, almost dismissive, implying it was the sort of thing that Szara had done a thousand times before. When he'd finished, Szara said, 'And if I simply vanish?'

'We are equals in this affair,' Von Polanyi said easily. 'If you don't want us, Herr Szara, then we don't want you. It's just that simple.'

They took him out of Germany in grand style, in a dark green Mercedes driven by a young man barely out of his teens, a naval officer, pink-cheeked, gangling, and endlessly solicitous. Every hour or so he would pull over, wait until the road was clear, then knock delicately on the lid of the boot and whisper loudly, 'All is well?' or some such thing.

All was well enough. Szara lay on a saddle blanket, his valise beside him, surrounded by assorted tack that smelled richly of old leather and horse. They had fed him sumptuously at the inn, a tray left in front of the door bearing poached eggs and buttered bread and jam tarts. And the naval officer – somewhere outside Vienna, he guessed – slipped him half a cold roast duck in a napkin and a bottle of beer. In the horsey-smelling darkness Szara felt a little seasick from the curves but picked at it for form's sake and drank the beer. There were three stops. Each time he imagined papers being presented to the accompaniment of Hitler salutes and a rough joke and a laugh. By nightfall they were rumbling up the avenues of a city and Szara was let out on a dark street in a pleasant neighbourhood. 'Welcome to Budapest,' said the young officer. 'The stamp is already in your passport. Good luck.' Then he drove away.

He was, in some sense, free.

Jean Bonotte was abroad in the world and lived much as Von Polanyi had suggested he might – in shabby hotels near railway stations or in the narrow streets by the harbour, where the air smelled like dead fish and diesel oil. He stayed nowhere very long. Joined a restless army of lost souls, men and women without countries, not so very different from his days in Kovno. He stood with them on the long lines for registration at the police stations – 'One more week, sir, then out you go' – ate at the same cheap restaurants, sat with them in the parks when the pale winter sun lit up the statue of the national hero. He changed. The cracked mirrors in the numberless hotel rooms told the story. He did not, as Von Polanyi had suggested, gain weight. He lost it, his face lean and haunted beneath his awkward, refugee haircut. He grew a natty moustache and trimmed it to perfection, the last vestige of self-respect in a world that had taken everything else away. A pair of faintly tinted eyeglasses gave him the look of a man who would be sinister if he dared, a weak, frightened man making a miserable pretence of strength. This message was not lost on the predators. Again and again the police of various cities took the little money he had in his pocket, and on two occasions he was beaten up.

The second day in Budapest, when he hadn't quite got the hang of life in the alleys, a little fellow with a cap down over his eyes and a stub of cigarette stuck to his lip demanded money for entry into a certain neighbourhood – or so Szara guessed from his gestures, for he understood not a word of Hungarian. Szara angrily brushed the impeding hand away and the next thing he knew he'd been hit harder than ever before in his life. He barely saw it happen, this dog didn't growl before it bit. Szara simply found himself lying in the street, ears ringing, blood running in his mouth, as he fumbled for money to offer. Fortunately he'd left his valise in a hotel or it would have been gone forever. The damage, when he saw it, was horrific. Both lips had been split to one side of his mouth, as well as the skin above and below. It healed poorly. A dark red scar remained. In his mismatched jacket and trousers, wearing a shirt bought purposely a size too large so that it stood out around his neck, he already looked like a man whose luck, if he ever had any, had run out a long time ago. The scar drew the eye, confirmed the image. If the NKVD was still hunting for André Szara, and he had to assume that they might be, they wouldn't look for him hiding inside this sad, battered fellow.

Budapest. Belgrade. The Roumanian port of Constanţa. Salonika, where he sold lottery tickets in the streets of the large, prosperous Jewish community. Athens. Istanbul. The new year of 1940 he welcomed in Sofia, staring at a light bulb on a cord that dangled from the ceiling and thinking of Nadia Tscherova.

As he did every day, sometimes every hour. To the address in Schillerstrasse he sent postcards. Signed *B*. *A* would have been for André, *B* was what he was now. She would understand this immediately, he knew. This *B* was a wealthy sort of cad, travelling about southern Europe on business, who now and then gave a thought to his old girlfriend Nadia who lived in Germany. 'The sea is quite lovely,' said *B* from a town on the Black Sea coast of Turkey. In Bucharest he'd 'finally got over a beastly cold.' In Zagreb, where he worked for two old Jewish brothers who had a market stall where they sold used pots and pans, *B* detected 'signs of spring in the air.' *I am alive,* he told her in this way. *I am not in Germany, not in Russia, I am free.* But living a life – in Varna, Corfu, Debrecen – that she could not possibly share. 'Love always,' said *B*, mailing his card an hour before he left a city. What *love always* really meant, the ten thousand words of it, he could only hope she understood. In the ruined beds of a hundred rooms spread across the lost quarters of Europe, her ghost lay with him every night.

When he worked, it was almost always in Yiddish. Even in the Sephardic communities where they spoke Ladino, somebody was sure to know it. In the outdoor markets, in the back streets of almost any city, he found Jews, and they almost always needed something done. He didn't ask very much, and they'd nod yes with a tight mouth, *probably you'll rob me.* It wasn't exactly charity, just something in the way they were that didn't like to say no. Maybe he was hungry. He didn't look strong enough to load or unload wagons but he did it once or twice. Mostly he cleaned up, or ran errands, or sold things. The dented, blackened pots and pans in Zagreb. Secondhand suits in Bucharest. Used dishes, sheets, tools, books – even eyeglasses. 'No?' he'd say. 'Then try these. Can you see that girl over there? Perfect! That's silver in those frames – you look ten years younger.' It was easy to pick up – he had to wonder if it hadn't been there all the time – and it had to be done, a premium for the customer. Who wanted to buy from a stone? In these streets, money was earned and spent in the cheapest coin there was, a whole dinar, a lek or a lev, that you never saw. But life was cheap. He lived on bread and tea, potatoes and onions, cabbage and garlic. A little piece of dried-up meat was a banquet. If it had a rim of fat at the edge, a feast. His skin grew red and rough from being outdoors in the winter, his hands hard as leather. He'd beckon a customer to him con-fidentially, look both ways to make sure no one was listening, slip a subtle finger beneath a lapel and say, 'Listen, you got to buy from me today, you're not going to anybody else. So make a price, I don't care, I'm a desperate man.' The owner of a stall that sold buttons and thread said to him in Constanţa, 'David' – for so he called himself that week – 'you're the best *luftmensch* I ever had. Maybe you'll stay awhile.'

He became, that spring, the other kind of *luftmensch* as well, the man as inconspicuous as air, the operative. Privately, at first, in the way he began to remember his past. It came back like an old love affair, the ashes of his former life a little warmer than he'd thought.

He found himself in Izmir, the old Greek city of Smyrna, now Turkish. Just by the old bazaar, on Kutuphane street, was a restaurant owned by a swarthy little Sephardic lady with shining black eyes. For her he scrubbed pots. It turned his hands and forearms crimson, and he earned almost nothing, but she was a provident feeder – he lived on lamb and pine nuts and groats, dried figs and apricots – and she had an unused room in the cellar with a dusty straw mattress on an old door that he could sleep on. There was even a table, the edges marked by forgotten cigarettes, and a paraffin lamp. Through a half window at pavement level he could see Kadifekele, the Velvet Fortress, perched on top of its hill. He had a strong, intuitive feeling about the room: a writer had worked there. The old lady's son was something or other in the administrative section of the Izmir police, and for the first time in his travels Jean Bonotte had an actual work permit, though not under that name. 'Write down,' she'd said. And he'd laboriously scrawled some concoction on a scrap of paper. A week later, a permit. 'My son!' she explained of the miracle. Fortune smiled. Izmir wasn't a bad place: a sharp wind blew across the docks off the Aegean, the harbour was full of tramp freighters. The people were reserved, slightly inward, perhaps because, not so many years earlier, the blood had literally run in the streets here, Turks slaughtering Greeks, and the town couldn't quite put it in the past.

From his meagre wages Szara bought a notebook and pencils and, once the huge iron pots were dried and put away for the evening, began to write. This was night writing, writing for himself, with no audience in mind. It was March, a good writer's month, Szara felt, because writers like abundant weather – thunder and lightning, wind and rain, surging spring skies – not particularly caring if it's good or bad just so there's a lot going on. He wrote about his life, his recent life. It was hard, he was surprised at the emotional aches and pains it cost him, but evidently he wanted to do it because he didn't stop. On the near horizon was what Von Polanyi had said about the executions of the 1936 purge and the secret courtship of Hitler and Stalin. But it was life he wrote about, not so much politics. Izmir, he sensed, was not a place where you would want to write about politics. It was almost too old for that, had seen too much, lived somewhere beyond those kinds of explanations – here and there the marble corner of a tumbled-down ruin had been worn to a curve by the incessant brush of clothing as people walked by for centuries. In such a place, the right thing to do was archaeology: archaeology didn't have to be about the ancient world, he discovered; you could scrape the dirt away and sift the sand of more recent times. The point was to preserve, not to lose what had happened.

Working down through his life, beneath the common anarchy of existence, the misadventures, dreams, and passions, he found pattern. Rather, two patterns. If every life is a novel, his had two plots. He discovered he had, often at the same moment, both served and resisted the Hitler–Stalin *affaire*, had worked for two masters, both in the Soviet special services. Bloch and Abramov.

What General Bloch had done was both daring and ingenious and, Szara came to believe, driven by desperation. He knew what was going on, he fought against it. And in this war André Szara had been one of his soldiers. To Szara, the depth of the operation and his part in it became clear only when he applied the doctrine of chronology – the exercise in a cellar in Izmir no different than the one he'd undertaken in a hotel room in Prague, when he'd worked through DUBOK's, Stalin's, history of betrayal.

Bloch had become aware of Stalin's move towards Hitler sometime before 1937 and had determined to prevent the alliance by naming Stalin as an Okhrana agent. He had somehow broken into Abramov's communication system and ordered Szara aboard the steamship taking Grigory Khelidze from Piraeus to Ostend. Khelidze was on his way to Czechoslovakia to collect the Okhrana file hidden sometime earlier in a left-luggage room in a Prague railway station. Szara had induced Khelidze to reveal his whereabouts in Ostend, then Bloch had ordered the courier's assassination. Then he'd used Szara as a substitute courier, used him to uncover Stalin's crimes in the Bolshevik underground, used him to publish the history of that treason in an American magazine. It had almost worked. The Georgian *khvost*, however, had somehow learned of the operation and prevented publication from taking place.

Here the chronology was productive: it revealed a mirror image of this event.

Szara, while in Prague, had written a story for *Pravda* about the agony of the Czech people as Hitler closed in for the kill. That story was suppressed. It was not in Hitler's interest for it to appear – evidently it was not in Stalin's interest, either. Ultimately, Britain and France were blamed for the loss of Czechoslovakia at Munich but, in the very same instant, Stalin and the Red Army stood quietly aside and permitted if to happen.

Abramov had then protected Szara, his old friend and sometime operative, by absorbing him directly into the intelligence *apparat* – what better place to hide from the devil than in a remote corner of hell? In Paris, Szara had become Baumann's case officer, in fact no more than one end of a secret communication system between Hitler and Stalin.

Then, a chance event that neither the Gestapo nor the NKVD could have foreseen.

The Paris OPAL network had broken through the screen of secrecy hiding their ongoing cooperation. Through Sénéschal's unwitting agent, the secretary Lötte Huber, Szara had discovered a meeting between Dershani, Khelidze's superior in the Georgian *khvost*, and Uhlrich, a known SD officer, and photographed it. Sénéschal had been murdered almost immediately because of this and Abramov had died for it a year or so later. Abramov, Szara now believed, had changed sides, attempted to use the photographs as leverage, and they had eliminated him as he attempted to escape.

There was more: Molotov's replacing Litvinov as the Hitler–Stalin courtship approached its moment of revelation, and Hitler's public approval of the change. Even Alexander Blok's poem 'The Scythians' seemed to have played a part in the operation. Here, the analysis depended on audience. If, on the night of the actor Poziny's recitation, the message was to the British and French diplomats in attendance, the poem served as a plea and a warning, which was how Blok had meant it: 'We ourselves henceforth shall be no shield of yours / we ourselves henceforth will enter no battle . . . Nor shall we stir when the ferocious Hun / rifles the pockets of the dead / Burns down cities . . .' To a German ear, however, at that particular moment in history, it might have meant something very different, something not unlike an invitation, from Stalin to Hitler, to do those very things. To bend Blok's poem to such a purpose was, to Szara, a particularly evil act, and it touched him with horror as nothing else had. He himself knew better, that compared to other evils the abuse of a poet's words oughtn't to have meant that much, yet somehow it did. Somehow it opened a door to what now happened in Europe, where, with Stalin's concurrence, the words became reality. The horror took place.

Late at night in Izmir, the spring wind blowing hard off the Aegean Sea, André Szara stared sightlessly out the window above his writing table. He would never understand the mysteries that these two peoples, the Russian and the German, shared between them. Blok had tried as only a poet could, applying images, the inexplicable chemistry at the borders of language. Szara would not presume to go deeper. He could see where answers might be hidden – somewhere in what happened between him and Marta Haecht, somewhere in what happened between Nadia Tscherova and her German general, somewhere in what happened between Hitler and Stalin, somewhere in what happened, even, between himself and Von Polanyi. Trust and suspicion, love and hate, magnetism and repulsion. Was there a magic formula that drew all this together? He could not find it, not that night in Izmir he couldn't. Perhaps he never would.

He could think only of Bloch's final act in the drama, in which he had manoeuvred Szara into the reach of de Montfried. It was as though Bloch, confronted by the certainty of failure – Beria ascendant, the murderers securely in power, a pact made with the devil – had sent one last message: *save lives.* Szara had done the best he could. And then the reality of circumstance had intervened.

And, soon enough, the reality of circumstance was that choices had to be made.

Szara filled a score of notebooks before he was done: messy, swollen things, pages front and back covered – entirely in disregard of the ruled lines – in pencilled Russian scrawl, erasures, scribbled-out words from moments when the great impatience was on him. In time, he began to live for the night, for the hours when the people of his life would come alive and speak. His memory astonished him: what Abramov said, the way Marta would put things, Vainshtok's sarcasms – and what may have been the final gesture of his life, which Szara never really did come to understand.

The potwasher's job took its toll. The skin of his hands dried out, cracked, and sometimes bled – occasionally he left a bloodspoor at the margin where his hand rested as he wrote. *Let them figure that out!* he thought. Them? He didn't know who that was. Russians had become secret writers, in camps and basements and cells and a thousand forms of exile, and they could only imagine secret readers. He was no different.

Otherwise, the world was unreasonably kind to him. The old lady developed a theory that his aptitude lay beyond scouring burned buckwheat crusts from the sides of pots and insisted, in the primitive one-word-at-a-time Yiddish they used between them, that he accompany her on the daily shopping expeditions – here she performed a fluent pantomime, lugging an invisible weight and blowing with fatigue – and when they attacked the markets, she took him to school. Onions were to be oblong and hard. You sniffed a melon here. With that thief you counted change twice. She had plans for him. He sensed a change of fortune, an improvement, a possible solution.

He was not the only one, that spring, who sought solutions. Far to the north of him, on Germany's western border, military intelligence officers were wondering exactly how they might penetrate France's Maginot Line or, if it could not be overrun, how to turn its flank. At first this seemed impossible. Even if the Wehrmacht were to violate Belgian neutrality, how were the Panzer tanks, so critical to the German attack scenario, to break through the dense Ardennes forest? To answer this question, the officers fixed lengths of pipe to the bonnets of their cars, making them the width of a tank, and drove through the forest. You had to go slow, they found, you had to weave in and out among the trees, you might have to knock down a few of them here and there, but it could be done.

It was done on 10 May. Along with glider and paratroop attacks to hold the Belgian bridges and subdue the Belgian forts. In the soft evening light on Izmir's seaside promenade Szara came upon a group of French people – perhaps commercial travellers or employees of French companies – gathered around a single copy of Le Temps. The Aeolus blew hard at that hour, and the men were holding their hats with one hand and the pages of the wind-whipped newspaper with the other. One of the women had tears on her face. Szara stood at the edge of the group and read over their shoulders. He understood immediately what had happened – he had seen Poland. One of the men was wearing a flat-brimmed straw boater. He let it go in order to flatten a recalcitrant page, the wind immediately blew it off and it rolled and skipped along the promenade.

Szara packed the notebooks that night, wrapping them carefully in brown paper and tying the package with string. An old sweater, a few novels – Balzac, Stendhal, Conrad in French – extra shirt and socks, a photograph of a Paris bistro torn from a magazine, a street map of Sofia; all of that went on top. It was time for the refugee to disappear, and a false-bottomed suitcase no longer served his purposes.

Early the following morning, sleepless and pale, he stood in a long line at the central post office. When he reached the grilled window he handed over a cable to be wired to de Montfried's office in Paris. He had an answer twenty-four hours later, was directed to a street of private banks where, beneath a vast, domed ceiling that assured a cool and perpetual dusk, a group of men in striped trousers counted out thousands of French francs. Outside, Szara blinked in the hard sunlight and made his way to the office of the Denizcilik Bankasi, the Turkish Maritime Lines, a venerable institution that had been calling at the ports of the Mediterranean for over a century. The clerks were deeply understanding. This French patriot would return to his homeland, sailing in a first-class stateroom to face his destiny in war. Each in turn, they shook his hand and looked into his eyes, then pointed out a hallway that led to the baggage room. Here too he found sympathy. A supervisor stood with hands clasped behind his back and watched as his young assistant wrote out a claim ticket. With ritual care, a tag was tied to the handle, then the supervisor tapped a bell and a man in a blue uniform appeared and carried the valise away. Szara got a glimpse of the baggage room when he opened the door; sturdy, wooden shelves climbed to the ceiling. He saw old-fashioned Gladstones, steamer trunks, portmanteaus, wooden crates, even a few metal dispatch boxes with stencilled printing. The supervisor cleared his throat. 'Do not trouble yourself,' he said. 'The trust of our clients is sacred, and this we maintain, even in the most difficult times.' Then he added, 'Good luck. Godspeed.' News of the German attack on France had flowed through the city like a current; war was now certain, it would surely be worse than 1914. All the citizens of Izmir Szara encountered that day were very formal and dignified; it was their particular way with tragedy.

He sailed on 14 May and reached Marseille five days later. On the voyage he kept to his cabin and had his meals brought up by the steward. Even though future sailings had been suspended, there were few travellers on the ship, only those who felt they had to return to a country at war. By the time they docked, Antwerp had been captured and the Wehrmacht had taken Amiens. Szara's steward told him confidentially that some of the passengers felt it was already too late, and they had decided not to disembark in France. The customs and passport officials took care of the first-class passengers in their state-rooms. They asked no questions of Jean Bonotte – there could be only one reason he was returning to France.

He was in Geneva a day later, travelling by hired car because the trains had become impossible, many of the locomotives and *wagons-lits* shifted north under French military control. Jean Bonotte was admitted to Switzerland on a five-day visa, in order to take care of banking business that had to be seen to in person. Again he wired de Montfried, again de Montfried responded immediately, and once again he was directed to a street of private banks. In this instance, the bankers were replaced, in an elaborately furnished sitting room, by lawyers. There were muted introductions, the fine weather was acknowledged, then the concept of *intervention* – a soft, subtle, even a graceful expression when purred a syllable at a time in French – was permitted to enter the conversation. Evidently it meant that certain officials would decide to intervene in Jean Bonotte's favour, for there could be no question but that he was the very sort of gentleman who should be resident in Switzerland. Szara said almost nothing; the Bonotte who sat at the table was virtually ignored, it was Bonotte the legal entity with whom they concerned themselves. These were gifted lawyers, with voices like cellos, who did not exactly ask questions; instead they provided answers, phrasing them for courtesy's sake in the interrogatory mood: 'Wouldn't it be much the best idea to inform the Préfecture that . . .' Szara followed along as best he could. Soothed by the distant clacking of typewriters, warmed by the sun pouring in a leaded-glass window, he might have fallen asleep if, every now and again, someone hadn't flourished a paper that needed signing. *This is how*, he thought, *you climb over barbed wire without cutting your hands.*

And so, it began again.

An eternal craft, Szara realized, in this warm and grey and placid city where the Rhône surged gently beneath stone bridges. Concessions were granted, money was earned, interest compounded, statements mailed in hand-addressed envelopes, and intelligence acquired, sold, traded, or simply locked away for later use. The city wasn't about secrecy, it was about privacy. Coat collars were worn flat. Szara found the usual small villa in the usual bland neighbourhood, on the chemin de Saussac, south of the city, and set aggressively about minding his own business, soon enough disappearing into the shadows of the daily and the expected. With his neighbours, he practised the single, stiff nod – no more, no less. He bought three brown suits, just barely different enough so the world might know he had more than one. Established a bank account, paid his bills, vanished. 'A most orderly and dignified city,' wrote the phantom *B* from Zürich. Something not unlike nostalgia attended Szara's hours on the train – all that effort to avoid a Geneva postmark while letting her know he was safe in Switzerland.

Safe was, of course, a relative term. He remained a fugitive. But somewhere, in his long odyssey through the back streets of southern Europe, Szara had learned to put aside his fear of inevitable retribution. Now he only hoped that if the NKVD discovered him he would not be kidnapped and interrogated. If they were going to kill him, let them get it over with quickly. He maintained some features of his previous disguise, in defence of chance recognition more than anything else. A woman journalist he knew, a Belgian, stared at him on a street one day. Szara acted like a man receiving an unexpected, though not at all unwelcome, sexual advance, and she hurried off. On another occasion an unknown man spoke to him, hesitantly, in Russian. Szara looked puzzled and asked, in French, if he needed assistance. The man apologized with a little bow and turned away.

What helped to protect him, Szara felt, was the attitude of the Swiss government towards the NKVD; the Soviet defector Ignace Reiss had been gunned down, quite openly, by NKVD operatives in Switzerland in 1937. The Swiss didn't like that sort of thing at all. What the Russians now maintained, he guessed, were quiet diplomatic affiliations and a few OPAL-style networks using former Communist party members as agents. Moscow thought it best to respect the limits of Swiss patience – any tolerance for revolutionary activity had long ago disappeared. The young Jews in flight from the Pale no longer argued the nights away – Hasidism! Socialism! Bolshevism! Zionism! – in Geneva cafés. Lenin, leaving exile in Switzerland in 1917, had left no statues of himself behind, and the Swiss seemed in no hurry to install them.

It would now be necessary to go to war.

This was his obligation, his heritage, it required no justification. 'I need,' Von Polanyi had said, 'a man who can do good and not get caught at it.' Very well, Szara was that man. In his desk drawer was the address of a certain drapery shop in Frankfurt. To complete the connection, he needed only a *poste restante* address, and this he obtained in Thonon, a pleasant train ride up the southern shore of Lac Leman. A communication line was now established out of Germany.

As to where Von Polanyi's information would go next, that depended on what he provided, and it was clearly Szara's choice to make: Geneva was rich with possibilities. Carefully, quietly, Szara built an inventory of candidates. The obvious – French and British political officers – and the not so obvious. Szara made contact with organizations interested in progressive political causes. He used the library, read old newspapers, identified journalists with strong contacts within the diplomatic community. Through one of de Montfried's attorneys, he managed an introduction to one of them, now retired, who had written about the Swiss political world with extraordinary insight. He took a vanilla cake and a bottle of kirschwasser to the man's home and they spent the afternoon in conversation. Yes, information was considered a crucial resource in Switzerland, a good deal of buying and selling went on. A certain Swedish businessman, a French oil executive, a professor of linguistics at the university. On hearing the last, Szara feigned surprise. The old journalist grinned. 'A terrific communist in the old days, but I guess he saw the light.' The look on the man's face – cynical, amused – told Szara everything he needed to know. He'd turned up the corner of a network.

Paris fell on 14 June.

Szara saw the famous photograph of the Wehrmacht marching past the Arc de Triomphe. He had hoped desperately for a miracle, a British miracle, an American miracle, but none had been performed. Because all eyes were on France, the USSR chose that moment for the military occupation of Latvia and Estonia, then took the Roumanian territories of Bessarabia and the northern Bukovina on the twenty-sixth. Szara mailed a postal card to a drapery shop in Frankfurt. 'My wife and I plan to return home on the third of July. Can new curtains be ready by that date?' Three weeks later, a letter to M. Jean Bonotte, Poste Restante, Thonon. In response to his inquiry, Herr Doktor Brückmann would arrive at the Hôtel Belvedere on the tenth of September. Patients wishing to consult with the doctor on neurological disorders should arrange appointments by reference from their local physicians.

'Dear, dear,' said the little man who'd driven him to the inn near Altenburg, 'you seem to have had a difficult time of it.'

Szara fingered the scar, now turned white. 'It could have been worse,' he said.

'We assume you are ready to cooperate with us.'

'I'm at your pleasure,' Szara said, and outlined how he wished to proceed, particularly in the matter of couriers. He implied that a certain individual in Berlin would regularly perform such services, but here he was deceptive. That individual, Szara swore to himself, once in Switzerland, would never leave it, not as long as war continued. *I will save that life at least*, he thought. Let them write it on his tomb. Von Polanyi would have to make other arrangements in the future.

'As you wish,' said the little man, accepting his choice. 'Now, I believe this will show our sincerity.' He handed Szara a brown envelope. 'Oh yes, one thing more. On turning over this document, Herbert asked me to say "Now lovers quarrel." I trust it makes some kind of sense to you.'

Until Szara, later that night, opened the envelope in his kitchen, it did not.

Then it took his breath away. In his hand he had two pages of single-spaced typewriting on plain white paper of indifferent quality. The first item concerned a Berlin photography studio on the Unter den Linden owned by a man named Hoffmann. Herr Hoffmann was Hitler's favourite photographer; he took portraits of Eva Braun, Hitler's mistress, and other Nazi dignitaries. The month before Hitler attacked Poland, Hoffmann had used a large map of that country to decorate his shop window. In April of 1940, he'd displayed maps of Holland and Scandinavia. Just one week before, the third of September, maps of the Ukraine, Byelorussia, and the Baltic countries had been posted.

The second item stated that the German transportation ministry had been ordered to make a study of east–west rail capacities leading to Germany's eastern border – the ministry had been told to assume that troops in excess of one million, plus artillery and horses, would have to be moved east.

The third item cited aviation fuel and maintenance requests for Luftwaffe reconnaissance aircraft operating over Liepāja, Tallinn, the island of Oesel, and the Moonzund archipelago – all Soviet defence lines in the Baltic – as well as the road network leading to Odessa, on the Black Sea.

The fourth item described the German General Staff's planning process for replacing border guard units in the region of the river Bug, the dividing line in Poland between German and Russian forces, with attack divisions. A study of evacuation plans for civilians in the area had been accelerated. Military staff was to replace civilian directors of all hospitals.

The final item stated simply that the operation was called Barbarossa: a full-scale attack on the Soviet Union, from the Baltic to the Black Sea, to take place in the late spring or early summer of 1941.

Szara had to go outside, into the air. He opened his front door cautiously, but all the houses on the street were dark, everyone was asleep. It was an overcast, warmish night, terribly still. He felt as though he'd been caught in amber, as though time had stopped dead on a wooded hill above Geneva. He had never in his life wanted so badly to walk, he realized. But he couldn't. He could not. To walk aimlessly up and down these empty streets would be to call attention to himself, and the paper lying on the yellow oilcloth that covered his kitchen table forbade such a thing; now more than ever he could not compromise the gentility that made him invisible. Just walking – it seemed so harmless. In fact he wanted more, much more. He wanted what he thought of as *life*, and by life he meant Paris, a crush of people in a narrow street, dusk, perfume, unwashed bodies, the sharp reek of Gauloises tobacco and frying potatoes. He wanted people, all kinds, laughing and arguing and posing, flirting, unconsciously touching their hair. He ached for it.

A lovers' quarrel, Von Polanyi called it. And wasn't he glib. No, that was wisdom speaking. A way of not exactly facing what it meant. It meant millions would die, and nobody, not anybody in the world, could stop it. *Madness*, he thought. Then corrected himself. He had seen a newsreel of Hitler dancing a jig outside the railway carriage in Compiègne, where the French had been forced to sign a peace treaty. A weird hopping little dance, like a madman. That was the line of the Western democracies – the man should be locked away somewhere. Szara had stayed to watch the newsreel a second time, then a third. The film had been altered, he was sure of it. One step of a jig had been turned into a lunatic's frenzy. Szara sensed an intelligence service at work. But Hitler wasn't mad, he was evil. And that was a notion educated people didn't like, it offended their sense of the rational world. Yet it was true. And just as true of his mirror image, Stalin. God only knew how many millions he had murdered. A decent, normal human being would turn away in sickness from either one of these monsters. But not Szara, not now. The luxury of damnation was not his. The accidents of time and circumstance demanded he rush to the side of one of the killers and hand him a sharpened axe. For now it had to be pretended that his crimes did not matter, and Szara, knowing the truth long before others, would have to be one of the first to pretend.

He did what had to be done. The linguistics professor was a short, angry man with a few brilliantined hairs pasted over a pink scalp. Szara understood him very well – combative, cocksure, vain, bathed in the arrogance of his theories. And, to be truthful, rather clever in his own devious way. The Communist party had always drawn such types, conferring importance on those denied it by their fellow humans. The man's eyes glittered with a sense of mission, and he was, Szara had to admit, terribly sly about what he was doing.

But Szara was the inheritor of a great tradition; Abramov's heir and Bloch's, one could trace it all the way back to the Okhrana officer and beyond, and he was more than a match for the professor. Szara wandered through the stacks of the university library, tracking his prey. Then he missed it the first time, but not the second. Just a slick little brush pass with a fortyish woman in a dark knit suit. Szara, nudging a Victorian study of phonemes out of his field of vision, saw a matchbox change hands, and that was enough for him. When the professor next visited his office, an envelope had been slipped beneath his door. Von Polanyi's second instalment was scheduled for October, and Szara knew there would be more to come. He took a rather malicious glee in all the variations he would visit upon the professor. Perhaps next time he would mail him a key to a storage locker.

But the professor would do his job, of that Szara was certain. Passing the information up the network until some Kranov would tap out code on his wireless in the dead of night. So it would come to Moscow. In Szara's imagination, a welcome was prepared for the Wehrmacht: Red Army units brought secretly to the border in goods wagons and covered trucks, tank traps dug in the dark hours when the Luftwaffe was blind, pillboxes reinforced, concrete poured. Until the lesser demon broke the greater, and the world could go on about its business.

18 October 1940.

André Szara stood among the autumn-coloured trees of a forest in the Alpine foothills and watched the waters of the Rhine curl white at the pillars of a bridge. On the other side of the river he could see the German village of Hohentengen; the red and black flag moved lightly in the wind above the town hall. A pretty place, at the southern extremity of the Black Forest, and quiet. On Szara's side of the Rhine, a few miles away, was the Swiss village of Kaiserstuhl, also pretty, also quiet. It was a peaceful border; not much happened there. At the German end of the bridge, two sentries stood guard over a wooden gate. A few log-and-barbed-wire barriers had been positioned at the edge of the village to thwart escape by a speeding car, but that was all.

He looked at his watch and saw that it was not yet four o'clock. Shifted his weight to lean against an oak tree, the dead leaves rustling at his feet as he changed position. It was deserted here. Only fifteen miles from Zürich, but another world. In his imagination he tracked the courier: from Berlin south towards Munich, crossing the Danube in the province of Württemberg, heading for Lake Constance, then drifting towards Basel, where the Rhine turned north, at last a left at Hohentengen, and across the Hohentengen bridge. Again he looked at his watch; the minute hand hadn't moved. A wisp of smoke curled from the chimney of a woodsman's hut that housed the Swiss border guard. They, unlike their German counterparts across the bridge, did not have to stand guard with rifles in the chill mountain air.

Now it came.

Szara stiffened when he saw it. A huge, shiny black car with long curves up the front fenders and little swastika flags set above the headlamps. It moved carefully around the barriers, rolled to a stop at the gate. One of the guards leaned down to the driver's window, then stood to attention and saluted briskly. The other guard lifted the latch, then walked the gate open until he stood against the railing of the bridge. The car moved forward; Szara could just hear it bump across the uneven wooden boards of the surface. The door of the woodsman's hut opened, and a guard came halfway out and casually waved the car forward into Switzerland.

Szara, hands thrust in pockets, set off on a dirt path that ran along the hillside, then descended to the road at a point where it left the view of the border guards. He had surveyed all the little bridges along this part of the Rhine and finally chosen the Hohentengen, walking through the operation a week earlier. He was now certain the meeting would be unobserved. Skidding on wet leaves, he reached the surface of the road and moved towards the idling car which had stopped by a road marker showing the distance to Kaiserstuhl. Through the windscreen Szara could just make out – the October light was fading quickly and the oblique angle made it difficult to see – the silhouette of a driver in uniform and military cap. The glass of the passenger windows was tinted for privacy. He saw only a reflected hillside, and then his own image, a hand reaching to open the back door, a face cold and neutral, entirely at war with what went on inside him.

The door swung open smoothly, but he did not find what he expected. He blinked in surprise. These were not pale blue eyes, and there was no affection in them. Curiosity, perhaps. But not much of that. These were the eyes of a hunter, a predator. They simply stared back at him, without feeling, without acknowledgment, as though he were no more than a moving shape in a world of moving shapes. 'Oh, Seryozha!' she said, and pulled the borzoi back on his silver chain.

Szara must have looked surprised because Nadia said, 'Why are you staring? I couldn't very well leave him in Berlin, now could I?'

They leaned across the dog's back to embrace. Szara's heart glowed within him. Seryozha's presence meant she had no intention of going back to Berlin. For her, life in the shadows was over.

Of that he was absolutely certain.

Afterword

This novel is based on a conversation held in a private clinic in Paris in February of 1937. While recovering from a car accident, the Soviet intelligence officer L. L. Feldbin – alias Alexander Orlov – was visited by his cousin Zinovy Katsnelson, a state security commissar for the Ukraine. Katsnelson claimed that members of the Ukrainian, principally Jewish, group within the special services intended to overthrow Stalin by denouncing him to the Communist party as a former agent of the Okhrana. Proof of the association lay in three copies of an Okhrana dossier held by the group. By March of 1937, Katsnelson had been recalled to Moscow and shot. Feldbin defected from an assignment in Spain in July of 1938, eventually reaching the United States. In the course of his debriefing, many years later, he reported what Katsnelson had told him.

Several characters in this book also appear in the novel *Night Soldiers*. I have tried to ensure that names, assignments, and locations are consistent in both books, with one exception: in *Night Soldiers*, the *rezident* Yadomir Ivanovich Bloch (Yaschyeritsa) is a colonel general, a rank of such high visibility that he would not have been able to operate as he does in *Dark Star*. Thus he has been demoted to lieutenant general in this novel.

Acknowledgments

I am grateful for the help of many individuals in the writing of *Dark Star*: historians of the period, librarians, booksellers, and friends – too many to name here. I would, however, like to thank Abner Stein and Anne Sibbald for their generous support and encouragement; manuscript editor Luise Erdmann for seeking clarity and precision in a chaotic world; and especially Joe Kanon, in particular for his confidence in my work, in general for making it possible for all sorts of writers to go on doing what they do best.

The Polish Officer

The Pilava
Local

In Poland, on the night of 11 September 1939, Wehrmacht scout and commando units – elements of Kuechler's Third Army Corps – moved silently around the defences of Novy Dvor, crossed the Vistula over the partly demolished Jablonka Bridge, and attempted to capture the Warsaw Telephone Exchange at the northern edge of the city. Meeting unexpected, and stubborn, resistance, they retreated along Sowacki Street and established positions on the roof and in the lobby of the Hotel Franconia, called for dive-bomber attacks on the exchange building, and settled in to wait for the light of dawn.

Mr Felix Malek, proprietor of the Franconia, put on his best blue suit, and, accompanied by a room-service waiter, personally served cognac to the German soldiers at their mortar and machine gun positions. He then descended to the wine cellar, opened the concealed door to an underground passage originally dug during the Prussian attack of 1795, hurried down Sowacki Street to the telephone exchange, and asked to see 'the gentleman in charge'.

He was taken up a marble staircase to the director's office on the fifth floor and there, beneath a sombre portrait of the director – pince-nez and brushed whiskers – presented to the officer in command, a captain. The captain was an excellent listener, and the questions he asked inspired Mr Malek to talk for a long time. Arms, unit size, insignia, the location of positions – he was surprised at how much he knew.

When he was done, they gave him tea. He asked if he might remain at the exchange, it would be an honour to fight the Germans. No, they said, perhaps another day. So Mr Malek made his way through the night to his sister's apartment in the Ochota district. 'And what,' she asked, 'were they like?'

Mr Malek thought a moment. 'Educated,' he said. 'Quite the better class of people.'

*

Mr Malek had not been thirty years an innkeeper for nothing: the defenders of the Warsaw Telephone Exchange, hastily recruited amidst the chaos of the German invasion, were officers of Polish Military Intelligence, known, in imitation of the French custom, as the Deux-ième Bureau. The Breda machine gun at the casement window was served by a lieutenant from the cryptographic service, a pair of spectacles folded carefully in his breast pocket. The spidery fellow reloading ammunition belts was, in vocational life, a connoisseur of the senior civil service of the USSR, while the commander of the machine gun, feet propped on the tripod, was Lieutenant Karlinski, heavy and pink, who in normal times concerned himself with the analysis of Baltic shipping.

The officer in charge, Captain Alexander de Milja, was professionally a cartographer; first a mapmaker, later assistant director of the bureau's Geographical Section. But Poland was at war – no, Poland had lost her war – and it was clear to the captain that nobody was going to be assistant director of anything for a long time to come.

Still, you couldn't just stop fighting. Captain de Milja stood at the open window; the night air, cool and damp, felt especially good on his hands. *Idiot!* He'd grabbed the overheated barrel of the machine gun to change it during the attack, and now he had red stripes on his palms that hurt like hell.

4:20 a.m. He swept the façade of the hotel with his binoculars, tried – based on the proprietor's intelligence – counting up floors to focus on certain rooms, but the Germans had the windows shut and all he could see was black glass. In Sowacki Square, a burned-out trolley, and the body of a Wehrmacht trooper, like a bundle of rags accidentally left in a doorway, weapon and ammunition long gone. To somebody's attic. De Milja let the binoculars hang on their strap and stared out into the city.

A refinery had been set on fire; a tower of heavy smoke rolled majestically into the sky and the clouds glowed a faint orange. A machine gun tapped in the distance, a plane droned overhead, artillery rumbled across the river. War – fire and smoke – had made autumn come early, dead leaves rattled along the cobblestones and caught in the iron drain covers.

Captain de Milja was a soldier, he knew he didn't have long to live. And, in truth, he didn't care. He was not in love with life. One or two things had to be taken care of, then matters could run their course.

The director's telephone was, naturally, of the very latest style; black, shiny, Bakelite plastic. De Milja dialled the military operator he had installed in the basement.

'Sir?'

'Sergeant, have you tried Tarnopol again?'

'Can't get through, sir. I've been up to Wilno, and down to Zakopane, just about every routing there is, but the whole region's down. We're pretty sure the lines have been cut, sir.'

'You'll keep trying.'

'Yes, sir.'

'Thank you, Sergeant.'

He replaced the receiver carefully on its cradle. He had wanted to say good-bye to his wife.

The Wehrmacht assault team got its air support at dawn; three Focke-Wulf 189s diving out of the clouds, engines screaming, cannon firing. But there was more drama than destruction; the 189 carried only one bomb. On the fifth floor of the telephone exchange, Lieutenant Karlinski swept the Breda across the sky and hammered off belt after belt of 7.35 ammunition. Grand streams of tracer, pale in the early light, showered up into the clouds, while hot casings ejected onto the director's Persian carpet and the office smelled like smouldering wool – until a bullet fired from the ballroom of the Hotel Franconia hit Karlinski in the collarbone and he collapsed back onto the floor and died of shock.

The lieutenant from the cryptographic service took over, while Captain de Milja steadied the tripod with his burning hands and the Russian bureaucracy expert fed belts into the gun. But by then the Focke-Wulfs had run dry of ammunition and headed back to Germany. At which point the telephone rang and somebody on the first floor, voice flat and controlled, informed de Milja that the building was on fire.

For a moment he went blank, the solution much too obvious. Then he said, 'Call the fire department.' Which they did and which, on 12 September, worked quite well because the city's water mains hadn't yet been destroyed. The firemen ran their hoses into the building on the side away from the fighting and pumped high-pressure streams on the flames, putting out the fire and, as water sluiced down into the switching stations, shutting down every telephone in Warsaw.

The Wehrmacht attack, from doorway to doorway up Sowacki Street, faltered, then collapsed. The support fire, machine gun and mortar, from the roof of the hotel lasted less than a minute, then the positions were abandoned. Just before dawn de Milja had sent sniper teams to the roofs of adjacent buildings, and when the fighting started they'd knocked down first a mortar man, then an officer. It was improvised –

the snipers were armed with hunting weapons and policemen's automatic pistols – but it worked.

De Milja watched through binoculars as an analyst from the economic intelligence section – the captain thought he specialized in feed grains – a man in his fifties wearing suspenders and a shirt turned up at the sleeves, suddenly appeared at a parapet on the roof of an apartment building and fired both barrels of an old shotgun, the sort of thing one found in the back halls of country houses, along with leather game bags and warped tennis rackets.

The sniper broke the shotgun and withdrew the empty cartridges. Smoke seeped from the barrels as he thrust new shells into the breech. *Get down*, the captain thought. He saw two German troopers at an upper window, bringing their rifles to bear. *Down*. The sniper lurched backwards, his face showed a moment of pain. But he kept his balance, braced one foot against the parapet and fired both barrels. His shoulder jerked with the recoil, then he fell to his knees, shaking his head grimly at whatever was going on inside him.

The Wehrmacht units retreated minutes later, trying to break through to German lines after dark. Most never made it, victims of small bands of soldiers, farmers, teenagers – Poles. And those who got as far as the Jablonka Bridge found that, on the second try, demolition had been complete. The ones who couldn't swim were found on the bank the following morning.

16 September, 5:40 p.m. Military Intelligence headquarters, Savka barracks. Order 3135-c: *With exception of special documents identified by department directors, all files to be destroyed by 1800 hours.*

Captain de Milja watched, motionless, one foot on a chair, as this work was done, as the department clerks burned eight thousand maps. Watched, apparently, without feeling. Perhaps he didn't care, or cared too much, or had gone off wherever he went when life was too cruel or too stupid. Whatever the truth, his eyes were cold, he could not be read.

The clerks had built a pinewood fire in the great hall, in a fireplace of heroic proportions with the date 1736 carved in the capstone, a fireplace built to roast spitted boar for a cavalry squadron. But this was a clerks' fire, it smoked and sputtered, and the maps, printed on linen and mounted on wooden rollers, did not burn well.

The office wit had always claimed that the department's chief clerk suffered from Talpidia, mole-face, a condition encountered in particularly subterranean bureaucracies. The man had been, certainly, a fierce obstructionist – everything had to be signed, and signed, and signed some more. Now, as his clerks ran by him with armloads of maps, he just seemed lost, poked dispiritedly at the ashes with a broom handle, the flames' reflections flickering on his eyeglasses.

Drawer 4088: Istanbul by street. Istanbul harbour with wharf and warehouse numbers. Surveyor's elevations of Üsküdar with shore batteries in scale. Bosphorus with depths indicated. Black Sea coast: coves, inlets, bridges, roads. Sea of Marmara coast: coves, inlets, bridges, roads.

In the fire.

Drawer 4098: Timber company surveys, 1935–1938; streams, logging paths, old and new growth trees, drainage, road access, river access. For forests in Poland, Byelorussia, and the Ukraine.

'That series aside, please,' de Milja said.

The clerk, startled, whirled and stared, then did as he was ordered. The timber surveys were stacked neatly atop maps, drawn in fine detail, of the Polish railway system.

16 September, 7:15 p.m. A message was brought by a young ensign, who saluted and stood stiffly at attention while the captain read it. Colonel Anton Vyborg requested his presence, in fifteen minutes, at the guard-house by the east gate; another officer had been sent to supervise the destruction of the files. The captain initialled the message carefully, then made sure he was on time.

They walked in the stables of the cavalry barracks, added to the Savka fortress when the Tenth Polish Hussars rode with Bonaparte in the Napoleonic Wars. The indoor riding ring – a floor of raked dirt below axe-hewn beams – was by tradition the regimental *champ d'honneur*, not just pistols at thirty paces, but duels on horseback with cavalry sabres. Beyond the riding ring, the horse barns. The horses stamped their hooves and whickered softly as the officers approached. The air smelled good to de Milja; manure and straw, autumn evening and Vyborg's cigar. Not the smell of burning buildings, not the smell of burning paper. A cloud of gnats hung in the still air, the light fading slowly from dusk into darkness.

There was something of the Baltic knight in Colonel Vyborg. In his forties, he was tall and lean and thin-lipped, with webbed lines at the corners of eyes made to squint into blizzards, and stiff, colourless hair cut short in the cavalry-officer fashion. He wore high leather boots, supple and dark, well-rubbed with saddle soap. His job was to direct the work of intelligence officers – usually but not always military attachés in foreign postings – who operated secret agents.

'Have one of these,' Vyborg said.

Vyborg lit the captain's small cigar, then spoke quietly as they walked.

'As of tonight, our situation is this: there are fifty-two German divisions in Poland, about a million and a half soldiers, led by thousands of tanks. Our air force was blown up on the ground the first morning. Our allies, France and England, have declared war, and made gestures – of course, we had hoped for more. America is neutral, and disinterested. So, as usual, we find ourselves alone. Worse, Stalin has forty divisions on the eastern border and all our intelligence indicates an attack within hours. Meanwhile, we have half a million men in uniform – or, rather, had. Our communications have broken down, but we know of a hundred thousand casualties and a hundred thousand taken prisoner. Probably it's worse than that. I suppose our view of the immediate future is implicit in the fact that we are burning the files. But it's not the first time, and this *is* Poland, and, for us at least, all is not necessarily lost. You agree?'

'I do, sir.'

'Good. We want to offer you a job, but I'm to emphasize that you have a choice. You can go out to one of the regular combat divisions – we're going to make a stand at the Bzura River, and, in addition, some units are going to try and hold out in the Pripet Marshes in the eastern provinces. The nation is defeated, but the *idea* of the nation mustn't be. So, if that's what you want to do, to die on the battlefield, I won't stop you.'

'Or?'

'Or come to work for us. Over on the west side of the building – at least that's where we used to be. It's no small decision, but time's the one thing we don't have. The city's almost completely cut off, and by tomorrow there'll be no getting out. The Germans won't try to break in, they know they'll pay in blood for that and they aren't quite so brave as their reputation makes them out. They'll continue to send the bomber flights, unopposed, and they'll sit out there where we can't get at them and shell the city. We'll take it as long as we can, then we'll sign something to get it stopped.'

'And then?'

'And then the war will begin.'

A horse leaned over the gate of its stall and the colonel stopped to run his hand through its mane. 'Wish I had an apple for you,' Vyborg said. 'What about it, Captain, shall we shoot these beasts? Or let the Germans have them?'

'Can they be hidden? In stables with cart horses, perhaps?'

'It's hard to hide valuable things from Germans, Captain. Very hard.'

They walked in silence for a time. A flight of Heinkel bombers passed overhead; both officers looked up, then waited. The bombs fell on the southern part of the city, a noise like rapid peals of thunder, then the planes turned away, a few anti-aircraft rounds burst well below and behind them, and the silence returned as the sound of engines faded.

'Well?' Vyborg said.

'The west side of the building, Colonel.'

'You know the sorts of things that go on if the Germans get hold of people like us, Captain.'

'Yes, sir.'

'A dossier has been prepared for you – we assumed that you would accept the offer. It will be delivered to your office when you return. It assigns a nom de guerre – we don't want anyone to know who you are. It has also some memoranda written over the last forty-eight hours, you will want to review that for a nine-fifteen meeting in my office. Questions?'

'No questions, sir.'

'There's a great deal of improvisation at the moment, but we're not going into the chaos business anytime soon. We're going to lose a war, not our minds. And not our souls.'

'Understood, sir.'

'Anything you want to say?'

'With regard to my wife—'

'Yes?'

'She's in a private clinic. In the countryside, near Tarnopol.'

'An illness?'

'She is – the doctor puts it that she has entered a private world.'

Vyborg shook his head in sympathy and scowled at the idea of illness attacking people he knew.

'Can she be rescued?'

Vyborg thought it over. Senior intelligence officers became almost intuitive about possibility – some miracles could be done, some couldn't. Once initiated, above a certain rank, you knew.

'I'm sorry,' the colonel said.

The captain inclined his head; he understood, it need not be further discussed. They walked in silence for a time, then the colonel said, 'We'll see you at nine-fifteen, then.'

'Yes, sir.'

'Officially, we're glad to have you with us.' They shook hands. The captain saluted, the colonel returned the salute.

A quarter moon, red with fire, over the Vilna station railyards.

The yard supervisor wore a bandage over one eye, his suit and shirt had not been changed for days, days of crawling under freight cars, of floating soot and oily smoke, and his hands were trembling. He was ashamed of that, so had wedged them in his pockets as though he were a street-corner tough who whistled at girls.

'This was our best,' he said sadly. Captain de Milja flicked the beam of his flashlight over a passenger car with its roof peeled back. A woman's scarf, light enough to float in the wind, was snagged on a shard of iron. 'Bolen Coachworks,' the supervisor said. 'Leaded-glass lamps in the first-class compartments. Now look.'

'What's back there?' de Milja asked.

'Nothing much. Just some old stock we pulled in from the local runs – the Pruszkow line, Wolomin.'

Cinders crunched under their feet as they walked. Yard workers with iron bars and acetylene torches were trying to repair the track. There were showers of blue sparks and the smell of scorched metal as they cut through the twisted rail.

'And this?'

The supervisor shrugged. 'We run little trains to the villages, on market days. This is what's left of the Solchow local. It was caught by a bombing raid on Thursday, just past the power station. The engineer panicked, he had his fireman uncouple the engine and they made a run for Vilna station. Maybe he thought he'd be safe under the roof, though I can't imagine why, because it's a glass roof, or it used to be. When the all clear sounded, the engine had been blown to pieces but the rest of the train was just left sitting out there on the track, full of angry old farm ladies and crates of chickens.'

De Milja and the supervisor climbed the steps into the coach. The captain's flashlight lit up the aisle; wooden floorboards, buckled and grey with age, frayed wicker seats – once yellow, now brown – chicken feathers, a forgotten basket. From the other end of the car came a deep, heavy growl. *What are you doing here?* de Milja thought. 'Come,' he said.

There was a moment of silence, then another growl. This time it didn't mean *prepare to die* – more like *not yet.*

'Come here.' *You know you have to.*

A huge head appeared in the aisle, thrust cautiously from a hiding place behind a collapsed seat. De Milja masked the flashlight beam and the dog came reluctantly, head down, to accept its punishment. To have deserved what had happened to it the last few days, it reasoned, it must have been very, very bad. De Milja went down on one knee and said, 'Yes, it's all right, it's all right.'

It was a male Tatra, a sheepdog related to the Great Pyrenees. De Milja sank his hands into the deep hair around the neck, gripped it hard and tugged the head towards him. The dog knew this game and twisted back against de Milja, but the man's hands were too strong. Finally the dog butted his head against the captain's chest, took a huge breath and sighed so deeply it was almost a growl.

'Perhaps you could find some water,' de Milja said to the supervisor.

His family had always had dogs, kept at the manor house of the estate in the Volhynia, in eastern Poland. They hunted with them, taking a wild boar every autumn in the great forest, a scene from a medieval tapestry. The Tatra was an off-white, like most mountain breeds, a preferred colour that kept the shepherd from clubbing his own dog when they fought night-raiding wolves. De Milja put his face into the animal's fur and inhaled the sweet smell.

The yard supervisor returned, a bowl filled to the brim with milk held carefully in his hands. This was a small miracle, but 'he must be hungry' was all he had to say about it.

'What's your name?' de Milja asked.

'Koski.'

'Can you keep a big dog, Mr Koski?'

The yard supervisor thought a moment, then shrugged and said, 'I guess so.'

'It will take some feeding.'

'We'll manage.'

'And this kind of coach?' The captain nodded at it. 'Have you got six or so?'

'All you want.'

'Same colour. Yellow, with red around the windows.'

Koski tried to conceal his reaction. The middle of a war, Germans at the outskirts of the city, and this man wanted 'the same colour'. Well, you did what you had to do. 'If you can wait for daylight, we'll freshen up the paint.'

'No, it's good just like that. We'll need a coal tender, of course, and a locomotive. A freight locomotive.'

Koski stared at his shoes. They had improvised, borrowed parts, kept running all sorts of stock that had no business running – but freight locomotives were a sore subject. Nobody had those. Well, he had *one*. Well and truly hidden. Was this the moment? 'Six red-and-yellow coaches,' he said at last. 'Tender, freight locomotive. That it?'

De Milja nodded. 'In about, say, an hour.'

Koski started to shout, something like *can't you see I'm doing the best I can*? But a covert glance at de Milja changed his mind – he wasn't someone you would say that to, much less shout it.

De Milja looked to be in his late thirties, but there was something about him, some air of authority, that was much older than that. He had dark hair, cut short and cut very well, and a pale forehead that people noticed. Eyes the colour – according to his wife – of a February sea, shifting somewhere between grey and green. His face was delicate, arrogant, hard; people said different things. In any event, he was a very serious man, that was obvious, with hands bigger than they ought to have been, and blunt fingers. He wore no insignia, just a brown raincoat over a grey wool sweater. There was a gun, somewhere. He stood, relaxed but faintly military, waiting for the yard supervisor to agree to make up his train in an hour. This man came, Koski thought, from the war, and when the war went away, if it ever did, so would he and all the others like him.

The supervisor nodded yes, of course he could have his train. The dog stopped lapping at the bowl, looked up and whined, a drop of milk falling from his beard. A yellow flame burst from the hillside above the yards and the flat crump of an explosion followed. The brush burned for a few seconds, then the fire died out as smoke and dust drifted down the hill.

Koski had flinched at the explosion, now he jammed his shaking hands deeper into his pockets. 'Not much left to bomb here,' he said.

'That wasn't a bomb,' de Milja said. 'It was a shell.'

17 September, 3:50 a.m. Freight locomotive, coal tender, six passenger cars from a market-day local. The yard supervisor, the Tatra by his side, watched as it left the railyards. Then it crossed Praga, a workers' suburb across the Vistula from Warsaw, and headed for the city on the single remaining railway bridge. Captain de Milja stood in the cab of the locomotive and stared down into the black water as the train clattered across the ties.

For a crew, Koski had done the best he could on short notice. A fireman, who would shovel coal into the steam engine's furnace, and a conductor would be joining the train in Warsaw. The engineer, stand-ing next to de Milja, had been, until that night, retired. He was a sour man, with a double chin and a lumpy nose, wearing an engineer's cap, well oiled and grimed, and a pensioner's blue cardigan sweater with white buttons.

'Fucking *shkopy*,' he said, using the Polish word for Germans equivalent to the French *boche*. He peered upriver at the blackened skeleton of the Poniatowski Bridge. 'I had all I wanted of them in 'seventeen.'

The Germans had marched into Warsaw in 1917, during the Great War. De Milja had been sixteen, about to enter university, and while his family had disliked the German entry into Poland, they'd seen one positive side to it: Russian occupiers driven back east where they belonged.

The firebox of the locomotive glowed faintly in the dark, just enough light to jot down a few figures on the iron wall. He had to haul a total of 88,000 pounds: 360 people – 43,000 pounds of them if you figured young and old, fat and thin, around 120 pounds a person. Sharing the train with 44,530 pounds of freight.

So, 88,000 pounds equalled 44 tons. Figuring two tons to a normal freight car, a locomotive could easily pull twenty cars. His six passenger coaches would be heavy, but that didn't matter – they had no suspension to speak of, they'd roll along if the locomotive could pull them.

'What are you scribbling?' The irritation of an old man. To the engineer's way of thinking, a locomotive cab wasn't a place for writing.

De Milja didn't answer. He smeared the soft pencil jotting with his palm, put the stub of pencil back in his pocket. The sound of the wheels changed as the train came off the bridge and descended to a right-of-way cut below ground level and spanned by pedestrian and traffic bridges: a wasteland of tracks, signals, water towers, and switching stations. Was the 44,530 correct? He resisted the instinct to do the figures again. Seven hundred and twelve thousand ounces *always* made 44,530 pounds, which, divided into five-pound units, *always* made 8,906. It is mathematics, he told himself, it is always the same.

'You said Dimek Street bridge?'

'Yes.'

The steam brake hissed and the train rolled to a stop. From a stairway that climbed the steep hillside came a flashed signal. De Milja answered with his own flashlight. Then a long line of shadowy figures began to move down the stairs.

17 September, 4:30 a.m. While the train was being loaded, the conductor and the fireman arrived and shook hands with the engineer. Efficiently, they uncoupled the locomotive and coal tender and used a switching spur to move them to the other end of the train, so it now pointed east.

There were two people waiting for de Milja under the Dimek Street bridge: his former commander, a white-moustached major of impeccable manners and impeccable stupidity, serving out his time until retirement while his assistant did all the work, and de Milja's former aide, Sublieutenant Nowak, who would serve as his adjutant on the journey south.

The Major shook de Milja's hand hard, his voice taut with emotion. 'I know you'll do well,' he said. 'As for me, I am returning to my unit.

They are holding a line at the Bzura River.' It was a death sentence and they both knew it. 'Good luck, sir,' de Milja said, and saluted formally. The major returned the salute and disappeared into a crowd of people on the train.

Guards with machine guns had positioned themselves along the track, while a dozen carpenters pried up the floorboards of the railway coaches and workers from the state treasury building installed the Polish National Bullion Reserve – $11,400,000 in five-pound gold ingots packed ten to a crate – in the ten-inch space below. Then, working quickly, the carpenters hammered the boards back into place.

At which point Nowak came running, his face red with anger. 'You had better see this,' he said. The carpenters were just finishing up. Nowak pointed at the shiny nailheads they'd hammered into the old grey wood.

'Couldn't you use the old nails?' de Milja said.

The head carpenter shrugged.

'Is there any lampblack?'

'Lampblack! No, of course not. We're carpenters, we don't have such things.'

17 September, 6:48 a.m. Gdansk station. The platforms and waiting rooms were jammed with people, every age, every class, babbling in at least seven languages, only one thing in common: they were too late. Unlucky or unwise didn't matter, the trains had stopped. A station-master's voice crackled through the public-address system and tried to convince them of that, but nobody was willing to believe it. In Poland, things happened in mysterious ways – authority itself was often struck speechless at life's sudden turns.

For instance:

The stationmaster's voice, 'Please, ladies and gentlemen, I entreat you, there will be no more service . . . ,' was slowly drowned out by the rumble of an approaching train. People surged to the edges of the platforms, police struggled to hold them back.

Then the crowd fell silent, and stopped pushing.

A war train. It had started raining, and water glistened on the iron plates in the twilight of the high-roofed station. The voice of the engine was deep and rhythmic, like a drum, and machine gun barrels thrust through firing ports traversed the platform. This was a Russian-style armoured train, a Bolshevik weapon, a peasant killer – it meant burnt villages and weeping women and everybody in Gdansk station knew it. The train, too heavy for its engine, moved at a crawl, so the crowd could see the faces, cold and attentive, of the anti-aircraft gunners in their sand-bagged nests on the roofs of the cars.

Then someone cheered. And then someone else. And then everybody. Poland had been brutally stabbed in the back, and so she bled, bled fiercely, but here was proof that she lived, and could strike back at those who tormented her.

But that was only part of the miracle. Because, only a few minutes later, another train appeared. And if the armoured train was an image of war, here was a phantom from the time of peace, a little six-car train headed south for – or so the signs on the sides of the coaches said – Pilava. The Pilava train! Only thirty miles south, but at least not in besieged Warsaw. Everybody had an aunt in Pilava, you went there on a Sunday afternoon and came home with half a ham wrapped in a cloth. Vladimir Herschensohn, pressed by the crowd against a marble column, felt his heart rise with joy. Somehow, from somewhere, a manifestation of normal existence: a train arrives in a station, passengers ascend, life goes on.

But Mr Herschensohn would not be ascending. He needed to, the Germans would make quick work of him and he knew it. But God had made him small, and as the crowd surged hungrily towards the empty train he actually found himself moving – helped along by a curse here, an elbow there – away from the track. After a moment or two of this, all he wanted to do was stay near enough to watch the train leave, to send some part of his spirit away to safety.

Watching from the cab of the locomotive, de Milja felt his stomach turn. The crowd was now a mob: if they got on this train, they would live. Babies howled, suitcases sprang open, men and women clawed and fought, policemen swung their batons. De Milja could hear the thuds, but he willed his face not to show what he felt and it didn't. A huge, brawny peasant shoved an old woman out of his way and started to climb onto the coupling between the engine and the coal car. The fireman waited until his weight hung on his hands, then kicked him full force under the chin. His head flew up and he went tumbling backwards into the crowd. 'Pig,' the fireman said quietly, as though to himself.

But, in the end, the ones who pushed to the front were the ones who got on.

When the train was good and full, people packed into the cars, when it looked like a refugee train should look, de Milja raised his hand. Then something stopped him. Out in the crowd, his eye found a little peanut of a man in a long black overcoat, with a black homburg hat knocked awry. He was holding some sort of a case and an old-fashioned valise in one hand, and pressing a handkerchief to his bloody nose with the other. The policeman standing next to de Milja was red in the face and breathing hard. 'Get me that man,' de Milja said, pointing.

The policeman whistled through his teeth, a couple of colleagues joined him, and the little man was quickly retrieved, virtually carried through the crowd by the elbows and hoisted up to de Milja in the locomotive cab.

'Better go,' the policeman said.

De Milja signalled to the conductor, who swung himself up onto the train. The engineer worked his levers and blew a long blast on the whistle as the heavily laden train moved slowly out of Gdansk station.

'Thank you,' said the little man. He was somewhere in his forties, de Milja thought, with the face of a Jewish imp. 'I am Vladimir Herschensohn.' He extended his hand, and de Milja shook it. Herschensohn saw that de Milja was staring at his battered violin case. 'I am,' he added, 'the principal violinist of the Polish National Symphony Orchestra.'

De Milja inclined his head in acknowledgment.

'So,' Herschensohn said. 'We are going to Pilava.' He had to raise his voice above the chuff of the locomotive, but he managed a tone of great politeness.

'South of there,' was all de Milja said.

At the 9:15 meeting with Colonel Vyborg, de Milja had brought up the issue: what to tell the passengers. 'What you like, when you like, you decide,' Vyborg had said.

Vyborg's room had been crowded – people sitting on desks, on the floor, everywhere. De Milja knew most of them, and what they had in common was a certain ruthless competence. Suddenly the days of office politics, family connections, the well-fed wink, were over. Now the issue was survival, and these officers, like de Milja, found themselves given command and assigned to emergency operations.

The agenda of the meeting was long and difficult and devoted to a single topic: the dispersion to safety of the national wealth. War cost money and Poland meant to keep fighting. And there wasn't that much. A country like Great Britain had a national wealth of two hundred million dollars, but Poland had only been alive as an independent nation since 1918 – this time around – and owned barely a tenth of that.

Stocks and bonds and letters of deposit on foreign banks were going to leave the port of Gdynia on a Danish passenger liner. British pounds, French francs, and American dollars were to be flown out at night by one of the last remaining air-force transports, while millions of Polish zlotys and German reichsmarks were being buried in secret vaults in Warsaw – they would be needed there. Senior code and cipher experts, the cream of Polish intelligence, had already left the country. And it was de Milja's job to take out the gold reserve, carrying it by train to Roumania, where another group would move it on to Paris, the time-honoured host to Polish governments-in-exile.

From Gdansk station they travelled slowly through the central districts of the city, where crews were filling bomb craters and repairing rail by the light of fires in oil drums. They crossed the railway bridge back into Praga, then turned south on the eastern bank of the Vistula. Soon the city was behind them, and the track left the river and curved gently south-east, towards the city of Lublin.

The conductor who'd boarded the train at the Dimek Street bridge was a man of old-fashioned manners and grave demeanour, with a droopy moustache, a conductor's hat one size too large, and a limp from wounds received when his train was dive-bombed in the first hours of the war. When he'd reported to de Milja at the bridge, he had stood at attention and produced from his belt a 9 mm Parabellum pistol – a 1914 cannon – and informed de Milja that he'd fought the Bolsheviks in 1921, and was prepared to send a significant number of Germans straight to hell if he got the opportunity.

As the train chugged through the Polish countryside, the conductor went from car to car and made a little speech. 'Ladies and gentlemen, your attention, please. Soon we will be stopping at Pilava; those who wish to get off the train are invited to do so. However, this train will not be returning to Warsaw, it is going all the way to Lvov, with brief stops at Lublin and Tomaszow. The military situation in the south is unclear, but the railway will take you as far as you wish to travel. Passage is without charge. Thank you.'

From the last car, de Milja watched the crowd carefully. But the reaction was subdued: a number of family conferences conducted in urgent whispers, an avalanche of questions that God himself, let alone a train conductor, couldn't have answered, and more than a little head shaking and grim smiling at the bizarre twists and turns that life now seemed to take. The Polish people, de Milja realized, had already absorbed the first shock of war and dislocation; now it was a question of survival; ingenuity, improvisation, and the will to live through catastrophe and see the other side of it. So when the train stopped at Pilava, only a few people got off. *The farther from Warsaw the better –* what consensus there was among the passengers seemed to follow that line of reasoning.

For a time, the countryside itself proved them right. South of Pilava there was no war, only a rainy September morning, a strip of pale sky on the horizon, harvested fields, birch groves, and tiny streams. The air smelled of damp earth and the coming October. The leaves a little dry now, and rustling in the wind.

De Milja's mother was the Countess Ostrowa, and her brothers, known always as 'the Ostrow uncles', had taken it upon themselves to teach him about life; about dogs and horses and guns, servants and mistresses. They were from another time – a vanished age, his father said – but his mother adored them and they lived hard, drunken, brutal, happy lives and never bothered to notice they were in the wrong century.

His father was an aristocrat of another sort: second son of a family occupied for generations with polite commerce, senior professor of economics at Jagiello university. He was an arid man, tall and spare, who had been old all his life and who, in his heart, didn't really think very much of the human mammal. The vaguely noble name de Milja, pronounced *de Milya*, he shooed away with his hand, admitting there was a village in Silesia, some forty miles from where the family originated, called Milja, but the aristocratic formation he ascribed to 'some Austro-Hungarian nonsense my grandfather meddled with' and would never say any more about it. Exiled to the top floor of the family house in Warsaw, he lived by the light of a green-glass lamp amid piles of German periodicals and stacks of woody paper covered with algebraic equations rendered in fountain pen.

So de Milja's world, from its earliest days, had a cold north and a hot south, and he spent his time going back and forth; as a boy, as a young man, maybe, he thought, forever. The uncles laughing and roaring downstairs, throwing chicken bones in the fire, grabbing the maids' bottoms, and passing out on the sofas with their boots on the pillows. Up two flights, a family of storks nested among the chimneys on the opposite roof and his father explained spiders and thunder.

They'd married de Milja off when he was nineteen. The families had known each other forever, he and Helena were introduced, left alone, and encouraged to fall in love. She probably saw the wisdom of all this much more clearly than he did – gazed at his belt buckle, kissed him with swollen lips and a hand on his jaw, and he was hers. Two weeks before the wedding, his favourite Ostrow uncle had taken him into a disused parlour, the furniture covered with sheets, where they fortified themselves with Armagnac, and his uncle – scarlet face, shaved head, glorious cavalry moustaches – had given him a premarital lovemaking lesson with the aid of a dressmaker's dummy. 'You're not a bull, dammit!' he'd bellowed. 'You don't mount her when she's at the kitchen stove.'

In the event, the problem did not arise: she never bent over to get the bread out of the oven because she never put it in – that was done by a series of country girls charitably called maids, more than one of whom had flipped the back of her skirt at him.

Over time, Helena changed. At first she would flirt, touch him accidentally with her breasts, and hold him between the legs with both hands. But something happened, she would only make love in the dark, sometimes cried, sometimes stopped. He learned to work his way through her defences, but in the process discovered what she was defending. He began to realize that the membrane that separated her from the world was too thin, that she could not tolerate life.

She'd gotten pregnant, then lost the baby during an influenza epidemic in the winter of 1925. That was the end. In the deepest part of himself he'd known it, known it the day it happened. For three years, everyone pretended that everything would be all right, but when little fires were started in the house she had to go to the doctors and they prescribed a stay at a private clinic near Tarnopol 'for a few weeks'.

Absence from the world cured her. He didn't say that back in Warsaw, but it was true. Visiting once a month, bouquet in hand, he could feel the calm she'd found. In fact she pitied him, having to live amid anger and meanness. In good weather they walked in the forest. She, wrapped in a shawl, said little, lived in a self-evident world – there was nothing to explain. Once in a great while she would reach over and take his hand, her way of saying thank you.

He woke suddenly, snapping his head erect just as his chin grazed his chest. He stood braced against the doorway of the last coach, track falling away through rolling fields, wheels in a steady clatter. When had he slept? Not for a long time.

He cleared his throat. Sublieutenant Nowak was pointedly looking elsewhere – no commanding officer of his, de Milja realized, would ever be seen to drift off.

'Coming into Deblin, Captain.'

De Milja nodded. Nowak was too young – fresh-faced and eager. Out of uniform, in his Sunday suit, he looked like a student. 'Map?'

Nowak unfolded it. Deblin was a river town, where the Wieprz flowed east into the Vistula. The route south continued into Pulawy, Krasnystaw, Zamosc, Tomaszow. Crossed the river Tanew into the Ukrainian districts of Poland at Rava-Russkaya. Then the major city of Lvov, down to Stryj, a sweep around the eastern tip of German-occupied Czechoslovakia – known as Little Ukraine – into Uzhgorod, and finally across the border into the Roumanian town of Sighet in the Carpathian Mountains.

Four hundred and fifty miles, more or less. With the locomotive making a steady thirty-five miles an hour, about fourteen hours. Nowak heard the aeroplanes at the same time as he did, and together they looked up into the clouds. A flight of Heinkel bombers, in V formation, headed a little east of due north. That meant they'd been working on one of the industrial cities in the south, maybe Radom or Kielce, and were on their way home, bomb bays hopefully empty, to an airfield in East Prussia, probably Rastenburg.

'Nothing for you down here,' de Milja said quietly.

He'd done the best he could: it was just a little train, yellow coaches with red borders on the windows and a locomotive puffing through the wheat fields. Pastoral, harmless.

The Heinkels droned on. Below and behind them, a fighter escort of ME-109s. The pilots were bored. Sneak attacks on Polish airfields had blown up the opposition on the first day – and stolen their war. Now their job had little to do with skill or daring. They were nursemaids. From the wing position, a fighter plane sideslipped away from the formation, swooped down a sharp angle in a long, steep dive, flattened out in perfect strafing attitude, and fired its 20 mm cannon into the annoying little train chugging along below as though it hadn't a care in the world. The pilot had just broken off the attack, soaring up through the smoke of the locomotive's stack, when the radio crackled furiously and the flight leader gave a short, sharp order. The plane slipped back into formation, maintaining rigid spacing and perfect airspeed discipline all the way home to East Prussia.

The engineer remembered his orders and followed them: slowed down, rolled to a stop. Flight excites hunting dogs and fighter pilots, nothing standing still interests them for very long.

De Milja called out to Nowak as he swung off the platform: 'Go through the cars, get the dead and wounded out, see if there's anybody who can help.'

He ran along the track, then climbed into the cab of the locomotive. A column of steam was hissing from a hole in the firebox, the engineer was kneeling by the side of the fireman, who was lying on his back, his face the colour of wood ash, a pale green shadow like a bruise already settled on his cheekbones. De Milja cursed to himself when he saw it.

The engineer was breathing hard; de Milja saw his chest rise and fall in the old cardigan. He went down on one knee and put a hand on the man's shoulder. 'That was done well,' he said. Then: 'You're all right.' More an order than a question, the *of course* unvoiced but clear.

The engineer pressed his lips together and shook his head – very close to tears. 'My sister-in-law's husband,' he said. 'My wife said not to ask him.'

De Milja nodded in sympathy. He understood, patted the man's shoulder twice, hard, before he took his hand away. The engineer said, 'She—,' but there was nothing more. It was quiet in the fields, the only sound the slow beat of the locomotive's pistons running with the engine at rest. A bird sang somewhere in the distance. The fireman raised his hands, palms up, like a shrug, then made a face. 'Shit,' he said. As de Milja leaned over him, he died.

Nowak had the casualties laid out in a beet field; a dark woman with hair braided and pinned worked over them. When de Milja arrived, she put him to work tearing cotton underdrawers into strips for bandages and sent Nowak running up to the locomotive for hot water.

'This man has been shot through the foot,' she said, carefully removing the shoe. 'Went in above the heel, came out the sole just here, behind the second toe.' She put the bloody shoe aside. 'Foot scares me, I'm unfamiliar with it.'

'You're a nurse?'

'Veterinarian. A paw or a hoof, there I can help. Grab his hand.' De Milja held the man's hand as the veterinarian swabbed on antiseptic from a big brown-glass bottle.

'A little girl is dead,' she said. 'She was about ten years old. And a man in his forties, over there. We looked and looked – there's not a mark on him. An old woman jumped out a window and broke her ankle. And a few others – cuts and bruises. But the angle of the gunfire was lucky for us – no glass, no fire. It's fire I hate.' She worked in silence a moment. 'It hurts?' she asked the patient.

'Go ahead, Miss. Do whatever you have to. Did I understand you to say that you were a veterinarian?'

'That's right.'

'Hah! My friends will certainly get a laugh when they hear that!' De Milja's fingers throbbed from the pressure of the wounded man squeezing his hand.

A grave-digging crew was organized, which took turns using the fireman's shovel, and a priest said prayers as the earth was piled on. The little girl had been alone on the train, and nobody could find her papers. A woman who'd talked to her said her name was Tana, so that name was carved on the wooden board that served as a gravestone.

*

De Milja ordered the train stopped at a village station between Pulawy and Lublin, then used the phone in the stationmaster's office – he could barely hear through the static – to report the attack to Vyborg, and to revise the estimated time of arrival 'in the southern city'.

'The Russian divisions have crossed the border,' Vyborg said. 'They may not reach your area for a day or so, but it's hard to predict. The Germans are headed west – giving up territory. We believe there's a line of demarcation between Hitler and Stalin, and the Russians will move up to occupy the new border.'

'Does that change anything for us?'

'No. But German aircraft have been attacking the line south of you. The railway people say they can keep it open another twenty-four hours, but that's about it. Still, we think you ought to find cover, then continue after dark. Understood?'

'Yes, sir.'

'All the roads out of Warsaw are now cut. This office is closing down, so you're on your own from now on. Consider that to have the status of a written order.'

'Understood, sir.'

'So, best of luck to you. To all of us.'

The connection was broken.

A corporal in the Geographical Section had made a speciality of hiding trains. Using his hand-drawn map, de Milja directed the engineer to a branch line south of Pulawy that wound up into the hills above the Vistula. There, twenty miles west of Lublin, a gypsum mining operation had gone bankrupt and been shut down some time in the 1920s. But the railway spur that ran to the site, though wildly overgrown, was still usable, and a roofed shed built for loading open railcars was still standing. Under the shed, with the engine turned off, they were very close to invisible.

17 September, 8:25 p.m. Over the years, the abandoned quarry had filled with water, and after dark de Milja could see the reflection of the rising moon on the still surface.

The engineer had patched the hole in the firebox, using tin snips, a tea tray, and wire. A big kid, about fifteen, from a farm village volunteered to work as the fireman – what he lacked in skill he'd make up with raw strength. Nowak took the opportunity to sight-in four rifles, which, with a few boxes of ammunition, had been hidden behind a panel in the last coach. He chose four men: a mechanic, a retired policeman, a student, and a man who didn't exactly want to say what he did, to be armed in case of emergency.

There wasn't much else they could do. The engine moved cautiously over the old track, heading east for the ancient city of Lublin, the countryside dark and deserted. The passengers were quiet, some doubtless having second thoughts about being cast adrift in a country at war. Maybe they would have been better off staying in Warsaw.

They reached Lublin a little after ten. Warehouses along the railway line had been blazing since that afternoon, and the city's ruptured water mains meant that the fire department could do little more than watch. The train crawled through thick black coils of heavy smoke, the passengers had to wet handkerchiefs and put them over their noses and mouths in order to breathe. A brakeman flagged them down. De Milja went up to the locomotive.

'We've been ordered to get you people through,' the brakeman said, 'and the crews are doing the best they can. But they bombed us just before sunset, and it's very bad up ahead.' The brakeman coughed and spat. 'We had all the worst things down here; wool, creosote, tarred rope. Now it's just going to burn.'

'Any sign of Russian troops?' de Milja asked.

'Not sure. We had a freight train disappear this morning. Vanished. What's your opinion about that?'

It took forever for them to work their way through Lublin. At one point, a shirtless work crew, bodies-black with soot, laid twenty-five feet of track almost directly beneath their wheels. The passengers gagged on the smoke, tried to get away from it by taking turns lying flat in the aisle, rubbed at the oily film that clung to their hands and faces, but that only made it burn worse. Farther down the line an old wooden bridge had collapsed onto the track and the huge, charred timbers were being hauled away by blindfolded farm horses. A saboteur – identified as such by a sign hung around his neck – had been hanged from a signal stanchion above the track. A group of passengers came to the last coach and pleaded with de Milja to get off the train. Nowak got the engine stopped, and a small crowd of people scurried away down the firelit lanes of the old city.

And then, once again, the war was gone.

The train climbed gently into the uplands east of the Carpathians. Warsaw, a northern city, seemed a long way from here – this was the ragged edge of Europe, border land. They ran dark, the lamps turned off in the coaches, only the locomotive light sweeping along the rails where, as the night cooled, land mist drifted through the beam. Beyond that, the steppe. Treeless, empty, sometimes a few thatched huts around a well and a tiny dirt road that ran off into the endless distance, to Russia, to the Urals. Now and then a village – a log station house with a Ukrainian name – but down here it was mostly the track and the wind.

De Milja stood beside the engineer and stared out into the darkness. The boy who'd taken the fireman's job fed coal to the firebox when the engineer told him to. His palms had blistered after an hour of shovelling, so he'd taken his shirt off and torn it in half and tied it around his hands. When he stepped away from the furnace he shivered in the night air, but he was a man that night and de Milja knew better than to say anything.

At some nameless settlement, the train stopped at a water tower, the engineer swung the spout into position and began to fill the tank. It was long after midnight, and deserted – only the sigh of the wind, moths fluttering in the engine light, and the splash of water. Then, suddenly, a girl was standing by the locomotive. She was perhaps sixteen, barefoot, wearing a soiled cotton shift, head scarf, and a thin shawl around her shoulders. She was the most beautiful girl that de Milja had ever seen. 'Please, Your Excellency,' she said – the dialect was ancient and de Milja barely understood her – 'may I be permitted to ride on the train?'

She raised her hand, opened her fingers to reveal a pair of tiny gold earrings resting on her palm.

De Milja was speechless. The engineer, standing atop the front of the locomotive, stared down at her, and the boy stopped shovelling coal. The hem of the shift was spattered with mud, her ankles thin above dirty feet. She is pregnant, de Milja thought. She stood patiently, her eyes not quite meeting his, a sign of submission, her other hand clutching the shawl at her throat. But when de Milja did not speak, she looked directly at him and, just for an instant, her eyes lit up green fire as they caught the light, then she hid them away.

'Please, Excellency?' The earrings must not be worth what she thought; her voice faded in defeat.

'You do not have to pay,' de Milja said.

Her face hid nothing, and it was plain how she had struggled, all her life, to understand things. She had never been on a train before, but she knew one or two people who had, and she had asked them about it, and one certainly had to pay. Atop the locomotive, the engineer swung the water spout away so that water splashed on the ground beside the tracks until he shut it off.

De Milja waited for her to ask where they were going, but she never did. 'You may ride on the train,' he said.

Still hesitant, she closed the earrings in her fist and held them to her throat. Then turned towards the passenger coaches. Did he mean what he said? Or was he just making fun of her? No, he meant it. Before he could change his mind she ran like a deer, climbed cautiously onto the iron step of the first coach, peered inside, then vanished.

Past Lvov, then Uzhgorod.

Sublieutenant Nowak took the watch for an hour, then a little after four in the morning de Milja returned. Now the train was climbing a grade that ran through a pine forest, then past Kulikov, then deeper into the mountains that marked the southern border of Poland.

Captain de Milja and the engineer saw the dim shape ahead at the same moment. De Milja wondered what it was, and squinted to bring it into focus. The old man swore and hauled on the brake with both hands. The wheels locked and screeched as they slid on the iron rails, and the train finally shuddered to a halt just short of the barrier, tree trunks piled across the track.

The light was strange at that hour – not night, not yet dawn – so the shapes coming towards them from the forest had no colour, and seemed to glide on mist, like phantoms in a dream, with white plumes steaming from the horses' nostrils in the cold mountain air.

The bandit leader – or ataman, or headman, whatever he called himself – was not to be hurried. Rifle at rest across his saddle, he walked his horse to the cab of the locomotive and stared at de Milja. 'Get out,' he said softly. This was Ukrainian, of which de Milja understood that much at least. The bandit was perhaps in his fifties, wore a peaked cap and a suit jacket. Two or three days' white bristle covered a stubborn jaw below the small, shrewd eyes of the farmer's most cherished pig.

De Milja jumped to the ground, the engineer followed, the boy did not. *Hiding*, de Milja thought. All along the train, passengers were filing out of the coaches, hands high above their heads, lining up at the direction of the bandits. The leader looked him over: where was the danger in him? Where the profit? De Milja met his gaze. Back by the coaches there was a rifle shot. The bandit watched to see what he would do, so he did not turn around to see what had happened.

'Who are you?' the leader asked.

'I work for the railway.'

The bandit did not quite believe that. 'You ready to die up in a tree?' Ukrainian executions lasted all day. De Milja did not react.

'Hardheaded, you people,' the leader said. 'You're finished,' he went on. 'Now it's the Germans and us.'

De Milja was silent.

'Carrying anything valuable on that train?'

'No. Just people heading for the border.'

The bandit glanced back at the passenger coaches, de Milja followed his eyes. The passengers had their hands on the sides of the railcars, their baggage was laid out on the ground so that the bandits could pick and choose what they wanted.

A bandit on a grey pony rode up beside the leader. 'Any good?' the leader asked.

'Not bad.'

'Gold?'

'Some. Polish money. Jewellery.'

'And the women?'

'Good. Four or five of them.'

The bandit leader winked at de Milja. 'You won't be seeing them again.' He paused, something about de Milja fascinated him. 'Come over here,' he said. De Milja stepped forward, stood beside the bandit's boot in a stirrup. 'Give me your watch. It would be a railway watch, of course.'

De Milja undid the strap, handed up his watch, long ago a present from his wife. The bandit glanced at it, then dropped it in his pocket. 'Not a railway watch, is it?'

'No.'

The leader was getting bored. With one hand he raised his rifle until de Milja was looking down the barrel. 'What do you see in there?' De Milja took a deep breath, the bandit was going to ask him to look closer. One of the passengers screamed, de Milja couldn't tell if it was a man or a woman. The bandit on the grey pony trotted a little way towards the sound. A rifle fired, a flat, dull crack like the earlier shot; then another, deeper. The bandit leader puffed out his cheek so hard it burst in a red spray, his horse shied and whinnied. De Milja grabbed the harness and pulled himself close to the horse's body. The barrel of the rifle probed frantically, looking for him. Somewhere above, the bandit was wailing and cursing like a child. De Milja hung on to the reins with one hand and snatched the rifle barrel with the other. The weapon fired but he didn't let go. Then the boy came out from behind a locomotive wheel and hit the bandit on the head with the shovel, which rang like a bell as the rifle came free in de Milja's hand and the horse tore away from him.

The other bandit danced his pony around and shot the boy again and again, de Milja could hear the bullets hit, and the boy grunted each time. He fumbled the rifle around to firing position but the bandit galloped away, jumped his horse over the coupling between cars and disappeared. De Milja flinched as something hissed by his ear. Then Nowak called to him from the coal car and he ran up the ladder mounted on the wall as a bullet struck a silver chip out of the iron and the locomotive's light went dark. Two horses thundered past, then a cluster of rapid rifle shots, a yell of triumph.

Nowak was lying on the coal at one end of the car, firing a rifle into the darkness. De Milja threw himself down beside him. Between the train and the forest, dark shapes were sprawled amid clothing and suitcases. A yellow spark from the trees – both he and Nowak swung their weapons. Nowak fired, but de Milja's clicked as the hammer fell on an empty chamber. He threw it aside and worked the pistol free from beneath his sweater. 'Who has the other rifles?' de Milja asked, meaning the weapons they had hidden behind a panel.

'Don't know, sir,' Nowak said. 'It's chaos.'

He couldn't permit chaos. Rolled over the lip of the car, slid down the ladder on the other side, stood between cars for a moment, then jumped to the ground and ran along the length of the train. The conductor ran by him going the other way, eyes white, teeth clenched, pistol held up in the safe position. Combat-mad, he never even saw de Milja, who wondered who he was chasing. Passengers were climbing through the coach windows; some of them had gotten a horse off its feet and it kicked and whinnied in terror as they tried to kill its rider, who howled for mercy. De Milja stepped on a body, then through a tangle of clothing that reeked of cloves – hair tonic from a shattered bottle. He tripped as he leaped for an open doorway, then went sprawling into the last coach.

The smell of gunpowder and urine hit him like a wall. Someone moaned softly, but mostly it was very dark and very quiet – the people packed together on the floor were breathing audibly, as though winded. A bullet from the forest went through the car and a triangle of glass fell on a seat without breaking. A silhouette rose suddenly in the middle of the car and returned the fire.

As de Milja crawled along the aisle, the train moved. Barely, only just making way, but he thought he could feel the logs being slowly forced off the track. The engineer is alive, he thought, using the locomotive like a bulldozer. The rifleman knelt quickly, moved on his knees to a neighbouring window, straightened up, and fired. It was Herschensohn, the violinist. The homburg was jammed down on his head, a muscle ticked in his jaw, and he was muttering under his breath – 'Stay still, you' – as he took aim.

ALAN FURST

De Milja reached the far end of the car – the back of the train – just as something seemed to give way and, with the sound of splintering wood, the train moved a little faster.

'Wait!'

A running shape burst from the forest – the peasant girl who'd begged to be let on the train at the water tower. 'She got away!' Herschensohn had appeared beside him. The girl ran in panic, tripped, went sprawling on her face, struggled back up again, limping now and much slower. She waved her hands and screamed as the train gradually picked up speed.

De Milja was abruptly shoved aside. A man in a grey suit, with carefully brushed hair, leaped off the train and ran towards the girl, circled an arm around her waist and tried to help her. No longer young, he could barely run fast enough to keep up with the injured girl. 'For God's sake don't leave us!' he yelled.

The bandits, on horseback and in the woods, saw what was happening. De Milja pinpointed the muzzle flashes in the half-light. The range was absurd but he aimed with both hands, changed the action to single-shot, and squeezed off round after round from his automatic. Herschensohn muttered angrily under his breath, talking to the target, as he fired his rifle. A young woman in a sweater and skirt jumped from a window, stumbled, came up running, took the girl around the waist from the other side. De Milja heard footsteps pounding above him as Nowak ran down the roof of the car, firing into the trees. Somebody yelled 'Save her, save her, save her,' like a chant, and others took up the cry. De Milja thrust his empty pistol into his pocket and stood on the lowest step as the three people gained on the car. Herschensohn was firing over his shoulder and Nowak was shouting something from the roof. The three faces were distorted with exhaustion, with tears of effort, mouths gasping for breath, hands clawing frantically at the railings beside the door. But as the last log rolled away, the locomotive accelerated, the three runners flailing and staggering as the platform moved away from them.

Then the train quivered – the shock slammed de Milja against the wall – and suddenly the runners were close. He reached out and grabbed handfuls of shirt, coat, hair, whatever he could get, and hung on desperately. Someone caught the back of his coat just as he started to fall onto the tracks, other hands reached over his shoulders, people yelled, shoes scraped on the boards as somebody fought for traction, and the two rescuers and the girl were hauled aboard with a cry of triumph.

De Milja ended up on hands and knees as the train – something

606

wrong with the way it ran now – slowly ground through a long, gentle curve. At the bottom of the embankment lay what was left of a truck: cab torn in half, petrol flames flickering over the radiator, a tyre spinning, a mounted machine gun aimed at the sky, and a man, arms flung wide, half-buried in a pile of broken brick.

When de Milja worked his way forward to the cab of the locomotive, he found bullet marks everywhere – the Ukrainian gunners had had their moment – and a very pale engineer. They'd mounted a machine gun on a brick truck and parked it on the tracks behind the log barrier. Just in case.

For the last hundred miles they were well up in the Carpathians, some of the passes at seven thousand feet, and the train switched back over ridges and granite outcrops, through sparse grass and forests of stunted pine where hawks floated on the mountain thermals. The train barely went now, maybe ten miles an hour, crawled along a trestle over a thousand-foot gorge as the passengers prayed silently and not-so-silently, oil trickling from beneath the engine. The sun didn't reach them until ten in the morning; they were cold, there was nothing to eat, and very little water.

They crossed the Tisza River; there'd been a fire on the bridge, but it still held. De Milja walked along in front of the engine, watching the track bow under the weight, trying not to hear the sounds the wooden girders made. They travelled for a time beside a deeply rutted dirt track, where stone mileposts gave the distance to Roumania. A burned-out Polish army car had been shoved into a ditch, a wagon and a pair of horses hit by a divebomber, a truck lay on its side in the middle of a mountain stream.

They worked at it all day, Nowak and de Milja taking turns standing with the engineer in the locomotive, sometimes running the train themselves since he was long past exhaustion. Slow as their progress was, there were no other trains. The stationmaster at Mukachevo told them the Germans had bombed the lines running south – the Polish railway system didn't really exist any longer.

They were what was left. De Milja and Nowak changed into officers' uniforms a few miles before they reached the frontier at Sighet. The train stopped at the Polish border station, but it had been abandoned: an empty hut, a bare flagpole. A mile farther on, at the Roumanian customs post, a tank was parked with its cannon facing down the track. 'So,' said the engineer, 'we are expected.' De Milja took a set of papers, prepared in Warsaw, to the Roumanian major who greeted him at the wooden barrier pole.

The two officers saluted, then shook hands. The major was dark, with a movie-hero moustache and excellent manners. Yes they were expected, yes everything was in order, yes they'd be processed through in a half-hour, yes, yes, yes. The sun dropped lower in the sky, the children cried because they were hungry, the truth was to be seen in the eyes of the passengers on the train: despair, boredom, fatigue – the refugee life had begun. Please be patient, the Roumanian major said. Please.

Two Polish diplomats materialized; eyeglasses, Vandyke beards, and overcoats with velvet collars. Negotiations continued, they reported, but a diplomatic solution had been proposed: the Polish passengers could enter Roumania – temporary immigrant status would be granted – the Polish train could not. A troublesome technicality, but . . . The hanging sentence meant *what can be done?* Poland could no longer insist on anything. It was a *former* nation now, a phantom of international law.

Meanwhile, de Milja used the diplomats to make contacts he'd been given in Warsaw, and with a few code words and secret signs, things started to happen, not the least of which was the delivery of hampers of bread and onions and wormy pears brought by Roumanian soldiers.

And eventually, long after dark, another Polish Captain Nom de Guerre showed up. They recognized each other from the meeting in Vyborg's office: shared a cigarette, a walk by the tracks, and the news of the day. Then a phone call was made and, an hour later, a train appeared at the Roumanian frontier post: a few freight cars, a small but serviceable locomotive, and Polish regular army soldiers with sub-machine guns. This train was moved up to the edge of the barrier on the Roumanian side, and the Antonescu government, an uncertain mistress to several lovers – England, Germany, Russia – agreed that the passengers could bring whatever baggage they had onto Roumanian soil.

It was very dark at the border, so pitch-pine torches were brought. And several volunteers among the passengers were given prybars. The floorboards in the coaches were prised up and, by flickering torchlight, the Polish National Gold Reserve, more than eleven million dollars, was carried into Roumania.

Standing with Nowak by the train, Captain de Milja felt his heart stir with pride. From the Pilava local, with its shattered windows and bullet gashes, its locomotive reeking of singed bearings and burnt oil, the passengers handed out crates stamped NATIONAL BANK OF POLAND. Blood had been shed for this; by a locomotive fireman, a ten-year-old girl, a boy from a country village. By a conductor of the Polish National Railways who, teeth clenched, pistol in hand, had disappeared into the darkness. De Milja did not believe it had been shed in vain and stood very nearly to attention as his little army struggled past with the heavy boxes: Vladimir Herschensohn, his violin carried off by Ukrainian bandits, the veterinarian who had treated the wounded, the pensioned engineer, the peasant girl, the man and woman – from some comfortable professional class – who had run onto a battlefield to save a life, a few country people, a few workers, women and children. Poland had lost a war, this was what was left.

Room 9

20 October 1939. Bucharest, Roumania.

Now the war was over, a pleasant autumn.

Hitler had what he wanted. Maybe he did, after all, have a right to it, a case could be made, you had to accept the reality of politics in central Europe. The days were cool and sunny, the harvest in, a little fog in the morning and geese overhead. Germany had Austria, Czechoslovakia, and Poland, and was, officially, *officially*, at war with England and France. But this was politics; eddies and swirls and tidal shifts in the affairs of diplomats. Slowly the sun warmed the squares and plazas, the boulevards and little winding streets and, by midmorning, all across Europe, it was just right for a coffee on the café terrace.

On the terrace of the Dragomir Niculescu restaurant, a man at leisure – or perhaps he simply has no place to go. A respectable gentleman, one would have to say. The suit not new, of course. The shirt a particular colour, like wheat meal, that comes from washing in the sink and drying on a radiator. The posture proud, but maybe, if you looked carefully, just a little lost. Not defeated, nothing that drastic. Haven't we all had a moment of difficulty, a temporary reversal? Haven't we all, at some time or another, washed out a shirt in the sink?

Still, it must be said, the times are not so easy. The police are seen a good deal lately in the neighbourhood of rooming houses that take in refugees, and the medical school does have all the, ah, *subjects* that its anatomy students might require, and the police launch on the nearby river almost always has a customer on the early-morning patrol, sometimes two. Difficult, these times. Discontent, dislocation, shifting power, uneasy alliance. The best way, nowadays, is to remain flexible, supple. Almost everybody would agree with that.

Speaking of the police: the gentleman on the terrace of the Niculescu is evidently of interest to at least three, one uniformed, two not, and they are in turn doubtless assisted by various barmen, drivers of horse-drawn trasuri cabs, and the rouge-cheeked girls left over from last night. Such a wealth of attention! But, frankly, whose fault is that? Poor Roumania, the flood comes to its door – Jews and socialists and misfits and Poles and spies and just about any damn thing you care to name. It's gotten so bad they've had to put little cards on the tables at the Plaza-Athénée. BY ORDER OF THE GOVERNMENT. POLITICAL DISCUSSION IS FORBIDDEN.

The gentleman on the terrace of the Niculescu ordered a second coffee. When it came, he took a handful of leu coins out of his pocket, then hesitated a moment, uncertain what was worth what. The waiter, the natural curl of his lip tightening just a bit, deftly plucked out the right ones and dropped them in his waiter's saucer. Here was the land of 'saruta mina pe care nu o poti musca' – kiss the hand you cannot bite – inhabited solely by the contemptuous and the contemptible, and those who had some doubt as to where they belonged could find instruction in the eyes of any café waiter.

If the gentleman on the terrace of the Niculescu didn't particularly care, it was, at least in part, because his head swam with hunger. Just behind him, lunchtime lobsters and crayfish were being set out on beds of shaved ice, the Niculescu's kitchen was preparing its famous hot-meat-and-fried-mushroom patties. Two peddlers with packs and long beards had stopped nearby to eat slices of white cheese and garlic on cold corn polenta, even the Gypsies, just across the square, were cooking a rabbit over a pot of burning tar. The gentleman on the terrace took a measured sip of coffee. Discipline, he told himself. Make it last.

The woman was stylish, somewhere in middle age, wearing a little hat with a half-veil. She arrived in a trasuri, bid it wait with a wave of a gloved hand, and accepted the doorman's arm to descend from the carriage. The gentleman on the terrace was pleased to see her. He stood politely while she settled herself on a chair. The waiter pushed the lank hair back from his forehead and said 'Service' in French as he went for her coffee.

She drank only a sip. They spoke briefly, then she whispered by his ear, and they held hands for a moment beneath the table. He stood, she rose, he took her hand, she presented her veil for a brush of his lips, said a parting word behind the back of her hand, walked quickly to her trasuri and was gone, leaving a cloud of lilac scent. 'God go with you, Captain,' was what she'd said.

The gentleman on the terrace touched the pocket of his jacket, making sure of the money she'd passed to him, then strolled slowly across the square, past the policemen, uniformed and not, and their helpers, past old women sweeping the cobblestones with twig brooms, past a flock of pigeons that rose into the air with beating wings.

Captain de Milja left that night. He'd had enough of Bucharest: the rooming house, the police, and the assorted ghosts and wolves who lived in the cafés. And more than enough of Roumania. The country, under German diplomatic pressure, had started to intern Polish army units crossing the border – as they had interned most of the senior ministers of the Polish government. Time to go.

He travelled under a cover he'd created for himself, using a blank identity card they'd left in his dossier the night he went to work for Vyborg. Name: Jan Boden. That made him a Silesian Pole – like his father – with a good knowledge of German and likely some German blood. Profession: Buyer of wood for coffins. That made it normal for him to travel, yet wasn't a profession that the Germans would want to draft – not, for example, like an expert machinist – for labour in Germany. He wore a leather coat so he wouldn't freeze, and carried a VIS, the Polish army automatic pistol, so he wouldn't be taken prisoner. If he had to drop it quickly somewhere, he could always get another. After six years of war, 1914–1918, then the 1920–1921 campaign against the Red Army, Poland was an armoury. Every barn, every cellar, every attic had its weapons and ammunition. And the Poles were not Russian peasants; they cleaned and oiled and maintained, because they liked things that worked.

He had some time to spare – the message that the courier delivered along with the money was *Room 9 at Saint Stanislaus Hospital on Grodny Street by 23 October* – and that probably saved his life. He took a train from Bucharest up to Sighisoara in the Transylvanian Alps, then another, going west, that crossed into Hungary near Arad. Changed again, this time going north to Kisvarda, in the Carpathians. As it grew dark, he caught a ride on a truck into a border village by a stream that fed into the Tisza, close to one of several passes over the mountains.

He entered the local tavern, ordered beer and sausage, and was approached by the local *passeurs* – smugglers – within the hour. He said he wished to be guided into Poland, a price was set, everybody spit on their palms and shook hands.

But soon after they started out, he realized that, contractual spits notwithstanding, they meant to kill him and take his money. It was black dark. The two *passeurs*, reeking of taverns, goats, and rancid fat, squatted on either side of him. They whispered, and touched his arms. Too much, as though familiarizing themselves with his physical capacity, and dissipating his protective magic. One of them had a knife in his belt – a dull, rusty thing, the idea of being stabbed with it gave de Milja a chill.

'I have to go behind a tree,' he said in Polish. Then he faded away in the darkness and just kept going. He found what he believed to be the south bank of the Tisza, then a dirt track that someone might have intended as a road, then a bridge, where he could hear the unmistakable sounds of Russian soldiers getting drunk: singing, then arguing, then fighting, then weeping, then snoring. As one of the Ostrow uncles used to say, 'Here is something a man can depend on – never mind some silly ball rolling down an inclined plane.'

De Milja crossed the bridge a little after two in the morning; he was then in Soviet-occupied Poland. He walked another hour, winter cold numbing his face at the high altitude, then came upon a deserted farm – no barking dogs – opened the milking shed, kicked together a straw bed for himself, and actually slept until dawn.

By midday on the twenty-first of October, he was in the town of Kosow, where the railway went to Tarnopol. He bought a ticket and caught the next train; his night in the milk shed had left him rumpled, unshaven, a little smelly, and thoroughly acceptable – proletarian – to the Russian guards at the railway station. He leaned his head against the cold glass of the window as the train crossed the Dniester: yes, he was under orders to go to Warsaw, but he meant to find his wife at the clinic, meant somehow to get her across the border into Roumania. Let them intern her if they liked – it was better than being at the mercy of the Russians.

In Tarnopol, the taxis had disappeared from the railway station, so he walked through the winding streets in late afternoon, found the way out of town, and was soon headed for the clinic down a rutted dirt path. He knew this country, the Volhynia, it was home to his mother's family estates, more than three thousand acres of rolling hills, part forest, part farmland, with bountiful hunting and poor harvests and no way to earn a zloty, a lost paradise where one could gently starve to death with a contented heart beneath a pale, lovely moon.

The birch trees shimmered in the wind as night came on, butterflies hovered over a still pond in a meadow, the shadowy woods ran on forever – a fine place to write a poem or be murdered or whatever fate might have in mind for you just then. The little boy in de Milja's heart was every bit as scared of this forest as he'd always been, the VIS pistol in his pocket affording just about as much protection from the local spirits as the rock he used to carry.

*

It was near twilight when he reached the clinic. The wicker wheelchairs stood empty on the overgrown lawns, the white pebble paths were unraked; it was all slowly going back to nature.

He walked up a long path lined with Lombardy poplars, was not challenged as he entered the hundred-year-old gabled house, formerly the heart of a grand estate. There were no bearded doctors, no brisk nurses, no local girls in white aprons to bring tea and cake, and there seemed to be fewer patients about than he remembered. But, on some level, the clinic still functioned. He saw a few old village women making soup in the kitchen, the steam radiators were cold but a fire had been built in the main parlour and several patients, wrapped in mufflers and overcoats, were staring into it and talking quietly among themselves.

His wife was sitting a little apart from the group, hands held between her knees – something she did when she was cold – face hidden by long, sand-coloured hair. When he touched her shoulder she looked startled, then recognized him and smiled for a moment. She had sharp features and generous, liquid eyes, the face of a person who could not hurt anything. Strange, he thought, how she doesn't seem to age.

'Helena,' he said.

She searched for something, then looked down, hiding her eyes.

'Let's sit over here,' he said. Often it was best just to go forward. He took her hand and led her to a sofa where they could be private. 'Are you all right?' he asked.

A little shrug, a wry smile.

'Have you seen soldiers? Russian soldiers?'

That bore thinking about – she simply did not hear things the way others did, perhaps she heard much more, echoes and echoes of meaning until no question could have an answer. 'Yes,' she said, hesitantly.

'Was anyone . . . hurt?'

'No.'

She was thinner, her eyes seemed bruised, but they always did. She disliked the Veronal they gave her to calm down and sleep, and so hid it somewhere and paced away the nights.

'Enough to eat?'

She nodded yes.

'So then?' he said, pretending to be gruff.

This never failed to please her. 'So then?' she said, imitating him.

He reached for her, resting his hand lightly on the soft hair that fell to her shoulder, it was something she allowed. 'Helena,' he said.

Her eyes wandered. What did he want?

'The Russians,' he continued, 'are here now, perhaps you know. I—'

'Please,' she said, eyes pleading. She would not stand for exegesis, could not bear it.

He sighed and took her hands. She took them back – gently, she didn't want to hurt his feelings, she simply wanted the hands – folded them in her lap and gave him a puzzled look. Usually he was so courteous.

'I have been thinking that I ought to take you away from here,' he said.

She considered it – he could see a certain shadow touch her face as she reasoned. Then she shook her head no. The way she did it was not vague, or crazy, but sharp, completely in control. She'd thought through *everything:* soldiers, what they did, how bad it was, that she was not vulnerable to whatever he feared might happen to her.

He dropped his hands into his lap. He felt completely helpless. He considered taking her away by force, but he knew it wouldn't work.

'To go where?' she asked, not unkindly.

He shook his head, defeated.

'Will you walk me to the lake house?' she asked. She could be soft and shy to a point where he came near tears – the ache in the back of the throat. He stood and offered her his arm.

What she called 'the lake house' had once been a pavilion, where guests were served cream cakes, and tea from a silver urn, and the doctors could speak frankly in peaceful surroundings. Now it was dark and abandoned and some bird out in the reed marsh beyond the lake repeated a low, evening call.

She stood facing him, almost touching, reluctant to speak at first, and, even for her, very troubled. 'I want you to make love to me as you used to,' she said. *One last time* – her unspoken words were clear as a musical note.

Looking around, he found a cane deckchair, grey with years of weather. He sat down, then invited her to sit on his lap with a flourish, as though it were a masterpiece of a bed, all silk and wool, in some grand hotel. She liked to play like this, raised her skirt just an inch, settled herself on his legs and laid her head against his shoulder. A little wind blew across the lake, the reeds bent, a few ducks flew over the marsh on the horizon. Idly, he stroked her dry lips with an index finger, she raised her face to it, and he saw that she had closed her eyes.

He took the hem of her sweater in his fingertips and lifted it to her shoulders, then lowered her slip, pulled her coat tight around her for warmth, wet his finger in her mouth and rubbed her breasts for a long time. They were heavier than he remembered but that had always been true of her, even when she was nineteen – her body full and round for a girl with a small face. She sighed, sentimental, yes, this was what she'd meant. Then she hummed softly and where her weight rested on him he could feel the *V* of her legs widen. When he slid his hand beneath her skirt she smiled. Covertly, he watched her face, wondered what sort of dream she was having. Her lips moved, drew back slowly, then parted; her breathing became louder, shallow and rhythmic, until her weight suddenly pressed into him.

'Stand up,' he said. He stepped behind her, slid her coat down her arms and spread it on the broad, dry planks of the pavilion floor. She took her skirt off, then stepped out of her underpants. He knelt, embraced her hips, hard, as though something in the sky meant to sweep her away. She smoothed his hair – it didn't matter, it didn't matter. Then she settled herself on the coat, and swung her knees to one side, hands clasped beneath her head, a girl in a soap ad. He laughed.

They made love for a while; like strangers, like husband and wife, eventually like lovers. 'I want to ask you,' she said quietly, almost to herself, as they lay curled around each other to keep warm. 'You didn't bring flowers, this time.' The words trailed off into the evening sounds by the lake.

'And you think, do I love you? Yes, I do.'

'But you always . . .'

'Left on the train,' he said. 'You have to forgive me.'

She burrowed closer to him, he could feel the tears on her face.

On the train back to Warsaw he made a mistake.

He went north from Tarnopol, to Rovno. Stayed overnight in the railway station – technically illegal but tolerated, because people had to wait for trains, yet dangerous, because security police knew that railway stations attracted fugitives.

A uniformed NKVD guard looked through his documents, reading with a slow index finger on each word, then handed them back silently. He got out of Rovno on a dawn train to Brzesc, near the east bank of the river that formed the dividing line between German and Russian occupation forces. On this train, two men in overcoats; one of them stared at him, and, foolishly, he stared back. Then realized what he'd done and looked away. At the very last instant. He could see from the posture of the man – his age, his build – that he was *somebody*, likely civilian NKVD, and was about to make a point of it.

De Milja's heart hammered in his chest, he felt prickly sweat break out under his arms, he did not even dare a glance to see if the man had accepted his 'surrender': breaking off eye contact. Could not put a hand on the VIS, just tried to shrink down into the seat without a single sign of bravado. He *was* strong. And unafraid. And the way he carried himself, people knew that, and it would bury him in a hurry if he didn't learn some other way to be in public.

The two men got off the train one station before Brzesc. From the platform, his enemy squinted at him through the window. De Milja stared at his shoes, a proud man subdued. The Russian didn't buy it; with a certain casual violence he turned to get back on the train and, de Milja was sure, haul him off. But his partner stopped him and grabbed the shoulder of his coat, pulling him, with a joke and a laugh, along the platform – they had more important things to do. From the corner of his eye, de Milja could see the Russian as he glanced back one last time. He was red in the face. The man, de Milja knew beyond a doubt, had intended to kill him.

In the German sector it was different. Much easier. The black-uniformed border police did not hate Poles as the Russians did. Poles to them were truly *untermenschen*, subhuman, beneath contempt. They were to be treated, like all Slavs, as beasts, controlled by '*zuckerbrot und peitsché*' – sweets and the whip. They checked his identity card, then waved him on. He was nothing, they never even saw him.

Of equal interest to de Milja was a siding some fifty miles south of Warsaw: eight German tank cars, pointed east, clearly going to the Soviet ally, marked NAPHTHALENE.

Yes, well, what couldn't one do with that.

23 October, Warsaw. Saint Stanislaus Hospital.

An excellent safe house: all sorts of people went in and out at all hours of the day and night. There were cots for sleeping, meals were served, yet it was far safer than any hotel ever could be.

Room 9 was in the basement, adjacent to the boilers that heated the hospital water. It had a bed, a steel sink, and plaster walls painted pale green in 1903. It had a military map of Poland, a street map – Baedeker – of Warsaw, two steel filing cabinets, a power-boosted radio receiver with an aerial disappearing through a drainpipe entry in an upper corner, three telephones, several tin ashtrays, a scarred wood table with three chairs on one side and one chair on the other. Illumination was provided by a fifteen-watt bulb in a socket in the middle of the ceiling.

Of the three people facing him, de Milja knew one by acquaintance: a Warsaw hellion called Grodewicz who was not, as far as he knew, in the military and who should have been, as far as most of his friends were concerned, in prison. One by reputation: Colonel Jozef Broza, the former military attaché to Belgium. And one not at all, a woman who introduced herself only as 'Agata'. She was in her late fifties, with a square jaw, a tip-tilted nose, and thick, dark-blonde hair shot with grey, pulled back in a tortoiseshell clip. She had the fine skin of a nun, a filigreed gold wedding band, nicotine stains on the fingers of both hands, and unpolished but well-buffed fingernails. De Milja could easily see her in a country house or on horseback, obviously a member of the upper gentry.

She lit a cigarette, blew smoke through her nostrils, and gave him a good long stare before she started to speak. What she told him was brief but to the point: an underground organization had been formed to fight the Germans and the Russians – it would operate independently in each of the occupied zones. His job would be in the western half of the country, the German half.

The underground was to be called the ZWZ, Zwiazek Walki Zbrojnej – the Union for Armed Struggle. The highest level of command, known as the Sixth Bureau, was based in Paris, part of the Polish government-in-exile now led by General Sikorski. In German-occupied Poland, the ZWZ was headquartered in Warsaw, with regional stations in Cracow, Lodz, Poznan – all the major cities. Operational sections included sabotage, propaganda, communications – couriers and secret mail – and an intelligence service. 'You,' she said to de Milja, 'are being considered for a senior position in the latter.' She stubbed out her cigarette, lit a fresh one.

'Of course it is folly to say *anything* in this country in the singular form – we are God's most plural people and losing wars doesn't change that. There are, in fact, undergrounds, run by the entire spectrum of political parties: the Communists, the Nationalists, the Catholic Nationalists, the Peasant Party, and so on. The Jews are attempting to organize in their own communities, also subject to political division. Still, the ZWZ is more than ninety per cent of the effort and will likely remain so.

'But, whatever name it's done under, we have several months of hard, dirty fighting ahead of us. We now estimate that the French, with England's help, are going to need six months to overrun Germany. It's our job to survive in the interim, and keep the national damage at the lowest possible level. When Germany's finished off, it will be up to the League of Nations to pry the USSR out of Poland and push it back to the August '39 borders. This will require diplomacy, patience, and perhaps divine intervention – Stalin cares for nothing but brute force. There will be claims for Ukrainian, Byelorussian, and Lithuanian sovereignty, the Jews will want restrictive laws repealed – it won't ever be what it was before, but that's maybe not such a bad thing as far as the people in this room are concerned. Any questions?'

'No questions,' de Milja said.

'Right now,' she continued, 'we have two problems: the Polish people are in a state of mourning – how could the country be beaten so badly? And we lack explosives, incendiaries, and medicines for the partisan effort. We're waiting to be supplied by air from Paris, but nothing's happened yet. They make promises, then more promises. Meanwhile all we can do is insist, and not lose faith.'

Colonel Broza opened a dossier and glanced through it. He was barely five and a half feet tall, with massive shoulders, receding curly hair, and a pugnacious face. When he put on reading glasses, he looked like a peasant turned into a chess master which, the way de Milja heard it, wasn't so far from the truth.

'Aren't you something to Eugeniusz Ostrow?'

'Nephew, sir.'

'Which side?'

'My mother's family.'

'Ah. The countess.'

'Yes, sir.'

'Your uncle . . .' The colonel tried not to laugh. 'You must forgive me, I shouldn't . . . Wasn't there a formal dinner? A trade minister's wife, something about a goat?'

'A sheep, I believe it was, sir.'

'In diplomatic sash.'

'Yes, sir.'

The colonel pinched the bridge of his nose. 'And then . . . a cook, wasn't she?'

'A laundress, sir.'

'My God, yes! He married her.'

'A large, formal wedding, sir.'

The woman called Agata cleared her throat.

'Yes, of course, you're right. You were at Jagiello university?'

'I was.'

'In mathematics?'

'Yes, sir.'

'How'd you do?'

'Very poorly. Tried to follow in my father's footsteps, but—'

'Tossed out?'

'Not quite. Almost.'

'And then?'

'My uncles helped me get a commission in the army, and an assignment to the military intelligence service, and they sent me off to study cartography.'

'Where was that?'

'First at staff college, then at the French military academy, Saint-Cyr.'

'Three years, it says here.'

'Yes, sir.'

'So you speak the language.'

'Yes, sir.'

'And German?'

'My father's from Silesia, I spent time there when I was growing up. My German's not too bad, I would say.'

Colonel Broza turned over a page, read for a moment. 'Vyborg recommends you,' he said. 'I'm going to run the ZWZ intelligence service, I need somebody to handle special operations – to work with all the sections. You'll report directly to me, but not too often. You understand what I'm saying?'

'Yes, sir.'

'Do you know Captain Grodewicz?'

'Yes, sir.'

'Spend a little while with him. He's going to run the ZO unit.'

'Sir?'

'Zwiazek Odwety. Reprisal. You understand?'

It snowed, early in November, and those who read signs and portents in the weather saw malevolence in it. The Germans had lost no time stealing Polish coal, the open railcars rattled ceaselessly across the Oder bridges into ancient, warlike Prussia. The men who ran the coal companies in ancient, warlike Prussia were astonished at how much money they made in this way – commercial logic had always been based on buying a little lower, selling a little higher. But buying for virtually nothing, well, perhaps the wife ought to have the diamond leaf-pin after all. Hitler was scary, he gave these huge, towering, patriotic speeches on the radio, that meant *war* for God's sake, and war ruined business, in the long run, and worse. But this, this wasn't exactly war – this was a form of mercantile heaven, and who got hurt? A few Poles?

The wind blew down from Russia, howled at the windows, piled snow against the door, found every crack, every chip and flaw, and came looking for you in your house. The old people started to die. 'This is war!' they shouted in France, but no planes came. Perhaps next week.

Cautiously, from a distance, Captain de Milja tried to keep an eye on his family. He knew where one of the maids lived, and waited for her at night. 'Your father is a saint,' the woman said at her kitchen table. 'Your mother and your sister are in Hungary, safe, away from the murderers. Your father managed it – I can guess how, there's barely a zloty in the house these days.'

'What is he doing?'

'He will not leave, he will not go to the country, he will not admit that anything has changed,' the woman said. 'Will not.' She shook her head, respect and apprehension mixed together. 'He reads and writes, teaches his classes. He is a rock—' She called de Milja by a childhood pet name and the captain looked at his knees. He took a sheaf of zloty notes out of his pocket and laid it on the table. The maid gave him a wry look: *How do I explain this?*

'Don't talk about it. Just go to the black market, put something extra on the table, he won't notice.'

He had the woman turn out her oil lamp, they sat in the dark for a time, listening to the wind whine against the old brick, then he whispered good-bye and slid out the door into the night. Because of the curfew he went doorway to doorway, alert for the sound of German patrol cars. It could be done – anything could be done – but you had to think it through, you had to concentrate. A life lived in flight from the police, a life of evasion, had the same given as always, it hadn't changed in centuries: they could make a thousand mistakes, you couldn't make one. Once upon a time, only criminals figured that out. By November 1939, every man, woman and child in Poland knew it.

Something had to be done. De Milja met with his directorate in Room 9 – he was living in a servant's garret in Mokotow that week and the sudden warmth of the hospital basement made him giddy. He sat in the chair and presented his case: the heart was going out of the people, he could sense it. Colonel Broza agreed, Agata wasn't sure, Grodewicz thought maybe it didn't, for the moment, matter. Broza prevailed. All sorts of actions were considered; some violent, some spectacular. Should they humiliate the Germans? What, for an underground army, constituted a resounding success? How would people find out about it? Cigarette smoke hung in the still air, the perpetual dusk in the room grew darker, one of the hospital nuns brought them tea. They made a decision, Agata suggested a name, the rest was up to him.

The name was a retired Warsaw detective called Chomak. De Milja went to see him; found a man with stiff posture, shirt buttoned at the throat but no tie, dark hair combed straight back. Young to be retired, de Milja thought, but the prewar politics of the Warsaw police department could hardly concern him now. Chomak accepted the assignment, a worried wife at his side, a dachshund with a white muzzle sitting alertly by his chair. 'Everybody thinks it's easy to steal,' Chomak said. 'But that isn't true.'

He seemed to take great pleasure in the daily repetitive grind of the work, and always had a certain gleam in his eye: *not so easy, is it, this kind of job?* They rode trains together, bicycled down snowy roads at the distant edges of Warsaw; following leads, checking stories, seeing for themselves. They needed to steal a plane. Not a warplane, that would have required a massive use of the ZWZ resources. Just a little plane. Working through a list of mechanics and fuel-truck drivers – these names coming from prewar tax records secreted by the intelligence services before the Germans took over – they discovered that the great majority of small aircraft, Fiesler-Storch reconnaissance planes for example, were well guarded by Luftwaffe security forces.

But the Germans did have a gentlemen's flying club.

Flying clubs had gained great popularity at the time of the record-setting flights of the 1920s and 1930s, and served as training grounds for future fighter pilots who had come to aviation as aeroplane-crazy teenagers. And so, a few days after German victory, the flying club had taken over a small airfield at Pruszkow, about ten miles west of Warsaw. De Milja and Chomak bicycled slowly along the little road past the field. There wasn't much to see; an expanse of brown grass, a nylon wind sock on a pole, a hut with a swastika flag, and six single-engine planes, of which two had had their engines taken down to small pieces in the lone hangar.

Part Two: The printer across the river in Praga had all the work he could handle. The Germans *loved* print; every sort of decree and form and official paper, signs and manuals and instruction sheets and direct-ives, they couldn't get enough of it. Especially that Gothic typeface. The Wehrmacht, as far as the printer could see, would rather publish than fight. Hell, he didn't mind. What with four kids and the wife pregnant and his old mother and her old mother and coal a hundred zlotys a sack on the black market, he had to do something. Don't misunderstand, he was a patriot, had served in the army, but there were mouths to feed.

This book? Yeah, he'd printed that. Where the hell had they ever found it? Look at that. Doesn't look too bad, does it? Quite a problem at first, didn't get a call for that sort of thing very often and he and his chief compositor – poor Wladek, killed in the war, rest in peace – had had to work it out together, combining different letters from a variety of fonts. Mostly it was just the usual thing but now and then you got a chance to be creative in this business and that made it all worthwhile did they know what he meant?

Do it again? Well, yes, shouldn't be a problem. He still had all, well almost all the letters he'd used for this book. He'd have to work at night, probably best to do the typesetting himself – if he remembered how. No, that was a joke. He remembered. What exactly did they need? Single sheet? A snap. Had to have it last week, he supposed. Wednesday soon enough? How many copies? *How* many? Jesus, the Germans kept him on a paper ration, there was no way he could – oh, well, if that was the way it was, no problem. As for the ink, he'd just add that into the German charges over the next few months, they'd never notice. Not that he habitually did that sort of thing, but, well . . .

It was December before all the other details could be sorted through and taken care of. Chomak spent two nights in the forest bordering the airfield, binoculars trained on the little hut. The light stayed on all night, a glow at the edges of the blackout curtain, and the watchman, a big, brawny fellow with white hair and a beer belly, was conscientious; made a tour of the field and the hangar twice a night.

They found a pilot – not so easy because Polish airmen who survived the war had gone to London and Paris to fight for the Allies. The man they located had flown mail and freight all around the Baltic, but poor eyesight had disqualified him for combat flying. When approached, he was anxious to take on the mission.

They picked up the printing in a taxi, storing the string tied bundles in Chomak's apartment. The mission was then scheduled for the ninth of December, but that night turned out cold and crisp, with a sky full of twinkling stars. Likewise the tenth and eleventh. The night of the twelfth, the weather turned bad, and the mission was on until an icy snow closed down every road out of Warsaw.

December fourteenth dawned warm and still, the snow turned to slush, and the sky was all fog and thick cloud. A wagon full of turnips transported the leaflets to a forest clearing near the airfield, then de Milja and the pilot arrived by bicycle an hour later. By 5:20 p.m. the field manager and the mechanic had gone home, and the night watchman had arrived. De Milja and his crew knocked on the door around seven. At first the watchman – a German it turned out – struggled and swore when they grabbed him and pulled a pillowcase over his head. Then he decided to cooperate and Chomak started to tie him up, but he changed his mind and got one hand loose and they had to hit him a few times before he'd calm down. Chomak and de Milja then rolled a plane to the gas pump and filled the tank. The pilot clambered in and studied the controls with a flashlight, while de Milja and Chomak pushed the plane to the edge of the grass runway.

At 8:20, Captain de Milja cranked the engine to life, the pilot made the thumbs-up sign, the plane bumped over the rocky field, picked up speed, then staggered up into the sky – airborne and flying a mission for free Poland.

The trick for the pilot was to get the plane *down* – quickly.

There certainly was hell to pay in the Warsaw air-defence sector – the Germans could hear something buzzing around up there in the clouds but they couldn't see it, the searchlight beams swept back and forth but all they found was grey mist. The anti-aircraft batteries let loose, the drone of the plane vanished to the west, the pilot headed around east on his compass until he picked up two petrol-in-a-barrel fires lit off by de Milja and Chomak, then wasted no time getting down on the lumpy field, since Luftwaffe nightfighters were just that moment slicing through the sky over Warsaw looking for something to shoot at.

Down below, hundreds of people broke the curfew to run outside and snatch up a leaflet. These were, with the aid of friends and dictionaries, soon enough deciphered – the English-style printing, as opposed to the usual Polish letters, made it just a little more difficult to read – and by breakfast time everybody in Warsaw and much of occupied Poland felt good the way one did when a friend came around to say hello.

To the Brave People of Poland

Greetings from your British allies. We are flying over your troubled land tonight to let you know that you are not forgotten. We'll be back soon, there will be lots more of us, and next time we won't be dropping leaflets. Until then, keep your chin up, and give the Germans hell any way you can.

Long live Poland!

Tenth Bomber Wing
RAF

'. . . but he changed his mind and they had to hit him a few times before he'd calm down.' Thus the night watchman at the Pruszkow airfield. But nothing more. De Milja had carried a small 9 mm automatic – there wasn't any point in not having something, not for him.

But Colonel Broza had said in their last meeting before the operation, 'Don't kill him, Captain. Let's not start that yet.'

Yet.

But then, it wasn't really up to them, of course it never had been, and the miracle was that fifty days or so of occupation had passed so – *peacefully*. Then it happened, out in Praga one Friday night, and that was that.

A workers' tavern in a workers' part of town. What was a Wehrmacht noncom even doing in such a place? Probably a worker himself, back in Dusseldorf or Essen or wherever it was. Not the classic Nazi – some fine-boned little blond shit quivering with rage and overbreeding, cursing Jews in a squeaky voice with saliva on his chin. The breed existed, but it didn't fight wars. Who fought wars was the guy in the Polish tavern: some big, blunt, slow-thinking German workingman, strong as an ox, common as dirt, and not such a bad type.

Here it was coming Christmas and he was stuck in Poland. He wasn't making out with the Polish girls, everything was a little grimier than he liked, there was garlic in his food, and people either wouldn't meet his eyes or glared with hatred. Hatred! Christ, he hadn't done anything. They put him in the army and they said go here, go there, and he went here and there. Who wouldn't? That was the way of the world; you did what the Wehrmacht told you to do, just like you did what Rheinmetall or Krupp told you to do.

And Friday night, like always, you went to a tavern, just to get out from underneath it a little. Ordered a beer, then another, and minded your own business.

But taverns were taverns, especially in working-class neighbour-hoods, and it was always the same: a word, a look, some little thing that just couldn't be ignored. And people who couldn't afford to lose their tempers brought them in here on Friday night in order to do exactly that. And then, some people didn't like Germans. Never had, never would. Maybe they thought that Hansi or Willi or whatever his name was was spoiling a good night's drinking. Just by being there. Maybe they told him to leave. Maybe Hansi or Willi had never been told to leave a tavern. Maybe he figured he was a conqueror. Maybe he refused.

Well, he wasn't a conqueror that night. Somebody took out a knife and put it just the right place and that was that. The Gestapo came running, hanged the tavern keeper over his own door and next day executed a hundred and twenty neighbourhood men. So there. The Germans were famous for reprisal long before they forced the Polish frontier. In 1914, stomping into Belgium, they encountered *franc-tireurs*

– snipers – and responded with heavy reprisals, shooting hundreds of Belgians when they couldn't get at the *franc-tireurs.* They didn't invent it – revenge killing was right up at the front of the Bible – but they believed in it.

And it was just about that time when Hans Frank, named governor-general of the swath of Poland around Warsaw not directly incorporated into Germany, wrote in his diary that 'the Poles will be the slaves of the German Reich'. Meanwhile they had the Jews sewing Stars of David on their breast pockets and hanging signs on the shops that said NICHT ARISCH, not Aryan.

The ZWZ was beseiged. Everybody wanted a piece of a German. De Milja didn't exactly recruit, but he did look over candidates before passing the name on to a committee, and the first two weeks of December he barely had time to do anything else.

Two days before Christmas, de Milja went to see the maid who was taking care of his father, a newspaper-wrapped parcel in hand: sausage, aspirin, and sewing needles, the latest items that had become impossible-to-get treasures. 'He wants to see you,' the woman said. 'He told me to tell you that.'

De Milja thought a moment; he was staying in the basement of a large apartment house in central Warsaw, just off Jerozolimskie Avenue, one of the city's main thoroughfares. 'There's a bar called Zofia, just by Solski Park, with a public room above it. Ten minutes after seven, tell him.' The maid nodded that she understood, but de Milja could see she disapproved of the idea that the professor would set foot in such a low place.

It *was* a low place, an after-curfew nightclub with a room upstairs that held three pool tables and an assortment of Warsaw lowlife – mostly black-market operators and pimps and their entourages. Tough guys; plenty of hair oil, overcoats with broad shoulders and ankle-length hems, a little bit of a cigarette stuck up in the corner of the mouth. They played pool, bet on the games, practised three-bank wizard shots, sold a tyre, bought a few pounds of sugar. De Milja liked it because someone was paying off the Germans to stay away, and that made it useful to people like him who'd had to learn one of the cardinal truths of secret life: anything clandestine is temporary. So the room above the Zofia was a welcome item on a list that could never be long enough.

Watching his father walk through the smoky poolroom, de Milja felt a pang in his heart. With hair combed faultlessly to one side, and round tortoiseshell spectacles, he looked like photographs of T.S. Eliot, the

English banker/poet. His face was thinner and brighter than de Milja remembered, and he wore a raincoat, not his winter overcoat. Where was that? de Milja wondered. Sold? Clutching his professorial briefcase tightly, he excused his way through the crowd, ignoring the stares of the poolroom toughs. Some of them would have liked to humiliate him – he was an inviting target, a large ungainly bird who cried out for insult – but he was moving faster than they realized and before the right words could be said, he was gone. He paused while a boy with a huge pompadour and a royal-blue suit squinted down his cue to line up a shot, and winked suddenly at his son: *there in a minute, must wait while Euclid here gets it all worked out.* Thus had his father survived years of the Ostrow uncles: the more his sensibilities were offended, the more he twinkled.

They shook hands, his father settled himself at the table, noting the rough wood with hearts and initials carved in it, the water glass of vodka, wilted beet slices on a plate, and a saltshaker. 'How've you been?' he asked.

De Milja smiled. 'Not so bad. You?'

That was ignored. 'Most thoughtful of you, that package. We ate the sausage, and sent the aspirin and the needles on to your mother and sister. They are in Hungary, I believe Sonya told you. Near Eger, in a sort of tumbledown castle – decrepit nobility wearing earmuffs at the dinner table, very Old World, I'm sure.'

'I think you should join them.'

'Me? What would I do for a library? Besides, I still have students, a few anyhow. As long as they show up, I will.'

'But Hungary is safe, you think.'

The professor hesitated. 'Yes. They're just now Germany's great friends. Maybe later it will turn out they loved England all along. In their secret heart, you see.'

'And the house?'

'Cold as a donkey's dick.' A sly smile bloomed for a moment – *shocked you, did I?* 'I've got newspapers stuffed in every crack, but it doesn't seem to help.'

'Look, why don't you let me find you an apartment—'

The professor cut him short. 'Really, you needn't bother.' Then he leaned closer and lowered his voice. 'But there is something I want you to do.' He paused, then said, 'Am I correct in assuming you've been recruited into the underground? That you remain under military orders?'

De Milja nodded yes.

'Are you anything important?'

No reaction, at first, then a slight shrug: *important?*

But the professor was not to be fended off. 'Don't be coy. Either you can talk to the leadership or you can't.'

'I can.' De Milja felt his ears getting warm.

His father searched his face, then decided he was telling the truth – it really was some other boy who'd thrown the chalk – reached into his briefcase and surfaced with three pages of densely written pen-and-ink script. 'For the right person, this would be of consequence,' he said.

'What is it?'

'A study.' His father stared at it a moment. 'The research is thin. I merely talked to a few of my old students, had a coffee, a little gossip. But they're smart – that I know for a certainty because I made them prove it more than once – and well placed. Not at the very top of the civil service but just below it, where they actually read the paper and make the decisions and tell the boss what to say. Anyhow, it's the best that I could do, an outline, but useful to the right people.'

He paused for effect. 'The point is, I'd like to be asked to do more.' He met de Milja's eyes. 'Is that clear? Because what I have in mind is far more ambitious, an ongoing study that—'

A sudden commotion interrupted him; two of the local princes had reversed their pool cues and were snarling at each other while friends held them back. When de Milja looked back at his father he caught him with a particular expression on his face: irritation, disappointment, why did he have to see his son in places like this? Why wasn't it a faculty dining room or an intellectuals' café? The response was irrational – he would have admitted that – but it was the truth of his heart and for a moment he'd forgotten to hide it.

De Milja took the papers from his father's hand. 'I can only promise that it will be read.'

'Well, naturally. I don't expect more than that.'

De Milja glanced at his watch. 'I'd like to spend more time, but if you're going to get back home before curfew . . .'

His father stood quickly. 'You'll be in touch?' he said.

'Through Sonya.'

They said good-bye; it was awkward, as their time together always was. They shook hands, both started to say something, shook hands again, then parted. At the door, his father turned and looked back; de Milja started to wave but he was too late. The raincoat and briefcase disappeared through the doorway, and de Milja never saw him again.

It was cold in Warsaw that night, there was ice in Captain de Milja's basement room; a rust-coloured stalactite that hung from a connection in the water pipe that ran across his ceiling. A janitor had once lived here, his church calendar – little girls praying with folded hands – and his French movie star torn from a magazine, a Claudette Colbert look-alike, were still stuck on nails in the wall. Cold enough to die, the captain thought. Wondered how cold that actually had to be. He wore an army greatcoat, a scarf, and wool gloves as he sat on the edge of a cot and by the light of a candle read the report his father had written.

He read it twice, then again. The writing was plain enough, and the facts were not obscure – just a listing of things governments did on a daily basis; a few administrative procedures, some new policies and guidelines. Really, not very interesting. But look again, he told himself. *Principles of the German Occupation of Poland: 10 December 1939.* There wasn't anything in the report that Colonel Broza and the directorate didn't know – all his father and his informants had done was to gather up what was available and synthesize it. Three pages. Four principles:

1) Calculated devaluation of the currency. 2) Replacement of the judiciary. 3) Direction of labour. 4) Registration. That was all – the real, arid horror of the thing lay in its simplicity. The essential mechanics of slavery, it turned out, weren't at all complicated. With registration you knew who and what and where everyone was – a Jew or a metallurgical engineer, it was all filed for future reference. With the direction of labour they worked where you wanted, and had to meet production norms you set. With your own judiciary, you controlled their behaviour with their own police. And with devaluation of the currency you 'bought' everything they owned or produced, and then you starved them to death.

De Milja passed the report to Colonel Broza in Room 9. The colonel put on his reading glasses and thumbed the pages over. 'Yes,' he said, and 'mmm,' and finally 'thank you.' That was all.

But there was something much more troubling on the agenda that day: the man who had printed the RAF leaflets had been arrested in his shop by the Gestapo. 'Find out about it,' Broza said. 'Then see Grodewicz.'

He went to visit the printer's wife. They lived in a quite good neighbourhood – surprisingly good for a man with a small job shop – broad avenues with trees, solid apartment houses with fire-escape ladders on the alley side, toilets in the apartments instead of the usual privies in the courtyard, and a building superintendent, a heavy woman in a kerchief, polite and not a bit drunk. De Milja asked her about the family. She took notice of his warm coat, and heavy, well-made shoes and raised her palms to heaven: didn't know, didn't want to get involved.

The apartment was on the seventh floor, the top of the building. De

Milja trudged up the endless staircase, the marble steps grey from years of scrubbing with Javel water. He stopped to get his breath at the door, then knocked. The wife was a small woman, tepid, harmless, in a faded apron. They sat at the kitchen table. 'I don't know what he did,' she said.

'What about the neighbours?'

'Mostly they only knew me. And I never made an enemy, Mister.'

He believed her. 'And him?'

'He was away, you know. Here and there. Some wives, they know when their husband breathes in, when he breathes out. Not me. You couldn't do that with him.'

'What did you imagine?'

'Imagine? I only know we had a lot – a lot for who he was and what he did. He was ambitious, my husband. And maybe rules weren't made for him, you know? But nothing serious. I swear it. Whoever you are, wherever you come from, go back and tell them he didn't do anything so wrong.'

She started to cry but she didn't care, didn't touch her face where the tears ran and didn't seem to notice it; everybody cried these days, so what?

'Are you in touch with the Gestapo?'

She nodded that she was. 'On Szucha Avenue.'

That wasn't good – Szucha Avenue was the central Gestapo head-quarters. 'I go every week to get his laundry,' she continued. 'Do the wash and bring it back.' Her eyes found his, just for an instant. 'There's blood on his underwear,' she said.

'We can stop the interrogation,' he said.

Just for a moment she believed him, and her eyes widened, then she realized it was a lie.

'He did something for us,' de Milja said. 'For the underground. Will he tell them?'

She wiped the tears away from her face with her hand. 'Not him,' she said. 'If only he would – but he won't.'

'A last question,' he said. 'How did they catch him?'

She thought for a time, stared out the window at the grey sky over the winter city. 'Betrayed,' she said. 'He never gave himself away.'

She was right, de Milja thought. He sensed it wasn't the jealous neighbour, or the business partner with a grudge. It wasn't a denuncia-tion in that sense. He went to see another detective, a man with a big stomach and white hair, who had a line into the Gestapo office on Szucha Avenue. A clerk, perhaps, or a janitor. Information was fragmentary, and uncertain – as though somebody saw an open register, or a list on a desk. Nonetheless, his question was answered: Chomak.

De Milja hadn't expected that. 'Why?' he asked.

The detective shrugged. 'A man reaches a certain time in life, and a certain conclusion. He's alone. For himself. At war with the world. So he'll do this for that one, and that for this one – he's a spider, this is his web. *Everybody* is corrupt, he thinks. So he'd better be the same.'

It wasn't much, de Milja thought. But there might never be any more, and they were at war, so it had to be enough. As Broza had directed, he went to see Grodewicz. They met at night in the office of a broom factory.

He had known Grodewicz for a long time, they belonged to the same social class, were not quite the same age but had overlapped for a year or two at university. While de Milja had laboured desperately – and, it turned out, fruitlessly – to be a mathematician, Grodewicz had thrown himself into drinking and fighting and whoring to such a degree that it had become an issue with the police, and eventually with the university authorities, who finally had to expel him. What bothered de Milja was that Grodewicz not only didn't care, he didn't suffer. He walked away from university life, served as a merchant seaman, was said to have smuggled emeralds into the Balkans from South America, killed a shipmate in a knife fight, screwed a movie star in Vienna. Too many rumours about Grodewicz were true, he thought.

De Milja watched Grodewicz as he spoke quietly into the telephone – making him wait, naturally. He had long, lank, yellow hair that hung over his forehead, was handsome in some indefinably unhealthy way, and arrogant in every bone in his body. Now *Captain* Grodewicz – perhaps a post-invasion commission. De Milja sensed he'd gone to war not because Poland had been attacked, but because Grodewicz had been insulted.

'We'll paint the south wall first,' Grodewicz said, obviously using code, from memory and with great facility. 'And extend the line of the roof over that window, the south window. Is it clear?'

Grodewicz met de Milja's glance and winked at him. 'Good,' he said. 'Just exactly. Plumb line, chisel, ripsaw and so forth. Can you manage?' The answer evidently pleased Grodewicz, who smiled and made a galloping rhythm with three fingers on the desk. 'I would think,' he said. 'Maybe we'll all move in.' He replaced the receiver on its cradle.

They talked for a few minutes. De Milja explained what he needed, Grodewicz said there would be no problem – he had people ready to do that sort of work. They smoked a cigarette, said nothing very important, and went off into the night. The following day de Milja went to a certain

telephone booth, opened the directory to a prearranged page, underlined a word on the second line, which set the rendezvous two days in
the future; circled a word on the eighteenth line: 6:00 p.m.; and crossed
through the twenty-second letter: 6:22 p.m. Very quickly, and very
painfully, the ZWZ had learned the vulnerability of personal contact.
Telephone books were safer.

It worked. The operative was on time, appearing suddenly in a heavy
snow of soft, wet flakes that muffled the streets and made it hard to see.
God, he was young, de Milja thought. Moonfaced, which made him
seem placid. Hands shoved in the pockets of a baggy overcoat.

Chomak's dachshund knew right away who he was. It exploded in a
fit of barking and skittered about at the detective's feet until his wife
gathered it up in her arms and went into another room.

They took the evening workers' train across the Vistula. The snow
was falling thickly now, and looking out the window, de Milja could just
see the iron-coloured river curling slowly around the piers of a bridge.
Nobody talked on this train; it had been a long day in the factories and
they didn't have the strength for it. De Milja and Chomak and the
operative stood together in the aisle, holding on to the tops of the seats
as the train swayed through the turns, the steamy windows white with
snow blown sideways by the wind. At the second stop, a neighbourhood
of red-brick tenements, they got off the train and found a small bar near
the station. They sat at a table and drank home-brewed beer.

'We're trying to find out about the printer,' de Milja said. 'The
Gestapo arrested him.'

Chomak shrugged. 'Inevitable,' he said.

'Why do you say that?'

'He was a thief,' Chomak said. 'A Jew thief.'

'Really? How do you know?'

'Everybody knew,' Chomak said. 'He was clever, very clever, just in
the way he went around, in the way he did things. He was always up to
something – you only had to look at him to see it.'

'And the Gestapo, you think, acted on that?'

Chomak thought for a time, then shrugged and lit a cigarette. De
Milja saw that his hand was shaking. 'Types like that get into trouble,'
he said after the silence had gone on a little too long. 'Sooner or later.
Then they get caught. It's a flaw they have.'

De Milja nodded slowly, the dark side of human nature making him
pensive. 'Well,' he said, 'we can't be late for our meeting.'

'You don't think *I* did anything, do you?'

'No.' Pause. 'Did you? Maybe by accident?'

'Not me.'

'Time to go,' de Milja said. Then to Chomak: 'You're armed?'

'You didn't tell me to bring anything, so I didn't. I have to tell you, I don't care for being suspected. That's not right.'

De Milja stood up and left, Chomak following, the operative waving Chomak out the door ahead of him. 'Don't worry about it,' de Milja said.

Hunched over in the cold and the snow, they hurried along a narrow street that wound back towards the railway. Chomak took a fast two steps and caught up with de Milja. 'Why would you ask me a thing like that?' He had to raise his voice a little because of the wind and it made him sound querulous and insulted. 'I served fourteen years in the detectives.' He was angry now. 'We knew who did what. That type, you're always on the short end of the deal – just once turn your back and then you'll see.'

A Gestapo car, a black Grosser Mercedes with headlights taped down to slits because of the blackout, honked at them to get out of the way. They stood with their backs against the wall, faces averted, as it bumped past, the red tail-lights disappearing into the swirling snow.

'You see?' Chomak said, when they were walking again. 'I could have flagged them down. But I didn't, did I?'

At an arched railway bridge, where the street dipped below the track, de Milja signalled to stop, and the three men stood by the curved wall and stamped their feet to keep warm. It was dark under the bridge and the snow was blowing right through it.

'Hell of a night for a meeting,' Chomak said, a good-natured laugh in his voice.

De Milja heard the sound of a train approaching in the distance. Bending over to protect the match from the wind, he lit a cigarette, then cupped his palm to shield the glow. 'Face the wall,' he said to Chomak.

'What did you say?'

'Face the wall.'

Chomak turned slowly and faced the wall. The approaching train was moving slowly because of the snowstorm. 'It's not right,' Chomak said. 'For a Jew thief. Some little sneak from the gutter. Not right.'

'Why would you do a thing like that?' de Milja said. 'Were you in trouble?'

De Milja could see that Chomak's legs were trembling, and he thought he might collapse. He looked at the operative and their eyes met for a moment as the train came closer. The sound of the wheels thundered in the tunnel as it passed overhead, Chomak bounced off the wall, then sagged back against it, his hand groping for a hold on the smooth surface. Very slowly, he slid down to his knees, then toppled over on his side. The operative straddled him and fired once into his temple.

January 1940. The French planes did not come. Perhaps, people thought, they are not going to come. Not ever. In the streets of Paris, the Communist party and its supporters marched and chanted for peace, for dignity, for an end to war. Especially this unjust war against Germany – Russia's ally. On the Maginot Line, quartered in a school-house near Strasbourg, Private Jean-Paul Sartre of the artillery's meteorological intelligence service sent balloons aloft, reported on the speed and direction of the wind to gunners who never fired a shot, and wrote in his journal that '*Life* is the transcendent, psychic object constructed by human reality in search of its own foundation.'

In Great Britain, German magnetic mines had taken a considerable toll of merchant shipping, and rationing had been established for butter, sugar, bacon, and ham. Winston Churchill spoke on the radio, and told the nations of Europe that 'each one hopes that if he feeds the crocodile enough, the crocodile will eat him last. All of them hope that the storm will pass before their turn comes to be devoured.'

As for the United States, it remained stern and unrelenting in the maintenance of a 'moral embargo' it had declared against Germany.

Meanwhile, Warsaw lived in ice. The calendar froze – a winter of ten thousand days was at hand. And as the hope of help from friends slowly waned, it became the time of the prophecies. Sometimes typed, some-times handwritten, they were everywhere and, whether casually dis-missed or secretly believed, were passionately followed. A battlefield of contending spectres: rune-casters and biblical kings, the Black Madonna of Czestochowa and Nostradamus, the fire at the centre of the earth, the cycles of the moon, the springs of magic water, the Apocrypha – the fourteen known books and the fifteenth, only just now revealed. The day was coming, it couldn't quite be said exactly when, but blood would flow from stones, the dead would rise from their graves, the lame would walk, the blind would see, and the fucking *shkopy* would get out of Poland.

At a time when national consolation was almost non-existent, the prophecies helped, strange as some of them were, and the intelligence service of the Polish underground certainly wrote their share. Mean-while, hiding in their apartments from winter and the Gestapo, the people of Warsaw listened – on pain of death if caught – to the BBC on illicit radios. And they also studied English. That winter in Warsaw, an English grammar couldn't be had for love or money. Even so, the joke everybody was telling around town went like this: the pessimists are learning German, the optimists are learning English, while the realists, in January of 1940, were said to be learning Russian.

In Room 9, Agata leaned back from the committee table, ran long fingers through her chopped-off hair, blew savage plumes of smoke from her nostrils, and said, 'Next. The eastern zone, and the need to do something about the Russians. As of yesterday, a courier reported six more arrests by the NKVD.'

It had been a long meeting, not a good one, with too many problems tabled for future consideration. Colonel Broza did not respond – he stared absently at a map of Poland tacked to the green wall, but there was certainly little comfort for him there.

'The efficiency of the NKVD,' Agata went on, 'seems only to increase. They are everywhere, how to say, *inside our lines.* In the professions, the peasantry – there is no social class we can turn to. People in the Russian zone have simply stopped talking to their friends – and I can't imagine anything that hurts us more than that. The fear is on the streets, in the air. Of our top echelon, political and military, nothing remains; those who are alive are in the Lubianka, and out of contact. From the officer camps in the Katyn forest it's the same thing: no escapes, no letters, silence. So, since it is Poland's great privilege to play host to both the NKVD and the Gestapo, it's time to admit we are not doing all that badly with the Germans, but have not yet learned how to operate against the Russians.'

Broza thought about it for a time. 'Why?' he said.

'Why are the Russians better at it?' Agata said.

'Yes.'

'Oh, tradition. A thousand years of espionage, the secret police of Ivan the Terrible – is that what you want to hear?'

Broza's expression was grim, almost despairing – wasn't there perhaps a little more to it? No? Maybe?

Agata tapped a pencil eraser against the open page of a notebook. 'There is a difference,' she said slowly, 'that interests me. Say that it is the difference between nationalism and, ah, what we might call social theory. For the Germans, nationalism is an issue of race, ethnicity. For example, they accept as their own the *Volksdeutsch* – descendents of German colonists, many of whom do not even speak German. But their blood is German blood – these Teutonic philosophers really believe in such things. Cut a vein, listen closely, you can hear the overture to *Lohengrin* – why, that's a *German* you've got there! The Bolsheviks are just the opposite – they recruit the mind, or so they like to pretend. And all the world is invited to join them; you can be a communist any time you like – "Good heavens! I just realized it's all in the dictatorship of the working class."

'Now as a practical matter, that difference serves the purposes of the NKVD very nicely. We all accept that every society has its opportunists – criminals, misfits, unrecognized geniuses, the pathologically disappointed – and when the conqueror comes, that's the moment to even the score. But, here in western Poland, the only job open is collaborator – you can't just get up in the morning and decide to be German. On the Soviet side, however, you can experience insight, then conversion, and you'll be welcomed. Oh, you may have to tattle a little; tell the NKVD whatever you happen to know – and everybody knows *something*. You can invite your former friends to join you in conspiracies, you can inform on your enemies. And what are you then? A traitor? No, a friend of peace and the working class. And, if you turn out to have a bit of a flair for the work, you can be a commissar.'

Agata paused a moment, lit a new cigarette. 'And if that's not bad enough,' she said, shaking out the match, 'the NKVD is very shrewd, and never in a hurry. They follow the spirit of resistance like a hidden current running through an ocean: they detain, interrogate, torture, turn a few to work for them, shoot the rest, and start over.'

Colonel Broza nodded slowly. 'Tyranny,' he said, 'has become a science.' He turned to de Milja. 'What do you think we can do, Captain?'

De Milja was in no hurry to answer. 'Perhaps, over time, we'll prove to be stronger than they are. But right now, I would say the important thing for us is to hammer at the links between the Germans and the Russians. For us, in this room, the worst would be if NKVD methods were to spread to the Gestapo.'

'We know they've been meeting in Cracow,' Grodewicz said, 'but the Russians aren't sharing much. They cooperate by handing over German communists who fled to Moscow in the thirties, but they don't talk about methods.'

'That is because,' Agata said, 'they are going to fight.'

'Yes. They must, eventually,' Broza said. He thought a moment, then his eyes met de Milja's. 'Take some time and a few people, Captain. See if you can get a sense of when that might be.'

A week later, he left the freezing basement. Life immediately improved, was certainly warmer, better in a number of ways. He moved to a room in the Mokotow district, down a long hallway in the apartment of a former customs official, now a clerk in a factory office and a great friend to the resistance. Since the occupation authority had closed the schools – Poles, as a slave race, needed only to understand simple directions and to count to twenty – the official's wife taught at a secret school in a church basement while the children attended classes.

That left de Milja alone in the apartment for much of the day. Alone, except for Madame Kuester. Fortyish, probably a little older, a distant cousin of one side of the family or the other, she had met and married a Dutch engineer – Herr Kuester – who had gone off to work on a bridge in Kuala Lumpur in 1938, then vanished. Madame Kuester, childless, had then come to stay with the family. Not quite a servant, not quite an equal, she had worked in fashionable women's shops before the war, lived quietly in her room, proud of not being a burden to anyone. The title 'madame' was a survival of the world of the shops, where she had been, evidently, a bad-tempered and difficult supervisor to a generation of young assistants.

Given the hours of proximity, a love affair seemed inevitable. But the captain resisted. A deep, almost haunted longing for the wife who wasn't there, a nominal – and sometimes not so nominal – Catholicism, and ZWZ security procedures: everything was against it. Including the attitude of Madame Kuester, haughty and cold, clearly meant to discourage familiarity between two people forced by war into the accidental intimacies of apartment life.

She was, de Milja came to understand, a snob to her very marrow. She set herself above the world, looking down on its unrefined excesses with small, angry eyes set in a great expanse of white brow. Her mouth was mean, down-curved, she wore her coarse hair elaborately pinned up, went about the apartment in grey blouse and long wool skirt – the prewar uniform of some of the better shops – that hung shapeless over a thick, heavy figure, and her walk, hard and definitive, told the world all it needed to know: *you have left me alone, now leave me alone.*

But it was cold, always cold.

The February snow hissed against the window, the afternoons were silent, and dark, and endless. Captain de Milja was now subject to increased ZWZ security constraints; stay out of the centre of Warsaw, where police patrols were abundant, try not to be on the streets during working hours – use the morning and evening travel periods as cover for getting around the city. He had to hold agent meetings as he probed for German intentions towards the USSR, but he scheduled them early in the morning and late in the afternoon, always in public places – libraries, railway stations, the thicker the crowd the better he liked it. But for much of the day he was a prisoner in the Mokotow apartment.

Where he discovered that he was keeping track of Madame Kuester by the sound of her presence: the scrape of the match as she lit the stove for midmorning tea, the rhythm of a carpet sweeper rolled relentlessly back and forth, the polite slam of a firmly closed door as she retired to her room for a midday rest, the creak of the bedspring as she lay down to nap.

Every afternoon at about 2:35, that was. She rather believed, he sensed, in the idea of routine, consistency. It was the way *her sort of people* – never defined, yet always with her – chose to live. After lunch she would sit primly in the corner of the sofa, then, after forty-five minutes of reading, rise majestically and disappear into her room. On Sunday, with the family present, everything was different, but six days a week her habit never varied, never changed.

Well, perhaps just once it did. On an otherwise unremarkable day in the middle of the week, she forgot her book. Ha! What absurdly spiteful joy he felt at such a lapse. He was immediately ashamed of himself, but there it lay, open, face down on the arm of the sofa, protected by the blue paper cover she fussily wrapped her books in. Curious, he had a look. French. Well, of course, he should have known. A French novel, the very thing *her sort of people* would amuse themselves with.

De Milja scanned the page to see what kept Madame so occupied that she hadn't a thought for the rest of the world. '. . . *dans une position en lequel ses places ombrées étaient, comme on dit, disponibles, mais c'était le sens de la caresse de l'aire sur elles, ces ouvertures, qui faisait battre fort son coeur . . .*'

What?

In pure astonishment and disbelief he slipped the cover off the novel: *La Belle Dominique*. Written by that well-known and time-honoured author, Vaguely Saucy Nom de Plume. The French novel was a French novel! He flipped the pages, and read some more, and flipped the pages, and read some more. It was the sheer contrast of the moment that struck his heart. The dying, ice-bound city, heavy with fear and misery and the exhaustion of daily life, set against these brittle pages of print, where gold passementerie was untied and heavy drapes flowed together, where pale skin flushed rose with excitement, where silk rustled to the floors of moonlit chambers.

De Milja's eyes sought the door to Madame Kuester's room, which, in defiance of her cherished routine, stood open a suggestive inch. He opened it the rest of the way and stepped inside. A small room in a Warsaw apartment, winter light yellow behind the drawn shade, an old steamer trunk used as a wardrobe, a shape curled up on a cot beneath a wool army blanket.

As in a dream, she drew her knees up, arched her back like a yawning cat, then rolled slowly onto her stomach and nestled against the bed. One hand snaked out of the covers and smoothed the loose hair off the side of her face. Now he could see that her eyes were closed, but she smiled a little smile for him; greedy and bittersweet and sure of itself all at once. And if, somehow, he still didn't get the point, she breathed a soft, interrogatory sigh. He stepped to the side of the bed and lowered the blanket to her bare heels. She moved a little, just the signature on an invitation, took the pillow in both hands, and slid it under her body until it rested beneath her hips. Which elevated her, he thought as he undid his belt, '*to such a position that her shadowed places were, as it is said, available, but it was the feeling of the touch of the air upon them, these openings, that made her heart beat hard.*'

They never spoke of it, not ever. *One doesn't* – that was her unspoken law and he obeyed it. So she remained, in the daily life of the apartment, as remote and distant as she had always been. He spent the middle part of the day with his notes and papers, mostly numbers and coded place names, while she, nose in the air, dusted, and ran the carpet sweeper over the rugs. She read every day after lunch, sitting properly in the corner of the sofa. Then, at 2:35, she went to her room. He followed a few minutes later, and found each time a different woman. In this bed, for this hour, everything was possible. It was as though, he thought, they owned in common a theatre under a blanket where, every after-noon, they rehearsed and performed for an audience of themselves. Only themselves. The city would not know of it – at the conclusion of each scene she stuffed the blanket into her down-curved mouth and screamed like a Fury.

Wizna, on the Narew River, 7 March 1940. Encampment of the Nine-teenth Infantry Division, Grenadierregiment, Wehrkreis XIV, Kassel. 5:30 a.m. The floodlights were turned out and the dawn fog pooled at the bases of the barbed-wire stanchions. The Russian troops were camped on the other side of the river; when they ran the engines of their tanks, the Wehrmacht soldiers could hear them.

Each day at dawn the garbage cans were brought out to the regi-mental dump on hand trucks; the contents spilled out with a spirited banging, the garbage detail working in shirtsleeves despite the bitter cold, cigarettes stuck in their mouths to mask the smell. First the dogs came, trotting, heads down, silent – precedence had been established in the first days of occupation and there were no more fights. Next came the old Polish women in their black shawls and dresses, each holding a stick to beat the dogs if they got too insistent.

Oberschützen Kohler and Stentz, the two privates first-class on guard duty, stood and watched the Polish women, dark figures in the morning fog, as they picked through the mounds of garbage. This guard duty was permanent, and they did it every morning. They didn't like it, but they knew nobody cared about that, so they didn't, either.

At the age of nineteen, though, it was a sad lesson. These women, fated to spend this early hour picking through the garbage of a German garrison in order to have something to eat – could they be so different from their own mothers and grandmothers? Kohler and Stentz were not barbarians, they were Wehrmacht riflemen, not so different from generations of infantry, Swedish or Prussian or Corsican or Austrian – the list was just too long – who had stood guard at camps on these Polish rivers back into the time of the Roman legions.

Kohler looked around, made sure there were no officers in the vicinity, then he tapped Stentz on the shoulder. Stentz whistled a certain clever way, and the crone showed up a few moments later like she always did. Her face, all seamed and gullied beneath wisps of thin, white hair, never stopped nodding, *thank you, Excellency, thank you, Excellency*, as she moved to the edge of the barbed wire. She reached out trembling hands and took the crusts of bread that Stentz got from a friend in the camp kitchen. These vanished into her clothing, kept separate from whatever was in the burlap sack she carried over her shoulder. She mumbled something – she had no teeth and was hard to understand, but it was certainly thankful. It wished God's mercy on them. Heaven had seen, she was certain, this kindness to an old woman.

Later that morning she walked to the edge of her village to meet the man who bought rags. For him too she thanked God, because these were not very good rags, they were used, worn-out rags with very little rubbing and cleaning left in them. Still, he paid. She had petrol-soaked rags from the motor pool, damp, foul rags that had been used to clean the kitchens, brown rags the soldiers used to polish their boots, a few shreds of yellow rag they used to shine brass with, and some of the oily little patches they used to clean their rifles.

The rag man bought everything, as he always did, and counted out a few coppers into her hand – just as he would for all the other old ladies who came to see him throughout the morning. Only a few coppers, but if you had enough of them they bought something. Everybody was in business now, she thought, it was always that way when the armies came. Too bad about the nice boys who gave her the bread. They would die, pretty soon, nice or not. Sad, she thought, how they never learned what waited for them in Poland.

7 March 1940, Budapest. The offices of Schlegel and Son, stock and commodity exchange brokers based in Zurich. Mr Teleky, the brisk

young transfer clerk, took the morning prices off the teletype just before noon and wrote them in chalk on a blackboard hung from the oak panelling in the customers' room. Behind a wooden railing a few old men sat and smoked, bored and desultory. War was bad for the brokerage business, as far as Mr Teleky could see. People put their money into gold coins and buried them in the basement – nobody believed in the futures market when nobody believed in the future.

Still, you acted as though everything would come out for the best – where would you go in the morning if you didn't go to work? Mr Teleky printed the morning numbers in a careful hand. A few customers were watching. Gottwald, the German Jew, trying to make the money he'd earned selling his wife's jewellery go a little further. Standing next to him was Schaumer, the Austrian Nazi party functionary, who came here to speculate with money stolen from Viennese Jews. Then there was Varski, the old Polish diplomat who walked with a cane, proud and poor, earning a few francs one day and losing them the next. Mr Teleky privately wondered why he bothered, but you couldn't talk to the Poles, they were hardheaded and did what they wanted, you might as well argue with the sea.

So, what did he have for these august gentlemen? Cairo cotton was up a point, Brazilian coffee unchanged, London wool down a quarter and so was flax, iron ore had gained half a point, coal was off an eighth. Trading in manganese was suspended – the Germans meddling, no doubt. Mr Teleky went on and on, rendering each symbol and number carefully, for whoever might want to come to the Schlegel offices and witness the fluctuations of world trade. Gottwald turned on his heel and left, then Schaumer. Varski the Pole stayed until the bitter end, then stood, nodded politely to Mr Teleky, and went on about his daily business.

The chemist and the commodity analyst.

The chemist in Lodz – the traditional home of industrial chemistry in Poland, where dyes for the fabric mills had been produced since the nineteenth century – wrote the most careful, the most studied report of his professional life. If he'd been an indifferent patriot before September, '39, before dead friends and vanished family, before his house was taken and his salary halved, he wasn't one now.

Now he was a patriot of reports. He had tested, and retested, used infinite care, worked to the very limit of his technical abilities. And his conclusion was:

No change.

An analysis of seventy-five samples selected from a range of over five thousand cotton patches bearing traces of the oil used to clean and maintain weapons showed no meaningful variation in the viscosity of the oil. Samples were obtained from disposal areas abandoned by Wehrmacht units in September of 1939 – in eastern, now Russian-occupied, Poland – and these were compared with samples from bases currently occupied in Silesia, East Prussia, and western Poland. The analysed material, a lightly refined petroleum-based oil also used in machine shops for lubrication and protection of bored and rifled metal surfaces, had not been significantly altered during the seven-month period in question. The viscosity of the oil was consistent to a low temperature of $-5°$ Fahrenheit, but below that point effectiveness was rapidly degraded. For the maintenance and cleaning of rifled weapons below $-5°$ Fahrenheit, a lower viscosity, lighter-weight oil would be required.

The commodity analyst in Warsaw was a Jew, and suspected he hadn't long to live. A few people he knew of had managed to leave Poland, but most hadn't. The German Jews had been attacked by means of taxation and bureaucratic constraint since the ascension of the Nazi government in 1933 – a six-year period. Two thirds of them, about four hundred thousand people, had gotten out of Germany before the borders closed. They had bribed South American consular officials, filled the British quotas in Palestine, deployed wealth and influence to evade immigration regulations in the United States and Great Britain. But in using those methods they had, in effect, worn out the administrative escape lines. For the three million Polish Jews, there was nothing.

So the commodity analyst, a yellow Star of David sewn to the breast pocket of a suit made by a London tailoring establishment in 1937, wrote what he believed to be his final report. Since the German occupation he had worked in a small factory that made needles and pins, sweeping up, running errands, whatever was needed, but even this little job was ending. And he had been told that he and his family would have to move into the old Polish ghetto just south of Gdansk station. The Germans meant to kill him, a forty-eight-year-old man with a wife and three children. If there was something he could do about that, some tactic of evasion, he had not been able to discover it. He had a good mind, trained in Talmud, trained in business, and recognized that some problems cannot be solved. What would happen next would happen next, it wasn't up to him.

He would have liked to be, in this analysis written at the request of an old friend, brilliant, at least ingenious. He had specialized in the behaviour of the wool markets for twenty years, and he thought he knew them just about as well as anyone could. But facts were facts, numbers worked a certain way, and after an intensive study of twelve

645

months of buying and selling activity in the commodity exchanges of London, Chicago, and Geneva, there was only one, rather dull but plainly evident, conclusion to be drawn:

No change.

Captain de Milja met privately with Colonel Broza in Room 9. Outside, the evening streets were awash with spring rain. 'There is no preparation to attack,' de Milja said.

'Hard to believe that,' Broza said.

'Yes. But that is what we found. Germany will have to deploy three million men to attack Russia, led by tanks as they were in Poland. Supplied by horse and wagon, and freight train. Attacking on a line from the Baltic to the Black Sea. As for the time of the attack, that too can be deduced. Today is the sixteenth of March. Russia must be invaded in the late spring, after the rivers crest and the floods recede, and it must be defeated by the middle of autumn, before the winter freeze. Napoleon learned that in 1812, and very little has changed since then. The temperature in Russia in December goes down, habitually and unremarkably, to minus thirty degrees Fahrenheit. It can go lower, and when the wind blows – which it does, for weeks on end – the cold is acutely intensified. You can't send three million men into that kind of weather without preparation.

'So, we have the sixteenth of March and three million men. As of a week ago, not a drop of low-viscosity oil had been issued at any Wehrmacht base we know about. And there has been no change in the international wool markets – which means no warm coats for the Wehrmacht. The Germans have been clever all along about covert logistics – disguised orders for chemicals and rubber – but you can't slaughter millions of sheep or buy up that much wool production without a reaction from the markets. So if the Wehrmacht goes east in April, they'll go without wool coats, and by January they'll freeze to death with useless rifles in their hands.'

Broza wasn't so sure. 'Perhaps. But Hitler thinks he'll be in Moscow by late October – that's the point of the blitzkrieg. They'll take their wool coats from the cloakroom at the Kremlin. What's to stop them? The Red Army is sick as a dog; officers shot in the purges, all the tactics they tried in Finland failed miserably.'

'The Russians *won't* stop them. They'll slow them down, bleed their strength – it will be some variation on defence-in-depth.'

Broza paused to consider that. Defence-in-depth was the ancient, traditional military doctrine of Russia. For a thousand years, they'd protected their cities by use of the abatis: trees cut down at the three-foot level, the logs hung up on the stumps and pointing out towards the enemy. Among the felled trees were pits camouflaged with cut brush – intended to break the ankle of a horse or a man. These defences were eighty miles deep. With raiding parties harassing their flanks, an invasion force would find itself exhausted when it finally reached the site the Russians had chosen as a battleground.

By 1938, building what was called the Stalin Line on the USSR's western boundary, various refinements had been added: artificial lakes – five feet deep, to tempt an invader to try a crossing – artificial marsh, cornfields cut to accommodate enfilading machine gun fire, concrete bunkers three feet thick, with barbed wire now tangled in the trunks of the fallen trees.

'Defence-in-depth doesn't happen overnight,' Broza said, thinking out loud. 'And the Stalin Line is being dismantled now that the Russians have moved up to the middle of Poland. That advance may cost them more than they suspect.'

'They will sacrifice lives,' de Milja said. 'And land. Burn the villages, blow up the bridges.'

Broza thumbed through a sheaf of papers in a dossier. 'Granted, they are not distributing light oil for the winter, and they are not buying sheepskins. But we know they are building large hospitals on the border. For who? Not for us, certainly. And we've seen important commanders and staff logistics people flown in to border camps for conferences.'

Both officers thought about that for a time. 'It is coming,' de Milja said. 'But not this spring. Perhaps in '41.'

'And this spring?'

'France.'

'Nobody believes such a thing can happen,' Broza said. 'You mean a major attack – tanks, assault planes, infantry, Paris in flames?'

'Yes,' de Milja said.

Broza shook his head. It wasn't possible.

The first winter of German occupation turned slowly to the rain and mud of a long, slow spring. Perhaps the Poles lost heart a little. The first rage was spent – a few SS officers assassinated, several hundred hostages shot. But when the smoke cleared the Germans weren't frightened and the Poles weren't intimidated. And so they settled down to fight.

The recommendation of the ZWZ intelligence service – to hammer at the links between Russia and Germany – was endorsed by the Sixth Bureau administration in Paris, and the logical area of attack turned out to be the Hitler/Stalin Pact trade agreements. German technology needed Russian raw materials; a million tons of animal fodder, a million tons of crude oil, tons of cotton, coal, phosphates, chromium, and iron ore. The Russians had the matériel – it was simply a matter of shipping it to Germany. By rail. Across Poland.

From the first days of occupation it was clear that all labour would be performed by Polish workers, under German supervision. So the Germans, when they decided to enlarge Prezmysl railway station, just on the German side of the border, hired ZWZ carpenters, ZWZ masons, and ZWZ helpers to hand them the proper tools. Broza, de Milja and company knew everything before it happened. The railway line Prezmysl/ Cracow/Breslau, entirely under the view of Polish underground intelligence, was soon ready to carry the goods that would keep Germany rich and powerful, while the Poles were itching to blow it all to hell, a small first step on the road to making Germany poor and weak.

The battle started with Polish Boy Scouts, adept at crawling under freight cars, opposed by German sentries, who shot anything and justified nothing. But it did not remain on that level. The initial Polish thrust – we can blow up whatever we want – was answered by a German counterthrust – we can fix whatever you blow up. The Poles soon realized the magnitude of the job they had taken on: the Germans *were* good fixers, and the strategic sector of the German/Polish economy was no small thing – it was going to require one hell of an effort to blow it all up. Not only that, the means to blow it up had to be stolen from these very Germans; at least until the French and British Allies found a way to fly in the explosives they needed. Not at all daunted, the Poles created a special blowing-up-and-stealing organization to do the job. They called it Komenda Dyversji – Sabotage and Diversion – Kedyv for short.

Like any organization, Kedyv measured its success in numbers. In 1940, a disabled locomotive was out of service for fourteen hours. Later, the period would rise to fourteen days. The increase in productivity was achieved by Polish chemists and engineers, opposed by German chemists and engineers. At which point the conflict had reached the level on which it would be decided: national intelligentsia versus national intelligentsia.

The Polish scientists took the offensive and never let up: they built incendiary devices that were swiftly and easily attachable to tank cars loaded with Russian crude oil, they then timed the fuse by the rhythm of the rails: x number of thumps would set off the explosion, sometimes in Poland, sometimes in Germany. Unable to determine the venue of the sabotage, the Germans found it impossible to investigate. Petroleum storage tanks were set afire by the introduction of cylinders of compressed hydrogen with open valves. Locomotives were disabled by the addition of an abrasive to the lubricating system. Russian iron ore was seeded with bombs that exploded while the ore was travelling down chutes into German smelters. When railway tracks were mined, the first mine blew up a train, the second a rescue train, the third a repair train.

The Germans didn't like it.

These *untermenschen* were not to be permitted to interfere with the harmonization of German Europe. A message was sent to the Poles: the faculty of Cracow University was called to a meeting, then arrested en masse. It was thought to be the first time an entire university had been arrested. But a few nights later, on the Silesian border, a blue flash, a fiery spray of tank-car metal, five vats of flame towed through the darkness by a terrified engineer. *Fuck you.*

28 March, 3:40 a.m. De Milja woke suddenly. He listened, concentrated. First the strange, whispery silence of a city under curfew. Then a board creaked in the hallway.

So, 9 mm from the nightstand, safety thumbed off. He sat up slowly, sighted on the crack where the door met the jamb. The knob turned delicately, a cautious hand on the other side. De Milja took a breath and held it.

Madame Kuester. In a silk robe, hair in a long braid. 'Don't kill me, please,' she said. He understood only by watching her mouth move, her voice barely made a sound. He lowered the gun. 'Germans,' she said. Gestured with her eyes. She walked down the hall to her room, he followed, in undershirt and shorts. He stood close to her in the small room, could smell the laundry soap she washed with. The shade moved slightly in the air, the window behind it open an inch. From the roof across the narrow street, a hushed '*Ocht-svansig, Ocht-svansig,*' then a brief hiss of radio static. *Eight-twenty, then,* he thought. Meaning I'm in place, or proceed to apartment, or they're all asleep, or whatever it meant. Now de Milja's decision had been made for him: orders were specific, the response detailed; and he was not to permit himself to be taken alive. 'Get dressed, please,' he said.

He walked down the hallway, tapped lightly at the door of the master bedroom. He heard the man and his wife breathing deeply inside, opened the door, had finally to lean over and touch the man on his bare shoulder. *They made love tonight* he thought. The man was immediately awake, saw de Milja and the 9 mm and understood everything.

He went back to Madame Kuester's room. When he opened the door she was naked, standing in front of an open bureau drawer. He knew this profile – the curve of her abdomen, flat bottom, heavy thighs. Her head turned towards him. She didn't exactly pause, skipped a single beat perhaps, then took underwear from the drawer and stepped into it. He wanted to hold her against him, something he had never done before. There were family noises in the hall; the children, the parents, an angry word. 'Best to say good-bye,' she said.

'Good-bye,' he said. He couldn't see her eyes in the darkened room.

He hurried back to his room, put on a sweater, wool trousers, heavy shoes, and a raincoat. The gun fit in the raincoat pocket. From inside a book he selected an *ausweis* – German work pass – and other identification meant for emergencies, as well as a packet of zloty notes and some gold coins. The family and Madame Kuester were waiting for him at the front door.

The bolt and lock mechanisms were heavily oiled, just a soft click and de Milja was looking out at the landing. A current of chilly air from the staircase meant that the street door was standing open. This was not normal. De Milja turned, silently let the others know what had happened. The reaction was calm; the father held a large military revolver, his thirteen-year-old son had its twin. The man smiled and nodded gravely. *I understand.*

Three flights below, somebody tried to walk silently through the lobby. Others followed, one of them stifled a cough. They could have climbed the stairs quietly if they'd taken off their boots, but the SS didn't do things like that, so de Milja and the family could hear them coming. When they came around the curve of the staircase onto the second floor, de Milja took the 9 mm out of his pocket and climbed the iron rungs of a ladder that led to a hatch that opened onto the roof. He tested the hatch with his gun hand, moving it only enough to make sure it wasn't secured from the other side. He was reasonably sure there were German police on the roof.

They reached the floor below. They weren't very careful about noise now, de Milja could hear the heels of their boots and the sound of leather belts and holster grommets and breathing deepened by excitement and anticipation. Then they pounded their fists on a door and yelled for somebody to open up, the guttural German rolled and echoed up the open staircase and rang on the tile landings. The door was flung open, knob hammering the wall, then there were shouts and running footsteps and a wail of terror as the downstairs neighbour was arrested.

They had, de Milja calculated, at most an hour.

The middle-aged couple who lived below would be taken to Szucha Avenue headquarters, a sergeant would put down basic information and fill out forms, and when the interrogators finally got busy they would realize that this was not Captain Alexander de Milja or *the man in the brown raincoat* or whatever description they had. Then they would come back.

There was, of course, at least the mathematical possibility that the police had not made an error, but those who indulged themselves in that kind of thinking were no longer alive in Poland in the spring of 1940.

A few minutes after five in the morning, when the curfew ended, the wife, both children, and Madame Kuester left the apartment with false identity cards and a wicker basket on wheels they used for shopping. Moments later, they came to the side street and turned right. Which meant, to de Milja looking out the window, that German police remained on guard in the lobby, checking papers as the tenants left the building. Five minutes later, de Milja was alone – the former customs official had walked out the door of his apartment, probably never to see it again. He too turned right at the side street, which confirmed the earlier signal, and touched his hair, which meant the Germans were checking closely. At 5:15, de Milja climbed the ladder, cautiously raised the hatch, then hoisted himself out onto the roof.

The dawn was a shock after the close apartment – cold air, dark blue sky, shattered red cloud in streaks that curved to the horizon. He took a moment to get his bearings, smelled cigarette smoke nearby, then knelt behind a plaster wall at the foot of a chimney. Somebody was up here with him, possibly a German policeman. He held the 9 mm in his right hand, pressed the fingertips of his left hand against the tar surface of the roof. He could feel somebody pacing: one, two, three, four, five. Pause. Then back again. Everything de Milja knew suggested a police guard on the roof – the raid, the document control at the front door. Germans were thorough, this was the sort of thing they did. He wanted to see for himself, but resisted the temptation to rise up and look around – the roof was cluttered; sheets hung on clotheslines, chimneys, ventilation pipe outlets, two tarpaper-roofed housings that covered the entries to staircases.

A few feet away, across a low parapet and above a narrow alley, was a fire escape on the sixth floor of the building next door. From there, he had several choices: climb in an apartment window, descend to the alley, or go up to the roof, which abutted two neighbouring buildings, one of them a factory with heavy truck traffic in and out. All he had to do was jump the space above the alley.

Down in the street, a tramcar arrived, ringing its bell, grinding to a stop, then starting up again. He heard the clop of hoofbeats – perhaps the wagon that delivered coal – and the high/low siren of German police wagons as they sped through the city streets. The air smelled of coal smoke and onions frying in fat, and he could see the morning star, still sharp, but fading in the gathering daylight. He heard the rasp of a window forced up, he heard a woman laugh – shrill, abandoned, it was so funny she didn't care how she sounded.

Turning his head, he saw a woman appear at an open window in an adjacent building. Her apartment was one storey above the roof, so he found himself looking up at her. She wore an old print dress with the sleeves rolled up, an apron, and a kerchief with the knot tied in the middle of her forehead. Her face was determined – here it was just after dawn and she was cleaning her house. She poked a dustmop out the window and gave it a good bang against the sill, then another, just so it remembered who was boss.

When she saw de Milja, she stared as though he were an animal in a zoo. Of course, he thought. What she sees is a man with an automatic pistol in his hand, kneeling behind the base of a chimney. *Hiding* behind the base of a chimney. Hmm. Probably a criminal. But he's not alone on the roof. From where she stood – she gave the mop a desultory rap just to keep up appearances – she could see another man. This man was pacing, and smoking a cigarette. Perhaps, if God wills, de Milja thought, he's wearing a uniform, or if he's in civilian clothes maybe he has on one of those stupid little hats with alpine brushes the Germans liked.

De Milja watched the woman, she stared back shamelessly, then looked away, probably at the pacing man. Then back at him. He sensed a motion behind her, and she was briefly distracted. She almost, he felt, turned away from the window and went back to cleaning the apartment – somebody in the room had told her to do that. Yes, de Milja thought, that was it. She turned her head and said something, something dismissive and sharp, then returned to watching the men on the roof below her. She had broad shoulders and big red hands – nobody told *her* what to do. De Milja now faced her directly and spread his arms, palms up in the universal interrogatory gesture: *what's going on?*

She didn't react. She wasn't going to help a thief – her expression was suspicious and hostile. But then, a moment later, she changed her mind. She held out a hand, fingers stiff: *stop*. De Milja put his hand back on the surface of the roof, three, four, five. Pause. The woman held her signal. Then, just as a new sequence of footsteps began, she beckoned abruptly, excitedly: *yes, it's all right now, he can't see you.* Three, four, five. Pause. *No, stop, he's facing your way.* Three, four, five. Pause. *Yes, it's . . .*

De Milja leaped up and ran for his life.

He almost got away with it.

But if he could feel the policeman pacing on the roof, the man could feel it when he ran. 'Halt!'

As de Milja reached the parapet he could see the woman's face with perfect clarity: her mouth rounded into an O, her hand came up and pressed the side of her face. She was horrified at what was about to happen. The first shot snapped the air next to his ear just as his foot hit the parapet. It was a long way across. Seven floors down, broken glass in the alley glittered up at him. And the parapet was capped with curved, slippery, ceramic tile. It was a bad jump, one foot slipped as he took off. He flailed at the empty air, and he almost cleared the railing, but then his left heel caught and that spilled him forward, his head hitting the iron floor of the fire escape as something pinged in the stairway above him and somebody shouted.

He had not felt the bullet, but he was on his knees, vision swimming, a rock in his chest that blocked his air. He went away. Came back. Looked down at a windowsill, worn and weathered grey. A big drop of blood fell on it, then another. His heart raced, he clawed at the iron fretwork, somehow stood up. The world spun around him; whistles, shouts – a brick exploded and he turned away from it. Saw the ladder to the floor below, made himself half slide, half tumble to the iron platform.

His escape – from everything, forever – was six storeys down into the alley and he knew it, he just had to get one leg over the railing and then the other and then the terrors of Szucha Avenue no longer existed. Hide under the ground, they will never touch you. He was going to do it – then he didn't. Instead, the window on the fire escape exploded into somebody's kitchen – glass, blood, and de Milja all showing up for breakfast.

A family around a table; a still life, a spoon frozen in air between bowl and mouth, a woman at a stove, a man in suspenders. Then he was in a parlour; a canary tweeted, in a mirror above a buffet a man with bright blood spattered on his face. He fumbled at the family's locks, somehow worked the right bolt the right way, the door opened, then closed behind him.

He froze. Then the door on the other side of the landing flew open and a man beckoned fiercely from the darkness of his hall. 'This way,' he said, voice thick with excitement. De Milja couldn't see – objects doubled, then faded into ghosts of themselves – then a bald man with a heavy face and small, restless eyes emerged from the fog. He wore an undershirt, and held his trousers up with his hand.

When de Milja didn't move, the man grabbed him – he had the strength of the mad, he may have been mad for all de Milja knew – and shoved him down a long, dark hallway. Once again de Milja started to fade out, he felt the wall sliding past on his right shoulder as the man half-carried him along. There was a sense of still air, the odour of closed rooms. A hallway made unlikely angles, sharp turns into blank walls, a wood panel swung wide, and he found himself in a box that smelled of freshly sawn planks. Then it was dark, with a heavy silence, and as he blacked out he realized that he had been entombed.

There was more. It went on from there, but he was less and less a part of it. Merely something of value. It was not so bad to be something of value, he discovered. He was fed into a Saving Machine – a mechanism that knew better than to expect anything of fugitives, the damaged and the hunted. It simply saved them. So all de Milja ever retained of the next few days were images, remnants, as he was moved here and there, an object in someone else's operation, hidden and rehidden, the treasure of an anxious miser.

He came to rest on a couch in a farmhouse, a place of palpable safety. It was drizzling, and he could smell wet earth and spring. It took him back to Tarnopol, to the Volhynia. There too they burned oak logs, wet dogs dried by the fire, somebody wore oilskins, and the smell of a stone house in the rain was cut by *bay rhum*, which the Ostrow uncles always used after shaving.

His head ached, his mouth was dry as chalk. A young woman doctor sat on the edge of the couch, looked in his eyes with a penlight, then put a delicate finger on a place above his forehead. 'Hurt?' she asked.

'Not much.'

'I'm the one who sewed you up,' she said. 'In a few days we'll take them out.'

He had six stitches in his hairline. He had not been hit by a bullet, but the fall on the fire escape had given him a concussion.

An hour later an adjutant took him upstairs, to an office in an old farm bedroom with a little fireplace. The man behind a long worktable had tousled grey hair and moustache and the pitted complexion of childhood smallpox. He wore a country jacket with narrow shoulders and a thick wool tie. When he stood to shake hands, de Milja saw that he was tall and thin. 'Captain,' he said quietly, indicating a chair.

He was called Major Olenik, and he was de Milja's new superior officer. 'You might as well hear all the bad news at once,' he said. 'The basement of Saint Stanislaus Hospital was raided by an SS unit, what files were there were taken. Colonel Broza was wounded, and captured. The woman you knew as Agata swallowed a cyanide capsule. You and Captain Grodewicz survived.'

For a moment, de Milja didn't say anything. Then, 'How did that happen?'

Olenik's shrug was eloquent: let's not waste our time with theories, we don't know and it's likely we won't ever know. 'Of course we are working on that,' Olenik said. 'Did you know who Agata was?' he asked.

'I didn't, no.'

'Biochemist. One of the best in Europe.'

Olenik cleared his throat. 'The Sixth Bureau in Paris informed us, a few days ago, that our senior intelligence officer in France has been relieved of duty. We are going to send you as his replacement, Captain. You studied at Saint-Cyr for three years, is that correct?'

'Yes. 1923 to 1926.'

'And your French is fluent?'

'It's acceptable. Good workable French spoken by a Pole. I've read in it, in order not to lose it, but conversation will take a few weeks.'

'We're sending you out, with couriers. Up to Gdynia, then by freighter across the Baltic to Sweden. We've created an identity and a legend for you. Once in France, you'll report to the Sixth Bureau Director of Intelligence in Paris. It's your decision, of course, but I want to add, parenthetically, that you are known to the German security services in Poland.' He paused, waiting for de Milja to respond.

'The answer is yes,' de Milja said.

The major acknowledged his response with a polite nod.

Later they discussed de Milja's escape from the Germans. He learned that the customs official, his family and Madame Kuester, had gotten away successfully and been taken to safety in the countryside.

As for the man who had hidden him in his apartment, he was not in the underground, according to Olenik. 'But he did have an acquaintance who he believed to be in the ZWZ, he confided in her, and she knew who to talk to. Word was passed to us, and the escape-and-evasion people picked you up, moved you around for a time, eventually brought you down here.'

'I owe that man my life,' de Milja said. 'But he was – perhaps he was not entirely sane.'

'A strange man,' Olenik said. 'Perhaps a casualty of war. But his hiding place, well, it's common now. People turning their homes into magicians' boxes, some of it is art, really. Double walls, false ceilings, secret stairways, sections of floorboard on hinges, drawer pulls that unlock hidden passageways to other buildings.'

Olenik paused and thought about it. 'Yes, I suppose he was a little crazy. What he built was bizarre, I went to see it, and it was, *byzantine*. Still, you were lucky – your mad carpenter was a good carpenter. Because the Gestapo did search that apartment, every apartment in that building, in fact. But to find you they would have had to rip out the walls, and that day they didn't bother. That's not always the case –

they've turned Jewish apartments into sawdust – but all they did was break up some furniture, and so here you are.'

Olenik smiled suddenly. 'We must look at the bright side. At least the *Kulturtrager*' – it meant culture-bringer, a cherished German notion about themselves – 'brought us "subhumans" some new and adventurous ideas in architecture.'

3 April 1940. The 'subhumans' turned out to be adept pupils, gathered attentively at the feet of the *Kulturtrager*. The Germans had, for example, a great passion for important paper. It was all prettily stamped and signed and franked and checked, order and discipline made manifest. Such impressive German habits, the Poles thought, were worthy of imitation.

So they imitated them, scrupulously and to the letter. As de Milja was moved north through occupied Poland, he was provided with a splendid collection of official paper. *Passierscheine, Durchlasscheine, Urlaubsscheine*, and *Dienstausweise* – general passes, transit permits, furlough passes, and work permits. The Poles had them all – stolen, imitated, doubled-up (if you had one legitimate citizen, why not two? – it's not unsanitary to share an identity), forged, secretly printed, altered, reused, and, every now and then, properly obtained. To the Germans, documentation was a fence; to the Poles, it was a ladder.

And they discovered a curious fact about the German security police: they had a slight aversion to combat soldiers. It wasn't serious, or even particularly conscious, it was just that they felt powerful when elbowing Polish civilians out of their way in a passenger train. Among German soldiers, however, whose enemies tended to be armed, they experienced some contraction of self-esteem, so avoided, in a general way, those situations.

The lowly *untermenschen* caught on to that little quirk in their masters right away: the new ZWZ intelligence officer for France reached the port of Gdynia by using *Sonderzuge* – special night trains taking Wehrmacht soldiers home to leave in Germany. These 'specials' were also used by railway workers, who rode them to and from trains making up in stations and railyards all over Poland. De Milja was one of them – according to his papers and permits a brakeman – headed to an assignment in Gdansk. Taken under the care of escape-route operators, he moved slowly north over a period of three nights.

Three April nights. Suddenly warm, then showery, crickets loud in the fields, apple trees in clouds of white blossom. It meant to de Milja that he would not see this country again – it was that strange habit of a thing to show you its loveliest face just before you lost it.

The trains clanked along slowly under the stars in the countryside. Across the river on the rebuilt bridge at Novy Dvor, back to the other side at Wyszogrod, then tracking the curves and bends of the Vistula as it headed for the sea. The railwaymen gathered in a few seats in the rear of the last car on the *Sonderzuge* trains, and the tired Wehrmacht soldiers left them alone. They were just working people, doing their jobs, not interested in politics. A heel of bread or a boiled potato wrapped in a piece of newspaper, a cigarette, a little quiet conversation with fellow workers – that was the disguise of the Polish train crews.

Captain de Milja rarely spoke, simply faded into the background. The escape-route operators were young – the boy who brought him to the town of Torun was sixteen. But the Germans had helped him to grow up quickly, and had sharpened his conspirative instincts to a fine edge. He'd never been an angel, but he should have been lying to some schoolteacher about homework, or bullshitting his girlfriend's father about going to a dance. Instead, he was saying 'Nice evening, Sergeant,' to the *shkopy* police Kontroll at the Wloclawek railway station.

'New man?' the sergeant said.

'Unh-huh,' said the teenager.

Polite, but pointless to seek anything further. The sergeant had had a teaspoon of human warmth in this godforsaken country, he'd have to make do with that. Stamped de Milja's papers, met his eyes for an instant, end of discussion.

In the daytime, he was hidden in apartments, and he'd grab a few hours sleep on a couch while young people talked quietly around him. The escape-route safe house in Torun was run by a girl no more than seventeen, snub-nosed, with cornsilk hair. De Milja felt tenderness and desire all mixed up together. Tough as a stick, this one. Made sure he had a place to sleep, a threadbare blanket, and a glass of beer. Christ, his heart ached for her, for them all because they wouldn't live the year.

Germans too thought in numbers, and their counter-espionage array was massive: Abwehr, KRIPO – criminal police, SIPO – security police, including the Gestapo – the SD intelligence units, Ukrainian gestapo, railway police, special detachments for roads, bridges, forests, river traffic, and factories. In Poland, it *rained* crossed leather belts and side arms. People got caught.

'There is soup for you,' Snub-nose said when he woke up.

'Thank you,' de Milja said.

'Are those glasses false?'

'Yes.' Because they had his photograph, he had grown a little moustache and wore clear glasses.

'You must not wear them in Torun. The Germans here know the

trick – they stop people on the street and if their lenses are clear they arrest them.'

People came in and out all day; whispered, argued, left messages, envelopes, intelligence collection. Young as she was, Snub-nose had the local authority and nobody challenged her. That night, another railwayman arrived, this one eighteen, and de Milja's journey continued.

Late in the evening, they left the train at Grudziaz. De Milja, wearing a railwayman's blue shirt and trousers, metal lunchbox in hand, walked through the rain down a street in front of the station. A whore in a doorway blew him a kiss, a half-peeled German poster on a wall showed a Polish soldier in tattered uniform, Warsaw in flames in the background. The soldier shook his fist in anger at a picture of Neville Chamberlain, the British prime minister. 'England, this is your work!' said the caption. Along with their propaganda, the Germans had put up endless proclamations, 'strictly forbidden' and 'pain of death' in every sentence.

They were stopped briefly by the police, but nothing serious. They played their part, eternally patient Poles. The Germans knew that Russia had owned the country for a hundred and twenty-three years, until 1918. They certainly meant to do better than that. The policeman said in slow German, 'Let's see your papers, boys.' Hell, who cared what the politicians did. Weren't they all just working folks, looking for a little peace in this life?

After midnight, the leave train slowly wound through the flat fields towards the coast, towards Gdynia and Gdansk. It kept on raining, the soldiers slept and smoked and stared out the windows of the darkened rail carriage.

The escape-route way station in Gdynia was an office over a bar down by the docks, run by the woman who owned the bar. Tough exterior – black, curly hair like wire, blood-red lipstick – but a heart like steel. 'Something's wrong here,' she grumbled. '*Shkopy*'s got a flea up his ass.'

In a room lit blue by a sign outside the window that said BAR, the couriers ran in and out. Most carried information on German naval activity in the port.

'Look out the window,' said the woman. 'What do you see?'

'Nothing.'

'Right. Eight German ships due in this week – two destroyers and the rest merchantmen. Where are they?'

'Where do you think?'

'Something's up. Troops or war supplies – ammunition and so forth. That's what they're moving. Maybe to Norway, or Denmark. It means invasion, my friend.'

'I have to get to Stockholm,' de Milja said.

'Oh, you'll be all right,' she said. An ironic little smile meant that he wouldn't be, not in the long run, and neither would she. 'The Swedes are neutral. And it's no technicality – they're making money hand over fist selling iron ore to the Germans, so they'll keep Hitler sweet. And he's not going to annoy them – no panzer tanks without Swedish iron.'

They were getting very rich indeed – de Milja had seen a report. Meanwhile they were righteous as parsons; issued ringing indictments at every opportunity and sat in judgment on the world. Pious hypocrites, he thought, yet they managed to get away with it.

'When do I go out?' de Milja asked.

'Tomorrow,' she said. 'On the *Enköping.*'

Two men in working clothes arrived before dawn. They handed de Milja an old greasy shirt, overalls, and cap. De Milja shivered when he put them on. One of the men took coal dust from a paper bag, mixed it with water, and rubbed it into de Milja's face and hands. Then they gave him a shovel to carry and walked him through the wire gates to the dock area. A German customs official, glancing at de Milja's pass to the port, held himself as far away as possible, his lip curled with distaste.

They joined other Polish stevedores working at two cranes loading coal into the hold of the *Enköping.* The Swedish seamen ignored them, smoking pipes and leaning on the rail. De Milja had a bag on a leather string around his neck, it held microfilm, a watch, some chocolate, and a small bottle of water. Casually, one of the workers climbed down a rope ladder into the hold. De Milja followed him. 'We're not going to fill this all the way up – we'll leave you a little space,' said the man. 'Just be sure you stay well to one side. All right?'

'Yes.'

Above them, a crane engine chugged and whined. 'Good luck,' the man said. 'Give the Swedish girls a kiss for me.' They shook hands and the man climbed back up the rope ladder. An avalanche of coal followed. De Milja pressed his back against the iron plates of the hold as it cascaded through the hatch and grew into a mountain. When it stopped, there were only three feet between de Milja and the decking above him as he lay on the lumpy coal. The hatch cover was fitted on, the screws squeaked as it was tightened down. Darkness was complete. Later in the morning he heard commands shouted in German and the barking of dogs as the ship was searched. Then the engines rumbled to life, and the freighter wallowed out into the Baltic.

*

It was seventy hours to Stockholm.

The deck plates sweated with condensation and acid coal-water dripped steadily and soaked him to the skin. At first, discomfort kept him alert – he turned and twisted, wet, miserable, and mad. But that didn't last. With the steady motion of the ship and the beat of the engines, the black darkness and the cold, dead air, de Milja fell into a kind of stupor. It was not unpleasant. Rather the reverse. He drifted down through his life, watched certain moments as they floated by. He saw dead leaves on a path in the forest in the Volhynia, his feet kicking them as he walked along, a little girl who'd come to stay with a neighbour that summer, a kiss, more than that. It made them giggle. This silly stuff – what did adults see in it? He had no idea he was dying, not for the longest time. Heavy snow fell past a window in Warsaw, Madame Kuester looked over her shoulder into a mirror, a red mark where he'd held her too tightly. He said he was sorry, she shrugged, her expression reflective, bittersweet. *It must be time to sleep*, he thought, because at last he did not feel the cold. He was relieved. His wife jammed her hands in the pockets of her coat, stood at the shore of the lake as evening came on. She looked a little rueful, that was all. If you stood far enough back, the world wasn't frightening. It wasn't anything. In the end, you were a little sad at what went on. Really, it ought to be better. Casement window at the manor house, the first gleam of the sun at the rim of a hill, two dogs trotting out of the forest onto the wet grass of the lawn. Finally, he became aware, for a moment, of what was happening. He did what he could – took long, deep breaths. *Coal*, he thought. *Sulphur, carbon monoxide, confined space, red blood cells.* It was all very confusing. One painful stab of regret: a crumpled body, Polish stowaway found on a mound of coal in a Swedish freighter. Captain Alexander de Milja hated that idea, simply one more senseless, muted death in time of war. He lay on his back at the foot of a poplar tree and looked up as the wind rattled the little leaves.

Every summer had one perfect day.

The green sea rose under the ship, held a moment, then fell away. Sometime later, the engines slowed, the iron walls shuddered, a tug tied on and nudged the *Enköping* against its pier. The rusty bolts squeaked as they were backed off, the hatch cover swung into the air, and a crane began to scoop the coal away. Later, under the dock lights, too bright against the pale evening sky of Sweden, a booming voice shouted recognition signals down into the echoing hold.

Lezhev's
Last Day

Was the third of June, 1940.

A springtime day in Paris and, last days being tricky this way, especially breezy and soft. No, Lezhev told himself, don't be seduced. *Le printemps*, like every other spectacle of the French theatre of life, was an illusion, a fraud. That was absurd, of course, and Lezhev knew it; spring was spring. But he chose to indulge himself in a little unjust spite, then smiled acidly at his intransigence. On this day above all he could say whatever he wanted – nobody contradicts a man writing a suicide note.

Stationed at the window of the smelly little garret room, he had watched spring come to the Parisian slums: to the tiny, dark street covered in horseshit and dire juices, to the fat women who stood with folded arms in doorways waiting to be insulted, and to the girls. Such girls. It would take the words of a Blok, a Bely, a Lezhev, to do them justice. 'In *Lights of a Lost Evening*, the tenth volume from Boris Lezhev, this fierce apostle of Yesenin reveals a more tender, more lyric voice than usual. In the title work, for instance, Lezhev . . .'

Now, *there* you had girls. Lithe, momentary, a flash in the corner of your eye, then gone. Nothing good lasted in the world, Lezhev thought, that's why you needed poets to grab it as it went flying by.

Well, now and then there was something good. For example, Genya Beilis. Genya. Yes, he thought, Genya. Lithe and momentary? Hah! You could never call her a girl. Girls had no such secret valleys and mysterious creases, girls did not contrive to occupy the nether mind quite as Genya did. He would miss her, up on his cloud or wherever he was going. Miss her terribly. She'd been his salvation – good thing in a bad life – the last few years of exile. Sometimes his lover, sometimes not, indomitable friend always, his brilliant bitch of a hundred breeds.

It was true, she was an extraordinary mixture. Her father, the publisher Max Beilis, was Russian, Jewish, and French. Her mother was Spanish, with some ancient Arab blood from Cordoba. Also an Irish grandmother on the maternal side. Lord, he thought, what wasn't she? You could feel the racial rivers that flowed through her. She had strange skin; sallow, olive, smooth and taut. Hair thick, dark, with reddish tints in full sunlight, and long enough so that she twined and wound it in complicated ways. Strong eyebrows, supple waist, sexy hands, eyes sharp with intelligence, eyes that saw through people. You were right to be a little afraid of Genya Beilis. The idea of some great, naked, flabby whale of a German hovering above her made Lezhev sick with rage, he would rise up and—

No, he wouldn't. The German panzer divisions were racing south from Belgium, French troops surrendering or running away as they advanced, the police were on the verge of arresting him – the closer the Germans got, the worse for all the Lezhevs of Paris. So he wasn't going to be anybody's protector, not even his own.

Fact was, they had finally hounded him to the edge of the grave. The Bolsheviks had chased him out of St Petersburg in 1922. He fled to Odessa. They ran him out of there in 1925. So he'd gone to Germany. Written for the émigré magazines, played some émigré politics. 1933, in came Hitler, out went Lezhev. So, off to sad Brussels; earnest, neutral Belgium. He hadn't much left by then – every time he ran, things flew away: clothes, money, poems, friends. 1936, off to fight in Spain – the NKVD almost got him there, he had to walk over the Pyrenees at night, in snow up to his knees. He barely made it into Liberié-Egalité-and-Fraternité, where they threw him in prison.

Amazing, Lezhev thought, the things he'd done. As a St Petersburg teenager in 1917, he'd torn a czarist policeman's club from his hands and cracked him on the nose. Stayed up all night, haunting the dark alleyways of the city and its women: talking to the whores, screwing the intellectuals. He saw a man executed with a leather cord as he sat in a kitchen chair at a busy intersection. He was a worker of the world. For a year or two, anyhow. Worked with a pen, which was mightier than the sword, he discovered, only when approximately the same size. He'd run from raging fires, crazed mobs, brawling Nazis, rumbling tanks, and the security police of at least six nations.

> *My valise, dark-eyes. Quick.*
> *It's under your bed.*
> *There's nothing in there,*
> *and nothing to pack,*
> *but I take it along.*

So, at last, after all that, who got him? The *ronds-de-cuir*. French bureaucrats, labouring all day on wooden chairs, were prone to a shine on the seat of the pants. The antidote was a chair-sized round of leather – *rond de cuir* – carried daily to work, placed ever so precisely beneath the clerical behind. The makers of Parisian slang were not slow to see the possibilities in this. To Lezhev, the *ronds-de-cuir* seemed, at first, a doleful but inevitable feature of French life but, in time, he came to understand them in a different way. Fussy, niggling, insatiable, they had some kinship with the infamous winds of Catalonia, which will not blow out a candle but will put a man in his grave. And now, he realized, they were going to do what all the Okhrana agents and Chekists and Nazis and pimps and machine gunners and Spanish cooks had failed to do.

They were going to kill him.

But maybe not.

On his rounds that night, in Le Chasseur Vert and the Jean Bart out in the Russian seventeenth arrondissement and Petrukhov's place up in Pigalle, he felt the life force surge inside him. He laid some little glovemaker's assistant among the mops and brooms in Petrukhov's storeroom. Tossed his last francs out on the zinc bars as a rich slice of émigré Paris got drunk on his money and told him what a fine fellow he was. Sometime near dawn he was with the acmeist playwright Yushin, too plastered to walk any farther, propped on a wall and staring down into the Seine by the Alexandre III bridge.

'Don't give up now,' Yushin said. 'You've been through too much. We all have.'

Lezhev belched, and nodded vigorously. Yushin was right.

'Remember the Cossacks chased you?'

'Mm,' Lezhev said. Cossacks had never chased him, Yushin had him confused with some other émigré poet from St Petersburg.

'How you ran!'

'Mm!'

'Still, they didn't catch you.'

'No.'

'Well, there it is.'

'You're right.'

'Don't weaken, Boris Ivanovich. Don't let these sanctimonious prigs stab your heart with their little quills.'

'Well said!'

'You think so?'

'Yes.'

'You're kind to say that.'

'Not at all.' Lezhev saw that the compliment had put Yushin to sleep, still standing, propped against the stone wall.

But then, on the morning of 4 June, he had to report to the Préfecture of Police and slid, like a man who cannot get a grip on an icy hillside, down into a black depression. The Parisian police, responsible for immigration, had placed him on what they called a Régime des Sursis. *Sursis* meant reprieves, but *régime* was a little harder to define. The authorities would have said system, but the word was used for a diet, implying control, and some discomfort. Lezhev would describe it as 'a very refined cruelty'.

In March, the French had declared Lezhev an undesirable alien, subject to deportation back to Germany – his last country of legal residence, since he'd entered Belgium, Spain, and France illegally. Of course all sorts of judicial nightmares awaited him in Berlin; he could expect concentration camp, beating, and probably execution. The French perfectly understood his predicament. You may, they told him, appeal the order of deportation.

This he did, and was granted a stay – for twenty-four hours. Since the stay would lapse at 5:00 p.m. the following afternoon, he had to go to the Préfecture at 1:00 p.m. to stand on the lines. At 4:20, they stamped his papers – this enabled him to stay in France an additional twenty-four hours. And so forth, and so on. For four months.

The lines at the Préfecture – across from Notre-Dame cathedral on the Île de la Cité – had a life of their own, and Lezhev grimly joined in. He'd been hit on the head in his life, missed plenty of meals, been tumbled about by fate. Standing in line every day held no terrors for him. He couldn't earn any money, but Genya Beilis had a little and she helped him out; so did others. He'd written behind barbed wire, on a sandbag, under a bridge, now he'd write while standing in line.

This defiance held for March and April, but in May he began to slip. The *ronds-de-cuir*, on the other side of their wire-grille partitions, did not become friendly over time – that astonished, then horrified, finally sickened Lezhev. What sort of human, he wondered, behaved this way? What sort of reptilian heart remained so cold to somebody in trouble? The sort that, evidently, lived in the hollow chest of the little man with the little man's moustache. That lived within the mountainous bosom of the woman with the lacquer hairdo and scarlet lips, or behind the three-point handkerchief of Coquelet the Rooster, with his cockscomb of wild hair and the triumphant crow of the dunghill. 'Tomorrow, then, Monsieur Lezhev. Bright and early, eh?' Stamp – *kachuck* – sign, blot, admire, hand over, and smile.

The line itself, snaking around the building, then heading up the quay, was a madhouse: Jews, Republican Spaniards, Gypsies, Hungarian artists, the lost and the dispossessed, criminals who hadn't yet got around to committing crimes, the full riptide of unwanted humanity – spring of 1940. They whispered and argued and bartered and conspired, laughed and cried, stole and shared, extemporized life from one hour to the next.

But slowly, inevitably, the Régime de Sursis gnawed away until it ate a life, took one victim, then another. Zoltan in the river, Petra with cyanide, Sygelbohm under a train.

Boris Lezhev, papers stamped for one more day of existence, returned to his room late at night on the fourth of June. He'd stopped at a café, listened to a report on the radio of the British Expeditionary Force's departure, in small boats, from the beaches of Dunkirk. But the population was to remain calm at all costs – Prime Minister Reynaud had demanded that President Roosevelt send 'clouds of warplanes.' Victory was a certainty.

Lezhev was temporarily distracted from writing by a drunken altercation in the tiny street below his window. One old man wanted to defend Paris, the other favoured the declaration of an open city – the treasures of the capital, its bridges, arcades, and museums, would be spared. Trading arguments, then insults, the old men worked themselves up into a fulminous rage. They slapped each other in the face – which made them both wildly indignant – they swore complicated oaths, threatened to kick each other, snarled and turned red, then strode off in opposite directions, threatening vengeance and shaking their fists.

When this was over, Lezhev sat on a broken chair in front of an upturned crate and wrote, on paper torn from a notebook, a long letter to Genya Beilis. He wanted her to be the custodian of his poetry. Over the years, he'd tinkered endlessly with his work, back and forth, this way and that. Now, tonight, he had to decide, so: here a birch was a poplar. The sea shattered, it didn't melt. Tania did not smell of cows or spring earth – she simply walked along the path where the ivy had pulled down the stake fence.

'I don't exactly thank you, Genya – my feelings for you are warmer than courtesy. I will say that I remember you. That I have spent considerable time and remembered you very carefully. It is a compliment, my love, the way you live in my imagination. The world should be that perfect.'

7 June 1940. Boulogne-Billancourt cemetery.

A few mourners for Lezhev: he'd made the enemies émigré poets make, some of the regulars had already fled south, and it was a warm, humid evening with the threat of a thunderstorm in the air. Those who did attend were those who, if they kept nothing else, kept faith with community: a dozen men with military posture, in dark suits, medals pinned to their breast pockets. There was a scattering of beards – Lezhev's colleagues, gloomy men with too much character in their faces. And the old women, well practised at standing before open graves, you could not be buried without them. The priest was, as always, Father Ilarion, forced once again to pray over some agnostic/ atheist/anarchist – who really knew? – by the exigencies of expatriate life.

Doz'vidanya, Boris Ivanovich.

There wasn't much in the way of flowers, but a generous spread awaited the funeral party in an upstairs room at the Balalaika – Efrimov's restaurant in St Petersburg had also been steps away from the cemetery – vodka, little sandwiches of sturgeon or cucumber, cookies decorated with half a candied cherry. Genya Beilis, lover, muse, nurse, editor, and practical goddess to the deceased, had, once again, been generous and openhanded. 'God bless you,' an old woman said to her as they walked down the gravel path towards the restaurant.

Genya acknowledged the blessing with a smile, and the old woman limped ahead to catch up with a friend.

'Madame Beilis, my sympathies.'

He crunched along the path beside her, and her first view of him was blurred by the black veil she wore. His French wasn't native, yet he did not speak to her in Russian.

'A friend of Monsieur Lezhev?' she asked.

'Unfortunately, no.'

Polite, she thought. Through the veil, she could see a strong, pale forehead. He was in his late thirties, hair expensively cut, faintly military bearing. *Aristocrat*, she thought. But not from here.

'An associate of Monsieur Pavel,' he said.

Oh.

She was, just for a moment, very angry. Boris was gone, she would never hear his voice again. For all his drinking and brawling he'd been a tender soul, accidentally caught up in flags and blood and honour and history, now dead of it. And here by her side was a man whose work lay in such things. *I am sick of countries*, she wanted to say to him. But she did not say it. They walked together on the gravel path as the first thunder of the storm grumbled in the distance.

'The help you've provided is very much appreciated,' he said quietly. She sensed he knew what she'd been thinking. 'The government has to leave Paris – but we wanted to set up a contact protocol for the future, if that is acceptable to you.'

She hesitated a moment, then said, 'Yes, it's acceptable.' Suddenly she was dizzy, thought she might faint. She stopped walking and put a hand on the man's forearm to steady herself. The thunder rumbled again and she pressed her lips together hard – she did not want to cry.

'There's a bench—' the man said.

She shook her head no, fumbled in her purse for a handkerchief. The other mourners circled around them. Yushin the playwright tipped his hat. 'So sorry, Genya Maximova, so sorry. Just the other night, he . . . my regrets.' He walked backwards for a step or two, tipped his hat again, then turned around and scurried away.

The man at her side handed her a clean white handkerchief and she held it to her eyes. It smelled faintly of *bay rhum* cologne. 'Thank you,' she said.

'You're welcome.' They started walking again. 'The protocol will mention the church of Saint-Etienne-du-Mont, and the view from the rue de la Montagne. Can you remember it?'

'Yes. I like that church.'

'The contact may come by mail, or in person. But it will come – sooner or later. As I said, we are grateful.'

His voice trailed away. She nodded yes, she understood; yes, she'd help; yes, it had to be done; whatever yes they needed to hear that day. He understood immediately. 'Again, our sympathies,' he said. Then: 'I'll leave you here – there are French security agents in a car at the bottom of the hill.'

He moved ahead of her, down the path. He wasn't so bad, she thought. It just happened that information flowed to her like waves on a beach, and he was an intelligence officer in time of war. Big drops of rain began to fall on the gravel path and one of the men in dark suits with medals on the breast pocket appeared at her side and opened a black umbrella above her head.

It was a long way from the Russian neighbourhoods in Boulogne to Neuilly – where he was staying in the villa of an industrialist who'd fled to Canada – and a storm was coming, but Captain Alexander de Milja decided to walk, and spent the evening headed north along the curve of the Seine, past factories and docks and rail sidings, past workers' neighbourhoods and little cafés where bargemen came in to drink at night.

They had dragged him, black with coal dust and more dead than alive, from the hold of the freighter *Enköping*, laid him on the back seat of a

Polish diplomatic car and sped off to the embassy. A strange time. Not connected with the real world at all, drifting among dim lights and hollow sounds, a sort of mystic's paradise, and when people said 'Stockholm' he could only wonder what they meant. Wherever he'd been, it hadn't been Stockholm.

And where was he now? A place called *poor Paris*, he thought. In *poor France*. He saw the posters on his walk, half torn, flapping aimlessly on the brick factory walls: NOUS VAINCRONS CAR NOUS SOMMES LES PLUS FORTS. Signed by the new prime minister, Paul Reynaud. 'We will win because we are the strongest.' *Yes, well*, was all de Milja could think. What could you say, even to yourself, about such empty huffing and puffing? Paris had been bombed twice, not heavily. But, while the Wehrmacht was still north of the Belgian border, France had quit. He knew it – it was what he and Colonel Broza had fought against in Warsaw – and he'd felt it happen here.

De Milja had arrived in Paris in late April and gone to work for Colonel Vyborg, the 'Baltic knight' who had recruited him into the ZWZ as the Germans began the siege of Warsaw. At first it was as though he'd returned to his old job – staff work in military intelligence. There were meetings, dinners, papers written and read, serious and urgent business but essentially the life of the military attaché. He had assisted in some of the intelligence collection, developed assets, liaised with French officers.

They were sympathetic – *poor Poland*. Clandestine flights with money and explosives for the underground would be starting any day now, any day now. There were technical problems, you needed a full moon, calm weather, extra gas tanks on the aeroplanes. That was true, de Milja knew, yet somehow he sensed it wouldn't happen even when conditions were right. 'Steady pressure,' Vyborg said. 'Representatives of governments-in-exile are patient, courteous men who do not lose their tempers.' De Milja understood, and smiled.

His counterpart, a Major Kercheval of the SR – Service des renseignements, the foreign intelligence operation that supplied data to the Deuxième Bureau of the French General Staff – invited him to tour the Maginot Line. 'Be impressed,' Vyborg told him. Well, he was, truly he was. A long drive through spring rains, past the Meuse, the Marne, the battlefields of the 1914 war. Then barbed wire, and an iron gate with a grille, opening into a tunnel dug deep in the side of a hill. Over the entrance, a sign: ILS NE PASSERONT PAS – They shall not pass. Three hundred feet down by elevator, then a cage of mice hung by the door as a warning – they'd keel over if gas were present – and a brilliantly lit tunnel traversed by a little train that rang a bell. In vast, concrete chambers there were offices, blackboards, and telephones – a huge fire-control centre staffed by sharp young soldiers dressed in white coveralls. A general officiated, demanding that de Milja choose a German target from a selection of black-and-white photographs. All he could see were trees and brush, but his cartographer's eye turned up a woodcutter's hut by a stream and he pinned it with his finger. '*Voilá*,' said the general, and great activity ensued – bells rang, soldiers talked on telephones, maps were unrolled, numbers written hurriedly on blackboards. At last, a dial in the wall was turned and the deep gong of a bell sounded again and again. 'The target has received full artillery fire. It is completely destroyed.' De Milja was impressed. He did wonder, briefly, why, since the French were officially at war with the Germans, they rang a bell instead of firing an actual gun, but that was, he supposed, a detail. In fact, the series of fortresses could direct enormous firepower at an enemy from underground bunkers. The Maginot Line went as far as the Belgian border. And there it stopped.

So on 10 May, when Hitler felt the time was ripe, the Wehrmacht went through Belgium. A French officer said to de Milja, 'But don't you see? They have violated Belgian neutrality! They have played into our hands!'

Just where the river rounded the Isle of Puteaux, de Milja came to a *tabac, a boulangerie,* and a cluster of cheap cafés: a little village. Because of the blackout the streetlamps of Paris had been painted blue, and now the city was suffused with strange, cold light. It made the street cinematic, surreal. Friday night, the cafés should have been jammed with Parisians – *to hell with the world, have a glass of wine! Can I see you home?* Now they were triste, half-empty. But these were workers. Out in Passy, in Neuilly, in Saint-Germain and Palais-Royal there wasn't anybody. They had all discovered a sudden need to go to the country; to Tante Giselle or their adored *grandmère* or their little house on the river whatever-it-was. Where they'd gone in 1914. Where they'd gone, for that matter, in 1789.

Meanwhile, in Poland, they were committing suicide. Vyborg had told him that, white lines of anger at the corners of his mouth. France was a kind of special heaven to the Poles, with its great depths of culture, its adept wit, and ancient, forgiving intelligence. To the Poles, it was simple: don't give in, fight on, when Hitler tangles with the French that'll be the end of him. But that wasn't what happened and now they knew it – they risked their lives listening to the BBC and they heard what the announcer tried not to say. The French ran. They didn't, wouldn't, fight. A wave of suicides washed over Warsaw, Cracow, the manor houses in the mountains.

A girl at a café table looked at de Milja. Beret and raincoat, curly, copper-coloured hair with a lock tumbled onto the forehead, a dark mole setting off the white skin on her cheek, lips a deep, solemn red. With her eyes she asked him some sort of question that could not quite be put into words. De Milja wanted her – he wanted all of them – but he kept walking and she turned back to her glass of wine. What was she after, he wondered. A little money? A husband for a little problem in her belly? A man to beat up the landlord? Something, something. Nothing was free here – he'd learned that in the 1920s when he was studying at Saint-Cyr. He turned and looked back at her; sad now, staring into her glass. She had a heavy upper lip with a soft curve to it, and he could imagine the weight of her breasts against her cotton blouse. Jesus, she was beautiful; they all were. They couldn't help it, it wasn't their fault. He stopped, half turned, then continued on his way. Probably she was a whore, and he didn't want to pay to make love.

Yes, well.

The industrialist who'd fled to Canada had not had time, apparently, to clean out his things in Neuilly. He'd left behind mounds of women's clothing, much of it still folded in soft tissue paper, a crate of twenty telephones, a stack of chic little boxes covered in slick gold paper, and dozens of etchings – animals of every sort; lions, zebras, camels – signed *Dovoz* in a fluid hand. De Milja had simply made a neat pile on the dining-room table and ignored it. The toothbrush left in the sink, the paste dried on it, he'd thrown away.

Hard to sleep in a city waiting for invaders. De Milja stared out the window into the garden of the neighbouring villa. So, the barbarians were due to arrive; plans were being made, the angles of survival calculated. He read for a time, a little Joseph Roth, a book he'd found on the night table – *The Radetzky March*. Roth had been an émigré who'd killed himself in Paris a year earlier. It was slow going in German, but de Milja was patient and dawn was long hours away.

The Trottas were not an old family. Their founder's title had been conferred on him after the battle of Solferino. He was a Slovene and chose the name of his native village, Sipolje. Though fate elected him to perform an outstanding deed, he himself saw to it that his memory became obscured to posterity.

An infantry lieutenant, he was in command of a platoon at Solferino. The fighting had been in progress for half an hour. He watched the white

backs of his men three paces in front of him. The front line was kneeling,
the rear standing. They were all cheerful and confident of victory. They
had . . .

Now it rained. Hard. De Milja had been lying on a long red-and-gold
couch with a brocade pillow under his head. He got to his feet, walked
to the French doors, index finger holding his place in the book, and
stared out into the night. Someone had stored pieces of old statuary
behind the villa, water glistened on the stone when the lightning
flickered. The wind grew stronger, rain blew in sheets over the garden,
then the air cooled suddenly and the sound of thunder rolled and
echoed down the deserted streets.

9 June 1940. 2, avenue de Tourville, Hôtel des Invalides.

De Milja was prompt for his eleven o'clock meeting with Major
Kercheval of the SR. The streets around the walled military complex at
the centre of the seventh arrondissement were quiet – the residents were
away – but in the courtyard they were busy loading filing cabinets onto
military trucks. It was hot, no air moved, the soldiers had their jackets
off, sleeves rolled up, suspenders dangling, making them look like
cannoneers from the Franco-Prussian war of 1870.

A fifteen-minute wait, then an elderly sergeant with plentiful decorations led him up long flights of stairs to Kercheval's office. The major's
greeting was friendly but correct. They sat opposite each other in
upholstered chairs. The office was impressive, a wall of leatherbound
volumes, historic maps in elaborate frames were hung on the walnut
boiserie.

'Not a happy moment,' Kercheval said, watching the trucks being
loaded in the courtyard below.

'No,' de Milja agreed. 'We went through it in Warsaw.'

Kercheval's eyebrow twitched – *this is not Warsaw.* 'We're thinking,'
he said, 'it won't be quite so difficult here. Some of our files are being
shifted for temporary safekeeping.'

De Milja made a polite sound of agreement. 'How is it up north?' he
asked.

Kercheval steepled his fingers. 'The Tenth Army's situation on the
Somme appears to have stabilized. At the river Oise we have a few
problems still – mostly logistics, supply and what-not. But we expect to
clear that up in seventy-two hours. Our current appreciation of the
position is this: we've got hell to pay for two or three days yet, we then
achieve a static situation – *une situation statique.* We can maintain that
indefinitely, of course, but I'd say give us two weeks of hard work and

then, in the first heat of summer, look for us to be going the other way. Germans are Nordic – they don't like hot weather.'

He shifted to the particular concerns they shared – the flow of information from open and clandestine sources, how much of it the Poles got to see. He spoke easily, at length, in confidential tones. The meaning of what he said, as far as de Milja could make out, was that the people above them, the diplomats and senior officers in the rarefied atmosphere of binational relations, had yet to complete work on a format of cooperation but they would soon do so, and at that time de Milja and his colleagues could look forward to a substantive increase of shared intelligence.

Kercheval was in his late forties, with dry skin, a corded underside to his jaw, and smooth, glossy hair combed flat. A turtle's head, de Milja thought. The small, mobile mouth, whether talking or eating, strengthened that impression. The exterior was flawless: courteous, confident, polished and hard as a diamond. If Kercheval lied, he lied, regrettably, for reasons of state – *raisons d'état* – and if you listened carefully you would hear a faint and deeply subtle signal inviting you to agree that deception was simply a part of life, as all very old cultures had learned, sadder but wiser, to acknowledge. *Come now, you must admit it's so.*

'It's an ordeal, and takes forever,' he went on, 'but experience has shown that relations go much more smoothly, indeed much more productively, when the initial understandings are thoroughly formulated.'

He smiled warmly at de Milja, perhaps a hint of apology in his face – *our friendship will surely survive all the nonsense I'm forced to tell you, you certainly won't hold it against me. Life's too short for resentment, my dear fellow.*

De Milja tried to nod agreement as enthusiastically as he could, an importunate smile nailed to his mouth. The *situation statique* on the Somme was that the Tenth Army had been encircled and destroyed, and de Milja knew it. To Kercheval, however, the fate of an army was of secondary importance to the conversation he was having with de Milja. Of primary concern was that adverse and humiliating information could not be stated in front of a foreigner, of lesser rank and lower social position. As for 'some of our files are being shifted', de Milja passed through the sentry gates, turned right towards the Métro, and passed sixty trucks lined up and waiting to enter the courtyard.

On the train he read the *Daily Telegraph* to see what the British were thinking about that morning. Asked if Paris would be declared an open city, a French spokesman replied, 'Never. We are confident that Hitler's mechanized hordes will never get to Paris. But should they come so far, you may tell your countrymen we shall defend every stone, every clod of earth, every lamp-post, every building, for we would rather have our city razed to the ground than fall into the hands of the Germans.'

Emerging at the Pont de Neuilly Métro stop, de Milja saw a group of white-haired garbagemen – veterans, wearing their decorations – working on a line of twelve garbage trucks. They were engrossed in mounting machine guns on the trucks and, by that afternoon, the Paris police were wearing tin-pot helmets and carrying rifles.

'The government's going to Tours,' Vyborg said.

'From what I saw this morning they were certainly going *somewhere*,' de Milja said.

Late afternoon, an anonymous café on the rue Blanche. Amber walls tinted brown with Gauloises smoke, etched glass between booths. An old lady with a small dog sat at the bar, the bored owner scowled as he read one of the single-sheet newspapers that had replaced the usual editions.

Vyborg and de Milja sat facing each other in a booth and sipped at glasses of beer. The afternoon was hot and still, a fly buzzing around a motionless fan in the ceiling. Sometimes, from the refugee columns trudging down the boulevards a block away, the sound of a car horn. Vyborg wore an old grey suit, with no tie and shirt collar open. He looked, de Milja thought, like a lawyer with unpaid office rent and no clients.

'Hard to believe that it's over here. That the French army lasted one month,' Vyborg said.

'It is over, then.'

'Yes. Paris will be declared an open city today or tomorrow. The Germans will be in here in a week or less.'

'But France will fight on.'

'No, it won't. Reynaud cabled Roosevelt and demanded American intervention, Roosevelt's response was a speech that dithered and said nothing. Pétain appeared before the cabinet in Tours and said that an armistice is, in his view, "the necessary condition for the survival of eternal France". That's that.'

De Milja was incredulous. France remained powerful, had a formidable navy, had army units in Morocco, Syria, Algeria, could have fought on for years. 'In Warsaw—'

'This isn't Warsaw,' Vyborg said. 'In Tours, they lost a top-secret cable, turned the whole chateau upside down looking for it. Finally a maid found it, crumpled up in Reynaud's mistress's bed. Now, that's not the first time in the history of the world that such a thing has happened, but you get the feeling it's the way things are. It's as though they've woken from a dream, discovered the house on fire, then shrugged and walked away rather than calling the fire department or looking for a bucket. If you read history, you know there are times when nations fail, that's what happened here.'

Vyborg took a pack of Gitanes from his pocket, offered it to de Milja, took one for himself, then lit both with a silver lighter. In the rue Blanche, a refugee family had become separated from the stream moving south across Paris. A man pulled a cart with quilts tied over the top of a mound of furniture; here and there a chair leg poked through. His wife led two goats on a rope. The farm dog, panting hard in the afternoon heat, walked in the shadow of the cart. Behind the cart were three small children, the oldest girl holding the hands of two little boys. The family had been on the road a long time; their eyes, glazed with fatigue, saw nothing of their surroundings.

The proprietor put his paper down for a moment and stared at the family as they laboured past. A tough Parisian, his only comment was to turn his head and make a spitting sound before going back to his newspaper with an almost imperceptible shake of the head. The old woman's lapdog barked fiercely at the goats. The farm dog glanced up, then ignored it – *some little woolly thing in Paris that thought it was a dog; the things you see when you travel.* The old woman shushed her dog, muttering something about 'unfortunates' that de Milja could barely make out.

'Fucking German pigs,' Vyborg said quietly, with resignation. 'The local bullyboys – come Friday night and they beat up the neighbours. Which is why, I guess, the French and the Poles have always been friends; they share the problem.'

'I suppose,' de Milja said, 'we're going to London. Unless there's a miracle.'

'There will be no miracle,' Vyborg said. 'And, yes, it is London. We've got a destroyer berthed at the mouth of the Loire, in Nantes, not too far from the government in Tours. I'm going down there tomorrow, we have to be where official France is. You're going to stay here – the last man out. Work on the reactivation programme, whatever you can manage to get done. Just don't stray too far from base, meaning Neuilly. That villa is now the French station of the Polish army's intelligence service. As for a time of departure, it's hard to predict exactly. It will be at the final hour – Polish honour demands at least that, with shells falling on the harbour and our fantail on fire. You'll be contacted when we know a little more, by telephone or courier. Given a cipher, probably. The BBC has agreed to broadcast signals for us – we're likely to do it that way, in the *Messages Personnels*, so get yourself a working radio and listen to it – ten, four and midnight. Myself, I like the garden programmes. Did you know that periwinkle can be used as a ground cover on a shady hillside?'

It was dark when de Milja returned to Neuilly. He carried with him a battered briefcase stuffed with French francs and a new list, in code, of Polish agents in Paris. People on the Genya Beilis level had been contacted, now there remained the small-fry, a surprisingly long list. But Poland had always had an aggressive, busy intelligence service – a characteristic of small countries with big enemies.

De Milja made a successful contact at 11:20 that night at a dance hall in Clichy – an ageing, embittered clerk in the French department of the Admiralty who was paid a small monthly stipend. Then he hurried to the Notre-Dame-de-Lorette Métro stop, but the woman he expected, an ethnic Pole running a group of engineers in the Hungarian armament industry, did not appear.

The following morning he awoke to find the air dark, the leaves of the tree outside his window covered in oily grime, and the spring birds fled. Later that day a taxi driver confirmed his suspicion: the Germans had bombed the petrol storage tanks at Levallois-Perret, the black cloud of soot had drifted down on the city.

At the fallback meeting of 2:25 p.m. – Notre-Dame-de-Lorette station replaced by Abbesses – the ethnic Pole appeared: Chanel scarf, clouds of perfume, and a refusal to meet his eyes when he handed her a payment of five thousand francs. She was gone, he thought. But he was doubly gracious, thanked her profusely, and passed her the Saint-Etienne-du-Mont protocol anyhow. The best he could do was to try to leave a positive impression – the world changed, luck went sour, he wanted her to feel that working for the Polish service was a life preserver in a stormy sea.

Paris dying.

Refugees streaming past, among them disarmed French soldiers, still in uniform. The city now silent, seemingly empty but for the shuffle of the refugee columns. The abandoned government offices had caused consternation – even the one-page newspapers were gone now, the kiosks were shut tight, and the garbage was no longer collected.

De Milja could not escape the sadness. Even when it rained death and fire, Warsaw had fought desperately to survive; improvising and improvising, ingenuity and courage set against iron and explosives. They'd had no chance, but they fought anyhow; brave, deluded, stubborn. Closing his eyes, he saw the passengers on the Pilava local, clothing dirty, here and there bloody, walking into Roumania with the heavy little crates of bullion.

He tried to keep his spirits up. The fight against despair was, he told himself, just another way of fighting Germany. But as the life of the streets faded away, he began to wonder why anybody cared so much about flags and nations. An old, old city, everything had happened here, people loved and people died and none of it mattered very much. Or maybe it was just him – maybe he was just tired of life. Sometimes that happened.

He'd scheduled a dawn contact out in the nineteenth arrondissement, at the Canal de l'Ourcq, the home dock of a Dutch barge captain with knowledge of the production capacities of petroleum refining centres along the upper Seine. Not much point at the moment – every ounce of French petrol was either in flames or pumped into government cars in full flight. But in the future it might be a useful thing to know.

At 2:00 a.m. he tossed and turned, unable to sleep. The silence of the little street was oppressive. He moved to an armchair, read *The Radetzky March*, dozed off, then woke suddenly – not knowing why until the fist hammered on the door a second time. He ran down the hall and looked out the judas hole. A Breton, he thought. Reddish hair clipped high on the sides, fair skin, a cold face, a silk tie, and a certain practised patience in the way he stood. De Milja left him and walked silently to the back door. The one waiting there had his hands in his pockets, was looking aimlessly up at the stars.

He returned to the bedroom, struggled into trousers, shirt, and shoes as the one in front knocked again. 'Are you in there?' If a voice could be good at calling through doors, this one was: *I'm being polite – don't test my patience. 'Allons,* eh!' Let's go! *Last warning.* De Milja opened the door.

The man made a soft grunt of satisfaction – at least we got that much done. 'Captain de Milja,' he said, polite in an official way. 'I am sorry to trouble you, but . . .'

But what? The Germans at the gates? The times we live in?

'Yes?' de Milja said.

'Perhaps you would get dressed, we're ordered to escort you to our office.'

'Where is that, please?'

'At the Préfecture of Police.'

'Could you identify yourself?'

'Of course. Forgive me.' He produced a small leather case with an identity card of the DST – *Direction de la Surveillance de la Territoire*, the French FBI – and held it up for de Milja to see. 'All right?' the man said.

'Come in,' de Milja said.

The man entered, whistling tunelessly, strolled through the villa and opened the back door. The one who'd waited there had a little moustache trimmed to the line of his upper lip. He looked around the villa curiously. 'It's quite a place here. Belong to you?'

'I'm just a tenant,' de Milja said.

'Ah.' A professional sceptic, it amused him to seem easily satisfied.

De Milja went into the bedroom; the man he thought of as the Breton stood in the doorway as he put on a tie, smoothed his hair to one side, put on a jacket. He had a weapon, he intended to use it, it was just a question of timing. 'Now I'm ready,' he said to the Breton.

In the blue shadow of the street, de Milja could make out a blocky Citroen, black and well polished. The Breton opened the back door, then went around the car while the other waited by de Milja's side. *Now*, he thought. The weaker one first.

'This is going to cause very serious difficulties,' de Milja said. The man looked at him sharply. Was he mad? 'In scheduling,' he hastened to add. 'I'm expected someplace else.'

'Well . . .' said the man, not unkindly. So the world went.

'The problem is, I'm supposed to deliver certain funds,' de Milja said. The Breton started the car, which rumbled to life, sputtering and missing. 'It's forty thousand francs – I'm reluctant to leave it here.'

The man was likely proud of his opacity – policemen don't react if they don't choose to – but de Milja saw it hit. At least two years' salary. 'I wonder,' he continued, 'if you could keep that money for me, at the Préfecture. Then I'll be along, later tonight, after my meeting.'

The man with the moustache opened the back door and said something to the driver. Then, to de Milja, 'Where is it?'

'Inside.'

'Let's go.'

He was on the streets for the rest of the night. They went out one door with a briefcase, he went out the other ten minutes later. He moved to cover, checked from a vantage point at 3:15, saw a car at each end of his street with silhouette of driver and passenger.

Au revoir.

He walked miles, headed east into Paris proper, and tried two hotels, but they were locked up tight, doors chained, windows shuttered. On the main thoroughfares, the stream of refugees flowed on; at the intersection of the boulevards Saint-Germain and Saint-Michel humanity collided and struggled as one column moved west, another south. On the north-south Métro lines – Porte d'Orléans – Clignancourt – people fought their way onto trains that would never move. De Milja walked and walked, hiding in chaos.

At least they hadn't killed him. But he had calculated they wouldn't go that far. He was nothing to them, probably just somebody to lock up until the Germans arrived. Welcome to Paris – we couldn't find any flowers but here's a Polish spy. The Breton and Pencil-Moustache had gone back wherever they came from and reported, simply enough, that he wasn't home, so the next shift came on and parked cars at either end of his street.

Dawn was warm, a little strange beneath a disordered sky of scudding purplish cloud. He saw a line of Flemish monks, faces bright red above their woollen robes, toiling along on women's bicycles. A city bus from Lille packed with families, a fire truck from Caen, a tank – a few pathetic twigs tied to its turret in attempted camouflage – an ambulance, a chauffeured Daimler; all of it moving one mile an hour along the choked boulevard. Past an abandoned parrot in a cage, a barrel organ, a hearse with smoke drifting from its blown engine and a featherbed tied to its roof.

He was tired; sat at the base of a plane tree by a bench somewhere and held his head in his hands. Deep instinct, survival, got him on his feet and headed north, towards Clichy and Pigalle, towards whores, who had hotel rooms where nobody asked questions.

Then, a better idea. The neighbourhood around the Gare Saint-Lazare railway station, deep in the ninth arrondissement, was a commercial stew of small, unrespectable enterprises of all kinds. A world of its own where the buildings, the streets, and the people were all a little crooked. You could get insurance from the Agence ABC at the top of the wooden stairway – who didn't need every sort of official documentation in this complex, modern age? – but had you asked them to actually pay a claim they would have fainted with surprise and fallen over onto the packed suitcases that stood by the door. The leather in the Frères Brugger company's chic belts and purses came, unquestionably, from an animal, and, frankly, who were you to demand that it be a cow? And probably you had no business being out in the rain in the first place. There was an agency for singing waiters, an import company for green bamboo, a union office for the drivers of wagons that hauled butchers' bones.

Even a publisher of books – Parthenon Press. There, see the little drawing with the broken columns? That's the Parthenon. They were proud, at the little suite of offices at 39 rue de Rome, to issue an extraordinarily wide and diverse list of books. The poetry of Fedyakov, Vainshtok, Sygelbohm, and Lezhev. The plays of Yushin and Var. And all sorts of novels, all sorts. *October Wheat*, which told of the nobility of peasant life in the Ukraine. *The Sea*, a saga which, through the lives of a family of fisherfolk in the eastern Crimea, suggested the ebb and flow of both oceanic and human tides. *The Baronsky Pearls* – a noble family loses its money and survives on love; *Letter from Smolensk* – experimental fiction about the machines in a tractor factory – no human character appears; *Natasha* – a girl of the streets rises to fame and fortune. There was *Private Chamber*, in English, by Henry Thomas; *The Schoolmistress of Lausanne*, about the need for discipline at a school for wealthy young women, by Thomas Henry; and *Slender Birch*, not, as you might imagine, about the romance of the Russian steppe, by Martin Payne. These novels in English had found an appreciative audience first among British and American soldiers after the Great War, then among tourists from those nations, pleased to find, during their trip to Paris, books in their own language about their own personal interests and hobbies.

The huge pair of ancient, ironbound doors at 39 rue de Rome was firmly locked, but de Milja knocked and refused to go away when nothing happened. Finally, in the first watery light of morning, a panel in the concierge's station by the doorway slid open and a large eye peered out. Clearly he wasn't the German army – just a man with his tie pulled down and sleepless eyes who'd been walking all night – and the door creaked open. The concierge, not a day under eighty, a Lebel rifle held in his trembling hands, said, 'We're closed. What do you want here?'

'Please tell Madame Beilis that a friend has come to call.'

'What friend?'

'A friend from the church of Saint-Etienne-du-Mont, tell her.'

'A priest? You?'

'No,' de Milja said. 'Just an old friend.'

14 June 1940. Dawn. It rained. But then, it would. Not a human soul to be seen in Paris. Out at the Porte d'Auteuil, untended cattle had broken through the fence at the stockyard pens and were wandering about the empty streets mooing and looking for something to eat.

At the northern edge of the city, the sound of a German motorcycle, engine perfectly tuned, approached from the suburbs. A young Wehrmacht soldier sped across the place Voltaire, downshifted, revved the engine a little – *here I am, girls* – put the gear back where it belonged, and disappeared, in a rising whine, up the rue Grenoble.

From the north-east, from the direction of Belgium and Luxembourg and Germany, a series of canvas-covered trucks drove through the Porte de la Villette. One broke off from the file and moved slowly down the rue de Flandre, headed towards the railway stations: the Gare de l'Est and the Gare du Nord and the Gare Saint-Lazare. The truck stopped every few blocks and a single German soldier jumped from the back. Like all the others, the one on the rue de Rome wore white gloves and a crossed white belt. A traffic policeman. When the armoured cars and the troop transports rolled past an hour later, he waved them on.

At seven-thirty in the morning, the German army occupied the Hôtel Crillon and set up an office for local administration in the lobby. Two officers showed up at the military complex just abandoned by Major Kercheval and his colleagues at Invalides and demanded the return of German battle flags captured in 1918. France had lost a war but it was still France. The battle flags, an officer explained, had been mislaid. Of course the gentlemen were more than welcome to look for them.

The Germans hung a swastika flag from the Eiffel Tower, and one from the Arc de Triomphe.

Over on the rue de Rome, Genya Beilis pushed a sheer curtain aside and watched the Wehrmacht traffic policeman at the corner. She lit a Lucky Strike and blew long plumes of smoke from her nostrils. 'What happens now?' she asked.

De Milja came and stood by her, gently pulled the fabric of the curtain from her fingers and let it fall closed. 'The fighting changes,' he said. 'And people hide. Hide in themselves, or hide from the war in enemy beds, or hide in the mountains. Sooner or later, they hide in the sewers. We learn, under occupation, that there's more rat in us than we knew.'

'They'll get rid of us, won't they?' she said.

'Us?'

'All the – what? The little bits and pieces that always seem to wash up in Paris: Russians, Jews, the Spaniards on the run from Franco, Poles and whatnot. Castaways. People who dance naked in ateliers and wave scarves, people who paste feathers and seashells on a board.'

'That "us",' de Milja said. 'The French, the real French, they'll be safe if they mind their manners. But the others, better for them to disappear.'

She left the window, settled herself in a chair at the dining-room table. It was never clear where the office stopped and the residence began. The mahogany table was piled high with stacks of a slim volume in a pale-blue dustjacket – *The Golden Shell*. 'You aren't supposed to be here, are you?' she said.

'Why do you say that?'

'Monsieur Pavel, your, ah, predecessor. One saw him for just a moment. Here or there, in a museum or a big brasserie, someplace public.'

'That's the recommended way.'

'But you don't care.'

'I care,' he said. He started to qualify that, then shrugged.

She got up and went into a pantry off the dining room and started to make coffee, cigarette hanging from her lips. Her blouse was a very flat red and she wore little gold-hoop earrings. In profile, she spooned out coffee, liberally, then fiddled with a nickel-plated coffee urn. Smoke rose around her face and hung in drifts below the brass ceiling lamp. He couldn't stop looking at her; the texture of her hair didn't go with the colour, he thought, so black it should have been coarse. But it hung loose and soft and moved as she did things with her hands.

He couldn't stop looking at her. He had been in the apartment since the previous day, had slept in a spare room, had wanted her so badly it hurt. Anyone would, he thought; man, woman, or tree. It wasn't that she was beautiful. More than that. Dark, and supple, with fingers that lingered on everything she touched for just a moment longer than they should. He wanted to carry her to the bed, put his hands in the waistbands of everything she was wearing and pull down. But then, at the same time, he was afraid to touch her.

On a wall above a desk hung a portrait of the publisher Max Beilis, her father, a small, handsome man with a sneer and angry, brilliant eyes. She would, of course, be his single weakness – *anything she wanted.*

She turned on the radio, let it warm up and tuned into the BBC. He moved closer, could smell a hint of perfume in the cigarette smoke. *People who dance naked in ateliers,* she'd said. Part of her world – the held breath of the audience, the brush of bare feet on cold floorboards. Her Parisian heart could not, of course, be shocked by such things.

On the BBC, modern music, atonal and discordant. Music for the fall of a city. It faded and returned, disappeared into the static, then came in strong. Not jammed, though, not yet – jamming came in rising and falling waves, they'd find that out soon enough. When the announcer came on, Genya leaned forward in concentration, lit a new cigarette, ran her hair back behind one ear.

'And now the news . . .'

The French government had left Tours and had set up shop in Bordeaux. Reynaud had stated that 'France can continue the struggle only if American intervention reverses the situation by making Allied victory certain.' In the USA, the chairman of the Senate Foreign

Relations Committee suggested that, since it was hopeless for the British to fight on alone, they should surrender to Germany. Fighting continued sporadically in France, the Maginot Line was now being abandoned. German troops had crossed the Marne. German forces in Norway this, in Denmark that, in Belgium and Holland the other thing. This morning, German troops had entered Paris and occupied the city.

When it was over, another symphony.

16 July 1940. Banque Nationale de Commerce, Orléans. 11:30 a.m.

Was he French?

Monsieur LeBlanc had a second, covert, look at the man waiting behind the railing that separated bank officers from the cashiers' windows. He was rather clever about people – who was who and what was what, as they said. Now this one had been, in his day, quite the fellow. An athlete or a soldier – a certain pride in the carriage of the shoulders indicated that. But lately, perhaps things weren't going so well. Inexpensive glasses, hat held in both hands – an unconscious gesture of submission – scuffed shoes. A drinker? No, some wine, like all the world, but no more than his share. Death of a loved one? A strong possibility. By now, most of the refugees who'd taken the road south had found their way home, but many had died – the delicate ones, some of the strong as well.

Not French.

Monsieur LeBlanc didn't know how he knew that, but he did. The set of the mouth or the angle of the head, a subtle gesture, revealed the foreigner, *the stranger.* Could he be a German? Hah! What an idea! No German would wait on the pleasure of Monsieur LeBlanc, he'd be served now, ahead of everyone else, and rightly so. Yes, you had to admire that. A shame about the war, a swastika flew over the Lycée where he'd gone to school, and German officers filled the better restaurants. On the other hand, one didn't say so out loud but this might not turn out to be the worst possible thing for France. Hard work, discipline – the German virtues, coupled with the traditional French flair. A triumphant combination for both countries, Monsieur LeBlanc thought, in the New Europe.

'Monsieur.' He gestured towards a chair by the side of his desk.

'*Bonjour, Monsieur,*' said the man.

Not French.

'And you are Monsieur—?'

'Lezhev. Boris Lezhev.'

'Very well, and you will require?'

'A safe-deposit box, Monsieur.'

'You've moved recently to Orléans?'

'Yes, sir.'

Was that all? He waited. Evidently that was all. 'And what size did you have in mind? We have three.'

'The least thick, would be best.'

Ignoramus. He meant the least *large,* but used the word *gros,* which meant thick, or heavy. Oh well, what could one do. He was tired of this shabby Russian. He reached in a drawer and took out a long sheet of yellow paper. He dipped his pen in the inkwell and began taking down Lezhev's particulars; birth and parentage and police card number and residence and work permits and all the rest of it. When he was done, he scratched his initials on the page and went off to retrieve the list of available boxes.

At the assistant cashier's office, a shock awaited him. This was a culturally interesting city but not a major one – Jeanne d'Arc was long gone from sleepy Orléans, now a regional business centre for the farming community. But when Monsieur LeBlanc obtained the list of available boxes, there was exactly one that remained unrented. A number of local residents evidently expected good fortune to be coming their way.

As Lezhev signed forms and accepted the keys, Monsieur LeBlanc took a discreet look at his watch. Only a few minutes until noon. Excellent. What was today? Wednesday. At Tante Marie that meant, uh, blanquette de veau and baby carrots.

'Thank you, Monsieur,' said the Russian.

'You are very welcome, we're pleased to have you, Monsieur, as our customer.'

Barbarian.

And Mildred Green wasn't much better – Monsieur LeBlanc, had he ever encountered her, likely would have clapped his hat on his head and run the other way.

She was squat, homely, and Texan, with sparse hair, a pursed mouth, and a short temper. Her redeeming qualities were, on the other hand, only narrowly known – to American soldiers wounded in the Great War, when she'd been an army nurse, and to the American military attaché in France, for whom she now worked as secretary, administrative assistant, and bull terrier.

The military attaché's office had moved down to Vichy on 5 July, panting hot on the tail of the mobile French government, which had pulled stakes in Bordeaux on the first of July and moved to Vichy on the river Allier, a stuffy old spa town with copious hotels and private houses to absorb the bureaucracy and those privileged souls allowed to kneel at its feet.

Life had not been easy for Mildred Green. The people running France now loathed the British and hated their American cousins. Better Germans, better *anything*, than Brits or Yanks. The assignment of housing space in Vichy rather reflected that point of view, so the villa would take, at least, some fixing up. Water bubbled from the pipes, the windows had last been opened in the heat wave of 1904, mice lived in one closet, squirrels in another, and God only knew what in the third because they could hear it in there but nobody could open the door.

Mildred Green did not lose her temper, staunch amid the hammering and banging, fits of artistic temperament and huge bills courteously presented for no known service or product. She had worked in France since 1937, she knew what to expect, how to deal with it, and how to maintain her own equilibrium in the process – some of the time, anyhow. She knew, for example, that all labourers stopped work around ten in the morning for *casse-croûte*, a piece of bread and some red wine to keep them going until lunchtime.

Thus she was surprised, sitting at her typewriter, when a man carrying a toolbox and wearing *bleu de travail* knocked at the door and asked if he could work on the wiring in her ceiling. She said yes, but had no intention of leaving the office – fearing not so much for the codebooks as for the typewriters. The electrician made a grand show of it, tapped on the wall with a screwdriver handle, then moved to her desk and handed her an envelope. Inside she could feel the outline of a key.

'I'm not an electrician,' the man said in French. 'I'm a Polish army officer and I need to get this letter to the Polish government-in-exile in London.'

Mildred Green did not react, simply tapped a corner of the envelope thoughtfully against her desk. She knew that the French counter-espionage services were aggressive, and fully versed in the uses of *agents provocateurs*. 'I'm not sure I can help you,' she said in correct, one-word-at-a-time French.

'Please,' he said. 'Please help me. Help *us*.'

She took a breath, let it out, face without expression. 'Can't promise you a thing, sir. I will speak to somebody, a decision will be made. If this isn't right, in the garbage it goes. That's the best I can do for you.'

'Read it,' he said. 'It just says that they should contact me, and tells them how to go about it, through a safe-deposit box in Orléans. It can't hurt you to give that information to the Poles in London. On the other hand if you give it to the French I'm probably finished.'

Mildred Green had a mean Texas eye, which now bored into the false electrician in *bleu de travail*. This was, perhaps, monkey business, but likely not. What the Pole didn't know was that when she returned home that night, the hotel desk would have a fistful of messages for her, all of them delivered quietly. From Jews, intellectuals, all sorts of people on the run from Hitler. A few left names, others left instructions – for ads in personal columns, for notes hidden in abandoned workshops, for contact through third parties. Every single one of them was urgent, sometimes desperate. Europe had festered for a long time, now the wound was open and running, and suddenly it seemed as if everybody in the neighbourhood wanted her to clean the damn thing up.

'We'll just have to see,' she said. 'Can't promise anything.' She said that for whatever little ears might be listening. Her real response was to slide the envelope into her big leather shoulder bag – a gesture her lost Pole immediately understood. He inclined his head to thank her – almost a bow – then saluted. Then vanished.

The nights of July were especially soft that Paris summer. All cars, taxis, and buses had been requisitioned by the Germans, and with curfew at 11:00 p.m., windows masked by blackout curtains, and the streetlamps painted over, the city glowed a deep, luminous blue, like Hollywood moonlight, while the steps of a lone policeman echoed for blocks in the empty streets. Nightingales returned and sang in the shrubbery, and the night-time breeze carried great clouds of scent from the flowers in the parks. Paris, like a princess in a folk tale, found itself ancient, enchanted, and chained. Hidden away on a side street in the seventh arrondisse-ment – the richest, and most aloof, of all Parisian neighbourhoods – the Brasserie Heininger was an oasis of life on these silent evenings. Started by competing beer breweries at the turn of the century, the brasseries of Paris had never abandoned their fin-de-siècle glitter. At Heininger, a white marble staircase climbed to a room of red-plush banquettes, mirrors trimmed in gold, painted cupids, and lamps lowered to a soft glow. Waiters with muttonchop whiskers ran across the carpet carrying silver trays of langouste with mayonnaise, sausage grilled black, and whole poached salmon in golden aspic. The brasserie spirit was refined madness; you opened your heart, you laughed and shouted and told your best secrets – tonight was the last night on earth and here was the best place to spend it.

And if the Heininger cuisine was rich and aromatic, the history of the place was even more so. In 1937, as storm clouds gathered over Europe, the Bulgarian headwaiter Omaraeff had been shot to death in the ladies' room by an NKVD assassin while two accomplices raked the mirrored walls with tommy-gun fire. A single mirror had survived the evening, its one bullet hole a monument, the table beneath it – number fourteen, seating ten – becoming almost immediately the favoured venue of the restaurant's preferred clientele. Lady Angela Hope, later exposed in *Le Matin* as an operative of the British Secret Intelligence Service, was said to have recruited the agent known as *Curate* – a Russian foreign correspondent – at that table. Ginger Pudakis, wife of the Chicago meat baron, had made it her evening headquarters, with Winnie and Dicky Beale, the American stove-pipe millionaires, the Polish Countess K – and her deerhound, and the mysterious LaReine Haric-Overt. Fum, the beloved clown of the Cirque Dujardin, was often seen there, with the tenor Mario Thoeni, the impresario Adelstein, and the dissolute British captain-of-the-night Roddy Fitzware. What times were had at table fourteen! Astonishing revelations, brilliant seductions, lost fortunes, found pleasures.

Then war came. And from the fourth of June to the twenty-eighth of June, the great brasserie slumbered in darkness behind its locked shutters.

But such a place could not die any more than the city of Paris could; it had come alive again, and table fourteen once again took centre stage at its nightly theatre. Some of the regulars returned; Mario Thoeni was often there – though his friend Adelstein had not been seen lately – Count Iava still came by, as did Kiko Bettendorf, the race-car driver and Olympic fencer for Germany, now serving in the local administration.

Kiko's stylish friends, on arriving in Paris from Hamburg or Munich, had made the Brasserie Heininger a second home. On this particular summer night, Freddi Schoen was there, just turned twenty-eight, wearing a handsomely tailored naval officer's uniform that set off his angular frame and pretty hazel eyes. Next to him sat his cousin, Traudl von Behr, quite scarlet with excitement, and her close friend, the Wehrmacht staff officer Paul Jünger. They had been joined at table fourteen by the White Russian general Vassily Fedin, who'd given the Red Army such a bad time outside Odessa in 1919; the general's longtime fellow-émigré, the world-wandering poet Boris Lezhev; and the lovely Genya Beilis, of the Parthenon Press publishing family. Completing the party were M. Pertot – whose Boucheries Pertot provided beef to all German installations in the Lower Normandy region – tonight accompanied by his beautiful niece; and the Baron Baillot de Coutry, whose company provided cement for German construction projects along the northern coasts of France and Belgium; tonight accompanied by his beautiful niece.

Just after midnight – the Brasserie Heininger was untroubled by the curfew, the occupation authorities had quickly seen to that – Freddi

Schoen tapped a crystal vase with his knife, and held a glass of Pétrus up to the light. 'A toast,' he said. 'A toast.'

The group took a moment to subside – not everybody spoke quite the same language, but enough people spoke enough of them – French, German, English – so that everybody more or less understood, with occasional help from a neighbour, most of what was going on. In this milieu one soon learned that a vague smile was appropriate to more than ninety per cent of what went on in the world.

'To this night,' Freddi said, turning the glass back and forth in front of the light. 'To these times.' There was more, everybody waited. M. Pertot, all silver hair and pink skin, smiled encouragement. 'To,' Freddi said. The niece of Baron Baillot de Coutry blinked twice.

'Wine and friendship?' the poet Lezhev offered.

Freddi Schoen stared at him a moment. This was *his* toast. But then, Lezhev was a man of words. 'Yes,' Freddi said, just the bare edge of a sulk in his voice. 'Wine and friendship.'

'Hear, hear,' said M. Pertot, raising his glass in approval. 'One must drink to such a wine.' He paused, then said, 'And friendship. Well, these days, that means something.'

Freddi Schoen smiled. That's what he'd been getting at – unities, harmonies.

'One Europe,' General Fedin said. 'We've had too many wars, too much squabbling. We must go forward together.' He had a hard face, the bones sharply evident beneath the skin, and smoked a cigarette in an ivory holder clenched between his teeth.

Jünger excused himself from the table, M. Pertot spoke confidentially to his niece, the waiter poured wine in Mademoiselle Beilis's glass.

'Is that what you meant, Herr Lezhev?' Freddi said quietly.

'Yes. We'll have one Europe now, with strong leadership. And strength is the only thing we Europeans understand.'

Freddi Schoen nodded agreement. He was fairly drunk, and seemed preoccupied with some interior dialogue. 'I envy you your craft,' he said after a moment.

'Mine?' Lezhev's smile was tart.

'Yes, yours. It is difficult.' Freddi said.

'It cannot be "easy" to be a naval officer, Lieutenant Schoen.'

'Pfft.' Freddi Schoen laughed to himself. 'Sign a paper, give an order. The petty officers, clerks, you know, tell me what to do. It can be technical. But people like yourself, who can see a thing, and can make it come alive.' He shook his head.

Lezhev squinted one eye. 'You write, Lieutenant.' A good-humoured accusation.

A pink flush spread along Freddi Schoen's jawline, and he shook his head.

'No? Then what?'

'I, ah, put some things on canvas.'

'You paint.'

'I try, sometimes . . .'

'Portraits? Nudes?'

'Country scenes.'

'Now that *is* difficult.'

'I try to take the countryside, and to express an emotion. To feel what emotion it has, and to bring that out. The melancholy of autumn. In spring, abandon.'

Lezhev smiled, and nodded as though confirming something to himself – *now this fellow makes sense, all night I wondered, but I couldn't quite put my finger on it.*

'Here is . . . guess who!' The wild shout came from Lieutenant Jünger, who had returned to the table with a tall, striking Frenchwoman in captivity. She was a redhead, fortyish, with a Cupid's-bow mouth, carmine lipstick, and a pair of enormous breasts corseted to sharp points in a black silk evening dress. Jünger held her tightly above the elbow.

'Please forgive the intrusion,' she said.

'Tell them!' Jünger shouted. 'You must!' He was a small-boned man with narrow shoulders and tortoiseshell eyeglasses. Very drunk and sweaty and pale at the moment, and swaying back and forth.

'My name is Fifi,' she said. 'My baptismal name is Françoise, but Fifi I am called.'

Jünger doubled over and howled with laughter. Pertot and Baillot de Coutry and the two nieces wore the taut smiles of people who just know the punchline of the joke will be hilarious when it comes.

Freddi Schoen said, 'Paul?' but Jünger gasped for breath and, shaking the woman by jerking on her elbow, managed to whisper, 'Say what you do! Say what you do!'

Her smile was now perhaps just a degree forced. 'I work in the cloakroom – take the customers' coats and hats.'

'The hatcheck girl! Fifi the French hatcheck girl!' Jünger whooped with laughter and grabbed at the table to steady himself; the cloth began to slide but Pertot – the cheerful, expectant smile on his face remaining absolutely fixed in place – shot out a hand and grabbed the bottle of Pétrus. A balloon glass of melon balls in kirsch tumbled off the edge of the table and several waiters came rushing over to clean up.

'Bad Paul, bad Paul.' Traudl von Behr's eyes glowed with admiration. She had square shoulders and straw hair and very white skin that had turned even redder at Lieutenant Jünger's performance. 'Well, *sit down,*' she said to the tall Frenchwoman. 'You must tell us all about those hats, and how you check them.'

Jünger shrieked with laughter. The corner of Fifi's mouth trembled and a man with grey hair materialized at her side and led her away. 'A problem in the cloakroom!' he called back over his shoulder, joining the mood just enough to make good their escape.

'Those two! They were like that in school,' Freddi Schoen said to Lezhev. 'We all were.' He smiled with amused recollection. 'Such a sweet madness,' he added. 'Such a special time. Do you know the University of Göttingen?'

'I don't,' Lezhev said.

'If only I had your gift – it is not like other places, and the students are not like other students. Their world has,' he thought a moment, 'a glow!' he said triumphantly.

Lezhev understood. Freddi Schoen could see that he did. Strange to find such sympathy in a Russian, usually blunt and thick-skinned. A pea hit him in the temple. He covered his eyes with his hand – what could you *do* with such friends? He glanced over to see Traudl von Behr using a page torn from the *carte des vins*, rolled up into a blowpipe. She was bombarding a couple at another table, who pretended not to notice.

'It's hopeless,' Freddi Schoen said to Lezhev. 'But I would like to continue this conversation some other time.'

'This week, perhaps?'

Freddi Schoen started to answer, then Jünger yelled his name so he shrugged and nodded yes and turned to see what his friend wanted.

Lezhev excused himself and went to the palatial men's room, all sage-coloured marble and polished brass fixtures. He stared at his face in the mirror and took a deep breath. He seemed to be ten thousand miles away from everything. From one of the stalls came the voice of General Fedin, a rough-edged voice speaking Russian. 'We're alone?'

'Yes.'

'Careful with him, Alexander.'

Noontime, the late July day hot and still. The German naval staff had chosen for its offices a financier's mansion near the Hotel Bristol, just a few steps off the elegant Faubourg St-Honoré. Lezhev waited in a park across the street as naval officers in twos and threes trotted briskly down the steps of the building and walked around the cobbled carriage path on their way to lunch. When Freddi Schoen appeared outside the door of the mansion and peered around, Lezhev waved.

'You're certain this will be acceptable?' Freddi Schoen asked, as they walked towards the river.

'I'm sure,' Lezhev said. 'Everything's going well?'

'Ach yes, I suppose it is.'

'Every day something new?' Lezhev said.

'No. You'd have to be in the military to understand. Sometimes a superior officer will really tell off a subordinate. It mustn't be taken to heart – it's just the way these things have always been done.'

'Well then, tomorrow it's your turn.'

'Of course. You're absolutely right to see it that way.'

They walked through the summer streets, crossed the Seine at the place de la Concorde. Parisians now rode about on bicycle-cart affairs, taxi-bicycles that advertised themselves as offering 'Speed, comfort, safety!' The operators – only yesterday Parisian cab-drivers – had changed neither their manners nor their style; now they simply pedalled madly instead of stomping on the accelerator.

'Are you hard at work writing?' Schoen asked.

'Yes, when I can. I have a small job at Parthenon, it takes up most of my time.'

'We all face that.' They admired a pair of French girls in frocks so light they floated even on a windless day. 'Good afternoon, ladies,' Schoen said with a charming smile, tipping his officer's cap. They ignored him with tosses of the head, but not the really serious kind. It seemed to make him feel a little better. 'May I ask what you are writing about these days?'

'Oh, all that old Russian stuff – passion for the land, Slavic melancholy, life and fate. You know.'

Schoen chuckled. 'You keep a good perspective, that's important, I think.'

They reached the Saint-Germain-des-Prés quarter, one of the centres of Parisian arts, and Parisian artiness as well. The cafés were busy; the customers played chess, read the collaborationist newspapers, argued, flirted, and conspired in a haze of pipe smoke. Freddi Schoen and Lezhev turned up a narrow street with three German staff cars parked half on the sidewalk. Schoen was nervous. 'It won't be crowded, will it?'

'You won't notice.'

They climbed five flights of stairs to an unmarked door that stood open a few inches. Inside they found nine or ten German officers, hands clasped behind their backs or insouciantly thrust into pockets, very intent on what they were watching. One of them, a Wehrmacht colonel, turned briefly to see who'd come in. The message on his face was clear:

do not make your presence evident here, no coughing or boot scraping or whispering or, God forbid, conversation.

At the far end of the room, lit by a vast skylight, Pablo Picasso, wearing wide trousers and rope-soled Basque espadrilles, was sketching with a charcoal stick on a large sheet of newsprint pinned to the wall. At first the shape seemed a pure abstraction, but then a horse emerged. One leg bent up, head turned sideways and pressed forward and down – it was not natural, not the way a horse's body worked. Lezhev understood it as tension: an animal form forced into an alien position. Understood it all too well.

'My God,' Freddi Schoen whispered in awe.

The colonel's head swivelled round, his ferocious eye turning them both to stone as Picasso's charcoal scratched across the rough paper.

2 August. Occupation or no occupation, Parisians left Paris in August: streets empty, heat flowing in waves from the stone city. A telephone call from Freddi Schoen cancelled lunch near the Parthenon Press office. Too busy.

4 August. Late-afternoon coffee. But not on the Faubourg St-Honoré. The addition of extra staff, he apologized, had forced his department to find new, likely temporary, quarters: a former college of pharmacy not far from the wine warehouses at the eastern end of the city.

7 August. A soirée to celebrate Freddi Schoen's new painting studio in the Latin Quarter. Cocktails at seven, supper to follow. Invitations had been sent out in late July, but now the arrival time was changed. Telephone calls from a German secretary set it for eight. Then nine-thirty. Freddi Schoen did not appear until eleven-fifteen, pale and sweaty and out of breath.

The paintings, hung around the room and displayed on three easels, weren't so bad. They were muddy, and dense. The landscapes themselves, almost exclusively scenes of canals, might have been, probably were, luminous. But light and shadow were unknown to Freddi Schoen. Here you had woods. So. There you had water. So. The former was green. The latter was blue. So.

After a few glasses of wine, Freddi shook his head sadly. He could see. 'In the countryside it is right there before you, right there,' he said to Lezhev. 'But then you try to make it on the canvas, and look what happens.'

'Oh,' said Lezhev, 'don't carry on so. We've all been down this road.'

It was, Lezhev could tell, the *we* that thrilled Freddi Schoen – he was one of them. 'It's time that helps,' he added, the kindly poet.

'Time!' Freddi said. 'I tell you I don't have it – some of these I did when everybody else was eating lunch.'

'Let me fill your glass,' Genya said. Her kindness was practised – she'd been soothing frantic writers since girlhood, by now it was second nature. She well knew the world where nothing was ever good enough. So, nothing was. So what?

Freddi Schoen smiled gratefully at her, then some German friends demanded his attention. Genya leaned close to Lezhev and said, 'Can you take me home when this is over?'

Clothes off, laid on a chair along with Lezhev's personality. A relief after a day that seemed a hundred hours long. De Milja stared at the ceiling above Genya's bed, picked over the evening, decided that he hadn't done all that well. I'm a *mapmaker*, he thought. I can't do these other things, these deceptions. All he'd ever wanted was to show people the way home – now look what he'd become, the world's most completely lost man.

Not his fault that he was cut off from the Sixth Bureau in London – he was improvising, doing the best he could, doing what he supposed they would have wanted done and waiting for them to re-establish contact. *Yes, but even so*, he said to himself. This wasn't an operation, it was an, an *adventure*. And he suspected it wasn't going to end well for anybody.

But, otherwise, what?

'Share this with me,' Genya said. He inhaled her breath and perfume mixed in the smoke. She had a dark shadow on her upper lip, and a dark line that ran from her navel to her triangle. Or at least that's where it disappeared, like a seam. He traced it gently with his fingernail.

She put the cigarette out delicately, took the ashtray off the bed and put it on the night table. Then she settled back, took his hand and put it between her legs and held it there. Then she sighed. It wasn't a passionate sigh, it simply meant she liked his hand between her legs, and not much else in the world made her happy, and the sigh was more for the second part of the thought than the first. 'Yes,' she said, referring to the state of affairs down below, 'that's for you.'

Of course in a few hours she would spy for him, if that was what he wanted. The *schleuh* – the Germans – couldn't just be allowed to, well, they couldn't just be allowed. This was France, she was French, she'd sung the national anthem in school with her little hand on her little breast – excuse her, her little heart. If the world demanded fighting, she'd fight. Just the instant they got out of bed. What? Not quite yet?

'France spreads her legs,' he'd once said in a moment of frustration.

Yes, she supposed it rather did, everybody had always said so. They'd said so in *Latin*, for God's sake, so it must be true. Did he not, after all, approve of spread legs? Did he not wish to spread her legs? Oh, pardon her, *évidemment* a mistake on her part. And did he also find France, like her, duck-assed? What did that mean? It meant this.

There was an English pilot, shot out of the sky in the early raids over France, they had heard about him. He'd been taken in by farmers up in Picardy, where they'd lost everything to the Germans in the last war. They knew that trained pilots were weapons, just like rifles or tanks. Not innocent up there. So they passed him along, from the curé to the schoolmistress to the countess to the postman, and he went to ground in Paris in late June, just after the surrender. Certainly he would be heading back to England, there to fight once more. How else could he arrange to be shot down and killed – a fate which had danced maddeningly out of reach on the previous try.

Only, he didn't want to be put on the escape route down to the Pyrenees, guided across to freedom by patriots, or sold to the Spanish police by realists – it all depended these days on whom one happened to meet. Then he met Sylvie or Monique or Francette or whoever it was, and he decided that Paris might be, even hidden out, just the very place to spend the war. Because he'd learned a terrible truth about the Germans: unless you were a Jew they wouldn't bother you if you didn't bother them. The French understood that right away.

So the pilot stayed hidden, and he chanced to gamble, and he chanced to win a racehorse. And, the second week in July, the racetracks opened. Goebbels had ordered that France return to merriment and gaiety or he'd have them all hanged, so the racetracks joined the whorehouses and the movie theatres, which had closed for twenty-four long hours the day the Germans arrived. The pilot's horse won. And won again. It ran like the wind – a good idea for a horse in a city with horsemeat butchers and rationed beef. And the English pilot was in no hurry at all to go home.

That was one answer to the question *what should we do about the Germans.* Genya Beilis stood naked at the window and pulled the blackout curtain aside so she could see the sky. 'My God, the stars,' she said.

He rolled off the damp sheet and stood by her, their bare skin touching. He bent his knees in order to see above the roof across the street, a mediaeval clutter of chimneys and broken slates and flowerpots, and there was the sky. There was no city light, the summer heavens were satin black with a sweep of white stars. 'Look,' she said.

*

15 August. Ninety-five degrees in the street. They had no idea what it was in the attic under the copper-sheeted roof, amid trunks and piles of gauze curtains, stacks of picture frames and a dressmaker's dummy, all of it the colour of dust. The BBC had a particular, very identifiable, sound to it, and they worried about neighbours, or people passing in the street. Some Parisians had seen right away that Germans should be treated like other visitors; groomed and fed and milked. The characteristic British voice, amid the static and hiss, meant there was a 'terrorist' or a 'Bolshevik' in the neighbourhood, and you could get a damn good price for one of those if you knew who to talk to down at the local police station.

It was too hot and dirty for clothes, so they stripped at the foot of the narrow staircase and climbed up in their underwear. They sat on a sprung old sofa that somebody had covered with a sheet, and put the radio on the floor, with picture wire run up into the eaves as an aerial. In the evening, when reception was marginally better, Genya would stare into space as she concentrated on the radio voice; bare brown arms clasping her knees, hair limp in the humid summer air, sweat glistening between her breasts.

Midnight in the century, someone called that time, and she was the perfect companion for it. He was lucky, he thought, that at the end he had a woman to be with. Because the end had pretty clearly come. First Czechoslovakia, then Poland, then Norway, Denmark, Belgium, and Holland. Then France. Now England. It wasn't a question of if, only how. And then a matter – not uncomplicated – of working out your personal arrangements with what was called the New Europe.

On the subject of the immediate future, two French generals had recently been heard from. Weygand, who'd helped the Poles beat the Russians in 1920, had said that the Germans would 'wring England's neck like a chicken'. De Gaulle, a former defence minister, had surfaced in London and was trying to sell the French the idea of resistance, while *L'Humanité*, the communist newspaper, called him a British agent, and advised French workers to welcome German soldiers and to make them feel at home.

On the sweltering evening of 15 August, the BBC had 'music for dancing, with the Harry Thorndyke Society Orchestra from Brighton', then the news: 'In the skies over Britain today, more than one thousand five hundred sorties were flown against various targets, met by hundreds of RAF fighter planes and turned back.'

Then, Harry Thorndyke himself: 'Good evening, everybody. Good evening, good evening. Tonight, we thought it might be just the thing to pay a call on Mr Cole Porter – thank you, thank you – and so now, without further ado, why don't we just . . . "Begin the Beguine"?'

Genya flopped over on her stomach, hands beneath her chin. They listened to the music in silence for a while, then she said, 'How long will it take?'

'A few weeks.'

'Perhaps the English planes can win.'

'Perhaps. But the German planes are probably better.'

'We French had fighter planes, you know. Made by a certain Monsieur Bloch – and very rich he got, too. They were known as "*cerceuils volants*", flying coffins, but nobody thought it mattered. An opportunity for the French pilots to show how much more skilful and courageous they were than their German opponents, who had superior machines.'

There was no answering that.

'It's hot,' she said. 'I smell.'

There was no answering that either. The music played, through the crackling night air, and they listened, preoccupied and silent. He unhooked her bra, and she pushed herself up so he could get it free of her. He rubbed his finger across the welt it had made on the skin of her back.

'Why does it do that?'

'Too tight,' she said. 'And cheap. I buy them from the Arab carts up on the boulevard Clichy.'

'What about these?'

'Silk.'

He slid her panties down.

'You like that?' she said.

'Yes.'

'French girls have the most beautiful asses in Europe.'

'Well, this French girl.'

'No, Alexander, I am serious. Women are cold on this point, there's no illusion. And we are just built the way we are. What I wonder is, do you suppose that it's why they always come here?'

'You mean this is what the conquerors are after?'

'Yes.'

'Perhaps they are. And the gold. Steel mills, castles. Bloodstock and paintings. Your watch.' He traced his finger along her curves.

'Alexander?'

'Yes?'

'Should we go to Switzerland?'

He thought for a time. 'They'd just kick us out. And everybody in Europe can't go to Switzerland.'

'Yes, but *we* can, I think. There's time to do that, for the moment. And if we stay here, I feel in my heart that they will kill us. We don't matter to anybody, my sweet boy, not to anybody at all.'

'I don't think,' he said slowly, 'that it's time to run.'

She closed her eyes, moved her hips a little, took a deep breath and exhaled slowly, a sorrowful sound. 'You know what it is, Alexander? I like to fuck. It's that simple. To drink a glass of wine. Just to watch the day go by in the most pointless way.'

'Really? You like those sorts of things?'

'All right, I give up. Go ahead and get me killed. But you know what will be my revenge? I'll leave a will and have a statue built in a public square: it will be you and I, just exactly as we are now, in polished stone. *Patriots in 1940* it will be called. A true-life monument for the tourists to visit. Ow! Yes, good, that's exactly what you'll be doing on the statue.'

'Lezhev, you must help me.'

It was just a manner of speaking, but when Freddi Schoen used the expression, even over the noisy line of a French telephone, the *must* had a way of lingering in the air.

'Of course. What is it?'

'First of all, please understand that I am in love.'

'Bravo.'

'No, Lezhev, I beg you, don't make light of it. She is, it is, just don't, all right?'

'You are smitten.'

'Yes. It's true. Cupid's arrow – it was an ambush, completely a surprise. A dinner in Passy, I didn't want to go. The man's in textiles, a vicomte he says, some sort of complicated business connection with my family. Expecting the worst, I went. And then . . .'

'She is French?'

'Very. And of the most elevated family – that's the problem.'

'Problem?'

'Well, here is what happened. I arrived late, and very excited. I had just taken a country estate; a lovely place and, great good luck for me, an open lease, so I can have it as long as I like. The owner was most accommodating. So naturally I talked about it at the dinner – where it was, and how old, and the river – and she was delighted. "*Ah, les collines d'Artois, mais qu'elles sont belles!*" she said. So I said, "But you must come and see it." And I could tell she wanted to but there was, how to say, a momentary sense of frost in the air. Then I realized! For me to ask her there alone would be most awkward, but with friends . . . So quickly I added that a couple I knew was coming on Sunday, wouldn't she join us for lunch? And Mama and Papa too, I insist! But no, as soon as they heard there was another couple, they were occupied. So, now . . .'

'We're the couple.'

'You must say yes!'

'Yes. And with pleasure.'

'Thank heaven. I'll have Fauchon do the picnic, in wicker hampers, with Dom Pérignon, and monogrammed champagne flutes, and lobsters, and the napkins they have that fit in the little leather loops in the hamper. What do you think?'

'Perfect.'

'Now, here is my scheme. My driver will take the two of us up there – it's a good morning's drive from Paris – and that way we'll be alone, but, of course, by happenstance, so all will be quite correct.'

'A natural situation.'

'Who could object? Meanwhile, you and Mademoiselle Beilis will take the train up to Boulogne – it gets in there from Paris about noon. And we'll pick you up. Did I mention the day? Sunday.'

'*Boulogne?*'

Genya, paying bills in the Parthenon office, looked up in surprise. 'Nobody's been there since 1890. Deauville, yes. Cabourg, well, maybe. But Boulogne?'

'What's it like?'

'It's all those *sur-la-plage* paintings – the French flag fluttering in the breeze, miles of sand because the tide's always out, little dogs, ladies with hats.'

'Actually, the way he spoke, it sounded as though the house was inland – "the hills of Artois".'

'Well I hope he doesn't dig in his garden – because what he'll find is bones and unexploded shells. That's *Flanders*, is what that is.'

The goddess was, as advertised, a goddess. Fine porcelain, with china-blue eyes and spots of colour in the cheeks, thick auburn hair with a flip that just touched the collar, and a porcelain heart. Freddi Schoen was lost – if he'd cantered about on his hands and knees and bayed it might, *might*, have been more obvious.

As for Lezhev and Genya, the porcelain doll wasted no time. She couldn't have been sweeter *but*: one could understand that a foreign gentleman might not have the knack of social relations in a new country; however, if she took possession of this particular spaniel, they could be sure that he'd seen the last of émigré poets and publishers' daughters. Rue de Rome publishers' daughters especially.

Lezhev found it damned hard to be Lezhev. The toasts, the snippets of poems, and all that whooping and carrying-on – his version of a Russian poet *loved and lived life to the hilt.* Sometimes he silently apologized to poor Lezhev's shade; clearly he hadn't loved life all that much, but Freddi Schoen seemed responsive to the performance so that's where he pitched it, with Genya loving life to the hilt right beside him.

De Milja, on the other hand, had an unforeseen reaction to the porcelain doll. To his considerable surprise, she offended the aristocrat in him, put him in mind of the Ostrow uncles, who would have made short work of such snobbery.

Still whatever his taste in French aristocrats, Freddi Schoen had been right about the estate. A very old Norman farmhouse – how it had survived the unending wars in that part of the world God only knew, but there it was. Ancient timber and cracked plaster, leaning left and right at once, with tiny windows to keep the arrows out and thick walls to keep the dampness in. It sat in a valley just over a low hill from the river Authie, which just there was quite pretty, winding its course past a network of canals. Naturally August would be its most sumptuous month, the woods a thousand shades of gold and green in the tender light of the French countryside, the banks of the canals cut back to stands of willow, leaves dancing in the little sea breeze. For they were only a few miles from La Manche, the French name for what was called, on the opposite shore some thirty miles away, the English Channel.

After lunch they went for a ride, Freddi Schoen's driver dressed up in a chauffeur's uniform for the day. The road ran through breathtaking countryside, forest to the left, meadow to the right. Surprising how the land had healed since 1918, but it had. The grass grew lush and deep green, and there was a cloud of orange butterflies at the edge of a canal where even the barges – some two hundred and forty of them at Lezhev's count, it took several minutes to drive past – seemed part of the natural beauty of the place. Or, at least, not alien to it; big, square hulls, dark and tarry from a thousand journeys, with only the painted names, Dutch, Belgian, German, or French, to disrupt the harmony of the handsome old wood.

Freddi Schoen, holding court on the leather seat of the big Mercedes, was at his best, charming and voluble and witty as only he could be; the porcelain doll smiled with delight and it was all Lezhev and Genya could do to keep up. Sitting next to the driver, Freddi hung his elbow over the seat and entertained them. 'Of course the admiral was a *Prussian,* with a big, red face like, oh, like . . . a ball!'

Ha ha, but was it eighteen tugboats tied in a row after the intersection of the Route Departmentale 34? No, twenty, Genya told him later.

'A deer!' Freddi Schoen cried out. Then, when the women turned to look at the forest side of the road, he winked at Lezhev. Wasn't this fine? These two French lovelies riding with them along a road in a Pissarro painting? From Lezhev, a poet's smile of vast sagacity, confirmed by a wise little shake of the head. No, life wasn't all bad, it had its moments of great purity, say on a summer day near the sea, rolling past a particularly charming little canal, where some good old soul a generation ago had planted borders of Lombardy poplar, where thirty-one seagoing tugs, tied up to cleats, bobbed lazily when the wind ruffled the surface of the still water.

'I saw it!' Genya Beilis cried out.

Freddi Schoen's eyes grew wide with amazement – his little joke had grown wings. Fate had put a real deer in the forest; even the gods of Chance were with them today.

19 August, Banque Nationale de Commerce, Orléans.

An old woman wearing a funeral hat had preceded him into one of the little rooms where one communed with one's safe-deposit box. He could hear her through the wall, mumbling to herself, then counting, each number articulated with whispered ferocity. '*Quatorze. Quinze. Seize. Dix-sept. Dix-huit.*'

Lezhev had less to whisper about. Only a small slip of paper: 'Hôtel Bretagne. 38, rue Lepic. Room 608. You are Monsieur Gris, from Lille.'

To hell and gone up an endless hill in the back streets of Montmartre, a hotel two windows wide and six floors tall, the smell of the toilet in the hall good and strong on the fiery August day.

He knocked.

'Yes?'

'Monsieur Gris. From Lille.'

She was five feet tall, blonde hair cut back to a boyish cap above a round face and a snub nose. Scared to death, intrepid, Polish.

'How old are you?' he asked in French. She just stood there. He tried again in Polish.

'Seventeen,' she said.

She went to the peeling armoire and opened the door. The suitcase radio was open and ready to transmit. 'You are not to be here when I send,' she explained. 'An order.'

He indicated that he understood.

She went on, a carefully memorized speech. 'Colonel Vyborg sends his regards. You are to occupy yourself with information pertinent to the German plan to attack Great Britain. Where, how, and when. He tells you that the English are the only hope now – aeroplane drops of ammunition and money and specialists are planned for Poland. For their part, they ask our help in France, in any way we are able. I am to transmit for you, whenever you like, as much as you like.'

'How did you come?'

'Fishing boat to the Brittany coast, from Scotland. Then on a train.'

'With the suitcase in hand.'

She shrugged. 'There is no control on the trains. It's very different here.'

'Where were you in Poland?'

'Lodz. I came to France as a courier, then we fled on the ship *Batory*, from Bordeaux. On the twenty-second of June, after the surrender. We were the last ship to leave France.'

'What name do I call you?' he asked.

'Janina,' she said. Her smile was radiant, they were comrades in arms, she was proud to serve at his side. She returned to the armoire, brought out a thick packet of French francs. 'We will beat them, Monsieur Gris. We will certainly beat them.'

The two brothers owned a garage in Saclay, in the poor southern suburbs of Paris. This was Wednesday, another three days until the Saturday shave, the white bristle on their cheeks was shiny with motor oil and dark with grime. Hidden somewhere in the complex of fallen-down sheds was a pig they were fattening for market; de Milja and Fedin could hear it grunting and snuffling in the mud.

'When will the pig be ready?' de Milja said.

'October,' one brother said. ' "Cannibal", we call him.'

'We need a little Citroen truck, a delivery truck.'

'Expensive, such things.'

'We know.'

'Could be fifteen thousand francs.'

'Maybe nine.'

'Fifteen, I think I said.'

'Eleven, then.'

'What money?'

'French francs.'

'We like those American dollars.'

'Francs is what we have.'

'Fourteen five – don't say we didn't give you a break. Have it with you?'

De Milja showed a packet of notes, the man nodded and grunted with satisfaction. When he leaned close, de Milja could smell the wine in his sweat. 'What country do you come from?' he asked. 'I want to hear about it.' The second brother had left the shack abruptly after the money was shown – de Milja had barely noticed that he'd gone. Now Fedin stood at the door, shaking his head in mock disillusion and pointing a Lüger out into the yard. 'Put that down,' he said.

The response was a whine. 'I was just going to cut up some firewood. To cook the lunch.'

They used what they had:

Whatever remained of the old Polish networks, sturdy White Russian operatives who'd put in their time for a variety of services, friends, friends of friends. They were not so concerned about being betrayed to the Germans. That would happen – it was just a question of when, and whether or not they would be surprised when they figured out who'd done it.

'As you get older, you accept venality. Then you learn to like it – a certainty in an uncertain world.' Fedin the skull, the Lüger under his worker's apron, cigarette holder clenched in his teeth as though he were a Chinese warlord in a Fu Manchu film.

Wearing workmen's smocks, they drove their little delivery van slowly through what remained of the streets of Dunkirk. Two hundred thousand weapons had been left on the oil-stained beaches, abandoned by the British Expeditionary Force and several French divisions making their escape across the Channel. All along the shore, German soldiers were trying to deal with the mess, stripping tyres from shot-up trucks, emptying ammunition from machine gun belts.

In the back streets they found a heavy woman who walked with a cane and kept a dollmaker's shop not far from the canals that ran out into the countryside. She painted eyebrows on tiny doll heads with a cat's whisker, and counted barges when she walked her elderly poodle. She was a Frenchwoman; her Polish coal-miner husband had gone off to fight in Spain in the Dabrowsky Brigade, and that was the last she'd heard of him. De Milja's predecessor had found her through a relief organization, and now the Polish service was her *petit boulot*, her little job. Before the Germans had come she'd been a postbox on a secret mail route, a courier, the owner of a discreet upstairs bedroom where one could get away from the world for a night or two without hotel – and therefore police – registration.

'A hard week, Monsieur,' she said as de Milja counted out francs.

'You're confident of your numbers?'

'Oh yes, Monsieur. One hundred and seven of the beastly things. It took four expeditions to find them all.'

'Well then, keep up the good work. This may go on for months.'

'Mmm? Poor Roquette.' The poodle's tail managed a single listless thump against the floorboards when she heard her name. Perhaps, de Milja thought, Rocket had been the right name for her at one time, but that was long ago. 'Having to walk all those miles on that cinder path,' the woman added.

'Buy her a lamb chop,' de Milja said, counting out some extra francs into the attentive hand.

Fedin was exactly right, de Milja thought, as a German sentry waved them away from a turn-off for the coastal road – the pleasure of venality was that Madame would be faithful as long as the francs held out.

The van rolled to a stop. De Milja climbed out and approached the sentry. 'Excuse, kind sir. This place?' He showed the soldier, who smiled involuntarily at de Milja's eccentric German, a commissary form. On the bottom, an inventory of Vienna sausage and tinned sardines; on top, an address.

'The airfield,' the sentry said. 'You must go down this road, but mind your own business.'

The Germans were of two minds, it seemed to him. Down the beach road, all preparations were defensive. Engineered – concrete – positions with heavy machine guns pointing out into the Channel. Rows of concrete teeth sunk into the sand at the low-tide mark, strung with generous coils of barbed wire. French POWs were digging trenches and building anti-aircraft gun emplacements, and clusters of artillery had been positioned just behind the sand dunes. This was nothing to do with an invasion of England: this was somebody worried that the British were coming back, unlikely as that seemed. But then somebody, *some-body* had screamed 'We will invade!' and so Freddi Schoen and all the rest of the Kriegsmarine, the German navy, had started moving barges up and down the canals of Europe. They must have stripped every river in northern Europe, de Milja thought. Stopped commerce dead. On the Danube and the Rhine, the Weser and the Mosel, the Yser, Escaut, Canche, and Somme, nothing moved.

Fedin laid it out for him. Quite a number of the Russian generals in Paris had never been in anyone's army, but Fedin was a real general who'd commanded real troops in battle and done well at it. De Milja watched with admiration as he planned the invasion of Britain on a café napkin.

'Twelve divisions,' he said. 'Hand-picked. With a hundred thousand men in the first wave, all along the English coastline for, say, two hundred miles. That's the Wehrmacht thinking – spread the invasion, thin down the British defence forces, dissipate energy, resources, every-thing. Lots of refugees moving on the roads, miles and miles for the ammunition trucks to cover, honking all the time to get Mrs Jones and her baby carriage out of the way.

'For the German navy, on the other hand, the two-hundred-mile spread is a nightmare, precisely what they don't want. They need a concentrated beachhead, ships hurrying back and forth across the Channel, multiplying their load capabilities by the hour, with aero-planes overhead to keep the British bombers away.'

'That's the key.'

'Yes, that's the key. If they can keep the RAF out of their business, the Germans can secure the beaches. That will do it. They hold out seventy-two hours, twenty-five divisions make the crossing, with the tanks, the big guns, all the stuff that wins wars. Churchill will demand that Roosevelt send clouds of warplanes, Roosevelt will give an uplifting speech and do nothing, the governments-in-exile will make a run for Canada, and that will be that. The New Europe will be in place; a sort of hard-headed trade association with German consultants making sure it all goes the way they want.'

'What will it take to get across the Channel?'

The café was on the seafront in Veulettes. General Fedin stared out at the calm sea for a moment, then started a new napkin. 'Well, let's say . . . about two thousand barges should do it. With their bows refitted with ramps that can be raised and lowered. They'll want motor launches, for speed, to get the beach-masters and the medical people and staff officers moved around. About twelve hundred of those. To move the barges back and forth – five hundred tugboats, seagoing or adapted for it. And two hundred transport ships. That's for the big stuff, tanks and heavy guns and repair shops – and for the horses, which still do eighty per cent of the army's haulage.'

'Four thousand ships. That's it?'

Fedin shrugged. War was logistics. You got your infantry extra socks, they marched another thirty miles.

'They'll need decent weather. They can't afford to wait for autumn, the Channel will swamp the barges. So, end of summer is the time.'

'And the date?'

Fedin smiled to himself. Flipped the pages of a French newspaper someone had left on a chair, then ran his finger down a column. 'Seventeen September,' he announced. 'Full moon.'

They drove into Belgium, into Holland. German occupation made it easier – northern Europe was more or less under a single government.

In the Belgian ports, Ostend and Blankenberge and Knokke-Le-Zoute, and up as far as Rotterdam, they talked to the dockyard workers, because the dockyard workers were the ones who knew what went on. The ordinary civilian saw 'invasion fleet' as something tied up on a beach, stretched out for miles, all in a row. But ports didn't work that way.

Ports wandered inland from the sea; secondary harbours and river docks, canals dug out a hundred years ago for something supremely important that nobody remembered any more. Waterways for this or that, rank weeds and dead, black water, where cats came for courtship in the moonlight and men got laid standing up. You could hide an invasion fleet in such places, in Zeebrugge and Breskens, and that's what the Germans had tried to do.

'Four tugboats,' said a Dutchman with a little pipe. 'Well fitted out and ready for the sea.'

'How do you know?' Fedin asked.

'We built them, is how.'

Back to Paris. Back to Janina.

In the sweltering room on the top floor of the Hôtel Bretagne, she enciphered the data, then settled in to wait for the night, the best time for radio waves. When it was dark, she climbed up on a chair and fed the aerial through a hole in the top of the armoire to a pipe that crossed the ceiling on its way from the roof to the toilet.

She stopped for a moment and, as they'd trained her to do, ran through a mental checklist, a kind of catechism, until she was satisfied that everything was right. Then she plugged the radio into the wall, turned it on, and settled the heavy earphones on her head. Using a delicate thumb and forefinger, she explored the width of her frequency. Her neighbour to the left was very far away, very faint, and keyed at a slower and more deliberate pace than she did. But always there, this neighbour, and still transmitting when she signed off. On her right, a deep bass hum, unchanging, some piece of equipment that ran all night long. A radio beam, she thought, used by the Germans or the English for some esoteric purpose – not her destiny to know about it. An electronic strategem; a beacon that guided, or a beacon that deceived. She wondered if whoever depended on it, to their triumph or their sorrow, listened to her transmission. Submariners, perhaps. Or pilots. All of them moving around in the dark ocean or the night sky.

119 675 she began. Her call sign. Janina in Paris.

In London, at the Sixth Bureau headquarters in the Rubens Hotel on Buckingham Palace Road, four officers and a radio operator waited in a dark room, cigarette smoke hanging thick in the air. They looked at their watches long before the minute hand advanced. 8:22 p.m. Paris time was one hour later; by now the August dusk had faded away into darkness. 8:24. One minute after the scheduled time of transmission. Of course, life was uncertain, they told themselves. Watches ran slow or fast, even Wireless/Telegraph operators missed trains or heard suspicious sounds, and sometimes equipment failed. 8:27. The operator wearing the headset had an annoying habit of biting his lower lip when he concentrated. 8:28. He fussed with his dial, eyes blank with concentration. Colonel Vyborg took the deep breath that steadied him for bad news. So soon? How could they have her this soon?

Then the operator's face relaxed, and they knew what had happened before he got around to saying 'Here she is.' He said it as though the worrying were beside the point – he had trained her, she could do no wrong.

The Sixth Bureau operator sent 202 855. *I know you have important things to say, my darling, let's go someplace where we can be alone.* He moved his dial from 43 metres down to 39 metres.

Sent 807 449.

Hello, Janina.

But not here. In the Hôtel Bretagne, the dial moved up to 49 metres.

Sent 264 962 – sent it several times, the way operators transmitted call signs until their base acknowledged. A false call sign, in essence, that actually said: *now we can talk.*

551 223. London agreed.

It wasn't a perfect night, the wet August evening brewed thunderstorms and the interference crackled as the Sixth Bureau operator bit his lip. The Germans didn't jam her frequency, but that might mean they were listening silently. That might mean a thousand things.

Meanwhile Janina, dependable, stolid Janina, sent her groups. The sweat ran down her sides and darkened the back of her shirt, the boards creaked as a large man walked down the hall to the toilet, a woman cried out. But for Janina there were only the numbers.

So many numbers. Canals, barges, towns, roads. Three freighters at anchor in Boulogne harbour with no cargo, ammunition train into Middlekerke, Wehrmacht Pioneer insignia seen at Point Gris Nez, phrase *Operation Sealion* reported by prostitute in Antwerp.

Fifteen minutes, Janina. Remember, I told you that.

But then: what to leave out? Which rivers, for example, did the RAF not really care to know about? No, Captain Alexander de Milja's improvised information machine shuddered and clanked, steam whistled from a rag knotted around a broken pipe, but somehow it worked, and it needed far more than fifteen minutes to report what it had found out.

The Funkabwehr – the signals intelligence unit of the Gestapo – maintained offices in the army barracks on the boulevard Suchet. They too had darkened rooms, and operators with headsets wandering among the night-time frequencies.

'What's this up at 49?' one of them said, making a note of the time, 9:42 p.m., in his log.

'They were there last night,' his colleague said.

They listened for thirty seconds. 'Same one,' he continued. 'Slow and steady – refuses to make a mistake, nothing bothers him.'

The first operator threw a switch that played the telegraphy through a speaker, listened a moment, then he picked up a telephone and dialled a single digit. A moment later, Sturmbannführer Grahnweis came through the door.

Grahnweis was a legend, and he didn't mind that. He was enormously fat – the shape of a Renaissance cherub grotesquely overblown – and moved with heavy dignity. He had been at dinner when the call came, a white damask napkin still tucked into the collar of his black Gestapo uniform, and a waiter followed him into the office carrying a plate of venison sausages and a half stein of beer. Grahnweis nodded to his operators and smiled benevolently. He forgave them the interrupted dinner.

Then he listened.

Perhaps he made a little more of it than necessary, but who was going to blame him for a touch of theatre? As the numbers tapped out, in the foreground of the atmospheric sighs and crackles, Grahnweis tilted his head to one side and puckered his mouth, then, slowly, nodded in confirmation. Yes, yes. No question about it. The diagnosis is as you suspected, gentlemen. Herr Doktor Grahnweis will take the case.

'Be so good as to serve the dinner in my office,' he said to the waiter.

The desk was vast, and contained his weapons.

There were five: a very good radio receiver, a street map of Paris, two celluloid discs calibrated zero to 360°, with silk threads attached to their precise centres, and a telephone.

Grahnweis had spent his life in radio: as a childhood ham operator in Munich, he'd built his own crystal sets. He had worked for the Marconi company, then enlisted in the army in 1914 and served as a signals NCO on the eastern front. That was followed by unemployment, then the Nazi party – which made great use of radio – in 1927, and finally the

Gestapo as a major. 'Send the trucks, please,' he said into the phone, cut a piece of venison sausage, swirled it in the chestnut puree, used his knife to top it with a dab of gooseberry jelly. As he chewed, his eyes closed with pleasure, a sigh rumbled deep in his chest, beads of sweat stood on his forehead.

Casually, without putting down his fork, he flicked on his radio receiver, then turned the dial with the side of his hand until he found the transmission on 49 metres.

236 775 109 805 429

'Take your time, my friend,' he said under his breath. 'No reason to rush on this warm summer night.'

The trucks drove out of the boulevard Suchet garage within seconds of Grahnweis' call. They were RDF – radio direction finding – vans built by the Loewe-Opta Radio Company for the practice of what was technically known as goniometry. They sped through the empty streets to their prearranged positions: one at place de la Concorde, the other in front of the Gare de l'Est railway station. Almost as soon as they arrived, they were on the radio to Grahnweis' office:

Place de la Concorde reports a radio beam at 66 degrees.

Gare de l'Est reports a radio beam at 131 degrees.

Grahnweis put down his fork, rubbed his hands on the napkin, took a sip of beer. He placed the celluloid discs on the street map of Paris, one at each of the truck locations. Then he ran the two silk threads along the reported angles. They crossed at Montmartre.

4 September, 6:30 p.m., Calais railway station.

De Milja and Genya Beilis said good-bye on the platform. She had been drafted as a courier, from the Channel ports to the Hôtel Bretagne, because de Milja and Fedin could no longer go back and forth. The full moon in September was too close, the fuel for the van took so many black-market ration coupons it potentially exposed the operation to the French police, and, as the German invasion plan gathered momentum, information began to flow so fast they could barely deal with it.

Genya's summery print dress stirred as the locomotive chugged into the station; she moved towards de Milja so that her breasts touched him. 'Do you know,' she said, her voice just above the noise of the train, 'you can ride with me to Amiens, and then come back here.'

'It's direct,' de Milja said. 'Express to Paris.'

'No, no,' Genya said. 'This train stops in Amiens. I'm certain of it.'

De Milja smiled ruefully.

Genya studied him. 'On second thought,' she said, looking down.

He stared at her, at first took what she said for a lover's joke. But she wasn't smiling. Her eyes shone in the dim light of the station platform, and her lips seemed swollen. He took her by the shoulders, gripped her hard for a moment. To tell her, without trying to have a conversation while a train waited to leave a station, that he had to do what he was doing, that he was exhausted and scared, that he loved her.

But she shrugged. 'Oh well,' she said. Picked up a string-tied bundle as the loudspeakers announced the departure of the train. The way Parisians survived the rationing system was to get food in the country-side – everybody on the crowded platform had a large suitcase or a package.

'A few days,' de Milja said.

She pushed him away and fled to the step of the coach just before it began to move. When she turned to him, her face had changed to a brainless, bourgeois mask, and she waved at him – the dumb ox, her poor excuse for a husband – and called out, '*Au revoir! Au revoir! À bientôt, chéri!*'

In silence Fedin and de Milja drove out of Calais on a little country road, the E2, headed for the village of Aire, where the Lys River met the Calais canal. They were to meet with a man called Martagne – formerly the director of the port of Calais, now an assistant to a German naval officer – at his grandfather's house in the village.

A few miles down the E2, a camouflage-painted Wehrmacht armoured car blocked the road. A soldier with a machine pistol slung over his shoulder held up a hand. 'Out of the car,' he said.

As Fedin moved to open the door he asked quietly, 'Who are they?'

'*Feldengendarmerie*,' de Milja said. 'Field police units. It means they're starting to secure the staging areas for the invasion.' He wondered where Fedin's Lüger was. Normally he hid it in the springs beneath the driver's seat.

'Papers, please.'

They handed them over.

'Ruzicki,' he said to de Milja. 'You're Polish?'

'French citizen.'

'Your work pass runs only to November, you know.'

'Yes. I know. I'm getting it renewed.'

He glanced at Fedin's papers, then gestured for them to open the back of the truck. He studied the crates of Vienna sausage and sardines, the name of the distributor stencilled on the rough wood. 'Unload it,' he said.

'All of it?'

'You heard me.'

He lit a cigarette as they worked, and another soldier joined him, watching them haul the crates out and stack them on the warm tarred gravel of the road. 'Did I see this truck up in Le Touquet last week?' the second soldier asked.

'Might have,' de Milja said. 'Sometimes we go up there.'

'Where do you go there?'

'Oh, Sainte Cecile's – you know, the orphanage.'

'French orphans eat Vienna sausage?'

'For the sisters, I think. The nuns.'

When they were done they stood aside. The first soldier slid a bayonet out of a case on his belt and neatly popped a slat loose from a crate of sardines. He speared one of the tins, held it away from his uniform to avoid the dripping oil, sniffed it, then flung it away, cleaning his bayonet on the weeds beside the road.

'Load it up,' he said.

While they worked, the soldier wandered around the van. Something displeased him, something wasn't right. He opened the passenger-side door, squatted on the road, stared into the cab. De Milja sensed he was a moment away from putting his hand beneath the front seat and finding Fedin's pistol.

'Do you know, sir, we took an extra crate of sausage from the storeroom? There's one more than we're supposed to have.'

The soldier stood and walked to the back of the truck. His face was dark with anger. 'What does that mean? Why do you tell me that?'

De Milja was completely flustered. 'Why, ah, I don't know, I didn't mean . . .'

His voice hung in the air, the soldier leaned close, saw the fear in his eyes. 'You do not offer bribes to German soldiers,' he said very softly. 'It is something you do not do.'

'Of course, I know, I didn't—' de Milja sputtered.

The soldier jerked his head towards the road: it meant *get moving*. Fedin grabbed the last two crates, carried them into the front seat with him. When he tried to start the car it stalled. The engine caught, Fedin made a grinding shift, the car lurched forward, almost stalled again. The soldier turned away from them, clasped his hands behind his back and stared down the road in the direction they'd come from.

4 September, 9:26 p.m.

In the Funkabwehr bureau on the boulevard Suchet, at the end of the hall where Sturmbannführer Grahnweis' personal office was located, there was a mood of great anticipation. Grahnweis was cool and businesslike in the summer heat. He could be seen through the open door doing a little late paperwork; studying reports, sometimes writing a comment in the margin. Work went on, he seemed to suggest, the glory and the drudge in turn, such was life.

A few senior officers had found it necessary to be in the Funkabwehr office that night, chatting in low voices with attentive junior staff, who busied themselves with the thousand little jobs that must be done every day in a military office. *The devil is in the details*, the Germans say.

Klaus was hunting for the CARNET file, Helmut needed a look at the July pay vouchers for the Strasbourg station, Walter asked Helmut if the Lyons relay tower plan was still locked up in committee in Berlin. Heinrich, at 9:27, nodded sharply to himself, held the headphones tightly to his ears for a moment to make absolutely sure, then dialled a single digit on his telephone. The crowd in the Funkabwehr office knew immediately that what had been a strong possibility was now confirmed: Grahnweis had caught a spy.

But the Sturmbannführer let the receiver rest on its cradle. He finished the final paragraph of his report, initialled the lower corner, and then answered the phone. The frequency was the same as last night, Heinrich reported. Grahnweis thanked him, turned on his receiver, fiddled with the dial until the transmitted numbers came through crisp and clear. Several of the senior officers and a few people on his own staff drifted into the large office, close enough to Grahnweis' desk to hear what went on.

The two Loewe-Opta radio trucks had been in position since early evening, strategically placed on either side of the Montmartre hill. Grahnweis gave them a few minutes to get a fix on the transmission, then called Truck Number One to come in on his communications radio.

'I can confirm the forty-nine metres – are you getting it?'

'We hear him, but the direction is a little blurred. The way we're receiving, he's bouncing between eighteen and twenty-three degrees.'

'I see.' Grahnweis studied his city map for a moment. 'Then go up to the rue Caulaincourt, try for a reading there and call me back.'

From the second truck, on the boulevard Barbès side of Montmartre, the news was better. Their signal was clear, just about precisely on 178.4 degrees. Grahnweis made certain the celluloid disc was perfectly centred, then ran the silk thread out along the degree line. 'Could be in Sacré-Coeur,' he said. 'Perhaps in the belfry. I wonder – have they also a hunchback, like Notre-Dame?'

The first RDF truck came over the radio a few minutes later. 'Not much better, Herr Sturmbannführer. Maybe it's the elevation – but something's deflecting here, something's hurting the reception.'

'But not in London, we hope.'

There was a pause as the radio technician tried to decide how to answer this. Grahnweis saved him the trouble. 'We're doing just fine. Stay where you are, I'll be back in a moment.'

The technician said *Yes sir* briskly and signed off in a hurry. This working for a legend required a steady nerve.

Grahnweis reached into his desk drawer and retrieved a special map of Paris, in book form, printed on heavy paper, showing every street, every alley, the number of every building. He then dialled his intercom and instructed his chief clerk to telephone the northern electrical power substation. Moments later he was talking to the French night supervisor, asking to be connected with the office of Leftenant Schillich.

As he waited, he could hear the deep hum of the station's giant turbines. Leftenant Schillich, he thought to himself, you had best be available for this call, and don't make a fool of Grahnweis.

'Leftenant Schillich,' said a youthful voice.

Grahnweis explained what he needed, starting at the rue Caulaincourt side of Montmartre and working along a certain line towards the east, street by street. Then he turned up the volume on his receiver and silently begged the W/T operator to keep on transmitting.

'Starting at Caulaincourt, *now*,' Schillich announced.

From the speaker: 562 511

'Next on the list is the avenue Junot, from number thirty to the end.' Grahnweis' audience was hushed and anticipatory, sensing that the moment of the kill was near. At the lieutenant's direction, the substation engineers worked their way east, across the grid of steep, crooked streets that made up the old village high above Paris.

'Next we have,' said Schillich, following his own edition of Grahnweis' map, 'the rue Lepic.'

Grahnweis found the street and marked it with his index finger.

From the receiver: 335.

Then 428.

Then silence.

In the Hôtel Bretagne, the room went dark. Janina's hand froze on the dead key and she tore the earphones from her head. But there was nothing, other than the evening hush of an occupied city, for her to hear. For a few seconds she sat there, then, before she could do anything, the lights came on, the red filaments in her radio tubes glowed back to life.

It was just a brief outage, she realized, some problem with the electricity.

A few miles south of the roadblock, Fedin pulled off the E2 and drove a little way down a farmer's dirt path. There was no need to discuss what had to be done – he simply took the weapon from beneath the seat and walked out into the strip of forest that separated two fields. Theoretically they would note where it had been dumped and, some day, return to collect it.

De Milja smoked pensively and stared out over the countryside. The peasants, working in the last light of the late summer dusk, were harvesting wheat with horse-drawn mowing machines. There was a haze of dust in the air, cicadas whirred madly, the mowing machines swayed as they cut through the ripe grain. He got out of the truck to stretch his legs and felt a slight vibration in the ground. For a moment, there was no sound. Then there was just the beginning of it, thunder in the distance. Fedin returned, stood by the side of the truck, and squinted up into the darkening sky.

The ground trembled, then shook. The sound swelled, then seemed to explode the air, growing louder and louder until de Milja could feel the waves of it hammering against his heart. In self-defence he knelt down, then tried to count the dark shapes that moved slowly across the sky, returning from London, or Liverpool. Perhaps fifty Heinkel-IIIs and maybe the same number of Ju-88s, the best of the German bombers, and their escort, possibly thirty Messerschmitt-110s.

He had seen it in Warsaw, how the fronts of the buildings slid into the street in a cloud of dust, the silhouette of a fireman on a roof – arms and legs thrown wide like a gingerbread man by the blast, white fire and blue fire, the young woman a block away from harm who sits down and dies without a mark on her. He knew the Germans for the fine engineers they were.

Above him, one of the bombers trailed a delicate strand of white smoke from beneath its wing. Another flew very low and far behind the formation, De Milja could hear its engine; ignition, then silence, ignition, silence. It seemed restless; a wing dipped, the nose of the plane lowered, then righted itself. Perhaps the plane and the pilot were both damaged, de Milja thought. But, two planes among a hundred – only two planes. Others in the sea, maybe. One in poor Mrs Brown's kitchen. But most of the bombers would be back at it the following day. Even fire hoses wore out eventually, de Milja knew, the white, frayed threads visible through the broken rubber.

The sound faded slowly to the south, towards the Luftwaffe base near Merville. The cicadas started up again, the huge horses plodded along and the mowers creaked as they rolled through the wheat. A Norman peasant walked beside his plough horse – walked slowly, head down, like an old man – one hand riding on the horse's shoulder.

It worked. Once you determined the street by turning off the electricity until the transmission stopped, your sound trucks could identify the building by strength of signal. They radioed back to Grahnweis: *Hôtel Bretagne.* The hunting party was hastily organized; two Gestapo detectives – thick-bodied types – a few senior officers with their side arms, and Walter and Helmut, who squeezed into the second car, encouraged by Grahnweis' wink. The two cars sped through the Paris night, arriving at the rue Lepic in good time – the W/T operator was still at it, according to the technicians in the Loewe-Opta trucks.

The actual entry into the hotel was restricted to the two detectives, along with two of the senior officers who could not be told no, as well as Walter – representing Grahnweis' faithful staff – and Grahnweis himself.

The night clerk, an old man with a white eye, trembled with fear when the Gestapo uniforms swept through the door. He showed them the registration book; they picked out, immediately, the woman 'Marie Ladoux,' who for ten days had occupied a top-floor room. Rented for her by a cousin, the man said, a week before she arrived. 'She doesn't sleep here at night,' he confided to one of the detectives. 'God only knows where she goes.'

They acknowledged later, quietly, among themselves, that she had been very brave. The young French girl or English girl or whoever she was – really very brave. When they kicked the door open she simply turned and stared at them as though they'd been impolite, her hand poised on the telegraph key. 'Strange she had no watchers,' Walter said later to the others in the Funkabwehr office on the boulevard Suchet.

'A patched-together business, I think,' Helmut said. 'Extemporized.' A sad little smile, and the shrug that went with it: the British were losing now, knocked silly by German bombs, waiting for the blow to fall as a tough, predatory army waited on the chalk cliffs at Boulogne. The same cliffs where Napoleon's Grande Armée had waited. And waited. But this wasn't Napoleon. And the junior officers quite properly read desperation in the girl's mission – one could say *sacrifice.* Clearly nobody had expected her to survive for very long.

She shocked them, though. The rules of the game specified that the W/T operator give up, accept interrogation, accept the consequences of spying, which hadn't changed in a hundred years – the courtyard, the blindfold. But though she did not struggle when they took her, they got her only as far as the back seat of the Gestapo Mercedes, securely handcuffed, with a detective on either side. Yet she managed to do what she had to do; they heard the crunch of bitten glass and a few seconds later her head fell over like a broken doll and that was the end of 'Marie Ladoux'.

Grahnweis stayed behind with one of the senior officers to examine the real prize – the clandestine radio. Which turned out to be the good old Mark XV transceiver – actually its first cousin, the Paraset – but, Grahnweis thought, standard MI-6 equipment. He nodded to himself with satisfaction and relief. The British scientists made him nervous – sometimes great bumblers, sometimes not. He feared that under pressure of war they might outperform themselves and conjure up some diabolical apparatus that would make his life a hell. But, so far, nothing like that, as far as he could tell, in the Hôtel Bretagne.

Standard stuff. Two transmission frequencies – from 3.3 to 4.5 megacycles and from 4.5 to 7.6 megacycles. Four to five watts of power – enough to get to London. Three American metal tubes, a 6V6 crystal-controlled pilot, cadmium steel box, silver finish. A calibration curve, to assist the operator, was mounted in the upper-left-hand corner, essentially a graph chart with a diagonal line. Grahnweis took a soft leather tool pouch from the pocket of his uniform jacket and selected a screwdriver for the task of getting behind the control panel. To the senior officer looking over his shoulder he said, 'Maybe something new inside.'

There was.

Grahnweis left the hotel by the Saint-Rustique side of the building; meanwhile, the senior officer exited on the rue Lepic – this parting company a mysterious event that nobody ever really explained. For a time it wasn't clear that Grahnweis was ever going to be found, but, with persistence and painstaking attention to detail, he was. Crown on the second bicuspid molar, fillings in upper and lower canines, a chipped incisor. Yes, that was Grahnweis, if a tattered charcoal log under a jumble of brick and tile could be called any name at all.

The junior officers of the Funkabwehr were extremely put out by this turn of events. It was, at its heart, rude. And rudeness of this sort they would never have ascribed to the British character. Had they known, of course, that it was the Poles who'd sent their leader from the room they would have thrown up their hands in angry recognition. *What could you expect?* But the British were different: Aryan, northern, civilized, and blessed with certain German virtues – honour in friendship, and love of learning.

The British were, in fact, perhaps a little worse than the Poles, but the Germans wouldn't come to understand that for some time. 'Personally,' said Heinrich, 'it is the very sort of thing I find I cannot forgive.'

*

7 September, 2:30 p.m.

Genya Beilis seated herself by a window in the Café Trois Reines, next to the St Pierre cemetery in Montmartre. She was a vision, even in the end-of-summer heat. A little white hat with a bow, set just to one side of her head, a little white suit, three dashes of Guerlain. Not the usual for this neighbourhood, but who knew what business royalty might have up here – maybe a call on a poor relative, or a bouquet for a former lover, who somehow wound up in the local boneyard. Whatever the truth, she shone, and her tea was served with every courtesy, and every drop still in the cup.

Very damn inspiring, the way she walked. Maybe you didn't believe in heaven but you certainly could believe in that. Chin and shoulders elevated, back like fine steel, the emphatic ring of high heels on the tile floor of a café. In the *cabinet de toilette*, Madame whipped off a lambskin glove and slipped a brown envelope behind a radiator. Then she returned to her tea.

A few blocks away, a number of Gestapo gentlemen read newspapers in cars and doorways all the livelong day as the mess in the rue Lepic was cleaned up, but that was hopeless and they knew it. Nobody was going to be coming around to see what happened to X. The abrupt halt in transmission, the absence of coded start-up signals – mis-sent call sign, incorrect date – and the London people would know their network communication had been cut. One sent the newspaper readers out to the cars and doorways, but one knew better.

The lovely lady in white returned to the *quartier* of the Café Trois Reines on two occasions, but she found no chalk mark on M. Laval's gravestone and the letter in the toilette mailbox went uncollected, so that, in the end, the latest news on canals and barges in the Channel ports went unread.

Though she had never seen her correspondent she felt sad, enough a veteran of the business to know what uncollected mail implied. Then too, she had walked past the spontaneous renovation at the Hôtel Bretagne, noted newspaper readers in the vicinity, noted the absolute silence of the Parisian press on the subject of local explosions, and wondered if it all might not somehow fit together.

But hers not to reason why. Hers to travel down to the Banque de Commerce Nationale in Orléans, humiliate the most vulgar, oily little bank man that God ever made, and collect a new set of procedures.

Now it was the sixteenth arrondissement.

Now it was the Café du Jardin.

Now the adjacent cemetery was in Passy.

Ghouls, she thought.

*

Starry night in the village of Aire. In 1430, the Roman bridge over the river Lys had been replaced and the Martagne family had built a fine house at the end of it, so the cool air that hung above the water made the stone rooms pleasant on summer evenings.

Martagne, the port supervisor from Calais, had a red face and black hair, a big cleft nose and a big moustache. He sat in the dark kitchen with de Milja – Fedin was waiting at the edge of the village – drinking farmer-made Calvados from a stone crock. 'Take another Calva,' he said. 'Uncle made that in 1903.' Martagne liked to spend his time in the bars with the Polish dockyard workers, and they put him on to Fedin and de Milja when he got frustrated with the Germans and threatened *to talk to somebody.*

Now he was drunk. He stared down at the scarred old table and brooded. Finally he said, 'You a spy?'

'Yes.'

Martagne made a face. 'I'm a Norman,' he said. 'Not French – whatever that means. But we fight their damn battles. They're good at insults, not so good at fighting. Bad combination, you'll agree.'

'Yes.'

'It's fighting – you'll find a Martagne. Crècy, Agincourt, Sedan, Poitiers, the Marne, Jena, Marengo. Probably went over the Channel with William the Conqueror – last time anybody managed to do that, by the way. Probably somebody looked like me, with my ugly face.' Martagne laughed at the idea. 'Can't stand the English,' he said. 'You care?'

'No,' de Milja said.

'They care?'

'No.'

Martagne laughed again. 'Me neither,' he said. He stood, swayed a moment, then left the room. Through a crack in the closed shutter de Milja could see that moon and starlight lit the old village and he could hear splashing water where the Lys ran over a small weir. Somewhere in the house Martagne was banging drawers open and shut. Finally he reappeared and handed de Milja three sheets of used carbon paper.

'Sorry I didn't bring the originals,' he said. 'We'll take one more Calva.' He poured generously, the fragrance of distant apples drifted up to de Milja. 'Now, Monsieur Spy, one little story before you go.'

De Milja sipped the Calvados.

'The last week in June, on the day of the surrender, when Pétain got on the radio about how he was preserving the honour of France, my grandfather put on a nightshirt he'd never worn in his life and got into his bed. He was a healthy old bird, pissed like a fountain. But now he stayed in bed, he didn't speak, he didn't smile, he just stared at the wall. The doctor came, a childhood friend. Didn't help. He made the old jokes, said the old things, left a tonic on the nightstand. But a week later, my grandfather was gone. "He has died of shame," the doctor said. So now, what you have in your hand, that is his revenge – and mine. Do you understand?'

'Yes, I understand,' de Milja said. He proved it by standing up to leave. Martagne looked away; angry at what he'd done, angry at the world for having made him do it. De Milja said good night and slipped out the door.

Gold in hand, it turned out.

12 September. In Nieuwpoort, just across the Belgian border, dust from the wheat harvest hung in the warm air and the fields shimmered in golden light; the docks were burning, the harbour smelled of dead fish, an RAF Blenheim-IVF came tearing over the jetty at fifty feet with its gunports twinkling. The windows of the Café Nieuwpoort fell in on a dead fisherman and a dead waiter and a German corporal came running out of the toilet with his trousers around his ankles. A mackerel boat caught fire and the cook jumped into the harbour. Eight rounds from the .303 guns, including an incendiary tracer, stitched up the side of the harbour petrol tank, thirty feet high, and absolutely nothing happened. The cook yelled he couldn't swim; a couple of taxi drivers ran to the edge of the pier, but when the Blenheim screamed around the town in a banked turn they threw themselves on their bellies and by the time they looked out at the water again there was nobody there.

The Germans had an anti-aircraft gun at the top of the hill, in the little garden behind the town hall, and red fireballs went whizzing through the port as they tried to hit the Blenheim. Flown by some species of madman – in fact a Rhodesian bush pilot – the Blenheim seemed enraged by the attack, tore out over the sea and came skimming back into Nieuwpoort, blazing away at the gun position and hitting two of the gunners and the mayor's secretary.

On the top floor of the dockside Hotel Vlaanderen, de Milja and a whore wearing a slip and a Turkish seaman wearing underpants watched the fight together through a cracked window. De Milja had come running in here when the attack started, but the whore and the sailor hardly seemed to notice him. The room quivered and a blast wave rang the window glass – high explosive going off on the other side of town. De Milja looked out the window to see, just over the town horizon, thick, curling smoke, black and ponderous, tumbling slowly upwards, implying the death of an industrial something or other that had lived on heavy oil. Then the hotel was hit, the sailor squawked and grabbed the whore in terror, knocking her blonde wig askew and revealing clipped dark hair beneath. 'Shh,' she said, and stroked the man's hair.

De Milja pressed his palm against the worn linoleum, testing for heat in case the floor below them was on fire. For the moment, he decided, he was about as safe as he was going to get. The bombers seemed to be working north of Nieuwpoort, near the railway yards. Puffs of dark smoke from spent ack-ack bursts drifted back over the town from that direction. Fedin should have been halfway down to Abbeville – de Milja could only hope he hadn't been killed in the raid.

The mackerel boat was fully ablaze now; a man ran up to it, threw a completely pointless bucket of water on the roof of the crackling wheelhouse, then ran away. 'My poor town,' the whore said under her breath. The sailor said something in Turkish and the whore, responding to the tone of his voice, said, 'Yes, that's right.'

As de Milja turned back to the window, the Blenheim flashed by, the wing tip no more than ten feet away, engines howling, rattling the window in its frame. The pilot circled low over the town and headed back out to sea, towards the Dover cliffs and home. The Germans had now gotten their anti-aircraft gun working again and sent him on his way with a volley that may have nicked the tail of the aeroplane. The pilot responded; put his plane in a violent climb, foot on the floor, then a steep bank at the top of the climb, where he vanished into the low cloud. A little bell rang in the street: the Nieuwpoort fire truck, stopped for a moment while two firemen struggled with a large chunk of concrete, dragging it to the edge of the dock by the bent rods sticking out at odd angles.

The men jumped back on the truck and it drove around the harbour to where the burning mackerel boat had now set the pier on fire. A *Feldengendarmerie* open car pulled up behind the truck and a soldier ran over to the driver's window and pointed back the other way. The soldier climbed into his car and both vehicles began the long process of getting themselves turned around without dropping a wheel over the edge of the pier.

Good, de Milja thought. Something's really gone up somewhere and the Germans are very unhappy about it. But even so, de Milja the realist had been watching German equipment go up in flames since September of 1939 and he had to admit that it didn't seem to slow them down. They patched and fixed and improvised and did without. *War's own children*, he thought. They find a way to get the job done and go on to the next town.

Another plane came tearing past the hotel, the clatter of gunfire echoing in the little room. No – the same Blenheim, de Milja realized. He'd been hiding out over the sea somewhere or a little way down the coast and this time, like magic, the huge petrol storage tank erupted in a great whuff of orange flame and boiling black smoke. The pilot circled the town, getting a good eyeful for his gun cameras and obviously very proud of what he'd done. He then waggled his wings – the AA gunners did everything but throw their lunch at him – and sped out over the sea towards the English coast.

A little rain that night. The Turkish seaman went off to sail away – if he still had a boat to sail away on – and de Milja paid the whore to stay with her in the room. Bernette, she was called. No longer young, short and sturdy, fiercely proud in the face of all the pranks that life had played her. She hung her blonde wig on the post at the foot of the bed and fussed over it and combed it out, calling it her *poor beaver*, entirely unselfconscious in her slip and half-inch salt-and-pepper hair.

De Milja gave her some money and she wriggled into a skirt and went off to a café she knew where they cooked on a wood-fired stove – the electricity in Nieuwpoort was out – and returned carrying a big plate of lentils and bacon with vinegar, still warm and covered with yesterday's newspaper, and two bottles of dark beer. Excuse them for not sending the lady and gentleman a glass, but their glassware had not survived the afternoon.

The rain pattered on the wharfside streets, cooling everything a little. In the distance the bells of the fire trucks never stopped. It smelled like Warsaw; charred plaster, burning oil, and cordite. Bernette wrinkled her nose and splashed herself with White Ginger perfume, so that the room smelled like bombs and gardenias. Would the gentleman, she wanted to know, care for a half-and-half when he'd finished his lentils? The money he'd given her entitled him to at least that. No, de Milja said. Somehow the events of the day had left him not much in the mood for such things. Strange, he thought, how much I like you. Like me a wanderer, somehow never home.

That was, it happened, true. She'd had a home, a child, a family, but, well, what did it all matter? God meant her not to have them and now she didn't. It wasn't much of a story anyhow.

Well the hell with everybody, he said. And he was getting tired of the four walls – could they go out for a walk? She agreed to go. Scared as she was, she agreed. Strange, he thought, how you stumble on the world's secret nobility when you're not even looking for them.

When she went down the hall to the toilet de Milja poured half a bottle of beer down his shirt. She made a sour face about that when she returned – she could wash it out in the sink. No, he said, turned away from her so she wouldn't smell that he'd washed his mouth with the rest of the beer and splashed some on his hair.

Outside it was quiet at first, the rain hissing on a few small fires here and there. Some of the townspeople were poking through the burnt-out café, lifting a blackened timber then dropping it quickly when they saw what was under it. The *patron*, the toughest man in Nieuwpoort, was sitting on the kerb and weeping into a dirty handkerchief, his shoulders shaking. 'Ach,' Bernette said, fought back the tears, then steadied. Soot drifted down on them as they walked, walked carefully because the sea fog hung over the town. Quiet water that night, just lapping at the foot of the quai. as the tide went out. Walking away from the centre of Nieuwpoort they were stopped by a pair of Wehrmacht sentries. Nervy and angry now that they'd been on the wrong end of the war for a moment – they hadn't liked that at all.

But what could they do with a beer-smelling slob and a whore headed down the beach for a blow job? He was now Rosny, Belgian of Czech descent, a long story. In the end the Germans waved them along, but for half a pfennig they would have run a rifle butt under his chin just to see his heels fly up in the air. Because they had dead friends and half-dead friends and would-have-been-better-off-dead friends – de Milja knew what bombing did to people – and they were full of rage, and quite dangerous. Bernette, good Bernette, looked at them a certain way, and maybe that bled out the fury just enough to keep de Milja's jaw from getting broken, but it was a close thing.

The sirens went off about an hour past midnight, and de Milja and Bernette moved off the beach and back into the dunes. They were in the town's shame pit – broken glass, old rags, a dead shoe – a hidden place for those Nieuwpoort citizens who had to do something private and couldn't afford to do it indoors. De Milja moved into the lee of a dune, they sat down on the damp sand, he put an arm around her shoulders and she clung to him, her protector.

Not much more than a gesture, with what came down on Nieuwpoort that night.

The Blenheim, it turned out, was merely an opening act, a juggler on roller skates. Now the full troupe of comedians came running out of the wings. Lancaster bombers, de Milja guessed. The beach shuddered as the bombs hit, to long rolls of thunder and flashes of orange fire in the darkness. Once or twice it was close, sand showered down on them and Bernette whimpered like a poodle and burrowed into him. The anti-aircraft people up at the mayor's office got on the scoreboard just as the raid began, hit a Lancaster with a full bomb load a little way out to sea from the harbour and de Milja swore he could see the night cloud for twenty miles around by the light of the explosion. But most of the rest got through, hitting the town and the sea and the villages nearby and God only knew what else. Pretty soon Nieuwpoort was truly on fire, the Hotel Vlaanderen no more than a pile of smoking brick.

The second British attack came at 3:30 in the morning. It seemed very quiet when they left. De Milja and Bernette dozed, then woke up at dawn, stiff and chilled and miserable. The sea had come alive in first light; white combers rolling in a long way, crying gulls hanging in the air above the breaking surf. De Milja walked down to the tideline to splash his face and there, riding to and fro in a foot of water, a thin trail of yellow foam traced up the back of his uniform, was the first German. Face-down, arms above his head. As de Milja watched, a wave a little more powerful than the ones before picked him up, rushed him in a few extra feet, and dumped him on the wet sand.

It wasn't clear how he had died – he hadn't burned, hadn't been hit by shellfire. Probably he had drowned. He wore a field-grey combat uniform, waist encircled by a belt with ammunition pouches and a commando knife, prepared to fight. *One of mine*, de Milja thought. But it wasn't one, it was three, no, a dozen. Hundreds. At first the grey of their uniforms blended with the colour of the sea, but as the light changed he could see more and more of them. Most wearing heavy packs, bobbing silently in the surf. Now and then the sea would leave another one on the beach, then, so it seemed to de Milja, go back out in order to bring in a few more.

Dependable port official reports security staff alerting coastal defence units to a landing exercise, to be carried out at division strength, using barges and seagoing tugs, at Westende on the Belgian coast on the night of 12 September.

So this was his kill.

It would have been suicide to try for Westende, so he'd settled for Nieuwpoort, to see what he could see. And here it was. Some of the dead were burned – perhaps a ship had been hit. Perhaps several ships. Invasion troops, from the packs and all the other equipment – the Germans had put on a dress rehearsal for a landing on the beaches of Britain.

And the British had put on a dress rehearsal of their own.

It was much too dangerous to stay where he was, there would be hell to pay on this beach once the Germans discovered what the tide was bringing in. But when he turned to look for Bernette he discovered she'd been standing by his side, bare feet splayed in the sand, arms crossed beneath her breasts.

He put a hand on her shoulder, but she did not respond so he let it drop. Then he knelt down, took a little slip of paper and a stub of pencil from his pocket and sketched the shoulder-patch insignia of one of the dead soldiers: a knight raised a sword above his head, his shield a crusader's cross. The legend above the knight: *Grenadierregiment 46*. Legend below: *21 Infanteriedivision Dresden.*

He tucked the slip of paper into his trousers cuff, then stood up. 'I know you are a patriot,' he said.

She had seen, and certainly understood, what he had just done. It was an act of war to learn who the dead were. 'Yes,' she said. 'I am.' Just one more secret, she thought. She kept them all.

15 September.

Martagne had stolen three carbons from the Port of Calais office; the German landing exercise was one of them.

De Milja made his way south to the village of Sangatte, on the road that ran by the sea from Boulogne to Calais. Fedin was waiting for him in a closed-up villa owned by a Russian baron – lately a toy manufacturer, formerly one of the czar's riding masters – in Paris. De Milja arrived a little after one in the afternoon, Genya Beilis came by taxi from the resort town of Le Touquet an hour later. All trains from Paris to Boulogne and Calais had been suspended, she said. Military traffic only. Railway guns. Field hospitals.

The time had come.

The roads were jammed with panzer tanks and 88 artillery pieces on carriers and fuel tankers with red crosses painted on them to fool the British attack aircraft. Wehrmacht invasion planners were playing chess now – big guns at Calais had engaged British artillery across the Channel, communications frequencies were being jammed, radio towers and radars attacked. *We're coming*, it meant.

'The enemy's ports are our first line of defence.' Lord Nelson, in 1805, and nothing had changed. Britain had its little piece of water that it hid behind. The princes of Europe could field huge land armies. But when they reached the coast of France, they stopped.

A Russian general, a publisher's daughter, a Polish cartographer. At the villa they sat on sheets that covered the furniture, in a dark room behind closed shutters. Finished, and they knew it. Fedin, at sixty, perhaps the strongest of them, de Milja thought. To survive Russia you had to fight for life – fight the cold, fight the sadness and its vodka. Those who lived were like iron. Genya, de Milja saw, had covered the dark circles beneath her eyes with powder. He thought the shadows decadent, sexy, but the attempted disguise made her look old, a woman attempting to deceive the world. As for himself, he felt numb, as though a nerve, pounded on by the hour, had gone dead.

The three of them smoked. It made up for food, for sleep.

'They've arrested Rijndal,' Fedin said. 'The Dutch barge captain. His wife let another friend of ours know about it.'

'Do they know why?' de Milja asked.

'No.'

'What can he tell them?'

'That he talked to émigrés – Russians, Poles, Czechs – working against the Germans.'

'I'm going to sleep,' Genya said. She assumed there was a bedroom on the second floor, so climbed the stairs. Fedin and de Milja could hear her up there, walking around in different rooms.

Fedin and de Milja left the house, walked to a café, telephoned another café. In silence, they drank coffee for an hour, then an ambulance pulled up outside. The driver joined them, ordered a marc, opened a newspaper, GERMAN STRENGTH AND FRENCH CULTURE TO INSPIRE NEW EUROPE, read the headline, quoting a French minister.

'How can you read that garbage?' Fedin asked.

The ambulance driver shrugged. 'I used to prefer PIG BORN WITH TWO HEADS, but this is all you get now.' He looked at his watch. 'I can let you have two hours, so if you're going you better go.'

Fedin handed over a stack of franc notes.

'What are you moving?' the driver asked.

'Hams,' Fedin said.

The driver raised his eyebrows in a way which meant *I wouldn't mind having one*. Fedin smiled a knave's smile and patted him on the arm. *Business is business*, he meant.

Fedin drove the ambulance, de Milja lay down on the stretcher in the back. The days when they could use the van were now over, only French emergency vehicles were allowed on the roads in the coastal region. Keeping to the farm routes, they reached the village of Colombert, on the D6. In the main square, a military policeman wearing white gloves was directing traffic. Fedin pointed at the road he wanted, the policeman waved him violently in that direction – *yes, go on, hurry!* An army truck in the square had a flat tyre; soldiers were standing around waiting for the driver to fix it. They wore the same uniform as the soldiers on the beach at Nieuwpoort, but their shoulder insignia was different. 'Commandos,' Fedin said, squinting to see the patches. 'To climb ropes up cliffs.'

'If they can get to the cliffs,' de Milja said.

Fedin nosed the wheel over gingerly and drove down a lane between two rows of linden trees. The trunks had grown for too many years, there was barely room for a vehicle. The road divided at a canal. Fedin turned off the ignition. Another lost, exquisite little place – still water, soft sky, leaves barely moving in the breeze. De Milja clambered out of the back of the ambulance. 'I hope nobody asks us what we're doing down here.'

Fedin shrugged. 'We'll say Van Gogh had a fainting spell.'

They walked along the canal for a time. Around a curve, fourteen barges were tied up end to end, roped to iron rings set at the edge of what had been, a century earlier, a towpath. By the water there were three blackened, splintered trunks of linden trees; several others had had their leaves blown off. A single sunken barge was lying halfway on its side in the still water. Fedin tapped a cigarette out of his pack, screwed it into his ivory holder, and lit it with a small silver lighter. 'Well,' he said, 'we did try.'

The villa at Sangatte, late afternoon. De Milja climbed the stairs, found the bedroom and opened the door quietly. Genya was sleeping in her underwear, hands beneath her head instead of a pillow, on top of a mattress covered with a sheet. He watched her for a time; she was dreaming. What she showed the world was hard and polished. But in her dream she was frightened, her breathing caught. Carefully, he lay down next to her, but she woke up. 'You're here,' she said.

'Yes.'

'How was it?'

'Not so good.'

'Really?'

'We managed to see three different places. There was one barge sunk, one transport damaged – the Germans had French shipfitters working on it. In Calais, an old man who fishes off the jetty said that a motor launch blew up the other night when the British came.'

Genya didn't answer. De Milja was tired. It was hot and airless on the upper floor, dark behind the shutters. Yet he could feel, just at that moment, summer slipping away. He could hear the ocean breaking on the rocky beach. Two girls on bicycles, talking as they pedalled side by side. Some kind of bird that sang a single, low note in a tree outside. He moved closer to Genya, her skin brown against the white sheet, touched her shoulder with his lips. She moved a little away from him. 'I'm asleep,' she said.

16 September. The invasion fleet began to assemble. It had been planned for Genya to make a courier run to the Passy W/T operator on the evening of the fifteenth. But the French police had blocked all the roads and the railway stations were off-limits to civilians. The region had been closed.

The Calais waterfront was a maze of dark, cobbled streets winding among brick warehouses and cargo sheds, small tenements where the dockworkers lived, a few cafés where they drank, and a crumbling hotel with a blue neon sign – HÔTEL NEPTUNE – a whorehouse for foreign sailors.

De Milja and Fedin went into one of the bars, ordered *ballons de rouge*, glasses of red wine, and spent an hour gossiping with the owner and his fat blonde wife. The owner wore a tweed cap, had his shirtsleeves rolled up above the elbows. Business was no good, he said, at this rate they wouldn't last much longer. The English dropped bombs on their customers, the Germans paid like drunkards on a spree or they didn't pay at all. One thought one had it tough before May of '40, *et alors*, what one didn't know! The wife had a rich laugh and red cheeks.

And what was that warehouse across the street?

Labard et Labard? Boarded up, now. They used to see the workers all day – first for an eye-opener, then lunch – a very nice plat du jour for a few francs and a coffee. Finally a little something at the end of the day when they gathered to get up their courage to go home and face their wives. So, life wasn't perfect but it went along. But then, the war. The young Monsieur Labard an officer, now a prisoner of war in Germany. The elder Labard was eighty-seven. He'd tried, but it hadn't worked out. *Tant pis*, too bad, oh well, that was life, what could one do, so it went. The owner shook his head grimly at the sorrow of it all while the wife winked at de Milja and rolled her hips when she walked down to the other end of the bar to refill their glasses.

They broke in to the Labard warehouse just after dark. Used an old piece of iron to pry a padlock off a side entry, groped their way up an ancient wooden staircase to the top floor. Found a window with a space between the board and the frame, kicked it a little wider, and got a view of the Calais harbour.

Fedin had been right about the date – full moon on the seventeenth. They counted forty troop transports anchored out in the harbour, six more in position for boarding on the wharf. Trucks pulled in, piled high with wooden ammunition boxes. The first invasion wave would be loaded the following morning, then, that night, they would sail for England.

'This is it,' Fedin said, staring intently at the activity in the harbour. 'I hope they have something ready on the other side.'

'The English abandoned a lot of weapons on the beach at Dunkirk,' de Milja said. 'That was three months ago – I wonder how much of it they've been able to replace. Some, not all. Every farmer has his shotgun, of course. Which is just what they thought would happen in France, but farmers with shotguns can't do much about artillery.'

A broad-beamed tugboat came chugging into the harbour from the direction of the Calais canals. It was pushing three barges from a position on the port side and almost to the stern of the last barge. The tug, built for moving bargeloads of coal among the Rhine ports, made rapid way into the harbour.

'They're going across in that?' Fedin said.

'If the water stays calm.'

'What about the Royal Navy?'

'The Germans must feel they can neutralize it for forty-eight hours – after that it doesn't matter. And if the Luftwaffe can get the advantage in the air over the Channel, the Royal Navy can't do a thing.'

De Milja watched the harbour in silence. The activity wasn't frantic, but there were thirty operations going on at once, ships moving about, trucks arriving and departing – all of it steady and certain, nobody was smoking or standing around. All non-military ships had been tied up in the small pleasure-boat harbour that adjoined the main dock areas of the city. The name of one of the ships was familiar – he had to think for a moment before he realized why. The rusty freighter with flaking black paint was, according to the letters fading away on her hull, the *Malacca Princess*. Grand name for an old tramp, de Milja thought. It had appeared on one of the carbons Martagne had given them – a schedule of commercial shipping traffic expected to enter or depart the port of Calais over the period 14/9/40 to 21/9/40, with a brief description of each cargo manifest.

The first British attack came at 10:15.

Assault aircraft – built to work near the ground – engines screaming as they flashed across the harbour. Beauforts, de Milja thought. Perhaps a dozen. One flew into the side of a warehouse, and by the yellow flash of that impact de Milja saw another, cartwheeling twice over the surface of the water. The Germans were waiting for this attack – the stutter of heavy machine guns and the deeper, two-stroke drumming of the anti-aircraft cannon rang in de Milja's ears, then deafened him. The Beauforts attacked at one hundred feet, carrying four five-hundred-pound bombs apiece, four dives each if they lasted that long.

There were ME-109s above them, nightfighters, one of them followed a Beaufort right down the chute, guns blazing, in such hot pursuit it chased its quarry through a cloud of machine gun tracer. Moments later, a pair of green flares came floating down, illuminating an airman hanging limp from a parachute, which settled gently on the calm sea then disappeared as the flares hit the water.

Two minutes, no more. The sound faded away, de Milja's hearing came back in time to make out the low wail of an all-clear siren. In the moonlight a single barge settled slowly into the water, a single transport steamer burned, firefighters with hoses silhouetted in its flames.

'Do you have a gun?' de Milja said to Fedin.

'This,' Fedin said. A Walther P-38, a German officer's side arm. De Milja extended his hand. Fedin, after a puzzled moment, gave him the pistol.

'What . . . ?'

De Milja didn't answer.

The second British attack came at 11:16.

A chess game somewhere, in offices below ground, linked to radio towers, British air controllers moving a castle here, a knight there. Blind chess. With command-and-control sometimes functioning, sometimes not. Now and then everybody simply had to improvise, to do whatever seemed best. De Milja had seen plenty of that in Poland, where it hadn't worked. A lot of dead, brave people is what you got from that.

The RAF pilots – British and South African, Canadian, Czech, and Polish – were something beyond brave. They flew into the firestorm a second time, and a number of them paid for it. Perhaps, this time out, the controllers had shifted a flight of Spitfires to keep the 109s away from the assault aircraft. Which left the docks in London unprotected when the Junkers and Heinkels flew over, and that was the chess game. The Calais docks on fire – the London docks on fire in exchange. As de Milja watched the raid play itself out, two searchlights nailed a wounded Beaufort trying to sneak home a few feet above the water. De Milja didn't see the 109 that did the job; the Beaufort simply grew a blossom of white fire behind the cockpit, then hit the water in a cloud of steam and spray.

De Milja's hands ached, he had to pull them free of the windowsill he'd been holding. Only a single siren now, a fire truck somewhere in Calais. Not needed at the docks because nothing was on fire. The transport had been saved – though the barge hit in the 10:15 attack had now apparently sunk into the harbour ooze. Probably it would be salvaged, raised and repaired, used to run ammunition across the Channel to the British beaches. Maybe in a week or so, de Milja thought, as London held out valiantly – as had Warsaw – while around the world people gathered close to their radios to hear, through the static and the sirens, the British pleading for help in their last hours.

De Milja stepped back from the window. 'One last thing to try,' he said.

General Fedin understood him perfectly – he'd been at war, one way or another, for forty years. 'I would be honoured to accompany you,' he said.

'Better if you stay here,' de Milja said.

Fedin nodded stiffly. He might have saluted, but how – the salute of which country, which army? De Milja moved towards the door, for a moment a dim shape in the darkness of the warehouse, then gone. The last Fedin heard of him was footsteps descending the old wooden staircase.

Not long, maybe fifteen minutes, from the Labard warehouse to the docks. He moved quickly, low and tight to the buildings, a strange elation in his heart. He circled a burning garage, avoided a street where flames rolled black and orange from the upper windows of a workers' tenement. Faded into a doorway when a German vehicle – a sinister armoured car, some kind of SS troop in black uniforms hanging off it – came rumbling slowly around a corner.

In the distance, a low, muttering thunder. Weather or bombs. Probably the latter. The RAF hammering away at Boulogne, or Ostende, or Dunkirk. Staggering its attacks, in and out like a boxer. They would be at it all night on this coast, as long as the planes and pilots held out.

The port was a maze – a jumble of streets, then harbours with rock jetties, miles of them, drydocks and spillways, sagging wood fence and high, stone walls. At the main entry, under the PORT DE CALAIS sign, the security people had cut through their own barbed wire and shoved the stanchions back against the brick walls of the guardhouse. It wasn't security they wanted that night, they wanted speed, fire trucks and ambulances in and out. Then, at first light, after the bomb damage was cleaned up, there were troops and ammunition and equipment to load up. As de Milja watched from cover, a truck sped through the gate, bouncing on the cobbles, never slowing down. Nonetheless, he waited. Saw the glint of a helmet through the window of the guardhouse. Moved off to try somewhere else.

He used the little streets, worked parallel to the harbour. A whore hissed at him from a doorway, swung her trench coat aside when she got his attention. He might need an assistant, he thought, and studied her for a moment. 'So,' she said, a little uncomfortable with the sort of attention he was paying her, 'something unusual we have in mind tonight?' De Milja grinned despite himself, *let her live*, just for a moment the choice was his. As he walked away she called after him, a sweet, husky French voice like a café singer – 'You never know if you don't ask, my love.'

Down the next street, he had what he needed. A Beaufort had opened the way for him. Arriving in France in flames and out of control, it had chosen to set up housekeeping on a street that bordered the harbour, had rolled up a hundred feet of wire fence, collected an empty bus and a little watchman's hut that happened to be lying around, then piled it all up against an ancient stone wall and set it on fire. A few French firemen had attempted to interfere with the project, but, as the Beaufort burned, it cooked off several belts of ammunition and chased them away. Water foamed white from the hoses they'd dropped in the street and they called out to one another from the doorways where they'd taken cover. Somebody yelled at de Milja as he ran through the opening torn in the fence, that was the only challenge. That, and something that sputtered and whizzed past his ear, as though to say *move along there*.

An area of open workshops, stone bays as big as barns – they'd likely worked on Napoleon's fleet here. 'Give me six hours' control of the Strait of Dover, and I will gain mastery of the world.' Napoleon had said that – de Milja had had to learn it when he'd studied at Saint-Cyr. The workshops were full of small engines, propeller shafts. De Milja's eye fell on a tank of acetylene and he smiled as he trotted past.

It seemed to take a long time – after midnight on his watch – but he finally stood on the old jetty that protected the pleasure-boat harbour; massive slabs of granite piled up a century earlier against the seas of the Pas de Calais – angry North Sea water trapped between the cliffs of England and France. Now it was calm in the September moonlight, just a quiet swell running diagonally to the shore; a slow, lazy ocean like a cat waking up. De Milja trotted past staunch little sailboats – *Atlantic Queen, Domino* – until the hulls of the commercial ships came into view. Banished here to be kept out of the way of the invasion fleet, allowed to sail into Calais on schedule so as not to give away the date and location of the invasion.

He stopped, looked anxiously into the sky. *Not yet.* No, it was only a flight of German bombers, at high altitude, droning towards England. Perhaps two hundred of them, he thought, they seemed to take forever to pass above him. It was too exposed on the skyline so he half-ran, half-slid to the foot of the jetty where the water lapped at the rocks. The green seaweed reeked in the summer heat and clouds of flies hung above it. He knelt, took the Walther from the back of his waistband, and had a look. The 7.65 mm version, a heavy, dependable weapon, for use, not for show. Eight rounds in the magazine, one in the chamber. He worked the safety, noted the film of oil that glistened on the slide. *Trust Fedin*, he thought, *to keep things in good order.*

The foot of the jetty lay in moon-shadow, so de Milja, invisible, used it as a pathway. Past a pair of Greek tankers, empty from the way they rode high in the water, and a flaking hulk called the *Nicaea*, a sheen of leaked oil coating the water at its stern. Then, last in line, as far away as the harbourmaster could berth it, the *Malacca Princess*. The smell! De Milja blinked and shook his head. How did the crew survive it, all the way from the port of Batavia?

He gripped the Walther firmly and thought *no surprises, please.* No stubborn captain who took the care and protection of his cargo as a sacred trust – no fanatics, no heroes. De Milja moved quickly, from the shadows of the jetty to the first step of an iron gangway covered with tattered canvas that climbed ten feet to the deck. On deck, he went down on one knee. *Deserted*, he thought. Only the creak of old iron plates as the ship rose and fell, and the grating of the hawser cable as it strained against its post on the jetty below. The smell was even stronger here, his eyes were tearing. De Milja listened intently, heard, no, didn't hear. Yes, did. Bare feet on iron decking. Then a voice – a native of the Dutch East Indies speaking British English – very frightened and very determined. 'Who is there?' A pause. 'Please?'

De Milja ran, low to the deck, and flattened himself against the base of a cargo crane. From here he could see a silhouette, standing hunched over, a few feet from the open door of the deck cabin, peering about, head moving left, then right. In one hand, a long shape. What? A rifle? It occurred to de Milja to point the Walther at the man and blaze away but he knew two things – he wouldn't hit him, and somebody, even in the tense, hushed interlude between bombing attacks, would hear a pistol shot and just have to stir up French or German security to go and see what it was all about.

De Milja stepped out where the man could see him, extended the pistol, and called, 'Stand still.'

The silhouette froze. De Milja worked out the next phrase in his uncertain English. 'Let fall.' He waggled the pistol once or twice, there followed the clatter of an object dropped on the iron deck. Whatever it was, it didn't sound like a rifle. He approached the man. He was young, wearing only a pair of cotton trousers cut off below the knee and a cloth tied around his forehead. De Milja stooped cautiously, retrieved what the man had dropped: a wooden club. 'Others?' he said.

'There are none, sir. No others,' the man said. 'Just me. To keep the watch.'

De Milja lowered the pistol. The watchman smiled, then made a certain motion with his hands and shoulders. *Whatever you want*, it meant, *to me it's not worth dying for.*

De Milja nodded that he understood. The young man had a family, in Sumatra or Java somewhere, and if circumstance carried him to the ends of the earth where people had gone mad, well, it was their war, not his.

At first, he didn't know how to do what de Milja needed but he knew where to look, and from there the solution to the problem was evident. Raise the large, metal arm beside the box to its *up* position, then move around the *Malacca Princess*, find its various equipment, for loading and anchorage and warning and identifying other ships and just about anything you could think of, and throw all those switches to the *on* position.

Then wait.

'Your things,' de Milja said.

'Sir?'

De Milja pointed to his own trousers, shirt, wallet, pistol. The man nodded vigorously and together they went below while he collected a small bundle, then moved back to the main deck.

Where they waited. The ship rocked gently and creaked, the nearby harbour felt deserted. In the dock area, activity continued; trucks, visible even with taped headlights, moving invasion matériel to be loaded onto barges. By 1:30, de Milja began to worry. What if the British had taken too many losses and decided to halt operations for the night? No, it wasn't possible.

It wasn't. At 1:50, the air-raid sirens began to wail, all along the wharf and from the city of Calais. De Milja smiled at the watchman, and pointed at the sky. The man nodded, returned the smile, tight and conciliatory. He understood fighting very well, he understood that de Milja was in the act of fighting; a sort of noble privilege. He just wasn't all that pleased to have been drawn into it – no insult intended, sir.

Poor Charles Grahame, not much success in life. Still young, but the pattern was set. Public school with a name that made people say 'Where?' A year at the University of Edinburgh, a year at the Scottish Widows Assurance Society in the City of London. Then, war on the way, an attempt to join the RAF. Well, yes, of course, what they needed just then were meteorologists.

So he joined the Royal Navy, and with grit and determination worked his way into the naval aviator school. He got through it, assigned to the aircraft carrier HMS *Avenger*.

Not to fly fighter-bombers, oh no, not Charley. Tall and gangly, curly hair that wouldn't stay, ears like jug handles, freckles everywhere, and a silly grin. The headmaster of his school used to say that God didn't quite get around to finishing Charles.

The Royal Navy assigned him to fly the Swordfish torpedo plane.

The Swordfish was a biplane – top and bottom wing and a fixed wheel – that looked like a refugee from World War I. It carried a single torpedo, slung beneath the cockpit. 'Quite serviceable, though,' the flight instructor said. Its airspeed was 150 miles an hour. 'But it *will* get you there, eventually,' the flight instructor said. Saying to himself immediately thereafter *now whether or not it will get you home is entirely another matter.*

Not much talent as a pilot. Charles's method of achievement was to learn the rules and follow them to the letter. Do this, then do this, then do that. A different age might have found this approach greatly to its liking but bad luck, Charles lived at a moment when spontaneity, the daring solution, and the flash of genius were particularly in fashion.

The carrier HMS *Avenger* was steaming in circles in Aldeburgh Bay in the first hours of 17 September, just after midnight. Charles Grahame climbed into the open cockpit beneath the top wing and his gunner/torpedo-man, Sublieutenant Higbee, sat in the gunner's cockpit behind him. They took off, then turned south, in a formation of six Swordfish assigned to attack Calais harbour.

The formation hugged the coastline, protected by coastal anti-aircraft defences. A single ME-109 might have done for all of them, so hiding, down at six thousand feet, was their best – in fact their only – defence. The night was warm and still, moonlight turned the clouds to silver and sparkled on the water below the planes. They flew past navigation beams at Shoeburyness and Sheerness, then turned east at Herne Bay, headed for Margate.

At Margate, a rendezvous with a flight of Hurricanes, well above them somewhere, godlike, lords of the high cloud. The Hurricane squadron leader came on his radio moments later. 'Hullo Hector, hullo Hector. This is Jupiter, we're above you right now, and we're going to keep you company on the way to destination. Radio silence from here on, but we did want to wish you good hunting. Roger and out.'

Charles Grahame knew that voice, it had a moustache and it drove a

Morgan and its friends called it Tony and it got the girl and, really, worst of all, it knew it. Oh well, he told himself. Just get on with it. Not everybody could be lord of the manor.

Coming into the Strait of Dover, the Germans started shooting at them. Puffs of anti-aircraft burst that hung in the air like painted smoke. Something tossed the Swordfish's port-side wings in the air, and something else flicked the plane's tail. Charles worked the controls to see if they still responded, and they did, as much as they ever did.

The Swordfish flight attacked in a three-and-three configuration, Charles the wingman on the left in the first wave. Higbee yelled 'Good luck, Charley,' above the singing of the wind in the struts, his voice at nineteen a high tenor. Then all hell broke loose – *somebody* down there took Charley Grahame pretty damn seriously after all because they tried to kill him. Tracer streamed past the cockpit, flak burst everywhere, a bullet hit the fuselage with an awful tinny rattle. 'Easy does it,' Charles said to himself. Now he concentrated on doing what he'd been taught. Step One, the approach. Well, they'd managed that well enough. Step Two, acquire the target. By now Higbee should be ready to fire. But Charles couldn't see a thing. Not a bloody thing. He was whipping along, three hundred feet above the water, below him, theoretically, the harbour at Calais. But what he could see was a dark, confused blur, the moon lit up water here and there, but it meant nothing to Charles. He'd been instructed to attack a troop transport, or, almost as good, a tugboat. A barge, which could carry eight hundred tons of supplies, was a very desirable third choice. But Charles couldn't find a harbour, a city, or indeed anything at all. Probably it was France, *probably* . . .

Good heavens!

Right in the middle of the torpedo run, somewhere over on his left, a ship had lit up like a Christmas tree; cabin lights, searchlights, docking lights, navigation lights – and in the muddy darkness of the blacked-out coast it looked, somehow, *celestial*. Higbee and Charles both gasped. 'Hold fire!' Charles yelled and threw the Swordfish into a tight left bank that made the plane shudder. Higbee had, just at that moment, been about to fire, a shot that would have sent a torpedo on its way to harrowing a mighty groove in the Protestant cemetery of Calais.

'Is it a trick?' Higbee's voice was dangerously close to soprano now but Charles never noticed. A trick! No, damn it, it wasn't a trick. That was a *ship* and he'd been reliably informed that this was *Calais* and his job was to shoot a ship in Calais and now that was exactly what he meant to do. To which end, he traversed the city of Calais, drawing the fire of every anti-aircraft gun in the place but, somehow, the Swordfish was too big and slow to hit.

Charles did it right – one-two-three right. Got enough distance away from the target before circling back, and adjusting his altitude to one hundred feet. The ship grew, bigger and bigger as they plunged towards it, its lights twinkled, then glared brightly. At the end it seemed enormous, a vast, glowing city. 'Torpedo away!' Higbee screamed, his voice wobbly with excitement. The plane bucked, then, freed of weight, accelerated. Charles pulled back on the stick, his training calling out *climb, climb.*

Emerging from a blizzard of lights and tracer and cannon fire, the clumsy Swordfish worked its way upwards through the thin night air. Then, suddenly, Charles felt the plane quiver and he was, for an instant, blinded. A flash, so intense and white it lit the clouds, and seemed to flicker, like lightning. Now you're shot, he thought. But he was wrong. The plane had been hammered, not by a shell but by a concussive blast.

Higbee had actually hit something.

He had hit the *Malacca Princess*, in its final moments a shining beacon in the harbour at Calais. The torpedo had done what it was supposed to do – run straight through the water, found its target, penetrated the rusty old plate amidships and, there, detonated. Causing the explosion, almost simultaneously, of the *Malacca Princess's* cargo: a hundred thousand gallons of volatile naphtha.

Now you could see Calais.

The *Malacca Princess* burned to the waterline in a half-hour – actually it melted – burned like a dazzling white Roman candle, burned so bright it lit up every troop transport and tugboat and barge in the harbour.

25 October 1940.

Only one couple at the auberge by the sea at Cayeux. They used to come up here from Paris in the autumn, the secret couples, park their cars so the licence plates couldn't be seen from the road, register as Monsieur and Madame Duval.

But, with the war, only one couple this year. They didn't seem to mind the barbed wire, and they didn't try to walk on the cliffs – where the German sentries would have chased them away. This couple apparently didn't care. They stayed in the room – though that quite often happened at the auberge at Cayeux – and what with all that staying in the room, they brought sharp appetites to the dinner table in the evening, and enough ration coupons so that no awkward explanations had to be made.

They made love, they ate dinner at the table in the bow window, they watched the sea, they paid cash. It made the owner feel sentimental. How nice life used to be, he thought.

The flan was made with fresh eggs from a nearby farm, and de Milja and Genya cleaned the plate quite shamelessly, then lit cigarettes. The waiter – also the owner and the cook; his wife did the accounts and made the beds – came to the table and said, 'Will Monsieur and Madame take a coffee?'

De Milja said they would.

While it was being made they looked out the window at the sea. Long, slow rollers ran into the shore, white spray flying off the crests in the driving wind. The dark water exploded as it hit the rocks at the base of the cliff, a pleasant thunder if you were warm and dry and having dinner.

'One wouldn't want to be out there now,' Genya said. She was in a sadder-but-wiser mood that evening, and it made her voice melancholy. What she'd said was normal dinner conversation, but the reference was deeper; to German invasion fleets, to the victory won by the British.

'No,' de Milja said. 'It's no time of year for boating.'

She smiled at that. *Canotage,* he'd said. A word that summoned up the man in straw hat and woman in frock, her hand trailing idly in the river as they floated past a lily pad.

Genya's cigarette glowed as she inhaled. She let the smoke drift from her nostrils. 'Probably,' she said, 'you haven't heard about Freddi Schoen.'

'Freddi.' De Milja smiled.

'His friend Jünger was leaving Paris and he took me to lunch. Freddi won an Iron Cross. To do with a naval exercise off the Belgian coast somewhere. There was disaster and he took command and, and – did all sorts of things, Jünger's French didn't really last through the whole story. But he was very brave, and they gave him a medal. Posthumously.'

'I always wondered,' de Milja said, 'why the Freddi Schoens of Germany didn't do something about Hitler before he manoeuvered them into war.'

'Honour,' Genya said. 'If I'm allowed only one word.'

The waiter came with coffee, real coffee, very hard to get in Paris these days unless you bought on the black markets.

'We're not serving sugar tonight,' the waiter explained.

'Oh, but we don't take sugar,' Genya said.

The waiter nodded appreciatively – a gracious and dignified lie, well told, was a work of art to a man who understood life.

The coffee was very good. They closed their eyes when they drank it. 'I've learned to like small things now,' de Milja said. 'War did that, at least.'

When he looked up from his coffee the light of the candles caught the ocean colour in his eyes and she took his hand on top of the table and held it tight.

'You are to be loved,' she said with a sigh. 'No doubt of that.'

'And you,' he said.

She shook her head; he'd got it wrong there.

Late that night it rained hard, water streamed down the windows and the sound of the sea was muffled as it broke against the cliff. It was cold and damp in the room. De Milja opened an armoire and found an extra blanket, then they wrapped themselves up and began to make love. 'We're on a boat,' she whispered. 'Just us. In the middle of the sea. And now it's a storm.'

'Then we better hang on to what's valuable,' he said.

She laughed. 'I've got what I want.'

Some time later he woke up and saw that her eyes were shining. She caught him staring and said, 'See what you did?' He got himself untangled from the coarse sheet and moved next to her. Her skin was very hot. Then she wiped at her eyes with her fingers. 'I hope you love me, whatever happens,' she said.

The letter came a week later. He was sitting at a table in a tiny apartment. She had gone to Switzerland, she would be married when she got there. Please forgive her, she would love him forever.

He read the letter again, it didn't say anything new the second time. He was changing his identity – once again – that week. Becoming someone else in order to do whatever they wanted him to do next, and papers were always a part of that. Still, poor old Lezhev might have lasted out another month if he'd been careful with him. But de Milja ached inside, so the passport and the work permit and all the rest of it went into the blackened little stove that sat in the corner of the room. There was no heat, it was snowing out, the papers burned in a few minutes, and that was the end of it.

Paris
Nights

Now he was valuable.

And when they brought him out, to neutral Spain, he was handled very carefully. De Milja knew what it took – people and money and time – and stood off and marvelled a little at what they thought him worth. The finest papers, delivered by courier. An invitation to dinner at the chateau of Chenonceaux, a castle that spanned the river Cher, which happened to be the boundary between German-occupied France and Vichy France. He arrived at eight, had a glass of champagne, strolled to the back of the grand house, and found a fisherman and a small boat on the other side of the river. Then a truck, then a car, then a silent, empty hotel in the hills above Marseilles, then a fishing boat after midnight.

No improvisation now.

Now he was *the Poles have someone in Paris,* also known as *I can't tell you how I know this, or forgive me, Colonel, but I must ask you to leave the room.* Or maybe he was *Proteus* or whatever code name they'd stuck on him – he was not to know. This kind of attention made him uncomfortable. First of all it was dangerous – he had learned, since 1939, how not to be noticed, so it had become second nature with him to fade away from attention, and he'd got so he could sense it *feeling* for him.

Second of all, he didn't like to be managed, or controlled, and that, with some delicacy, was exactly what they were doing. And third, all this was based on the assumption that he was good, and that wasn't quite the word for it. He was, perhaps, two things: unafraid to die, and lucky so far – if they had an unafraid-to-die-and-lucky-so-far medal, he would take it.

He and the watchman, for instance, sprinting for their lives down the slippery jetty, had survived by sheer, eccentric chance. Burning planes zooming over their heads, anti-aircraft fallback, then a shattering explosion that cut the *Malacca Princess's* neighbour, the *Nicaea,* in half and showered down burning metal. They jumped into the harbour, like

741

reasonable men anywhere, where bits and pieces of tramp freighter steamed as they hit the water. When German and French police ran by, cursing and with guns drawn, they ducked below the water. Who wouldn't? Later, in the jumble of streets around the docks, he and the watchman knew it was time for them to go their separate ways. De Milja shook his hand, and the man smiled, then ran like the wind. All this wasn't, to de Milja's way of thinking, definable by the word *good*.

The fishing boat that took de Milja from Marseilles landed on the coast of Spain at night, aided by Sixth Bureau operatives who signalled with flashlights from the beach. Yes, Spain was neutral, but not all *that* neutral. He was hustled into a shiny black sedan and driven at speed to the outskirts of Barcelona. There, in a bedroom on the third floor of a villa with heavy drapes drawn across the window, he was served a chicken and a bottle of wine. His keepers were young Poles – fresh-faced, earnest, well conditioned, and cheerfully homicidal. There was a pile of books on the table – *put a pile of books on his table, damn it.* He read one of them for an hour; *In spring, the Alpine lakes of Slovenia are a miracle of red sunsets and leaping trout* – then fell asleep.

Various terrors he had avoided feeling now returned in force, and he woke up eighteen hours later having sweated through a wool blanket. He remembered only a few fragments of those dreams and forgot them as soon as he could. He staggered into the bathroom, shaved, showered, had a good long look at himself in the mirror. So, this was who he was now, well, that was interesting to know. Older, leaner, marked with fatigue, rather remote, and very watchful. On a chair he found clean slacks, a shirt, and a sweater. He put them on. Shifted the drape an inch aside from the window and stared out at the brown autumn hills. Just the motion of the drape apparently caused a restless footstep or two on the gravel path below his room, so he let it fall back into place. Why didn't they just bar the window and put him in stripes and stop all the pretence?

Vyborg showed up that morning. In a good brown suit and a striped British tie. Had there always been a gentleman under that uniform, or was it just a trick that London tailors did? They could do nothing, however, about the face: the Baltic knight, squinting into a blizzard and ready to cut down a company of Russian pikemen, was still very much in evidence. He suggested a walk in the hills and they did that, with guards following a little way down the path. November, de Milja thought, was a strange time in dry countries; faded colours, sky grey and listless. Vyborg told de Milja that his wife had died. They walked in silence for a long time after that. Finally de Milja was able to say, 'Where is she?'

'A small cemetery in the town where the spa is. A mass was said for her. It had to be done quietly, but it was done.' They walked for a moment, through a stand of low pines. 'My sympathies, Alexander,' Vyborg said softly. 'It comes from all of us, from everyone who knows you.'

'How, please?'

'Influenza.'

De Milja was again unable to speak.

'She was working in the kitchen,' Vyborg went on. 'Some of us do best in bad times, and that was true of her. She had a high fever for three days, and then she died in her sleep.'

'I think I would like to go back to the house,' de Milja said.

He visited Barcelona once or twice, but it was just another conquered city. It had the silence that passed for peace, the courtesy of fear. The police state was in place, people in the street avoided his eyes. There were still bullet chips and shell holes in the buildings, but the masons were at work, and there were glaziers, their glass sheets balanced on the sides of their mules, shouting up the sides of apartment houses to announce their presence.

He spent a lot of time walking in the hills, sometimes with two men from the Sixth Bureau; one clerkish, a man who sat behind a desk, the other with a hard, bald head, a well-groomed moustache, and small, angry eyes. They needed to know about various things in France and de Milja told them what he could. The bald-headed man, though he did not come out and say it, was clearly concerned with the construction of new and better wireless/telegraphy sets, and de Milja didn't feel he was able to help much. The other man asked questions about French political life under the Germans and de Milja helped him, if possible, even less. But they were decent men who tried to make things easy for him – *as long as we all happen to find ourselves in Spain, why not spend a moment chatting about the views of the French Communist Party* – and de Milja did the best he could for them.

Again and again, he thought about his wife. He had, in October of 1939, said good-bye to her, left her in charge of her destiny, as she'd asked. Maybe he shouldn't have done that. But then he had never once been able to make her, crazy or sane, do anything she did not want to do.

Down the road from the villa was a tiny café in the garden of an old woman's house. She had a granddaughter who said *gracias* when she served coffee, and when it wasn't raining de Milja and Vyborg would sit at a rusty iron table and talk about the war.

'Operation Sealion has failed,' Vyborg said. 'The first time Hitler's been beaten.'

'Do we know what actually happened?' de Milja asked.

'We know some of it. It wasn't a total victory, of course, nothing like that. The RAF sank 21 out of 170 troop transports. That's a loss, but not a crippling loss for people contemplating an invasion from the sea. Out of 1,900 barges, 214 were destroyed. Only five tugboats out of 368; only three motorboats out of more than a thousand.'

'Three, did you say?'

'Yes.'

'Then what made them quit?'

Vyborg shrugged. 'An invasion is more than ships. A five-hundred-ton ammunition dump was blown up at Den Helder, in Holland. On the sixth of September, a rations depot was burned out. In Belgium, an ammunition train was destroyed. Then down at Le Havre, where a number of German divisions were based, the waterworks were put out of commission. There was also the training exercise – you saw some of the results at Nieuwpoort, and German hospital trains crossed Belgium all that night. Therefore, if the RAF could hit a practice run through that hard, what would they do once the real thing got started? Funny thing about the German character, they're very brave, not at all afraid to die, but they are afraid to fail. In some ways, our best hope for Germany is the Wehrmacht – the generals. If Germany loses again, and then again, perhaps they can be persuaded that honour lies in a change of government.'

'Can that really happen?'

Vyborg thought about it.' 'Maybe,' he said. 'With time.'

It drizzled, then stopped. The little girl came and put up a faded umbrella and wiped the table with a cloth and said, '*Gracias.*' She smiled at de Milja, then ran away.

'One last time, the people who knew you as Lezhev?' Vyborg said.

'Freddi Schoen.'

'Dead.'

'Jünger, the Wehrmacht staff officer.'

'Transferred. In Germany at the OKW headquarters.'

'Traudl von Behr.'

'She's in Lille, at the moment. Aide to a staff major running transports from northern France to Germany.'

'There were more Germans, but they didn't know who I was. Somebody they saw here and there, perhaps Russian.'

'Be absolutely certain,' Vyborg said.

De Milja nodded that he was.

12 January 1941.

In the cold, still air of the Paris winter, smoke spilled from the chimneys and hung lifeless above the tiled rooftops.

Stein crunched along the snow-covered rue du Château-d'Eau, head down, hands jammed deep in the pockets of his overcoat. Cold in the 5:00 p.m. darkness, colder with the snow turned blue by the lamplight, colder with the wind that blew all the way from the Russian steppe. You can feel it, Parisians said, you can feel the bite. Eighteen degrees, the newspaper said that morning.

Stein walked fast, breath visible. Here was 26, rue du Château-d'Eau. Was that right? He reached into an inside pocket, drew out the typewritten letter with the exquisite signature. Office of the notary LeGros, yes, this was the building. Notaries and lawyers and *huissiers* – officers of the court – all through this quarter. It wasn't that it was pleasant, because it wasn't. It was simply where they gathered. Probably, as usual, something to do with a Napoleonic decree – a patent, a licence, a dispensation. A special privilege.

The concierge was sweeping snow from the courtyard entry with a twig broom, two mufflers tied around her face, her hands wound in flannel cloths. 'Notaire LeGros? Third floor, take the stairs to your left, Monsieur.'

LeGros opened the door immediately. He was an old man with a finely made face and snow-white hair. He wore a cardigan sweater beneath his jacket and his hand was like ice when Stein shook it.

The business was done in the dining room, at an enormous chestnut table covered with official papers. Huysmanns, a Belgian with broad shoulders and a thick neck, was waiting for him, stood and grunted in guttural French when they shook hands. Stein sat down, kept his coat on – the apartment was freezing and he could still see his breath. 'Hard winter,' Huysmanns said.

'Yes, that's true,' Stein said.

'Gentlemen,' said the notary.

He gathered papers from the table, which he seemed to understand by geology: the Stein-Huysmanns matter buried just below the Duval matter. The two men signed and signed, writing *read and approved*, then dating each signature, their pens scratching over the paper, their breathing audible. Finally LeGros said, 'I believe the agreed payment is forty thousand francs?'

Stein reached into the inner pocket of his overcoat and withdrew a sheaf of five-hundred-franc notes. He counted out eighty, passed them to the notary, who counted and gave them to Huysmanns, who wet his thumb in order to count and said the numbers in a whisper. LeGros then coughed – a cough of delicacy – and said, 'A call of nature, gentlemen. You will excuse me for a moment.'

He left the room, as notaries had been leaving rooms, Stein imagined, since the days of Richelieu. The remainder of the money would now be paid, theoretically out of sight of the honest notary, theoretically out of sight of the tax authorities. Stein counted out an additional hundred and twenty-five thousand francs. Huysmanns wet his thumb and made sure.

The notary returned, efficiently, just as Huysmanns stuffed the money in his pocket. 'Shall we continue?' he chirped. They signed more papers, the notary produced his official stamp, made an impression in wax, then certified the documents with his magnificent signature.

'I would like,' Stein said, 'to make certain of the provision that specifies the name of the business is to continue as Huysmanns. To assure that the goodwill of established customers is not lost to me.'

As the notary rattled papers, Huysmanns stared at him. Goodwill? He had an opaque face, spots of bright colour in his cheeks, a face from a Flemish military painting. LeGros found the relevant paragraph and pointed it out; the two men read it with their index fingers and grunted to confirm their understanding.

Then the notary said, 'Congratulations, gentlemen.' And wished them success and good fortune. In other times, they might have adjourned to a café, but those days were gone.

Stein walked back to the Métro, paid his fourteen centimes for a ticket, and rode the train back to the avenue Hoche, where he had a grand apartment, just around the corner from Gestapo headquarters on the rue de Courcelles. He was now the owner of a business, a *dépôt de charbon* – coal yard – out by the freight tracks near the Porte de la Chapelle. The train was crowded with Parisians, their expressions empty, eyes blank as their minds turned away from the world.

It was seven; Stein had an appointment in an hour. He took off the disguise: the dark overcoat, the black suit, the olive silk tie, the white shirt, the diamond ring, the gold watch. De Milja sighed with exhaustion and put the Stein costume on a chair. Except for the Clark Gable moustache, he was rid of the disguise. He lay down on a big featherbed in a pale-blue bedstead flecked with gold. The walls were covered in silk fabric, sombre red, burgundy, with a raised pattern. Facing the bed, a marble fireplace. On the wall by the doorway, a large oil painting in the manner of Watteau – *school of Watteau*. An eighteenth-century swain in a white wig, a lady with gown lowered to reveal powdered bosoms and pink nipples, a King Charles spaniel playing on the couch between them. The swain has in hand a little ball; when he tosses it, the dog will leap off the couch, the space between the lovers will be clear. Both are at that instant when the stratagem has occurred to them; they are delighted with the idea of it, and with what will inevitably follow. Below the painting, a Louis XVI chiffonier in pale blue flecked with gold, its drawers lined with silk, its top drawer holding mother-of-pearl tuxedo studs in a leather box and a French army 7.65 automatic – in fact a Colt .45 rechambered for French military ammunition. De Milja didn't expect to last out the winter.

He hated Anton Stein, but Anton Stein made for a useful disguise in the winter of 1941. A *Volksdeutsch*, ethnic German, from Czechoslovakia, the Slovakian capital of Bratislava. So he spoke, in the natural way of things, de Milja's rough German and de Milja's bad but effective French. He had even, according to Vyborg, existed. The records were there in case anybody looked – the tack on the teacher's chair and the punch on the policeman's nose lived on, in filing cabinets somewhere in Bratislava. But that was all, that was the legacy of Stein. 'He's no longer with us,' Vyborg had said.

Anton Stein came to Paris in the wake of the German occupation. A minor predator, he knew an opportunity when he saw one. The Nazis had a sweet way with the Anton Steins of the world, they'd had it since 1925: *too bad nobody ever gave you a chance*. A kind of ferocious, law-of-the-jungle loyalty was, once that took hold, theirs to command.

De Milja slept. The apartment was warm, the quilt soft against his skin. There was, in his dreams, no war. An Ostrow uncle carved a boat in a soft piece of wood, Alexander's eyes followed every move. Then he woke up. What was, was. Every Thursday, Madame Roubier made love at twilight.

'Take a mistress,' Vyborg had said. After he'd rented the apartment on the avenue Hoche, the woman at the rental agency had suggested one Madame Roubier to see to the decoration and furnishing. The money made de Milja's heart ache – in Warsaw they were starving and freezing, heating apartments with sticks of wood torn from crates, working all day, then spending the night making explosives or loading bullets. And here he was, amid pale blue flecked with gold.

'Pale blue, flecked with gold.'

Madame Roubier was a redhead, with thin lips, pale skin, a savage temper, and a daintily obscure history that changed with her mood. She was that indeterminate age where French women pause for many years – between virginal girlhood (about thirty-five) and wicked-old-lady-hood – a good long run of life. Yes, she was a natural redhead, but she was most certainly *not* a Breton, that impossibly rude class of people. She was, at times, from Mâcon. Or perhaps Angers.

To supervise the furnishings, she had visited the apartment. Made little notes with a little gold pen on a little gold pad. 'And this window will take a jabot and festoon,' she said.

Suddenly, their eyes met. And met.

'. . . a jabot . . . and . . . festoon . . .'

Her voice faded away to a long Hollywood silence – *they suddenly understand they are fated to become lovers.* They stood close to each other by the window, snow falling softly on the grey stone of the avenue Hoche. Madame Roubier looked deep into his eyes, a strange magnetism drawing her to him as the consultation slowly quivered to a halt: '. . . jabot . . . and . . . festoon . . .'

She had a soft, creamy body that flowed into its natural contours as her corsets were removed. 'Oh, oh,' she cried. She was exquisitely tended, the skin of her ample behind kept smooth by spinning sessions on a chamois-covered stool, the light of her apartment never more than a pink bulb in a little lamp. 'I know what you like,' she would say. 'You are a dirty-minded little boy.' Well, he thought, if nothing else I know what dirty-minded little boys like.

They would make love through the long Paris dusk – *l'heure bleue* – then Stein would be banished from the chamber, replaced by Maria, the maid. Sometime later, Madame Roubier would appear, in emerald-green taffeta, for example – whatever made her red hair blaze redder and her skin whiter, and Stein would say *Oh, mais c'est Hedy Lamarr!* and she would shush him and pooh-pooh him as he helped her wrestle into a white ermine coat.

Then dinner. Then a tour of the night. Then business.

Thursday night. Chez Tolo.

All the black-market restaurants were in obscure streets, down alleys, you had to know somebody in order to find them. Chez Tolo was at the end of a narrow lane – nineteenth-century France – reached through fourteen-foot-high wooden doors that appeared to lead into the court-yard of a large building. The lane had been home to tanneries in an earlier age, but the workshops had long since been converted to workers' housing and now, thanks to war and scarcity, and the vibrant new life that bobbed to the surface in such times, it found itself at the dawn of a new age.

Wood-burning taxicabs pulled up to the door, then a De Bouton with its tulipwood body, a Citroen *traction-avant* – the favoured car of the Gestapo – a Lagonda, a black Daimler. Madame Roubier took note of the last. 'The Comte de Rieu,' she said.

Inside it was dark and crowded. Stein and Madame Roubier moved among the diners; a wave, a nod, a smile, acknowledging the new aristocracy – the ones who, like Anton Stein, had never been given a chance. A fistful of francs to the headwaiter – formerly a city clerk – and they were seated at a good table.

Madame Roubier ate prodigiously. Stein could never quite catch her doing it, but somehow she made the food disappear. Oysters on shaved ice, veal chops in the shape of a crown, sauced with Madeira and heavy cream and served with walnut puree, a salad of baby cabbage, red and green, with raisins and vinegar and honey. Then a cascade of Spanish orange sections soaked in Cointreau and glistening in the candlelight. Stein selected a vintage Moët & Chandon champagne to accompany the dinner.

With the cognac, came visitors. The Comte de Rieu, and his seventeen-year-old Roumanian mistress, Isia, fragile and lovely, who peered out at the world through curtains of long black hair. The count, said to be staggeringly rich, dealt in morphine, diamonds, and milk.

'You must take a cognac with us,' Stein said.

A waiter brought small gilt chairs. Jammed together at the table they were pleasantly crowded, breathing an atmosphere of cigarette smoke and perfume and body heat and breaths of oranges and mints and wine. The count's white-and-black hair was combed back smoothly and rested lightly atop his ears.

'A celebration tonight,' Stein said.

'Oh?' said the count.

'I became, today, a *charbonnier.*'

'You did?'

'Yes.'

'A coal merchant, eh? Well, you must permit us to be your customers. Shall you haul the sacks down the cellar stairs?'

'Absolutely, you may depend on it.'

'A Polack!'

'Exactly!'

'Stein?'

'Yes?'

'You're an amusing fellow.'

They sipped at their balloon glasses of cognac. 'What year?' said the count.

'Nineteen ten.'

'Alas, before your time,' the count said to Madame Roubier.

'Yes? It's your guess?'

'My certain knowledge!'

'Dear me, how is one to repay such a compliment?'

The taxi that served as limousine took them home from a nightclub at dawn, the snow turned grey in the January light. Madame Roubier snored by his side in the back seat. She slept snuggled up to him, the ermine warm against his cheek.

Success purchased investment.

Perhaps you fought, with luck you won, then came the little men with the money. Vyborg had made a point of telling him that, because Vyborg knew exactly who de Milja really was. Vyborg knew how happy he'd been fussing over his maps, knew about his academic papers, worked over endlessly, on the signalization of braiding, or aggrading, rivers. He'd spent his daily life occupied with the Lehman system of hachuring, the way in which the angle of slope is shown on military surveys – important knowledge for artillery people – contour intervals, hydrographic symbolism. He was, in Vyborg's words to Sixth Bureau staff meetings, 'his father's very own son'. He was, in fact, a man whose physical presence to some degree betrayed his personality. He wanted to be a mole who lived in libraries, but he didn't look like that, and the world didn't take him that way.

His mother, de Milja thought, would have made a good spy. She was deceptive, manipulative, attractive – people wanted to talk to her. The world she lived in was a corrupt and cynical place where one had to keep one's guard up at all times, and the probable truth of her opinions had often been the subject of a sort of communal sigh privately shared by de Milja and his father.

But the chief resident intelligence officer for France had to be an executive, not a cartographer. De Milja's quarterly budget was 600,000 francs; rental of safe houses, agents' pay, railway tickets, hotels, endless expenses. Bribes were extra. The money for Huysmanns was extra – and it had been made clear to de Milja that the company had to succeed and profit.

Instinctively, de Milja knew what he would find at Huysmanns Coal. He knew Huysmanns – phlegmatic, northern, Belgian. Profit earned a franc at a time, dogged patience, do we really need all these lights on? Would such a man employ a troupe of merry philosophers?

Never. Thus the man de Milja needed was already in place, right there in Huysmanns' office overlooking the coal yard by the railway tracks.

Monsieur Zim-*maire* it was said. Zimmer, an Alsatian, fifty or so, who wore a clean, grey dustcoat every day, buttoned all the way to the knees. At one time or another he'd taken a hand in everything the company did. He'd driven the trucks, hauled sacks of coal, a job that turned the deliveryman black by the second or third call. He talked to the suppliers, the mines in northern France, and he knew the important customers: hospitals and office buildings and workshops. There were two secretaries who kept the books and sent out the bills, Helene and Cybeline. At Zimmer's suggestion, they fired Cybeline. She was a distant relation of Huysmanns – that didn't matter to Zimmer or de Milja but she insisted it meant she didn't have to work. She filed her nails, sipped coffee, gossiped on the phone and flirted with the drivers. As for Helene, who actually did the work, she got a raise.

Zimmer, too, got a raise. He would, in fact, be running the company. 'I'll be seeking out new customers,' was the way de Milja put it. 'So I expect to be travelling a good part of the time.'

That was true. The Sixth Bureau had directed him to assist in certain British operations against Luftwaffe units based in France. The nightly bombing was relentless. Something had to be done.

8 March 1941.

West of Bourges, de Milja pedalled a bicycle down a cow path. Early spring morning, raw and chilly, the ground mist lying thick on the fields. Leading the way, a Frenchman called Bonneau. Perhaps thirty, a tank officer wounded and captured in late May of 1940. Sent to a POW camp, a munitions factory near Aachen. Escaped. Recaptured. Escaped again, this time reached France and made it stick.

Riding just ahead of de Milja, Bonneau's sister Jeanne-Marie, perhaps twenty, thin and intense and avid to fight the Germans. Through a prewar association – something commercial, Bonneau had sold British agricultural equipment in central France – he'd gotten in touch with somebody in London, and his name had been passed to the special services.

De Milja liked him. Forthright, handsome, with a scrupulous sense of honour. The best of the French, de Milja thought, were the incarnations of heroes in boys' books. Or girls' books – because the principle was twice as true for the French women. De Milja had seen them face down the Germans more than once; iron-willed idealists, proud and free, and quite prepared to die to keep it that way.

'*Bonjour*, Monsieur Gache,' Bonneau called out, coasting on his bicycle. Jeanne-Marie echoed the greeting.

Monsieur Gache was a fourteenth-century peasant. He'd loomed up through the milky-grey mist holding a long switch, surrounded by a half-dozen cows, their breaths steaming, bells clanking. He squinted at de Milja from beneath a heavy brow, his glance suspicious and hostile. He knew every pebble and cowpie in these fields – perhaps this stranger was aiming to help himself to a few. Well, he'd know about it soon enough.

It's spring, start of the war season in Europe, de Milja thought. And Monsieur Gache knew, in some ancient, intuitive sense, exactly who he was and what his appearance meant. Nothing good, certainly. Caesar likely sent somebody up here in the spring of 56 BC to take a look at the Gauls – and there was Monsieur Gache and his six cows.

'That's old Gache,' Bonneau called back to him. 'It's his uncle's land we'll be using.'

De Milja grunted assent, implying that it seemed a good idea. He hoped it was. This was something worked out between people in the countryside, such rural arrangements being typically far too complicated to be successfully explained to outsiders.

They pedalled on for fifteen minutes, threading their way among great expanses of ploughed black earth separated by patches of old-growth forest, oak and beech, left standing as windbreak. The cow path ended at a small stream and Bonneau dismounted like a ten-year-old, riding a little way on one pedal, then hopping off.

'Oop-la!' he said with a laugh. He grinned cheerfully, a man who meant to like whatever life brought him that day. Wounded during the German attack, he had fought on for twelve hours with only a gunner left alive in his tank.

'Now, sir, we shall have to walk,' Jeanne-Marie said. 'For, perhaps, twenty-five minutes.'

'Exactly?' de Milja said.

'In good weather, close to it.'

'If she says it, it's probably true,' Bonneau said wearily, admiring his sister and teasing her in the same breath.

'Here is the Creuse,' she said, pointing across a field.

They could see it from the hill, a ribbon of quiet water that flowed through brush-lined banks and joined, a few miles downstream near the town of Tournon, the Gartempe. This in turn became part of the Loire, and all of it eventually emptied into the Atlantic at the port of Saint-Nazaire.

What mattered was the confluence of the rivers – a geographical feature visible from an aeroplane flying on a moonlit night. They walked on in silence. The field was a good distance from any road, and therefore a good distance from German motorized transport. If the

Germans saw parachutes floating from the sky, they were going to have to organize an overland expedition to go see about the problem.

The field itself had been chosen, de Milja thought, with great care. 'It's Jeanne-Marie's choice,' Bonneau explained. 'She is a serious naturalist – turns up everywhere in the countryside, so nobody notices what she does.'

'I've paced it more than once,' Jeanne-Marie said. 'It is as suggested, about 650 by 250 yards.'

They walked its perimeter. 'There were stumps, but I had our workmen haul them out with the plough horses.' Silently, on behalf of a descending parachutist, de Milja was grateful for her forethought. He saw also that somebody had moved big stones to one side of the field.

'How many people will you have?' de Milja asked.

'Four, perhaps. Six altogether.'

'You'll need brushwood for your fires. It's best to store it under canvas to keep it dry. Then the fires should be set in the shape of an arrow, giving wind direction.'

'Yes,' Jeanne-Marie said. 'We know that.'

De Milja smiled at her. The mysterious foreigner who came from nowhere and told them things they already knew. She stood, holding her bicycle by the handlebars, in front of a huge French spring sky; a few strands of hair had escaped from the front of her kerchief and she brushed them back impatiently.

'Shall we have something before we go back?' Bonneau said.

Jeanne-Marie grinned to herself and nodded yes. She untied a cloth-wrapped packet from the back of her bicycle. They sat on the rim of the field – true to the suggested standard, Jeanne-Marie had located a slightly concave area – and ate bread and crumbly farm cheese and last fall's apples, dried-out and sweet.

'Something must be done, and we hope it is soon,' Bonneau said. 'The people here don't like the Germans, but they are drifting. Pétain speaks on the radio and says that all this has happened to us because France was immoral and self-indulgent. A number of people believe that, others will do whatever makes them comfortable at that moment. One lately hears the word *attentisme* – the philosophy of waiting. Do nothing, we'll see what happens next. This is dangerous for France, because here we don't really live in a country, you know. We live in our houses with our families, that's our true nationality, and what's best is determined from that point of view.'

It was Jeanne-Marie who answered her brother. 'The English will do what they can,' she said, a snap in her voice. 'But not from any tender feeling for the French. We're allies, not friends.'

'Again she's right,' de Milja said.

*

A local train west, then to Nantes, then north on a series of locals. *Very, very careful now*, he told himself. Where he was going the Germans were sensitive, because they had a secret.

As the train rolled to a stop at each little town, de Milja could see he was in the country of Madame Roubier. Brittany. Tall redheads with fair, freckled skin. Sharp-eyed – not easily fooled. Often venal, because it was them against the world, had always been so, and this unending war was fought with wealth.

It was late afternoon when he reached the town of Vannes, down the coast of Brittany from L'Orient, one of the bomber fields used in the Luftwaffe campaign against Britain. North from Vannes was Brest – on the south shore of the widening English Channel, across from Plymouth, on the Cornish coast. No doubt about the bomber field, Vannes railway station was full of German airmen, returning from leave or heading off to sinful Paris for ten days.

De Milja kept his eyes down. Cheap leather briefcase in hand, felt hat with brim turned down, well-worn blue suit. A provincial lawyer, perhaps, snuffling out a living from feuding heirs and stubborn property owners and the tax indiscretions of *petits comerçants*. He walked for a long time, towards the edge of town. No more Germans. Pavements that narrowed, then vanished. Old women with string bags, a few cats. The neighbourhood darkened – buildings crumbling softly into genteel poverty, a grocery store with a sign on the boarded window: FERMÉ.

Finally, a *confiserie* – a candy shop, the miniature gold-foil packets of chocolates in the window covered with a layer of fine dust. A bell jangled above the door as he entered and a young girl stood to attention behind the counter. She was very plain, skin and hair the same washed-out colour, and wore a tight sweater that was more hopeful than seductive. The smell of candied violets and burnt sugar was intense in the dark interior of the shop. It made de Milja feel slightly queasy.

'Mademoiselle Herault?' he asked the clerk.

'In back, Monsieur.' Her voice was tiny.

Mademoiselle Herault sat at a desk in the office. She was in her forties, he guessed. But older than her years. A hard face, lined and severe. As though she dealt in candy from contempt for human appetite, not a desire to sell the world something sweet. Or maybe it was the silent store, the trays of stale orange drops, a small business failing by slow, agonizing degrees.

He identified himself – *Guillaume* for this meeting, and her eyes searched his, to see if he could be trusted. She was, he thought, not a particularly attractive woman, but she had probably never lacked for lovers, being one of those women who understands that attraction hasn't much to do with it.

'May I take a minute of your time?' he asked.

She looked at him a little sideways – minutes, hours, she had nothing but time. Very slowly she worked a Gauloise free of its pack, tapped one end against her thumbnail, held it in her mouth with thumb and forefinger, handed de Milja a box of matches and leaned towards him so he could light it. 'Thank you,' she said.

She opened a drawer in the desk, searched through papers, found an unsealed envelope and handed it to him. 'Here it is,' she said.

He took out what looked like a polite note, written in purple ink on bordered paper sold in stationery stores. His eyes ran along the lines, trying to decipher the penmanship. Then, when he realized what he had, he read it through again.

'This is – this is extremely important,' he said.

She nodded in a sort of vague agreement – *yes, so it seemed to her*. She drew on her Gauloise and blew a plume of smoke at the ceiling.

'Was there a reason you did so much? The occupation?'

'No,' she said. 'I am not French,' she added.

'What then?'

'I'm a Pole, though I've lived here a long time.'

De Milja came close to responding in Polish. He wanted to – then raged at himself for being so stupid. Guillaume was Guillaume – nobody. 'Herault?' he said.

She shrugged. 'That was my father's attempt to fit in.'

'Did he fit in?'

'No,' she said. They were silent for a moment. 'I don't think I'll tell you any reasons,' she said. 'For what I've done, that is. I don't especially believe in reasons.'

De Milja ran his eyes back over the paper. *Kampfgeschwader 100, Pathfinder, Knickbein beam.* De Milja was stunned at the quality of what he had in hand. He'd gotten the woman's name from Fedin – an old contact from the late '30s, nothing very productive, but an address that placed her, quite by accident, on the front line of the German offensive against Britain. Fedin had made the initial contact, then a signal from Vannes reached Paris that meant *I have something for you*. But this was well beyond anything de Milja had expected.

'Please, Mademoiselle. I must ask you to tell me how you managed this.'

A ghost of a smile passed over the woman's face. She found his urgency a little bit pleasing. She nodded her head towards the front of the shop. 'Veronique,' she said.

'Who?'

'My little clerk.'

She almost laughed out loud, so stupid and lost did he look. Then, when she saw the mist clear, she said, 'Yes, that.'

'By design?'

She made a face: *who could say?* Paused a moment, leaned closer, lowered her voice. 'Ugly as sin, poor thing. But for everyone there is someone, and for poor Veronique there is poor Kurt. Eighteen, away from home for the first time, short, homely, with bad teeth and bad eyes. In his unit the lowest of the low: he helps the mechanics who fix the aircraft. I believe engine parts are washed in petrol. Is that so?'

'Yes.'

'He does mostly that. Red hands the result. But he is a *conqueror*, Monsieur Whatever-you-call-yourself. And he has discovered, in this shapeless lump of a child, *le vrai passion*. He drives her, I assure you, to the very edge of sanity. No, beyond.'

'And in bed, he tells her things?'

'No, Monsieur. Men don't tell women things in bed. Men tell women things when they are trying to get them into bed. To let women know how important they are. Once in bed, the time for telling things is over.'

'But Veronique continues.'

'Yes. She loves Kurt. He is her man, hers alone. National borders are here transcended. You understand?'

'Yes.'

'Of course they do chatter, in the way people do, and she tells me things – just to gossip, just to have something to say. They are innocent. Monsieur.'

De Milja nodded sympathetically.

'Someday, you might be asked to do something for Veronique.'

'What is that?'

'Well, national borders are never transcended. Love doesn't conquer all. In Veronique's mind, the Germans will be here for forty years. Should she wait until she's fifty-nine to go on with life? Of course not. Unfortunately for her, I suspect the end of this war may come sooner than forty years. And then, the women who have made love with the enemy will not fare well. The people here who have collaborated silently, *skilfully*, the ones who talk but do nothing, they will take it out on the poor Veroniques of the world. And they can be very cruel. When this happens, perhaps I will find you, or somebody like you, and you will try to do something for poor Veronique.'

'How do you know these things?'

'I know. I'm a Pole – it came to me in my mother's milk. Will you help?'

'If I can, I will,' he said. 'In the meantime, *stop*. Don't do anything – and don't permit her to do anything – that could lead to exposure. The most important thing now is that nobody finds out what was discovered.'

It rained in Paris. Slowly, endlessly. The bare branches of the chestnut trees dripped water in the grey light. At five in the afternoon, Anton Stein stared out the window above his coal yard. A freight train moved slowly along the track. Its couplings rattled and banged as it manoeuvred – stopped, jerked ahead a few feet, stopped, backed up. The board siding of the freight cars and the cast-iron wheels glistened in the rain.

On his desk, March earnings. They were doing well – Zimmer was implacable. All day long, in his clean grey smock, he tended the business. Spillage. Theft. Truck fuel. Suppliers' invoices with added charges. Defaulting customers. Margin of profit, date of delivery. Anton Stein made money.

And Captain Alexander de Milja spent it.

Rental of the apartment on the rue A, where a W/T operator enciphered and transmitted, moving like a butterfly among a hundred different bands to elude the Funkabwehr technicians. Rental of the apartment on the rue B, where an alternate W/T operator was based. Rental of the villa in the suburb of C, where a wounded British pilot was in hiding. Not to mention the apartment on the avenue Hoche, each window dressed with jabot and festoon.

He was tired now. Spirit worn away by the tide. Clandestine war since September of 1939 – it had gone on too long, there'd been too much of it.

He forced his eyes away from the freight cars, back to a sheet of cheap paper on the desk. Huysmanns' desk. Scarred oak, burns on the edge where somebody had rested a cigarette, little drawers full of used rubber bands and thumbtacks and dried-out inkpads for stamps.

On the paper, in his own informal code, the first draft of a report to London: at the Luftwaffe base at Vannes was *Kampfgeschwader 100*, a unit of Pathfinders – pilots who flew along a radio beam, called a *Knickbein beam* because it had the shape of a dog leg. The job of these Pathfinders was to lead flights of bombers to the target, then drop incendiaries, to light fires for the guidance of the planes behind them.

What Veronique the shop clerk had found out was this: the pilots of

Kampfgeschwader 100 did not live on the base in barracks, they lived in various billets in the town of Vannes, and on the afternoon before a mission they travelled to the field by bus. All together, maybe thirty of them, slated to lead various night attacks against British targets. De Milja knew what happened next. He went to the movie theatres on the Champs-Élysées where they showed German newsreels – always with the lights on, because in darkness the French audience made rude noises – of the bombing raids. So he had seen the burning factories, and the bridges down in the rivers, and the firemen weeping with exhaustion.

All together, maybe thirty of them, travelled to the field by bus.

On the Route Nationale – the RN18 – that traced the coast of Brittany: from Brest south to Quimper, L'Orient, then Vannes. The airfield was twelve miles from the outskirts of Vannes, and there were several points of interest along the way. A curve with a rock out-cropping to the east, a grove of stunted beach pine to the west, between the road and the sea. Or perhaps the old fish cannery, abandoned in '38, with rows of dark windows, the glass long ago broken out.

Block the road. A coal truck – somebody else's coal truck – would do that nicely. You'd want six – no eight – operatives. Take the driver and the tyres. Then you had leisure for the pilots. Fragmentation grenades in the windows, then someone with a carbine in the bus. Short range, multiple rounds.

Thirty Pathfinder pilots. All that training, experience, talent. Hard to replace. The ratio of bravado to skill was nearly one to one. Flying an aeroplane along a transmitted beam meant constant correction as you drifted and the signal tone faded. Flying at the apex of the attack meant searchlights and flak – you had to have a real demon in you to want to do that.

'Monsieur Stein?'

He looked up from the wood-flecked paper, initials and numbers; a curving line for a road, a rectangle for a blocking truck. Helene was holding a large leatherbound book. 'Monsieur Zimmer asked that these be sent out today, Monsieur.' She left the book on Stein's desk and returned to work.

Inside the leather cover were cheques for him to sign – a typical practice in a French office. He made sure his pen had ink and went to work – *Anton Stein, Anton Stein*. The payees were coal mines up in Metz, mostly. He was permitted to buy what was left over after the Germans, paying with absurdly inflated currency, took what they wanted and shipped it east. Just after the New Year the Germans had returned the ashes of Napoleon's son, L'Aiglon, to France. Thus the joke of the week: they take our coal and send us back ashes.

Two more to sign. One a *donation*, to the Comité France-Allemagne, in business since 1933 to foster Franco-German harmony and understanding. Well, they'd fostered it all right – now the French had just about all the harmony and understanding anybody could want. The other cheque was made out to Anton Stein for ten thousand francs. His night money.

At the avenue Matignon, the evening performance with Madame Roubier. 'Oh, oh,' she cried out. Under the guise of nuzzling her pale neck he got a view of his watch. 8:25. Outside, the air-raid sirens began. Gently, he unwound himself from her, stood by the bed and turned off the pink bed-table lamp that made her skin glow. Opened the window, then the shutter, just a crack.

Circles of light against the clouds, then arching yellow flames and golden fire that seemed to drip back down towards the dark earth. Kids would be in the parks tomorrow, he thought, adding to their shrapnel collections. A sharp fingernail travelled across his bare backside.

'*Bonjour, Monsieur*,' Madame Roubier said. It amused her to pretend to be his language teacher. '*Comment allez-vous?* The fingernail headed back in the other direction.

He turned away from the fiery lights, looked over his shoulder. She was sprawled on her stomach, reaching out to touch him. 'He ignores me,' she pouted like a little girl. 'Yes he does.' He turned back to the sky. A sudden stutter, bright yellow. Then a slow, red trail, curving down towards the earth. It made his heart sick to see that. 'Yes he *does*.'

Brasserie Heininger. 11:30.

At table, a party of seven: the Comte de Rieu and his little friend Isia. Isia had paid a visit that afternoon to the milliner Karachine, who had fashioned, for her exclusively, a hat of bright cherries and pears with a red veil that just brushed the cheekbones.

At her left, the coal dealer Stein, his mood heavy and quiet, his cigar omnipresent. His companion, the fashionable Lisette Roubier, wore emerald silk. Next to her, the art dealer Labarthe, hair shiny with brilliantine, who specialized in Dutch and Flemish masters and jailed relatives. He could, for a price, produce any loved one from any prison in France. His companion was called Bella, a circus acrobat of Balkan origins.

At her side, the amusing Willy – *w* pronounced *v* – Kappler. The silliest-looking man: a fringe of colourless hair, a long, pointed nose like a comic witch, ears to catch the wind; a face lit up by a huge melon slice of a smile, as though to say *well then what can I do about it?*

'Coal!' he said to Stein. 'Well, that's a lucky job these days.' Then he laughed – melodious, infectious. You couldn't resist joining in; if you didn't get the joke, maybe you would later.

'I can sell as much as they'll let me have,' Stein admitted. 'But,' he added, 'the stocks are often low.'

'Yes, it's true. This ridiculous war drags on – but go talk sense to the English. Then too, Herr Stein, those rascals up there in the mines don't like to work.' With fist and extended thumb he imitated a bottle, tilted it up to his mouth and made glug-glug sounds. Stein laughed. 'Oh but it's true, you know,' Kappler said.

'And you, Herr Kappler,' Stein said. 'What is it that keeps you in Paris?'

'Hah! What a way to put it. I hardly need anything to keep me *here*.'

'In business?'

'Jah, jah. Business, all right.'

Across the table, the Comte de Rieu could barely suppress a laugh – he knew what Kappler did.

'The truth is,' Kappler said, 'I'm just an old cop from Hamburg – like my poppa was before me. I was born to it. A cop under the kaiser, a cop during the Weimar time. So now I work for Heini and Reini, but believe me, Herr Stein, it's the same old thing.'

Heini and Reini meant Heinrich Himmler and Reinhard Heydrich. Which put Kappler somewhere in the RSHA empire – most likely the Gestapo or one of the SD intelligence units. Stein puffed at his cigar but it had gone out.

'Here, let me,' Kappler said. He snapped a silver lighter and Stein turned the cigar in the flame before inhaling.

'Tell them what you heard today, darling,' Labarthe said to his friend Bella.

She looked confused. 'In beauty salon?'

'Yes, that's right.'

She nodded and smiled – now she knew what was wanted. She wore a military-style soft cap with a black feather arching back from one side, and theatrical circles of rouge on her cheeks.

'It was, it was . . .' She turned to Labarthe for help, whispered in his ear, he spoke a phrase or two behind his hand and she nodded with relief. 'Hairdresser was telling me about *death ray*,' she said brightly.

'Death ray?' Madame Roubier said.

'Yes. Was made by man who invented telegraph.'

'Marconi,' Labarthe prompted.

'Yes, Marconi. Now for Mussolini he build death ray. So, war is over.' She smiled enthusiastically.

Willy Kappler shook with silent laughter, then pressed a hand against the side of his face. 'People love a rumour,' he said. 'The stranger it is, the better they like it. Did you hear last week? How de Gaulle was killed in an air raid in London and British spies smuggled his ashes into Paris and buried them in Napoleon's tomb?'

'I did hear that,' said the comte. 'From my dentist. And on the last visit he'd told me the British had invented a powder that set water on fire. Told me in strictest confidence, mind you.'

'Mesdames . . . et . . . monsieurs!'

The waiter made sure he had their attention, then, with a flourish, he presented a *foie gras blond en bloc*, at least two pounds of it. In a basket, a mountain of toast triangles, crusts trimmed off. For each person at the table a tiny chilled dish of Charentais butter. The champagne-coloured aspic quivered as the waiter carved slabs off the block and slid them deftly onto monogrammed plates. '*Et alors!*' said the comte, when the first cut was made and the size of the black truffle within revealed. Then the table was quiet as knives worked foie gras on toast and little sips of Beaune were taken to wash it down. 'I tell you,' said Willy Kappler, eyes glazed with rapture, 'the best is really very good.'

The headwaiter appeared at Stein's chair.

'Yes?' Stein said.

'A telephone call for you, Monsieur.'

The phone was on a marble table in an alcove by the men's toilet. 'Stein,' he said into the receiver. But the line just hissed, there was nobody on the other end.

The men's room attendant opened the door a few inches and said, 'Monsieur Stein?' Stein went into the small tiled foyer that led to the urinals. The attendant's table held a stack of white towels, scented soaps, and combs. A little dish of coins stood to one side. The white-jacketed attendant was called Voyschinkowsky, a man in his sixties, with the red-rimmed, pouchy eyes and hollow cheeks of the lifelong insomniac. Rumour had it that he had, at one time, been one of the richest men in Paris, a brilliant speculator, known as the Lion of the Bourse. But now, with his gravel-voiced Hungarian accent and white jacket, he was just an amusing character.

'I have your message. Monsieur Stein,' Voyschinkowsky said. 'A young man is waiting downstairs, looking at newspapers at the stand just east of the restaurant. He needs to see you urgently.'

De Milja peeled a hundred-franc note from a roll in his pocket and laid it in Voyschinkowsky's dish. 'What next, I wonder,' he grumbled under his breath.

Voyschinkowsky's face remained opaque. 'Thank you, Monsieur,' he said. De Milja went downstairs. It was a warmish April night, the street smelled like fish – a waiter in a rubber apron was shucking oysters over a hill of chipped ice. The young man reading the headlines at the newspaper stand wore a thin jacket and a scarf. 'Yes? You're waiting for me?' de Milja said.

The young man looked him over. 'Fedin needs to see you right away,' he said.

'Where?'

'Up at Boulogne-Billancourt.' Boulogne meant the factory district at the edge of Paris, not the seaside town.

De Milja stared at the young man. It could be anything – an emergency, a trap. There was nothing he could do about it. 'All right,' he said. 'I'll be back.'

The young man looked at his watch. 'Twenty minutes to curfew.'

'I'll hurry,' de Milja said. He had a pass that allowed him to be out any time he wished, but he didn't want to go into that now.

Back at the table he said, 'An emergency.'

'What happened?' Madame Roubier said.

'An accident at the yard. A man is injured.' He turned to the comte. 'Would you see Madame home?'

'Yes, of course.'

'May I help?' said Willy Kappler, very concerned. 'Not much I can't do in this city.' De Milja seemed to consider. 'Thank you,' he said. 'I think the best thing is for me to go, but I appreciate the offer.'

Kappler nodded sympathetically. 'Another time,' he said.

They rode the Métro to the Quai d'Issy station. The train stopped there because the tunnel up ahead had flooded but the police wouldn't let anybody exit to the street. So they crossed over, took a train back one stop, and walked. The quarter was a snarl of freight tracks and old factories surrounding the Renault plant and the large docks on the Seine. On the other side of the river was a Russian neighbourhood – émigrés packed into brick tenements and working on the car assembly lines.

Under German occupation, Renault manufactured military vehicles for the Wehrmacht, so the British bombed the plant. De Milja and Fedin's messenger crunched broken glass underfoot as they walked. Water flooded from broken mains, black smoke that smelled like burning rubber made de Milja's eyes run and he kept wiping at them with his hand. An ambulance drove by, siren wailing. Where a building had collapsed into the street, de Milja stepped over a smouldering mattress, picking his way among scattered pans and shoes and sheet music.

At the Eastern Orthodox Church of Saint Basil, the young man stood back. Tears ran from his eyes and cut tracks in the soot on his face. 'He's in there,' he said to de Milja.

'The church?'

The young man nodded and walked away quickly.

The church was being used as an emergency room. General Fedin was lying on a blanket on the stone floor, a second blanket was drawn up to his chin. When de Milja stood over him he opened his eyes. 'Good,' he said. 'I hoped they'd find you.'

De Milja knelt by his side. Fedin's face, once fierce and skull-like, had collapsed, and his skin was the colour of wax. Suddenly, an old man. He lowered the blanket a little – gauze bandage was taped across his chest – and made a sour face that meant *no good*.

'Better for you to be in the hospital,' de Milja said. 'Fastest way is a taxi, you'll lie on the back seat.'

'Let's not be stupid,' Fedin said gently. 'I know this wound very well, I've seen it many times.'

'Vassily Alexandrovich . . .'

Fedin gripped his arm, he meant to grip it hard, but he couldn't. 'Stop it,' he said.

De Milja was silent for a time: 'How did this happen?'

'I was at the Double Eagle, a Russian club, people playing chess and drinking tea. The sirens went off, like always. We shrugged and ignored them, like always. The next thing, somebody pulled me out from under some boards. Then I woke up here.'

He paused a moment, lips pressed tight. 'I'm sixty-three years old,' he said.

It was dark in the church, a few candles the only light. People were talking in low voices, taking care to walk quietly on the stone floors. Like actors in a play, de Milja thought. Some still wore the costumes – cabdrivers, cleaning women – that exile had assigned them, but in this church they were themselves, and spoke and gestured like the people they had once been. Outside, the last sirens of police cars and ambulances faded away and it was quiet again.

'I always thought I'd die on a horse, on a battlefield,' Fedin said. 'Not in a chess club in Paris. You know I fought at Tannenberg, in 1914? Then with Brusilov, in Galicia. Against the Japanese, in 1905. In the Balkans, 1912 that was, I was on the staff of the Russian military attaché to Serbia. 1912. I was in love.'

He smiled at that. Thought for a time, with his eyes closed. Then looked directly at de Milja and said, 'Jesus, the world's a slaughterhouse. Really it is. If you're weak they're going to cut your throat – ask the Armenians, ask the Jews. The bad people want it their way, my friend. And how badly they want it is the study of a lifetime.'

He shook his head with sorrow. 'So,' he said, 'so then what. You step into it, if you're a certain sort. But then you're taking sides, and you've written yourself down for an appointment with the butchers. There's a waiting list – but they'll get around to you, never fear. Christ, look at me, killed by my own side.' He paused a moment, then said, 'Damn fine bomb, though, even so. Made in Birmingham or somewhere. Didn't hit any factories, this one didn't. But it settled with the Double Eagle club once and for all. And it settled with General Fedin.'

Fedin laughed, then his mood changed. 'Listen, I know all about what you did on the docks that night. Running off to die because you couldn't stand to live in a bad world. What the hell did you think you were doing? You can't do that, you can't *resign*.' He thought a moment, then said sternly, 'That's not for you, boy. Not for you.'

He sighed, wandered a little, said something, but too quietly for de Milja to hear. De Milja leaned closer. 'What did you say?'

'I want to rest for a minute, but don't let me go yet,' Fedin said.

De Milja sat back, hands on knees, in the gloom of the darkened church. He looked at his watch: just after one in the morning. Now the night was very quiet. He sensed somebody nearby, turned to see a woman standing next to him. She had grey hair, hastily pinned up, wore a dark, ill-fitting suit, had a stethoscope around her neck. She stared at Fedin for a long moment, knelt by his side and drew the blanket up over his face.

'Wait,' de Milja said. 'What are you doing?' She stood, then put a hand on his shoulder. He felt warmth enter him, as though the woman had done this so often she had contrived a single gesture to say everything that could be said. Then, after a moment, she took her hand off and walked away.

17 April. 3:20 a.m. West of Bourges.

Bonneau drove the rattletrap farm truck, Jeanne-Marie sat in the middle, de Milja by the window. They drove with the headlights off, no more than twenty miles an hour over the dirt farm roads. The truck bounced and bucked so hard de Milja shut his mouth tight to keep from cracking a tooth.

Three-quarter moon, the fields visible once the eyes adjusted. With aeroplanes on clandestine missions, you fought the war by the phases of the moon. 'The Soulier farm,' Jeanne-Marie said in a whisper. Bonneau hauled the wheel over and the old truck shuddered and swayed into a farmyard. The dogs were on them immediately, barking and yelping and jumping up to leave muddy paw marks on the windows.

A huge silhouette appeared in the yard, the shadows of dogs dancing away from its kicking feet as the barking turned to whining. A shutter banged open and a kerosene lamp was lit in the window of the farmhouse. The silhouette approached the truck. 'Bonneau?'

'Yes.'

'We're all ready to go, here. Come and take a coffee.'

'Perhaps later. The rendezvous is in forty minutes and we've got to walk across the fields.'

The silhouette sighed. 'Don't offend my wife, Bonneau. If you do, I can reasonably well guarantee you that the Germans will be here for generations.'

Jeanne-Marie whispered a curse beneath her breath.

'What? Who is that? Jeanne-Marie? *Ma biche* – my jewel! Are you going to war?' The silhouette laughed, Bonneau put his forehead on his hands holding the steering wheel. To de Milja he said, 'Soulier was my sergeant in the tank corps.' Then, to the silhouette at the truck window, 'You're right, of course, a coffee will be just the thing.'

They entered the farmhouse. The stove had been lit to drive off the night chill. On a plank table there was a loaf of bread and a sawtooth knife on a board, butter wrapped in a damp cloth, and a bottle of red wine. Madame Soulier stood at the stove and heated milk in a black iron pot 'We just got this from Violet,' she said.

De Milja teetered dangerously on the edge of asking who Violet was – then from the corner of his eye caught Jeanne-Marie's discreet signal, a two-handed teat-pulling gesture.

Madame Soulier gathered the skin off the top of the milk with a wooden spoon, then whacked the spoon on the rim of the zinc-lined kitchen sink to send it flying. 'That's for the devil,' she muttered to herself.

De Milja knew this coffee – it was the same coffee, black, bitter, searing hot, he'd drunk in the Volhynia before going hunting on autumn mornings. He held the chipped cup in both hands. The cities were different in Europe; the countryside was very much the same.

'And the Clarais cousins? They're coming?' Bonneau said.

Soulier shrugged. It scared de Milja a little, the quality of that shrug. He understood it, he feared, all too well – the Clarais cousins hadn't shown up where they'd promised to be since the spring of 1285, likely tonight would be no different. Jeanne-Marie's face remained immobile, perhaps the Clarais cousins were not crucial to the enterprise but had been asked for other reasons.

'Townspeople,' Soulier said to him, a confidential aside that explained everything.

'Better without them?' de Milja asked.

'Oh yes, no question of that.'

Soulier sucked up the last of his coffee and emitted a steamy sigh of pleasure. He rose from the table, pushing with his hands on the plank surface, then said, 'Must have a word with the pig.'

When he returned, the aroma came with him. He stopped at the open door, wiped the muck off his boots, then entered, his arms full of rifles. He laid them out on the kitchen table and proceeded to strip off the oiled paper that had protected them. He dumped an old tin can on the table, moving bullets with a thick forefinger, and counted to eighteen. 'Souvenirs of the war,' he said to de Milja.

There were four rifles, Soulier and Bonneau each took one. Jeanne-Marie wasn't expected to use such things, and de Milja declined. He carried a 9 mm Italian automatic that had found its way to him, part of the Anton Stein persona, but he had no intention of shooting at anybody.

Soulier examined one of the rifles. 'We kept these with us in the tank just in case,' he said.

Just in case, de Milja thought, the 1914 war started up again. They were bolt-action rifles, with five-round magazines, and far too many soldiers in the French infantry had carried them in 1940.

De Milja looked meaningfully at his watch. Soulier said fondly, 'Ah my friend, do not concern yourself too much. We're not in the city now, you know. Life here happens in its own time.'

'We'll have to explain that to the pilot,' de Milja said.

Soulier laughed heartily – sarcasm was of absolutely no use with him. 'There's no point in worrying about that,' he said. 'These contraptions have never yet been on time.'

The BBC *Message Personnel* – delivered in a cluster of meaningless phrases to deny the Germans analysis of traffic volume – had been broadcast forty-eight hours earlier. *In the afternoon, visit the cathedral at Rouen.* Then confirmed, a day later, by the BBC's playing Django Reinhardt's 'In a Sentimental Mood' at a specified time.

They had avoided offending the hospitality of Madame Soulier, but the Bonneau reception committee was now behind schedule. They tried riding their bicycles across the countryside, but it was too dark, and most of the time they had to walk, following cattle paths that wound around the low hills, soaking their feet when the land turned to marsh, sweating with effort in the cold night air.

De Milja had been right, they were late getting to the field Jeanne-Marie had chosen. But Soulier was right too – the contraption had not been on time. A triumph of what was called *System D*, *D* for the verb *débrouiller*, to muddle through, to manage somehow. First used to describe the French railway system's response to supply obligations in the war of 1914, it explained, in a few syllables, the French method of managing life.

They got to the field late, four instead of the expected six, and had to hurry to arrange the brush piles. Somehow they managed, although the head of the arrow that indicated wind direction was missing one side. Then Bonneau stopped dead, looked up, signalled for quiet. A low, distant hum. Getting louder, a drone. Then, clearly, the sound of aeroplane engines. '*Les flambeaux!*' Soulier cried.

It was Jeanne-Marie who actually had matches. The torches were lit. Rags, smeared thickly with pitch-pine resin and knotted at the ends of branches, they crackled and sputtered and threw wild shadows across the meadow as the reception party ran from brush pile to brush pile. Jeanne-Marie and de Milja raced past each other on the dead run – by firelight he saw her face, close to tears with anger and pride, with fierce joy.

In the clouds above them, a Whitley bomber, slow and cumbersome.

The pilot banked gently to get a better view of the land below him. He had sifted through the air defences on the Brittany coast – a few desultory rounds of ack-ack, nothing more, the gunners not sorry to hear him droning off to somebody else's sector. Then he'd followed the Loire, just about due east, the shadow of his plane cast by moonlight running next to the river. He picked up the Vienne – he hoped – branching south, then found the confluence of the Creuse and the Gartempe. Here he adjusted his bearing, a few degrees south of east, and' watched the seconds tick away. *Now*, he thought.

Nothing there, dark and peaceful fields. Then came the voice of his navigator, 'Here we are. Just a little north of us, sir.'

An orange fire appeared below – then another and another as the pilot watched. He pushed a button, a green light went on in the cargo hold but the drop-master could see as well as he could. First the crates, shoved out the door, white parachutes flaring off into the darkness before they caught the wind and jerked upright, swaying down towards the fires in the field below.

'Best of luck to you, gentlemen,' said the drop-master and the four French paratroopers jumped in rapid succession. They had been given little paper French flags to take down with them and one of them, Lucien, the leader, actually managed to hold one aloft as he floated to earth. He had left France from the port of Dunkirk, not quite a year earlier, by swimming towards a British fishing boat. His trousers and shirt and officer's cap were left on the beach, his pistol was at the bottom of the Channel. He thought, as the wind rushed past him, he heard someone cry out down below.

That was Soulier, crazed with excitement. 'It worked! By God it worked!' He might have said *Vive la France* – the paratroopers would certainly have appreciated the sentiment – but, for the moment, surprise had exceeded patriotism. The paratroopers wrestled free of their harness, then menaced the night with their Sten guns, but there was only the reception committee in the field, so they greeted each other formally, embraced, and talked in whispers. Then the officer excused himself to Jeanne-Marie, turned away, undid his fly, watered a rock, and mumbled something relieved and grateful under his breath – thus, at last, was *Vive la France* said on that occasion.

As the fires burned themselves out, they took Soulier's pry bar and tore open the crates. Unpacked two dozen Sten guns – rapid-firing carbines of no particular range but brutal effect up close, the British solution to the problem of a weapon for clandestine war. There were W/ T sets, maps printed on silk, cans of a nasty green jelly that British scientists had concocted to burn down Europe.

Everything took longer than they'd calculated. With dawn came a cold, dirty drizzle, the wind blowing the smell of raw spring earth off the fields. Using the bicycles as carts they hauled the shipment off to Soulier's farm. Were suitably impressed when Soulier reached down through the pig shit and opened a trapdoor in the earth, as the tenant of the sty looked on, slit-eyed and suspicious, from the fence where he'd been tied up.

Once again, on local trains to Vannes.

De Milja had appointed Jeanne-Marie liaison officer for the Kampf-geschwader 100 attack. Bonneau and Soulier to handle logistics and supply, the paratroopers to do the actual shooting.

They rode together in the first-class compartment. Jeanne-Marie, with open shirt collar spread across the lapels of a dark suit and mannish hat with feather, looked exactly like what she was – a part of the high bourgeois or petit nobility – the French landowning class. De Milja, briefcase in hand, hat with brim snapped down – her provincial lawyer.

Two German officers entered their compartment at Poitiers, very polite and correct. From their insignia, they were involved with engineering – perhaps construction. Essentially they were German businessmen, on leave from daily life in Frankfurt or Düsseldorf or wherever it was in order to fight a war. Still, a great deal of silence in the compartment. Jeanne-Marie, living just below the Vichy line, had not seen many Germans and wasn't really used to moving around among them. For their part, the Germans found French women irresistible, and Jeanne-Marie, pale and reserved with small, fine features and aristo-cratic bearing, was of a type particularly attractive to the officer class.

'Would Madame care to have the window open?' one of them said, using vacation French.

'No, thank you.'

'Not too warm for you, in here?'

'Quite comfortable, thank you.'

'Well then . . .'

The train chugged along, the fields of the Poitou plain falling away slowly behind them.

'I wonder, sir, if you can tell me what time we arrive in Nantes?'

'I'm not really certain,' de Milja said.

'Just after two, perhaps?'

'I believe that's right.'

The man smiled at Jeanne-Marie: isn't it satisfying, in some deliri-ously mysterious way, for us all to be rolling through the French countryside together? Not actually an *adventure*, not quite that. But, surely, not the usual thing either. Wouldn't you agree?

In this rising tide of banality, de Milja sensed danger. Just such moments, he knew, could turn fatal. You did not see it coming.

With a sigh, a sigh of apology, he set to unbuckling the briefcase that lay across his knees. Providently, he had fitted it out with its own false identity in case it was searched: mostly land deeds, obtained from clerks in an office of registry just outside Paris.

'What have you there, Duval?' Jeanne-Marie said.

De Milja found a name on the deed. 'The Bredon papers. I'm afraid we'll have to go over them together sometime before tomorrow.'

Jeanne-Marie took the deed and began to read it.

The German folded his hands across his middle and turned towards the window – an admission of defeat.

In Vannes, Jeanne-Marie was checked in at the better hotel by the railway station. De Milja set off towards the street where Mademoiselle Herault kept a *confiserie*. The mood of the neighbourhood hadn't changed, perhaps it had grown darker, quieter. Five o'clock on a spring afternoon, it should have been hopeful. Paris, hungry and cold and beginning to fray badly after a year of occupation, somehow kept its hopes up. But not here.

Then he came around the corner, saw what had happened, and just kept walking. There wasn't much to see – a lowered shutter, a chain, and a padlock.

It was what he would have seen at eight that evening, when mademoiselle herself had locked up the money and locked up the office and sent her clerk home. Her final act of the day would have been to lower the shutter and chain it to a ring set in the sill. But she had not done this.

De Milja couldn't defend his intuition. Perhaps the padlock was slightly better, slightly newer than the one she had used, but otherwise there was nothing. Absence. Five on a spring afternoon, even in a sad little town, even in a shadowy street, somebody buys candy. But Mademoiselle Herault was closed. And she wouldn't, de Milja knew in his heart, be reopening.

He didn't stop walking, he didn't slow down. Just glanced at the rolled-down shutter, then made certain he was in the right street. That was all. Somebody might be watching the street, but he thought not. There wouldn't be anything here for them now, they would simply lock it up and think about it for a time – *here a spy worked*. That was an instinct of policemen. Perhaps evidence could be retrieved, perhaps something had been forgotten.

So de Milja knew what had happened – but of course that kind of knowing wasn't acceptable. He could not return to Paris and have his operator cipher up some bedtime story for the Sixth Bureau: *Officer instinctively sensed* . . . He returned to the hotel, made sure Jeanne-Marie was where he'd left her. Normally he would not have said anything to her, would have kept her where she belonged, with a high brick wall between her and Mademoiselle Herault. In one of the first French attempts at an underground network, earlier that year, a single arrested individual had compromised a hundred and sixty-five people. So, you compartmentalized. And if they didn't know about that over here, they sure as hell knew it in the eastern part of Europe, where nobody had any illusions about what went on in the basements of police stations. What people knew, they told.

No, that was wrong. Some people never told. Some people, only the bravest, or perhaps the angriest, let the interrogation run its course, and died in silence. He suspected, again an intuition, that Mademoiselle Herault had not given the operation away. What she was, she was – a soured sort of life, he believed. Ignoring the spiteful neighbours, squeezing every sou, hating the world, but strong. Stronger than the people who would try to dominate her. That was it, he realized, that was what he knew about her. She would not be dominated, no matter how they made her suffer.

He went to the not-so-good hotel at the railway station, across the square from Jeanne-Marie, and checked in. The lawyer Benoit from Nantes, a boring little man on a boring little errand – please God let them believe that. Below his window, freight cars rolled past all night. The Germans were building here: massive defences to repel an invasion, and submarine pens to attack British shipping.

De Milja couldn't sleep. He smoked, sat in a chair by the window, and stared out into the darkened square. Some nights he could travel like a ghost skimming over the landmass of Europe, the bloody cellars and the silent streets, the castles and the princes and the assassins who waited for them. Wolves in the snow – at the edge of town, where the butchers made sausage.

At seven he stood in front of the sink, bare-chested, suspenders dangling from the waistband of his trousers. He washed himself with cold water, then rubbed his skin with a towel.

In the lobby of the hotel, an old man was sweeping the tile floor, moving slowly among the ancient velvet chairs and sofas. De Milja went out in the street. Better there – the sun just up, the cobblestones of the square sluiced down with water. Around the corner he found an open café, ordered a coffee, stood at the bar and chatted with the *patron*.

The *patron* had a friend called Henri, who could get him anything he wanted. A pair of bicycles? No problem. An arching eyebrow indicated that the resources available to Henri went much deeper than that. Henri himself appeared an hour later, pushing the bicycles. De Milja paid him handsomely, then mentioned *truck tyres*, price no object, perhaps at the end of the week? No problem! Henri nodded, gestured, winked. What de Milja really wanted was seventy-two hours during which Henri would refrain from selling him to the police, and he thought he'd accomplished that. First tyres, then betrayal, so read the heart of Henri.

The following day, at five in the morning, in a patter of spring rain, they were on the road. They pedalled out of Vannes with some forty other cyclists, all headed to work at the fish-oil plant, at the small machine shops and boat-repair yards found in every port, some of them no doubt going the twelve miles to the air base, where the pilots of the Kampfgeschwader 100 also worked. The riders were silent – it was too early in the morning to be among strangers. Now and then a bicycle bell rang, two or three times a car, no doubt carrying somebody important and German, went roaring past.

De Milja let the crowd get ahead of them so they could talk. 'Now this curve,' he said, 'is a possibility. To the right, the pine forest provides some cover. To the left, the rock makes it impossible for the bus to swerve, to simply drive away from the attack.'

They rode on, Jeanne-Marie making mental notes about the road, the terrain, the time of day – everything that would have to be factored into an assault plan. 'Of course,' de Milja said, 'it will be up to the officer leading the attack to make the decision – exactly where to conceal his firing points and everything else. But there are locations along the route that he ought to at least consider.'

Up ahead, a warning bell rang and a railwayman lowered a safety gate. Then a locomotive sounded its whistle and a slow freight came rumbling across the road. De Milja and Jeanne-Marie pulled up to the crowd of cyclists, standing patiently on one foot while the boxcars rolled past. A dark green sports car, its hood secured by a leather strap, stopped next to de Milja. The driver and his companion were young men, wearing good tweed jackets and pigskin gloves. *'Ach du lieber!'* the driver said, his hand clapped over his eyes. What had struck him blind was a girl in a tight skirt astride a bicycle seat. The other man shook his head in wonder, said in German, 'Sweet sugar – come fly through the clouds with me.' The girl ignored them.

The freight train moved off into the distance, the railwayman raised the gate. The driver of the sports car gunned his engine, the cyclists scurried out of the way, and the two Germans went tearing down the road, an echo of speed shifts and screaming engine lingering after them.

5:30 p.m. The first minutes of darkness. Outlines blurred, faces indistinct. People were out; coming home from work, going visiting, shopping. A couple, even strangers, moved easily along the street, unremarkable, nobody really saw them.

De Milja took Jeanne-Marie by the arm for a moment, guided her into a long alley, a crooked lane no more than three feet wide with lead-sheathed drain tiles running down both sides and crumbling stone arches above. It was chaos back here; stake fences concealing garden plots, leaning sheds and rusty tin roofs, curved tiles stacked against walls, dripping pipes, sheets hung to dry on lines spanning the alley – a thousand years of village life concealed from the public street.

Finding the back entrance to a particular shop should have been a nightmare, but no, in fact the Germans had done him a favour. The back door of the *confiserie* was chained and padlocked – the same equipment they'd used for the front door.

The chain ran from a rusty cleat in the wall to the iron door handle. It wasn't a system Mademoiselle Herault had ever used, and it didn't work now. De Milja took an iron bar from under his coat, slotted one end next to the chain in the wall cleat, used a piece of broken brick as a fulcrum, and put his weight against it. Out came the cleat with a puff of dust, a chunk of old masonry still attached to it. Next the door lock. He threw a shoulder into the door, but nothing happened. Drew a foot up and drove his heel against the lock plate – same result. Finally he worked the sharp end of the bar into the dried-out wood between the door and the jamb, levered it apart until he could get the end of the bar past the inside edge of the door, used every bit of strength he had. Nothing at first, then it gave a little, finally there was a loud squeak and the sound of ripping wood as the lock tore free. He swung the door open, waited a beat, stepped inside.

What he needed to see he saw immediately – the dusk of closed spaces was broken up by shadowy light from the doorway, and the last two years had taught him to see in the dark. There was no malice or evil in the *confiserie*, just a professional job, cold and thorough.

They had searched: dumped the canisters of flour into the stone sink, then the sugar, the salt, the baking soda, whatever else had been on the shelf, stirring through each new addition. They would have used a thin metal rod, sifting, probing, hunting the spool of microfilm or the miniature camera, the book marked for ciphering or a set of crystals for a radio. De Milja walked into the office, every step a brittle crunch – they'd spilled a bin of hard candies on the floor, and their boots had ground them into powdery shards of red and green.

Mademoiselle Herault's office was torn to pieces. Not a piece of paper to be seen, upholstery fabric sliced from the bottom of an upside-down chair, drawers pulled from the desk, then the desk flipped over, smashing the drawers beneath it. In the store itself, the glass had been kicked out of the counters and the wooden frame torn apart – spies were diabolical when it came to hiding things. The searchers had unwrapped the chocolates and squashed them – ants were at work on the result, tossed atop the shards of glass.

By the cash register, where Veronique the clerk had spent her days, de Milja smelled something strange. Even amid the orange essence and vanilla and peppermint and God knew what else – something strong and particular, like flowers. He knelt, the smell got stronger. A small glass bottle, in pieces, half-hidden by the leg of a counter. Candy clerk's perfume, he thought. They had stood her against a wall, searched through her purse, and it had fallen out, or perhaps they'd thrown it on the floor.

No more than a minute inside the shop, but too long.

Jeanne-Marie called in a whisper, de Milja was up and out in one motion. A flashlight bobbed at the other end of the alley. He kicked the door shut with his foot and embraced Jeanne-Marie in the same instant. Passionately, pressing his mouth against hers. She made a small sound of distaste, stiffened, tried to pull away from him just as the flashlight pinned them both.

The voice was a growl. 'What's this?'

It was the eternal voice of the *flic*, the cop, tired and sour beyond redemption. 'Romance?' it wondered.

De Milja shielded his eyes from the light, squinting helplessly as he did so, a profoundly virtuous gesture: 'We have no place to meet,' he said.

A moment while that was considered. 'Well, you can't *meet* here.'

The light was lowered. De Milja heard the little pop of a holster flap snapped back into place. 'Take a walk,' the cop said. He sensed something, but he wished not to know about it. He simply made it vanish so it no longer troubled him.

They took local trains out of Vannes that night. Jeanne-Marie back to the country house, de Milja to the avenue Hoche.

It was, inevitably, spring in Paris. The first chestnut trees bloomed at the entrances to the Métro, where warm air flowed up the staircases. Greece was taken in April, so was Yugoslavia. Belgrade, pressured by tank columns on three sides, was surrendered to a German captain and nine enlisted men who had bluffed their way through the defence lines. The United States had frozen German and Italian assets held in American banks.

For Parisians, daily existence was a struggle, and people simply tried to stay out of the way of the Germans. There had, in the first year of occupation, been one execution – Jacques Bonsergent, shot for jostling a German officer in the Gare Saint-Lazare.

The mood in the cafés was now resignation, the defeat by the Germans called *the debacle*. De Milja found this a curious expression once he thought about it – just the sort of linguistic trap that the French liked to construct. It meant a complete rout, a total collapse. But somewhere in the spirit of the word was a touch of the absurd, the comic: it wasn't anyone's fault, no point in assigning blame, it was just that everything went wrong all at once – a moment of Divine slapstick and poof, we lost the country.

For de Milja, contacts in the Polish community had finally begun to pay off. He had enlisted a railway clerk and a miner's daughter from Alsace – both contacts made through Polish clergy at local churches.

The value of priests now became particularly apparent. They had political views, strong ones often enough, and were the keepers of community secrets. They knew who drank, who made money, and who lost it. They knew who the collaborators were, and who the patriots were. People, perhaps resisting an urge to gossip over the back fence, told the priest everything. Sometimes in church, more often in the parlour or at the vegetable stall. That couldn't be wrong, could it? Heaven knew all your secrets anyhow.

The Alsatian girl, very studious and shy, in her early twenties, came to live in Paris at de Milja's request. He assigned her the code name *Vera*, then, in a slow and curiously difficult effort, tried to place her in a job in a German bureau. She spoke excellent German, perfect French, it should have been easy. 'I have never felt French, exactly,' she told her interviewers. 'Always we spoke German in my house.' She was offered two jobs, both clerical and meaningless, in the office that handled payments flowing from France to Germany – 400 million francs a day, the cost of the German military and civilian administration. After all, one couldn't expect one's country to be occupied for free.

With de Milja's coaching. *Vera* extracted herself from those offers, moved to a *pension*, and waited patiently.

26 April 1941. 3:20 a.m. Le Chabanais.

Paris's finest brothel. Draperies, broacades, velvets, and cut crystal – such weight as to suggest a thick and impenetrable wall of discretion. Waitresses in golden slippers served osetra caviar. In one of the private rooms, the Slovakian coal dealer Anton Stein had invited the Comte de Rieu and the art dealer Labarthe to be his guests for a late supper and whatever other diversions they might enjoy. They had a peaceful, relaxed, gentlemen's evening of it.

The count had been entertained, in one of the upstairs bedrooms, by a 'Hungarian countess' and her 'Spanish maid' – the glass of wine tipped over, the slipper applied, then forgiveness, at length and in many ways. The count returned, shaking his head in wonder at what the world had to offer him. Lit a Camel cigarette, drank a sip of champagne, rested his head on the back of a chair and blew two seemingly endless plumes of smoke at the chandelier.

No need to talk, a grand silence – a moment to contemplate human desire and the masks it wore. De Milja had seen the countess; hair dark red, Magyar cheekbones, long, delicate fingers. But a temper, as you might expect. Not the one to stand for a maid's clumsy behaviour.

The count smiled at his host by way of saying thank you. 'The pleasures of excess,' he said quietly. Labarthe snored lightly on a settee, head fallen to one side.

Stein raised his glass in a silent toast to the count's words. He drank, then after a moment said, 'I was in Alsace recently. Stumbled on treasure.'

'Let me guess: a Rhine maiden?'

'Oh no. Completely the opposite.'

'Really?'

Stein nodded yes. Opened a tortoiseshell case and selected a small, pale-leafed cigar. He rolled it between his fingers, then snapped a silver lighter until a flame appeared. 'Mmm,' he said, putting the lighter away. 'Spinster type – to look at her you'd never imagine.'

'Oh, I can imagine.'

'Little more champagne?'

'Not just yet, thanks.'

'Anyhow, I have her here. In a *pension.*'

'Can't get enough?'

'That's it.' He paused a moment. 'Thing is, she's bored. Nothing to do all day.'

'Why not a job? Coming from there, she must speak German.'

'She does, she does. Wants to work for *Jeder Einmal.*'

'Why there?'

'I think she worked at Eszterhazy, the travel agency, before the war.'

'Well, that shouldn't be a problem. I don't know anyone there, exactly, but Kappler can do it in a minute. I'll call him Monday, if you like.'

'Would you? That would certainly help me out.'

'Consider it done.'

From somewhere in the vast building came the sound of a violin. It was playing a folk melody, slow and melancholy, something eastern, perhaps Russian. Both men listened attentively. Labarthe stopped snoring, mumbled something, then fell back asleep. 'Remarkable, the way life is now,' the count said. 'Untold stories.' Then, after a moment, he said, 'A spinster?' He meant, in a rather delicate way, that such an appetite in Stein was unexpected.

Stein shrugged. 'Quite religious,' he said. 'She is like a storm.'

Transmission of 12 May. 1:25 a.m.

To Director. Source: Albert

Railway Bureau designates departures 21 May/26 May. 3rd class and livestock cars making up at Reims yards. Route: Reims/Metz/Trier/

Würzburg/Prague/Breslau/Cracow/Tarnow. Including: Artillery regiment 181, Fusilier Regiment 202 (Stettin), Grenadier Regiments 80, 107, 253 (Wiesbaden). Grenadier regiments 151, 162, and 176 (Wehrkreis X, Hamburg).

Of 21 Divisions in France as of 22/4/41, total of 9 (135,000 men) now moved east.

De Milja's railway clerk. Fussy little man, fierce patriot. Dead-drop at the Église Sainte Thérèse – Albert to the six o'clock mass, de Milja at ten. The take from Wehrmacht rail scheduling made de Milja's heart lift. Great numbers of troops – and their vehicles, weapons, files, and draught horses – on the move from conquered France and Belgium to conquered Poland. That meant Russia. And that meant the end. There was in Wilno a historical marker, alongside the Moscow road, that read 'On 28 June, 1812, Napoleon Bonaparte passed this way with 450,000 men.' Then, on the other side, approached from the east, was a different message: 'On 9 December, 1812, Napoleon Bonaparte passed this way with 900 men.'

Could Adolf Hitler – shrewd, cunning – do such a foolish thing? Maybe not. De Milja had observed that the failed Operation Sealion had been undertaken without a feint, without deception. If the Germans were going to try again, June would be the time to lay a false trail, such as the shipment of men and arms to the east.

To find out, de Milja had Albert on the one hand, Vera on the other. The Comte de Rieu had been true to his word. Vera was hired as a clerk – 'But in six months, we'll see about something better' – by the *Jeder Einmal in Paris* organization. This was Goebbels at work, the phrase meant *Paris for Everybody Once*. A morale builder for the military, and a spy's dream. *Everybody* meant just that – from privates to generals, two weeks' leave in romantic, naughty Paris. The brothels and the nightclubs were fully staffed, the inflated Occupation Reichsmark would buy an astonishing mound of gifts for Momma and Poppa and the ever-faithful Helga.

The German empire now ran from Norway to North Africa, from Brest, France, to Brest Litovsk in Poland. Getting all those people in and out of Paris was a logistical nightmare, but not for the efficient *Jeder* organization, a vast travel agency coordinating hotels, barracks, and train reservations. They simply had to know – thus Vera had to know – where everybody was: the location of every unit in the German war machine. Where it was strong, and where it wasn't.

French students still went to university – a privilege not enjoyed in

Poland, where by Himmler's order the slave population was to learn to count on its fingers and acknowledge orders with affirmative grunts. De Milja's response was to hide one of his W/T operators in a tiny room in the student quarter of the fifth arrondissement. The agent seemed to belong there, with a beard tracing the outline of his jaw, a piercing student gaze and hair he cut himself.

It was in the tiny room, with pictures of philosophers pinned to the walls, that de Milja learned, from a Sixth Bureau transmission on 17 May, that the operation in Vannes had to be completely reworked. The Pathfinder pilots of Kampfgeschwader 100 now drove their own cars to the airfield rather than going by bus.

And it was in the tiny room that de Milja learned, from a Sixth Bureau transmission of 19 May, that he'd been fired.

It wasn't put that way – the word *relieved* was not used – but that was what it meant. De Milja's reaction was first shock, then anguished disbelief. Why? How could this happen? What had he done wrong?

'Is this correct?' he asked the operator.

'I believe so,' the man said. He was embarrassed, did not meet de Milja's eyes. 'Of course I can request retransmission. Or clarification.'

But it was already quite dear. The reference to de Milja by his assigned cipher, rendezvous on a certain beach on a certain night, to be transported back to Sixth Bureau London headquarters for reassignment. Prepare all field agents and technical staff for a change of resident officer.

He did that. Vera didn't like it. Albert nodded grimly, war was war. He could say nothing to Lisette Roubier, to Zimmer at the coal company, to the people who were simply there in his life as he was in theirs. The French placed great store by daily encounters, small friendships carried on a few minutes at a time, and he would have liked to have said good-bye.

Lost people, lost money. Huysmanns coal, probably the apartment on the avenue Hoche, gone. Abandoned. Intelligence services had to operate in that fashion, build and walk away, it was in the nature of their existence. But de Milja knew, in a hungry city, what that money would buy.

A certain night in June, sweet and sad, he chased Madame Roubier around the bed with real conviction. 'Oh my,' she said, and scowled with pleasure. Then it was time to go and he kissed her on the lips and she put her arms around him and squeezed him tight. Pulling back a little to have a look at him, her eyes were shiny in the peach light that made her pretty. She knew, she knew. What, exactly? Could you fool a woman you made love to? Well, of course you could, he thought. Well, of course you couldn't.

The tears never quite came. A French woman understood love. Its beginning, and its ending. 'Shall I see you tomorrow?'

'Not quite sure,' he said. 'I'll telephone in the afternoon.'

'If not, then some other time,' she said.

'Yes,' he said. '*Au revoir.*' *I'll see you again.*

'*Adieu,*' she said. *Not in this life.*

Later he stood at the door of the apartment on the avenue Hoche. Dawn just breaking, the sky in the window a dozen shades of blue.

He had to ride the trains for long days across the springtime fields. He tried, again and again, to find a reason for what had happened, and was shocked at how broken his heart was. Over the months in Paris he had thought he hated what he did. Maybe not. Out the train window: spring earth, flowering apple trees, villages with bakeries and town halls. He had lost a lot of people, he realized. The obvious ones; Janina the telegraphist, Mademoiselle Herault, Veronique. And the not-so-obvious ones; Genya Beilis, and Fedin. Could someone else do better? Is that what the Sixth Bureau thought? You should be happy to be alive, he told himself savagely. But he wasn't.

Four nights on the beach at Saint-Jean-de-Luz, just north of the Spanish border, where the last Polish ship, the *Batory*, had departed in June of 1940, twelve months earlier. He pretended to be a tourist, a spectre from another time, strolled down to the beach at night, then uncovered a hidden bicycle and worked his way north, to a deserted stretch of rocky shore miles from a road. There he sat amid the dune grass, waiting, as the ocean crashed against the beach, but no light signalled. He stayed at a boardinghouse run by a Portuguese couple who had lived in France for thirty years and barely acknowledged that a war was in progress. There were other guests, but they averted their eyes, and there were no conversations. Everybody on the run now, he thought, in every possible direction.

Then at last, on 28 May, a light.

A rubber boat gliding over a calm sea. Two sailors with their faces lamp-blacked, and a man he'd never seen before, perhaps his replacement brought into shore. Older, heavy-set, distinguished, with thick eyebrows. They shook hands and wished each other well.

The sailors worked hard, digging their paddles into the water. The land fell away, France disappeared into the darkness. De Milja knelt in the stern of the little boat. Above the sound of the waves lapping against the beach he could hear a dog barking somewhere on the shore. Two barks, deep and urgent, repeated over and over again.

In London, people seemed pale, cold and polite, bright-eyed with fatigue. They spent their days running a war, which meant questions with no answers and ferocious, bureaucratic infighting. Then at night the bombs whistled down and the city burned.

De Milja was quartered in a small hotel just north of Euston Station. He had braced himself for criticism, or chilly disapproval, even accusations, but none of that happened. Some of the British liaison staff seemed not entirely sure why he'd shown up. Colonel Vyborg was 'away'. The Polish officers he reported to that May and early June he had never met before. The ZWZ, he realized, had grown up. Had become an institution, with a bottom, a middle and a top. Poles had found their way to England by every conceivable means, ordinary and miraculous. And they all wanted to shoot at somebody. But getting them to that point – fed, dressed, assigned, transported – took an extraordinary effort, a price paid in meetings and memoranda.

This was the war they wanted de Milja to fight. In the course of his debriefing he was told, in a very undramatic way, why he'd been relieved. Somebody somewhere, in the infrastructure that had grown up around the government-in-exile, had decided he'd lost too many people. The senior staff had taken his part, particularly Vyborg and his allies, but that battle had eventually been lost and there were others that had to be fought.

De Milja didn't say a word. The people around the table looked down, cleared their throats, squared the papers in front of them. Of course he'd done well, they said, nobody disputed that. Perhaps he'd just been unlucky. Perhaps it had become accepted doctrine in some quarters that his stars were bad. De Milja was silent, his face was still. Somebody lit a cigarette. Somebody else polished his spectacles. Silence, silence. 'What we need you to do now,' they said, 'is help to run things.'

He tried. Sat behind a desk, read reports, wrote notes in the margins, and sent them away. Some came back. Others appeared. A very pleasant colonel, formerly a lawyer in Cracow, took him to an English pub and let him know, very politely, that he wasn't doing all that well. Was something wrong? He tried harder. Then, one late afternoon, he looked up from A's analysis of XYZ and there was Vyborg, framed in the doorway.

Now at least he would have the truth, names and faces filled in. But it wasn't so very different from what he'd been told. This was, he came to realize, not the same world he'd lived in. The Kampfgeschwader 100 operation, for instance, had been cancelled. The RAF leadership felt that such guerrilla tactics would lead the Germans to brutalize downed and captured British airmen – the game wasn't worth the candle.

'You're lucky to be out of it,' Vyborg said one day at lunch. They ate in a military canteen in Bayswater Road. Women in hairnets served potatoes and cauliflower and canned sausage.

De Milja nodded. Yes, lucky.

Vyborg looked at him closely. 'It takes time to get used to a new job.'

De Milja nodded again. 'I hate it,' he said quietly.

Vyborg shrugged. *Too bad.* 'Two things, Alexander. This is an army – we tell people what to do and they do it the best they know how. The other thing is that the good jobs are taken. You are not going to Madrid or to Geneva.'

Vyborg paused a moment, then continued. 'The only person who's hiring right now runs the eastern sector. We have four thousand panzer tanks on the border and prevailing opinion in the bureau says they will be leaving for Moscow on 21 June. Certainly there will be work in Russia, a great deal of work. Because those operatives will not survive. They will be replaced, then replaced again.'

'I know,' de Milja said.

The Forest

On 21 June 1941, by the Koden bridge over the river Bug, Russian guards – of the Main Directorate of Border Troops under the NKVD – were ordered to execute a spy who had infiltrated Soviet territory three days earlier as part of a provocation intended to cause war. The man, a Wehrmacht trooper, had left German lines a few miles to the west, swum the river just after dark, and asked to see the officer in charge. Through an interpreter he explained he was from Munich, a worker and a lifelong communist. He wished to join the Soviet fighting forces, and he had important information: his unit had orders to attack the Soviet Union at 0300 hours on the morning of 22 June.

The Russian officer telephoned superiors, and the information rose quickly to very senior levels of the counter-espionage *apparat*. Likely the Kremlin itself was consulted, likely at very high, the highest, levels. Meanwhile, the deserter was kept in a barracks jail on the Soviet side of the river. The guards tried to communicate with him – sign language, a few words of German. He was one of them, he let them know, and they shared their cigarettes with him and made sure he had a bowl of barley and fat at mealtime.

Late in the afternoon of 21 June, an answer came down from the top: the German deserter is a spy and his mission is provocation: shoot him. The officer in charge was surprised but the order was clear, and he'd been told confidentially that the British Secret Service had orchestrated similar incidents all along the Soviet/German border – formerly eastern Poland – to foster suspicion, and worse, between the two nations.

The sergeant assigned to take care of the business sighed when he came to collect the deserter. He'd felt some sympathy for the man, but, it seemed, he'd been tricked. Well, that was the world for you. '*Podnimaisa zvieshchami*,' he said to the German. This was formula, part of a ritual language that predated the Revolution and went back to czarist times. *Get going, with things*, it meant. You are going to be executed. If he'd said *Get going, with overcoat, without things*, for example, it would have meant the man was going to be deported, and his blanket and plate should be left behind.

The German didn't understand the words, but he could read the sergeant's expression and could easily enough interpret the significance of the Makarov pistol thrust in his belt. *At least I tried*, he thought. He'd known where this all might lead, now it had led there, now he had to make peace with his gods and say good-bye, and that was that.

They walked, with a guard of three soldiers, to the edge of the river. It was a warm evening, very still, thousands of crickets racketing away, flickers of summer lightning on the horizon. The deserter glanced back over his shoulder as they walked – *anything possible?* The sergeant just shook his head and gave him a fraternal little push in the back – *be a man*. The German took a deep breath, headed where the sergeant pointed and the sergeant shot him in the back of the head.

And again, a coup de grâce in the temple. Then the sergeant signalled to the troopers and they came and took the body away. The sergeant found a stub of cigarette deep in his pocket and lit it in cupped hands, staring across the river. What the hell *were* they doing over there? This was the third night in a row they'd fired up the panzer tank engines – a huge roar that drowned out the crickets – then changed positions, treads clanking away as the iron plates rolled over the dirt.

The sergeant finished his cigarette, then headed back to his barracks. Too bad about the German. That was fate, however, and there was no sense trying to get in its way. But the sergeant was in its way anyhow, some instinct – the rumbling of German tanks – may have been telling him that, and he himself had less than seven hours to live.

3:00 a.m. The sergeant asleep. The sound of German boots thumping across the wooden bridge, calls of 'Important business! Important business!' in Russian. The Soviet sentry signalled to the German messengers to wait one moment, and shook the sergeant awake. Grumbling, he worked his feet into his boots and, rubbing his eyes, walked onto the bridge. A brief drumming, orange muzzle flares – the force of the bullets took him and the sentry back through a wooden railing and down into the river.

The sergeant didn't die right away. He lay where he'd fallen, on a gravel bank in the slow, warm river. So he heard running on the bridge, heard the explosions as the barracks were blown apart by hand grenades, heard machine gun fire and shouts in German as the commandos finished up with the border guards. Dim shapes – German combat engineers – swung themselves beneath the bridge and crawled among the struts, pulling wires out of the explosive charges. *Tell headquarters,* the sergeant thought. A soldier's instinct – *I'm finished but command must know what's happened.* It had, in fact, been tried. A young soldier bleeding on the floor of the guardhouse had managed to get hold of the telephone, but the line was dead. Other units of Regiment 800, the Brandenburgers – the Wehrmacht special-action force – some of them Russian-speaking, had been at work for hours, and telegraph and telephone wires had been cut all along the front lines.

The sergeant lost consciousness, then was brought back one last time. By a thousand artillery pieces fired in unison; the riverbed shook with the force of it. Overhead, hundreds of Luftwaffe fighters and bombers streaked east to destroy the Soviet air force on its airfields. Three million German troops crossed the border, thousands of Soviet troops, tens of thousands, would join the sergeant in the river by morning.

Soviet radio transmissions continued. The German Funkabwehr recorded an exchange near the city of Minsk. To headquarters: 'We are being fired on. What should we do?' The response: 'You must be insane. And why is this message not in code?'

The sergeant died sometime after dawn. By then, hundreds of tanks had rolled across the Koden bridge because it was the Schwerpunkt – the spearpoint – of the blitzkrieg in the region of the Brest fortress. Just to the south, the Koden railway bridge, also secured by the Brandenburgers, was made ready to serve in an immense resupply effort to fighting units advancing at an extraordinary rate. By the following evening young Russian reservists were boarding trains, cardboard suitcases in hand, heading off to report to mobilization centres already occupied by Wehrmacht troops.

Days of glory. The Germans advanced against Soviet armies completely in confusion. Hitler had been right – 'Just kick in the door and the whole thing will come tumbling down.' Soviet air cover was blown up, ammunition used up, no food, tanks destroyed. Russians attacked into enfilading machine gun fire and were mown down by the thousands. Nothing stopped the panzer tanks, great engines rumbling across the steppe. Some peasants came out of their huts and stared. Others, Ukrainians, offered bread and salt to the conquerors who had come to free them from the Bolshevik yoke.

Yet, here and there, every now and again, there were strange and troublesome events. Five commissars firing pistols from a schoolhouse until they were killed. A single rifleman holding up an advance for ten minutes. When they found his body, his dog was tied to a nearby tree with a rope, as though he had, somehow, expected to live through the assault. A man came out of a house and threw two hand grenades. Somehow this wasn't like the blitzkriegs in western Europe. They found a note folded into an empty cartridge case and hidden in a tree by the highway to Minsk. 'Now there are only three of us left. We shall stand firm as long as there's any life left in us. Now I am alone, wounded in my arm and my head. The number of tanks has increased. There are twenty-three. I shall probably die. Somebody may find my note and remember me: I am a Russian from Frunze. I have no parents. Good-bye, dear friends. Your Alexander Vinogradov.'

The German advance continued, nothing could stop it, whole armies were encircled. Yet, still, there was resistance, and something in its nature was deeply disturbing. They had attacked the USSR. But it was Russia that fought back.

10 October 1941. 11:45 p.m. Near the Koden bridge.

The Wehrmacht was long gone now. They were busy fighting to the east, on the highway to Moscow. Now it was quiet again – quiet as any place where three nations mixed. The Ukraine, Byelorussia, and Poland. 'Thank heaven,' Razakavia would say, 'we are all such good friends.' People laughed when he said that – a little tentatively at first until they were sure he meant them to, then a big, loud, flattering laugh. He was tall and bony, with the blowing white hair and white beard of an Old Testament prophet. But the similarity ended there. A pucker scar marked the back of his neck – bullet in 1922 – and a rifle was slung across his back. Razakavia was a leader – of outcasts, of free men and women, of bandits. It depended who you asked.

Razakavia pulled his sheepskin jacket tight around him and leaned closer to his horse's neck. 'Cold, Miszka. Hurry up a little.' The pony obliged, the rhythm of his trot a beat or two faster. It was cold – Razakavia could smell winter hiding in the autumn air, and the moonlight lay hard on the white-frosted fields. He reached into a pocket and pulled out a railway watch. Getting towards midnight. Up ahead of him he could hear Frantek's pony. Frantek was fourteen, Razakavia's best scout. He carried no rifle, only a pistol buried in his clothing – so he could play the innocent traveller as long as possible, should they chance to meet a stranger on the trails they rode. Somewhere behind Razakavia was Kotior, his second-in-command, a machine gun resting across his saddle.

They had ridden these fields before. This operation had been attempted twice since the end of September. Razakavia didn't like it, but he had no choice. The people who had arrived in the wake of the Wehrmacht – the SS, German administrators, murder squads hunting Jews, all sorts really, were not much to his taste. He was used to fighting the Polish gendarmerie, not themselves so very appealing, frankly, but a fact of life and something he'd got used to. These new lords and masters were worse. They were also temporary. They didn't understand what was going to happen to them, and that made them more dangerous as allies than they were as enemies. So he needed some new allies.

Frantek appeared just ahead of him, his horse standing still with breath steaming from its nose and mouth. The river was visible from here, not frozen yet but very slow and thick. Razakavia pulled his pony up, twenty seconds later Kotior arrived. The three sat in a row but did not speak – voices carried a long way at night. The wind sighed here as it climbed the hillside above the river, and Razakavia listened carefully to it for a time until he could make out the whine of an aeroplane engine. So, perhaps this time it would work. Frantek pointed: a few degrees west of north, a mile or so from where the river Bug met the Lesna. A triangle of fires suddenly appeared, sparks flying up into the still air. Frantek looked at him expectantly, waiting for orders.

Razakavia didn't move – always he weighed the world around him for a moment before he did anything – then chucked the reins and the three of them trotted off in the direction of the fires.

He had six men in the meadow, where the hay had been cut a month earlier. They stood with rifles slung, warming their hands over the signal fires, faces red in the flickering light. The sound of the plane's engines grew louder and louder, then it faded and moved away into the distance. Above, three white flowers came floating to earth.

At Razakavia's right hand, Frantek watched avidly. Such things intrigued him – aeroplanes, parachutes. The world had come here along with the war, and Frantek was being educated by both at once. Kotior just glanced up, then scanned the perimeter. He was not quick of mind, but he killed easily and good-naturedly, and he was remorselessly loyal.

The white flowers were just overhead now and Razakavia could see what they were. As he'd been promised, a Polish officer and two crates of explosives. It is a long life, Razakavia thought, one takes the bad with the good.

Captain Alexander de Milja was the last to leave the plane, the other two operatives – an explosives expert and a political courier – had jumped when they got to the outskirts of Warsaw. His body ached from the ride, six and a half hours in a four-engine Halifax, every bolt and screw vibrating, and the cold air ferocious as it flowed through the riveted panels. He hoped this was the right triangle of fires below him – and that the builders of these brush piles had not changed sides while the Halifax droned across Europe. He was, in truth, a rich prize: $18,000 in czarist gold roubles, $50,000 in American paper money. A fortune once converted to zlotys or occupation currency. German cigarettes and German razor blades, warm clothing, two VIS pistols – WZ 35s with the Polish eagle engraved on the slide, and a hundred rounds of ammunition. He might very well do them more good simply murdered and stripped, he thought. No, he *would* do them more good that way, because he was not here to do them good.

He had been forced to wait four months to return to Poland, because the distance from London to Warsaw was 900 miles – in fact Route One, over Denmark, was 960 miles and de Milja had to go a hundred miles farther east. Route Two, over Göteberg, Sweden, was even longer. The normal range of the Halifax bomber was 1,500 miles, the normal load capacity, 4,180 pounds. With the addition of an extra fuel tank, the range increased to 2,100 miles – the bomber could now fly home after dropping its cargo – but the load capacity decreased to 2,420 pounds; of guns, ammunition, medical supplies, people: and the crew had to be reduced from nine to seven.

The airspeed of the Halifax was 150 miles an hour, thus a trip of 2,000 miles was going to take thirteen hours – discounting the wind as a factor. Those thirteen hours had to be hours of darkness, from 5:00 p.m. in London to 6:00 a.m. the following morning. And that was cutting it close. The flight could only be made when there was enough of a moon to see the confluence of rivers that would mark the drop zone. This period, the second and third phases of the moon, was code-named *Tercet.* So the first Tercet with sufficient darkness was 7 October – in fact it was 10 October before he actually took off. That was the moment when there was just enough autumn darkness and just enough moonlight to give the operation a chance of success.

They'd taken him by car to Newmarket racecourse, where the special services had built a secret airfield to house the 138th Squadron – British and Polish aircrews. A final check of his pockets: no London bus tickets, no matchboxes with English words. He was now Roman Brzeski, a horse breeder from Chelm. As he waited to board the plane, a jeep drove across the tarmac and stopped by his side. Vyborg climbed out, holding on to his uniform cap in the backwash from the Halifax's propellers. The engines were very loud, and Vyborg had to shout as he shook hands. 'You'll be careful?'

'I will.'

'Need anything?'

'No.'

'Well . . . No end to it, is there?'

De Milja gave him a mock salute.

'Good luck,' Vyborg said. 'Good luck.'

De Milja nodded that he understood.

One of the partisans came into the hut well before dawn, nudging de Milja and the others with his boot. 'Work today. Work today,' he said. De Milja got one eye open. 'Move your bones, dear friends. Prove you're not dead.' He gave de Milja, the honoured guest, an extra little kick in the ankle and left the hut.

De Milja shuddered in the cold as he worked himself free of the blanket. Through the open door he could see black night, a slice of moon. There would be a skim of ice on the water barrel, white mist hanging in the birch trees. Beside him, Kotior rolled over and sat up slowly, held his face in his hands, cursed the cold, the Russians, the Germans, what women had between their legs, the guard, the forest, and life itself. De Milja forced his swollen feet into his boots, sat up, touched his face – two weeks' growth of beard, chapped skin – and scratched his ankles where he'd been bitten the night before.

There was a small iron stove in a hut where food was cooked. A young woman handed him a metal cup of powerful, scalding tea; it warmed him and woke him up when he drank it. The woman was dark, muffled in kerchiefs and layers of clothing. 'Another cup, sir?'

Educated, he thought, from the pitch of the voice. Perhaps a Jew. 'Please,' de Milja said. He held the cup in both hands and let the steam warm his face. Razakavia's band, about forty men and fifteen women, came from everywhere: a few Russian soldiers, escaped from Wehrmacht encirclement; a few Jews, escaped from the German round-ups; a few criminals, escaped from Ukrainian and Byelorussian jails; a few Poles, who'd fled from the Russian deportations of 1939; a few Byelorussians – army deserters, nationalists – who'd fled Polish administration before the Russian occupation. To de Milja it seemed as though half the world had nowhere to go but the forest. He finished the tea and handed the cup back to the young woman. 'Thank you,' he said. 'It was very good.'

Later he rode beside Razakavia – as always, Kotior somewhere behind them. They had given him, as the honoured guest, a Russian *panje* horse to ride. She was small, with a thick mane and shaggy coat. When the band stopped for a moment, she grazed on whatever weeds happened to be there, apparently she could eat anything at all. They had also given him, as the honoured guest who brought explosives and gold coins, one of the better weapons in their armoury: a Simonov automatic rifle with a ten-shot magazine box forward of the trigger guard, and two hundred rounds of 7.62 ammunition.

As they rode two by two on a forest trail, Razakavia explained that a courier had reached them with intelligence from local railwaymen: a small train was due, late in the day, carrying soldiers being rotated back for leave in Germany, some of them walking wounded. There would also be flatcars of damaged equipment, scheduled for repair at the Pruszkow Tank Works outside Warsaw. The train was from the Sixth Panzer Division, fighting 400 miles east at Smolensk.

'We watched them brought up to the line in late summer,' Razakavia told him. 'A hundred and sixty trains, we counted. About fifty cars each. Tanks and armoured cars and ammunition and horses – and the men. Very splendid, the Germans. Nothing they don't have, makes you wonder what they want from us.'

At noon they left the forest, and rode for a time along the open steppe. It was cold and grey and wet; they rode past smashed Russian tanks and trucks abandoned during the June retreat, then moved back into the forest for an hour, watered the horses at a stream, and emerged at a point where the railway line passed about a hundred yards from the birch groves. The line was a single track that seemed to go from nowhere to nowhere, disappearing into the distance on either end. 'This goes north-west to Baranovici,' Razakavia told him. 'Then to Minsk, Orsha, Smolensk, and Viazma. Eventually to Mozhaisk, and Moscow. It is the lifeline of the Wehrmacht Army Group Centre. Our Russians tell us that a German force cannot survive more than sixty miles from a railhead.'

A man called Bronstein assembled the bomb for the rails. A Soviet army ammunition box, made of zinc, was filled with cheddite. British, in this case, from the honoured guest, though the ZWZ in Poland also manufactured the product. A compression fuse, made of a sulphuric-acid vial and paper impregnated with potassium chloride, was inserted beneath the lid of the box.

De Milja sat by Bronstein as the bomb was put together. 'Where did you learn to do that?' he asked.

'I was a teacher of science,' Bronstein said, 'in Brest Litovsk.' He took the cigarette from his mouth and set it on a stone while he packed cheddite into the box. 'And this is science.'

They dug a hole beneath the rail and inserted the mine, the weight of the locomotive would do the rest. A scout – Frantek – came galloping up to Razakavia just as it began to get dark. 'It comes now,' he said.

The band settled into positions at the edge of the forest. De Milja lay on his stomach, using a rotten log for cover, feeling the cold from the earth seeping up into his body. The train came slowly, ten miles an hour, in case the track was sabotaged. It was. Bronstein's device worked

– a dull bang, a cloud of dirt blown sideways from beneath the creeping locomotive, wheels ripping up the ties, then the locomotive heeling over slowly as a jet of white steam hissed from its boiler. A man screamed. A German machine gun crew on a platform mounted towards the rear of the train began to traverse the forest.

De Milja sighted down the barrel of the Simonov. From the slats of a cattle car he could see pinpricks of rifle fire. He returned it, squeezing off ten rounds, then changing magazines as bullets rattled in the branches above his head. One of Razakavia's men leaped from a depression in the earth on the other side of the track and threw a bomb into the last car on the train. The walls blew out and the wooden frame started to burn. German riflemen, some wearing white bandages, jumped out of the train on the side away from the gunfire and began to shoot from behind the wheels of the cars. De Milja heard a cry from his left, a bullet smacked into his log. He aimed carefully and fired off his magazine, then looked up. A figure in field grey had slumped beneath the train, the wind flapping a bandage that had come loose from his head. De Milja changed magazines again. Some of the German soldiers were shooting from behind a tank chained to a flatcar, de Milja could hear the ricochet as gunfire from the forest hit the iron armour.

Another group of Germans began firing from the coal tender, half on, half off the rails where the locomotive had dragged it, and the machine gun came back to life. De Milja heard the sharp whistle that meant it was time to break off the engagement and head back into the forest.

He ran with the others, his breath coming in harsh gasps, up a slight rise to where several young women were guarding the ponies. They left immediately on orders from Kotior, two wounded men slung sideways across the backs of the horses. A third man was shot too badly to move, and Razakavia had to finish him off with a pistol. The rest of the band rode off at a fast trot, vanishing into the forest as the railcar burned brightly in the grey evening.

'The Germans, they always counterattack,' Kotior told him. 'Always.' He pointed up at several Fiesler-Storch reconnaissance planes, little two-seater things that buzzed back and forth above the forest. 'This is how partisans die,' Kotior added.

They were up there all night, crisscrossing the dark sky. So there could be no fires, no smoking outside the huts. De Milja pulled the blanket tight around his shoulders and loaded box magazines. The cold made his fingers numb, and the springs, like everything Russian, were too strong, tended to snap the feeder bar back into place, ejecting the bullet two feet in the air and producing a snarl of laughter from Kotior.

Four hundred miles to the east, on the line Smolensk/Roslavl/Bryansk, the Wehrmacht was fighting. How the hell did they manage in this kind of cold? he wondered. And it was only October. At night the temperature fell and the puddles froze and huge clouds gathered in the sky, but it did not snow. And in the morning it was blue and sunny: *winter isn't coming this year.*

At dawn, an alert. De Milja in position on the camp perimeter, aiming into the forest gloom. Somewhere south, perhaps a mile away, he could hear the faint popping of riflery, then the chatter of a light machine gun. Two scouts arrived at midday – they'd had a brush with a Ukrainian SS unit. 'They shot at us,' the scout said. 'And we shot back. So they fired the machine gun.' He was about fifteen, grinned like a kid. 'Frantek went around and he got one of them, we think. They were screaming and yelling "fucking Bolsheviks" and every kind of thing like that. Calling for God.'

'Where is Frantek?' Razakavia said.

The boy shrugged. 'He led them away into the marsh. He'll be back.'

'*Banderovsty.*' Razakavia spat the word.

He meant Ukrainian nationalists under the command of the leader Bandera, absorbed into an SS regiment called the Nachtigall. Kotior turned to de Milja and explained. 'They do what the SS won't.'

With Razakavia and Kotior he went to a town on the outskirts of Brest Litovsk. The owner of a bakery sold them milled oats and rye flour for bread. 'We pay for this,' Razakavia told him as they knocked at the back door. 'Not everyone does.' There was an ancient relationship in these lands, de Milja knew, between groups of armed men and keepers of granaries. Both sides had to survive, together they defined where honour might lie.

The iron door swung open and a hot wind, heavy with the smell of baking bread, swept over de Milja. 'Come in,' the baker said. He had a pink face, and a big belly in an undershirt. They sat at a marble-top table, there was flour everywhere. The baker wiped his hands on his shirt and accepted a cigarette from Razakavia. Behind him the brick ovens were at work, with sometimes a lick of flame where the furnace doors didn't quite meet. A black bread was brought over and cut up with a sawtooth knife.

Razakavia and the baker talked about the weather. The baker shook his head grimly. 'All the old *babas* have been reading the signs. Caterpillars and geese and bear scat. Probably nonsense, but even if it is, they're all saying the same thing: it's going to freeze your balls off.'

Razakavia nodded and chewed on a piece of bread. He reached into a pocket and counted out zlotys he'd bought with the gold roubles. The money lay in stacks on the marble table.

'It's in the barn in the village of Krymno,' the baker said. 'You know where I mean? The same as last spring. In wooden bins.'

'I remember,' Razakavia said.

'You want to take care on the roads, over there.'

'What's going on?'

'I don't know. Somebody goes out and doesn't come back. Somebody else has to give up a horse. People moving around in the forest.'

'A partisan band?'

'Who knows? These days it could be anything.' He nodded at de Milja. 'Who's your friend?'

'One of us. He's from down in the Volhynia.'

'Polish?'

'Yes,' de Milja said.

'One of my grandmothers was Polish,' the baker said. 'Crazy, she was. All with spells and potions and times of the moon, but good to us. Always jam or a little cake.' The baker's face softened as he remembered. He put out a hand and de Milja shook it. 'Times change, maybe we can have something to drink,' he said.

De Milja smiled. 'Better have it now,' he said.

The baker laughed. 'Well,' he said.

The dirt track back to the forest went through a little settlement called Gradh. They smelled smoke a mile away, walked the horses in a wide circle around the village. Near the old Jewish cemetery was a great scar of newly packed earth, they saw a lost shoe and a bloody shirt. Above the village, ravens circled in a haze of dirty grey smoke.

'It was a Jewish town,' Razakavia said.

The weather. At first you didn't notice. A leaf fell. You put on a jacket, took it off later. Then suddenly it tried to kill you, you hid from it as best you could but it seemed to search, to seek you out. In the swamps and woodlands there was mist, snow showers, a freeze, a thaw, heavy rain; then impossible, unimaginable mud. Like dull-minded peasants, de Milja and Frantek would stand by the road – the 'road', the 'Moscow highway' – and stare at the German columns. Some days the equipment could move, some days it ground the lightly frozen earth into the mud below, and sank. At night they could hear the panzer tanks – every four hours the engines had to be run to a hundred and forty degrees Fahrenheit, which took about fifteen minutes. Then they had to move the tanks around, to use the transmissions – because the oil was of too low a viscosity to protect the gears. Razakavia's forest was well behind the front lines, a night attack was unlikely. But the Germans could not be sure, and the Soviet air force sent over a plane to harass them now and then, to stir up the defences on icy nights.

The partisans attacked a repair train the following week. This time Bronstein's bomb derailed all seven cars, and some of the railway workers tried to surrender, as did a Wehrmacht railway officer. But every German was shot down, as well as most of the Poles and Ukrainians who worked on the track. The partisans looted the train, taking tools and coal and cigarettes and ammunition. One of the Polish labourers, lightly wounded, pleaded for mercy. Frantek worked the bolt on his rifle, but de Milja stepped between them. 'Leave him to me,' he said.

The man fell on his knees and tried to wrap his arms around de Milja's legs. 'Mercy,' he said.

De Milja took him by the shoulder of his jacket and hauled him to his feet. 'Stop it,' he hissed in Polish. The man wept. 'I have children,' he said. 'Four children, little girls.'

De Milja saw Razakavia staring at him coldly: take him as a gift, but don't ask for another. 'It's all right,' de Milja said. 'You can come with us.'

All around him, in the smoking wreckage of the repair train – a tangle of coaches with smashed windows, a flatcar with a crane bent at right angles – single shots rang out as the crew was finished off.

The man de Milja had saved was, by trade, a cobbler, and spent his first days in the encampment sewing boots and improvising repairs of all kinds. De Milja took him, late one afternoon, to a village near the forest, where a young widow sold vodka. If you paid a little extra you could drink it in a toolshed behind her house – she would even supply a few sticks of wood for the stove.

'My family is from Rovno, south of the Pripet marsh,' the man explained. 'Life wasn't so bad. The Poles had to watch it down there, but there was plenty of work, the police protected us, we had everything we needed. Maybe a little more.'

He took a pull from the vodka bottle, wiped his moustache with his fingers. Outside it was growing dark, and rain drummed on the roof of the shed. 'Then, September of '39. The Russians came and occupied the town. We were working people, didn't put on airs, and we'd always been decent to the peasants, so when the commissars appointed a council of workers, they spared us, and let us go on with our lives. Very honestly, a lot of them had boots for the first time – it was the deportees who went barefoot – so they needed us and they knew it.

'Still, some of my family didn't fare so well. One of my sisters was a nun, she disappeared. Another sister was married to a clerk in the district administration – they were sent east in freight cars. Gone. Door of the house banging in the wind, dinner rotting on the table. Make your heart sick to see it. My brother was a sergeant in the army. He'd been captured in the first days of the invasion, but maybe that was better for him. At least he wasn't arrested, and he came from a unit that had laid down their guns when the Soviet troops said they'd arrived to fight the Germans.

'So him they sent to a prisoner-of-war camp, an NKVD camp called Ostashkov, not far from Smolensk. They really didn't seem to know what they wanted to do with them. The officers – mostly reserve officers; engineers, teachers, doctors – they took them away, rumour was to a camp in the Katyn forest. Stefan, that's my brother, and the other enlisted men, they just sat there and starved. Finally, they sent him to Moscow.'

'*Moscow!* It's true?'

'It's true, I swear it. What happened to Stefan was, the Russians thought he was one of them. Almost by accident – but then, that's how he is. He's not like me, doesn't matter what I try it goes wrong. But Stefan's not like that – if the world had gone on like it always did, he'd be doing very well now.'

The cobbler took another pull at the vodka. He looked off into the dusk, watching fondly as his brother did well.

'What happened?' de Milja said. 'At the camp.'

'Oh. He befriended one of the NKVD men.'

'A political officer?'

'No! Nothing like that – a sergeant, just like him. This man had a hunting dog, a spaniel bitch, and his pleasure was to go into the marsh with this dog and perhaps shoot a duck or two and the dog would go into the reeds and bring them back. But the dog got hurt, and it wouldn't eat, and it was dying. Stefan found out about it, and he told the NKVD man what to do, and the dog got better. And that was the end of it – except that it wasn't. One day the man came to where he was kept and said, "You're going to have a choice. Everybody here is going to a new camp, in the Katyn forest. For you, it's better to tell them that you want to go to school, in Moscow." And that's what Stefan did.'

'And then?'

'Well, he came home.'

'Just like that?'

The cobbler shrugged. 'Yes.'

'A free man?'

'Well, yes. For a time, anyhow.'

'What happened?'

'Poor Stefan.'

'Another drink? There's a little left.'

'Yes, all right, thank you. I owe you my life, you know.'

'Oh, anyone would have done what I did. But, ah, what happened to Stefan?'

'Too strong, Stefan. Sometimes it isn't for the best. He went into the town, I don't know why. And some German didn't like his looks, and they asked for his papers, and Stefan hit him.'

'In Rovno, this was?'

'Yes. He managed to run away – a friend saw it and told us. But then they caught him. They beat him up and took him off in one of those black trucks, and now he's in Czarny prison.' The cobbler looked away, his face angry and bitter. 'They are going to hang him.'

'He has a family?'

'Oh yes. Just like me.'

'Name the same as yours?'

'Yes. Krewinski, just like mine. Why wouldn't it be?'

'Don't get angry.'

'Shameful thing. It's the Russians' fault, they won't leave us alone.' He paused a moment, took another sip of vodka. 'You think there's hope? I mean, we're told to pray for this and for that. We're told there's always hope. Do you think that's true?'

De Milja thought it over. 'Well,' he said at last, 'there's always hope. But I think you ought to pray for his soul. That might be the best thing.'

The cobbler shook his head in reluctant agreement. 'Poor Stefan,' he said, wiping the tears from his eyes.

Kotior commanded the unit sent off to Krymno to retrieve the grain. He was accompanied by Frantek, his fellow scout Pavel, an older man called Korbin, de Milja, and two Ukrainian peasant girls who drove the farm wagons. The rifles were hidden under burlap sacks in the wagons.

They rode all morning, along a track that wound through water meadows, fields of reeds rustling as they swayed in the wind, the air chill and heavy. The village was no more than fifteen miles from Brest but it lay beyond the forest, some distance into the marshland along a tributary of the river Pripet. A few wooden huts, a farm with stone barns, then reeds again, pools of black, still water, and windswept sky to the horizon on every side.

The farm dogs snarled at them as they rode up and the peasant who tended the farm came out of his house with a battered shotgun riding the crook of his arm. The man spoke some form of local dialect de Milja could barely understand but Kotior told him to call the dogs off, dismounted, and explained slowly who they were and what they had come for. Then they all went into the barn – warmed by a cow, smelling of dung and damp straw, the dogs drinking eagerly at pools of water where grain stalks had fermented.

'Where is the rest?' Kotior asked, standing in front of empty wooden bins.

The peasant, agitated now, seemed to be telling Kotior a long and complicated story. Kotior nodded, a reasonable man who would accept whatever he was told, then suddenly barred a forearm across the peasant's throat and forced him back against a wall. A Russian bayonet – four-edged, it made a cross-shaped wound – had appeared in his hand and he held the point under the man's chin. The shotgun dropped to the floor. The dogs went wild, but Frantek kicked one and it ran away with the rest following.

The peasant didn't struggle, his face went passive as he prepared to die. Then Kotior let him go. 'He says the grain was taken away. By a detachment of partisans. He thinks they intend to come back for the rest of it.' After some discussion they decided to wait, at least until morning. They pulled the wagons into the barn, posted Frantek and Pavel at the two ends of the settlement, and took turns sleeping.

They came at dawn. Pavel sounded the alarm in time for them to set up an ambush. At Kotior's direction, de Milja was in the hayloft of the barn, the Simonov covering the road below.

The column appeared from the grey mist, silent but for the sound of hooves on the muddy road. There were forty of them, well armed. He saw several automatic rifles, several *pepechas* – Russian submachine guns – a few weapons he could not identify. Otherwise they looked like the Razakavia band. They wore wool jackets and peaked caps and boots, sometimes a military coat or trousers. The leader, de Milja guessed he was the leader, had a pair of binoculars on a strap and a holstered pistol.

The peasant came out of the barn and raised his hand. The column stopped. The leader – de Milja had been right – climbed off his horse and led it forward. De Milja sighted on him. He was perhaps forty, a Slav, clean-shaven, something of the soldier in the way he held his shoulders. He talked with the peasant for a time. Then Kotior came out of the barn and joined the conversation, eventually signalling to de Milja that he should come down.

They were joined by another man, who the leader referred to as *politruk*. The conversation was very tense. 'He has told me they are taking the grain,' Kotior said evenly. 'Requisitioned,' the leader said in Russian. 'For partisan operations.'

'We are also partisans,' Kotior said.

'Not bandits, perhaps?'

'Polish partisans.'

'Then we are friends,' the politruk said. 'Poland and the Soviet Union. Allies.' He wore a leather coat, had cropped fair hair and albino colouring. His hands were deep in his pockets – de Milja could almost see the NKVD-issue Makarov in there. 'This matter of the grain, a misunderstanding,' he said.

Kotior and de Milja were silent.

'Best to come back to our camp, we can sit down and talk this out.'

'Another time, perhaps,' de Milja said.

The politruk was angry. 'War doesn't wait,' he said.

De Milja saw no signal, but the mounted partisans shifted, some of them moving out of de Milja's line of sight.

'I think it would be best . . .' The politruk stopped in mid-sentence. De Milja watched his eyes, then turned to see what he was looking at. One of the wagons was moving slowly out of the barn, the pair of shaggy horses trudging through the mud. The Ukrainian girl held the reins in the crook of her knee and was pointing a rifle at the two Russians. The leader made a gesture – *enough*, let it go. Frantek rode up, pistol in one hand, face pinched like an angry child. In his other hand, the reins of de Milja's and Kotior's horses. When he spat, meaningfully, down into the dirt, the politruk blinked.

De Milja put a foot in the stirrup and swung up on the pony. The politruk and the leader stared without expression as the unit rode off, walking the horses at wagon speed. The skies over the marsh were alive, broken grey cloud blown west, and a few dry flakes of snow drifting down.

'We'll need a rear guard,' de Milja said to Kotior as the settlement fell behind them.

'Yes, I know. You stay, with Frantek.' He paused. 'I can understand most Russians when they speak, we all can in this place. But what is a *politruk?*'

'It means *political officer*.'

Kotior shrugged – that was to raise life to a level where it only pretended to exist. 'We'll need an hour,' he said, gesturing at the wagons. 'At least that.'

'You will have it,' de Milja said.

There wasn't much cover. Frantek and de Milja rode at the back of the column until they found a low hill with a grove of pine trees that marked the edge of the forest east of Brest. There they waited, watching the dirt road below them, the cold working its way through their sheepskins.

Frantek seemed, to de Milja, to have been born to the life he lived. His parents had gone to market one Saturday morning and never come home. So, at the age of twelve, he had gone to the forest and found Razakavia. The forest bands always needed scouts, and Frantek and his friends knew it. Now he leaned back against a tree, folded his arms around his rifle and across his chest, and pulled his knees up, completely at rest except for his eyes, slitted against the snow, watching the approaches to the hilltop.

'Do you like the life in the forest?' de Milja asked him, tired of listening to the wind.

Frantek thought it over. 'I miss my dog,' he said. 'Her name was Chaya.'

The Russians came thirty minutes later, four scouts riding single file. One of them dismounted, squatted, determined that the horse droppings were fresh, and climbed back on his horse. They moved slowly, at wagon speed, waiting for the band to leave the steppe and enter the forest.

'Do not fire,' de Milja said to Frantek as they flattened out behind the pine trees. 'That is an order,' he added.

Frantek acknowledged it – barely. To him, de Milja seemed cautious, even hesitant, and he'd killed enough to know how attentive it made people. But he'd also come across many inexplicable things in his short life and he'd decided that de Milja was just one more.

De Milja sighted down the Simonov at four hundred yards. *Ping.* That animated the Russians and drew an appreciative chuckle from Frantek. They leaped off their horses and went flat on the ground. Disciplined, they did not fire their rifles. They waited. Ten long minutes.

'Mine is on the far left,' Frantek said, squinting through his gunsight.

'Not yet,' de Milja said.

One of the Russian scouts rose to one knee, rifle at his hip swinging back and forth across the axis of the road. Then he stood.

'Now?' said Frantek.

'No.'

The scout retrieved his horse. Climbed up in the saddle. *Ping.*

At first, de Milja was afraid he'd miscalculated and killed him, because he seemed to fly off the horse, which shied and galloped a few yards. And the other three scouts returned fire, including a long staccato rattle, at least half a drum of pepecha rounds. Some of it in their direction – a white mark chipped in a tree trunk, the sound of canvas ripping overhead – but not the sort of enthusiastic concentration that would mean the scouts knew where they were. Then the man de Milja had fired at moved, changed positions, scuttling along low to the ground and throwing himself flat.

De Milja's greatest worry was Frantek, an excellent shot with young eyes. But discipline held. De Milja extended his left hand, palm flat, fingers slightly spread: *hold on, do nothing*. Frantek pressed himself against the earth, outraged he had to endure this insulting gunfire but, for the moment, under control.

The wind rose, snowflakes spun through the air, swirling like dust and whitening the dirt road. It saved their lives, Razakavia said later. 'Russians read snow like priests read Bibles.' Or, perhaps, that day, nobody wanted to die.

The Russians mounted their horses, slow and deliberate under the eyes of the unseen riflemen, and rode back the way they came.

De Milja had been ice inside for a long time – there wasn't any other way for him to do what he had to do – but Rovno scared him. The Germans had it all their own way in Rovno. The SS were everywhere, death's-head insignia and lightning flashes, a certain walk, a certain smile. The Einsatzgruppen came through, on the way to murder Jews in another ghetto somewhere, there were Ukrainian SS, Latvian SS, and German criminals, alley killers the Nazi recruiters had quarried from the prisons since 1927. As well as those ordinary Germans, always liked by their neighbours, who, given the opportunity, turned out to be not so very mild-mannered after all. They were the worst, and one taste of blood was all it took.

De Milja met their eyes in Rovno. He dared not be furtive. So he returned the stares, trudged along in the snow, cold and absentminded and absorbed in his business. And armed. It went against the current wisdom – one street search and you were finished. But he would not be taken alive. The cyanide capsule sewn in the point of his shirt collar was the last resort, but the VIS snugged against the small of his back gave him at least the illusion of survival.

The ZWZ secret mail system operated all over Poland, mostly out of dress shops, with couriers carrying letters from city to city. De Milja had used it to report the Russian contact and that had produced a request – delivered in a park in Brest Litovsk – for a meeting in Rovno. With Major Olenik, his former superior in Warsaw and, now that he was no longer under the direct orders of the Sixth Bureau in London, his superior once again.

Rovno had always been a border city – a Polish possession, claimed by Russia, populated by Ukrainians. Narrow streets, brick buildings darkened by factory smoke, November ice, November fog, Gestapo cars with chains on the tyres.

'They will yet take Moscow,' Olenik said. 'Or maybe not. The Russians have introduced a weapon they call the Katyusha rocket, also known as the Stalin Organ – multiple rockets fired simultaneously from a launcher that can be towed by a truck. The Germans don't like it. They are afraid of it – they ran away from it up in Smolensk. And the Russians have a new tank, the T-34. German shells bounce off. If they can produce enough of them, they'll shut the panzer divisions down. There's that, and the fact that our weather people predict December temperatures outside Moscow of sixty-five degrees below zero. We'll see what *that* does to their *Wehrwille*.'

The word meant *war will*, a cherished German idea: who wants most to win, wins.

De Milja and Olenik sat in the parlour of a safe house in Rovno, a small apartment, old-fashioned, as though a couple had grown old there and never changed anything. It was all curtains and doilies and clocks with loud ticks – a certain musty smell, a certain silence. De Milja wondered what it would be like in the forest at sixty-five degrees below zero. Olenik apparently read his mind. 'We expect you'll finish up before then,' he said.

Olenik hadn't changed. Narrow shoulders, tousled grey hair and moustache, pockmarked skin – triumphantly seedy in a worn grey cardigan, you'd walk past him and never see him on any street in the world. He rummaged in a briefcase, found a pipe, fussed with it until he got it lit, then searched again until he found a single sheet of yellowish newsprint. 'Have a look,' he said.

The newspaper was called *Miecz i Mlot – Sword and Hammer*. It was published in Polish by the League of Friends of the Soviet Union and the PPR, the Polska Partia Robotnicza, the Polish Workers' Party.

'It comes from Bialystok,' Olenik said. 'From Stryj and Brody and Wilno. From Brest and Rovno. All over the eastern districts. Curious, with a hundred and sixty-five newspapers issued by underground presses in Poland, including every prewar party, socialist, and peasant and all the rest of it, we now see this. Reference to a *communist* underground in Poland. If it exists, we don't know about it. If it exists, it does nothing *but* exist, but that may be just precisely to the point. Its existence will make it easier for them to say, later on, that the communist state of Poland was preceded by a communist underground.'

De Milja handed the newspaper back and Olenik returned it to his briefcase. 'Of course,' Olenik said, 'we're not spending life and money to find out what the Russians think about us. They enslaved us for a hundred and twenty years. Attacked in 1920. Attacked again in 1939. And they'll be coming back this way, pushing a wave of Wehrmacht grey in front of them. We have to decide what to do then.

'If they go all the way to the Oder, to the Rhine, we're done for – they'll occupy the country. It's that simple. So what we may have to do is, at the right moment, throw the Germans out by ourselves and declare a free Polish state, recognition by the British and the Americans to follow. That means a rising, and a terrible price to pay in blood.

'The alternative: reveal Soviet intentions – stick a knife in Stalin before he can get to the conference table. Britain won't give him Poland, but the Americans are blind to life beyond their oceans.' He stopped for a moment and seemed to drift, then spoke again in a softer voice. 'If you're a small country and you have a bully for a neighbour, God help you, because nobody else will. You're alone. You'll cry out in the night, but nobody will come.'

He stopped abruptly, had said more of what was in his heart than he'd meant to. He cleared his throat. 'What matters now,' he went on, 'are the particular and demonstrable intentions of the Soviet state. If their partisan units take food without paying for it – and they do. If those partisan units have political officers – and they do. If they are forcing Poles to fight in those units and burning down villages that resist, and we know they are doing that, too, then they are acting, according to their own rules, like people fighting in an enemy country among enemies.'

'It was certainly that way in Krymno,' de Milja said. 'And we were asked – that's not really the word for the way it was put – to follow them to their camp.'

'Two of our people, in the northern Polesian district, did just that. They believed they were going somewhere to sit down and work out an agreement. One is dead. The other, we're told, is in the Lubianka. So we are both fighting the Germans, but we are not allies.'

He stopped a moment, considered what he would say next. 'So,' he said. 'We, I mean London and Warsaw, we are interested in the story of Sergeant Krewinski, the brother of the man captured in the attack on the repair train.'

'The man in Rovno prison?'

'Yes. What we want you to do now, Captain, is to force Rovno prison. Liberate Krewinski – and two ZWZ officers who are also being held there. All are going to be executed.'

De Milja met the major's eyes, but his look was opaque and distant.

There'd been three attempts on German prisons that de Milja knew about, all had failed. Then he understood: this was a committee at work, and if they assigned what was in effect a suicide mission, there was nothing Olenik could do about it.

'It's right away, then?' de Milja said.

Olenik spread his hands: *of course.*

That completed Major Olenik's work and he left the city by train the following evening. As a notional waterworks engineer, his papers allowed him to travel anywhere within German-occupied lands. He handed over to de Milja a group of code and contact procedures: ZWZ officers and operatives in the district were at his disposal. Explosives, weapons, whatever he needed was available.

De Milja returned to the forest, explaining to Razakavia what had to be done. The first step was to move the encampment, from huts in a clearing to an abandoned farm at the edge of a wood about ten miles from Rovno. The farm would serve as a reception base for the freed prisoners and some members of the attack commando. A doctor and nurse would set up an aid station at the farmhouse twenty-four hours before the attack.

Back in Rovno he made contact with a local ZWZ operative known as Vlach, a man in his late twenties, with tipped-up nose, carefully combed blond hair and a wise-guy curl to his lip. The ZWZ ran, in general, to more sober and stable personalities – Vlach had replaced one of those very gentlemen in late July. Had survived, had impressed Major Olenik; those were his credentials. At Vlach's suggestion they met in a tearoom in Rovno's central square, a very proper place, where German officials' wives and girlfriends could drink tea with extended pinkies and nibble at mounds of pale-green petits fours. 'Ha ha,' Vlach laughed. 'Who would look for us here?'

Then he grew serious. 'We can get you anything you like,' he said. 'Cars, trucks, you say what.'

'How can you do that?'

'We all do the same thing here, everybody who you-know-what. See, the Luftwaffe and the panzer tanks, they can really do the job. Whatever the Russians had here is flat, gone. I never saw such a mess; staff cars on top of each other, railway tracks peeled straight up into the air, airfields turned into junkyards. So now it's conquered, so now it all has to be rebuilt.

'So, just about the time the Wehrmacht shot the last sniper and hanged the last commissar, the big German construction companies came in. Ho, ho – Ve gonna make money now, Fritz! The military authority told them what they needed – airfields, barracks, aeroplane hangars, oil-storage tanks – exactly what they just finished blowing up. Plus, as long as they were at it, roads, which they never had here.

'So, the construction companies get all these contracts, but when they finished rubbing their hands and winking at each other, it begins to dawn on them that they're going to have to find somebody to do the work. Ah, not so easy. Can't bring in people from Germany, either they're building aeroplanes and submarines back in Essen, or they're shooting more Russians, six hundred miles east of here. See, when you shoot a Russian, somebody puts another one down, but they haven't figured that out yet.

'Anyhow, they're going to have to use local labour. We started by getting one guy hired. Every German's dream of what a Pole should be – cooperative, friendly, religious, trustworthy. A fifty-five-year-old man, a machinist all his life, Henryk. So all the Germans loved Henryk. They could count on him, he never drank, he never stole, he never answered back, and you said be at the job site at five-thirty in the morning, and there he was.'

Vlach blew out his cheeks to make a fat German face. ' "Henryk, mein friend, maybe you haff a cousin?" ' Well, guess what, he does. He has also an uncle, an aunt, a long-lost friend, a nephew – that's me – and about eighteen more, one way and another. We go anywhere we like, we have company trucks, two Opel cars. If we want to carry something that's – unusual, you understand, we can request a Wehrmacht driver. When they're behind the wheel, nobody even pretends to look.'

Respectable little man, tortoiseshell spectacles gave him a slight resemblance to the American comedian Harold Lloyd. Except that Harold Lloyd would have bought new glasses if he'd cracked a lens.

'The Russians put him in a camp in '39,' Vlach said.

'How did you get out?' de Milja asked.

'I escaped,' the man said.

He sat with de Milja and Vlach in the apartment, a map of Rovno unfolded on the kitchen table. 'From the central telephone exchange, which is here, there are three lines that leave Rovno.' He pointed, his hands cracked and peeling from working as a dishwasher in a restaurant. The main line goes west, to Lutsk. Then we had a branch north, to Klesow, and one south, to Ostrog. From there a line went to Kiev – but it was often cut, or blocked. The Russians interfered any way they could.'

'And the wireless telegraph – is that something you knew about?' The man had been the regional accounting supervisor for the telephone system before the war.

'There were five stations,' he said.

'So if we disabled those, and cut the telephone lines—'

'They would use the military wireless. I don't think you can silence them, sir.'

The prison guard had never liked his work. They paid him slave wages to sit on the lid of a garbage can, the way he saw it. But it was better than nothing, so he did what he had to do. A mean existence; everything had to be watched, saved, rationed: light bulbs, soap, coal, meat. He'd never, not once, had a lot of something he liked. His kids were gone, had their own sorry lives. His wife was still with him, mostly the Church to thank for that, but whatever had once been inside her had died years ago. For himself, he sat in a bar after work and soaked up vodka until he was numb enough to go home. He would have liked, once he got older, to go back to the countryside where he'd been raised. Since the war you could buy a small farm, it didn't take much, just more than he'd ever had.

So when the offer came, he didn't say no. They'd probably watched him, the way he looked, the misery in his step. The old man who made the offer wasn't such a bad sort. Polish, with the sharp cheekbones like they had sometimes. And educated, maybe very educated. 'You've had enough bad weather,' the old man said. 'Time to take a walk in the sunshine.' Then he mentioned an amount of money, and the guard just nodded.

'You don't have to do anything,' the old man said. 'Just draw what's inside, the corridors and the offices and the cells, and show me how it's numbered.'

'What's going to happen?'

'They don't tell me. It's the Russians gave me this job.'

'Bandits. We have some of them locked up.'

'Just draw and number.'

'I'll take care of it at home,' the guard said.

The old man put a sheet of paper and a pencil in front of him. 'Why not right now? There's nobody here.'

So the guard did it. And when his mind raced as he lay in bed that night – should he tell, could he sell the old man to the Germans, should he have demanded more money? – he realized that his childish drawing was as good as a signed confession. That scared him. So he hid the money under the mattress and kept quiet.

Vlach and de Milja shivered in the cold of the unheated garage. Outside the snow whispered down, the air frozen and still. Henryk was exactly as Vlach had described him, square-jawed and square-shouldered, sleeves and collar buttoned up. An honest man, not a crooked bone in his body. It just happened that he was a patriot, and the construction executives hadn't really thought that through.

Henryk was lying on his back under a large German truck, working with a wrench. His face reddened as one of the rusty bolts refused to give, then squeaked, and turned. He pulled the muffler, laid it on the floor, and slid from beneath the truck, wiping his hands on a rag. 'Start it up,' he said.

De Milja climbed into the cab and turned the key. The roar was deafening, it shook the windowpanes in the garage. Vlach appeared at the truck window, hands pressed against his ears, and de Milja had to read his lips even though he appeared to be shouting. 'Turn, that, fucking, thing, off.'

In the silent apartment with the ticking clock, the sofas had been pushed back to the walls to make room on the floor. The doilies on the backs of the chairs were creased and stained where too many people had rested their heads, and the carpet, pale blue with a pattern of roses and vines, was also ruined, spotted with cosmoline and oil.

The armoury was laid out on the rug: three Simonovs, three Russian PPD submachine guns – the pepecha, crude and lethal, named after the rhythm of its fire. Two German machine pistols, all-steel MP34s. Known as the Bergmann, the weapon had been manufactured outside German borders to evade the armament limits of the Treaty of Versailles. There were the two VIS automatics that accompanied de Milja from London, the ones with the Polish eagle on the slide, and four VIS automatics made since the German occupation – no eagle. There were two American Colt .45s. A Hungarian Gepisztoly 39M, a very fast machine pistol that fired Mauser Export cartridges. For hand grenades, they had the variety called Sidolowki – manufactured in clandestine ZWZ workshops and named after the cans of Sidol polish they resembled – logically, since the workshops were hidden in the Sidol factory.

The brothers were nineteen and seventeen, big and broad-shouldered and towheaded. They walked around Rovno all day looking for a candidate. They saw an SS major outside the movie theatre – German romantic films and newsreels of the victorious Wehrmacht on the

Russian front. An SS sergeant, extremely tall and thin, leaving a restaurant. Two SS corporals, ogling girls on the bridge over the small stream
that ran through Rovno.

Then, late in the afternoon, they found another SS sergeant, of
medium build, looking at the stills posted on the outside of the movie
theatre. After some consideration, he paid and went inside. They did
too. He wandered down the aisle, they took seats near the back. Not
much of an audience, mostly German soldiers on their off-duty hours.
On the screen, a man in a tuxedo sitting in an elegant nightclub,
speaking rapid German to a blonde woman with tight curls and a
black dress with a white bib collar. She looked down and bit her lip, he
had smooth black hair and a thin moustache. The brothers didn't speak
much German but they could tell the man was apologizing.

The woman wasn't really sure how she felt. She kept giving the man
shy glances from beneath her dark eyelashes. *I'm supposed to love darling
Helmut – what could be the matter with me?* is what she seemed to be
saying to herself. Then, a commotion at the entrance to the room,
where a maître d' stood guard over a velvet rope. A handsome fellow
wearing a yachting cap wanted to go down the steps but the burly
waiters wouldn't let him, and they struggled in front of some potted
palms.

The SS sergeant came up the aisle and the older brother nudged the
younger. They let some time lapse, then went into the men's room. The
SS sergeant was buttoning his fly. Up close, he was bigger than they'd
thought. He had several medals and ribbons, and a scar on his forehead,
but the brothers were practised and adept and they had him strangled in
short order. They stripped off his uniform and left him on the floor
with his mouth wide open against the stained tile, still wearing the old
green tie they'd used.

The Czarny prison, on Zamkova Street. Quiet enough in the late
afternoon. The weather had warmed up, leaving the cobbles awash in
wet, dirty slush. The prison had been built in 1878, a series of courtyards
behind a wall, ten feet high, with plaster peeling off the granite block.
The neighbourhood was deserted. Boarded-up clothing store, a burned-
out tenement: people avoided Zamkova Street. De Milja walked along
briskly, as though he had business nearby. The windows visible from the
street were opaque green glass covered by steel mesh – *dungeon* was the
word that came to mind. A sentry box with a big swastika flag stood to
one side of the main gate. An old woman in black came through the
door in the gate, pulling her shawl up over her head, then folding her
arms around herself for warmth. A large brown truck with its canvas

top closed at the back came rumbling down the street and rolled to a stop in front of the sentry box. The driver joked with the guard. He was German, while the guard, they knew, was part of a Latvian SS unit used for duty outside the cell blocks. Day-to-day supervision inside the prison was managed by local Ukrainian warders.

'Hey, you, what are you staring at?'

De Milja turned to see who it was. Two Germans in black-and-silver uniforms. De Milja smiled hesitantly and started to move away when one of them kicked him in the back of the leg. He fell hard, comically, his feet flying up in the air, into the cold slush. The Germans laughed and walked off. De Milja got to his feet and limped in the opposite direction.

26 November, 4:30 p.m.

The assault commando gathered in the apartment. Group One had four men – de Milja, Vlach, and two whom he'd never met until that night; one with the nom de guerre *Kolya*, in his twenties, lean and hard-eyed, and the other called *Bron*, the armourer, heavier and older with a deceptively soft face. Group Two, six men, was led by a ZWZ officer who had parachuted into the Lodz area in late October, formerly an officer in a special reconnaissance unit of the Polish army. He had a full beard and was known as Jan.

They all smoked nervously, looking at their watches, talking in low voices, going over the pencilled maps of the prison again and again. Bron said, 'I had better get busy,' stood up and left the room. One of Jan's men was working the mechanism of a Bergmann machine pistol, the sound of the slide and lock, oiled steel on steel, cutting through the quiet voices. 'Hey, Bron,' the man called to the armourer.

Bron came out of the kitchen; he was wearing underpants, his bare legs red from the cold, had a cigarette stuck in the corner of his mouth, and was buttoning up an SS sergeant's tunic. 'What is it?' he said.

The man worked the Bergmann bolt and said, 'Is this right?'

'I had it apart this morning. It works.'

The man tried it one last time, then laid the weapon across his knees. De Milja looked at his watch, the minute hand was where it had been the last time he'd looked. His side hurt from where he'd fallen in the street the day before. Strong, that German. They liked to kick, it added insult to injury, the way they saw it, and they were good at it, probably from all the soccer they played.

'So?' Vlach said, and raised his eyebrows. He smiled a wise-guy smile, but his face was very white.

'Eleven of,' de Milja said.

Vlach didn't answer. Somebody was tapping his foot rhythmically against the leg of the sofa. Bron came back in the room. Now in SS uniform, he put out the stub of one cigarette and lit another. De Milja stood. 'It's time to go,' he said. 'Good luck to you all.' Two of the men crossed themselves. Jan adjusted a fedora in front of the hall mirror. De Milja opened the apartment door and the men flowed out quickly, automatic weapons held beneath overcoats, hats pulled down over their eyes.

One of the men in Jan's unit patted de Milja on the shoulder as he went past and said, 'Good luck.' A neighbour heard people in the hallway, opened his door a crack, then closed it quickly.

De Milja turned to look back into the dark apartment, then shut the door. On the doorframe was a pen-sized outline with two empty screw holes where something had been removed. De Milja knew that Jews often kept a metal device by their front doors, though he couldn't remember what it was called. The people who had lived in the apartment had apparently taken it off, thinking perhaps that nobody would notice the outline where it had once been fastened.

With Bron driving, they looked like three Gestapo executives with an SS chauffeur. The Opel turned into Zamkova Street, almost dark at 5:00 p.m., an hour before the Rovno curfew, a few people hurrying home with heads down. The second Opel and the truck, Jan's unit, continued on, heading for the entrance that led to the prison offices.

The first Opel pulled up to the sentry box. Bron opened the door, stood half in, half out of the front seat so the guard got a good look at the SS uniform. He started yelling orders in very fast German, angry and impatient and dangerous. The guard had seen such behavior before, and hastened to open the gate. The car shot through, then one of the civilians rolled out of the back and headed for the sentry box on the run. The guard was puzzled. The running man, Kolya, put an automatic pistol against his temple. 'Hand over your weapon,' he said.

The Latvian guard did as he was told. Kolya emptied the chamber and the magazine and returned the rifle. 'Now stand guard, do everything as usual,' he said, sitting down in the sentry box below the level of the window. He pressed the VIS against the base of the man's spine. 'As usual,' he said. The guard nodded.

The second Opel and the truck pulled into the street that ran perpendicular to Zamkova. Two ladders were taken from the truck and placed against the wall. The prison had been built to keep people from getting out – very little thought had been given to keeping them from getting in. As Jan's unit climbed the ladders, the truck was driven fifty yards farther down the street and parked, its engine idling loud enough to cover the sound of gunfire from behind the prison wall.

The street sentry box was visible from the interior guard station, so Bron drove the Opel at normal speed, then stopped and shouted angrily in German. The guard didn't understand what all the fuss was about: 'What's the matter?' he asked the SS sergeant. Dimly, he could see two men in civilian suits in the car – that meant important security types. Evidently the poor bastard driving the car had been bullied by his superiors – but why take it out on him? The SS sergeant sputtered and turned red. The guard shrugged and opened the gate. The car sped through, one of the men in civilian clothes got out and ran towards him.

Not right.

He went for his rifle.

De Milja readied himself, his fist tight on the door handle. The Opel jerked to a stop, he shoved the back door open and jumped out. All he could see of the Latvian guard was a pale face in the darkness. The face seemed puzzled, and faintly offended. Three paces from the sentry box their eyes locked, and everyone knew everything. The guard reacted, snatched for a rifle in the sentry box. De Milja brought the VIS up and pulled the trigger as he ran. It bent the guard in two, arms folded across his stomach. De Milja moved around him, took a moment to steady his hand, then shot him four times in the side of the head. The man dropped to his knees, then pitched forward on his face.

De Milja ran back to the car and climbed in. 'All right, go to the next gate.'

Jan and three of his men climbed over the wall into the administrative courtyard of the prison. A trained commando, Jan had memorized every detail of the guard's sketch. He looked around the courtyard and saw that each doorway and gate was where the map had said it was. A young clerk coming down the stairway from the prison office dropped an armload of files when he saw the machine pistols and the men in the hats with the brims pulled down. He choked off a yell, threw his hands in the air, stood absolutely still.

Jan opened a door at the top of the stairs. There were three more clerks – the German warden and his German assistant had separate offices at the end of the room. 'Raise your hands,' Jan said. The clerks did as they were told. Two of Jan's men pulled the Germans from their office chairs and stood them against a wall. The warden had been a Nazi streetfighter in the 1930s and the Rovno prison was his reward for faithful service. He'd put on weight since those days, and wore a fine suit, but he met Jan's stare with defiance. 'Are you Herr Kruger? The warden?' Jan asked.

'Yes.'

'Please give me the keys to blocks four and six.'

'I cannot.'

Jan raised the machine pistol so Kruger could look down the barrel. Kruger closed his eyes, pressed his lips closed, and drew himself up to his full height. The Hungarian weapon fired a heavy, high-velocity bullet; the warden was thrown back against the wall so hard the plaster cracked, and he left a long red smear as he slid to the floor.

Jan turned the weapon towards the assistant warden. 'Please give me the keys to blocks four and six,' he said. The assistant trembled with fear but he would not give in. 'Is that your answer?' Jan asked.

The man made a sound. Resistance? Assent? Jan shrugged and fired a long burst. The man screamed once before he died. One of the clerks yelled, 'Here, here are keys. In this drawer. Take them, please.'

In a room down the corridor, a clerk hid behind a bank of filing cabinets. He heard gunfire, heard the assistant warden cry out, heard several minutes of silence, and carefully lifted the receiver off a telephone and held it to his ear, tapping the disconnect bar impatiently with his finger, but the line was dead.

A darkened courtyard bordered by cell blocks, cobblestones worn smooth by half a century of prisoners' felt slippers. At the centre, an iron grating sparkling with frost. De Milja and Vlach ran across the courtyard, bent low to the ground. They reached an entry marked *South* in Cyrillic and used the arched doorway as cover. Czarny prison was silent, the inmates forbidden to talk, so they could hear the jangle of keys as warders moved along the corridors, the idling truck on the other side of the wall, the high-low sirens of German and Ukrainian police in the streets of Rovno. A voice called, another answered, a third laughed – guards on one of the cell blocks. Then footsteps, three or four running men, and Jan and two others came out of the darkness.

'Everybody all right?' de Milja whispered.

Jan nodded. 'We shot the wardens.'

'Keys?'

'Yes.'

Jan was breathing hard, he rummaged through a ring of keys, peering at the stamped markings. He removed two keys and handed them to de Milja. 'Block four,' he said.

'Good. We go out as planned.'

'No change. See you in better times.'
'Yes. See you then,' de Milja said.

De Milja turned the key and opened the grille that led to Block Four. It creaked when it opened, then clanged shut. A warder came around the corner and said, 'Tomek?' Vlach had the machine pistol pressed against his chest before he knew what was happening. He gasped with surprise, dropped a wooden club with a clatter that echoed down the corridor. De Milja pulled the man's arms behind him and wound a piece of wire around his wrists. He'd thought at first that the warder was a fat man, but he wasn't. The muscles in his shoulders and back were massive, and the smell of him, like stale garlic, cut through the prison odour of open drains and crumbling stone.

'Prisoner Krewinski,' Vlach whispered.
'Which?'
'*Krewinski.*'
'Yes, wait. It's that corridor. Second to the last, on the left. You see, I don't give you a problem.'
'On the floor,' de Milja said.
The guard gave a nervous laugh, went to one knee, then both. 'Like this? You see, sirs, no trouble from me.'
De Milja pushed him over on his side and began wiring his ankles together. 'Sirs?' The guard's voice was very high now. 'You're going to let men out of these cells, don't leave me tied up here, I beg you.'
De Milja didn't answer. He ripped the keys off the warder's belt, held them in front of the man's eyes, and began going through them. 'Yes, there,' the man said. He was fading now – drifting towards death before anyone touched him, de Milja could see it.

The prisoners, in cells lining the twilit corridor, came to their barred doors and watched with curiosity: two men with weapons, moving quickly. No uniforms, no warder. For the moment, de Milja and Vlach ignored them. In the second cell from the end on the left, a man sat on a bed – a wood frame suspended from the wall by two chains. He was tall and wiry, with a mournful face and hair shaved to a colourless stubble – a hard head and soft eyes. He was clean-shaven, but a cavalry moustache would not have been out of place. *Sergeant* Krewinski, de Milja now saw. The man stared at de Milja and Vlach without much interest, they were only the most recent in a long line of men with guns who'd come for him.

'Are you Sergeant Krewinski?'
'Yes,' the man said – meaning *if you like.*

*

As the three left the cell block, the keys were passed to other prisoners. In Block Six, Jan and his group freed the two ZWZ officers, a group of Russian partisans, all the political prisoners, and the women in the adjoining wing. The pandemonium was just getting started when de Milja and Vlach and the sergeant reached the Opel. Ukrainian guards running for their lives, prisoners running out into the streets of Rovno. Some would escape, and police units would be busy for days. At the Zamkova Street intersection, they saw Jan's truck, rocking from side to side as it sped away from the prison.

The Opel wound through the back alleys of Rovno – there were sirens now, as the attack on Czarny prison began to draw in security elements. They first dropped Kolya at a hideout, a room above a pharmacy. Then Vlach, on the outskirts of the city, at a lumberyard. A few miles down the road, the Opel stopped at the edge of a small village. Bron tapped the horn three times and an ancient farm truck rolled out of a snow-covered lane. The driver of the truck joined Bron in the Opel, they waved good-bye, and drove off in the direction of Rovno. De Milja and the sergeant sat in the cab of the truck, changed into sheepskin jackets, old boots, and new identity papers.

They waited until dawn, then in first light headed for the Razakavia band in the farmhouse at the edge of the forest. De Milja never went more than twenty miles an hour – the tyres were old and battered, the road ice over frozen mud, and patches of ground fog turned the windshield white. As they drove along, Krewinski told his story. 'The NKVD sergeant, the man whose dog had been sick, he came to the wire one day and told me, "You go to Moscow, to the training school, because if you stay here, well . . ." I understood what he meant. I never saw him again, but he saved my life. The major who had run my regiment was still in the camp at that time, and he told me how to go about it. He was a reserve officer, a chemist from Lodz, an important man.

'Well, it was just like he said it would be. I asked for a book about communism, and I read it and I discussed it with a guard. A political type called me into his office, and he gave me another book. That went on for a month or two, then they moved me to a separate part of the camp, and they left a gate open.' Krewinski laughed. 'I'd been told they would do that, and they did. I ignored it. Then, a week later, the provocateur. A little man that worked around the office. Came to me and said, "I know your game. Let's you and me work together and get ourselves out of here."'

'What did you do?'

'Went directly to the camp commandant and turned him in. And *that* really seemed to make a difference, that earned their trust. About two weeks later I went east.

'It was a kind of school. On Arbat Street, in an old mansion. And also at the university. A school for guerrilla fighting. Nothing like that in Poland – oh, maybe for officers, but not for an enlisted man like me. They had all kinds of people there, from everywhere in Europe – we could barely talk to one another. Estonians and Lithuanians and Hungarians, Frenchmen and Belgians. All kinds. They taught us how to blow up a train, how to ambush a column. But they also spent time on political matters – putting out a newspaper, and getting it into people's hands; by leaving it on trains, or mailing it to addresses in the phone book. They taught assassination. How to force peasants to fight for you, how to infiltrate organizations. Then, in August, after the German attack on Russia, they dropped me by parachute into the Tsuman forest. I was to search out a certain band, and work to bring them under the control of the Znamensky Street centre – the GRU – in Moscow.'

'What happened?'

'I went home,' Krewinski said. 'It wasn't that simple or easy, and it took time and luck, but that's what I did.'

They reached the farm at dusk, were given something to eat, the sergeant spent some time with his brother, then they were given blankets and taken to a hayloft on the second floor of an old stone stable. There they fell into a dead sleep, awakened at 5:00 a.m. when German anti-partisan units and Ukrainian militia, acting on a tip from an informer, attacked the farm.

They got very close, killing the sentries silently as they came. Three hundred of them, Ukrainian militia led by a special SS unit – men imprisoned for poaching game in Germany recruited to hunt humans, partisans, in the forests of Poland.

It was a hand grenade that woke Captain de Milja.

It blew a hole in the corner of the stable and set the beams on fire. By the flickering light he saw militia running across a frozen pond. He kicked himself free of his blanket and ran to a window, Simonov in hand. Down below, on the ground floor of the stable, some of the partisans were shouting to one another, trying to organize a defence. But the guards out in the forest were lying in the leaves with their throats cut, and it was too late to organize much of anything.

The Germans had a heavy machine gun in the woods. They traversed window to window across the outbuildings, the main house, then the stable. Only Frantek's final cry alerted de Milja to the gunfire and he dived below the sill just as it reached him. He crawled over to help, but Frantek simply stared at him upside down, eyes wide, a look of indignation frozen on his face.

Sergeant Krewinski knew how to do these things. He waited until the machine gun moved to the next building, then fired a long burst at its muzzle flare with a machine pistol. This occasioned a change of gunners – a few moments of reorganization, but nothing more. By then, the fire in the beams had taken hold and it was getting hard to see, and to breathe, on the upper floor. One of the defenders from down below rushed halfway up the stairway, yelled something, then tumbled, dead weight, back down. A moment later a rifle was poked up from the stairs and fired blind. A partisan reached down and pulled it up, a very surprised Ukrainian hanging on the other end. The sergeant shot him. Then Krewinski and de Milja exchanged a certain look – *the time we always knew would come has come* – and led the others on the second floor in running down the open stairway. Nobody really wanted to burn to death in a stable. Krewinski was shot, but the impulse turned out to have been a good one. There were only five or six militia gathered at the foot of the stairway. Triumphant – blood on the walls, dead militia, dead partisans – but undermanned, a successful attack that had spent its strength en route.

Two Ukrainians leaped on de Milja – partisans taken alive were worth gold to the Germans. He fell over backwards under the weight but had had the foresight to jump with a VIS in his hand, so he shot each one in the abdomen and they rolled off him in a hurry. He struggled to his feet, saw Krewinski staggering around with blood on his shirt, grabbed him by the collar and pulled him outside.

Into a cloud of hot, black smoke from the burning farmhouse. They both went flat. The smoke made it hard to breathe, but it gave them a moment's camouflage, a moment to think. De Milja, VIS in one hand, Krewinski's collar in the other, decided to crawl into the farmhouse, hoping that Razakavia, or somebody, was holding out there.

It was deserted, except for Kotior. He had been wounded. Badly. He was sitting on a couch holding a light machine gun by its tripod, the feeder belt snaked around his shoulders, the barrel pointed at the front door. His face was white, he would not live much longer. 'Out the back door,' he said. 'They have retreated.'

'Good-bye, Kotior,' de Milja said.

'Good-bye,' Kotior said.

He dragged Krewinski towards the back door, was almost there when a shadow flew at him from behind an overturned table. He swung the

VIS, then saw it was the Jewish woman who had given him coffee one morning when he'd first arrived in the forest. 'I ask you to shoot me,' she said formally.

He had no time to think about it. Krewinski's weight was beginning to pull hard, not a good sign. The woman put her hands on his forearm. 'Please,' she said. 'I don't want to be tortured.' She was right, the militia liked the screams of women. He pointed the VIS at her forehead, she looked at him, closed her eyes, then lifted her face.

But he couldn't. His hand would not kill her. 'No,' he said. 'Come with me.' He dragged Krewinski forward and she followed, holding on to his shirt in the billowing smoke.

The truck.

De Milja had driven it a little way into the forest the night before, now it saved their lives.

The starter failed, four or five times, then he forced himself to a slow and determined effort, pulled the choke out where it belonged, and babied the truck to life. It sputtered and coughed, but it did not die. It took all his strength to ease the big clutch up slowly enough not to stall the engine, his teeth ground with effort and concentration, but he did it. The truck crawled forward, slow but steady, moving down a narrow path into the forest. Branches broke off against the windshield, the wheels climbed over downed logs and rocky outcrops. Occasionally the tyres spun on the ice, de Milja let some air out and that enabled them to grip better, somehow finding traction on the frozen earth.

He saw Razakavia once more.

A few miles west of the farmhouse the forest divided – low hills rising from either bank of a small river. De Milja took the right fork, then, an hour after sunrise, found himself on a section of road where foresters had long ago built a corduroy track of cut logs. He stopped the truck to let the engine cool down and there, three hundred yards away, his horse moving at a brisk walk along the bank of the frozen river, was Razakavia.

A scout, riding well in advance of the main party, disappeared into the trees as de Milja watched. The main body of riders was strung out a long way, some of them riding double, many of them slumped over, perhaps wounded, certainly exhausted. Razakavia rode at the front, his white hair and beard stark against the grey-green forest, a rifle slung across his back.

They stopped at midday. There was still petrol in the truck, and the corduroy track had continued without interruption. Perhaps they had happened on one of the vast estates owned by the Polish nobility in the nineteenth century, the road maintained by the count's foresters for the use of wagons during the hunting season.

The woman he had saved had told him her name was Shura. She had, since they'd fled the burning farmhouse, tried to make Krewinski comfortable as best she could, but at last she said to de Milja, 'I think now we must stop for a little time.'

He knew what she meant, and turned off the engine. 'Thank you,' Krewinski whispered, grateful for a few moments of peace. The slow, jolting progress of the truck over the log road had been agony for him, though he had never once complained. When the ignition was turned off, the forest was immediately a very different place. Cold and clean, with a small wind; quiet except for the creak of frozen branches. With Shura's help he settled Krewinski on the matted pine needles beneath a tree and covered him with an old blanket they'd found on the seat of the truck. When Shura tucked the blanket beneath his chin Krewinski closed his eyes and smiled. 'Much better,' he said.

He went to sleep, and a half-hour later he was gone. There was no question of burial in the frozen ground, so they folded his hands on his chest and scratched his name on a rock and set it by his head as a gravestone.

Contrary to de Milja's fears, the truck started, and moved forward along the corduroy road. The loss of Krewinski hurt – a life that should have continued. And de Milja wondered at the cost of the rescue when he considered the result. Nonetheless, in its own terms, the operation had succeeded. Olenik had been specific: they wanted the sergeant, but, if that proved impossible, they wanted the sergeant's story. Well, that at least they would have, *if* he managed to get back to Warsaw. He was, he calculated, a hundred miles south-east of the town of Biala, and from there it was another hundred and twenty-five miles to Warsaw.

In a leather passport case he had two pairs of railway tickets – for himself and Krewinski – along with the necessary documents for travel from the Rovno area to Biala, and from there on to Warsaw. His papers were good, and he had money in various forms. But he had no water, no food, and no petrol. He had a pistol with three rounds, and no idea what he was going to do with the woman sitting next to him. He stared at her a moment. Wrapped in a long black coat and a black shawl, she sat up properly, back straight, bounced around by the motion of the truck.

Even wearing the shawl like a Ukrainian peasant – drawn across the brow so that it hid the hairline – she had a certain look; curved nose, dark eyes, thick eyebrows, and shadowy, sombre skin. Someone who could have blended into the Byelorussian or Ukrainian population would not have been a problem, but Shura looked exactly like what she was, a Jew. And in that part of the world, people would see it. The forest bands preyed on Jews, especially on Jewish women. And the only alternative to the forest was a railway system crawling with SS guards and Gestapo. De Milja knew they would demand papers at every stop.

'Shura,' he said.

'Yes?' Her voice seemed resigned, she knew what this was about.

'What am I to do with you?'

'I do not know,' she said.

'Do you have identity papers?'

'I burned them. Better to be a phantom than a Jew.'

'A family?'

'They were forced into the ghetto, in Tarnopol. After that, I don't know. By accident I wasn't there the day the Germans came, and I fled to the forest with my cousin – he was seventeen. Razakavia agreed to take us in. I cooked, carried water, made myself useful any way I could. My cousin was killed a few weeks later, during an attack on a German train.'

I'm sorry,' de Milja said. 'And were you married, in Tarnopol?'

'No. And no prospects – though I suppose eventually something would have been arranged. They sent me away to study music when I was twelve years old. They thought I was a prodigy. But I wasn't. So then, I had to do something respectable, and I became a piano teacher. A bad piano teacher, I should add. Children mostly didn't like me, and I mostly didn't like them.' They rode in silence for a time. 'See?' she said. 'I am everything you ever dreamed of.'

She let him know, without saying it directly, that he could have her if he liked, she would not resist. But that wasn't what he wanted – a woman taken by some right of sanctuary. Still, by the time it was dark that night it was evident that they would have to sleep holding each other or die. They lay on the seat of the truck in each other's arms, the blanket wrapped around them, the windows closed tight and clouded over with their breath. Outside, the November moon – the hunter's moon – was full, a cold, pale light on the frozen river.

A clear night, the million stars were silver. She was warm to hold, her breath on his temple. When she dreamed, her hands moved. It brought him memories, the embrace with Shura. Long ago. The girls of his twenties. His wife. He missed love, he wondered if war had made it impossible for him. In the drift of his mind he paused on what it would be like to slide her skirt up to her waist. He sighed, shifted his weight, the springs creaked. Where the cold, sharp air touched his skin it actually hurt, and he pressed his face against her shoulder. Sometimes she slept, and sometimes he did.

The road ended.

They let the truck roll down the hill – a foot at a time, it took forever – and out onto the grey ice of the river. They managed five or six miles an hour that way, headed east of north by his calculations. They discovered a tiny settlement on the shore, pole-built docks coated with ice in the morning sun. They bought some black bread and salt from a woman who came down to the river to stare at them. From an old ferryman they bought a jar to melt ice in so they could have water. 'Brzesc nad Bugiem' he said, pointing north. Brest Litovsk. He smiled and rubbed his whiskers. They were on, he told them, a tributary of the river Bug.

The grey clouds came in that afternoon and a white fog rose off the ice. Now they drove even slower, because it was hard to see. He worried about fuel, but the truck had a large tank, and a hundred miles wasn't too much to ask of it when they could only go a few miles an hour.

Then there were no more settlements. The rise of the hills above them grew steep, the woods thicker, no trails to be seen. And the river narrowed with every mile. Finally, when it was only ten feet wide, the ice changed. The truck wouldn't go any more. The tyres spun, the engine roared, and the back slid sideways, but that was all. Slipping on the ice, they tried to pile sticks beneath the back wheels. But the truck would not go forward. 'So,' Shura said. She meant it was finished, but she was glad they had tried it. What awaited them was at least peaceful, no more than going to sleep. He agreed. For him it was enough that somebody was there, that he would not have to be alone.

He turned off the ignition. The sky was fading above the hills, night was an hour away. It was colder now, much colder. They lay down on the seat and held each other beneath the worn blanket. 'I am so cold,' she said. The wind that night made it even colder, but the fog blew away, and a vast white moon rose above the hillside. A field of reeds sparkled with frost, and they saw a wolf, a grey shadow trotting along the river. It stopped and looked at them, then went on, pads silent on the ice. At last the world has frozen, he thought. A winter that would never end.

They tried in every way not to go to sleep, but they were very tired, and there was nothing more they could do. She fell asleep first, then him.

The truck stood silent on the ice. A few flakes of snow drifted down, then more. The cloud began to gather and the moon faded away until there was hardly any light at all. The snow fell heavier now; hissed down, a white blanket on the river, and the hills, and the truck.

He woke up suddenly. The window of the truck was opaque, and it was not so cold as it had been. He touched her, but she did not move. Then he held his hand against her face, and she stirred, actually managed a smile, putting her hand on top of his.

'We're going,' he said.

She opened one eye.

He didn't move his hand. 'Shura, look at the window,' he said. 'Sometimes you can't drive on ice. But you can drive on snow.'

They drove through the war that night, but it didn't want them just then.

They saw panzer tanks and armoured cars positioned on a bridge. An SS officer, a dark silhouette leaning on the railing, watched the truck as it passed beneath him, but nothing happened. A few miles north of there a village had been burned down, smoke still rising from the charred beams. And twice they heard gunfire, machine gun answering machine gun, tracer rounds in the darkness like sparks blown across the sky.

Sometimes the snow fell in squalls; swirling, windblown. Then it cleared, the clouds rolling east, the frozen river shimmering in the moonlight. De Milja drove with both hands gripping the wheel, coaxing the truck along the ice, riding the snow that gave them traction. Shura pointed out a small road that led up a hill from the river; perhaps an abandoned ferry crossing. De Milja stopped the truck and climbed the hill. He found a well-used dirt road and an ancient milestone that pointed the way to Biala.

It took a long time to get the truck off the river. De Milja and Shura knelt by the tyres and studied the surface like engineers, finally building a track of branches to the edge of the shore. It worked. Engine whining, wheels spinning, the truck lurched, swayed sideways, then climbed.

Once on the upper road, de Milja let the engine idle while he got his breath back. 'Where are we?' Shura asked.

'Not far from Biala. A few hours, if nothing goes wrong.' He eased the clutch into first gear, moved off slowly on the rutted road.

Midnight passed, then 1:00 a.m. They drove through snow-covered forest, boughs heavy and white bent almost to the ground. Shura fell into an exhausted sleep, then woke suddenly as they bounced over a rock. 'I'm sorry,' she said. 'I didn't mean to abandon you.'

'I'm all right,' de Milja said.

'I should have helped to keep you awake. I can sing something, if you like.'

'You don't have to.'

'I can discuss – oh, well certainly music. Chopin. Or Rachmaninoff.'

The engine steamed as the truck climbed a long hill. At the crest, de Milja braked gently to a stop. They were on a wooded height above Biala. Directly below, a poor neighbourhood at the edge of town. Crooked one-storey houses, crooked dirt streets, white with frost. Wisps of wood smoke hung above the chimneys in the still air. De Milja drove the truck to the side of the road and turned off the ignition. 'Now we wait for dawn, for the end of the curfew. Then we can go into the open-air market with the produce trucks from the countryside. Once we get there we can make contact with the local ZWZ unit – our luck, it's a good one. Very good. They'll move us the rest of the way, into Warsaw. In a freight train, maybe. Or hidden in a vegetable wagon.'

They sat and stared out the window. It seemed very quiet with the engine off.

'Perhaps it would be best if I stayed here,' Shura said.

'You know somebody here?'

'No.'

'You wouldn't last long.'

'No, probably not. But at least . . .'

'You'd have it over with?' De Milja shook his head angrily. 'No, no. That isn't right. We'll hide you,' he said. 'Not in the ghetto – somewhere in Warsaw, one of the working-class neighbourhoods. With friends of ours. It won't be easy, but if you're able to stay in the apartment, if you avoid people, in other words if you can live in hiding, you'll survive. You'll need some luck, but you'll see the end of the war.'

'And you?'

'Me?' De Milja shrugged. 'I have to keep fighting,' he said. 'The Germans, the Russians. Perhaps both. Perhaps for years and years. But I might live through it, you never know. Somebody always seems to survive, no matter what happens. Perhaps it will be me.'

He was silent for a time, staring at the sleeping town. 'There was a moment, about a year ago. Someone I knew in Paris, "Let's just go to Switzerland," she said. I could have, maybe I should have, but I didn't. I missed my chance, but I don't really know why. I had a friend, a Russian, he had theories about these things – a world of bad people and good people, a war that never seems to end, you have to take sides. I don't know, maybe that's the way it is.'

He paused, then smiled to himself. 'Honestly, Shura, right now I will be happy when the sun comes up. The marketplace will be full of people – there'll be a fire in a barrel, a way to get a hot cup of coffee. It's possible!' he laughed.

'Hot coffee,' Shura said.

'And some bread. Why not?'

They sat close together in the truck, trying to stay warm. He held her tightly, she pressed against his side. In time the darkness faded and the first sunlight hit the rooftops, a flock of pigeons flew up in the air, a dog barked, another answered.